30

D1151381

Freed

James is a former TV executive, wife and mother of two, in West London. Since early childhood she dreamed of stories that readers would fall in love with, but put those on hold to focus on her family and career. She finally d up the courage to put pen to paper with her first novel, lti-million-copy bestseller, *Fifty Shades of Grey* which, r with its sequels, *Fifty Shades Darker* and *Fifty Shades* became a worldwide phenomenon.

August 2012 Amazon announced that E L James had Amazon's bestselling author ever on amazon.co.uk, and on 2012 *Fifty Shades of Grey* became the bestselling novel in since records had begun in 1998. *Publishers Weekly* also ted her their Publishing Person of the Year, 2012.

Dy!

BOOKS BY E L JAMES

Fifty Shades of Grey

Fifty Shades Darker

Fifty Shades Freed

Grey

Darker

E L James
Fifty Shades
Freed

arrow books

3 5 7 9 10 8 6 4 2

Arrow Books
20 Vauxhall Bridge Road
London SW1V 2SA

Arrow Books is part of the Penguin Random House group of companies
whose addresses can be found at global.penguinrandomhouse.com.

Penguin
Random House
UK

First published in Great Britain by Arrow Books in 2012
This film tie-in edition published by Arrow Books in 2018

The author published an earlier serialised version of this story
online with different characters as *Master of the Universe* under the
pseudonym Snowqueen's Icedragon

www.penguin.co.uk

A CIP catalogue record for this book is available from the British Library.

ISBN 9781784757762

Book design by Claudia Martinez

Printed and bound in Great Britain by Clays Ltd, St Ives Plc

Para mi Mamá con todo mi amor y gratitud

And for my beloved Father

Daddy, I miss you every day

ACKNOWLEDGMENTS

Thanks to Niall, my rock.

To Kathleen for just being a great sounding board, friend, confidante, and a technical wiz.

To Bee for endless moral support.

To Taylor (also a technical wiz), Susi, Pam, and Nora for showing a girl a good time.

And for their advice and tact I'd really like to thank:

Dr. Raina Sluder for help with all matters medical; Anne Forlines for the financial advice; Elizabeth de Vos for her kind counsel regarding the American adoption system.

Thanks to Maddie Blandino for her exquisite, inspirational art.

And to Pam and Gillian for Saturday morning coffee and hauling me back to real life.

Also thanks to my editing team, Andrea, Shay, and the ever lovely and only occasionally frothing Janine, who tolerates my frothing with patience, fortitude, and a great sense of humor.

Lastly a huge thank-you to everyone at Vintage.

Fifty Shades
Freed

PROLOGUE

Mommy! Mommy! Mommy is asleep on the floor. She has been asleep for a long time. I brush her hair because she likes that. She doesn't wake up. I shake her. Mommy! My tummy hurts. It is hungry. He isn't here. I am thirsty. In the kitchen I pull a chair to the sink, and I have a drink. The water splashes over my blue sweater. Mommy is still asleep. Mommy wake up! She lies still. She is cold. I fetch my blankie, and I cover Mommy, and I lie down on the sticky green rug beside her. Mommy is still asleep. I have two toy cars. They race by the floor where Mommy is sleeping. I think Mommy is sick. I search for something to eat. In the freezer I find peas. They are cold. I eat them slowly. They make my tummy hurt. I sleep beside Mommy. The peas are gone. In the freezer is something. It smells funny. I lick it and my tongue is stuck to it. I eat it slowly. It tastes nasty. I drink some water. I play with my cars, and I sleep beside Mommy. Mommy is so cold, and she won't wake up. The door crashes open. I cover Mommy with my blankie. He's here. *Fuck. What the fuck happened here? Oh, the crazy fucked-up bitch. Shit. Fuck. Get out of my way, you little shit.* He kicks me, and I hit my head on the floor. My head hurts. He calls somebody and he goes. He locks the door. I lay down beside Mommy. My head hurts. The lady policeman is here. No. No. No. Don't touch me. Don't touch me. Don't touch me. I stay by Mommy. No. Stay away from me. The lady policeman has my blankie, and she grabs me. I scream. Mommy! Mommy! I want my mommy. The words are gone. I can't say the words. Mommy can't hear me. I have no words.

"Christian! Christian!" Her voice is urgent, pulling him from the depths of his nightmare, the depths of his despair. "I'm here. I'm here."

He wakes and she's leaning over him, grasping his shoulders, shaking him, her face etched with anguish, blue eyes wide and brimming with tears.

"Ana." His voice is a breathless whisper, the taste of fear tarnishing his mouth. "You're here."

"Of course I'm here."

"I had a dream . . ."

"I know. I'm here, I'm here."

"Ana." He breathes her name, and it's a talisman against the black choking panic coursing through his body.

"Hush, I'm here." She curls around him, her limbs cocooning him, her warmth leeching into his body, forcing back the shadows, forcing back the fear. She is sunshine, she is light . . . she is his.

"Please let's not fight." His voice is hoarse as he wraps his arms around her.

"Okay."

"The vows. No obeying. I can do that. We'll find a way." The words rush out of his mouth in a tumble of emotion and confusion and anxiety.

"Yes. We will. We'll always find a way," she whispers, and her lips are on his, silencing him, bringing him back to the now.

CHAPTER ONE

I stare up through gaps in the sea-grass parasol at the bluest of skies, summer blue, Mediterranean blue, with a contented sigh. Christian is beside me, stretched out on a sun lounge. My husband—my hot, beautiful husband, shirtless and in cut-off jeans—is reading a book predicting the collapse of the Western banking system. By all accounts, it's a page-turner. I haven't seen him sit this still, ever. He looks more like a student than the hotshot CEO of one of the top privately owned companies in the United States.

On the final leg of our honeymoon, we laze in the afternoon sun on the beach of the aptly named Beach Plaza Monte Carlo in Monaco, although we're not actually staying in this hotel. I open my eyes and gaze out at the *Fair Lady* anchored in the harbor. We are staying, of course, on board a luxury motor yacht. Built in 1928, she floats majestically on the water, queen of all the yachts in the harbor. She looks like a child's wind-up toy. Christian loves her—I suspect he's tempted to buy her. Honestly, boys and their toys.

Sitting back, I listen to the Christian Grey mix on my new iPod and doze in the late afternoon sun, idly remembering his proposal. Oh, his dreamy proposal in the boathouse . . . I can almost smell the scent of the meadow flowers . . .

—— · ——

"Can we marry tomorrow?" Christian murmurs softly in my ear. I am sprawled on his chest in the flowery bower in the boathouse, sated from our passionate lovemaking.

"Hmm."

"Is that a yes?" I hear his hopeful surprise.

"Hmm."

"A no?"

"Hmm."

I sense his grin. "Miss Steele, are you incoherent?"

I grin. "Hmm."

He laughs and hugs me tightly, kissing the top of my head. "Vegas, tomorrow, it is then."

Sleepily I raise my head. "I don't think my parents would be very happy with that."

He thrums his fingertips up and down my naked back, caressing me gently.

"What do you want, Anastasia? Vegas? A big wedding with all the trimmings? Tell me."

"Not big . . . Just friends and family." I gaze up at him, moved by the quiet entreaty in his glowing gray eyes. *What does he want?*

"Okay." He nods. "Where?"

I shrug.

"Could we do it here?" he asks tentatively.

"Your folks' place? Would they mind?"

He snorts. "My mother would be in seventh heaven."

"Okay, here. I'm sure my mom and dad would prefer that."

He strokes my hair. Could I be any happier?

"So, we've established where, now the when."

"Surely you should ask your mother."

"Hmm." Christian's smile dips. "She can have a month, that's it. I want you too much to wait any longer."

"Christian, you have me. You've had me for a while. But okay—a month it is." I kiss his chest, a soft chaste kiss, and smile up at him.

———

"You'll burn," Christian whispers in my ear, startling me from my doze.

"Only for you." I give him my sweetest smile. The late afternoon sun has shifted, and I am under its full glare. He smirks and in one swift move pulls my sun lounge into the shade of the parasol.

"Out of the Mediterranean sun, Mrs. Grey."

"Thank you for your altruism, Mr. Grey."

"My pleasure, Mrs. Grey, and I'm not being altruistic at all. If you burn, I won't be able to touch you." He raises an eyebrow, his eyes shining with mirth, and my heart expands. "But I suspect you know that and you're laughing at me."

"Would I?" I gasp, feigning innocence.

"Yes, you would and you do. Often. It's one of the many things I love about you." He leans down and kisses me, playfully biting my lower lip.

"I was hoping you'd rub me down with more sunscreen." I pout against his lips.

"Mrs. Grey, it's a dirty job . . . but that's an offer I can't refuse. Sit up," he orders, his voice husky. I do as I'm told, and with slow meticulous strokes from strong and supple fingers, he coats me in sunscreen.

"You really are very lovely. I'm a lucky man," he murmurs as his fingers skim over my breasts, spreading the lotion.

"Yes, you are, Mr. Grey." I gaze coyly up at him through my lashes.

"Modesty becomes you, Mrs. Grey. Turn over. I want to do your back."

Smiling, I roll over, and he undoes the back strap of my hideously expensive bikini.

"How would you feel if I went topless, like the other women on the beach?" I ask.

"Displeased," he says without hesitation. "I'm not very happy about you wearing so little right now." He leans down and whispers in my ear. "Don't push your luck."

"Is that a challenge, Mr. Grey?"

"No. It's a statement of fact, Mrs. Grey."

I sigh and shake my head. *Oh, Christian . . . my possessive, jealous, control freak Christian.*

When he's finished, he slaps my behind.

"You'll do, wench."

His ever-present, ever-active BlackBerry buzzes. I frown and he smirks.

"My eyes only, Mrs. Grey." He raises his eyebrow in playful warning, slaps my backside once more, and sits back down on his lounger to take the call.

My inner goddess purrs. Maybe tonight we could do some kind of floor show for his eyes only. She smirks knowingly, arching a brow. I grin at the thought and drift back into my afternoon siesta.

"*MAM'SELLE? UN PERRIER POUR moi, un* Coca-Cola light *pour ma femme, s'il vous plait. Et quelque chose a manger . . . laissez-moi voir la carte.*"

Hmm . . . Christian speaking fluent French wakes me. My eyelashes flutter in the glare of the sun, and I find Christian watching me while a liveried young woman walks away, her tray held aloft, her high blonde ponytail swinging provocatively.

"Thirsty?" he asks.

"Yes," I mutter sleepily.

"I could watch you all day. Tired?"

I flush. "I didn't get much sleep last night."

"Me neither." He grins, puts down his BlackBerry, and stands. His shorts fall a little and hang . . . in that way so his swim trunks are visible beneath. Christian takes his shorts off, stepping out of his flip-flops. I lose my train of thought.

"Come for a swim with me." He holds out his hand while I look up at him, dazed. "Swim?" he says again, cocking his head to one side, an amused expression on his face. When I don't respond, he shakes his head slowly.

"I think you need a wake-up call." Suddenly he pounces and lifts me into his arms while I shriek, more from surprise than alarm.

"Christian! Put me down!" I squeal.

He chuckles. "Only in the sea, baby."

Several sunbathers on the beach watch with that bemused disinterest so typical, I now realize, of the French, as Christian carries me to the sea, laughing, and wades in.

I clasp my arms around his neck. "You wouldn't," I say breathlessly, trying to stifle my giggling.

He grins. "Oh, Ana, baby, have you learned nothing in the short time we've known each other?" He kisses me, and I seize my opportunity, running my fingers through his hair, grasping two handfuls and kissing him back while invading his mouth with my tongue. He inhales sharply and leans back, eyes smoky but wary.

"I know your game," he whispers and slowly sinks into the cool, clear water, taking me with him as his lips find mine once more. The chill of the Mediterranean is soon forgotten as I wrap myself around my husband.

"I thought you wanted to swim," I murmur against his mouth.

"You're very distracting." Christian grazes his teeth along my lower lip. "But I'm not sure I want the good people of Monte Carlo to see my wife in the throes of passion."

I run my teeth along his jaw, his stubble tickly against my tongue, not caring a dime for the good people of Monte Carlo.

"Ana," he groans. He wraps my ponytail around his wrist and tugs gently, tilting my head back, exposing my throat. He trails kisses from my ear down my neck.

"Shall I take you in the sea?" he breathes.

"Yes," I whisper.

Christian pulls away and gazes down at me, his eyes warm, wanting, and amused. "Mrs. Grey, you're insatiable and so brazen. What sort of monster have I created?"

"A monster fit for you. Would you have me any other way?"

"I'll take you any way I can get you, you know that. But not right now. Not with an audience." He jerks his head toward the shore.

What?

Sure enough, several sunbathers on the beach have abandoned their indifference and now regard us with interest. Suddenly, Christian grabs me around my waist and launches me into the air, letting me fall into the water and sink beneath the waves to the soft sand below. I surface, coughing, spluttering, and giggling.

"Christian!" I scold, glaring at him. I thought we were going to make love in the sea . . . and chalk up yet another first. He bites his lower lip to stifle his amusement. I splash him, and he splashes me right back.

"We have all night," he says, grinning like a fool. "Laters, baby." He dives beneath the sea and surfaces three feet away from me, then in a fluid, graceful crawl, swims away from the shore, away from me.

Gah! Playful, tantalizing Fifty! I shield my eyes from the sun as I watch him go. He's such a tease . . . what can I do to get him back? While I swim to the shore, I contemplate my options. At the lounges our drinks have arrived, and I take a quick sip of Diet Coke. Christian is a faint speck in the distance.

Hmm . . . I lie down on my front and, fumbling with the straps, take my bikini top off and toss it casually onto Christian's sun lounge. There . . . see how brazen I can be, Mr. Grey. Put this in your pipe and smoke it. I shut my eyes and let the sun warm my skin . . . warm my bones, and I drift away under its heat, my thoughts turning to my wedding day.

"You may kiss the bride," Reverend Walsh announces.

I beam at my husband.

"Finally, you're mine," he whispers and pulls me into his arms and kisses me chastely on the lips.

I am married. I am Mrs. Christian Grey. I am giddy with joy.

"You look beautiful, Ana," he murmurs and smiles, his eyes glowing with love . . . and something darker, something hot. "Don't let anyone take that dress off but me, understand?" His smile heats a hundred degrees as his fingertips trail down my cheek, igniting my blood.

Holy crap . . . How does he do this, even here with all these people staring at us?

I nod mutely. Jeez, I hope no one can hear us. Luckily Reverend Walsh has discreetly stepped back. I glance at the throng gathered in their wedding finery . . . My mom, Ray, Bob, and the Greys are all applauding—even Kate, my maid of honor, who looks stunning in pale pink as she stands beside Christian's best man, his brother Elliot. Who knew that even Elliot could scrub up so well? All wear huge, beaming smiles—except Grace, who weeps graciously into a dainty white handkerchief.

"Ready to party, Mrs. Grey?" Christian murmurs, giving me his shy smile. I melt. He looks divine in a simple black tux with silver waistcoat and tie. He's so . . . *dashing.*

"Ready as I'll ever be." I grin, a totally goofy smile on my face.

Later the wedding party is in full swing . . . Carrick and Grace have gone to town. They have the tent set up again and beautifully decorated in pale pink, silver, and ivory with its sides open, facing the bay. We have been blessed with fine weather, and the late afternoon sun shines over the water. There's a dance floor at one end of the tent, a lavish buffet at the other.

Ray and my mother are dancing and laughing with each other. I feel bittersweet watching them together. I hope Christian and I last longer. I don't know what I'd do if he left me. *Marry in haste, repent at leisure.* The saying haunts me.

Kate is beside me, looking so beautiful in her long silk gown. She glances at me and frowns. "Hey, this is supposed to be the happiest day of your life," she scolds.

"It is," I whisper.

"Oh, Ana, what's wrong? Are you watching your mom and Ray?"

I nod sadly.

"They're happy."

"Happier apart."

"You're having doubts?" Kate asks, alarmed.

"No, not at all. It's just . . . I love him so much." I freeze, unable or unwilling to articulate my fears.

"Ana, it's obvious he adores you. I know you had an unconventional start to your relationship, but I can see how happy you've both been over the past month." She grasps my hands, squeezing them. "Besides, it's too late now," she adds with a grin.

I giggle. Trust Kate to point out the obvious. She pulls me into a Katherine Kavanagh Special Hug. "Ana, you'll be fine. And if he hurts one hair on your head, he'll have me to answer to." Releasing me, she grins at whoever is behind me.

"Hi, baby." Christian puts his arms around me, surprising me, and kisses my temple. "Kate," he acknowledges. He's still cool toward her even after six weeks.

"Hello again, Christian. I'm off to find your best man, who happens to be my best man, too." With a smile to us both, she heads over to Elliot, who is drinking with her brother, Ethan, and our friend José.

"Time to go," Christian murmurs.

"Already? This is the first party I've been to where I don't mind being the center of attention." I turn in his arms to face him.

"You deserve to be. You look stunning, Anastasia."

"So do you."

He smiles, his expression heating. "This beautiful dress becomes you."

"This old thing?" I blush shyly and pull at the fine lace trim of the simple, fitted wedding dress designed for me by Kate's mother. I love that the lace is just off the shoulder—demure, yet alluring, I hope.

He bends and kisses me. "Let's go. I don't want to share you with all these people anymore."

"Can we leave our own wedding?"

"Baby, it's our party, and we can do whatever we want. We've cut the cake. And right now, I'd like to whisk you away and have you all to myself."

I giggle. "You have me for a lifetime, Mr. Grey."

"I'm very glad to hear that, Mrs. Grey."

"Oh, there you two are! Such lovebirds."

I groan inwardly . . . Grace's mother has found us.

"Christian, darling—one more dance with your grandma?"

Christian purses his lips. "Of course, Grandmother."

"And you, beautiful Anastasia, go and make an old man happy—dance with Theo."

"Theo, Mrs. Trevelyan?"

"Grandpa Trevelyan. And I think you can call me Grandma. Now, you two seriously need to get working on my great-grandkids. I won't last too much longer." She gives us both a simpering smile.

Christian blinks at her in horror. "Come, Grandmother," he says, hurriedly taking her hand and leading her to the dance floor. He glances back at me, practically pouting, and rolls his eyes. "Laters, baby."

As I walk toward Grandpa Trevelyan, José accosts me.

"I won't ask you for another dance. I think I monopolized too much of your time on the dance floor as it is . . . I'm happy to see you happy, but I'm serious, Ana. I'll be here . . . If you need me."

"José, thank you. You're a good friend."

"I mean it." His dark eyes shine with sincerity.

"I know you do. Thank you, José. Now if you'll please excuse me—I have a date with an old man."

He furrows his brow in confusion.

"Christian's grandfather," I clarify.

He grins. "Good luck with that, Annie. Good luck with everything."

"Thanks, José."

After my dance with Christian's ever-charming grandfather, I stand by the French doors, watching the sun sink slowly over Seattle, casting bright orange and aquamarine shadows across the bay.

"Let's go," Christian urges.

"I have to change." I grasp his hand, meaning to pull him

through the French windows and upstairs with me. He frowns, not understanding, and tugs gently on my hand, halting me.

"I thought you wanted to be the one to take this dress off," I explain. His eyes light up.

"Correct." He gives me a lascivious grin. "But I'm not undressing you here. We wouldn't leave until . . . I don't know . . ." He waves his long-fingered hand, leaving his sentence unfinished but his meaning quite clear.

I flush and let go of his hand.

"And don't take your hair down either," he murmurs darkly.

"But—"

"No buts, Anastasia. You look beautiful. And I want to be the one to undress you."

Oh. I frown.

"Pack your going-away clothes," he orders. "You'll need them. Taylor has your main suitcase."

"Okay." What has he got planned? He hasn't told me where we're going. In fact, I don't think anyone knows where we're going. Neither Mia nor Kate has managed to inveigle the information out of him. I turn to where my mother and Kate are hovering nearby.

"I'm not changing."

"What?" my mother says.

"Christian doesn't want me to." I shrug as if this should explain everything. Her brow furrows briefly.

"You didn't promise to obey," she reminds me tactfully. Kate tries to disguise her snort as a cough. I narrow my eyes at her. Neither she nor my mother have any idea of the fight Christian and I had about that. I don't want to rehash that argument. *Jeez, can my Fifty Shades sulk . . . and have nightmares.* The memory is sobering.

"I know, Mom, but he likes this dress, and I want to please him."

Her expression softens. Kate rolls her eyes and tactfully moves away to leave us alone.

"You look so lovely, darling." Carla gently tugs at a loose tendril of my hair and strokes my chin. "I am so proud of you, honey. You're going to make Christian a very happy man." She pulls me into a hug.

Oh, Mom!

"I can't believe how grown-up you look right now. Beginning a new life . . . Just remember that men are from a different planet, and you'll be fine."

I giggle. Christian is from a different universe, if only she knew.

"Thanks, Mom."

Ray joins us, smiling sweetly at both Mom and me.

"You made a beautiful baby girl, Carla," he says, his eyes glowing with pride. He looks so dapper in his black tux and pale pink waistcoat. Tears prick the backs of my eyes. Oh no . . . so far I have managed not to cry.

"And you watched her and helped her grow up, Ray." Carla's voice is wistful.

"And I loved every single minute. You make one hell of a bride, Annie." Ray tucks the same loose strand of hair behind my ear.

"Oh, Dad . . ." I stifle a sob, and he hugs me in his brief, awkward way.

"You'll make one hell of a wife, too," he whispers, his voice hoarse.

When he releases me, Christian is back at my side.

Ray shakes his hand warmly. "Look after my girl, Christian."

"I fully intend to, Ray. Carla." He nods at my stepdad and kisses my mom.

The rest of the wedding guests have formed a long human arch for us to travel through, leading around to the front of the house.

"Ready?" Christian says.

"Yes."

Taking my hand, he leads me under their outstretched arms while our guests shout good luck and congratulations and shower us with rice. Waiting with smiles and hugs at the end of the arch are Grace and Carrick. They hug and kiss us both in turn. Grace is emotional again as we bid them hasty good-byes.

Taylor is waiting to whisk us away in the Audi SUV. As Christian holds the car door open for me, I turn and toss my bouquet of white and pink roses into the crowd of young women that has gathered. Mia triumphantly holds it aloft, grinning from ear to ear.

As I slide into the SUV, laughing at Mia's audacious catch, Christian bends to gather the hem of my dress. Once I'm safely in, he bids the waiting crowd farewell.

Taylor holds the car door open for him. "Congratulations, sir."

"Thank you, Taylor," Christian replies as he seats himself beside me.

As Taylor pulls away, our wedding guests shower the vehicle with rice. Christian grasps my hand and kisses my knuckles.

"So far so good, Mrs. Grey?"

"So far so wonderful, Mr. Grey. Where are we going?"

"Sea-Tac," he says simply and smiles a sphinxlike smile.

Hmm . . . what is he planning?

Taylor does not head for the departure terminal as I expect but through a security gate and directly onto the tarmac. What? And then I see her—Christian's jet . . . *Grey Enterprises Holdings, Inc.* in large blue lettering across her fuselage.

"Don't tell me you're misusing company property again!"

"Oh, I hope so, Anastasia." Christian grins.

Taylor halts the Audi at the foot of the steps leading up to the plane and leaps out to open Christian's door. They have a brief discussion, then Christian opens my door—and rather than stepping back to give me room to climb out, he leans in and lifts me.

Whoa! "What are you doing?" I squeak.

"Carrying you over the threshold," he says.

"Oh." *Isn't that supposed to be at home?*

He carries me effortlessly up the steps, and Taylor follows with my small suitcase. He leaves it on the threshold of the plane before returning to the Audi. Inside the cabin, I recognize Stephan, Christian's pilot, in his uniform.

"Welcome aboard, sir. Mrs. Grey." He grins.

Christian puts me down and shakes Stephan's hand. Beside Stephan stands a dark-haired woman in her—what? Early thirties? She's also in uniform.

"Congratulations to you both," Stephan continues.

"Thank you, Stephan. Anastasia, you know Stephan. He's our captain today, and this is First Officer Beighley."

She blushes as Christian introduces her and blinks rapidly. I want to roll my eyes. Another female completely captivated by my too-handsome-for-his-own-good husband.

"Delighted to meet you," gushes Beighley. I smile kindly at her. After all—he is mine.

"All preparations complete?" Christian asks them both as I glance around the cabin. The interior is all pale maple and pale cream leather. It's lovely. Another young woman in uniform stands at the other end of the cabin—a very *pretty* brunette.

"We have the all clear. Weather is good from here to Boston."

Boston?

"Turbulence?"

"Not before Boston. There's a weather front over Shannon that might give us a rough ride."

Shannon? Ireland?

"I see. Well, I hope to sleep through it all," says Christian matter-of-factly.

Sleep?

"We'll get underway, sir," Stephan says. "We'll leave you in the capable care of Natalia, your flight attendant." Christian glances in her direction and frowns, but turns to Stephan with a smile.

"Excellent," he says. Taking my hand, he leads me to one of the sumptuous leather seats. There must be about twelve of them in total.

"Sit," he says as he removes his jacket and undoes his fine sliver brocade vest. We sit in two single seats facing each other with a small, highly polished table between us.

"Welcome aboard, sir, ma'am, and congratulations." Natalia is at our side, offering us each a glass of pink champagne.

"Thank you," Christian says, and she smiles politely at us and retreats to the galley.

"Here's to a happy married life, Anastasia." Christian raises his glass to mine, and we clink. The champagne is delicious.

"Bollinger?" I ask.

"The same."

"The first time I drank this it was out of teacups." I grin.

"I remember that day well. Your graduation."

"Where are we going?" I'm unable to contain my curiosity any longer.

"Shannon," Christian says, his eyes alight with excitement. He looks like a small boy.

"In Ireland?" We're going to Ireland!

"To refuel," he adds, teasing.

"Then?" I prompt.

His grin broadens and he shakes his head.

"Christian!"

"London," he says, gazing intently at me, trying to gauge my reaction.

I gasp. *Holy cow.* I thought maybe we'd be going to New York or Aspen or maybe the Caribbean. I can hardly believe it. My lifetime ambition has been to visit England. I'm lit up from within, incandescent with happiness.

"Then Paris."

What?

"Then the South of France."

Whoa!

"I know you've always dreamed of going to Europe," he says softly. "I want to make your dreams come true, Anastasia."

"You are my dreams come true, Christian."

"Back at you, Mrs. Grey," he whispers.

Oh my . . .

"Buckle up."

I grin and do as I'm told.

As the plane taxis out onto the runway, we sip our champagne, grinning inanely at each other. I can't believe it. At twenty-two years old, I'm finally leaving the United States and going to Europe—to *London* of all places.

Once we're airborne, Natalia serves us yet more champagne and prepares our wedding feast. And what a feast it is—smoked salmon, followed by roast partridge with a green bean salad and *dauphinoise* potatoes, all cooked and served by the ever-efficient Natalia.

"Dessert, Mr. Grey?" she asks.

He shakes his head and runs his finger across his bottom lip as he looks questioningly at me, his expression dark and unreadable.

"No, thank you," I murmur, unable to break eye contact with him. His lips curl up in a small, secret smile, and Natalia retreats.

"Good," he murmurs. "I'd rather planned on having you for dessert."

Oh . . . here?

"Come," he says, rising from the table and offering me his hand. He leads me to the back of the cabin.

"There's a bathroom here." He points to a small door, then leads me on down a short corridor and through a door at the end.

Jeez . . . a bedroom. The cabin is cream and maple and the small double bed is covered in gold and taupe cushions. It looks very comfortable.

Christian turns and pulls me into his arms, gazing down at me.

"I thought we'd spend our wedding night at thirty-five thousand feet. It's something I've never done before."

Another first. I gape at him, my heart pounding . . . the mile high club. I've heard about this.

"But first I have to get you out of this fabulous dress." His eyes glow with love and something darker, something I love . . . something that calls to my inner goddess. He takes my breath away.

"Turn around." His voice is low, authoritative, and sexy as hell. How can he infuse so much promise into those two words? Willingly I comply and his hands move to my hair. Gently he pulls out each hairpin one at a time, his expert fingers making short work of the task. My hair falls in swaths over my shoulders, one lock at a time, covering my back and down to my breasts. I try to stand still and not squirm, but I'm aching for his touch. After our long, tiring but exciting day, I want him—all of him.

"You have such beautiful hair, Ana." His mouth is close to my ear and I feel his breath, though his lips don't touch me. When my hair is free of pins, he runs his fingers through it, gently massaging my scalp . . . *oh my* . . . I close my eyes and savor the sensation. His fingers travel on down, and he tugs, tilting my head back to expose my throat.

"You're mine," he breathes, and his teeth tug my ear lobe.

I groan.

"Hush now," he admonishes. He sweeps my hair over my shoulder and trails a finger across the top of my back from shoulder to shoulder, following the lace edge of my dress. I shiver in anticipation. He plants a tender kiss on my back above the first button on my dress.

"So beautiful," he says as he deftly undoes the first button. "You have made me the happiest man alive today." With infinite slowness, he unfastens each button, all the way down my back. "I love you so much." Trailing kisses from the nape of my neck to the edge of my shoulder. Between each kiss he murmurs, "I. Want. You. So. Much. I. Want. To. Be. Inside. You. You. Are. Mine."

Each word is intoxicating. I close my eyes and tilt my head, giving him easier access to my neck, and I fall further under the spell that is Christian Grey, my husband.

"Mine," he whispers once more. He peels my dress down my arms so that it pools at my feet in a cloud of ivory silk and lace.

"Turn around," he whispers, his voice suddenly hoarse. I do so and he gasps.

I'm dressed in a tight, blush-pink satin corset with garter straps, matching lacy briefs, and white silk stockings. Christian's eyes travel greedily down my body, but he says nothing. He just gazes at me, his eyes wide with want.

"You like?" I whisper, aware of the shy blush creeping across my cheeks.

"More than like, baby. You look sensational. Here." He holds out his hand and, taking it, I step out of my dress.

"Keep still," he murmurs, and without taking his darkening eyes off mine, he runs his middle finger over my breasts, following the line of my corset. My breath shallows, and he repeats the journey over my breasts once more, his tantalizing finger sending tingles down my spine. He stops and twirls his index finger in the air, indicating that he wants me to turn around.

For him, right now, I'd do anything.

"Stop," he says. I'm facing the bed, away from him. His arm encircles my waist, pulling me against him, and he nuzzles my neck. Gently he cups my breasts, toying with them, while his thumbs circle over my nipples so that they strain against the fabric of my corset.

"Mine," he whispers.

"Yours," I breathe.

Leaving my breasts bereft he runs his hands down my stomach, over my belly, and down to my thighs, his thumbs skimming my sex. I stifle a moan. His fingers skate down each garter, and with his usual dexterity, he simultaneously unhooks each one from my stockings. His hands travel around to my behind.

"Mine," he breathes as his hands spread across my backside, the tips of his fingers brushing my sex.

"Ah."

"Hush." His hands travel down the backs of my thighs, and once more he unclips my garters.

Leaning down, he pulls back the cover on the bed. "Sit down."

In his thrall, I do as I'm told, and he kneels at my feet and gently tugs off each of my white bridal Jimmy Choos. He grasps the top of my left stocking and slowly peels it off, running his thumbs down my leg . . . He repeats the process with my other stocking.

"This is like unwrapping my Christmas presents." He smiles up at me through his long dark lashes.

"A present you've had already . . ."

He frowns in admonishment. "Oh no, baby. This time it's really mine."

"Christian, I've been yours since I said yes." I scoot forward, cupping his beloved face in my hands. "I'm yours. I will always be yours, husband of mine. Now, I think you're wearing too many clothes." I bend to kiss him, and suddenly he leans up, kisses my lips, and grasps my head with his hands, his fingers threading into my hair.

"Ana," he breathes. "My Ana." His lips claim mine once more, his tongue invasively persuasive.

"Clothes," I whisper, our breath mingling as I push back his vest and he struggles out of it, releasing me for a moment. He pauses, gazing at me, eyes wide, eyes wanting.

"Let me, please." My voice is soft and cajoling. I want to undress my husband, my Fifty.

He sits back on his heels, and leaning forward I grasp his tie— his silver-gray tie, my favorite tie—and slowly undo it and pull it free. He raises his chin to let me tackle the top button of his white shirt; then once it's undone, I move on to his cuffs. He's wearing platinum cuff links—engraved with an entwined A and C—my wedding present to him. When I've removed them, he takes the cuff links from me and fists them in his hand. Then he kisses his fist and shoves them into his pants pocket.

"Mr. Grey, so romantic."

"For you Mrs. Grey—hearts and flowers. Always."

I take his hand and, glancing up through my lashes, kiss his plain platinum wedding ring. He groans and closes his eyes.

"Ana," he whispers, and my name is a prayer.

Reaching up to his second shirt button and mirroring him from earlier, I plant a soft kiss on his chest as I undo each of them and whisper between each kiss, "You. Make. Me. So. Happy. I. Love. You."

He groans, and in one swift move, he clasps me around the waist and lifts me onto the bed, following me down on it. His lips find mine, his hands curling around my head, holding me, stilling me as our tongues glory in each other. Abruptly Christian kneels up, leaving me breathless and wanting more.

"You are so beautiful . . . wife." He runs his hands down my legs, then grasps my left foot. "You have such lovely legs. I want to kiss every inch of them. Starting here." He presses his lips against my big toe and then grazes the pad with his teeth. Everything south of my waistline convulses. His tongue glides up my instep and his teeth skim my heel and up to my ankle. He trails kisses up the inside of my calf; soft wet kisses. I wriggle beneath him.

"Still, Mrs. Grey," he warns, and suddenly he flips me onto my stomach and continues his leisurely journey with his mouth up the backs of my legs, to my thighs, my behind, and then he stops. I groan.

"Please . . ."

"I want you naked," he murmurs and slowly unhooks my corset, one hook at a time. When it's flat on the bed beneath me, he runs his tongue up the length of my spine.

"Christian, please."

"What do you want, Mrs. Grey?" His words are soft and close to my ear. He's almost lying on top of me . . . I can feel him hard against my behind.

"You."

"And I you, my love, my life . . . ," he whispers, and before I know it, he's flipped me onto my back. He stands swiftly and in one efficient move dispenses with his pants and boxer briefs so that he's gloriously naked and looming large and ready over me. The small cabin is eclipsed by his dazzling beauty and his want and need of me. He leans down and peels off my panties, then gazes at me.

"Mine," he mouths.

"Please," I beg and he grins . . . a salacious, wicked, tempting, all-Fifty grin.

He crawls back onto the bed and trails kisses up my right leg this time . . . until he reaches the apex of my thighs. He pushes my legs wider apart.

"Ah . . . wife of mine," he murmurs, and then his mouth is on me. I close my eyes and surrender to his oh-so-adroit tongue. My hands fist in his hair as my hips swing and sway, slave to his rhythm, then buck off the small bed. He grabs my hips to still me . . . but doesn't stop the delicious torture. I'm close, so close.

"Christian." I moan.

"Not yet," he breathes, and he moves up my body, his tongue dipping into my navel.

"No!" *Damn!* I sense his smile against my belly as his journey continues north.

"So impatient, Mrs. Grey. We have until we touch down on the Emerald Isle." Reverentially he kisses my breasts and tugs my left nipple between his lips. Gazing up at me, his eyes are dark like a tropical storm as he teases me.

Oh my . . . I'd forgotten. *Europe.*

"Husband, I want you. Please."

He looms up over me, his body covering mine, resting his weight on his elbows. He runs his nose down mine, and I run my hands down his strong, supple back to his fine, fine backside.

"Mrs. Grey . . . wife. We aim to please." His lips brush. "I love you."

"I love you, too."

"Eyes open. I want to see you."

"Christian . . . ah . . . ," I cry, as he slowly sinks into me.

"Ana, oh Ana," he breathes, and he starts to move.

"WHAT THE HELL DO you think you're doing?" Christian shouts, waking me from my very pleasant dream. He's standing all wet and beautiful at the end of my sun lounge and glaring down at me.

What have I done? *Oh no . . . I'm lying on my back* . . . Crap, crap, crap, and he's mad. Shit. He's really mad.

CHAPTER TWO

I am suddenly very awake, my erotic dream forgotten.

"I was on my front. I must have turned over in my sleep," I whisper weakly in my defense.

His eyes blaze with fury. He reaches down, scoops up my bikini top from his sun lounge, and tosses it at me.

"Put this on!" he hisses.

"Christian, no one is looking."

"Trust me. They're looking. I'm sure Taylor and the security crew are enjoying the show!" he snarls.

Holy shit! Why do I keep forgetting about them? I grasp my breasts in panic, hiding them. Ever since *Charlie Tango*'s sabotaged demise, we are constantly shadowed by damned security.

"Yes," Christian snarls. "And some sleazy fucking paparazzi could get a shot of you, too. Do you want to be all over the cover of *Star* magazine? Naked this time?"

Shit! The paparazzi! Fuck! As I hurriedly scramble into my top, all thumbs, the color drains from my face. I shudder. The unpleasant memory of being besieged by the paparazzi outside Seattle Independent Publishing after our engagement was leaked comes unwelcome to mind—all part of the Christian Grey package.

"*L'addition!*" Christian snaps at the passing waitress. "We're going," he says to me.

"Now?"

"Yes. Now."

Oh shit, he's not to be argued with.

He pulls on his shorts, even though his trunks are dripping wet, then his gray T-shirt. The waitress is back in a moment with his credit card and the check.

Reluctantly, I wriggle into my turquoise sundress and step into my flip-flops. Once the waitress has left, Christian snatches up his book and BlackBerry and masks his fury behind mirrored aviator sunglasses. He's bristling with tension and anger. My heart sinks. Every other woman on the beach is topless—it's not that big a crime. In fact, I look odd with my top *on*. I sigh inwardly, my spirits sinking. I thought Christian would see the funny side . . . sort of . . . Maybe if I'd stayed on my front, but his sense of humor has evaporated.

"Please don't be mad at me," I whisper, taking his book and BlackBerry from him and placing them in my backpack.

"Too late for that," he says quietly—too quietly. "Come." Taking my hand, he signals up to Taylor and his two sidekicks, the French security officers Philippe and Gaston. Weirdly, they are identical twins. They have been patiently watching us and everyone else on the beach from the veranda. Why do I keep forgetting about them? How? Taylor is stony-faced behind his dark glasses. Shit, he's mad at me, too. I'm still not used to seeing him so casually dressed, in shorts and a black polo shirt.

Christian leads me into the hotel, through the lobby, and out onto the street. He remains silent, brooding and bad-tempered, and it's all my fault. Taylor and his team shadow us.

"Where are we going?" I ask tentatively, gazing up at him.

"Back to the boat." He doesn't look at me.

I have no idea of the time. I think it must be about five or six in the afternoon. When we reach the marina, Christian leads me onto the dock, where the motorboat and Jet Ski belonging to the *Fair Lady* are moored. As Christian unties the Jet Ski, I hand my backpack to Taylor. I glance nervously up at him, but like Christian, his expression gives nothing away. I flush, thinking about what he's seen on the beach.

"Here you go, Mrs. Grey." Taylor passes me a life vest from the motorboat, and I dutifully put it on. Why am I the only one who has to wear a life jacket? Christian and Taylor exchange some kind of look. Jeez, is he angry with Taylor, too? Christian then checks the straps on my life jacket, cinching the middle one tightly.

"You'll do," he mutters sullenly, still not turning to look at me. *Shit.*

He climbs gracefully onto the Jet Ski and holds out his hand for me to join him. Grasping it tightly, I manage to throw my leg over the seat behind him without falling into the water while Taylor and the twins clamber into the motorboat. Christian kicks the Jet Ski away from the dock, and it floats gently into the marina.

"Hold on," he orders, and I put my arms around him. This is my favorite part of traveling by Jet Ski. I hug him closely, my nose nuzzling into his back, marveling that there was a time when he would not have tolerated me touching him this way. He smells good . . . of Christian and the sea. *Forgive me, Christian, please?*

He stiffens. "Steady," he says, his tone softer. I kiss his back and rest my cheek against him, looking back toward the dock where a few holidaymakers have gathered to watch the show.

Christian turns the key and the motor roars to life. With one twist of the accelerator, the Jet Ski bucks forward and speeds across the cool dark water, through the marina, and out to the center of the harbor toward the *Fair Lady*. I hold him tighter. I love this— it's so exciting. Every muscle in Christian's lean frame is evident as I cling to him.

Taylor pulls alongside in the motorboat. Christian glances at him, then accelerates again, and we shoot forward, whipping over the top of the water like an expertly tossed pebble. Taylor shakes his head in resigned exasperation and heads straight to the yacht, while Christian shoots past the *Fair Lady* and heads out toward the open water.

The sea spray is splashing us, the warm wind buffeting my face and flaying my ponytail crazily around me. This is so much *fun.* Maybe the thrill of this ride will dispel Christian's bad mood. I can't see his face, but I know he's enjoying himself—carefree, acting his age for a change.

He steers in a huge semicircle and I study the shoreline—the boats in the marina, the mosaic of yellow, white, and sand-colored offices and apartments, and the craggy mountains behind. It looks so disorganized—not the regimented blocks that I am used to—

but so picturesque. Christian glances over his shoulder at me, and there's the ghost of a smile playing on his lips.

"Again?" he shouts over the noise of the engine.

I nod enthusiastically. His answering grin is dazzling, and he opens the throttle and speeds around the *Fair Lady* and on out to sea once more . . . and I think I'm forgiven.

"YOU'VE CAUGHT THE SUN," Christian says mildly as he undoes my life vest. I anxiously try to assess his mood. We are on deck aboard the yacht, and one of the stewards is standing quietly nearby, waiting for my life vest. Christian passes it to him.

"Will that be all, sir?" the young man asks. I love his French accent. Christian glances at me, takes off his shades, and slips them into the collar of his T-shirt, letting them hang.

"Would you like a drink?" he asks me.

"Do I need one?"

He cocks his head to one side. "Why would you say that?" His voice is soft.

"You know why."

He frowns as if weighing something in his mind.

Oh, what is he thinking?

"Two gin and tonics, please. And some nuts and olives," he says to the steward, who nods and quickly vanishes.

"You think I'm going to punish you?" Christian's voice is silky.

"Do you want to?"

"Yes."

"How?"

"I'll think of something. Maybe when you've had your drink." And it's a sensual threat. I swallow, and my inner goddess squints from her sun lounge where she's trying to catch rays with a silver reflector fanned out at her neck.

Christian frowns once more.

"You want to be?"

How does he know? "Depends," I mutter, flushing.

"On what?" He hides his smile.

"If you want to hurt me or not."

His mouth presses into a hard line, humor forgotten. He leans forward and kisses my forehead.

"Anastasia, you're my wife, not my sub. I don't ever want to hurt you. You should know that by now. Just . . . just don't take your clothes off in public. I don't want you naked all over the tabloids. You don't want that, and I'm sure your mom and Ray don't want that, either."

Oh! Ray. Holy shit, he'd have a coronary. What was I thinking? I mentally castigate myself.

The steward appears with our drinks and snacks and places them on the teak table.

"Sit," Christian commands. I do as he says and settle into a director's chair. Christian takes a seat beside me and passes me a gin and tonic.

"Cheers, Mrs. Grey."

"Cheers, Mr. Grey." I take a welcome sip. It's thirst-quenching, cold, and delicious. When I gaze at him, he's watching me carefully, his mood unreadable. It's very frustrating . . . I don't know if he's still mad at me. I deploy my patented distraction technique.

"Who owns this boat?" I ask.

"A British knight. Sir Somebody-or-Other. His great-grandfather started a grocery store. His daughter's married to one of the crown princes of Europe."

Oh. "Super-rich?"

Christian looks suddenly wary. "Yes."

"Like you," I murmur.

"Yes."

Oh.

"And like you," Christian whispers and pops an olive into his mouth. I blink rapidly . . . a vision of him in his tux and silver waistcoat comes to mind . . . his eyes burning with sincerity as he gazes down at me during our wedding ceremony.

"All that is mine is now yours," he says, his voice ringing out clearly, reciting his vows from memory.

All mine? "It's odd. Going from nothing to"—I wave my hand to indicate our opulent surroundings—"to everything."

"You'll get used to it."

"I don't think I'll ever get used to it."

Taylor appears on deck. "Sir, you have a call." Christian frowns but takes the proffered BlackBerry.

"Grey," he snaps and rises from his seat to stand at the bow of the yacht.

I gaze out at the sea, tuning out his conversation with Ros—I think—his number two. I am rich . . . stinking rich. I have done nothing to earn this money . . . just married a rich man. I shudder as my mind drifts back to our conversation about prenups. It was the Sunday after his birthday, and we were seated at the kitchen table enjoying a leisurely breakfast . . . all of us. Elliot, Kate, Grace, and I were debating the merits of bacon versus sausage, while Carrick and Christian read the Sunday paper . . .

————

"Look at this," squeals Mia as she sets her netbook on the kitchen table in front of us. "There's a gossipy item on the Seattle Nooz Web site about you being engaged, Christian."

"Already?" Grace says in surprise. Then her mouth purses as some obviously unpleasant thought crosses her mind. Christian frowns.

Mia reads the column out loud. "Word has reached us here at the Nooz that Seattle's most eligible bachelor, *the* Christian Grey, has finally been snapped up and wedding bells are in the air. But who is the lucky, lucky lady? The Nooz is on the hunt. Bet she's reading one helluva prenup."

Mia giggles, then stops abruptly as Christian glares at her. Silence descends, and the atmosphere in the Grey kitchen plunges to below zero.

Oh no! A prenup? The thought has never crossed my mind. I swallow, feeling all the blood drain from my face. *Please ground, swallow me up now!* Christian shifts uncomfortably in his chair as I glance apprehensively at him.

"No," he mouths at me.

"Christian," Carrick says gently.

"I'm not discussing this again," he snaps at Carrick, who glances at me nervously and opens his mouth to say something.

"No prenup!" Christian almost shouts at him and broodingly goes back to reading his paper, ignoring everyone else at the table. They look alternately at me and then him . . . then anywhere but at the two of us.

"Christian," I murmur. "I'll sign anything you and Mr. Grey want." Jeez, it wouldn't be the first time he's made me sign something. Christian looks up and glares at me.

"No!" he snaps. I blanch once more.

"It's to protect you."

"Christian, Ana—I think you should discuss this in private," Grace admonishes us. She glares at Carrick and Mia. Oh dear, looks like they're in trouble, too.

"Ana, this is not about you," Carrick murmurs reassuringly. "And please call me Carrick."

Christian narrows cold eyes at his father and my heart sinks. *Hell . . . He's really mad.*

Everyone erupts into animated conversation, and Mia and Kate leap up to clear the table.

"I definitely prefer sausage," exclaims Elliot.

I stare down at my knotted fingers. Crap. I hope Mr. and Mrs. Grey don't think I'm some kind of gold digger. Christian reaches over and grasps both my hands gently in one of his.

"Stop it."

How does he know what I'm thinking?

"Ignore my dad," Christian says so only I can hear him. "He's really pissed about Elena. That stuff was all aimed at me. I wish my mom had kept her mouth shut."

I know Christian is still smarting from his "talk" with Carrick about Elena last night.

"He has a point, Christian. You're very wealthy, and I'm bringing nothing to our marriage but my student loans."

Christian gazes at me, his eyes bleak. "Anastasia, if you leave me, you might as well take everything. You left me once before. I know how that feels."

Holy fuck! "That was different," I whisper, moved by his intensity. "But . . . you might want to leave me." The thought makes me sick.

He snorts and shakes his head with mock disgust.

"Christian, you know I might do something exceptionally stupid—and you . . ." I glance down at my knotted hands, pain lancing through me, and I'm unable to finish my sentence. Losing Christian . . . *fuck*.

"Stop. Stop now. This subject is closed, Ana. We're not discussing it anymore. No prenup. Not now—not ever." He gives me a pointed give-it-up-now look, which silences me. Then he turns to Grace. "Mom," he says. "Can we have the wedding here?"

————

And he's not mentioned it again. In fact at every opportunity he's tried to reassure me about his wealth . . . that it's mine, too. I shudder as I recall the crazy shopping fest Christian demanded I go on with Caroline Acton—the personal shopper from Nieman Marcus—in preparation for this honeymoon. My bikini alone cost five hundred and forty dollars. I mean, it's nice, but really—that's a ridiculous amount of money for four triangular scraps of material.

"You will get used to it," Christian interrupts my reverie as he resumes his place at the table.

"Used to it?"

"The money," he says, rolling his eyes.

Oh, Fifty, maybe with time. I push the small dish of salted almonds and cashews toward him.

"Your nuts, sir," I say with as straight a face as I can manage, trying to bring some humor to our conversation after my dark thoughts and my bikini top faux pas.

He smirks. "I'm nuts about you." He takes an almond, his eyes sparkling with wicked humor as he enjoys my little joke. He licks his lips. "Drink up. We're going to bed."

What?

"Drink," he mouths at me, his eyes darkening.

Oh my, the look he gives me could be solely responsible for global warming. I pick up my gin and drain the glass, not taking my eyes off him. His mouth drops open, and I glimpse the tip of his tongue between his teeth. He smiles lewdly at me. In one fluid move, he stands and bends over me, resting his hands on the arms of my chair.

"I'm going to make an example of you. Come. Don't pee," he whispers in my ear.

I gasp. *Don't pee? How rude.* My subconscious looks up from her book—*The Complete Works of Charles Dickens, volume 1*—with alarm.

"It's not what you think." Christian smirks, holding his hand out to me. "Trust me." He looks so sexy and genial. How can I resist?

"Okay." I place my hand in his, because quite simply, I'd trust him with my life. What has he got planned? My heart starts pounding in anticipation.

He leads me across the deck and through the doors into the plush, beautifully appointed main salon, along a narrow corridor, through the dining room, and down the stairs to the master cabin.

The cabin has been cleaned since this morning and the bed made. It's a lovely room. With two portholes on both the starboard and port sides, it's elegantly decorated in dark walnut furniture with cream walls and soft furnishings in gold and red.

Christian releases my hand, pulls his T-shirt over his head, and tosses it onto a chair. He steps out of his flip-flops and removes his shorts and trunks in one graceful move. *Oh my. Will I ever tire of looking at him naked?* He is utterly gorgeous and all mine. His skin glows—he's caught the sun, too, and his hair is longer, flopping over his forehead. I am one lucky, lucky girl.

He grasps my chin, pulling slightly so that I stop biting my lip, and runs his thumb along my lower lip.

"That's better." He turns and strides over to the impressive armoire that houses his clothes. He produces two pairs of metal handcuffs and an airline eye mask from the bottom drawer.

Handcuffs! We've never used handcuffs. I glance quickly and nervously at the bed. Where the hell is he going to attach those? He turns and gazes steadily at me, his eyes dark and luminous.

"These can be quite painful. They can bite into the skin if you pull too hard." He holds up one pair. "But I really want to use them on you now."

Holy fuck. My mouth goes dry.

"Here." He stalks gracefully forward and hands me a set. "Do you want to try them first?"

They feel solid, the metal cold. Vaguely, I hope I never have to wear a pair of these for real.

Christian is watching me intently.

"Where are the keys?" My voice wavers.

He holds out his palm, revealing a small metallic key. "This does both sets. In fact, all sets."

How many sets does he have? I don't remember seeing any in the museum chest.

He strokes my cheek with his index finger, trailing it down to my mouth. He leans in as if to kiss me.

"Do you want to play?" he says, his voice low, and everything in my body heads south as desire unfurls deep in my belly.

"Yes," I breathe.

He smiles. "Good." He plants a featherlight kiss on my forehead. "We're going to need a safeword."

What?

"'*Stop*' won't be enough because you will probably say that, but you won't mean it." He runs his nose down mine—the only contact between us.

My heart starts pounding. *Shit* . . . How can he do this with just words?

"This is not going to hurt. It will be intense. Very intense, because I am not going to let you move. Okay?"

Oh my. This sounds so hot. My breathing is too loud. *Fuck, I am panting already.* Thank heavens I'm married to this man, otherwise this would be embarrassing. My eyes flick down to his arousal.

"Okay." My voice is barely audible.

"Choose a word, Ana."

Oh . . .

"A safeword," he says softly.

"Popsicle," I say, panting.

"Popsicle?" he says, amused.

"Yes."

He grins as he leans back to gaze down at me. "Interesting choice. Lift up your arms."

I do, and Christian grasps the hem of my sundress, lifts it over my head, and tosses it on the floor. He holds out his hand, and I give him back the handcuffs. He places both sets on the bedside table along with the blindfold and yanks the quilt off the bed, letting it fall to the floor.

"Turn around."

I turn, and he undoes my bikini top so that it falls to the floor.

"Tomorrow, I will staple this to you," he mutters and tugs on my hair tie, freeing my hair. He gathers it into one hand and yanks gently so I step back against him. Against his chest. Against his erection. I gasp as he pulls my head to one side and kisses my neck.

"You were very disobedient," he murmurs in my ear, sending delicious shivers through me.

"Yes," I whisper.

"Hmm. What are we going to do about that?"

"Learn to live with it," I breathe. His soft languid kisses are driving me wild. He grins against my neck.

"Ah, Mrs. Grey. You are ever the optimist."

He straightens. Taking my hair, he carefully parts it into three strands, braids it slowly, and then fastens my hair tie to the end. He tugs my braid gently and leans down to my ear. "I am going to teach you a lesson," he murmurs.

Moving suddenly, he grabs me by the waist, sits down on the bed, and yanks me across his knee so that I feel his erection pressed against my belly. He smacks my backside once, hard. I yelp, then I'm on my back on the bed, and he's gazing down at me, his eyes molten gray. I'm going to combust.

"Do you know how beautiful you are?" He trails his fingertips up my thigh so that I tingle . . . everywhere. Without taking his eyes off me, he gets up from the bed and gathers both sets of hand-cuffs. He grasps my left leg and snaps one cuff around my ankle. *Oh!*

Lifting my right leg, he repeats the process so I have a pair of handcuffs attached to each ankle. I still have no idea where he's going to attach them.

"Sit up," he orders, and I comply immediately.

"Now hug your knees."

I blink at him, then draw my legs up so they are bent in front of me and wrap my arms around them. He reaches down, lifts my chin, and plants a soft wet kiss on my lips before slipping the blindfold over my eyes. I can see nothing; all I can hear is my rapid breathing and the sound of the water lapping against the sides of the yacht as she bobs gently on the sea.

Oh my. I am so aroused . . . already.

"What's the safeword, Anastasia?"

"Popsicle."

"Good." Taking my left hand, he snaps a cuff around my wrist then repeats the process with my right. My left hand is tied to my left ankle, my right hand to my right leg. I cannot straighten my legs. *Holy fuck.*

"Now," Christian breathes, "I'm going to fuck you till you scream."

What? And all the air leaves my body.

He grasps both of my heels and tips me back so that I fall backward on the bed. I have no choice but to keep my legs bent. The cuffs tighten as I pull against them. He's right . . . they cut into me almost to the point of pain . . . This feels weird—being trussed up and helpless—on a boat. He pulls my ankles apart, and I groan.

He kisses my inner thigh, and I want to squirm beneath him, but I can't. I have no purchase to move my hips. My feet are suspended. I cannot move.

"You're going to have to absorb all the pleasure, Anastasia. No moving," he murmurs as he crawls up my body, kissing me along the edge of my bikini bottoms. He pulls the strings on each side, and the scraps of material fall away. I am now naked and at his mercy. He kisses my belly, nipping my navel with his teeth.

"Ah," I sigh. This is going to be tough . . . I had no idea. He traces soft kisses and little bites up to my breasts.

"Shhh . . . ," he soothes. "You are so beautiful, Ana."

I groan, frustrated. Normally I'd be grinding my hips, responding to his touch with a rhythm of my own, but I cannot move. I moan, pulling on my restraints. The metal bites into my skin.

"Argh!" I cry. But I really don't care.

"You drive me crazy," he whispers. "So I am going to drive you crazy." He's resting on me now, his weight on his elbows, and he turns his attention to my breasts. Biting, sucking, rolling my nipples between his fingers and thumbs, driving me wild. He doesn't stop. It's maddening. *Oh. Please.* His erection pushes against me.

"Christian," I beg and feel his triumphant smile against my skin.

"Shall I make you come this way?" He murmurs against my nipple, causing it to harden some more. "You know I can." He suckles me hard and I cry out, pleasure lancing from my chest directly to my groin. I pull helplessly on the cuffs, swamped by the sensation.

"Yes," I whimper.

"Oh, baby, that would be too easy."

"Oh . . . please."

"Shh." His teeth scrape my chin as he trails his lips to my mouth, and I gasp. He kisses me. His skilled tongue invades my mouth, tasting, exploring, dominating, but my tongue meets his challenge, writhing against his. He tastes of cool gin and Christian Grey, and he smells of the sea. He grasps my chin, holding my head in place.

"Still, baby. I want you still," he whispers against my mouth.

"I want to see you."

"Oh no, Ana. You'll feel more this way." And, agonizingly slowly, he flexes his hips and pushes partway into me. I would normally tilt my pelvis up to meet him but I can't move. He withdraws.

"Ah! Christian, please!"

"Again?" he teases, his voice hoarse.

"Christian!"

He pushes fractionally into me again, then withdraws while kissing me, his fingers tugging at my nipple. It's pleasure overload.

"No!"

"Do you want me, Anastasia?"

"Yes," I beg.

"Tell me," he murmurs, his breathing harsh, and he teases me once more—in . . . and out.

"I want you," I whimper. "Please."

I hear his soft sigh against my ear.

"And have me you will, Anastasia."

He rears up and slams into me. I scream, tilting my head back, pulling on the restraints as he hits my sweet spot, and I am all sensation, everywhere—a sweet, sweet agony, and I cannot move. He stills, then circles his hips, and the motion radiates deep inside me.

"Why do you defy me, Ana?"

"Christian, stop . . ."

He circles deep inside me again, ignoring my plea, easing out slowly and then slamming into me again.

"Tell me. Why?" he hisses, and I'm vaguely aware that it's through gritted teeth.

I cry out in an incoherent wail . . . this is too much.

"Tell me."

"Christian . . ."

"Ana, I need to know."

He slams into me again, thrusting so deep, and I'm building . . . the feeling is so intense—it swamps me, spiraling out from deep within my belly, to each limb, to each biting metal restraint.

"I don't know!" I cry out. "Because I can! Because I love you! Please, Christian."

He groans loudly and thrusts deep, again and again, over and over, and I am lost, trying to absorb the pleasure. It's mind-blowing . . . body blowing . . . I long to straighten my legs, to control my imminent orgasm, but I can't . . . I'm helpless. I'm his, just his, to do with as he wills . . . Tears spring to my eyes. This is too intense. I can't stop him. I don't want to stop him . . . I want . . . I want . . . oh no, oh no . . . this is too . . .

"That's it," Christian growls. "Feel it, baby!"

I detonate around him, again and again, round and round, screaming loudly as my orgasm rips me apart, scorching through me like a wildfire, consuming everything. I am wrung ragged, tears streaming down my face—my body left pulsing and shaking.

And I'm aware that Christian kneels, still inside me, pulling me upright onto his lap. He clutches my head with one hand and my back with the other, and he comes violently inside me while my insides continue to tremble with aftershocks. It's draining, it's exhausting, it's hell . . . it's heaven. It's hedonism gone wild.

Christian tears off the blindfold and kisses me. He kisses my eyes, my nose, my cheeks. He kisses away the tears, clutching my face between his hands.

"I love you, Mrs. Grey," he breathes. "Even though you make me so mad—I feel so alive with you." I don't have the energy to open either my eyes or my mouth to respond. Very gently, he lays me back on the bed and eases out of me.

I mouth some wordless protest. He climbs off the bed and undoes the handcuffs. When I'm free, he gently rubs my wrists and ankles, then lies down beside me again, pulling me into his arms. I stretch out my legs. Oh my, that feels good. I feel good. That was, without doubt, the most intense climax I have ever endured. Hmm . . . a Christian Grey Fifty Shades punishment fuck.

I really must misbehave more often.

A PRESSING NEED FROM my bladder wakes me. When I open my eyes, I'm disoriented. It's dark outside. *Where am I?* London? Paris? Oh—the boat. I feel her pitch and roll, and hear the quiet hum of the engines. We're on the move. *How odd.* Christian is beside me, working on his laptop, casually dressed in a white linen shirt and chino trousers, his feet bare. His hair is still wet, and I can smell his body wash fresh from the shower and his Christian smell . . . *Hmm.*

"Hi," he murmurs, gazing down at me, his eyes warm.

"Hi." I smile, feeling suddenly shy. "How long have I been asleep?"

"Just an hour or so."

"We're moving?"

"I figured since we ate out last night and went to the ballet and the casino that we'd dine on board tonight. A quiet night *à deux.*"

I grin at him. "Where are we going?"

"Cannes."

"Okay." I stretch, feeling stiff. No amount of training with Claude could have prepared me for this afternoon.

I rise gingerly, needing the bathroom. Grabbing my silk robe, I hastily put it on. Why am I so shy? I feel Christian's eyes on me. When I glance at him, he returns to his laptop, his brow furrowed.

As I absentmindedly wash my hands at the vanity unit, recalling last night at the casino, my robe falls open. I stare at myself in the mirror, shocked.

Holy fuck! What has he done to me?

CHAPTER THREE

I gaze in horror at the red marks all over my breasts. Hickeys! I have hickeys! I am married to one of the most respected businessmen in the United States, and he's given me goddamn hickeys. How did I not feel him doing this to me? I flush. The fact is I know exactly why—Mr. Orgasmic was using his fine-motor sexing skills on me.

My subconscious peers over her half-moon specs and tuts disapprovingly, while my inner goddess slumbers on her chaise longue, out for the count. I gape at my reflection. My wrists have red welts around them from the handcuffs. No doubt they'll bruise. I examine my ankles—more welts. Holy hell, I look like I've been in some sort of accident. I gaze at myself, trying to absorb how I look. My body is so different these days. It's changed subtly since I've known him . . . I've become leaner and fitter, and my hair is glossy and well cut. My nails are manicured, my feet pedicured, my eyebrows threaded and beautifully shaped. For the first time in my life, I'm well groomed—except for these hideous love bites.

I don't want to think about grooming at the moment. I'm too mad. How dare he mark me like this, like some teenager. In the short time we've been together, he's never given me hickeys. I look like hell. I know why he's done this. Damn control freak. *Right!* My subconscious folds her arms beneath her small bosom—he's gone too far this time. I stalk out of the en suite bathroom and into the walk-in closet, carefully avoiding even a glance in his direction. Slipping out of my robe, I pull on my sweatpants and a camisole. I undo the braid, pick up a hairbrush from the small vanity unit, and brush out my tangles.

"Anastasia," Christian calls and I hear his anxiety. "Are you okay?"

I ignore him. *Am I okay? No, I am not okay.* After what he's done to me, I doubt I'll be able to wear a swimsuit, let alone one of my ridiculously expensive bikinis, for the rest of our honeymoon. The thought is suddenly so infuriating. How *dare* he? I'll give him *are you okay.* I seethe as fury spikes through me. I can behave like an adolescent, too! Stepping back into the bedroom, I hurl the hairbrush at him, turn, and leave—though not before I see his shocked expression and his lightning reaction as he raises his arm to protect his head so that the brush bounces ineffectively off his forearm and onto the bed.

I storm out of our cabin, bolt upstairs and out on deck, fleeing toward the bow. I need some space to calm down. It's dark and the air is balmy. The warm breeze carries the smell of the Mediterranean and the scent of jasmine and bougainvillea from the shore. The *Fair Lady* glides effortlessly through the calm cobalt sea as I rest my elbows on the wooden railing, gazing at the distant shore where tiny lights wink and twinkle. I take a deep, healing breath and slowly begin to calm. I'm aware of him behind me before I hear him.

"You're mad at me," he whispers.

"No shit, Sherlock!"

"How mad?"

"Scale of one to ten, I think I'm at fifty. Apt, huh?"

"That mad." He sounds surprised and impressed at once.

"Yes. Pushed to violence mad," I say through gritted teeth.

He stays silent as I turn and scowl at him, watching me with wide and wary eyes. I know from his expression and because he's made no move to touch me that he's out of his depth.

"Christian, you have to stop unilaterally trying to bring me to heel. You made your point on the beach. Very effectively, as I recall."

He shrugs minutely. "Well, you won't take your top off again," he murmurs petulantly.

And this justifies what he's done to me? I glare at him. "I don't like you leaving marks on me. Well, not this many, anyway. It's a hard limit!" I hiss at him.

"I don't like you taking your clothes off in public. That's a hard limit for me," he growls.

"I think we've established that," I hiss through my teeth. "Look at me!" I pull down my camisole to reveal the top of my breasts. Christian gazes at me, his eyes not leaving my face, his expression wary and uncertain. He's not used to seeing me this mad. Can't he see what he's done? Can't he see how ridiculous he is? I want to shout at him, but I refrain—I don't want to push him too far. Heaven knows what he'd do. Eventually, he sighs and holds his palms up in a resigned, conciliatory gesture.

"Okay," he says, his voice placating. "I get it."

Hallelujah!

"Good!"

He runs his hand through his hair. "I'm sorry. Please don't be mad at me." Finally, he looks contrite—using my own words back at me.

"You are such an adolescent sometimes," I scold him, mulishly, but the fight has gone out of my voice, and he knows it. He steps closer and tentatively raises his hand to tuck my hair behind my ear.

"I know," he acknowledges softly. "I have a lot to learn."

Dr. Flynn's words come back to me . . . *Emotionally, Christian is an adolescent, Ana. He bypassed that phase in his life totally. He's channeled all his energies into succeeding in the business world, and he has beyond all expectations. His emotional world has to play catch-up.*

My heart thaws a little.

"We both do." I sigh and cautiously raise my hand, placing it over his heart. He doesn't flinch like he used to, but he stiffens. He rests his hand over mine and smiles his shy smile.

"I've just learned that you've a good arm and a good aim, Mrs. Grey. I would never have figured that, but then I constantly underestimate you. You always surprise me."

I arch my eyebrow at him. "Target practice with Ray. I can throw and shoot straight, Mr. Grey, and you'd do well to remember that."

"I will endeavor to do that, Mrs. Grey, or ensure that all potential projectile objects are nailed down and that you don't have access to a gun." He smirks.

I smirk back, narrowing my eyes. "I'm resourceful."

"That you are," he whispers and releases my hand to circle his arms around me. Pulling me into an embrace, he buries his nose in my hair. I wrap my arms around him, holding him close, and feel the tension leave his body as he nuzzles me.

"Am I forgiven?"

"Am I?"

I feel his smile. "Yes," he answers.

"Ditto."

We stand holding each other, my pique forgotten. He does smell good, adolescent or not. How can I resist him?

"Hungry?" he says after a while. I have my eyes closed and my head against his chest.

"Yes. Famished. All the . . . er . . . activity has given me an appetite. But I'm not dressed for dinner." I'm sure my sweatpants and camisole would be frowned upon in the dining room.

"You look good to me, Anastasia. Besides, it's our boat for the week. We can dress how we like. Think of it as dress down Tuesday on the Cote D'Azur. Anyway, I thought we'd eat on deck."

"Yes, I'd like that."

He kisses me—an earnest forgive-me kiss—then we wander hand in hand toward the bow, where our gazpacho awaits.

THE STEWARD SERVES OUR crème brulée and discreetly retires.

"Why do you always braid my hair?" I ask Christian out of curiosity. We're sitting adjacent to each other at the table, my lower leg curled around his. He pauses as he's about to pick up his dessertspoon and frowns.

"I don't want your hair catching in anything," he says quietly, and for a moment, he's lost in thought. "Habit, I think," he muses. Suddenly he frowns and his eyes widen, his pupils dilating with alarm.

What's he remembered? It's something painful, some early childhood memory, I guess. I don't want to remind him of that. Leaning over, I put my index finger over his lips.

"No, it doesn't matter. I don't need to know. I was just curious." I give him a warm, reassuring smile. His look is wary, but after a moment he visibly relaxes, his relief evident. I lean over to kiss the corner of his mouth.

"I love you," I murmur, and he smiles his heart-achingly shy smile, and I melt. "I will always love you, Christian."

"And I you," he says softly.

"In spite of my disobedience?" I raise my eyebrow.

"Because of your disobedience, Anastasia." He grins.

I crack my spoon through the burned sugar crust of my dessert and shake my head. Will I ever understand this man? Hmm—this crème brulée is delicious.

ONCE THE STEWARD HAS cleared our dessert plates, Christian reaches for the bottle of rosé and refills my glass. I check that we're alone and ask, "What's with the no going to the bathroom thing?"

"You really want to know?" He half smiles, his eyes alight with a salacious gleam.

"Do I?" I gaze at him through my lashes as I take a sip of my wine.

"The fuller your bladder, the more intense your orgasm, Ana." I blush. "Oh. I see." Holy cow, that explains a lot.

He grins, looking far too knowing. Will I always be on the back foot with Mr. Sexpertise?

"Yes. Well . . ." I desperately hunt around for a change of subject. He takes pity on me.

"What do you want to do for the rest of the evening?" He cocks his head to one side and gives me his lopsided grin.

Whatever you want, Christian. Put your theory to the test again? I shrug.

"I know what I want to do," he murmurs. Grabbing his glass of wine, he rises and holds his hand out to me. "Come."

I take his hand and he leads me into the main salon.

His iPod is in the speaker dock on the dresser. He switches it on and selects a song.

"Dance with me." He pulls me into his arms.

"If you insist."

"I insist, Mrs. Grey."

A slinky, cheesy melody starts. Is this a Latin rhythm? Christian grins down at me and starts to move, sweeping me off my feet and taking me with him around the salon.

A man with a voice like warm melted caramel croons. It's a song I know but can't place. Christian dips me low, and I yelp in surprise and giggle. He smiles, his eyes filled with humor. Then he scoops me up and spins me under his arm.

"You dance so well," I say. "It's like I can dance."

He gives me a sphinxlike smile but says nothing, and I wonder if it's because he's thinking of her . . . Mrs. Robinson, the woman who taught him how to dance—and how to fuck. She hasn't crossed my mind for a while. Christian has not mentioned her since his birthday, and as far as I'm aware, their business relationship is over. Reluctantly though, I have to admit—she was some teacher.

He dips me low again and plants a swift kiss on my lips.

"I'd miss your love," I murmur, echoing the lyrics.

"I'd more than miss your love," he says and spins me once more. Then he sings the words softly in my ear, making me swoon.

The track ends and Christian gazes down at me, his eyes dark and luminous, all humor gone, and I'm suddenly breathless.

"Come to bed with me?" he whispers, and it's a heartfelt plea that tugs at my heart.

Christian, you had me at "I do"—two and half weeks ago. But I know this is his way of apologizing and making sure all is well between us after our spat.

WHEN I WAKE, THE sun is shining through the portholes and the water reflects shimmering patterns onto the cabin ceiling. Christian is nowhere to be seen. I stretch out and smile. Hmm . . . I'll take a punishment fuck followed by makeup sex any day. I marvel at what it is to go to bed with two different men—angry Christian and sweet let-me-make-it-up-to-you-in-any-way-I-can Christian. It's tricky to decide which of them I like the best.

I rise and head for the bathroom. Opening the door, I find Christian inside shaving, naked except for a towel wrapped around his waist. He turns and beams, not fazed that I am interrupting him. I have discovered that Christian will never lock the door if he is the only person in the room—the reason is sobering, and not one I want to dwell on.

"Good morning, Mrs. Grey," he says, radiating his good mood.

"Good morning yourself." I grin back as I watch him shave. I love watching him shave. He pulls up his chin and shaves beneath it, taking long deliberate strokes, and I find myself unconsciously mirroring his actions. Pulling my upper lip down just as he does, to shave his philtrum. He turns and smirks at me, one half of his face still covered in shaving soap.

"Enjoying the show?" he asks.

Oh, Christian, I could watch you for hours. "One of my all-time favorites," I murmur, and he leans down and kisses me quickly, smearing shaving soap on my face.

"Shall I do this to you again?" he whispers wickedly and holds up the razor.

I purse my lips at him. "No," I mutter, pretending to sulk. "I'll wax next time." I remember Christian's joy in London when he'd discovered that during his one meeting there, I'd shaved off my pubic hair out of curiosity. Of course I hadn't done it to Mr. Exacting's high standards . . .

"What the hell have you done?" Christian exclaims. He cannot keep his horrified amusement to himself. He sits up in bed in our suite at Brown's Hotel near Piccadilly, switches on the bedside

light, and gazes down at me, his mouth a startled O. It must be
midnight. I blush the color of the sheets in the playroom and try
to pull down my satin nightdress so he can't see. He grabs my
hand to stop me.

"Ana!"

"I—er . . . shaved."

"I can see that. Why?" He's grinning from ear to ear.

I cover my face with my hands. Why am I so embarrassed?

"Hey," he says softly and pulls my hand away. "Don't hide."
He's biting his lip so that he won't laugh. "Tell me. Why?" His
eyes dance with merriment. Why does he find this so funny?

"Stop laughing at me."

"I'm not laughing at you. I'm sorry. I'm . . . delighted," he says.

"Oh . . ."

"Tell me. Why?"

I take a deep breath. "This morning, after you left for your
meeting, I took a shower and was remembering all your rules."

He blinks. The humor in his expression has vanished, and he
regards me cautiously.

"And I was ticking them off one by one and how I felt about
them, and I remembered the beauty salon, and I thought . . . this
is what you'd like. I wasn't brave enough to get a wax." My voice
disappears into a whisper.

He stares at me, his eyes glowing—this time not with mirth at
my folly, but with love.

"Oh, Ana," he breathes. He leans down and kisses me tenderly.
"You beguile me," he whispers against my lips and kisses me once
more, clasping my face in both his hands.

After a breathless moment, he pulls back and leans up on one
elbow. The humor is back.

"I think I should do a thorough inspection of your handiwork,
Mrs. Grey."

"What? No." *He has to be kidding!* I cover myself, protecting
my recently deforested area.

"Oh, no you don't, Anastasia." He grasps my hands and pries

them away, moving nimbly so he's between my legs and pinning my hands to my sides. He gives me a scorching look that could light dry tinder, but before I combust, he bends and skims his lips down my naked belly directly to my sex. I squirm beneath him, reluctantly resigned to my fate.

"Well, what have we here?" Christian plants a kiss where, until this morning, I had pubic hair—then scrapes his bristly chin across me.

"Ah!" I exclaim. *Wow . . . that's sensitive.*

Christian's eyes dart to mine, full of salacious longing. "I think you missed a bit," he mutters and tugs gently, right underneath.

"Oh . . . Damn," I mutter, hoping this will put an end to his frankly intrusive scrutiny.

"I have an idea." He leaps naked out of bed and heads to the bathroom.

What on earth is he doing? He returns moments later, carrying a glass of water, a mug, my razor, his shaving brush, soap, and a towel. He puts the water, brush, soap, and razor on the bedside table and gazes down at me, holding the towel.

Oh no! My subconscious slams down her *Complete Works of Charles Dickens,* leaps up from her armchair, and puts her hands on her hips.

"No. No. No," I squeak.

"Mrs. Grey, if a job's worth doing, it's worth doing well. Lift your hips." His eyes glow summer storm gray.

"Christian! You are not shaving me."

He tilts his head to one side. "Why ever not?"

I flush . . . isn't it obvious? "Because . . . It's just too . . ."

"Intimate?" he whispers. "Ana, I crave intimacy with you— you know that. Besides, after some of the things we've done, don't get all squeamish on me now. And I know this part of your body better than you do."

I gape at him. Of all the arrogant . . . true, he does—but still. "It's just wrong!" My voice is prissy and whiny.

"This isn't wrong—this is hot."

Hot? Really? "This turns you on?" I can't keep the astonishment out of my voice.

He snorts. "Can't you tell?" He glances down at his arousal. "I want to shave you," he whispers

Oh, what the hell. I lie back, throwing my arm over my face so I don't have to watch.

"If it makes you happy, Christian, go ahead. You are so kinky," I mutter, as I lift my hips, and he slips the towel beneath me. He kisses my inner thigh.

"Oh, baby, how right you are."

I hear the slosh of water as he dips the shaving brush in the glass of water, then the soft swirl of the brush in the mug. He grasps my left ankle and parts my legs, and the bed dips as he sits between my legs. "I'd really like to tie you up right now," he murmurs.

"I promise to keep still."

"Good."

I gasp as he runs the lathered brush over my pubic bone. It's warm. The water in the glass must be hot. I squirm a little. It tickles . . . but in a good way.

"Don't move," Christian admonishes and applies the brush again. "Or I *will* tie you down," he adds darkly, and a delicious shiver runs down my spine.

"Have you done this before?" I ask tentatively when he reaches for the razor.

"No."

"Oh. Good." I grin.

"Another first, Mrs. Grey."

"Hmm. I like firsts."

"Me, too. Here goes." And with a gentleness that surprises me, he runs the razor over my sensitive flesh. "Keep still," he says distractedly, and I know he's concentrating hard.

It's only a matter of minutes before he grabs the towel and wipes all the excess lather off me.

"There—that's more like it," he muses, and I finally lift my arm to look at him as he sits back to admire his handiwork.

"Happy?" I ask, my voice hoarse.

"Very." He grins wickedly and slowly eases a finger inside me.

———·——

"But that was fun," he says, his eyes gently mocking.

"For you maybe." I try to pout—but he's right . . . it was . . . arousing.

"I seem to recall the aftermath was very satisfying." Christian returns to finishing his shave. I glance quickly down at my fingers. Yes, it was. I had no idea that the absence of pubic hair could make such a difference.

"Hey, I'm just teasing. Isn't that what husbands who are hopelessly in love with their wives do?" Christian tips my chin up and gazes at me, his eyes suddenly filled with apprehension as he endeavors to read my expression.

Hmm . . . payback time.

"Sit," I mutter.

He stares, not understanding. I push him gently toward the lone white stool in the bathroom. Perplexed, he sits down, and I take the razor from him.

"Ana," he warns as he realizes my intention. I lean down and kiss him.

"Head back," I whisper.

He hesitates.

"Tit for tat, Mr. Grey."

He stares at me with wary, amused disbelief. "You know what you're doing?" he asks, his voice low. I shake my head slowly, deliberately, trying to look as serious as possible. He closes his eyes and shakes his head, then tilts it back in surrender.

Holy shit, he's going to let me shave him. Tentatively I slide my hand into the damp hair at his forehead, gripping tightly to hold him still. He clenches his eyes closed and parts his lips as he inhales. Very gently, I stroke his razor up from his neck to his chin, revealing a path of skin beneath the lather. Christian exhales.

"Did you think I was going to hurt you?"

"I never know what you're going to do, Ana, but no—not intentionally."

I run the razor up his neck again, clearing a wider path in the lather.

"I would never intentionally hurt you, Christian."

He opens his eyes and circles his arms around me as I gently drag the razor down his cheek from the bottom of his sideburn.

"I know," he says, angling his face so I can shave the rest of his cheek. Two more strokes and I've finished.

"All done, and not a drop of blood spilled." I grin proudly.

He runs his hand up my leg so that my nightdress rides up my thigh and pulls me onto his lap so that I'm astride him. I steady myself with my hands on his upper arms. He's really very muscular.

"Can I take you somewhere today?"

"No sunbathing?" I arch a caustic brow at him.

He licks his lips nervously. "No. No sunbathing today. I thought you might prefer something else."

"Well, since you've covered me in hickeys and effectively put the kibosh on that, sure, why not?"

Wisely he chooses to ignore my tone. "It's a drive, but it's worth a visit from what I've read. My dad recommended we visit. It's a hilltop village called Saint-Paul-de-Vence. There are some galleries there. I thought we could pick out some paintings or sculptures for the new house, if we find anything we like."

I lean back and gaze at him. Art . . . he wants to buy art. *How can I buy art?*

"What?" he asks.

"I know nothing about art, Christian."

He shrugs and smiles at me indulgently. "We'll buy only what we like. This isn't about investment."

Investment? Jeez.

"What?" he says again.

I shake my head.

"Look, I know we only got the architect's drawings the other day—but there's no harm in looking, and the town is an ancient, medieval place."

Oh, the architect. He had to remind me of *her* . . . Gia Matteo, a friend of Elliot's who worked on Christian's place in Aspen. During our meetings, she'd been all over Christian like a rash.

"What now?" Christian exclaims. I shake my head. "Tell me," he urges.

How can I tell him that I don't like Gia? My dislike is irrational. I don't want to come across as a jealous wife.

"You're not still mad about what I did yesterday?" He sighs and nuzzles his face between my breasts.

"No. I'm hungry," I mutter, knowing full well that this will distract him from this line of questioning.

"Why didn't you say?" He eases me off his lap and stands.

SAINT-PAUL-DE-VENCE IS A FORTIFIED medieval hilltop village, one of the most picturesque places I have ever seen. I stroll arm in arm with Christian through the narrow cobblestone streets with my hand in the back pocket of his shorts. Taylor and either Gaston or Philippe—I can't tell the difference between them— trail behind us. We pass a tree-covered square where three old men, one wearing a traditional beret in spite of the heat, are playing boules. It's quite crowded with tourists, but I feel comfortable tucked under Christian's arm. There is so much to see—little alleys and passageways leading to courtyards with intricate stone fountains, ancient and modern sculptures, and fascinating little boutiques and shops.

In the first gallery, Christian gazes distractedly at the erotic photographs in front of us, sucking gently on the arm of his aviator specs. They are the work of Florence D'elle—naked women in various poses.

"Not quite what I had in mind," I mumble disapprovingly. They make me think of the box of photographs I found in his closet, our closet. I wonder if he ever did destroy them.

"Me neither," Christian says, grinning down at me. He takes my hand, and we stroll to the next artist. Idly, I wonder if I should let him take photos of me.

The next display is by a female painter who specializes in still lifes—fruit and vegetables super close up and in rich, glorious color.

"I like those." I point to three paintings of peppers. "They remind me of you chopping vegetables in my apartment." I giggle. Christian's mouth twists as he tries and fails to hide his amusement.

"I thought I managed that quite competently," he mutters. "I was just a bit slow, and anyway"—he pulls me into an embrace—"you were distracting me. Where would you put them?"

"What?"

Christian is nuzzling my ear. "The paintings—where would you put them?" He bites my earlobe and I feel it in my groin.

"Kitchen," I murmur.

"Hmm. Nice idea, Mrs. Grey."

I squint at the price. Five thousand euros each. *Holy shit!*

"They're really expensive!" I gasp.

"So?" He nuzzles me again. "Get used to it, Ana." He releases me and saunters over to the desk where a young woman dressed entirely in white is gaping at him. I want to roll my eyes, but turn my attention back to the paintings. Five thousand euros . . . jeez.

WE HAVE FINISHED LUNCH and are relaxing over coffee at the Hotel Le Saint Paul. The view of the surrounding countryside is stunning. Vineyards and fields of sunflowers form a patchwork across the plain, interspersed here and there with neat little French farmhouses. It's such a clear, beautiful day we can see all the way to the sea, glinting faintly on the horizon. Christian interrupts my reverie.

"You asked me why I braid your hair," he murmurs. His tone alarms me. He looks . . . guilty.

"Yes." *Oh, shit.*

"The crack whore used to let me play with her hair, I think. I don't know if it's a memory or a dream."

Whoa! His birth mom.

He gazes at me, his expression unreadable. My heart leaps into my mouth. What do I say when he says things like this?

"I like it when you play with my hair." My voice is hesitant.

He regards me with uncertainty. "Do you?"

"Yes." It's the truth. I grasp his hand. "I think you loved your birth mother, Christian." His eyes widen and he stares at me impassively, saying nothing.

Holy shit. Have I gone too far? *Say something, Fifty—please.* But he remains resolutely mute, gazing at me with fathomless gray eyes while the silence stretches between us. He looks lost.

He glances down at my hand on his and he frowns.

"Say something," I whisper, because I cannot bear the silence any longer.

He shakes his head, exhaling deeply.

"Let's go." He releases my hand and stands, his expression guarded. Have I overstepped the mark? I have no idea. My heart sinks and I don't know whether to say anything else or just let it go. I decide on the latter and follow him dutifully out of the restaurant.

In the lovely narrow street, he takes my hand.

"Where do you want to go?"

He speaks! And he's not mad at me—thank heavens. I exhale, relieved, and shrug. "I am just glad you're still speaking to me."

"You know I don't like talking about all that shit. It's done. Finished," he says quietly.

No, Christian, it isn't. The thought saddens me, and for the first time I wonder if it will ever be finished. He'll always be Fifty Shades . . . my Fifty Shades. Do I want him to change? No, not really—only insofar as I want him to feel loved. Peeking up at him, I take a moment to admire his captivating beauty . . . and he's *mine.* And it's not just the allure of his fine, fine face and his body that has me spellbound. It's what's behind the perfection that draws me, that calls to me . . . his fragile, damaged soul.

He gives me that look, down his nose, half amused, half wary, wholly sexy, then tucks me under his arm, and we make our way through the tourists toward the spot where Philippe/Gaston has parked the roomy Mercedes. I slip my hand back into the back pocket of Christian's shorts, grateful that he isn't mad. But, honestly, what four-year-old child doesn't love his mom, no matter how bad a mom she is? I sigh heavily and hug him closer. I know behind us the security team lurks, and I wonder idly if they've eaten.

Christian stops outside a small boutique selling fine jewelry and gazes in the window, then down at me. He grasps my free hand and runs his thumb across the faded red line of the handcuff mark, inspecting it.

"It's not sore," I reassure him. He twists so that my other hand is freed from his pocket. He clasps that hand, too, turning it gently over to examine my wrist. The platinum Omega watch he gave me at breakfast on our first morning in London obscures the red line. The inscription still makes me swoon.

Anastasia
You Are My More
My Love, My Life
Christian

In spite of everything, all his Fiftyness, my husband can be so romantic. I gaze down at the faint marks on my wrist. Then again, he can be savage sometimes. Releasing my left hand, he tilts my chin up with his fingers and scrutinizes my expression, his eyes troubled.

"They don't hurt," I repeat. He pulls my hand to his lips and plants a soft apologetic kiss on the inside of my wrist.

"Come," he says and leads me into the shop.

"HERE." CHRISTIAN HOLDS OPEN the platinum bracelet he's just purchased. It's exquisite, so delicately crafted, the filigree in the shape of small abstract flowers with small diamonds at their hearts. He fastens it around my wrist. It's wide and cufflike and hides the red marks. *It also cost thirty thousand euros*, I think, though I couldn't really follow the conversation in French with the sales assistant. I have never worn anything so expensive.

"There, that's better," he murmurs.

"Better?" I whisper, gazing into luminous gray eyes, conscious that the stick-thin sales assistant is staring at us with a jealous and disapproving look.

"You know why," Christian says uncertainly.

"I don't need this." I shake my wrist and the cuff moves. It catches the afternoon light streaming through the boutique window and small sparkling rainbows dance off the diamonds all over the walls of the store.

"I do," he says with utter sincerity.

Why? Why does he need this? Does he feel guilty? About what? The marks? His birth mother? Not confiding in me? *Oh, Fifty.*

"No, Christian, you don't. You've given me so much already. A magical honeymoon, London, Paris, the Cote D'Azur . . . and you. I'm a very lucky girl," I whisper, and his eyes soften.

"No, Anastasia, I'm a very lucky man."

"Thank you." Stretching up on tiptoes, I put my arms around his neck and kiss him . . . not for giving me the bracelet but for being mine.

BACK IN THE CAR he's introspective, gazing out at the fields of bright sunflowers, their heads following and basking in the afternoon sun. One of the twins—I think it's Gaston—is driving and Taylor is beside him up front. Christian is brooding about something. I clasp his hand, giving it a reassuring squeeze. He glances at me before releasing my hand and caressing my knee. I'm wearing a short, full, blue and white skirt, and a blue, fitted, sleeveless shirt. Christian hesitates, and I don't know if his hand is going to travel up my thigh or down my leg. I tense with anticipation at the gentle touch of his fingers and my breath catches. *What's he going to do?* He chooses down, suddenly grasping my ankle and pulling my foot onto his lap. I swivel my backside so I am facing him in the back of the car.

"I want the other one, too."

I glance nervously toward Taylor and Gaston, whose eyes are resolutely on the road ahead, and place my other foot on his lap. His eyes cool, he reaches over and presses a button located on his door. In front of us, a lightly tinted privacy screen slides out of a panel, and ten seconds later we are effectively on our own. Wow . . . no wonder the back of this car has so much legroom.

"I want to look at your ankles," Christian offers his quiet explanation. His gaze is anxious. The cuff marks? *Jeez* . . . I thought we'd dealt with this. If there are marks, they are hidden by my sandal straps. I don't recall seeing any this morning. Gently, he strokes his thumb up my right instep, making me wriggle. A smile plays on his lips and deftly he undoes one strap, and his smile fades as he's confronted with the darker red marks.

"Doesn't hurt," I murmur. He glances at me and his expression is sad, his mouth a thin line. He nods once as if he's taking me at my word while I shake my sandal loose so it falls to the floor, but I know I've lost him. He's distracted and brooding again, mechanically caressing my foot while he turns away to gaze out the car window once more.

"Hey. What did you expect?" I ask softly. He glances at me and shrugs.

"I didn't expect to feel like I do looking at these marks," he says.

Oh! Reticent one minute and forthcoming the next? How . . . *Fifty!* How can I keep up with him?

"How *do* you feel?"

Bleak eyes gaze at me. "Uncomfortable," he murmurs.

Oh no. I unbuckle my seat belt and scoot closer to him, leaving my feet in his lap. I want to crawl into his lap and hold him, and I would, if it were just Taylor in the front. But knowing Gaston is there cramps my style despite the partition. If only it were darker. I clutch his hands.

"It's the hickeys I don't like," I whisper. "Everything else . . . what you did"—I lower my voice even further—"with the handcuffs, I enjoyed that. Well, more than enjoyed. It was mindblowing. You can do that to me again anytime."

He shifts in his seat. "Mind-blowing?" My inner goddess looks up, startled, from her Jackie Collins.

"Yes." I grin. I flex my toes into his hardening crotch and see rather than hear his sharp intake of breath, his lips parting.

"You should really be wearing your seat belt, Mrs. Grey." His voice is low, and I curl my toes around him once more. He inhales and his eyes darken, and he clasps my ankle in warning. Does he want me stop? Continue? He pauses, scowls, then fishes his ever-present BlackBerry out of his pocket to take an incoming call while glancing at his watch. His frown deepens.

"Barney," he snaps.

Crap. Work interrupting us again. I try to remove my feet, but he tightens his fingers around my ankle.

"In the server room?" he says in disbelief. "Did it activate the fire suppression system?"

Fire! I take my feet off his lap and this time he lets me. I sit back in my seat, buckle my seat belt, and fiddle nervously with the thirty-thousand-euro bracelet. Christian presses the button on his door armrest again and the privacy glass slides down.

"Anyone injured? Damage? I see . . . When?" Christian glances at his watch again, then runs his fingers through his hair. "No. Not the fire department or the police. Not yet anyway."

A fire? At Christian's office? I gape at him, my mind racing. Taylor shifts so he can hear Christian's conversation.

"Has he? Good . . . Okay. I want a detailed damage report. And a complete rundown of everyone who had access over the last five days, including the cleaning staff . . . Get hold of Andrea and get her to call me . . . Yeah, sounds like the argon is just as effective, worth its weight in gold."

Damage report? Argon? It rings a distant bell from chemistry class—an element, I think.

"I realize it's early . . . E-mail me in two hours . . . No, I need to know. Thank you for calling me." Christian hangs up, then immediately punches a number into the BlackBerry.

"Welch . . . Good . . . When?" Christian glances at his watch yet again. "An hour then . . . yes . . . Twenty-four-seven at the off-site data store . . . good." He hangs up.

"Philippe, I need to be onboard within the hour."

"*Monsieur.*"

Shit, it's Philippe, not Gaston. The car surges forward.

Christian glances at me, his expression unreadable.

"Anyone hurt?" I ask quietly.

Christian shakes his head. "Very little damage." He reaches over and clasps my hand, squeezing it reassuringly. "Don't worry about this. My team is on it." And there he is, the CEO, in command, in control, and not flustered at all.

"Where was the fire?"

"Server room."

"Grey House?"

"Yes."

His responses are clipped, so I know he doesn't want to talk about it.

"Why so little damage?"

"The server room is fitted with a state-of-the-art fire suppression system."

Of course it is.

"Ana, please . . . don't worry."

"I'm not worried," I lie.

"We don't know for sure that it was arson," he says, cutting to the heart of my anxiety. My hand clutches my throat in fear. *Charlie Tango* and now this?

What next?

CHAPTER FOUR

I'm restless. Christian has been holed up in the onboard study for over an hour. I have tried reading, watching TV, sunbathing—fully dressed sunbathing—but I can't relax, and I can't rid myself of this edgy feeling. After changing into shorts and a T-shirt, I remove the ludicrously expensive cuff and go to find Taylor.

"Mrs. Grey," he says, startled from his Anthony Burgess novel. He's sitting in the small salon outside Christian's study.

"I'd like to go shopping."

"Yes ma'am." He stands.

"I'd like to take the Jet Ski."

His mouth drops open. "Erm." He frowns, at a loss for words.

"I don't want to bother Christian with this."

He represses a sigh. "Mrs. Grey . . . um . . . I don't think Mr. Grey would be very comfortable with that, and I'd like to keep my job."

Oh, for heaven's sake! I want to roll my eyes at him, but I narrow them instead, sighing heavily and expressing, I think, the right amount of frustrated indignation that I am not mistress of my own destiny. Then again, I don't want Christian to be mad at Taylor—or me, for that matter. Striding confidently past him, I knock on the study door and enter.

Christian is on his BlackBerry, leaning against the mahogany desk. He glances up. "Andrea, hold please," he mutters into phone, his expression serious. His gaze is politely expectant. Shit. Why do I feel like I've entered the principal's office? This man had me in handcuffs yesterday. I refuse to be intimidated by him, he's my husband, damn it. I square my shoulders and give him a broad smile.

"I'm going shopping. I'll take security with me."

"Sure, take one of the twins and Taylor, too," he says, and I know that whatever's happening is serious because he doesn't question me further. I stand staring at him, wondering if I can help.

"Anything else?" he asks. He wants me gone.

"Can I get you anything?" I ask. He smiles his sweet shy smile.

"No, baby, I'm good," he says. "The crew will look after me."

"Okay." I want to kiss him. Hell, I can—he's my husband. Strolling purposefully forward, I plant a kiss on his lips, surprising him.

"Andrea, I'll call you back," he mutters. He puts the Black-Berry down on the desk behind him, pulls me into his embrace, and kisses me passionately. I am breathless when he releases me. His eyes are dark and needy.

"You're distracting me. I need to sort this out, so I can get back to my honeymoon." He runs an index finger down my face and caresses my chin, tilting my face up.

"Okay. I'm sorry."

"Please don't apologize, Mrs. Grey. I love your distractions." He kisses the corner of my mouth.

"Go spend some money." He releases me.

"Will do." I smirk at him as I exit his study. My subconscious shakes her head and purses her lips. *You didn't tell him you were going on the Jet Ski,* she chastises me in her singsongy voice. I ignore her . . . *Harpy.*

Taylor is patiently waiting.

"That's all cleared with high command . . . Can we go?" I smile, trying to keep the sarcasm out of my voice. Taylor doesn't hide his admiring smile.

"Mrs. Grey, after you."

TAYLOR PATIENTLY TALKS ME through the controls on the Jet Ski and how to ride it. He has a calm, gentle authority about him; he's a good teacher. We are in the motor launch, bobbing and weaving on the calm waters of the harbor beside the *Fair Lady*. Gaston looks on, his expression hidden by his shades, and one of the *Fair Lady*'s crew is at the controls of the motor launch. Jeez—three people with me, just because I want to go shopping. It's ridiculous.

Zipping up my life jacket, I give Taylor a beaming grin. He holds out his hand to assist me as I climb onto the Jet Ski.

"Fasten the strap of the ignition key around your wrist, Mrs. Grey. If you fall off, the engine will cut out automatically," he explains.

"Okay."

"Ready?"

I nod enthusiastically.

"Press the ignition when you've drifted about four feet away from the boat. We'll follow you."

"Okay."

He pushes the Jet Ski away from the launch, and it floats gently into the main harbor. When he gives me the okay sign, I press the ignition button and the engine roars into life.

"Okay, Mrs. Grey, easy does it!" Taylor shouts. I squeeze the accelerator. The Jet Ski lurches forward, then stalls. *Crap!* How does Christian make it look so easy? I try again, and once again, I stall. *Double crap!*

"Just steady on the gas, Mrs. Grey," Taylor calls.

"Yeah, yeah, yeah," I mutter under my breath. I try once more, very gently squeezing the lever, and the Jet Ski lurches forward— but this time it keeps going. *Yes!* It goes some more. *Ha ha! It still keeps going!* I want to shout and squeal in excitement, but I resist. I cruise gently away from the yacht into the main harbor. Behind me, I hear the throaty roar of the motor launch. When I squeeze the gas further, the Jet Ski leaps forward, skating across the water. With the warm breeze in my hair and a fine sea spray on either side of me, I feel free. This *rocks!* No wonder Christian never lets me drive.

Rather than head for the shore and curtail the fun, I veer

around to do a circuit of the stately *Fair Lady*. Wow—this is so much *fun*. I ignore Taylor and the crew behind me and speed around the yacht for a second time. As I complete the circuit, I spot Christian on deck. I think he's gaping at me, though it's difficult to tell. Bravely, I lift one hand from the handlebars and wave enthusiastically at him. He looks like he's made of stone, but finally he raises his hand in the semblance of a stiff wave. I can't work out his expression, and something tells me I don't want to, so I head to the marina, speeding across the blue water of the Mediterranean, which shimmers in the late afternoon sun.

At the dock, I wait and let Taylor pull up ahead of me. His expression is bleak, and my heart sinks, though Gaston looks vaguely amused. I wonder briefly if something has happened to chill Gallic-American relations, but deep down I suspect the problem is probably me. Gaston leaps out of the motorboat and ties it to the moorings while Taylor directs me to come alongside. Very gently I ease the Jet Ski into position beside the boat and line up beside him. His expression softens a little.

"Just switch off the ignition, Mrs. Grey," he says calmly, reaching for the handlebars and holding out a hand to help me into the motorboat. I nimbly climb aboard, impressed that I don't fall in.

"Mrs. Grey," Taylor says nervously, his cheeks pink once more. "Mr. Grey is not entirely comfortable with you riding on the Jet Ski." He's practically squirming with embarrassment, and I realize he's had an irate call from Christian. *Oh, my poor, pathologically overprotective husband, what am I going to do with you?*

I smile serenely at Taylor. "I see. Well, Taylor, Mr. Grey is not here, and if he's not *entirely comfortable*, I'm sure he'll give me the courtesy of telling me himself when I'm back on board."

Taylor winces. "Very good, Mrs. Grey," he says quietly, handing me my purse.

As I climb out of the boat, I catch a glimpse of his reluctant smile, and it makes me want to smile, too. I cannot believe how fond I am of Taylor, but I really don't appreciate being scolded by him—he's not my father or my husband.

I sigh. Christian's mad—and he has enough to worry about at the moment. What was I thinking? As I stand on the dock waiting for Taylor to climb up, I feel my BlackBerry vibrate in my purse and fish it out. Sade's "Your Love Is King" is my ring tone for Christian—only for Christian.

"Hi," I murmur.

"Hi," he says.

"I'll come back on the boat. Don't be mad."

I hear his small gasp of surprise. "Um . . ."

"It was fun, though," I whisper.

He sighs. "Well, far be it for me to curtail your fun, Mrs. Grey. Just be careful. Please."

Oh my! Permission to have fun! "I will. Anything you want from town?"

"Just you, back in one piece."

"I'll do my best to comply, Mr. Grey."

"I'm glad to hear it, Mrs. Grey."

"We aim to please," I respond with a giggle.

I hear the smile in his voice. "I have another call—laters, baby."

"Laters, Christian."

He hangs up. *Jet Ski crisis averted*, I think. The car is waiting, and Taylor holds the door open for me. I wink at him as I climb in, and he shakes his head in amusement.

In the car, I fire up the e-mail on my BlackBerry.

From: Anastasia Grey
Subject: Thank You
Date: August 17 2011 16:55
To: Christian Grey

For not being too grouchy.

Your loving wife

xxx

From: Christian Grey
Subject: Trying to Stay Calm
Date: August 17 2011 16:59
To: Anastasia Grey

You're welcome.

Come back in one piece.

This is not a request.

x

Christian Grey
CEO & Overprotective Husband, Grey Enterprises
Holdings, Inc.

His response makes me smile. My control freak.

WHY DID I WANT to go shopping? I hate shopping. But deep down I know why, and I walk determinedly past Chanel, Gucci, Dior, and the other designer boutiques and eventually find the antidote to what ails me in a small, overstocked, touristy store. It's a little silver ankle bracelet with small hearts and little bells. It tinkles sweetly and it costs five euros. As soon as I've bought it, I put it on. This is me—this is what I like. Immediately I feel more comfortable. I don't want to lose touch with the girl who likes this, ever. Deep down I know that I'm not only overwhelmed by Christian himself but also by his wealth. Will I ever get used to it?

Taylor and Gaston follow me dutifully through the late afternoon crowds, and I soon forget they are there. I want to buy something for Christian, something to take his mind off what's happening in Seattle. But what do I buy for the man who has everything? I pause in a small modern square surrounded by stores and gaze at each one in turn. When I spy an electronics store, our visit to the gallery earlier today and our visit to the Louvre come back to me. We were looking at the *Venus de Milo* at the time . . . Christian's words echo in my head, *"We can all appreciate the female form. We love to look whether in marble or oils or satin or film."*

It gives me an idea, a daring idea. I just need help choosing the right one, and there's only one person who can help me. I wrestle my BlackBerry out of my purse and call José.

"Who . . . ?" he mumbles sleepily.

"José, it's Ana."

"Ana, hi! Where are you? You okay?" He sounds more alert now, concerned.

"I'm in Cannes in the South of France, and I'm fine."

"South of France, huh? You in some fancy hotel?"

"Um . . . no. We're staying on a boat."

"A boat?"

"A big boat." I clarify, sighing.

"I see." His tone chills . . . Shit, I should not have called him. I don't need this right now.

"José, I need your advice."

"My advice?" He sounds stunned. "Sure," he says, and this time he's much more friendly. I tell him my plan.

TWO HOURS LATER, TAYLOR helps me out of the motor launch onto the steps up to the deck. Gaston is helping the deckhand with the Jet Ski. Christian is nowhere to be seen, and I scurry down to our cabin to wrap his present, feeling a childish sense of delight.

"You were gone some time." Christian startles me just as I am applying the last piece of tape. I turn to find him standing in the doorway to the cabin, watching me intently. *Am I still in trouble over the Jet Ski?* Or is it the fire at his office?

"Everything in control at your office?" I ask tentatively.

"More or less," he says, an annoyed frown flitting across his face.

"I did a little shopping," I murmur, hoping to lighten his mood, and praying his annoyance is not directed at me. He smiles warmly, and I know we're okay.

"What did you buy?"

"This," I put my foot up on the bed and show him my ankle chain.

"Very nice," he says. He steps over to me and fondles the tiny bells so that they jingle sweetly around my ankle. He frowns again and runs his fingers lightly along the mark, sending tingles up my leg.

"And this." I hold out the box, hoping to distract him.

"For me?" he asks in surprise. I nod shyly. He takes the box and shakes it gently. He grins his boyish, dazzling smile and sits down beside me on the bed. Leaning over, he grasps my chin and kisses me.

"Thank you," he says with shy delight.

"You haven't opened it yet."

"I'll love it, whatever it is." He gazes down at me, his eyes glowing. "I don't get many presents."

"It's hard to buy you things. You have everything."

"I have you."

"You do." I grin at him. *Oh, you so do, Christian.*

He makes short work of the wrapping paper. "A Nikon?" He glances up at me, puzzled.

"I know you have your compact digital camera but this is for . . . um . . . portraits and the like. It comes with two lenses."

He blinks at me, still not understanding.

"Today in the gallery you liked the Florence D'elle photographs. And I remember what you said in the Louvre. And, of course, there were those other photographs." I swallow, trying my best not to recall the images I found in his closet.

He stops breathing, his eyes widening as realization dawns, and I continue hurriedly before I lose my nerve.

"I thought you might, um . . . like to take pictures of . . . me."

"Pictures. Of you?" He gapes at me, ignoring the box on his lap.

I nod, desperately trying to gauge his reaction. Finally he gazes back down at the box, his fingers tracing over the illustration of the camera on the front with fascinated reverence.

What is he thinking? Oh, this is not the reaction I was expecting, and my subconscious glares at me like I'm a domesticated farm animal. Christian *never* reacts the way I expect. He looks back up, his eyes filled with, what, pain?

"Why do you think I want this?" he asks, bemused.

No, no, no! You said you'd love it . . .

"Don't you?" I ask, refusing to acknowledge my subconscious, who is questioning why anyone would want erotic photographs of me. Christian swallows and runs a hand through his hair, and he looks so lost, so confused. He takes a deep breath.

"For me, photos like those have usually been an insurance policy, Ana. I know I've objectified women for so long," he says and pauses awkwardly.

"And you think taking pictures of me is . . . um, objectifying me?" All the air leaves my body, and the blood drains from my face.

He scrunches up his eyes. "I am so confused," he whispers. When he opens his eyes again, they are wide and wary, full of some raw emotion.

Shit. Is it me? My questions earlier about his birth mom? The fire at his office?

"Why do you say that?" I whisper, panic rising in my throat. I thought he was happy. I thought we were happy. I thought I made him happy. I don't want to *confuse* him. Do I? My mind starts racing. He hasn't seen Flynn in nearly three weeks. Is that it? Is that the reason he's unraveling? Shit, should I call Flynn? And in a possibly unique moment of extraordinary depth and clarity, it comes to me—the fire, *Charlie Tango*, the Jet Ski . . . He's scared, he's scared for me, and seeing these marks on my skin must bring that home. He's been fussing about them all day, confusing himself because he's not used to feeling uncomfortable about inflicting pain. The thought chills me.

He shrugs and once more his eyes move down to my wrist, where the cuff he bought me this afternoon used to be. *Bingo!*

"Christian, these don't matter." I hold up my wrist, revealing the fading welt. "You gave me a safeword. Shit—yesterday was *fun*. I enjoyed it. Stop brooding about it—I like rough sex, I've told you that before." I blush scarlet as I try to quash my rising panic.

He gazes at me intently, and I have no idea what he's thinking. Maybe he's measuring my words. I stumble on.

"Is this about the fire? Do you think it's connected some-how to *Charlie Tango*? Is this why you're worried? Talk to me, Christian—please."

He stares at me, saying nothing, and the silence expands between us again as it did this afternoon. *Holy fucking crap!* He's not going to talk to me, I know.

"Don't overthink this Christian," I scold quietly, and the words echo, disturbing a memory from the recent past—his words to me about his stupid contract. I reach over, take the box from his lap, and open it. He watches me passively as if I'm a fascinating alien creature. Knowing that the camera is prepped by the overly help-ful salesman in the store, and ready to go, I fish it out of the box and remove the lens cap. I point the camera at him so his beau-tiful anxious face fills the frame. I press the button and keep it pressed, and ten pictures of Christian's alarmed expression are captured digitally for posterity.

"I'll objectify you then," I murmur, pressing the shutter again. On the final still his lips twitch almost imperceptibly. I press again, and this time he smiles . . . a small smile, but a smile nevertheless. I hold down the button once more and see him physically relax in front of me and pout—a full-on, posed, ridiculous, "Blue Steel" pout, and it makes me giggle. *Oh, thank heavens.* Mr. Mercurial is back—and I've never been so pleased to see him.

"I thought it was *my* present," he mutters sulkily, but I think he's teasing.

"Well, it was supposed to be fun, but apparently it's a symbol of women's oppression." I snap away, taking more pictures of him, and watch the amusement grow on his face in super close-up. Then his eyes darken, and his expression changes to predatory.

"You want to be oppressed?" he murmurs silkily.

"Not oppressed. No," I murmur back, snapping again.

"I could oppress you big-time, Mrs. Grey," he threatens, his voice husky.

"I know you can, Mr. Grey. And you do, frequently."

His face falls. *Shit.* I lower the camera and stare at him.

"What's wrong, Christian?" My voice oozes frustration. *Tell me!*

He says nothing. *Gah!* He's so infuriating. I lift the camera to my eye again.

"Tell me," I insist.

"Nothing," he says and abruptly disappears from the viewfinder. In one swift, smooth move, he sweeps the camera box onto the cabin floor, grabs me, and pushes me down onto the bed. He sits astride me.

"Hey!" I exclaim and take more photographs of him, smiling down at me with dark intent. He grabs the camera by the lens, and the photographer becomes the subject as he points the Nikon at me and presses the shutter release down.

"So, you want me to take pictures of you, Mrs. Grey?" he says, amused. All I can see of his face is his unruly hair and a broad grin on his sculptured mouth. "Well, for a start, I think you should be laughing," he says, and he tickles me ruthlessly under my ribs, making me squeal and giggle and squirm beneath him until I grasp his wrist in a vain attempt to make him stop. His grin widens, and he renews his efforts while snapping pictures.

"No! Stop!" I scream.

"Are you kidding?" he growls and puts the camera down beside us so that he can torture me with both hands.

"Christian!" I splutter and gasp my laughing protest. He has never ever tickled me before. *Fuck—stop!* I thrash my head from side to side, trying to wiggle out from under him, giggling and pushing both of his hands away, but he's unrelenting—grinning down at me, enjoying my torment.

"Christian, stop!" I plead and he stops suddenly. Grabbing both of my hands, he holds them down on either side of my head while looming over me. I am panting and breathless with laughter. His breathing mirrors mine, and he gazes down at me with . . . what? My lungs stop functioning. Wonder? Love? Reverence? *Holy cow. That look!*

"You. Are. So. Beautiful," he breathes.

I stare up at his dear, dear face bathed in the intensity of his gaze, and it's as if he's seeing me for the first time. Leaning down, he closes his eyes and kisses me, enraptured. His response is a wake-up call to my libido . . . seeing him like this, undone, by me. *Oh my.* He releases my hands and curls his fingers around my head and into my hair, holding me gently in place, and my body rises and fills with my arousal, responding to his kiss. And suddenly the nature of his kiss alters, no longer sweet, reverential, and admiring, but carnal, deep, and devouring—his tongue invading my mouth, taking not giving, his kiss possessing a desperate, needy edge. As desire courses through my blood, awakening every muscle and sinew in its wake, I feel a frisson of alarm.

Oh, Fifty, what's wrong?

He inhales sharply and groans. "Oh, what you do to me," he murmurs, lost and raw. He moves suddenly, lying down on top of me, pressing me into the mattress—one hand cupping my chin, the other skimming over my body, my breast, my waist, my hip, and around my behind. He kisses me again, pushing his leg between mine, raising my knee, and grinding against me, his erection straining against our clothes and my sex. I gasp and moan against his lips, losing myself to his fervent passion. I dismiss the distant alarm bells in the back of my mind, knowing that he wants me, that he needs me, and that when it comes to communicating with me, this is his favorite form of self-expression. I kiss him with renewed abandon, running my fingers through his hair, fisting my hands, holding tight. He tastes so good and smells of Christian, my Christian.

Abruptly, he stops, stands up, and pulls me off the bed so that

I am standing in front of him, dazed. He undoes the button on my shorts and kneels quickly, yanking them and my panties down, and before I can breathe again, I am back on the bed beneath him and he's unbuttoning his fly. Whoa! He's not taking off his clothes or my T-shirt. He holds my head and with no preamble whatsoever he thrusts himself inside me, making me cry out—more in surprise than anything else—but I can still hear the hiss of his breath forced through his clenched teeth.

"Yessss," he hisses close to my ear. He stills, then swivels his hips once, pushing deeper, making me groan.

"I need you," he growls, his voice low and husky. He runs his teeth along my jaw, nipping and sucking, and then he's kissing me again, hard. I wrap my legs and arms around him, cradling and holding him hard against me, determined to wipe out whatever's worrying him, and he starts to move . . . move like he's trying to climb inside me. Over and over, frantic, primal, desperate, and before I lose myself in the insane rhythm and pace he's setting, I briefly wonder once more what's driving him, worrying him. But my body takes over, obliterating the thought, climbing and building so I am awash with sensation, meeting him thrust for thrust. Listening to his harsh breathing, labored and fierce at my ear. Knowing that he's lost in me . . . I groan loudly, panting. It's so erotic—his need for me. I am reaching . . . reaching . . . and he's driving me higher, overwhelming me, taking me, and I want this. I want this so much . . . for him and for me.

"Come with me," he gasps, and he rears up over me so I have to break my hold around him.

"Open your eyes," he orders. "I need to see you." His voice is urgent, implacable. My eyes flicker open momentarily, and the sight of him above me—his face taut with ardor, his eyes raw and glowing. His passion and his love is my undoing, and on cue I come, throwing my head back as my body pulses around him.

"Oh, Ana," he cries and he joins my climax, driving into me, then stilling and collapsing onto me. He rolls over so that I'm sprawled on top of him, and he's still inside me. As I surface from my orgasm and my body steadies and calms, I want to make some quip about being objectified and oppressed, but hold my tongue, uncertain of his mood. I glance up from Christian's chest to examine his face. His eyes are closed and his arms are wrapped around me, clinging tight. I kiss his chest through the thin fabric of his linen shirt.

"Tell me, Christian, what's wrong?" I ask softly, and wait anxiously to see if even now, sated by sex, he'll tell me. I feel his arms tighten around me further, but it's his only response. He's not going to talk. Inspiration hits me.

"I give you my solemn vow to be your faithful partner in sickness and in health, to stand by your side in good times and in bad, to share your joy as well as your sorrow," I murmur.

He freezes. His only movement is to open wide his fathomless eyes and gaze at me as I continue my wedding vows.

"I promise to love you unconditionally, to support you in your goals and dreams, to honor and respect you, to laugh with you and cry with you, to share my hopes and dreams with you, and bring you solace in times of need." I pause, willing him to talk to me. He watches me, his lips parted, but says nothing.

"And to cherish you for as long as we both shall live." I sigh.

"Oh, Ana," he whispers and moves again, breaking our precious contact so that we're lying side by side. He strokes my face with the backs of his knuckles.

"I solemnly vow that I will safeguard and hold dear and deep in my heart our union and you," he whispers, his voice hoarse. "I promise to love you faithfully, forsaking all others, through the good times and the bad, in sickness and in health, regardless of where life takes us. I will protect you, trust you, and respect you. I will share your joys and sorrows and comfort you in times of need. I promise to cherish you and uphold your hopes and dreams and keep you safe at my side. All that is mine is now yours. I give you my hand, my heart, and my love from this moment on for as long as we both shall live."

Tears spring to my eyes. His face softens as he gazes at me.

"Don't cry," he murmurs, his thumb catching and dispatching a stray tear.

"Why won't you talk to me? Please, Christian."

He closes his eyes as if in pain.

"I vowed I would bring you solace in times of need. Please don't make me break my vows," I plea.

He sighs and opens his eyes, his expression bleak. "It's arson," he says simply, and he looks suddenly so young and vulnerable.

Oh fuck.

"And my biggest worry is that they are after me. And if they are after me—" He stops, unable to continue.

" . . . They might get me," I whisper. He blanches, and I know that I have finally uncovered the root of his anxiety. I caress his face.

"Thank you," I murmur.

He frowns. "What for?"

"For telling me."

He shakes his head and a ghost of a smile touches his lips. "You can be very persuasive, Mrs. Grey."

"And you can brood and internalize all your feelings and worry yourself to death. You'll probably die of a heart attack before you're forty, and I want you around far longer than that."

"*You'll* be the death of me. The sight of you on the Jet Ski—I nearly did have a coronary." He flops back on the bed and puts his hand over his eyes, and I feel him shudder.

"Christian, it's a Jet Ski. Even kids ride Jet Skis. Can you imagine what you'll be like when we visit your place in Aspen and I go skiing for the first time?"

He gasps and turns to face me, and I want to laugh at the horror on his face.

"Our place," he says eventually.

I ignore him. "I'm a grown-up, Christian, and much tougher than I look. When are you going to learn this?"

He shrugs and his mouth thins. I decide to change the subject.

"So, the fire. Do the police know about the arson?"

"Yes." His expression is serious.

"Good."

"Security is going to get tighter," he says matter-of-factly.

"I understand." I glance down his body. He's still wearing his shorts and his shirt, and I still have my T-shirt on. Jeez—talk about *wham, bam, thank you ma'am*. The thought makes me giggle.

"What?" Christian asks, bemused.

"You."

"Me?"

"Yes. You. Still dressed."

"Oh." He glances down at himself, then back at me, and his face erupts into an enormous smile.

"Well, you know how hard it is for me to keep my hands off you, Mrs. Grey—especially when you're giggling like a schoolgirl."

Oh yes—the tickling. *Gah!* The tickling. I move quickly so that I'm straddling him, but immediately understanding my evil intent, he grabs both of my wrists.

"No," he says, and he means it.

I pout at him but decide that he's not ready for this.

"Please don't," he whispers. "I couldn't bear it. I was never tickled as a child." He pauses and I relax my hands so he doesn't have to restrain me.

"I used to watch Carrick with Elliot and Mia, tickling them, and it looked like such fun, but I . . . I . . ."

I place my index finger on his lips.

"Hush, I know," I murmur and plant a soft kiss on his lips where my finger has just been, then curl up on his chest. The familiar painful ache swells inside me, and the profound sadness that I hold in my heart for Christian as a little boy seizes me once more. I know I would do anything for this man because I love him so.

He puts his arms around me and presses his nose into my hair, inhaling deeply as he gently strokes my back. I don't know how long we lie there, but eventually I break the comfortable silence between us.

"What is the longest you've gone without seeing Dr. Flynn?"

"Two weeks. Why? Do you have an incorrigible urge to tickle me?"

"No." I chuckle. "I think he helps you."

Christian snorts. "He should; I pay him enough." He pulls my hair gently, turning my face to look up at him. I lift my head and meet his gaze.

"Are you concerned for my well-being, Mrs. Grey?" he asks softly.

"Every good wife is concerned for her beloved husband's well-being, Mr. Grey," I admonish him teasingly.

"Beloved?" he whispers, and it's a poignant question hanging between us.

"Very much beloved." I scoot up to kiss him, and he smiles his shy smile.

"Do you want to go ashore to eat?"

"I want to eat wherever you're happiest."

"Good." He grins. "Aboard is where I can keep you safe. Thank you for my present." He reaches over and grabs the camera, and holding it at arm's length, he snaps the two of us in our post tickling, postcoital, postconfessional embrace.

"The pleasure is all mine." I smile and his eyes light up.

We wander through the opulent, gilt splendor of the eighteenth-century Palace of Versailles. Once a humble hunting lodge, it was transformed by the Roi Soleil into a magnificent, lavish seat of power, but even before the eighteenth century ended it saw the last of those absolute monarchs.

The most stunning room by far is the Hall of Mirrors. The early afternoon light floods through windows to the west, lighting up the mirrors that line the east wall and illuminating the gold leaf decor and the enormous crystal chandeliers. It's breathtaking.

"Interesting to see what becomes of a despotic megalomaniac

who isolates himself in such splendor," I murmur to Christian as he stands at my side. He gazes down and cocks his head to one side, regarding me with humor.

"Your point, Mrs. Grey?"

"Oh, merely an observation, Mr. Grey." I wave my hand airily at the surroundings. Smirking, he follows me to the center of the room, where I stand and gawk at the view—the spectacular gardens reflected in the looking glass and the spectacular Christian Grey, my husband, reflected back at me, his gaze bright and bold.

"I would build this for you," he whispers. "Just to see the way the light burnishes your hair, right here, right now." He tucks a strand of hair behind my ear. "You look like an angel." He kisses me just below my earlobe, takes my hand in his, and murmurs, "We despots do that for the women we love."

I flush at his compliment, smiling shyly, and follow him through the vast room.

———

"What are you thinking about?" Christian asks softly, taking a sip of his after-dinner coffee.

"Versailles."

"Ostentatious, wasn't it?" He grins. I glance around the more understated grandeur of the *Fair Lady*'s dining room and purse my lips.

"This is hardly ostentatious," Christian says, a tad defensively.

"I know. It's lovely. The best honeymoon a girl could want."

"Really?" he says, genuinely surprised. And he smiles his shy smile.

"Of course it is."

"We've got only two more days. Is there anything you'd like to see or do?"

"Just be with you," I murmur. He rises from the table, comes around, and kisses me on the forehead.

"Well, can you do without me for about an hour? I need to check my e-mails, find out what's happening at home."

"Sure," I say brightly, trying to hide my disappointment that I'll be without him for an hour. Is it freaky that I want to be with him all the time?

"Thank you for the camera," he murmurs and heads for the study.

BACK IN OUR CABIN I decide to catch up on my own correspondence and open my laptop. There are e-mails from my mom and from Kate, giving me the latest gossip from home and asking how the honeymoon is going. Well, great, until someone decided to burn down GEH, Inc. . . . As I finish my response to my mom, an e-mail from Kate hits my in-box.

From: Katherine L. Kavanagh
Date: August 17 2011 11:45
To: Anastasia Grey
Subject: OMG!!!!

Ana, just heard about the fire at Christian's office.

Do you think it's arson?

K xox

Kate is online! I jump onto my newfound toy—Skype messaging—and see that she's available. I quickly type a message.

Ana: Hey are you there?
Kate: YES, Ana! How are you? How's the honeymoon? Did
      you see my e-mail? Does Christian know about the
      fire?

Ana: I'm good. Honeymoon's great. Yes, I saw your e-mail. Yes, Christian knows.

Kate: I thought he would. News is sketchy on what happened. And Elliot won't tell me anything.

Ana: Are you fishing for a story?

Kate: You know me too well.

Ana: Christian hasn't told me much.

Kate: Elliot heard from Grace!

Oh no—I'm sure Christian doesn't want this broadcast all over Seattle. I try my patented distract-tenacious-Kavanagh technique.

Ana: How are Elliot and Ethan?

Kate: Ethan has been accepted into the psych course at Seattle for his master's degree. Elliot is adorable.

Ana: Way to go, Ethan.

Kate: How's our favorite ex-dom?

Ana: Kate!

Kate: What?

Ana: YOU KNOW WHAT!

Kate: K. Sorry

Ana: He's fine. More than fine. ☺

Kate: Well, as long as you're happy, I'm happy.

Ana: I'm blissfully happy.

Kate: ☺ I have to run. Can we talk later?

Ana: Not sure. See if I am online. Time zones suck!

Kate: They do. Love you, Ana.

Ana: Love you, too. Laters. x

Kate: Laters. <3

Trust Kate to be on the trail of this story. I roll my eyes and shut Skype down before Christian sees the chat. He wouldn't appreciate the ex-Dom comment, and I'm not sure he's entirely ex . . .

I sigh loudly. Kate knows everything, since our tipsy evening three weeks before the wedding when I finally succumbed to the Kavanagh inquisition. It was a relief to finally talk to someone.

I glance at my watch. It's been about an hour since dinner, and I am missing my husband. I head back on deck to see if he's finished his work.

———— · ————

I am in the Hall of Mirrors and Christian is standing beside me, smiling down at me with love and affection. *You look like an angel.* I beam back at him, but when I glance into the looking glass, I'm standing on my own and the room is gray and drab. *No!* My head whips back to his face, to find his smile is sad and wistful. He tucks my hair behind my ear. Then he turns wordlessly and walks away slowly, the sound of his footsteps echoing off the mirrors as he paces the enormous room to the ornate double doors at the end . . . a man on his own, a man with no reflection . . . and I wake, gasping for air, as panic seizes me.

"Hey," he whispers from beside me in the darkness, his voice filled with concern.

Oh, he's here. He's safe. Relief courses through me.

"Oh, Christian," I mumble, trying to bring my pounding heartbeat under control. He wraps me in his arms, and it's only then that I realize I have tears streaming down my face.

"Ana, what is it?" He strokes my cheek, wiping away my tears, and I can hear his anguish.

"Nothing. A silly nightmare."

He kisses my forehead and my tearstained cheeks, comforting me. "Just a bad dream, baby," he murmurs. "I've got you. I'll keep you safe."

Drinking in his scent, I curl around him, trying to ignore the loss and devastation I felt in my dream, and in that moment, I know that my deepest, darkest fear would be losing him.

CHAPTER FIVE

I stir, instinctively reaching for Christian only to feel his absence. Shit! I wake instantly and look anxiously around the cabin. Christian is watching me from the small, upholstered armchair by the bed. Stooping down, he places something on the floor, then moves and stretches out on the bed beside me. He's dressed in his cut-offs and a gray T-shirt.

"Hey, don't panic. Everything's fine," he says, his voice gentle and soothing—like he's talking to a cornered wild animal. Tenderly, he smooths the hair back from my face and I calm immediately. I see him trying and failing to hide his own concern.

"You've been so jumpy these last couple of days," he murmurs, his eyes wide and serious.

"I'm okay, Christian." I give him my brightest smile because I don't want him to know how worried I am about the arson incident. The painful recollection of how I felt when *Charlie Tango* was sabotaged and Christian went missing—the hollow emptiness, the indescribable pain—keeps resurfacing; the memory nagging me and gnawing at my heart. Keeping the smile fixed on my face, I try to repress it.

"Were you watching me sleep?"

"Yes," he says, gazing at me steadily, studying me. "You were talking."

"Oh?" *Shit! What was I saying?*

"You're worried," he adds, his eyes filled with concern. Is there nothing I can keep from this man? He leans forward and kisses me between my brows.

"When you frown, a little V forms just here. It's soft to kiss. Don't worry, baby, I'll look after you."

"It's not me I'm worried about, it's you," I grumble. "Who's looking after you?"

He smiles indulgently at my tone. "I'm big enough and ugly enough to look after myself. Come. Get up. There's one thing I'd like to do before we head home." He grins at me, a big boyish yes-I'm-really-only-twenty-eight grin, and swats my behind. I yelp, startled, and realize that today we're going back to Seattle and my melancholy blossoms. I don't want to leave. I've relished being with him 24/7, and I'm not ready to share him with his company and his family. We've had a blissful honeymoon. With a few ups and downs, I admit, but that's normal for a newly married couple, surely?

But Christian cannot contain his boyish excitement, and despite my dark thoughts, it's infectious. When he rises gracefully off the bed, I follow, intrigued. What has he got in mind?

CHRISTIAN STRAPS THE KEY to my wrist.

"You want me to drive?"

"Yes." Christian grins. "That's not too tight?"

"It's fine. Is that why you're wearing a life jacket?" I arch my eyebrow.

"Yes."

I can't help my giggle. "Such confidence in my driving capabilities, Mr. Grey."

"As ever, Mrs. Grey."

"Well, don't lecture me."

Christian holds his hands up in a defensive gesture, but he's smiling. "Would I dare?"

"Yes, you would, and yes, you do, and we can't pull over and argue on the sidewalk here."

"Fair point well made, Mrs. Grey. Are we going to stand on this platform all day debating your driving skills or are we going to have some fun?"

"Fair point well made, Mr. Grey." I grasp the handlebars of the Jet Ski and clamber on. Christian climbs on behind me and kicks us away from the yacht. Taylor and two of the deckhands look on in amusement. Sliding forward, Christian wraps his arms around me and snuggles his thighs against mine. *Yes, this is what I like about this form of transport.* I insert the ignition key and push the start button, and the engine roars into life.

"Ready?" I shout to Christian over the noise.

"As I'll ever be," he says, his mouth close to my ear.

Gently, I pull on the lever and the Jet Ski moves away from the *Fair Lady*, far too sedately for my liking. Christian tightens his embrace. I pull on the gas some more, we shoot forward, and I'm delighted when we don't stall.

"Whoa!" Christian calls from behind, but the exhilaration in his voice is palpable. I speed past the *Fair Lady* toward the open sea. We're anchored outside the Saint-Laurent-du-Var, and Nice Côte d'Azur Airport is nestled in the distance, built into the Mediterranean, or so it seems. I've heard the odd plane landing since we arrived last night. I decide we need to take a closer look.

We shoot toward it, skipping rapidly over the waves. I love this, and I'm thrilled Christian's letting me drive. All the worry I've felt over the past two days melts away as we skim toward the airport.

"Next time we do this we'll have two Jet Skis," Christian shouts. I grin because the thought of racing him is thrilling.

As we zoom over the cool blue sea toward what looks like the end of the runway, the thundering roar of a jet overhead suddenly startles me as it comes in to land. It's so loud I panic, swerving and hitting the throttle at the same time, mistaking it for a brake.

"Ana!" Christian shouts, but it's too late. I'm catapulted off the side of the Jet Ski, arms and legs flailing, taking Christian with me in a spectacular splash.

Screaming, I plunge into the crystal blue sea and swallow a nasty mouthful of the Mediterranean. The water is cold this far from the shore, but I surface within a split second, courtesy of my life jacket. Coughing and spluttering, I wipe the seawater from my eyes and look around for Christian. He's already swimming toward me. The Jet Ski floats inoffensively a few feet away from us, its engine silent.

"You okay?" His eyes are full of panic as he reaches me.

"Yes," I croak, but I cannot contain my elation. *See, Christian? That's the worst that can happen on a Jet Ski!* He pulls me into his embrace, then grabs my head between his hands, examining my face closely.

"See, that wasn't so bad!" I grin as we tread water.

Eventually he smirks at me, obviously relieved. "No, I guess it wasn't. Except I'm wet," he grumbles, but his tone is playful.

"I'm wet, too."

"I like you wet." He leers.

"Christian!" I scold, trying for faux righteous indignation. He grins, looking gorgeous, then leans in and kisses me hard. When he pulls away, I'm breathless.

"Come. Let's head back. Now we have to shower. I'll drive."

We laze in the British Airways first class lounge at Heathrow outside London, waiting for our connecting flight to Seattle. Christian is engrossed in the *Financial Times*. I pull out his camera, wanting to take some photographs of him. He looks so sexy in his trademark white linen shirt and jeans, with his aviator specs tucked into the V of his open shirt. The flash disturbs him. He blinks up at me and smiles his shy smile.

"How are you, Mrs. Grey?" he asks.

"Sad to be going home," I murmur. "I like having you to myself."

He clasps my hand and, lifting it to his lips, grazes my knuckles with a sweet kiss. "Me, too."

"But?" I ask, hearing that small word unsaid at the end of his simple statement.

He frowns. "But?" he repeats disingenuously. I tilt my head to one side, gazing at him with the *tell me* expression I have been perfecting over the last couple of days. He sighs, putting his newspaper down. "I want this arsonist caught and out of our lives."

"Oh." That seems fair enough, but I'm surprised by his bluntness.

"I'll have Welch's balls on a platter if he lets anything like that happen again." A shiver runs down my spine at his menacing tone. He gazes at me impassively, and I don't know if he's daring me to be flippant or what. I do the only thing I can think of to ease the sudden tension between us and raise the camera and snap another photograph.

"Hey, sleepyhead, we're home," Christian murmurs.

"Hmm," I mumble, reluctant to leave my tantalizing dream of Christian and me on a picnic blanket at Kew Gardens. I am so tired. Traveling is exhausting, even in first class. We've been up for more than eighteen hours straight, I think—in my fatigue I've lost track. I hear my door open, and Christian is leaning over me. He unbuckles my seat belt and lifts me into his arms, waking me.

"Hey, I can walk," I protest sleepily.

He snorts. "I need to carry you over the threshold."

I put my arms around his neck. "Up all thirty floors?" I give him a challenging smile.

"Mrs. Grey, I am very pleased to announce that you've put on some weight."

"What?"

He grins. "So if you don't mind, we'll use the elevator." He narrows his eyes at me, though I know he's teasing.

Taylor opens the doors to the Escala lobby and smiles. "Welcome home, Mr. Grey, Mrs. Grey."

"Thanks, Taylor," says Christian.

I give Taylor the briefest of smiles and watch him head back to the Audi, where Sawyer waits at the wheel.

"What do you mean I've put on weight?" I glare at Christian.

His grin broadens, and he clasps me closer to his chest as he carries me across the lobby.

"Not much," he assures me, but his face darkens suddenly.

"What is it?" I try to keep the alarm in my voice under control.

"You've put on some of the weight you lost when you left me," he says quietly as he summons the elevator. A bleak expression crosses his face.

His sudden, surprising anguish tugs at my heart. "Hey." I curl my fingers around his face and into his hair, pulling him toward me. "If I hadn't gone, would you be standing here, like this, now?"

His eyes melt, the color of a storm cloud, and he smiles his shy smile, my favorite smile. "No," he says and steps into the elevator still holding me. He leans down and kisses me gently. "No, Mrs. Grey, I wouldn't. But I would know I could keep you safe, because you wouldn't defy me."

He sounds vaguely regretful . . . *Shit*.

"I like defying you." I test the waters.

"I know. And it's made me so . . . happy." He smiles down at me through his bemusement.

Oh, thank heavens. "Even though I'm fat?" I whisper.

He laughs. "Even though you're fat." He kisses me again, more heated this time, and I fist my fingers in his hair, holding him against me, our tongues twisting in a slow sensual dance with each other. When the elevator pings to a halt at the penthouse, we are both breathless.

"Very happy," he murmurs. His smile is darker now, his eyes hooded and full of salacious promise. He shakes his head as if to recover himself and carries me into the foyer.

"Welcome home, Mrs. Grey." He kisses me again, more chastely this time, and gives me the patented-Christian-Grey-full-gigawatt smile, his eyes dancing with joy.

"Welcome home, Mr. Grey." I beam, my heart answering his call, brimming with my own joy.

I think Christian's going to put me down, but he doesn't. He carries me through the foyer, across the corridor, into the great room, and deposits me on the kitchen island, where I sit with my legs dangling. He retrieves two champagne flutes from the kitchen cupboard and a bottle of chilled champagne from the fridge—our favorite, Bollinger. He deftly opens the bottle, not spilling a drop, pours the pale pink champagne into each glass, and hands one to me. Taking up the other, he gently parts my legs and moves forward to stand between them.

"Here's to us, Mrs. Grey."

"To us, Mr. Grey," I whisper, conscious of my shy smile. We clink glasses and take a sip.

"I know you're tired," he whispers, rubbing his nose against mine. "But I'd really like to go to bed . . . and not to sleep." He kisses the corner of my mouth. "It's our first night back here, and you're really mine." His voice drifts off as he plants soft kisses down my throat. It's early evening in Seattle, and I am dog-tired, but desire blooms deep in my belly.

CHRISTIAN IS SLUMBERING PEACEFULLY beside me as I stare at the pink and golden streaks of the new dawn through the vast windows. His arm is draped loosely over my breasts, and I try to match his breathing in an effort to get back to sleep, but it's hopeless. I'm wide-awake, my body clock on Greenwich mean time, my mind racing.

So much has happened in the last three weeks—*who am I kidding, the last three months*—that I feel that my feet haven't touched the ground. And now here I am, Mrs. Christian Grey, married to the most delicious, sexy, philanthropic, absurdly wealthy mogul a woman could meet. How did this all happen so fast?

I shift onto my side to gaze at him. I know he watches me sleep, but I rarely get the opportunity to repay the compliment. He looks young and carefree in his sleep, his long lashes fanned against his cheek, a light smattering of stubble covering his jaw, and his sculptured lips slightly parted, relaxed as he breathes deeply. I want to kiss him, to push my tongue between his lips, run my fingers over his soft yet prickly stubble. I really have to fight the urge not to touch him, not to disturb him. Hmm . . . I could just tease his earlobe with my teeth and suck. My subconscious glares up at me over her half-moon spectacles, distracted from volume two of the *Complete Works of Charles Dickens*, and mentally chastises me. *Leave the poor man alone, Ana.*

I am back to work on Monday. We have today to get back into our routine. It will be odd not seeing Christian for a whole day after spending almost every minute together for the last three weeks. I lie back and stare at the ceiling. One would think that spending so much time together would be suffocating, but that's just not the case. I've loved each and every minute, even our fighting. Every minute . . . except the news of the fire at Grey House.

My blood chills. Who could want to harm Christian? My mind gnaws at this mystery again. Someone in his business? An ex? A disgruntled employee? I have no idea, and Christian remains tight-lipped about it all, drip-feeding me the minimum information he can get away with in a bid to protect me. I sigh. My shining white-and-dark knight always trying to protect me. How am I going to make him open up more?

He stirs and I still, not wanting to wake him, but it has the opposite effect. *Damn!* Two bright eyes gaze at me.

"What's wrong?"

"Nothing. Go back to sleep." I try my reassuring smile. He stretches, rubs his face, and then grins at me.

"Jet lag?" he asks.

"Is that what this is? I can't sleep."

"I have the universal panacea right here, just for you, baby." He grins like a schoolboy, making me roll my eyes and giggle at the same time. And just like that my dark thoughts are swept aside and my teeth find his earlobe.

CHRISTIAN AND I CRUISE north on I-5 toward the 520 bridge in the Audi R8. We are going to have lunch at his parents', a welcome-home Sunday lunch. All the family will be there, plus

Kate and Ethan. It will be strange to be in company when we've been on our own all this time. I haven't had an opportunity to talk to Christian most of the morning. He was holed up in his study while I unpacked. He said I didn't have to, that Mrs. Jones would do it. But that's something else I need to get used to—having domestic help. I run my fingers absentmindedly over the leather upholstery of the door to distract my wandering thoughts. I feel out of sorts. Is it the jet lag? The arson?

"Would you let me drive this?" I ask, surprised that I say the words out loud.

"Of course," Christian replies, smiling. "What's mine is yours. If you dent it, though, I will take you into the Red Room of Pain." He glances swiftly at me with a malicious grin.

Shit! I gape at him. Is this a joke?

"You're kidding. You'd punish me for denting your car? You love your car more than you love me?" I tease.

"It's close," he says and reaches across to squeeze my knee. "But she doesn't keep me warm at night."

"I'm sure it could be arranged. You could sleep in her," I snap.

Christian laughs. "We haven't been home one day and you're kicking me out already?" He seems delighted. I gaze at him and he gives me a face-splitting grin, and although I want to be mad at him, it's impossible when he's in this kind of mood. Now that I think about it, he's been in a better frame of mind ever since he left his study this morning. And it dawns on me that I'm being petulant because we have to go back to reality, and I don't know if he's going to revert to the more closed pre-honeymoon Christian, or if I'll get to keep the new improved version.

"Why are you so pleased?" I ask.

He flashes yet another grin at me. "Because this conversation is so . . . normal."

"Normal!" I snort. "Not after three weeks of marriage! Surely." His smile slips.

"I'm kidding, Christian," I mutter quickly, not wanting to kill his mood. It strikes me how unsure he is of himself sometimes.

I suspect that he's always been like this, but has just hidden his uncertainty beneath an intimidating exterior. He's very easy to tease, probably because he's not used to it. It's a revelation, and I marvel again that we still have so much to learn about each other.

"Don't worry, I'll stick to the Saab," I mutter and turn to stare out the window, trying to shake off my bad mood.

"Hey. What's wrong?"

"Nothing."

"You're so frustrating sometimes, Ana. Tell me."

I turn and smirk at him. "Back at you, Grey."

He frowns. "I'm trying," he says softly.

"I know. Me, too." I smile and my mood brightens a little.

CARRICK LOOKS RIDICULOUS IN his chef's hat and *Licensed to Grill* apron as he stands at the barbecue. Every time I look at him, it makes me smile. In fact, my spirits have lifted considerably. We are all sitting around the table on the terrace of the Grey family home, enjoying the late summer sun. Grace and Mia are setting various salads out on the table, while Elliot and Christian trade friendly insults and discuss plans for the new house, and Ethan and Kate grill me about our honeymoon. Christian keeps hold of my hand, his fingers toying with my wedding and engagement rings.

"So if you can get the plans finalized with Gia, I have a window September through to mid-November and can get the whole crew on it," Elliot says as he stretches and drops an arm around Kate's shoulder, making her smile.

"Gia is due to come over to discuss the plans tomorrow evening," replies Christian. "I hope we can finalize everything then." He turns and looks expectantly at me.

Oh . . . this is news.

"Sure." I smile at him, mostly for the benefit of his family, but my spirits take a nosedive again. Why does he make these decisions without telling me? Or is it the thought of Gia—all lush hips, full breasts, expensive designer clothes, and perfume—

smiling too provocatively at my husband? My subconscious glares at me. *He's given you no reason to be jealous.* Shit, I am up and down today. What's wrong with me?

"Ana," Kate exclaims, snapping me out of my reverie. "You still in the South of France?"

"Yes," I reply with a smile.

"You look so well," she says, though she frowns as she says it.

"You both do." Grace beams while Elliot refills our glasses.

"To the happy couple." Carrick grins and raises his glass, and everyone around the table echoes the sentiment.

"And congratulations to Ethan for getting into the psych program at Seattle," chips in Mia proudly. She gives him an adoring smile, and Ethan smirks at her. I wonder idly if she's made any headway with him. It's difficult to tell.

I listen to the banter around the table. Christian is running through our extensive itinerary over the last three weeks, embellishing here and there. He sounds relaxed and in control, the worry of the arsonist forgotten. I, on the other hand, don't seem to be able to shake my mood. I pick at my food. Christian said I was fat yesterday. *He was joking!* My subconscious glares at me again. Elliot accidentally knocks his glass onto the terrace, startling everyone, and there's a sudden flurry of activity to get it cleaned up.

"I am going to take you to the boathouse and finally spank you in there if you don't snap out of this mood," Christian whispers to me.

I gasp with shock, turn, and gape at him. *What?* Is he teasing me?

"You wouldn't dare!" I growl at him, and from deep inside I feel a familiar, welcome excitement. He cocks an eyebrow at me. Of course he would. I glance quickly at Kate across the table. She's watching us with interest. I turn back to Christian, narrowing my eyes at him.

"You'd have to catch me first—and I'm wearing flats," I hiss.

"I'd have fun trying," he whispers with a licentious grin, and I *think* he's joking.

I blush. Confusingly, I feel better.

As we finish our dessert of strawberries and cream, the heavens open. We all leap up to clear the plates and glasses from the table, depositing them in the kitchen.

"Good thing the weather held off till we finished," Grace says, pleased, as we drift into the back room. Christian sits down at the shiny black upright piano, presses the quiet pedal, and starts to play a familiar tune that I can't immediately place.

Grace asks me for my impressions of Saint-Paul-de-Vence. She and Carrick had gone years ago during their honeymoon, and it occurs to me that this is a good omen, seeing how happy they are together now. Kate and Elliot are cuddling on one of the large overstuffed couches, while Ethan, Mia, and Carrick are deep in a conversation about psychology, I think.

Suddenly, as one, all the Greys stop talking and gape at Christian.

What?

Christian is singing softly to himself at the piano. Silence descends on us all as we strain to hear his soft, musical voice and the lyrics of "Wherever You Will Go." I've heard him sing before; haven't they? He stops, suddenly conscious of the deathly hush that's fallen over the room. Kate glances questioningly at me and I shrug. Christian turns on the stool and frowns, embarrassed to realize he's become the center of attention.

"Go on," Grace urges softly. "I've never heard you sing, Christian. Ever." She stares at him in wonder. He sits on the piano stool, looking absently at her, and after a beat, he shrugs. His eyes flicker nervously to me, then over to the French windows. The rest of the room suddenly erupts in self-conscious chatter, and I'm left watching my dear husband.

Grace distracts me, grasping my hands then suddenly folding me in her arms.

"Oh, darling girl! Thank you, thank you," she whispers, so only I can hear. It brings a lump to my throat.

"Um . . ." I hug her back, not really sure why I am being

thanked. Grace smiles, her eyes shining, and kisses my cheek. *What have I done?*

"I am going to make some tea," she says, her voice hoarse with unshed tears.

I amble over to Christian, who is now standing, staring out through the French windows.

"Hi," I murmur.

"Hi." He puts his arm around my waist, pulling me to him, and I slip my hand into the back pocket of his jeans. We gaze out at the rain.

"Feeling better?"

I nod.

"Good."

"You certainly know how to silence a room."

"I do it all the time," he says, and he grins at me.

"At work, yes, but not here."

"True, not here."

"No one's ever heard you sing? Ever?"

"It appears not," he says dryly. "Shall we go?"

I gaze up at him, trying to gauge his mood. His eyes are soft and warm and slightly bemused. I decide to change the subject.

"You going to spank me?" I whisper, and suddenly there are butterflies in my stomach. Perhaps this is what I need . . . this is what I have been missing.

He gazes down at me, his eyes darkening.

"I don't want to hurt you, but I'm more than happy to play."

I glance nervously around the large room, but we are out of earshot.

"Only if you misbehave, Mrs. Grey." He bends and murmurs in my ear.

How can he put so much sensual promise into six words?

"I'll see what I can do." I grin.

ONCE WE'VE SAID OUR good-byes, we walk over to the car.

"Here." Christian throws me the keys to the R8. "Don't bend it"—he adds in all seriousness—"or I will be fucking pissed."

My mouth goes dry. He's letting me drive his car? My inner goddess whips on her leather driving gloves and flat shoes. *Oh yes!* she cries.

"Are you sure?" I mouth, stunned.

"Yes, before I change my mind."

I don't think I have ever grinned so hard. He rolls his eyes and opens the driver's door so that I can climb in. I start the engine before he's even reached the passenger side, and he jumps in quickly.

"Eager, Mrs. Grey?" he asks with a wry smile.

"Very."

Slowly, I ease the car backward and turn it in the driveway. I manage not to stall it, surprising myself. Boy, is the clutch sensitive. Carefully navigating the driveway, I glance in my rearview mirror and see Sawyer and Ryan climb into the Audi SUV. I had no idea our security had followed us here. I pause before I set out onto the main road.

"You're sure about this?"

"Yes," Christian says tightly, telling me he's not sure about this at all. *Oh, my poor, poor Fifty.* I want to laugh at both him and myself because I'm nervous and excited. A small part of me wants to lose Sawyer and Ryan just for the kicks. I check for traffic then inch the R8 out onto the road. Christian curls up with tension and I can't resist. The road is clear. I put my foot down on the gas and we shoot forward.

"Whoa! Ana!" Christian shouts. "Slow down—you'll kill us both."

I immediately ease off the gas. Wow, can this car move!

"Sorry," I mutter, trying to sound contrite and failing miserably. Christian smirks at me, to hide his relief, I think.

"Well, that counts as misbehaving," he says casually, and I slow right down.

I glance in the rearview mirror. No sign of the Audi SUV, just a solitary dark car with tinted windows behind us. I imagine Sawyer and Ryan flustered, frantic to catch up, and for some reason this gives me a thrill. But not wanting to give my dear husband a coronary, I decide to behave and drive steadily, with growing confidence, toward the 520 bridge.

Suddenly, Christian swears and struggles to pull his Black-Berry from the pocket of his jeans.

"What?" he snaps angrily at whoever it is on the other end of the line. "No," he says and glances behind us. "Yes. She is."

I briefly check the rearview mirror, but I don't see anything odd, just a few cars behind us. The SUV is about four cars back, and we're all cruising at an even pace.

"I see." Christian sighs long and hard and rubs his forehead with his fingers; tension radiates off him. *Something's wrong.*

"Yes . . . I don't know." He glances at me and lowers the phone from his ear. "We're fine. Keep going," he says calmly, smiling at me, but the smile doesn't touch his eyes. *Shit!* Adrenaline spikes through my system. He picks the phone up again.

"Okay on the 520. As soon as we hit it . . . Yes . . . I will."

He slots the phone into the speaker cradle, putting it on hands-free.

"What's wrong, Christian?"

"Just look where you're going, baby," he says softly.

I'm heading for the on-ramp of the 520 in the direction of Seattle. When I glance at Christian, he's staring straight ahead.

"I don't want you to panic," he says calmly. "But as soon as we're on the 520 proper, I want you to step on the gas. We're being followed."

Followed! Holy shit. My heart lurches into my mouth, pounding, my scalp prickles and my throat constricts with panic. Followed by whom? My eyes dart to the rearview mirror and, sure enough, the dark car I saw earlier is still behind us. *Fuck! Is that it?* I squint through the tinted windshield to see who's driving, but I see nothing.

"Keep your eyes on the road, baby," Christian says gently, not in the truculent tone he normally uses where my driving is concerned.

Get a grip! I mentally slap myself to subdue the dread that's threatening to swamp me. Suppose whoever's following us is armed? Armed and after Christian! *Shit!* I'm hit by a wave of nausea.

"How do we know we're being followed?" My voice is a breathy, squeaky whisper.

"The Dodge behind us has false license plates."

How does he know that?

I signal as we approach the 520 from the on-ramp. It's late afternoon, and although the rain has stopped, the roadway is wet. Fortunately, the traffic is reasonably light.

Ray's voice echoes in my head from one of his many self-defense lectures. *"It's the panic that's gonna kill you or get you seriously hurt, Annie."* I take a deep breath, trying to bring my breathing under control. Whoever is following us is after Christian. As I take another deep steadying breath, my mind begins to clear and my stomach settles. I have to keep Christian safe. I wanted to drive this car, and I wanted to drive it fast. *Well, here's my chance.* I grip the steering wheel and take a final glance in my rearview mirror. The Dodge is closing on us.

I slow right down, ignoring Christian's sudden panicked glance at me, and time my entrance on to the 520 so that the Dodge has to slow and stop to wait for a gap in the traffic. I drop a gear and floor it. The R8 shoots forward, slamming us both into the backs of our seats. The speedometer whips up to seventy-five miles per hour.

"Steady, baby," Christian says calmly, though I'm sure he's anything but calm.

I weave between the two lanes of traffic like a black piece in a game of checkers, effectively jumping the cars and trucks. We're so close to the lake on this bridge, it's as if we're driving on the water. I studiously ignore the angry, disapproving looks from other drivers. Christian clutches his hands together in his lap, keeping as still as possible, and in spite of my fevered thoughts, I wonder vaguely if he's doing it so he doesn't distract me.

"Good girl," he breathes in encouragement. He glances behind him. "I can't see the Dodge."

"We're right behind the unsub, Mr. Grey." Sawyer's voice comes through the hands-free. "He's trying to catch up with you, sir. We're going to try and come alongside, put ourselves between your car and the Dodge."

Unsub? What does that mean?

"Good. Mrs. Grey is doing well. At this rate, provided the traffic remains light—and from what I can see it is—we'll be off the bridge in a few minutes."

"Sir."

We flash past the bridge control tower, and I know we're halfway across Lake Washington. When I check my speed, I'm still doing seventy-five.

"You're doing really well, Ana," Christian murmurs again as he gazes out the back of the R8. For a fleeting moment, his tone reminds me of our first encounter in his playroom when he patiently encouraged me through our first scene. The thought is distracting, and I dismiss it immediately.

"Where am I headed?" I ask, moderately calmer. I have the feel of the car now. It's a joy to drive, so quiet and easy to handle it's hard to believe how fast we are going. Driving at this speed in this car is easy.

"Mrs. Grey, head for I-5 and then south. We want to see if the Dodge follows you all the way," Sawyer says over the hands-free. The traffic lights on the bridge are green—thank heavens—and I race onward.

I glance nervously at Christian, and he smiles reassuringly. Then his face falls.

"Shit!" he swears softly.

There is a line of traffic ahead as we come off the bridge, and I have to slow down. Glancing anxiously in the mirror once more, I think I spot the Dodge.

"Ten or so cars back?"

"Yeah, I see it," Christian says, peering through the narrow rear window. "I wonder who the fuck it is?"

"Me too. Do we know if it's a man driving?" I blurt out toward the cradled BlackBerry.

"No, Mrs. Grey. Could be a man or woman. The tint is too dark."

"A woman?" Christian says.

I shrug. "Your Mrs. Robinson?" I suggest, not taking my eyes off the road.

Christian stiffens and lifts the BlackBerry out of its cradle. "She's not my Mrs. Robinson," he growls. "I haven't spoken to her since my birthday. And Elena wouldn't do this. It's not her style."

"Leila?"

"She's in Connecticut with her parents. I told you."

"Are you sure?"

He pauses. "No. But if she'd absconded, I'm sure her folks would have let Flynn know. Let's discuss this when we're home. Concentrate on what you're doing."

"But it might just be some random car."

"I'm not taking any risks. Not where you're concerned," he snaps. He replaces the BlackBerry in its cradle so we're back in contact with our security team.

Oh shit. I don't want to rattle Christian right now . . . later maybe. I hold my tongue. Fortunately, the traffic is thinning a little. I am able to speed over the Mountlake intersection toward the I-5, weaving through the cars again.

"What if we get stopped by the cops?" I ask.

"That would be a good thing."

"Not for my license."

"Don't worry about that," he says. Unexpectedly, I hear humor in his voice.

I put my foot down again, and hit seventy-five. Boy, this car can move. I love it—she's so easy. I touch eighty-five. I don't think I have ever driven this fast. I was lucky if my Beetle ever hit fifty miles an hour.

"He's cleared the traffic and picked up speed." Sawyer's disembodied voice is calm and informative. "He's doing ninety."

Shit! Faster! I press down on the gas and the car purrs to ninety-five miles per hour as we approach the I-5 intersection.

"Keep it up, Ana," Christian murmurs.

I slow momentarily as we glide onto I-5. The interstate is fairly quiet, and I'm able to cross straight over to the fast lane in a split second. As I put my foot down, the glorious R8 zooms forward, and we tear down the left lane, lesser mortals pulling over to let us pass. If I wasn't so frightened, I might really enjoy this.

"He's hit one hundred miles per hour, sir."

"Stay with him, Luke," Christian barks at Sawyer.

Luke?

A truck lurches into the fast lane—*Shit!*—and I have to slam on the brakes.

"Fucking idiot!" Christian curses the driver as we lurch forward in our seats. I am grateful for our seat belts.

"Go around him, baby," Christian says through clenched teeth. I check my mirrors and cut right across three lanes. We speed past the slower vehicles and then cut back to the fast lane.

"Nice move, Mrs. Grey," Christian murmurs appreciatively. "Where are the cops when you need them?"

"I don't want a ticket, Christian," I mutter, concentrating on the highway ahead. "Have you had a speeding ticket driving this?"

"No," he says, but glancing quickly at him, I can see his smirk.

"Have you been stopped?"

"Yes."

"Oh."

"Charm. It all comes down to charm. Now concentrate. Where's the Dodge, Sawyer?"

"He's just hit one hundred and ten, sir." Sawyer says.

Holy fuck! My heart leaps once more into my mouth. Can I drive any faster? I push my foot down once more and streak past the traffic.

"Flash the headlights," Christian orders when a Ford Mustang won't move.

"But that would make me an asshole."

"So be an asshole!" he snaps.

Jeez. Okay! "Um, where are the headlights?"

"The indicator. Pull it toward you."

I do it, and the Mustang moves aside, though not before the

driver waves his finger at me in a none-too-complimentary manner. I zoom past him.

"He's the asshole," Christian says under his breath, then barks
at me, "Get off on Stewart."

Yes, sir!

"We're taking the Stewart Street exit," Christian says to Sawyer.

"Head straight to Escala, sir."

I slow, check my mirrors, signal, then move with surprising
ease across four lanes of the highway and down the off-ramp.
Merging onto Stewart Street, we head south. The street is quiet,
with few vehicles. *Where is everyone?*

"We've been damned lucky with the traffic. But that means
the Dodge has, too. Don't slow down, Ana. Get us home."

"I can't remember the way," I mutter, panicked by the fact that
the Dodge is still on our tail.

"Head south on Stewart. Keep going until I tell you when."
Christian sounds anxious again. I zoom past three blocks but the
lights change to yellow on Yale Avenue.

"Run them, Ana," Christian shouts. I jump so hard I floor the
gas pedal, throwing us both back in our seats, speeding through
the now red light.

"He's taking Stewart," Sawyer says.

"Stay with him, Luke."

"Luke?"

"That's his name."

A quick glance and I can see Christian glaring at me as if I'm
crazy. "Eyes on the road!" he snaps.

I ignore his tone. "Luke Sawyer."

"Yes!" He sounds exasperated.

"Ah." How did I not know this? The man has been following
me to work for the last six weeks, and I didn't even know his first
name.

"That's me, ma'am," Sawyer says, startling me, though he's
speaking in the calm, monotone voice he always uses. "The
unsub is heading down Stewart, sir. He's really picking up speed."

"Go, Ana. Less of the fucking chitchat," Christian growls.

"We're stopped at the first light on Stewart," Sawyer informs us.

"Ana—quick—in here," Christian shouts, pointing to a parking lot on the south side of Boren Avenue. I turn, the tires screeching in protest as I swerve into the crowded lot.

"Drive around. Quick," Christian orders. I drive as fast as I can to the back, out of sight of the street. "In there." Christian points to a space. *Shit!* He wants me to park it. *Crap!*

"Just fucking do it," he says. So I do . . . perfectly. Probably the only time I have ever parked perfectly.

"We're hidden in the parking lot between Stewart and Boren," Christian says into the BlackBerry.

"Okay, sir." Sawyer sounds irritated. "Stay where you are; we'll follow the unsub."

Christian turns to me, his eyes searching my face. "You okay?"

"Sure," I whisper.

Christian smirks. "Whoever's driving that Dodge can't hear us, you know."

And I laugh.

"We're passing Stewart and Boren now, sir. I see the lot. He's gone straight past you, sir."

Both of us sag simultaneously with relief.

"Well done, Mrs. Grey. Good driving." Christian gently strokes my face with his fingertips, and I jump at the contact, inhaling deeply. I had no idea I was holding my breath.

"Does this mean you'll stop complaining about my driving?" I ask. He laughs—a loud cathartic laugh.

"I wouldn't go so far as to say that."

"Thank you for letting me drive your car. Under such exciting circumstances, too." I try desperately to keep my voice light.

"Maybe I should drive now."

"To be honest, I don't think I can climb out right now to let you sit here. My legs feel like Jell-O." Suddenly I'm shuddering and shaking.

"It's the adrenaline, baby," he says. "You did amazingly well, as usual. You blow me away, Ana. You never let me down." He touches my cheek tenderly with the back of his hand, his face full of love, fear, regret—so many emotions at once—and his words are my undoing. Overwhelmed, a strangled sob escapes from my constricted throat, and I start to cry.

"No, baby, no. Please don't cry." He reaches over and, despite the limited space we have, pulls me over the handbrake console to cradle me in his lap. Smoothing my hair off my face, he kisses my eyes, then my cheeks, and I curl my arms around him and sob quietly into his neck. He buries his nose in my hair and wraps me in his arms, holding me tight, and we sit, neither of us saying anything, just holding each other.

Sawyer's voice startles us. "The unsub has slowed outside Escala. He's casing the joint."

"Follow him," Christian snaps.

I wipe my nose on the back of my hand and take a deep steadying breath.

"Use my shirt." Christian kisses my temple.

"Sorry," I mutter, embarrassed by my crying.

"What for? Don't be."

I wipe my nose again. He tips my chin up and plants a gentle kiss on my lips. "Your lips are so soft when you cry, my beautiful, brave girl," he whispers.

"Kiss me again."

Christian stills, one hand on my back, the other on my behind.

"Kiss me," I breathe, and I watch his lips part as he inhales sharply. Leaning across me, he takes the BlackBerry out of its cradle, and tosses it onto the driver's seat beside my sandaled feet. Then his mouth is on me as he moves his right hand into my hair, holding me in place, and lifts his left to cradle my face. His tongue invades my mouth, and I welcome it. Adrenaline turns to lust and streaks through my body. I clasp his face, running my fingers over his sideburns, relishing the taste of him. He groans at my fevered response, low and deep in his throat, and my belly tightens swift and hard with carnal desire. His hand moves down my body, brushing my breast, my waist, and down to my backside. I shift fractionally.

"Ah!" he says and breaks away from me, breathless.

"What?" I mutter against his lips.

"Ana, we're in a car lot in Seattle."

"So?"

"Well, right now I want to fuck you, and you're shifting around on me . . . it's uncomfortable."

My craving spirals out of control at his words, tightening all my muscles below my waist once more.

"Fuck me then." I kiss the corner of his mouth. I want him. Now. That car chase was exciting. Too exciting. Terrifying . . . and the fear has jump-started my libido. He leans back to gaze at me, his eyes dark and hooded.

"Here?" His voice is husky.

My mouth goes dry. How can he turn me on with one word? "Yes. I want you. Now."

He tilts his head to one side and stares at me for a few moments. "Mrs. Grey, how very brazen," he whispers, after what feels like an eternity. His hand tightens around my hair at my nape, holding me firmly in place, and his mouth is on mine again, more forcefully this time. His other hand skims down my body, down over my behind and lower still to my mid-thigh. My fingers curl into his overlong hair.

"I'm so glad you're wearing a skirt," he murmurs as he slips his hand beneath my blue-and-white-patterned skirt to caress my thigh. I squirm once more on his lap and the air hisses between his teeth.

"Keep still," he growls. He cups my sex with his hand, and I still immediately. His thumb brushes over my clitoris, and my breath catches in my throat as pleasure jolts like electricity deep, deep, deep inside me.

"Still," he whispers. He kisses me once more as his thumb circles gently around me through the sheer fine lace of my designer underwear. Slowly he eases two fingers past my panties and inside me. I groan and flex my hips toward his hand.

"Please," I whisper.

"Oh. You're so ready," he says, sliding his fingers in and out, torturously slowly. "Do car chases turn you on?"

"You turn me on."

He smiles a wolfish grin and withdraws his fingers suddenly, leaving me wanting. He scoops his arm under my knees and, taking me by surprise, he lifts me and swings me around to face the windshield.

"Place your legs either side of mine," he orders, putting his legs together in the middle of the footwell. I do as I'm told, placing my feet on the floor on either side of his. He runs his hands down my thighs, then back, pulling up my skirt.

"Hands on my knees, baby. Lean forward. Lift that glorious ass in the air. Mind your head."

Shit! We really are going to do this, in a public parking lot. I quickly scan the area in front of us and see no one, but feel a thrill coursing through me. I'm in a public lot! This is so *hot!* Christian shifts beneath me, and I hear the telltale sound of his zipper. Putting one arm around my waist and with his other hand tugging my lacy panties sideways, he impales me in one swift move.

"Ah!" I cry out, grinding down on him, and his breath hisses through his teeth. His arm snakes around me up to my neck and he grasps me under my chin. His hand spreads across my neck, pulling me back and tilting my head to one side so he can kiss my throat. His other hand grips my hip and together we start to move.

I push up with my feet, and he tilts himself into me—in and out. The sensation is . . . I groan loudly. It's so deep this way. My left hand curls around the hand brake, my right hand braced against the door. His teeth graze my earlobe and he tugs—it's almost painful. He bucks again and again into me. I rise and fall, and as we establish a rhythm, he moves his hand around beneath my skirt to the apex of my thighs, and his fingers gently tease my clitoris through the sheer finery of my panties.

"Ah!"

"Be. Quick," he breathes into my ear through gritted teeth, his hand still curled around my neck beneath my chin. "We need to do this quick, Ana." And he increases the pressure of his fingers against my sex.

"Ah!" I feel the familiar build of pleasure, bunching deep and thick inside me.

"Come on, baby," he rasps at my ear. "I want to hear you."

I moan again, and I am all sensation, my eyes tightly closed. His voice at my ear, his breath on my neck, pleasure radiating out from where his fingers tease my body and where he slams deep inside me, and I am lost. My body takes control, craving release.

"Yes," Christian hisses in my ear, and I open my eyes briefly, staring wildly at the cloth roof of the R8, and I scrunch them closed again as I come around him.

"Oh, Ana," he murmurs in wonder, and he wraps his arms around me and rams into me one last time and stills as he climaxes deep inside.

He runs his nose along my jaw and softly kisses my throat, my cheek, my temple as I lie on him, my head lolling against his neck.

"Tension relieved, Mrs. Grey?" Christian closes his teeth around my earlobe again and tugs. My body is drained, totally exhausted, and I mewl. I feel his smile against me.

"Certainly helped with mine," he adds, shifting me off him. "Lost your voice?"

"Yes," I murmur.

"Well, aren't you the wanton creature? I had no idea you were such an exhibitionist."

I sit up immediately, alarmed. He tenses. "No one's watching, are they?" I glance anxiously around the car lot.

"Do you think I'd let anyone watch my wife come?" He strokes his hand down my back reassuringly, but the tone of his voice sends shivers down my spine. I turn to gaze at him and grin impishly.

"Car sex!" I exclaim.

He grins back and tucks a strand of hair behind my ear. "Let's head back. I'll drive."

He opens the door to let me climb off his lap and out into the parking lot. When I glance down he's quickly doing up his fly. He follows me out and then holds the door open for me to climb back in. Strolling quickly around to the driver's side, he climbs in beside me, retrieves the BlackBerry, and makes a call.

"Where's Sawyer?" he snaps. "And the Dodge? How come Sawyer's not with you?"

He listens intently to Ryan, I assume.

"Her?" he gasps. "Stick with her." Christian hangs up and gazes at me.

Her! The driver of the car? Who could that be—Elena? Leila?

"The driver of the Dodge is female?"

"So it would appear," he says quietly. His mouth presses into a thin angry line. "Let's get you home," he mutters. He starts up the R8 with a roar and reverses smoothly out of the space.

"Where's the, er . . . unsub? What does that mean by the way? Sounds very BDSM."

Christian smiles briefly as he eases the car out of the lot and back onto Stewart Street.

"It stands for Unknown Subject. Ryan is ex-FBI."

"Ex-FBI?"

"Don't ask." Christian shakes his head. It's obvious he's deep in contemplation.

"Well, where is this female unsub?"

"On the I-5, heading south." He glances at me, his eyes grim.

Whoa—from passionate to calm to anxious in the space of a few moments. I reach over and caress his thigh, running my fingers leisurely up the inside seam of his jeans, hoping to improve his mood. He takes his hand off the steering wheel and stops the slow ascent of my hand.

"No," he says. "We've made it this far. You don't want me to have an accident three blocks from home." He raises my hand to his lips and plants a cool kiss on my index finger to take the sting out of his rebuke. Cool, calm, authoritative . . . My Fifty. And for the first time in a while he makes me feel like a wayward child. I withdraw my hand and sit quietly for a moment.

"Female?"

"Apparently so." He sighs, turns into the underground garage at Escala, and punches the access code into the security keypad. The gate swings open and he drives on, smoothly parking the R8 in its designated space.

"I really like this car," I murmur.

"Me too. And I like how you handled it—and how you managed not to break it."

"You can buy me one for my birthday." I smirk at him.

Christian's mouth drops open as I climb out of the car.

"A white one, I think," I add, leaning down and grinning at him.

He smiles. "Anastasia Grey, you never cease to amaze me."

I shut the door and walk to the end of the car to wait for him. Gracefully he climbs out, watching me with that look . . . that look that calls to something deep inside me. I know this look well. Once he's in front of me, he leans down and whispers, "You like the car. I like the car. I've fucked you in it . . . perhaps I should fuck you on it."

I gasp. And a sleek silver BMW pulls into the garage. Christian glances at it anxiously, then with annoyance and gives me a sly smile.

"But it looks like we have company. Come." He grabs my hand and heads for the garage elevator. He pushes the "call" button and as we wait, the driver of the BMW joins us. He's young, casually dressed, with long, layered, dark hair. He looks like he works in the media.

"Hi," he says, smiling warmly at us.

Christian puts his arm around me and nods politely.

"I've just moved in. Apartment sixteen."

"Hello." I return his smile. He has kind, soft brown eyes.

The elevator arrives and we all walk in. Christian glances down at me, his expression unreadable.

"You're Christian Grey," the young man says.

Christian gives him a tight smile.

"Noah Logan." He holds out his hand. Reluctantly, Christian takes it. "Which floor?" Noah asks.

"I have to input a code."

"Oh."

"Penthouse."

"Oh." Noah smiles broadly. "Of course." He presses the button for the eighth floor and the doors close. "Mrs. Grey, I presume."

"Yes." I give him a polite smile and we shake hands. Noah flushes a little as he gazes at me a fraction too long. I mirror his flush and Christian's arm tightens around me.

"When did you move in?" I ask.

"Last weekend. I love the place."

There's an awkward pause before the elevator stops at Noah's floor.

"Great to meet you both," he says, sounding relieved, and steps out. The doors close silently behind him. Christian taps in the entry code and the elevator ascends again.

"He seemed nice," I murmur. "I've never met any of the neighbors before."

Christian scowls. "I prefer it that way."

"That's because you're a hermit. I thought he was pleasant enough."

"A hermit?"

"Hermit. Stuck in your ivory tower," I state matter-of-factly. Christian's lips twitch with amusement.

"Our ivory tower. And I think you have another name to add to the list of your admirers, Mrs. Grey."

I roll my eyes. "Christian, you think everyone is an admirer."

"Did you just roll your eyes at me?"

My pulse quickens. "I sure did," I whisper, my breath catching in my throat.

He cocks his head to one side, wearing his smoldering, arrogant, amused expression. "What shall we do about that?"

"Something rough."

He blinks to hide his surprise. "Rough?"

"Please."

"You want more?"

I nod slowly. The doors to the elevator open and we're home.

"How rough?" he breathes, his eyes darkening.

I gaze at him, saying nothing. He closes his eyes for a moment, and then grabs my hand and hauls me into the foyer.

When we burst through the double doors, Sawyer is standing in the hallway, looking expectantly at the two of us.

"Sawyer, I'd like to be debriefed in an hour," Christian says.

"Yes, sir." Turning, Sawyer heads back into Taylor's office.

We have an hour!

Christian glances down at me. "Rough?"

I nod.

"Well, Mrs. Grey, you're in luck. I'm taking requests today."

CHAPTER SIX

D o you have anything in mind?" Christian murmurs, pinning me with his bold gaze. I shrug, suddenly breathless and agitated. I don't know if it's the chase, the adrenaline, my earlier bad mood—I don't understand, but I want this, and I want it badly. A puzzled expression flits across Christian's face. "Kinky fuckery?" he asks, his words a soft caress.

I nod, feeling my face flame. Why am I embarrassed by this? I have done all manner of kinky fuckery with this man. *He's my husband, damn it!* Am I embarrassed because I want this and I'm ashamed to admit it? My subconscious glares at me. *Stop overthinking.*

"Carte blanche?" He whispers the question, eyeing me speculatively as if he's trying to read my mind.

Carte blanche? Holy fuck—what will that entail? "Yes," I murmur nervously, as excitement blooms deep inside me. He smiles a slow, sexy smile.

"Come," he says and tugs me toward the stairs. His intention is clear. *Playroom!*

At the top of the stairs, he releases my hand and unlocks the playroom door. The key is on the *Yes Seattle* keychain that I gave him not so long ago.

"After you, Mrs. Grey," he says and swings the door open.

The playroom smells reassuringly familiar, of leather and wood and fresh polish. I blush, knowing that Mrs. Jones must have been in here cleaning while we were away on our honeymoon. As we enter, Christian switches on the lights and the dark red walls are illuminated with soft, diffused light. I stand gazing at him, anticipation running thick and heavy through my veins.

What will he do? He locks the door and turns. Inclining his head to one side, he regards me thoughtfully and then shakes his head, amused.

"What do you want, Anastasia?" he asks gently.

"You." My response is breathy.

He smirks. "You've got me. You've had me since you fell into my office."

"Surprise me then, Mr. Grey."

His mouth twists with repressed humor and carnal promise. "As you wish, Mrs. Grey." He folds his arms and raises one long index finger to his lips while he appraises me. "I think we'll start by ridding you of your clothes." He steps forward. Grasping the front of my short denim jacket, he opens it and pushes it over my shoulders so it falls to the floor. He clasps the hem of my black camisole.

"Lift your arms."

I obey, and he peels it off over my head. Leaning down, he plants a soft kiss on my lips, his eyes glowing with an alluring mix of lust and love. The camisole joins my jacket on the floor.

"Here," I whisper, gazing nervously at him as I remove the hair tie from around my wrist and hold it up for him. He stills, and his eyes widen briefly but give nothing away. Finally, he takes the small band.

"Turn around," he orders.

Relieved, I smile to myself and oblige immediately. Looks like we've overcome that little hurdle. He gathers my hair and braids it quickly and efficiently before fastening it with the tie. He tugs the braid, pulling my head back.

"Good thinking, Mrs. Grey," he whispers in my ear, then nips my earlobe. "Now turn around and take your skirt off. Let it fall to the floor." He releases me and steps back as I turn to face him. Not taking my eyes off his, I unbutton the waistband of my skirt and ease the zipper down. The full skirt fans out and falls to the floor, pooling at my feet.

"Step out from your skirt," he orders. As I step toward him, he kneels swiftly down in front of me and grasps my right ankle.

Deftly, he unbuckles my sandals one at a time while I lean forward, balancing myself with a hand on the wall under the pegs that used to hold all his whips, crops, and paddles. The flogger and the riding crop are the only implements that remain. I eye them with curiosity. *Will he use those?*

Having removed my shoes so I'm just in my lacy bra and panties, Christian sits back on his heels, gazing up at me. "You're a fine sight, Mrs. Grey." Suddenly he kneels up, grabs my hips, and pulls me forward, burying his nose in the apex of my thighs. "And you smell of you and me and sex," he says, inhaling sharply. "It's intoxicating." He kisses me through my lace panties, while I gasp at his words—my insides liquefying. He's just so . . . *naughty.* Gathering up my clothes and sandals, he stands in one swift, graceful move, like an athlete.

"Go and stand beside the table," he says calmly, pointing with his chin. Turning, he strides over to the museum chest of wonder.

He glances back and smirks at me. "Face the wall," he commands. "That way you won't know what I'm planning. We aim to please, Mrs. Grey, and you wanted a surprise."

I turn away from him, listening acutely—my ears suddenly sensitive to the slightest sound. He's good at this—building my expectations, stoking my desire . . . making me wait. I hear him put my shoes down and, I think, my clothes on the chest, followed by the telltale clatter of his shoes as they drop to the floor, one at a time. Hmm . . . love barefoot Christian. A moment later, I hear him pull open a drawer.

Toys! Oh, I love, love, love this anticipation. The drawer closes and my breathing spikes. How can the sound of a drawer render me a quivering mess? It makes no sense. The subtle hiss of the sound system coming to life tells me it's going to be a musical interlude. A lone piano starts, muted and soft, and mournful chords fill the room. It's not a tune I know. The piano is joined by an electric guitar. *What is this?* A man's voice speaks and I can just make out the words, something about not being frightened of dying.

Christian pads leisurely toward me, his bare feet slapping on the wooden floor. I sense him behind me as a woman starts to sing . . . wail . . . sing?

"Rough, you say, Mrs. Grey?" he breathes in my left ear.

"Hmm."

"You must tell me to stop if it's too much. If you say stop, I will stop immediately. Do you understand?"

"Yes."

"I need your promise."

I inhale sharply. *Shit, what is he going to do?* "I promise," I murmur breathlessly, recalling his words from earlier: *I don't want to hurt you, but I'm more than happy to play.*

"Good girl." Leaning down, he plants a kiss on my naked shoulder, then hooks a finger beneath my bra strap and traces a line across my back beneath the strap. I want to moan. How does he make the slightest touch so erotic?

"Take it off," he whispers in my ear, and hurriedly I oblige and let my bra fall to the floor.

His hands skim down my back, and he hooks both of his thumbs into my panties and slides them down my legs.

"Step," he orders. Once more I do as I'm told, stepping out of my panties. He plants a kiss on my backside and stands.

"I am going to blindfold you so that everything will be more intense." He slips an airline eye mask over my eyes, and my world is plunged into darkness. The woman singing moans incoherently . . . a haunting, heartfelt melody.

"Bend down and lie flat on the table." His words are softly spoken. "Now."

Without hesitation, I bend over the side of the table and rest my torso on the highly polished wood, my face flush against the hard surface. It's cool against my skin and it smells vaguely of beeswax with a citrus tang.

"Stretch your arms up and hold on to the edge."

Okay . . . Reaching forward, I clutch the far edge of the table. It's quite wide, so my arms are fully extended.

"If you let go, I will spank you. Do you understand?"

"Yes."

"Do you want me to spank you, Anastasia?"

Everything south of my waist tightens deliciously. I realize I've wanted this since he threatened me during lunch, and neither the car chase nor our subsequent intimate encounter has sated this need.

"Yes." My voice is a hoarse whisper.

"Why?"

Oh . . . do I have to have a reason? I shrug.

"Tell me," he coaxes.

"Um . . ."

And from out of nowhere he smacks me hard.

"Ah!" I cry out.

"Hush now."

He gently rubs my behind where he's hit me. Then he leans over me, his hips digging into my backside, plants a kiss between my shoulder blades, and trails kisses across my back. He's taken his shirt off, so his chest hair tickles my back, and his erection presses against me through the rough fabric of his jeans.

"Open your legs," he orders.

I move my legs apart.

"Wider."

I groan and spread my legs wider.

"Good girl," he breathes. He traces his finger down my back, along the crack between my buttocks, and over my anus, which shrinks at his touch.

"We're going to have with some fun with this," he whispers.

Fuck!

His finger continues down over my perineum and slowly slides into me.

"I see you're very wet, Anastasia. From earlier or from now?"

I groan and he eases his finger in and out of me, over and over. I push back on his hand, relishing the intrusion.

"Oh, Ana, I think it's both. I think you love being here, like this. Mine."

I do—oh, I do. He withdraws his finger and smacks me hard once more.

"Tell me," he whispers, his voice hoarse and urgent.

"Yes, I do," I whimper.

He smacks me hard once more so I cry out, then sticks two fingers inside me. He withdraws them immediately, spreading the moisture up, over, and around my anus.

"What are you going to do?" I ask, breathless. *Oh my . . . is he going to fuck my ass?*

"It's not what you think," he murmurs reassuringly. "I told you, one step at time with this, baby." I hear the quiet spurt of some liquid, presumably from a tube, then his fingers are massaging me *there* again. Lubricating me . . . *there!* I squirm as my fear collides with my excitement of the unknown. He smacks me once more, lower, so he hits my sex. I groan. It feels . . . so good.

"Keep still," he says. "And don't let go."

"Ah."

"This is lube." He spreads some more on me. I try not to wriggle beneath him, but my heart is pounding, my pulse haywire, as desire and anxiety pump through me.

"I have wanted to do this to you for some time now, Ana."

I groan. And I feel something cool, metallically cool, run down my spine.

"I have a small present for you here," Christian whispers.

An image from our show-and-tell springs to mind. *Holy crap.* A butt plug. Christian runs it down the parting between my buttocks.

Oh my.

"I am going to push this inside you, very slowly."

I gasp, anticipation and anxiety charging through me.

"Will it hurt?"

"No, baby. It's small. Once it's inside you, I'm going to fuck you real hard."

I practically convulse. Bending over me, he kisses me once more between my shoulder blades.

"Ready?" he whispers.

Ready? Am I ready for this?

"Yes," I mutter quietly, my mouth dry. He runs another finger down past my ass and perineum and slips it inside me. Fuck, it's his thumb. He cups my sex and his fingers gently caress my clitoris. I moan . . . it feels . . . good. And gently, while his fingers and thumb work their magic, he pushes the cold plug slowly into me.

"Ah!" I groan loudly at the unfamiliar sensation, my muscles protesting at the intrusion. He circles his thumb inside me and pushes the plug harder, and it slips in easily, and I don't know if it's because I'm so turned on or if he's distracted me with his expert fingers, but my body seems to accept it. It's heavy . . . and strange . . . *there!*

"Oh, baby."

And I can feel it . . . where his thumb swirls inside me . . . and the plug presses against . . . oh, ah . . . He slowly twists the plug, eliciting a long drawn-out moan from me.

"Christian," I mumble, his name a garbled mantra, as I adjust to the sensation.

"Good girl," he murmurs. He runs his free hand down my side until it reaches my hip. Slowly he withdraws his thumb, and I hear the telltale sound of his zipper opening. Grasping my other hip, he pulls me back and parts my legs farther, his foot pushing against mine. "Don't let go of the table, Ana," he warns.

"No," I gasp.

"Something rough? Tell me if I'm too rough. Understand?"

"Yes," I whisper, and he slams into me and pulls me onto him at the same time, jolting the plug forward, deeper . . .

"Fuck!" I cry out.

He stills, his breathing harsher, and my panting matches his. I try to assimilate all the sensations: the delicious fullness, the tantalizing feeling that I am doing something forbidden, the erotic pleasure that spirals outward from deep within me. He pulls gently on the plug.

Oh my . . . I moan, and I hear his sharp intake of breath—a gasp of pure, unadulterated pleasure. It heats my blood. Have I ever felt so wanton . . . so—

"Again?" he whispers.

"Yes."

"Stay flat," he orders. He eases out of me and rams into me again.

Oh . . . I wanted this. "Yes," I hiss.

And he picks up the pace, his breathing more labored, matching my own as he thrashes into me.

"Oh, Ana," he gasps. He moves one of his hands from my hips and twists the plug again, tugging it slowly, pulling it out and pushing it back in. The feeling is indescribable, and I think I'm going to pass out on the table. He never misses a beat as he takes me, again and again, moving strong and hard inside me, my insides tightening and quivering.

"Oh fuck," I moan. This is going to rip me apart.

"Yes, baby," he hisses.

"Please," I beg him, and I don't know what for—to stop, to never stop, to twist the plug again. My insides are tightening around him and the plug.

"That's right," he breathes, and he slaps me hard on my right buttock, and I come—again and again, falling, falling, spinning, pulsing around and around—and Christian gently pulls the plug out.

"Fuck!" I scream, and Christian grabs my hips and climaxes loudly, holding me still.

THE WOMAN IS STILL singing. Christian always puts songs on repeat in here. Strange. I am curled in his arms on his lap, our legs tangled together, with my head resting against his chest. We're on the floor of the playroom by the table.

"Welcome back," he says, peeling the blindfold off me. I blink as my eyes adjust to the muted light. Tipping my chin back, he plants a soft kiss on my lips, his eyes focused on and anxiously searching mine. I reach up to caress his face. He smiles.

"Well, did I fulfill the brief?" he asks, amused.

I frown. "Brief?"

"You wanted rough," he says gently.

I grin, because I just can't help it. "Yes. I think you did . . ."

He raises his eyebrows and grins back at me. "I'm very glad to hear it. You look thoroughly well fucked and beautiful at this moment." He caresses my face, his long fingers stroking my cheek.

"I feel it," I purr.

He reaches down and kisses me tenderly, his lips soft and warm and giving against mine. "You never disappoint." He leans back to gaze down at me. "How do you feel?" His voice is soft with concern.

"Good," I murmur, feeling a flush creep across my face. "Thoroughly well fucked." I smile shyly.

"Why, Mrs. Grey, you have a dirty, dirty mouth." Christian feigns an offended expression, but I can hear his amusement.

"That's because I'm married to a dirty, dirty boy, Mr. Grey."

He grins a ridiculously stupid grin and it's infectious. "I'm glad you're married to him." He gently takes hold of my braid, lifts it to his lips, and kisses the end with reverence, his eyes glowing with love. Oh my . . . did I ever have a chance of resisting this man?

I reach for his left hand and plant a kiss on his wedding ring, a plain platinum band matching my own. "Mine," I whisper.

"Yours," he responds. He curls his arms around me and presses his nose into my hair. "Shall I run you a bath?"

"Hmm. Only if you join me in it."

"Okay," he says. He sets me onto my feet and stands up beside me. He's still wearing his jeans.

"Will you wear your . . . er . . . other jeans?"

He frowns down at me. "Other jeans?"

"The ones you used to wear in here."

"Those jeans?" he murmurs, blinking with perplexed surprise.

"You look very hot in them."

"Do I?"

"Yeah . . . I mean, really hot."

He smiles shyly. "Well, for you, Mrs. Grey, maybe I will." He bends to kiss me, then grabs the small bowl on the table that contains the butt plug, the tube of lubricant, the blindfold, and my panties.

"Who cleans these toys?" I ask as I follow him over to the chest.

He frowns at me, as if not understanding the question. "Me. Mrs. Jones."

"What?"

He nods, amused and embarrassed, I think. He switches off the music. "Well—um . . ."

"Your subs used to do it?" I finish his sentence. He gives me an apologetic shrug.

"Here." He hands me his shirt and I put it on, wrapping it around myself. His scent still clings to the linen, and my chagrin about butt plug washing is forgotten. He leaves the items on the chest. Taking my hand, he unlocks the playroom door, then leads me out and downstairs. I follow him meekly.

The anxiety, the bad mood, the thrill, fear, and excitement of the car chase have all gone. I'm relaxed—finally sated and calm. As we enter our bathroom, I yawn loudly and stretch . . . at ease with myself for a change.

"What is it?" Christian asks as he turns on the faucet.

I shake my head.

"Tell me," he asks softly. He spills jasmine bath oil into the running water, filling the room with its sweet, sensual scent.

I flush. "I just feel better."

He smiles. "Yes, you've been in a strange mood today, Mrs. Grey." Standing, he pulls me into his arms. "I know you're worrying about these recent events. I'm sorry you're caught up in them. I don't know if it's a vendetta, an ex-employee, or a business rival. If anything were to happen to you because of me—" His voice drops to a pained whisper. I curl my arms around him.

"What if something happens to you, Christian?" I voice my fear.

He gazes down at me. "We'll figure this out. Now let's get you out of this shirt and into this bath."

"Shouldn't you talk to Sawyer?"

"He can wait." His mouth hardens, and I feel a sudden pang of pity for Sawyer. What's he done to upset Christian?

Christian helps me out of his shirt, then frowns as I turn to him. My breasts still bear faded bruises from the love bites he gave me during our honeymoon, but I decide not to tease him about them.

"I wonder if Ryan has caught up with the Dodge?"

"We'll see, after this bath. Get in." He holds his hand out for me. I climb into the hot, fragrant water and sit tentatively.

"Ow." My ass is tender, and the hot water makes me wince.

"Easy, baby," Christian warns, but as he says it, the uncomfortable sensation melts away.

Christian strips and climbs in behind me, pulling me against his chest. I nestle between his legs, and we lie idle and content in the hot water. I run my fingers down his legs, and gathering my braid in one hand, he twirls it gently between his fingers.

"We need to go over the plans for the new house. Later this evening?"

"Sure." That woman is coming back again. My subconscious gazes up from volume three of *The Complete Works of Charles Dickens* and glowers. I'm with my subconscious. I sigh. Unfortunately, Gia Matteo's designs are breathtaking.

"I must get my things ready for work," I whisper.

He stills. "You know you don't have to go back to work," he murmurs.

Oh no . . . not this again. "Christian, we've been through this. Please don't resurrect that argument."

He tugs my braid so my face tilts up and back. "Just saying . . ." He plants a soft kiss on my lips.

I PULL ON SWEATPANTS and a camisole and decide to fetch my clothes from the playroom. As I make my way across the hallway, I hear Christian's raised voice from his study. I freeze.

"Where the fuck were you?"

Oh shit. He's shouting at Sawyer. Cringing, I dash upstairs to the playroom. I really don't want to hear what he has to say to him—I still find shouty Christian intimidating. Poor Sawyer. At least I get to shout back.

I gather up my clothes and Christian's shoes, then notice the small porcelain bowl with the butt plug still on top of the museum chest. *Well . . . I suppose I should clean it.* I add it to the pile and make my way back downstairs. I glance nervously through the great room, but all is quiet. Thank heavens.

Taylor will be back tomorrow evening, and Christian is generally calmer when he's around. Taylor is spending some quality time today and tomorrow with his daughter. I wonder idly if I'll ever get to meet her.

Mrs. Jones comes out of the utility room. We startle each other.

"Mrs. Grey—I didn't see you there." *Oh, I'm Mrs. Grey now!*

"Hello, Mrs. Jones."

"Welcome home and congratulations." She smiles.

"Please call me Ana."

"Mrs. Grey, I wouldn't feel comfortable doing that."

Oh! Why must everything change just because I have a ring on my finger?

"Would you like to run through the menus for the week?" she asks, looking at me expectantly.

Menus?

"Um . . ." This is not a question I have ever anticipated being asked.

She smiles. "When I first worked for Mr. Grey, every Sunday evening I would run through the menus for the upcoming week with him and list anything he might need from the grocery store."

"I see."

"Shall I take those for you?"

She holds out her hands for my clothes.

"Oh . . . um. Actually I haven't finished with these." *And they are hiding the bowl with the butt plug in it!* I turn crimson. It's a

wonder I can look Mrs. Jones in the eye. She knows what we do—
she cleans the room. Jeez, it's just weird having no privacy.

"When you're ready, Mrs. Grey. I'd be more than happy to run
through things with you."

"Thank you." We are interrupted by an ashen-faced Sawyer;
he stalks out of Christian's study and briskly crosses the great
room. He gives us both a brief nod, not looking either of us in the
eye, and slinks into Taylor's study. I'm grateful for his intervention,
as I don't wish to discuss menus or butt plugs with Mrs. Jones right
now. Offering her a brief smile, I scurry back to the bedroom.
Will I ever get used to having domestic staff at my beck and call?
I shake my head . . . one day, maybe.

I dump Christian's shoes on the floor and my clothes on the
bed, and take the bowl with the butt plug into the bathroom. I eye
it suspiciously. It looks innocuous enough, and surprisingly clean.
I don't want to dwell on that, and I wash it quickly with soap and
water. Will that be enough? I'll have to ask Mr. Sexpert if it should
be sterilized or something. I shudder at the thought.

I LIKE THAT CHRISTIAN has turned the library over to me. It
now houses an attractive white wooden desk I can work at. I take
out my laptop and check my notes on the five manuscripts I read
on our honeymoon.

Yep, I have everything I need. Part of me dreads going back to
work, but I can never tell Christian that. He'd seize on the opportunity to make me quit. I remember Roach's apoplectic reaction
when I told him I was getting married and to whom, and how,
shortly afterward, my position was confirmed. I realize now it was
because I was marrying the boss. The thought is unwelcome. I am
no longer acting editor—I am Anastasia Steele, editor.

I haven't yet plucked up the courage to tell Christian that I
am not going to change my name at work. I think my reasons are
solid. I need some distance from him, but I know there will be a
fight when he finally realizes that. Perhaps I should discuss this
with him tonight.

Sitting back in my chair, I start my final chore of the day. I glance at the digital clock on my laptop, which tells me it's seven in the evening. Christian still hasn't emerged from his study, so I have time. Taking the memory card out of the Nikon camera, I load it into the laptop to transfer the photographs. As the pictures upload, I reflect on the day. Is Ryan back? Or is he still on his way to Portland? Has he caught up with the mystery woman? Has Christian heard from him? I want some answers. I don't care that he's busy; I want to know what's going on, and I suddenly feel a tad resentful that he's keeping me in the dark. I rise, intending to go and confront him in his study, but as I do the photos from the last few days of our honeymoon pop up onscreen.

Holy crap!

Picture after picture of me. Asleep, so many of me asleep, my hair over my face or fanned out across the pillow, lips parted . . . shit—sucking my thumb. I haven't sucked my thumb for years! So many photos. I had no idea he'd taken these. There are a few candid long shots, including one of me leaning over the rail of the yacht, staring moodily into the distance. How did I not notice him taking this? I smile at the photos of me curled up beneath him and laughing—my hair flying as I struggle, fighting his tickling, tormenting fingers. And there's the one of him and me on the bed in the master cabin that he took at arm's length. I am cuddled on his chest and he gazes at the camera, young, wide-eyed . . . in love. His other hand cups my head, and I am smiling like a love-struck fool, but I cannot take my eyes off Christian. Oh, my beautiful man, his ruffled just-fucked hair, his gray eyes glowing, his lips parted and smiling. My beautiful man who cannot bear to be tickled, who could not bear to be touched just a short while ago, yet now he tolerates my touch. I must ask him if he likes it, or whether he lets me touch him for my pleasure rather than his.

I frown, gazing down at his image, suddenly overwhelmed by my feelings for him. Someone out there wants to harm him—first *Charlie Tango*, then the fire at GEH, and that damned car chase. I gasp, putting my hand to my mouth as an involuntary sob escapes. Abandoning my computer, I leap up to find him—not to confront him now—just to check that he's safe.

Not bothering to knock, I barge into his study. Christian is sitting at his desk and talking on the phone. He looks up in surprised annoyance, but the irritation on his face disappears when he sees it's me.

"So you can't enhance it further?" he says, continuing his phone conversation, though he doesn't take his eyes off me. Without hesitation, I walk around his desk, and he turns in his chair to face me, frowning. I can tell he's thinking, *What does she want?* When I crawl onto his lap, his eyebrows shoot up in surprise. I put my arms around his neck and cuddle into him. Gingerly, he puts his arm around me.

"Um . . . yes, Barney. Could you hold one moment?" He cups the phone against his shoulder.

"Ana, what's wrong?"

I shake my head. Tipping my chin up, he gazes into my eyes. I pull my head free from his hold, tuck it beneath his chin, and curl up smaller on his lap. Bemused, he wraps his free arm more tightly around me and kisses the top of my head.

"Okay, Barney, what were you saying?" He continues, wedging the phone between his ear and his shoulder, and taps a key on his laptop. A grainy black-and-white CCTV image appears on the screen. A man with dark hair wearing pale coveralls comes on the screen. Christian presses another key, and the man walks toward the camera, but with his head bowed. When the man is closer to the camera, Christian freezes the frame. He's standing in a bright white room with what looks like a long line of tall black cabinets to his left. This must be GEH's server room.

"Okay Barney, one more time."

The screen springs to life. A box appears around the head of the man in the CCTV footage and suddenly we zoom in. I sit up, fascinated.

"Is Barney doing this?" I ask quietly.

"Yes," Christian answers. "Can you sharpen the picture at all?" he says to Barney.

The picture blurs, then refocuses moderately sharper on the man consciously gazing down and avoiding the camera. As I stare at him, a chill of recognition sweeps up my spine. There is something familiar in the line of his jaw. He has scruffy short black hair that looks odd and unkempt . . . and in the newly sharpened picture, I see an earring, a small hoop.

Holy crap! I know who it is.

"Christian," I whisper. "That's Jack Hyde."

CHAPTER SEVEN

Y ou think?" Christian asks, surprised.
"It's the line of his jaw." I point at the screen. "And the earrings and the shape of his shoulders. He's the right build, too. He must be wearing a wig—or he's cut and dyed his hair."

"Barney, are you getting this?" Christian puts the phone down on his desk and switches to hands-free. "You seem to have studied your ex-boss in some detail, Mrs. Grey," he murmurs, sounding none too pleased. I scowl at him, but I'm saved by Barney.

"Yes, sir. I heard Mrs. Grey. I'm running face recognition software on all the digitized CCTV footage right now. See where else this asshole—I'm sorry ma'am—this man has been within the organization."

I glance anxiously at Christian, who ignores Barney's expletive. He's studying the CCTV picture closely.

"Why would he do this?" I ask Christian.

He shrugs. "Revenge, perhaps. I don't know. You can't fathom why some people behave the way they do. I'm just angry that you ever worked so closely with him." Christian's mouth presses into a hard, thin line and he encircles my waist with his arm.

"We have the contents of his hard drive, too, sir," Barney adds.

"Yes, I remember. Do you have an address for Mr. Hyde?" Christian says sharply.

"Yes, sir, I do."

"Alert Welch."

"Sure will. I'm also going to scan the city CCTV and see if I can track his movements."

"Check what vehicle he owns."

"Sir."

"Barney can do all this?" I whisper.

Christian nods and gives me a smug smile.

"What was on his hard drive?" I whisper.

Christian's face hardens and he shakes his head. "Nothing much," he says, tight-lipped, his smile forgotten.

"Tell me."

"No."

"Was it about you, or me?"

"Me." He sighs.

"What sort of things? About your lifestyle?"

Christian shakes his head and puts his index finger against my lips to silence me. I scowl at him. But he narrows his eyes, and it's a clear warning that I should hold my tongue.

"It's a 2006 Camaro. I'll send the license details to Welch, too," Barney says excitedly from the phone.

"Good. Let me know where else that fucker has been in my building. And check this image against the one from his SIP personnel file." Christian gazes at me skeptically. "I want to be sure we have a match."

"Already done, sir, and Mrs. Grey is correct. This is Jack Hyde."

I grin. *See?* I can be useful. Christian rubs his hand down my back.

"Well done, Mrs. Grey." He smiles, his earlier rancor forgotten. To Barney he says, "Let me know when you've tracked all his movements at HQ. Also check out any other GEH property he may have had access to, and let the security teams know so they can make another sweep of all those buildings."

"Sir."

"Thanks, Barney." Christian hangs up.

"Well, Mrs. Grey, it seems that you are not only decorative, but useful, too." Christian's eyes light up with wicked amusement. I know he's teasing.

"Decorative?" I scoff, teasing him back.

"Very," he says quietly, pressing a soft, sweet kiss on my lips.

"You're much more decorative than I am, Mr. Grey."

He grins and kisses me more forcefully, winding my braid around his wrist and wrapping his arms around me. When we come up for air, my heart is racing.

"Hungry?" he asks.

"No."

"I am."

"What for?"

"Well—food actually."

"I'll make you something." I giggle.

"I love that sound."

"Of me offering you food?"

"Your giggling." He kisses my hair, then I stand.

"So what would you like to eat, Sir?" I ask sweetly.

He narrows his eyes. "Are you being cute, Mrs. Grey?"

"Always, Mr. Grey . . . Sir."

He smiles a sphinxlike smile. "I can still put you over my knee," he murmurs seductively.

"I know." I grin. Placing my hands on the arms of his office chair, I lean down and kiss him. "That's one of the things I love about you. But stow your twitching palm—you're hungry."

He smiles his shy smile and my heart clenches. "Oh, Mrs. Grey, what am I going to do with you?"

"You're going to answer my question. What would you like to eat?"

"Something light. Surprise me," he says, mirroring my words from the playroom earlier.

"I'll see what I can do." I sashay out of his study and into the kitchen. My heart sinks when I see Mrs. Jones is there.

"Hello, Mrs. Jones."

"Mrs. Grey. Are you ready for something to eat?"

"Um . . ."

She is stirring something in a pot on the stove that smells delicious.

"I was going to make subs for Mr. Grey and me."

She pauses for a heartbeat. "Sure," she says. "Mr. Grey likes French bread—there is some in the freezer cut to sub length. I'd be happy to make it for you, ma'am."

"I know. But I'd like to do this."

"I understand. I'll give you some room."

"What are you cooking?"

"This is a Bolognese sauce. It can be eaten anytime. I'll freeze it." She smiles warmly and turns the heat right down.

"Um—so what does Christian like in a, um . . . sub?" I frown, struck by what I've just said. Does Mrs. Jones understand the inference?

"Mrs. Grey, you could put just about anything in a sandwich, and as long as it's on French bread, he'll eat it." We grin at each other.

"Okay, thank you." I skip to the freezer and find the French bread cut to size in Ziploc bags. I place two of them on a plate, pop them in the microwave, and set it to defrost.

Mrs. Jones has disappeared. I frown as I return to the fridge to search for ingredients. I suppose it will be up to me to set the parameters by which Mrs. Jones and I will work together. I like the idea of cooking for Christian on the weekends. Mrs. Jones is more than welcome to do it during the week—the last thing I'll want to do when I come home from work is cook. Hmm . . . a bit like Christian's routine with his submissives. I shake my head. I mustn't overthink this. I find some ham in the fridge, and in the crisper a perfectly ripe avocado.

As I am adding a touch of salt and lemon to the mashed avocado, Christian emerges from his study with the plans for the new house in his hands. He puts them on the breakfast bar, saunters toward me, and wraps his arms around me, kissing my neck.

"Barefoot and in the kitchen," he murmurs.

"Shouldn't that be barefoot and pregnant in the kitchen?" I smirk.

He stills, his whole body tensing against me. "Not yet," he declares, apprehension clear in his voice.

"No! Not yet!"

He relaxes. "On that we can agree, Mrs. Grey."

"You do want kids though, don't you?"

"Sure, yes. Eventually. But I'm not ready to share you yet." He kisses my neck again.

Oh . . . *share?*

"What are you making? Looks good." He kisses me behind my ear, and I know it's to distract me. A delicious tingle travels down my spine.

"Subs." I smirk, recovering my sense of humor.

He smiles against my neck and nips my earlobe. "My favorite."

I poke him with my elbow.

"Mrs. Grey, you wound me." He clutches his side as if in pain.

"Wimp," I mutter disapprovingly.

"Wimp?" he utters in disbelief. He slaps my behind, making me yelp. "Hurry up with my food, wench. And later I'll show you how wimpy I can be." He slaps me playfully once more and goes to the fridge.

"Would you like a glass of wine?" he asks.

"Please."

CHRISTIAN SPREADS GIA'S PLANS out over the breakfast bar. She really has some spectacular ideas.

"I love her proposal to make the entire downstairs back wall glass, but . . ."

"But?" Christian prompts.

I sigh. "I don't want to take all the character out of the house."

"Character?"

"Yes. What Gia is proposing is quite radical, but . . . well . . . I fell in love with the house as it is . . . warts and all."

Christian's brow furrows as if this is anathema to him.

"I kind of like it the way it is," I whisper. Is this going to make him mad?

He regards me steadily. "I want this house to be the way you want. Whatever you want. It's yours."

"I want you to like it, too. To be happy in it, too."

"I'll be happy wherever you are. It's that simple, Ana." His gaze holds mine. He is utterly, utterly sincere. I blink at him as my heart expands. *Holy cow, he really does love me.*

"Well"—I swallow, fighting the small knot of emotion that catches in my throat—"I like the glass wall. Maybe we could ask her to incorporate it into the house a little more sympathetically."

Christian grins. "Sure. Whatever you want. What about the plans for upstairs and the basement?"

"I'm cool with those."

"Good."

Okay . . . I steel myself to ask the million-dollar question. "Do you want to put in a playroom?" I feel the oh-so-familiar flush creep up my face as I ask. Christian's eyebrows shoot up.

"Do you?" he replies, surprised and amused at once.

I shrug. "Um . . . if you want."

He regards me for a moment. "Let's leave our options open for the moment. After all, this will be a family home."

I'm surprised by the stab of disappointment I feel. I guess he's right . . . although when are we going to have a family? It could be years.

"Besides, we can improvise."

"I like improvising," I whisper.

He grins. "There's something I want to discuss." Christian points to the master bedroom, and we start a detailed discussion on bathrooms and separate walk-in closets.

WHEN WE FINISH, IT'S nine thirty in the evening.

"Are you going back to work?" I ask as Christian rolls up the plans.

"Not if you don't want me to." He smiles. "What would you like to do?"

"We could watch TV." I don't want to read, and I don't want to go to bed . . . yet.

"Okay," Christian agrees willingly, and I follow him into the TV room.

We have sat here three, maybe four times total, and Christian usually reads a book. He's not interested in television at all. I curl up beside him on the couch, tucking my legs beneath me and resting my head against his shoulder. He switches on the flat-screen television with the remote and flicks mindlessly through the channels.

"Any specific drivel you want to see?"

"You don't like TV much, do you?" I mutter sardonically.

He shakes his head. "Waste of time. But I'll watch something with you."

"I thought we could make out."

He whips his face to mine. "Make out?" He gazes at me as if I've grown two heads. He stops the endless flicking, leaving the TV on an overlit Spanish soap opera.

"Yes." *Why is he so horrified?*

"We could go to bed and make out."

"We do that all the time. When was the last time you made out in front of the TV?" I ask, shy and teasing at the same time.

He shrugs and shakes his head. Pressing the remote again, he flicks through another few channels before settling on an old episode of *The X-Files.*

"Christian?"

"I've never done that," he says quietly.

"Never?"

"No."

"Not even with Mrs. Robinson?"

He snorts. "Baby, I did a lot of things with Mrs. Robinson. Making out was not one of them." He smirks at me and then narrows his eyes with amused curiosity. "Have you?"

I flush. "Of course." Well, kind of . . .

"What! Who with?"

Oh no. I do not want to have this discussion.

"Tell me," he persists.

I gaze down at my knotted fingers. He gently covers my hands with one of his. When I glance up at him, he's smiling at me.

"I want to know. So I can beat whoever it was to a pulp."

I giggle. "Well, the first time . . ."

"The first time! There's more than one fucker?" He growls.

I giggle again. "Why so surprised, Mr. Grey?"

He frowns briefly, runs a hand through his hair, and looks at me as if seeing me in a completely different light. He shrugs. "I just am. I mean—given your lack of experience."

I flush. "I've certainly made up for that since I met you."

"You have." He grins. "Tell me. I want to know."

I gaze into patient gray eyes, trying to gauge his mood. Is this going to make him mad, or does he genuinely want to know? I don't want him sulking . . . he's impossible when he's sulking.

"You really want me to tell you?"

He nods slowly once, and his lips twitch with an amused, arrogant smile.

"I was briefly in Texas with Mom and Husband Number Three. I was in tenth grade. His name was Bradley, and he was my lab partner in physics."

"How old were you?"

"Fifteen."

"And what's he doing now?"

"I don't know."

"What base did he get to?"

"Christian!" I scold—and suddenly he grabs my knees, then my ankles, and tips me up so I fall back onto the couch. He slides smoothly on top of me, trapping me beneath him, one leg between mine. It's so sudden that I cry out in surprise. He grabs my hands and raises them above my head.

"So, this Bradley—did he get to first base?" he murmurs, running his nose down the length of mine. He plants soft kisses at the corner of my mouth.

"Yes," I murmur against his lips. He releases one of his hands so that he can clasp my chin and hold me still while his tongue invades my mouth, and I surrender to his ardent kissing.

"Like this?" Christian breathes when he comes up for air.

"No . . . nothing like that," I manage as all the blood in my body heads south.

Releasing my chin, he runs his hand down over my body and back up to my breast.

"Did he do this? Touch you like this?" His thumb skims over my nipple, through my camisole, softly, repeatedly, and it hardens under his expert touch.

"No." I writhe beneath him.

"Did he get to second base?" he murmurs in my ear. His hand moves down across my ribs, past my waist to my hip. He takes my earlobe between his teeth and gently tugs.

"No," I breathe.

Mulder blurts from the television something about the FBI's most unwanted.

Christian pauses, leans up, and presses "mute" on the remote. He gazes down at me.

"What about Joe Schmo number two? Did he make it past second base?"

His eyes are smoldering hot . . . angry? Turned on? It's difficult to say which. He shifts to my side and slides his hand beneath my sweatpants.

"No," I whisper, trapped in his carnal gaze. Christian smiles wickedly.

"Good." His hand cups my sex. "No underwear, Mrs. Grey. I approve." He kisses me again as his fingers weave more magic, his thumb skimming over my clitoris, tantalizing me, as he pushes his index finger inside me with exquisite slowness.

"We're supposed to be making out." I groan.

Christian stills. "I thought we were?"

"No. No sex."

"What?"

"No sex . . ."

"No sex, huh?" He withdraws his hand from my sweatpants. "Here." He traces my lips with his index finger, and I taste my slick saltiness. He pushes his finger into my mouth, mirroring what he was doing a moment earlier. Then he shifts so he's between my legs, and his erection pushes against me. He thrusts, once, twice, and again. I gasp as the material of my sweatpants rubs in just the right way. He pushes once more, grinding into me.

"This what you want?" he murmurs and moves his hips rhythmically, rocking against me.

"Yes." I moan.

His hand moves back to concentrate on my nipple once more and his teeth scrape along my jaw. "Do you know how hot you are, Ana?" His voice is hoarse as he rocks harder against me. I open my mouth to articulate a response and fail miserably, groaning loudly. He captures my mouth once more, tugging at my bottom lip with his teeth before plunging his tongue into my mouth again. He releases my other wrist and my hands travel greedily up his shoulders and into his hair as he kisses me. When I pull on his hair, he groans and raises his eyes to mine.

"Ah . . ."

"Do you like me touching you?" I whisper.

His brow furrows briefly as if he doesn't understand the question. He stops grinding against me. "Of course I do. I love you touching me, Ana. I'm like a starving man at a banquet when it comes to your touch." His voice hums with passionate sincerity.

Holy cow . . .

He kneels between my legs and drags me up to haul off my top. I'm naked beneath it. Grabbing the hem of his shirt, he yanks it over his head and tosses it on the floor, then pulls me onto his kneeling lap, his arms clasped just above my behind.

"Touch me," he breathes.

Oh my . . . Tentatively I reach up and brush the tips of my fingers through the smattering of chest hair over his sternum, over his burn scars. He inhales sharply and his pupils dilate, but it's not with fear. It's a sensual response to my touch. He watches me intently as my fingers float delicately over his skin, first to one nipple and then the other. They pucker beneath my caress. Leaning forward, I plant soft kisses on his chest, and my hands move to his shoulders, feeling the hard, sculptured lines of sinew and muscle. Whoa . . . he's in good shape.

"I want you," he murmurs, and it's a green light to my libido.

My fingers move into his hair, pulling his head back so I can claim his mouth, fire licking hot and high in my belly. He groans and pushes me back onto the couch. He sits up and rips off my sweatpants, undoing his fly at the same time.

"Home run," he whispers, and swiftly he fills me.

"Ah . . ." I groan and he stills, grabbing my face between his hands.

"I love you, Mrs. Grey," he murmurs and very slowly, very gently, he makes love to me until I come apart at the seams, calling his name and wrapping myself around him, never wanting to let him go.

I LAY SPRAWLED ON his chest. We're on the floor of the TV room.

"You know, we completely bypassed third base." My fingers trace the line of his pectoral muscles.

He laughs. "Next time." He kisses the top of my head.

I look up to stare at the television screen, where the end credits for The X-Files play. Christian reaches for the remote and switches the sound back on.

"You liked that show?" I ask.

"When I was a kid."

Oh . . . Christian as a kid . . . kickboxing and X Files and no touching.

"You?" he asks.

"Before my time."

"You're so young." Christian smiles fondly. "I like making out with you, Mrs. Grey."

"Likewise, Mr. Grey." I kiss his chest, and we lie silently watching as The X-Files finish and the commercials come on.

"It's been a heavenly three weeks. Car chases and fires and psycho ex-bosses notwithstanding. Like being in our own private bubble," I mutter dreamily.

"Hmm," Christian hums deep in his throat. "I'm not sure I'm ready to share you with the rest of the world yet."

"Back to reality tomorrow," I murmur, trying to keep the melancholy from my voice.

Christian sighs and runs his other hand through his hair. "Security will be tight—" I put my finger over his lips. I don't want to hear this lecture again.

"I know. I'll be good. I promise." Which reminds me . . . I shift, propping myself up on my elbows to see him better. "Why were you shouting at Sawyer?"

He stiffens immediately. *Oh shit.*

"Because we were followed."

"That wasn't Sawyer's fault."

He gazes at me levelly. "They should never have let you get so far in front. They know that."

I blush guiltily and resume my position, resting on his chest. It was my fault. I wanted to get away from them.

"That wasn't—"

"Enough!" Christian is suddenly curt. "This is not up for discussion, Anastasia. It's a fact, and they won't let it happen again."

Anastasia! I am Anastasia when I am in trouble just like at home with my mother.

"Okay," I mutter, placating him. I don't want to fight. "Did Ryan catch up with the woman in the Dodge?"

"No. And I'm not convinced it was a woman."

"Oh?" I look up again.

"Sawyer saw someone with their hair tied back, but it was a brief look. He assumed it was a woman. Now, given that you've identified that fucker, maybe it was him. He wore his hair like that." The disgust in Christian's voice is palpable.

I don't know what to make of this news. Christian runs his hand down my naked back, distracting me.

"If anything happened to you . . . ," he murmurs, his eyes wide and serious.

"I know," I whisper. "I feel the same about you." I shiver at the thought.

"Come. You're getting cold," he says, sitting up. "Let's go to bed. We can cover third base there." He smiles a lascivious smile, as mercurial as ever, passionate, angry, anxious, sexy—my Fifty

Shades. I take his hand and he pulls me to my feet, and without a stitch on, I follow him through the great room to the bedroom.

THE FOLLOWING MORNING, CHRISTIAN squeezes my hand as we pull up outside SIP. He looks very much the powerful executive in his dark navy suit and matching tie, and I smile. He's not been this smart since the ballet in Monte Carlo.

"You know you don't have to do this?" Christian murmurs. I am tempted to roll my eyes at him.

"I know," I whisper, not wanting Sawyer and Ryan to overhear me from the front of the Audi. He frowns and I smile.

"But I want to," I continue. "You know this." I lean up and kiss him. His frown doesn't disappear. "What's wrong?"

He glances uncertainly at Ryan as Sawyer climbs out of the car. "I'll miss having you to myself."

I reach up to caress his face. "Me, too." I kiss him. "It was a wonderful honeymoon. Thank you."

"Go to work, Mrs. Grey."

"You, too, Mr. Grey."

Sawyer opens the door. I squeeze Christian's hand once more before I climb out onto the sidewalk. As I head into the building, I give him a little wave. Sawyer holds open the door and follows me in.

"Hi, Ana." Claire smiles from behind the reception desk.

"Claire, hello." I smile back.

"You look wonderful. Good honeymoon?"

"The best, thank you. How's it been here?"

"Old man Roach is the same, but security has been stepped up and our server room is being overhauled. But Hannah will tell you."

Sure she will. I give Claire a friendly smile and head to my office.

Hannah is my assistant. She is tall, slim, and ruthlessly efficient to the point that sometimes I find her a little intimidating. But she's sweet to me, in spite of the fact that she's a couple of years older. She has my latte waiting—the only coffee I let her get for me.

"Hi, Hannah," I say warmly.

"Ana, how was your honeymoon?"

"Fantastic. Here—for you." I pop the small bottle of perfume I bought for her onto her desk, and she claps her hands with glee.

"Oh, thank you!" she says enthusiastically. "Your urgent correspondence is on your desk, and Roach would like to see you at ten. That's all I have to report for now."

"Good. Thank you. And thanks for the coffee." Wandering into my office, I rest my briefcase on my desk and gaze at the piled up letters. I have a lot to do.

JUST BEFORE TEN THERE'S a timid tap on my door.

"Come in."

Elizabeth looks around the door. "Hi, Ana. I just wanted to say welcome back."

"Hey. I have to say, reading through all this correspondence, I wish I was back in the South of France."

Elizabeth laughs, but her laughter is off, forced, and I cock my head to one side and gaze at her like Christian does to me.

"Glad you're back safely," she says. "I'll see you in a few minutes at the meeting with Roach."

"Okay," I murmur, and she shuts the door behind her. I frown at the closed door. *What was that about?* I shrug it off. My e-mail pings—it's a message from Christian.

From: Christian Grey
Subject: Errant Wives
Date: August 22 2011 09:56
To: Anastasia Steele

Wife

I sent the e-mail below and it bounced.

And it's because you haven't changed your name.

Something you want to tell me?

Christian Grey
CEO, Grey Enterprises Holdings, Inc.

Attachment:

From: Christian Grey
FW Subject: Bubble
Date: August 22 2011 09:32
To: Anastasia Grey

Mrs. Grey
Love covering all the bases with you.
Have a great first day back.
Miss our bubble already.
x

Christian Grey
Back in the Real World CEO, Grey Enterprises Holdings, Inc.

Shit. I hit reply immediately.

From: Anastasia Steele
Subject: Don't Burst the Bubble
Date: August 22 2011 09:58
To: Christian Grey

Husband

I am all for a baseball metaphor with you, Mr. Grey.

I want to keep my name here.

I'll explain this evening.

I am going in to a meeting now.

Miss our bubble, too . . .

PS: Thought I had to use my BlackBerry?

Anastasia Steele
Editor, SIP

This is going to be such a fight. I can feel it. Sighing, I gather up my papers for the meeting.

THE MEETING LASTS FOR two hours. All the editors are there, plus Roach and Elizabeth. We discuss personnel, strategy, marketing, security, and year-end. As the meeting progresses, I grow more and more uncomfortable. There's a subtle change in how my colleagues are treating me—a distance and deference that wasn't there before I left for my honeymoon. And from Courtney, who heads up the nonfiction division, there's downright hostility. Maybe I'm just being paranoid, but it goes some way to explaining Elizabeth's odd greeting this morning.

My mind drifts back to the yacht, then to the playroom, then to the R8 speeding away from the mystery Dodge on I-5. Perhaps Christian's right . . . perhaps I can't do this anymore. The thought is depressing—this is all I've ever wanted to do. If I can't do this, what will I do? As I walk back to my office, I try to dismiss these dark thoughts.

When I sit down at my desk, I quickly check my e-mails. Nothing from Christian. I check my BlackBerry . . . Still nothing. Good. At least there's been no adverse reaction to my e-mail. Perhaps we'll discuss this tonight per my request. I find that hard to believe, but ignoring my uneasy feeling, I open the marketing plan I was given at the meeting.

AS IS OUR RITUAL on a Monday, Hannah comes into my office with a plate for my packed lunch courtesy of Mrs. Jones, and we sit and eat our lunches together, discussing what we want to achieve during the week. She brings me up to date with the office gossip, too, which—considering I've been away for three weeks—is sorely lacking. As we're chatting, there's a knock on the door.

"Come in."

Roach opens the door, and standing beside him is Christian. I'm momentarily struck dumb. Christian shoots me a blazing look and stalks in, before smiling politely at Hannah.

"Hello, you must be Hannah. I'm Christian Grey," he says. Hannah scrambles to her feet and holds out her hand.

"Mr. Grey. H-how nice to meet you," she stutters as they shake hands. "Can I fetch you a coffee?"

"Please," he says warmly. With a quick puzzled glance at me, she scuttles out of the office past Roach, who stands as dumb-struck as me on the threshold of my office.

"If you'll excuse me, Roach, I'd like a word with Ms. Steele." Christian hisses the S sibilantly . . . sarcastically.

This is why he's here . . . Oh shit.

"Of course, Mr. Grey. Ana," Roach mutters, shutting the door to my office as he departs. I recover my power of speech.

"Mr. Grey, how nice to see you." I smile, far too sweetly.

"Ms. Steele, may I sit down?"

"It's your company." I wave at the chair Hannah vacated.

"Yes, it is." He smiles wolfishly at me, the smile not reaching his eyes. His tone is clipped. He's bristling with tension—I can feel it all around me. *Fuck.* My heart sinks.

"Your office is very small," he says as he sits down facing my desk.

"It suits me."

He regards me neutrally, but I know he's mad. I take a deep breath. This is not going to be fun.

"So what can I do for you, Christian?"

"I'm just looking over my assets."

"Your assets? All of them?"

"All of them. Some of them need rebranding."

"Rebranding? In what way?"

"I think you know." His voice is menacingly quiet.

"Please—don't tell me you have interrupted your day after three weeks away to come over here and fight with me about my name." *I am not a freaking asset!*

He shifts and crosses his legs. "Not exactly fight. No."

"Christian, I'm working."

"Looked like you were gossiping with your assistant to me."

My cheeks heat. "We were going through our schedules," I snap. "And you haven't answered my question."

There's a knock on the door. "Come in!" I shout, too loudly.

Hannah opens the door and brings in a small tray. Milk jug, sugar bowl, coffee in a French press—she's gone all out. She places the tray on my desk.

"Thank you, Hannah," I mutter, embarrassed that I have just shouted so loudly.

"Do you need anything else, Mr. Grey?" she asks, all breathless. I want to roll my eyes at her.

"No, thank you. That's all." He smiles his dazzling, panty-dropping smile at her. She flushes and exits simpering. Christian turns his attention back to me.

"Now, Ms. Steele, where were we?"

"You were rudely interrupting my work day to fight with me about my name."

Christian blinks once—surprised, I think, by the vehemence in my voice. Deftly, he picks at an invisible piece of lint on his knee with long skilled fingers. It's distracting. He's doing it on purpose. I narrow my eyes at him.

"I like to make the odd impromptu visit. It keeps management on their toes, wives in their place. You know." He shrugs, his mouth set in an arrogant line.

Wives in their place! "I had no idea you could spare the time," I snap.

His eyes frost. "Why don't you want to change your name here?" he asks, his voice deathly quiet.

"Christian, do we have to discuss this now?"

"I'm here. I don't see why not."

"I have a ton of work to do, having been away for the last three weeks."

His eyes are cool and assessing—distant even. I marvel that he can appear so cold after last night, after the last three weeks. *Shit.* He must be mad—really mad. When will he learn not to overreact?

"Are you ashamed of me?" he asks, his voice deceptively soft.

"No! Christian, of course not." I scowl. "This is about me— not you." Jeez, he's exasperating sometimes. Silly overbearing megalomaniac.

"How is this not about me?" He cocks his head to one side, genuinely perplexed, some of his detachment slipping as he stares at me with wide eyes, and I realize that he's hurt. *Holy fuck.* I've hurt his feelings. Oh no . . . he's the last person I want to hurt. I have to make him see my logic. I have to explain my reasoning for my decision.

"Christian, when I took this job, I'd only just met you," I say patiently, struggling to find the right words. "I didn't know you were going to buy the company—"

What can I say about that event in our brief history? His deranged reasons for doing so—his control freakery, his stalker tendencies gone mad, given completely free rein because he is so wealthy. I know he wants to keep me safe, but it's his owner-ship of SIP that is the fundamental problem here. If he'd never interfered, I could continue as normal and not have to face the disgruntled and whispered recriminations of my colleagues. I put my head in my hands just to break eye contact with him.

"Why is it so important to you?" I ask, desperately trying to hold on to my fraying temper. I look up at his impassive stare, his eyes luminous, giving nothing away, his earlier hurt now hidden. But even as I ask the question, deep down I know the answer before he says it.

"I want everyone to know that you're mine."

"I am yours—look." I hold up my left hand, showing my wed-ding and engagement rings.

"It's not enough."

"Not enough that I married you?" My voice is barely a whisper.

He blinks, registering the horror on my face. Where can I go from here? What else can I do?

"That's not what I mean," he snaps and runs a hand through his overlong hair so that it flops onto his forehead.

"What *do* you mean?"

He swallows. "I want your world to begin and end with me," he says, his expression raw. His comment completely derails me. It's like he's punched me hard in the stomach, winding and wounding me. And the vision comes to mind of a small, frightened, copper-haired, gray-eyed boy in dirty, mismatched, ill-fitting clothes.

"It does," I say without guile, because it's the truth. "I'm just trying to establish a career, and I don't want to trade on your name. I have to do *something*, Christian. I can't stay imprisoned at Escala or the new house with nothing to do. I'll go crazy. I'll suffocate. I've always worked, and I enjoy this. This is my dream job; it's all I've ever wanted. But doing this doesn't mean I love you less. You are the world to me." My throat swells and tears prick the backs of my eyes. I must not cry, not here. I repeat it over and over in my head. *I must not cry. I must not cry.*

He stares at me, saying nothing. Then a frown crosses his face as if he's considering what I've said.

"I suffocate you?" His voice is bleak, and it's an echo of a question he's asked me before.

"No . . . yes . . . no." This is such an exasperating conversation—not one that I want to have now, here. I close my eyes and rub my forehead, trying to fathom how we got to this.

"Look, we were talking about my name. I want to keep my name here because I want to put some distance between you and me . . . but only here, that's all. You know everyone thinks I got the job because of you, when the reality is—" I stop when his eyes widen. *Oh no . . . it is because of him?*

"Do you want to know why you got the job, Anastasia?"

Anastasia? Shit. "What? What do you mean?"

He shifts in his chair as if steeling himself. Do I want to know?

"The management here gave you Hyde's job to babysit. They didn't want the expense of hiring a senior executive when the company was mid-sale. They had no idea what the new owner would do with it once it passed into his ownership, and wisely, they didn't want an expensive redundancy. So they gave you Hyde's job to caretake until the new owner"—he pauses, and his lips twitch in an ironic smile—"namely me, took over."

Holy crap! "What are you saying?" So it *was* because of him. *Fuck!* I'm horrified.

He smiles and shakes his head at my alarm. "Relax. You've more than risen to the challenge. You've done very well." There's the tiniest hint of pride in his voice, and it's almost my undoing.

"Oh," I murmur incoherently, reeling from this news. I sit right back in my chair, open-mouthed, staring at him. He shifts again.

"I don't want to suffocate you, Ana. I don't want to put you in a gilded cage. Well . . ." He pauses, his face darkening. "Well, the rational part of me doesn't." He strokes his chin thoughtfully as his mind concocts some plan.

Oh, where is he going with this? Christian looks up suddenly, as if he's had a eureka moment. "So one of the reasons I'm here—apart from dealing with my errant wife," he says, narrowing his eyes, "is to discuss what I am going to do with this company."

Errant wife! I am not errant, and I'm not an asset! I scowl at Christian again and the threat of tears subsides.

"So what are your plans?" I incline my head to one side, mirroring him, and I can't help my sarcastic tone. His lips twitch with the hint of a smile. Whoa—change of mood, again! How can I ever keep up with Mr. Mercurial?

"I'm changing the name of the company—to Grey Publishing."
Holy shit.

"And in a year's time, it will be yours."

My mouth drops open once more—wider this time.

"This is my wedding present to you."

I shut my mouth then open it, trying to articulate something—but there's nothing there. My mind is blank.

"So, do I need to change the name to Steele Publishing?"

He's serious. Holy fuck.

"Christian," I whisper when my brain finally reconnects with my mouth. "You gave me a watch . . . I can't run a business."

He tilts his head to one side and gives me a censorious frown. "I ran my own business from the age of twenty-one."

"But you're . . . you. Control freak and whiz-kid extraordinaire. Jeez, Christian, you majored in economics at Harvard before you dropped out. At least you have some idea. I sold paint and cable ties for three years on a part-time basis, for heaven's sake. I've seen so little of the world, and I know next to nothing!" My voice rises, growing louder and higher, as I complete my tirade.

"You're also the most well-read person I know," he counters earnestly. "You love a good book. You couldn't leave your job while we were on our honeymoon. You read how many manuscripts? Four?"

"Five," I whisper.

"And you wrote full reports on all of them. You're a very bright woman, Anastasia. I'm sure you'll manage."

"Are you crazy?"

"Crazy for you," he whispers.

And I snort because it's the only expression I can manage. He narrows his eyes.

"You'll be a laughingstock. Buying a company for the little woman, who has only had a full-time job for a few months of her adult life."

"Do you think I give a fuck what people think? Besides, you won't be on your own."

I gape at him. He really has lost his marbles this time. "Christian, I . . ." I put my head in my hands—my emotions have been through a wringer. *Is he crazy?* And from somewhere dark and deep inside I have the sudden, inappropriate need to laugh. When I look up at him again, his eyes widen.

"Something amusing you, Ms. Steele?"

"Yes. You."

His eyes widen further, shocked but also amused. "Laughing at your husband? That will never do. And you're biting your lip." His eyes darken . . . in that way. Oh no—I know that look. Sultry, seductive, salacious . . . No, no, no! Not here.

"Don't even think about it," I warn, alarm clear in my voice.

"Think about what, Anastasia?"

"I know that look. We're at work."

He leans forward, his eyes glued to mine, molten gray and hungry. *Holy shit!* I swallow instinctively.

"We're in a small, reasonably sound-proofed office with a lock-able door," he whispers.

"Gross moral turpitude." I enunciate each word carefully.

"Not with your husband."

"With my boss's boss's boss," I hiss.

"You're my wife."

"Christian, no. I mean it. You can fuck me seven shades of Sunday this evening. But not now. Not here!"

He blinks and narrows his eyes once more. Then, unexpectedly, he laughs.

"Seven shades of Sunday?" He arches an eyebrow, intrigued. "I may hold you to that, Ms. Steele."

"Oh, stop with the Ms. Steele!" I snap and thump the desk, startling us both. "For heaven's sake, Christian. If it means so much to you, I'll change my name!"

His mouth pops open as he inhales sharply. And then he grins, a radiant, all-teeth-showing, joyous grin. *Wow* . . .

"Good." He claps his hands, and all of a sudden he stands. *What now?*

"Mission accomplished. Now, I have work to do. If you'll excuse me, Mrs. Grey."

Gah—this man is so maddening! "But—"

"But what, Mrs. Grey?"

I sag. "Just go."

"I intend to. I'll see you this evening. I'm looking forward to seven shades of Sunday."

I scowl.

"Oh, and I have a stack of business-related social engagements coming up, and I'd like you to accompany me."

I gape at him. *Will you just go?*

"I'll have Andrea call Hannah to put the dates in your calendar. There are some people you need to meet. You should get Hannah to handle your schedule from now on."

"Okay," I mumble, completely bemused, bewildered, and shell-shocked.

He leans over my desk. *What now?* I am caught in his hypnotic gaze.

"Love doing business with you, Mrs. Grey." He leans in closer as I sit paralyzed, and he plants a soft tender kiss on my lips. "Laters, baby," he murmurs. He stands abruptly, winks at me, and leaves.

I lay my head on my desk, feeling like I've been run over by a freight train—the freight train that is my beloved husband. He has to be the most frustrating, annoying, contrary man on the planet. I sit up and frantically rub my eyes. *What have I just agreed to?* Okay, Ana Grey running SIP—I mean, Grey Publishing. The man is insane. There's a knock on the door, and Hannah pokes her head around.

"You okay?" she asks.

I just stare at her. She frowns.

"I know you don't like me doing this—but can I make you some tea?"

I nod.

"Twinings English Breakfast, weak and black?"

I nod.

"Coming right up, Ana."

I stare blankly at my computer screen, still in shock. How can I make him understand? E-mail!

From: Anastasia Steele
Subject: NOT AN ASSET!
Date: August 22 2011 14:23

To: Christian Grey

Mr. Grey

Next time you come and see me, make an appointment, so
I can at least have some prior warning of your adolescent
overbearing megalomania.

Yours

Anastasia Grey <——please note name.
Editor, SIP

From: Christian Grey
Subject: Seven Shades of Sunday
Date: August 22 2011 14:34
To: Anastasia Steele

My Dear Mrs. Grey (emphasis on My)

What can I say in my defense? I was in the neighborhood.

And no, you are not an asset, you are my beloved wife.

As ever, you make my day.

Christian Grey
CEO & Overbearing Megalomaniac, Grey Enterprises
Holdings, Inc.

He's trying to be funny, but I am in no mood to laugh. I take a
deep breath and go back to my correspondence.

CHRISTIAN IS QUIET WHEN I climb into the car that evening.
"Hi," I murmur.

"Hi," he responds, warily—as he should.

"Disrupt anyone else's work today?" I ask too sweetly.

A ghost of a smile crosses his face. "Only Flynn's."

Oh.

"Next time you go to see him, I'll give you a list of topics I want covered," I hiss.

"You seem out of sorts, Mrs. Grey."

I glare steadily at the backs of Ryan's and Sawyer's heads in front of me. Christian shifts beside me.

"Hey," he says softly and reaches for my hand. All afternoon, when I should have been concentrating on work, I was trying to figure out what to say to him. But I became angrier and angrier with each passing hour. I've had enough of his cavalier, petulant, and, frankly, childish behavior. I snatch my hand out of his—in a cavalier, petulant, and childish manner.

"You're mad at me?" he whispers.

"Yes," I hiss. Folding my arms protectively across my body, I gaze out my window. He shifts beside me once more, but I will not let myself look at him. I don't understand why I'm so mad at him—but I am. Really fucking mad.

As soon as we pull up outside Escala, I break protocol and leap out of the car with my briefcase. I stomp into the building, not checking to see who is following. Ryan scuttles into the foyer behind me and dashes to the elevator to press the "call" button.

"What?" I snap when I'm alongside him. His cheeks redden.

"Apologies, ma'am," he mutters.

Christian comes and stands beside me to wait for the elevator, and Ryan retreats.

"So it's not just me you're mad at?" Christian murmurs dryly. I glare up at him and see a trace of a smile on his face.

"Are you laughing at me?" I narrow my eyes.

"I wouldn't dare," he says, holding his hands up like I'm threatening him at gunpoint. He's in his navy suit, looking crisp and clean with floppy sex hair and a guileless expression.

"You need a haircut," I mutter. Turning away from him, I step into the elevator.

"Do I?" he says while brushing his hair off his forehead. He follows me in.

"Yes." I tap the code for our apartment into the keypad.

"So you're talking to me now?"

"Just."

"What exactly are you mad about? I need an indication," he asks cautiously.

I turn and gape at him.

"Do you really have no idea? Surely, for someone so bright, you must have an inkling? I can't believe you're that obtuse."

He takes an alarmed step back. "You really are mad. I thought we had sorted all this in your office," he murmurs, perplexed.

"Christian, I just capitulated to your petulant demands. That's all."

The elevator doors open and I storm out. Taylor is standing in the hallway. He takes a step back and quickly shuts his mouth as I steam past him.

"Hi, Taylor," I mutter.

"Mrs. Grey," he murmurs.

Dropping my briefcase in the hallway, I head into the great room. Mrs. Jones is at the stove.

"Good evening, Mrs. Grey."

"Hi, Mrs. Jones," I mutter. I head straight to the fridge and pull out a bottle of white wine. Christian follows me into the kitchen and watches me like a hawk as I take a glass down from the cupboard. He removes his jacket and casually places it on the countertop.

"Do you want a drink?" I ask super sweetly.

"No thanks," he says, not taking his eyes off me, and I know that he's helpless. He does not know what to do with me. It's comical on one level and tragic on another. *Well, screw him!* I am having trouble locating my compassionate self since our meeting this afternoon. Slowly, he removes his tie and then opens the top button of his shirt. I pour myself a large glass of sauvignon blanc, and Christian runs a hand through his hair. When I turn around, Mrs.

Jones has disappeared. *Shit!* She's my human shield. I take a slug of wine. *Hmm.* It tastes good.

"Stop this," Christian whispers. He takes the two steps between us so he's standing in front of me. Gently he tucks my hair behind my ear and caresses my earlobe with his fingertips, sending a shiver through me. Is this what I've missed all day? His touch? I shake my head, causing him to release my ear and gaze up at him.

"Talk to me," he murmurs.

"What's the point? You don't listen to me."

"Yes I do. You're one of the few people I do listen to."

I take another swig of wine.

"Is this about your name?"

"Yes and no. It's about how you dealt with the fact that I disagreed with you." I glare up at him, expecting him to be angered.

His brow furrows. "Ana, you know I have . . . issues. It's hard for me to let go where you're concerned. You know that."

"But I'm not a child, and I'm not an asset."

"I know." He sighs.

"Then stop treating me as though I am," I whisper, imploring him.

He brushes the backs of his fingers down my cheek and runs the tip of his thumb across my bottom lip.

"Don't be mad. You're so precious to me. Like a priceless asset, like a child," he whispers, a somber reverent expression on his face. His words distract me. *Like a child.* Precious like a child . . . a child would be precious to him!

"I'm neither of those things, Christian. I'm your wife. If you were hurt that I wasn't going to take your name, you should have said."

"Hurt?" He frowns deeply, and I know that he's exploring the possibility in his mind. He straightens suddenly, still frowning, and glances quickly at his wristwatch. "The architect will be here in just under an hour. We should eat."

Oh no. I groan inwardly. He hasn't answered me, and now I have to deal with Gia Matteo. My shitty day just got shittier. I scowl at Christian.

"This discussion isn't finished," I mutter.

"What else is there to discuss?"

"You could sell the company."

Christian snorts. "Sell it?"

"Yes."

"You think I'd find a buyer in today's market?"

"How much did it cost you?"

"It was relatively cheap." His tone is guarded.

"So if it folds?"

He smirks. "We'll survive. But I won't let it fold, Anastasia. Not while you're there."

"And if I leave?"

"And do what?"

"I don't know. Something else."

"You've already said this is your dream job. And forgive me if I'm wrong, but I promised before God, Reverend Walsh, and a congregation of our nearest and dearest to 'cherish you, uphold your hopes and dreams, and keep you safe at my side.'"

"Quoting your wedding vows to me is not playing fair."

"I've never promised to play fair where you're concerned. Besides," he adds, "you've wielded your vows at me like a weapon before."

I scowl. This is true.

"Anastasia, if you're still angry with me, take it out on me in bed later." His voice is suddenly low and full of sensual longing, his eyes heated.

What? Bed? How?

He smiles indulgently down at my expression. Is he expecting me to tie him up? *Holy crap!*

"Seven shades of Sunday," he whispers. "Looking forward to it."

Whoa!

"Gail!" he shouts abruptly, and four seconds later, Mrs. Jones appears. Where was she? Taylor's office? Listening? Oh no.

"Mr. Grey?"

"We'd like to eat now, please."

"Very good, sir."

Christian doesn't take his eyes off me. He watches me vigilantly as if I'm some exotic creature about to bolt. I take a sip of my wine.

"I think I'll join you in a glass," he says, sighing, and runs a hand through his hair again.

"YOU'RE NOT GOING TO finish?"

"No." I gaze down at my barely touched plate of fettuccini to avoid Christian's darkening expression. Before he can say anything, I stand and clear our plates from the dining table.

"Gia will be with us shortly," I mutter. Christian's mouth twists in an unhappy scowl, but he says nothing.

"I'll take those, Mrs. Grey," says Mrs. Jones as I walk into the kitchen.

"Thank you."

"You didn't like it?" she asks, concerned.

"It was fine. I'm just not hungry."

Giving me a small sympathetic smile, she turns to clear my plate and put everything in the dishwasher.

"I'm going to make a couple of calls," Christian announces, giving me an assessing look before he disappears into his study.

I let out a sigh of relief and head to our bedroom. Dinner was awkward. I'm still mad at Christian, and he doesn't seem to think he's done anything wrong. *Has he?* My subconscious cocks an eyebrow at me and gazes benignly over her half-moon glasses. Yes, he has. He's made it even more awkward for me at work. He didn't wait to discuss this issue with me when we were in the relative privacy of our own home. How would he feel if I came barging into his office, laying down the law? And to cap it all, he wants to give me SIP! How the hell could I run a company? I know next to nothing about business.

I gaze out at the Seattle skyline bathed in the pearly pink light of dusk. And as usual, he wants to solve our differences in the bedroom . . . um . . . foyer . . . playroom . . . TV room . . . kitchen countertop . . . *Stop!* It always comes back to sex with him. Sex is his coping mechanism.

I wander into the bathroom and scowl at my reflection in the mirror. Coming back to the real world is hard. We managed to skate over all our differences while we were in our bubble because we were so wrapped up in each other. But now? Briefly I am dragged back to my wedding, remembering my concerns that day—marry in haste . . . No, I mustn't think like this. I knew he was Fifty Shades when I married him. I just have to hang in there and try to talk this through with him.

I squint at myself in the mirror. I look pale, and now I have that woman to deal with.

I'm wearing my gray pencil skirt and a sleeveless blouse. *Right!* My inner goddess gets out her harlot-red nail polish. I undo two buttons, exposing a little cleavage. I wash my face, then carefully redo my makeup, applying more mascara than usual and putting extra gloss on my lips. Bending down, I brush my hair vigorously from root to tip. When I stand, my hair is a chestnut haze around me that tumbles to my breasts. I tuck it artfully behind my ears and go in search of my pumps, rather than my flats.

When I reemerge into the great room, Christian has the house plans spread out on the dining table. He has music playing through the sound system. It stops me in my tracks.

"Mrs. Grey," he says warmly, then looks quizzically at me.

"What's this?" I ask. The music is stunning.

"Fauré's Requiem. You look different," he says, distracted.

"Oh. I've not heard it before."

"It's very calming, relaxing," he says and raises an eyebrow. "Have you done something to your hair?"

"Brushed it," I mutter. I'm transported by the haunting voices. Abandoning the plans on the table, he walks toward me, a slow saunter in time to the music.

"Dance with me?" he murmurs.

"To this? It's a requiem." I squeak, shocked.

"Yes." He pulls me into his arms and holds me, burying his

nose in my hair and swaying gently from side to side. He smells his heavenly self.

Oh . . . I've missed him. I wrap my arms around him and fight the urge to cry. *Why are you so infuriating?*

"I hate fighting with you," he whispers.

"Well, stop being such an arse."

He chuckles and the captivating sound reverberates through his chest. He tightens his hold on me. "Arse?"

"Ass."

"I prefer *arse.*"

"You should. It suits you."

He laughs once more and kisses the top of my head.

"A requiem?" I murmur, a little shocked that we are dancing to it.

He shrugs. "It's just a lovely piece of music, Ana."

Taylor coughs discreetly at the entranceway, and Christian releases me.

"Miss Matteo is here," he says.

Oh joy!

"Show her in," Christian says. He reaches over and clasps my hand as Miss Gia Matteo enters the room.

CHAPTER EIGHT

Gia Matteo is a good-looking woman—a tall, good-looking woman. She wears her short, salon-blonde, perfectly layered and coiffed hair like a sophisticated crown. She's dressed in a pale gray pantsuit; the slacks and fitted jacket hug her lush curves. Her clothes look expensive. At the base of her throat, a solitary diamond glints, matching the single-carat studs in her ears. She is well groomed—one of those women who grew up with money and breeding, though her breeding seems to be lacking this evening; her pale blue blouse is undone too far. Like mine. I flush.

"Christian. Ana." She beams, showing perfect white teeth, and holds out a manicured hand to shake first Christian's, then my hand. It means I have to release Christian's hand to reciprocate. She's a fraction shorter than Christian, but then she's in killer heels.

"Gia," Christian says politely. I smile coolly.

"You both look so well after your honeymoon," she says smoothly, her brown eyes gazing at Christian through long mascaraed lashes. Christian puts his arm around me, holding me close.

"We had a wonderful time, thank you." He brushes his lips against my temple, taking me by surprise.

See . . . he's mine. Annoying—infuriating, even—but mine. I grin. *Right now I really love you, Christian Grey.* I slip my hand around his waist, then into his rear pocket of his pants and squeeze his behind. Gia gives us a thin smile.

"Have you managed to look over the plans?"

"We have," I murmur. I gaze up at Christian, who grins down at me, one eyebrow raised in wry amusement. Amused at what? My reaction to Gia or my squeezing his butt?

"Please," Christian says. "The plans are here." He gestures toward the dining table. Taking my hand, he leads me to it, Gia following in our wake. I finally remember my manners.

"Would you like something to drink?" I ask. "A glass of wine?"

"That would be lovely," Gia says. "Dry white if you have it."

Shit! Sauvignon blanc—that's a dry white, isn't it? Reluctantly leaving my husband's side, I head over to the kitchen. I hear the iPod hiss as Christian switches off the music.

"Would you like some more wine, Christian?" I call.

"Please, baby," he croons, grinning at me. Wow, he can be so swoon-worthy at times yet so aggravating at others.

Reaching up to open the cupboard, I'm aware his eyes are on me, and I'm gripped by the uncanny feeling that Christian and I are putting on a show, playing a game together—but this time we're on the same side pitted against Ms. Matteo. Does he know that she's attracted to him and is being too obvious about it? It gives me a small rush of pleasure when I realize maybe he's trying to reassure me. Or maybe he's just sending a message loud and clear to this woman that he's taken.

Mine. *Yeah, bitch—mine.* My inner goddess is wearing her gladiatrix outfit, and she's taking no prisoners. Smiling to myself I collect three glasses from the cupboard, take the opened bottle of sauvignon blanc from the fridge, and place them all on the breakfast bar. Gia is leaning over the table while Christian stands beside her and points at something on the plans.

"I think Ana has some opinions on the glass wall, but generally we're both pleased with the ideas you've come up with."

"Oh, I'm glad," Gia gushes, obviously relieved, and as she says it, she briefly touches his arm in a small, flirty gesture. Christian stiffens immediately but subtly. She doesn't even seem to notice.

Leave him the fuck alone, lady. He doesn't like to be touched.

Stepping casually aside so he's out of her reach, Christian turns to me. "Thirsty here," he says.

"Coming right up." He *is* playing the game. She makes him uncomfortable. Why didn't I see that before? That's why I don't like her. He's used to how women react to him. I've seen it often enough, and usually he thinks nothing of it. Touching is something else. Well, Mrs. Grey to the rescue.

I hastily pour the wine, gather all three glasses in my hands, and hurry back to my knight in distress. Offering a glass to Gia, I deliberately position myself between them. She smiles courteously as she accepts it. I hand the second to Christian, who takes it eagerly, his expression one of amused gratitude.

"Cheers," Christian says to us both, but looking at me. Gia and I raise our glasses and answer in unison. I take a welcome sip of wine.

"Ana, you have some issues with the glass wall?" Gia asks.

"Yes. I love it—don't get me wrong. But I was hoping that we could incorporate it more organically into the house. After all, I fell in love with the house as it was, and I don't want to make any radical changes."

"I see."

"I just want the design to be sympathetic, you know . . . more in keeping with the original house." I glance up at Christian, who is gazing at me thoughtfully.

"No major renovations?" he murmurs.

"No." I shake my head to emphasize my point.

"You like it as it is?"

"Mostly, yes. I always knew it just needed some TLC."

Christian's eyes glow warmly.

Gia glances at the pair of us, and her cheeks pink. "Okay," she says. "I think I get where you're coming from, Ana. How about if we retain the glass wall, but have it open out onto a larger deck that's in keeping with the Mediterranean style. We have the stone terrace there already. We can put in pillars in matching stone, widely spaced so you'll still have the view. Add a glass roof, or tile it as per the rest of the house. It'll also make a sheltered *alfresco* dining and seating area."

Got to give the woman her due . . . she's good.

"Or instead of the deck, we could incorporate a wood color

of your choice into the glass doors—that might help to keep the Mediterranean spirit," she continues.

"Like the bright blue shutters in the South of France," I murmur to Christian, who is watching me intently. He takes a sip of wine and shrugs, very noncommittal. *Hmm.* He doesn't like that idea but he doesn't overrule me, shoot me down, or make me feel stupid. God, this man is a mass of contradictions. His words from yesterday come to mind: *"I want this house to be the way you want. Whatever you want. It's yours."* He wants me to be happy—happy in everything I do. Deep down I think I know this. It's just—I stop myself. *Don't think about our argument now.* My subconscious glares at me.

Gia is looking at Christian, waiting for him to make the decision. I watch as her pupils dilate and her glossed lips part. Her tongue darts quickly over her top lip before she takes a sip of her wine. When I turn to Christian, he's still looking at me—not at her at all. *Yes!* I am going to have words with Ms. Matteo.

"Ana, what do you want to do?" Christian murmurs, very clearly deferring to me.

"I like the deck idea."

"Me, too."

I turn back to Gia. *Hey, lady, look at me, not him. I'm the one making the decisions on this.* "I think I'd like to see revised drawings showing the bigger deck and pillars that are in keeping with the house."

Reluctantly, Gia drags her greedy eyes away from my husband and smiles down at me. Does she think I'm not going to notice?

"Sure," she acquiesces pleasantly. "Any other issues?"

Other than you eye-fucking my husband? "Christian wants to remodel the master suite," I murmur.

There's a discreet cough from the entrance to the great room. We three turn as one to find Taylor standing there.

"Taylor?" Christian asks.

"I need to confer with you on an urgent matter, Mr. Grey."

Christian clasps my shoulders from behind and addresses Gia.

"Mrs. Grey is in charge of this project. She has absolute carte blanche. Whatever she wants, it's hers. I completely trust her instincts. She's very shrewd." His voice alters subtly. In it I hear pride and a veiled warning—a warning to Gia?

He trusts my instincts? Oh, this man's exasperating. My instincts let him run roughshod over my feelings this afternoon. I shake my head in frustration but I'm grateful that he's telling Miss Provocative-and-Unfortunately-Good-at-Her-Job just who's in charge. I caress his hand as it rests on my shoulder.

"If you'll excuse me." Christian squeezes my shoulders before following Taylor. I wonder idly what's going on.

"So . . . the master suite?" Gia asks nervously.

I gaze up at her, pausing for a moment to ensure that Christian and Taylor are out of earshot. Then, calling on all my inner strength and the fact that I've been seriously piqued for the last five hours, I let her have it.

"You're right to be nervous, Gia, because right now your work on this project hangs in the balance. But I'm sure we'll be fine as long as you keep your hands off my husband."

She gasps.

"Otherwise, you're fired. Understand?" I enunciate each word clearly.

She blinks rapidly, utterly stunned. She cannot believe what I've said. *I* cannot believe what I've just said. But I hold my ground, gazing impassively into her widening brown eyes.

Don't back down. Don't back down! I've learned this maddening impassive expression from Christian, who does impassive like no one else. I know that renovating the Greys' main residence is a prestigious project for Gia's architectural firm—a resplendent feather in her cap. She can't lose this commission. And right now I don't give a hoot that she's Elliot's friend.

"Ana—Mrs. Grey . . . I-I'm so sorry. I never—" She flushes, unsure what else she can say.

"Let me be clear. My husband is not interested in you."

"Of course," she murmurs, the blood draining from her face.

"As I said, I just wanted to be clear."

"Mrs. Grey, I sincerely apologize if you think . . . I have—" She stops, still floundering for something to say.

"Good. As long as we understand each other, we'll be fine. Now, I'll let you know what we have in mind for the master suite, then I'd like a run down on all the materials you intend to use. As you know, Christian and I are determined that this house should be ecologically sustainable, and I'd like to reassure him as to where all the materials are coming from and what they are."

"Of c-course," she stutters, wide-eyed and frankly a little intimidated by me. This is a first. My inner goddess runs around the arena, waving to the frenzied crowd.

Gia pats her hair into place, and I realize this is a nervous gesture.

"The master suite?" she prompts anxiously, her voice a breathless whisper. Now that I have the upper hand, I feel myself relax for the first time since my meeting with Christian this afternoon. I can do this. My inner goddess is celebrating her inner bitch.

CHRISTIAN JOINS US JUST as we're finishing up.

"All done?" he asks. He puts his arm around my waist and turns to Gia.

"Yes, Mr. Grey." Gia smiles brightly, though her smile looks brittle. "I'll have the revised plans to you in a couple of days."

"Excellent. You're happy?" he asks me directly, his eyes warm and probing. I nod and blush for some reason that I don't understand.

"I'd better be going," Gia says, again too brightly. She offers her hand to me first this time, then to Christian.

"Until next time, Gia," I murmur.

"Yes, Mrs. Grey. Mr. Grey."

Taylor appears at the entrance of the great room.

"Taylor will see you out." My voice is loud enough for him to hear. Patting her hair once more, she turns on her high heels and leaves the great room, followed closely by Taylor.

"She was noticeably cooler," Christian says, looking quizzically at me.

"Was she? I didn't notice." I shrug, trying to remain neutral. "What did Taylor want?" I ask, partly because I'm curious and partly because I want to change the subject.

Frowning, Christian releases me and begins to roll up the plans on the table. "It was about Hyde."

"What about Hyde?" I whisper.

"It's nothing to worry about, Ana." Abandoning the plans, Christian draws me into his arms. "It turns out he hasn't been in his apartment for weeks, that's all." He kisses my hair, then releases me and finishes his task.

"So what did you decide on?" he asks, and I know it's because he doesn't want me to pursue the Hyde line of inquiry.

"Only what you and I discussed. I think she likes you," I say quietly.

He snorts. "Did you say something to her?" he asks, and I flush. How does he know? At a loss for what to say, I stare down at my fingers.

"We were Christian and Ana when she arrived, and Mr. and Mrs. Grey when she left." His tone is dry.

"I may have said something," I mumble. When I peek up at him, he's regarding me warmly, and for an unguarded moment he looks . . . pleased. He drops his gaze, shaking his head, and his expression changes.

"She's only reacting to this face." He sounds vaguely bitter, disgusted even.

Oh, Fifty, no!

"What?" He's bemused by my perplexed expression. His eyes grow wide in alarm. "You're not jealous, are you?" he asks, horrified.

I blush and swallow, then stare down at my knotted fingers. *Am I?*

"Ana, she's a sexual predator. Not my type at all. How can you be jealous of her? Of anyone? Nothing about her interests me."

When I glance up, he's gaping at me as if I've grown an additional limb. He runs a hand through his hair. "It's only you, Ana," he says quietly. "It will only ever be you."

Oh my. Abandoning the plans once more, Christian moves toward me and clasps my chin between his thumb and forefinger.

"How can you think otherwise? Have I ever given you any indication that I could be remotely interested in anyone else?" His eyes blaze as he stares into mine.

"No," I whisper. "I'm being silly. It's just today . . . you . . ." All my conflicting emotions from earlier resurface. How can I tell him how confused I am? I've been confounded and frustrated by his behavior this afternoon in my office. One minute he wants me to stay at home, the next he's gifting me a company. How am I supposed to keep up?

"What about me?"

"Oh, Christian"—my bottom lip trembles—"I'm trying to adapt to this new life that I had never imagined for myself. Everything is being handed to me on a plate—the job, you, my beautiful husband, who I never . . . I never knew I'd love this way, this hard, this fast, this . . . indelibly." I take a deep, steadying breath, as his mouth drops open.

"But you're like a freight train, and I don't want to get railroaded because the girl you fell in love with will be crushed. And what'll be left? All that would be left is a vacuous social X-ray, flitting from charity function to charity function." I pause once more, struggling to find the words to convey how I feel. "And now you want me to be a company CEO, which has never even been on my radar. I'm bouncing between all these ideas, struggling. You want me at home. You want me to run a company. It's so confusing." I stop, tears threatening, and I force back a sob.

"You've got to let me make my own decisions, take my own risks, and make my own mistakes, and let me learn from them. I need to walk before I can run, Christian, don't you see? I want some independence. That's what my name means to me." There, that's what I wanted to say this afternoon.

"You feel railroaded?" he whispers.

I nod.

He closes his eyes, agitated. "I just want to give you the world, Ana, everything and anything you want. And save you from it, too. Keep you safe. But I also want everyone to know you're mine. I panicked today when I got your e-mail. Why didn't you tell me about your name?"

I flush. He has a point.

"I only thought about it while we were on our honeymoon, and well, I didn't want to burst the bubble, and I forgot about it. I only remembered yesterday evening. And then Jack . . . you know, it was distracting. I'm sorry, I should have told you or discussed it with you, but I could never seem to find the right time."

Christian's intense gaze is unnerving. It's as if he's trying to will his way into my skull, but he says nothing.

"Why did you panic?" I ask.

"I just don't want you to slip through my fingers."

"For heaven's sake, I'm not going anywhere. When are you going to get that through your incredibly thick skull? I. Love. You." I wave my hand in the air like he does sometimes to emphasize my point. "More than . . . 'eyesight, space, or liberty.'"

His eyes widen. "A daughter's love?" He gives me an ironic smile.

"No." I laugh, despite myself. "It's the only quote that came to mind."

"Mad King Lear?"

"Dear, dear mad King Lear." I caress his face, and he leans into my touch, closing his eyes. "Would you change your name to Christian Steele so everyone would know that you belong to me?"

Christian's eyes fly open, and he gazes at me as if I've just said the world is flat. He frowns. "Belong to you?" he murmurs, testing the words.

"Mine."

"Yours," he says, repeating the words we spoke in the playroom only yesterday. "Yes, I would. If it meant that much to you."

Oh my.

"Does it mean that much to you?"

"Yes." He is unequivocal.

"Okay." I will do this for him. Give him the reassurance he still needs.

"I thought you'd already agreed to this."

"Yes, I have, but now that we've discussed it further, I'm happier with my decision."

"Oh," he mutters, surprised. Then he smiles his beautiful, boyish yes-I-am-really-kinda-young smile, and he takes my breath away. Grabbing me by the waist, he swings me around. I squeal and start to giggle, and I don't know if he's just happy or relieved or . . . what?

"Mrs. Grey, do you know what this means to me?"

"I do now."

He leans down and kisses me, his fingers moving into my hair, holding me in place.

"It means seven shades of Sunday," he murmurs against my lips, and he runs his nose along mine.

"You think?" I lean back to gaze at him.

"Certain promises were made. An offer extended, a deal brokered," he whispers, his eyes sparkling with wicked delight.

"Um . . ." I am still reeling, trying to follow his mood.

"You reneging on me?" he asks uncertainly, and a speculative look crosses his face. "I have an idea," he adds.

Oh, what kinky fuckery is this?

"A really important matter to attend to," he continues, suddenly all serious once more. "Yes, Mrs. Grey. A matter of the gravest importance."

Hang on—he's laughing at me.

"What?" I breathe.

"I need you to cut my hair. Apparently it's overlong, and my wife doesn't like it."

"I can't cut your hair!"

"Yes, you can." Christian grins and shakes his head so his overlong hair covers his eyes.

"Well, if Mrs. Jones has a pudding bowl." I giggle.

He laughs. "Okay, good point well made. I'll get Franco to do it."

No! Franco works for the bitch troll! Maybe I could give him a trim. After all, I cut Ray's hair for years, and he never complained.

"Come." I grab his hand. His eyes widen. I lead him all the way to our bathroom, where I release him and grab the white wooden chair that stands in the corner. I place it in front of the sink. When I look at Christian, he's gazing at me with ill-disguised amusement, thumbs tucked in the front belt loops of his pants, but his eyes are smoking hot.

"Sit." I gesture to the empty chair, trying to maintain the upper hand.

"Are you going to wash my hair?"

I nod. He arches one brow in surprise, and for a moment I think he's going to back down. "Okay." Slowly he begins to undo each button of his white shirt, starting with the one beneath his throat. Nimble, deft fingers move to each button in turn until his shirt hangs open.

Oh my . . . My inner goddess pauses in her celebratory jaunt around the arena.

Christian holds out a cuff with an "undo this now" gesture, and his mouth twitches in that challenging, sexy way he has.

Oh, cuff links. I take his proffered wrist and remove the first one, a platinum disc with his initials engraved in a simple italic script—and then remove its matching twin. As I finish I glance at him, and his amused expression is gone, replaced by something hotter . . . much hotter. I reach up and push his shirt off his shoulders, letting it fall to the floor.

"Ready?" I whisper.

"For whatever you want, Ana."

My eyes stray from his eyes to his lips. Parted so that he can inhale more deeply. Sculptured, chiseled, whatever, it is a beautiful mouth and he knows exactly what to do with it. I find myself leaning up to kiss him.

"No," he says and places both of his hands on my shoulders. "Don't. If you do that, I'll never get my hair cut."

Oh!

"I want this," he continues. And his eyes are round and raw for some inexplicable reason. It's disarming.

"Why?" I whisper.

He stares at me for a beat, and his eyes grow wider. "Because it'll make me feel cherished."

My heart practically lurches to a halt. *Oh, Christian . . . my Fifty.* And before I know it I've circled him in my arms, and I kiss his chest before nuzzling my cheek into his tickly chest hair.

"Ana. My Ana," he whispers. He wraps his arms around me and we stand immobile, holding each other in our bathroom. Oh, how I love to be in his arms. Even if he is an overbearing, megalomaniac arse, he's *my* overbearing megalomaniac arse in need of a lifetime dose of TLC. I lean back without releasing him.

"You really want me to do this?"

He nods and gives me his shy smile. I grin back at him and step out of his embrace.

"Then sit," I repeat.

He dutifully does, sitting with his back to the sink. I take off my shoes and kick them over to where his shirt lies crumpled on the bathroom floor. From the shower I retrieve his Chanel shampoo. We bought it in France.

"Would Sir like this?" I hold it up in both hands like I'm selling it on QVC. "Hand-delivered from the South of France. I like the smell of this . . . it smells of you," I add in a whisper, slipping out of my television presenter mode.

"Please." He grins.

I grab a small towel off the towel warmer. Mrs. Jones sure knows how to keep the towels supersoft.

"Lean forward," I order, and Christian complies. Draping the towel around his shoulders, I then turn on the taps and fill the sink with a mix of warm water.

"Lean back." Oh, I like being in charge. Christian leans back, but he's too tall. He shifts the seat forward, then tilts back the entire chair until the top rests against the sink. Perfect distance. He tips back his head. Bold eyes gaze up at me, and I smile. Taking one of the drinking glasses we keep on the vanity, I dip it into the water and tip it over Christian's head, soaking his hair. I repeat the process, leaning over him.

"You smell so good, Mrs. Grey," he murmurs and closes his eyes.

As I methodically wet his hair, I freely gaze at him. *Holy cow.* Will I ever tire of this? Long dark lashes fan across his cheeks; his lips part a little, creating a small, dark diamond shape, and he inhales softly. Hmm . . . how I long to poke my tongue—

I splash water into his eyes. *Shit!* "Sorry!"

He grabs the corner of the towel and laughs as he wipes the water out of his eyes.

"Hey, I know I'm an arse, but don't drown me."

I lean down and kiss his forehead, giggling. "Don't tempt me."

He curls his hand behind my head and shifts so that he captures my lips with his. He kisses me briefly, making a low contented sound in his throat. The noise connects to the muscles deep in my belly. It's a very seductive sound. He releases me and lies back obediently, gazing up at me with expectation. For a moment he looks vulnerable, like a child. It tugs at my heart.

I squirt some shampoo into my palm and massage it into his scalp, beginning at his temples and working over the top of his head and down the sides, circling my fingers rhythmically. He closes his eyes and makes that low humming sound again.

"That feels good," he says after a moment and relaxes beneath the firm touch of my fingers.

"Yes, it does." I kiss his forehead once more.

"I like it when you scratch my scalp with your fingernails." His eyes are still closed, but his expression is one of blissful contentment—no trace of his vulnerability remains. Jeez, how much his mood has changed, and I take comfort knowing it's me that's done this.

"Head up," I command, and he obeys. Hmm—a girl could get used to this. I rub the suds into the back of his hair, scraping my nails into his scalp.

"Back."

He leans back, and I rinse off the lather, using the glass. This time I manage not to splash him.

"Once more?" I ask.

"Please." His eyes flutter open and his serene gaze finds mine. I grin down at him.

"Coming right up, Mr. Grey."

I turn to the sink that Christian normally uses and fill it with warm water.

"For rinsing," I say when his look turns quizzical.

I repeat the process with the shampoo, listening to his deep even breaths. Once he's all lathered up, I take another moment to appreciate the fine face of my husband. I cannot resist him. Tenderly, I caress his cheek, and he opens his eyes, watching me almost sleepily through his long lashes. Leaning forward I plant a soft, chaste kiss on his lips. He smiles, closes his eyes, and breathes out a sigh of utter contentment.

Who would have thought after our argument this afternoon he could be this relaxed? Without sex? I lean right over him.

"Hmm," he murmurs appreciatively as my breasts brush his face. Resisting the urge to shimmy, I pull the plug so the sudsy water drains away. His hands move to my hips and around to my behind.

"No fondling the help," I murmur, feigning disapproval.

"Don't forget I'm deaf," he says, keeping his eyes closed, as he runs his hands down past my behind and starts to hitch up my skirt. I swat his arm. I'm enjoying playing hairdresser. He grins, big and boyish, like I've caught him doing something illicit that he's secretly proud of.

I reach for the glass again, but this time use the water from the neighboring sink to carefully rinse all the shampoo from his hair. I continue to lean over him, and he keeps his hands on my backside, thrumming his fingers back and forward, up and down . . . back and forth . . . hmm. I wiggle. He growls low in his throat.

"There. All rinsed."

"Good," he declares. His fingers tighten on my behind, and

all at once he sits up, his soaked hair dripping all over him. He pulls me down onto his lap, his hands moving from my behind up to the nape of my neck, then to my chin, holding me in place. I gasp with surprise and his lips are on mine, his tongue hot and hard in my mouth. My fingers curl around his wet hair, and drops of water run down my arms; and as he deepens the kiss, his hair bathes my face. His hand moves from my chin down to the top button of my blouse.

"Enough of this primping. I want to fuck you seven shades of Sunday, and we can do it in here or in the bedroom. You decide."

Christian's eyes blaze, hot and full of promise, his hair dripping water onto us both. My mouth goes dry.

"What's it to be, Anastasia?" he asks as he holds me in his lap.

"You're wet," I respond.

He bends his head suddenly, running his dripping hair all down the front of my blouse. I squeal and try to wriggle off him. He tightens his grip around me.

"Oh, no you don't, baby." When he raises his head he's grinning salaciously at me, and I am Miss Wet Blouse 2011. My top is soaked and totally see-through. I'm wet . . . everywhere.

"Love the view," he murmurs and leans down to run his nose around and around one wet nipple. I squirm.

"Answer me, Ana. Here or the bedroom?"

"Here," I whisper frantically. To hell with the haircut—I'll do it later. He smiles slowly, his lips curling into a sensuous smile full of licentious promise.

"Good choice, Mrs. Grey," he breathes against my lips. He releases my chin and his hand moves to my knee. It glides smoothly up my leg, lifting my skirt and skating over my skin, making me tingle. His lips trail soft kisses from the base of my ear along my jaw.

"Oh, what shall I do to you?" he whispers. His fingers halt at my stocking tops. "I like these," he says. He runs a finger underneath the top and skims it around to my inner thigh. I gasp and squirm once more in his lap.

He groans, low in his throat. "If I'm going to fuck you seven shades of Sunday, I want you to keep still."

"Make me," I challenge, my voice soft and breathy.

Christian inhales sharply. He narrows his eyes and regards me with a hot, hooded expression.

"Oh, Mrs. Grey. You have only to ask." His hand moves from my stocking tops up to my panties. "Let's divest you of these." He tugs gently and I shift to help him. His breath hisses through his teeth as I do.

"Keep still," he grumbles.

"I'm helping," I pout, and he seizes my lower lip gently between his teeth.

"Still," he growls. He slides my panties down my legs and off. Tugging my skirt up so that it's bunched around my hips, he moves both hands to my waist and lifts me. He still has my panties in his hand.

"Sit. Astride me," he orders, staring intently into my eyes. I shift, straddling him, and regard him provocatively. *Bring it on, Fifty!*

"Mrs. Grey," he warns. "Are you goading me?" He gazes at me, amused but aroused. It's a seductive combination.

"Yes. What are you going to do about it?"

His eyes light up with salacious delight at my challenge, and I feel his arousal beneath me. "Clasp your hands together behind your back."

Oh! I comply obediently, and he deftly binds my wrists together with my panties.

"My panties? Mr. Grey, you have no shame," I admonish.

"Not where you're concerned, Mrs. Grey, but you know that." His look is intense and hot. Putting his hands around my waist, he shifts me so I am sitting a little farther back on his lap. Water still drips down his neck and over his chest. I want to bend forward and lick the drips off, but it's trickier now that I am restrained.

Christian caresses both of my thighs and skims his hands down to my knees. Gently he pushes them farther apart and widens his own legs, holding me in that position. His fingers move to the buttons of my blouse.

"I don't think we need this," he says. He starts methodically undoing each button on my clinging wet blouse, his eyes never leaving mine. They get darker and darker as he finishes the task, taking his own sweet time about it. My pulse quickens and my breathing shallows. I can't believe it—he's hardly touched me, and I feel like this—hot, bothered . . . ready. I want to squirm. He leaves my damp blouse hanging open and, using both hands, he caresses my face with his fingers, his thumb skimming across my bottom lip. Suddenly, he thrusts his thumb into my mouth.

"Suck," he orders in a whisper, stressing the s. I close my mouth around him and do exactly that. Oh . . . I like this game. He tastes good. What else would I like to suck? The muscles in my belly clench at the thought. His lips part when I scrape my teeth and bite the soft pad of his thumb.

He groans and slowly extracts his wet thumb from my mouth and trails it down my chin, down my throat, over my sternum. He hooks it into the cup of my bra and yanks the cup down, freeing my breast.

Christian's gaze never leaves mine. He's watching each reaction that his touch elicits from me, and I'm watching him. It's hot. Consuming. Possessive. I love it. He mirrors his actions with his other hand so both my breasts are free and, cupping them gently, he skims each thumb over a nipple, circling slowly, teasing and taunting each one so that they harden and distend beneath his skillful touch. I try, I really try not to move, but my nipples are hotwired to my groin, so I moan and throw my head back, closing my eyes and surrendering to the sweet, sweet torture.

"Shh." Christian's soothing voice is at odds with the teasing, even-tempo rhythm of his wicked fingers. "Still, baby, still." Releasing one breast, he reaches up behind me and splays his hand around the nape of my neck. Leaning forward, he takes my now bereft nipple into his mouth and sucks hard, his wet hair tickling me. At the same time, his thumb stops skimming across

my other elongated nipple. Instead, he takes it between his thumb
and forefinger and tugs and twists it gently.

"Ah! Christian!" I groan and buck forward on his lap. But he
doesn't stop. He continues the slow, leisurely, agonizing tease.
And my body is burning as the pleasure takes a darker turn.

"Christian, please," I whimper.

"Hmm," he hums low in his chest. "I want you to come like
this." My nipple gets a brief respite as his words caress my skin,
and it's like he's calling to a deep, dark part of my psyche that only
he knows. When he resumes with his teeth this time, the pleasure
is almost intolerable. Moaning loudly, I writhe on his lap, trying
to find some precious friction against his pants. I pull uselessly
against my restraining panties, itching to touch him, but I'm lost—
lost in this treacherous sensation.

"Please," I whisper, pleading, and pleasure flies through my
body, from my neck, right down to my legs, to my toes, tightening
all in its wake.

"You have such beautiful breasts, Ana." He groans. "One day
I'll fuck them."

What the hell does that mean? Opening my eyes, I gape down
at him as he suckles me, my skin singing under his touch. I no
longer feel my sodden blouse, his wet hair . . . nothing except the
burn. And it burns deliciously hot and low, deep inside me, and
all thought evaporates as my body tightens and clenches . . . ready,
reaching . . . pining for release. And he doesn't stop—teasing, pulling, driving me wild. I want . . . I want . . .

"Let go," he breathes—and I do, loudly, my orgasm convuls-
ing through my body, and he stops his sweet torture and wraps his
arms around me, clutching me to him as my body spirals down
from my climax. When I open my eyes, he is gazing down at me
where I rest against his chest.

"God, I love to watch you come, Ana." His voice is full of wonder.

"That was . . ." Words fail me.

"I know." He leans forward and kisses me, his hand still at the nape of my neck, holding me just so, angling my head so he can kiss me deeply—with love, with reverence.

I am lost in his kiss.

He pulls away to draw breath, his eyes the color of a tropical storm.

"Now I'm going to fuck you, hard," he murmurs.

Holy cow. Grabbing me around the waist, he lifts me from his thighs down to the edge of his knees and reaches with his right hand for the button on the waistband of his navy pants. He runs the fingers of his left hand up and down my thigh, stopping at my stocking tops each time. He's watching me intently. We're face to face and I'm helpless, trussed up in my bra and by my panties, and this has to be one of the most intimate times we've had—me sitting on his lap, staring into his beautiful gray eyes. It makes me feel wanton, but also so connected to him—I am not embarrassed or shy. This is Christian, my husband, my lover, my overbearing megalomaniac, my Fifty—the love of my life. He reaches for his zipper, and my mouth goes dry as his erection springs free.

He smirks. "You like?" he whispers.

"Hmm," I murmur appreciatively. He wraps his hand around himself and moves it up and down . . . *Oh my.* I gaze up at him through my lashes. Fuck, he's so sexy.

"You're biting your lip, Mrs. Grey."

"That's because I'm hungry."

"Hungry?" His mouth opens in surprise, and his eyes widen a fraction.

"Hmm . . ." I agree and lick my lips.

He gives me his enigmatic smile and bites his lower lip as he continues to stroke himself. Why is the sight of my husband pleasuring himself such a turn-on?

"I see. You should have eaten your dinner." His tone is mocking and censorious at once. "But maybe I can oblige." He puts his hands on my waist. "Stand," he says softly, and I know what he's going to do. I get to my feet, my legs no longer shaking.

"Kneel."

I do as I'm told and kneel down on the cool tiled floor of the bathroom. He slides forward on the seat of the chair.

"Kiss me," he utters, holding his erection. I glance up at him, and he runs his tongue over his top teeth. It's arousing, very arousing, to see his desire, his naked desire for me and my mouth. Leaning forward, my eyes on his, I kiss the tip of his erection. I watch him inhale sharply and clench his teeth. Christian cups the side of my head, and I run my tongue over the tip, tasting the small bead of dew on the end. Hmm . . . he tastes good. His mouth drops open farther as he gasps and I pounce, pulling him into my mouth and sucking hard.

"Ah—" The air hisses through his teeth, and he flexes his hips forward, thrusting into my mouth. But I don't stop. Sheathing my teeth behind my lips, I push down and then pull up on him. He moves both hands so that he fully cups my head, burying his fingers in my hair, and slowly eases himself in and out of my mouth, his breathing quickening, growing harsher. I twirl my tongue around his tip and push down again in perfect counterpoint to him.

"Jesus, Ana." He sighs and screws his eyes shut tightly. He's lost and it's heady, his response to me. *Me*. And very slowly I draw my lips back, so it's just my teeth.

"Ah!" Christian stops moving. Leaning forward he grabs me and pulls me up onto his lap.

"Enough!" he growls. Reaching behind me, he frees my hands with one tug on my panties. I flex my wrists and stare from under my lashes into scorching eyes that gaze back at me with love and longing and lust. And I realize it's me that wants to fuck him seven shades of Sunday. I want him badly. I want to watch him come apart beneath me. I grab his erection and scoot over him. Placing my other hand on his shoulder, very gently and slowly, I ease myself onto him. He makes a guttural, feral noise deep in his throat and, reaching up, pulls off my blouse, letting it fall to the floor. His hands move to my hips.

"Still," he rasps, his hands digging into my flesh. "Please, let me savor this. Savor you."

I stop. *Oh my . . .* he feels so good inside me. He caresses my face, his eyes wide and wild, his lips parted as he breathes. He flexes beneath me and I moan, closing my eyes.

"This is my favorite place," he whispers. "Inside you. Inside my wife."

Oh fuck. Christian. I cannot hold back. My fingers glide into his wet hair, my lips seek his, and I start to move. Up and down on my toes, savoring him, savoring me. He groans loudly, and his hands are in my hair and around my back, and his tongue invades my mouth greedily, taking all that I willingly give. After all our arguing today, my frustration with him, his with me—we still have this. We will always have this. I love him so much, it's almost overwhelming. His hands move to my backside and he controls me, moving me up and down, again and again, at his pace—his hot, slick tempo.

"Ah," I groan helplessly into his mouth as I'm carried away.

"Yes. Yes, Ana," he hisses, and I rain kisses on his face, his chin, his jaw, his neck. "Baby," he breathes, capturing my mouth once more.

"Oh, Christian, I love you. I will always love you." I'm breathless, wanting him to know, wanting him to be sure of me after our battle of wills today.

He moans loudly and wraps his arms around me tightly as he climaxes with a mournful sob, and it's enough—enough to push me over the brink once more. I clutch my arms around his head and let go, and I come around him, tears springing to my eyes because I love him so.

"HEY," HE WHISPERS, TIPPING my chin back and gazing at me with quiet concern. "Why are you crying? Did I hurt you?"

"No," I mutter reassuringly. He smoothes my hair off my face, wipes away a lone tear with his thumb, and tenderly kisses my lips. He is still inside me. He shifts, and I wince as he pulls out of me.

"What's wrong, Ana? Tell me."

I sniff. "It's just . . . it's just sometimes I'm overwhelmed by how much I love you," I whisper.

After a beat, he smiles his special shy smile—reserved for me, I think. "You have the same effect on me," he whispers, and kisses me once more. I smile, and inside my joy unfurls and stretches lazily.

"Do I?"

He smirks. "You know you do."

"Sometimes I know. Not all the time."

"Back at you, Mrs. Grey."

I grin and gently place feather light kisses over his chest. I nuzzle his chest hair. Christian caresses my hair and runs a hand down my back. He unclasps my bra and pulls the strap down one arm. I shift, and he tugs the strap down the other arm and drops my bra on the floor.

"Hmm. Skin on skin," he murmurs appreciatively and folds me in his arms again. He kisses my shoulder and runs his nose up to my ear. "You smell like heaven, Mrs. Grey."

"So do you, Mr. Grey." I nuzzle him again and inhale his Christian smell, which is now mixed with the heady scent of sex. I could stay wrapped in his arms like this, sated and happy, forever. It's just what I need after a full day of back-to-work, arguing, and bitch-slapping. This is where I want to be, and in spite of his control freakery, his megalomania, this is where I belong. Christian buries his nose in my hair and inhales deeply. I let out a contented sigh, and I feel his smile. And we sit, arms clasped around each other, saying nothing.

Eventually reality intrudes.

"It's late," Christian says, his fingers methodically stroking my back.

"Your hair still needs cutting."

He chuckles. "That it does, Mrs. Grey. Do you have the energy to finish the job you started?"

"For you, Mr. Grey, anything." I kiss his chest once more and reluctantly stand.

"Don't go." Grabbing my hips, he turns me around. He straightens then undoes my skirt, letting it drop to the floor. He holds his hand out to me. I take it and step out of my skirt. Now I am dressed solely in stockings and garter belt.

"You are a mighty fine sight, Mrs. Grey." He sits back in the chair and crosses his arms, giving me a full and frank appraisal.

I hold out my hands and twirl for him.

"God, I'm a lucky son of a bitch," he says admiringly.

"Yes, you are."

He grins. "Put my shirt on and you can cut my hair. Like this, you'll distract me, and we'll never get to bed."

I can't help my answering smile. Knowing that he's watching my every move, I sashay over to where we left my shoes and his shirt. Bending slowly, I reach down, pick up his shirt, smell it—*hmm*—then shrug it on.

Christian's eyes are round. He's redone his fly and is watching me intently.

"That's quite a floor show, Mrs. Grey."

"Do we have any scissors?" I ask innocently, batting my eyelashes.

"My study," he croaks.

"I'll go search." Leaving him, I walk into our bedroom and grab my comb from the dressing table before heading to his study. As I enter the main corridor, I notice the door to Taylor's office is open. Mrs. Jones is standing just beyond the door. I stop, rooted to the spot.

Taylor is running his fingers down her face and smiling sweetly at her. Then he leans down and kisses her.

Holy shit! Taylor and Mrs. Jones? I gape in astonishment—I mean, I thought . . . well, I kind of suspected. But obviously they are together! I flush, feeling like a voyeur, and manage to get my feet to move. I scamper across the great room and into Christian's study. Switching on the light, I walk to his desk. Taylor and Mrs. Jones . . . Wow! I'm reeling. I always thought Mrs. Jones was older than Taylor. Oh, I have to get my head around this. I open the top drawer and am immediately distracted when I find a gun. *Christian has a gun!*

A revolver. *Holy fuck!* I had no idea Christian owned a gun. I take it out, slip the release, and check the cylinder. It's fully loaded, but light . . . too light. It must be carbon fiber. What does Christian want with a gun? Jeez, I hope he knows how to use it. Ray's perpetual warnings about handguns run quickly through my mind. His army training was never lost. *These will kill you, Ana. You need to know what you're doing when you're handling a firearm.* I put the gun back and find the scissors. Retrieving them quickly, I bolt back to Christian, my head buzzing. Taylor and Mrs. Jones . . . the revolver . . .

At the entrance to the great room, I run into Taylor.

"Mrs. Grey, excuse me." His face reddens as he quickly takes in my attire.

"Um, Taylor, hi . . . um. I'm cutting Christian's hair!" I blurt out, embarrassed. Taylor is as mortified as I am. He opens his mouth to say something, then closes it quickly and stands aside.

"After you, ma'am," he says formally. I think I'm the color of my old Audi, the submissive special. Could this be more embarrassing?

"Thank you," I mutter and dash down the hallway. *Crap!* Will I ever get used to the fact that we're not alone? I dash into the bathroom, breathless.

"What's wrong?" Christian is standing in front of the mirror, holding my shoes. All of my scattered clothes are now neatly piled beside the sink.

"I just ran into Taylor."

"Oh." Christian frowns. "Dressed like that."

Oh shit! "That's not Taylor's fault."

Christian's frown deepens. "No. But still."

"I'm dressed."

"Barely."

"I don't know who was more embarrassed, me or him." I try my distraction technique. "Did you know he and Gail are . . . well, together?"

Christian laughs. "Yes, of course I knew."

"And you never told me?"

"I thought you knew, too."

"No."

"Ana, they're adults. They live under the same roof. Both unattached. Both attractive."

I flush, feeling foolish for not having noticed.

"Well, if you put it like that . . . I just thought Gail was older than Taylor."

"She is, but not by much." He gazes at me, perplexed. "Some men like older women—" He stops abruptly and his eyes widen.

I scowl at him. "I know that," I snap.

Christian looks contrite. He smiles fondly at me. Yes! My distraction technique was successful! My subconscious rolls her eyes at me—but at what cost? Now the unmentionable Mrs. Robinson is looming over us.

"That reminds me," he says brightly.

"What?" I mutter petulantly. Grabbing the chair, I turn it to face the mirror above the sinks. "Sit," I order. Christian regards me with indulgent amusement, but does as he's told and sits back down in the chair. I start to comb through his now merely damp hair.

"I was thinking we could convert the rooms over the garages for them at the new place," Christian continues. "Make it a home. Then maybe Taylor's daughter could stay with him more often." He watches me carefully in the mirror.

"Why doesn't she stay here?"

"Taylor's never asked me."

"Perhaps you should offer. But we'd have to behave ourselves." Christian's brow furrows. "I hadn't thought of that."

"Perhaps that's why Taylor hasn't asked. Have you met her?"

"Yes. She's a sweet thing. Shy. Very pretty. I pay for her schooling."

Oh! I stop combing and stare at him in the mirror.

"I had no idea."

He shrugs. "Seemed the least I could do. Also, it means he won't quit."

"I'm sure he likes working for you."

Christian stares at me blankly, then shrugs. "I don't know."

"I think he's very fond of you, Christian." I resume combing and glance at him. His eyes don't leave mine.

"You think?"

"Yes. I do."

He snorts a dismissive yet content sound as if he's secretly pleased that his staff may like him.

"Good. Will you talk to Gia about the rooms over the garage?"

"Yes, of course." I don't feel the same irritation I did before at the mention of her name. My subconscious nods sagely at me. *Yes . . . we done good today.* My inner goddess gloats. Now she'll leave my husband alone and not make him uncomfortable.

I am ready to cut Christian's hair. "You sure about this? Your last chance to bail."

"Do your worst, Mrs. Grey. I don't have to look at me, you do."

I grin. "Christian, I could look at you all day."

He shakes his head, exasperated. "It's just a pretty face, baby."

"And behind it is a very pretty man." I kiss his temple. "My man."

He grins shyly.

Lifting the first lock, I comb it upward and snare it between my index and middle finger. I put the comb in my mouth, take the scissors, and make the first snip, cutting an inch off the length. Christian closes his eyes and sits like a statue, sighing contentedly as I continue. Occasionally he opens his eyes, and I catch him watching me intently. He doesn't touch me while I work, and I'm grateful. His touch is . . . distracting.

Fifteen minutes later, I'm done.

"Finished." I'm pleased with the result. He looks as hot as ever, his hair still floppy and sexy . . . just a bit shorter.

Christian gazes at himself in the mirror, looking pleasantly surprised. He grins. "Great job, Mrs. Grey." He turns his head from side to side and snakes his arm around me. Pulling me to him, he kisses and nuzzles my belly.

"Thank you," he says.

"My pleasure." I bend and kiss him briefly.

"It's late. Bed." He gives my behind a playful slap.

"Ah! I should clean up in here." There is hair all over the floor.

Christian frowns, as if the thought would never have occurred to him. "Okay, I'll get the broom," he says wryly. "I don't want you embarrassing the staff with your lack of appropriate attire."

"Do you know where the broom is?" I ask innocently.

This stops Christian in his tracks. "Um . . . no."

I laugh. "I'll go."

AS I CLIMB INTO bed and wait for Christian to join me, I reflect on how differently this day could have ended. I was so mad at him earlier, and he with me. How am I going to deal with this running-a-company nonsense? I have no desire to run my own company. I am not him. I need to head this off at the pass. Perhaps I should have a safeword for when he's being overbearing and domineering, for when he's being an arse. I giggle. Perhaps the safeword should be *arse*. I find the thought very appealing.

"What?" he says as he climbs into bed beside me wearing only his pajama pants.

"Nothing. Just an idea."

"What idea?" He stretches out beside me.

Here goes nothing. "Christian, I don't think I want to run a company."

He props himself up on his elbow and gazes down at me. "Why do you say that?"

"Because it's not something that has ever appealed to me."

"You're more than capable, Anastasia."

"I like to read books, Christian. Running a company will take me away from that."

"You could be the creative head."

I frown.

"You see," he continues, "running a successful company is all about embracing the talent of the individuals you have at your disposal. If that's where your talents and your interests lie, then you structure the company to enable that. Don't dismiss it out of hand, Anastasia. You're a very capable woman. I think you could do anything you wanted if you put your mind to it."

Whoa! How can he possibly know that I'd be any good at this?

"I'm also worried it will take up too much of my time."

Christian frowns.

"Time I could devote to you." I deploy my secret weapon.

His gaze darkens. "I know what you're doing," he murmurs, amused.

Damn it!

"What?" I feign innocence.

"You're trying to distract me from the issue at hand. You always do that. Just don't dismiss the idea, Ana. Think about it. That's all I ask." He leans down and kisses me chastely, then skims his thumb down my cheek. This argument is going to run and run. I smile up at him—and something he said earlier today pops unbidden into my mind.

"Can I ask you something?" My voice is soft, tentative.

"Of course."

"Earlier today you said if I was angry with you, I should take it out on you in bed. What did you mean?"

He stills. "What did you think I meant?"

Holy shit! I should just say it. "That you wanted me to tie you up."

His eyebrows shoot up in surprise. "Um . . . no. That's not what I meant at all."

"Oh." I'm surprised by my slight twinge of disappointment.

"You want to tie me up?" he asks, obviously reading my expression correctly. He sounds shocked. I blush.

"Well . . ."

"Ana, I—" he stops, and something dark crosses his face.

"Christian," I whisper, alarmed. I move so that I am lying on my side, propped up on my elbow like him. I caress his face. His eyes are large and fearful. He shakes his head sadly.

Shit! "Christian, stop. It doesn't matter. I thought that's what you meant."

He takes my hand and places it on his pounding heart. *Fuck!* What is it?

"Ana, I don't know how I'd feel about you touching me if I were restrained."

My scalp prickles. It's like he's confessing something deep and dark.

"This is still too new." His voice is low and raw.

Fuck. It was just a question, and I realize that he's come a long way, but he still has a long way to go. *Oh, Fifty, Fifty, Fifty.* Anxiety grips my heart. I lean over and he freezes, but I plant a soft kiss at the corner of his mouth.

"Christian, I got the wrong idea. Please don't worry about it. Please don't think about it." I kiss him. He closes his eyes, groans, and reciprocates, pushing me down into the mattress, his hands clasping my chin. And soon we're lost . . . lost in each other again.

CHAPTER NINE

When I wake before the alarm the following morning, Christian is wrapped around me like ivy, his head on my chest, his arm around my waist, and his leg between mine. And he's on my side of the bed. It's always the same, if we argue the night before, this is how he ends up, coiled around me, making me hot and bothered.

Oh, Fifty. He is so needy on some level. Who would have thought? The familiar vision of Christian as a dirty, wretched little boy haunts me. Gently, I stroke his shorter hair and my melancholy recedes. He stirs, and his sleepy eyes meet mine. He blinks a couple of times as he wakes.

"Hi," he murmurs and smiles.

"Hi." I love waking to that smile.

He nuzzles my breasts and hums appreciatively deep in his throat. His hand travels down from my waist, skimming over the cool satin of my nightgown.

"What a tempting morsel you are," he mutters. "But, tempting though you are," he glances at the alarm, "I have to get up." He stretches out, untangles himself from me, and rises.

I lie back, put my hands behind my head, and enjoy the show—Christian stripping for his shower. He is perfect. I wouldn't change a hair on his head.

"Admiring the view, Mrs. Grey?" Christian arches a sardonic brow at me.

"It's a mighty fine view, Mr. Grey."

He grins and throws his pajama pants at me so they almost land on my face, but I catch them in time, giggling like a school-girl. With a wicked grin, he pulls the duvet off, puts one knee on the bed, grabs my ankles, and drags me toward him so that my nightdress rides up. I squeal, and he crawls up my body, trailing little kisses on my knee, my thigh . . . my . . . oh . . . *Christian!*

"GOOD MORNING, MRS. GREY," Mrs. Jones greets me. I flush, embarrassed, remembering her tryst with Taylor the night before.

"Good morning," I respond as she hands me a cup of tea. I sit on the barstool beside my husband, who just looks radiant: freshly showered, his hair damp, wearing a crisp white shirt and that silver-gray tie. My favorite tie. I have fond memories of that tie.

"How are you, Mrs. Grey?" he asks, his eyes warm.

"I think you know, Mr. Grey." I gaze up at him through my lashes.

He smirks. "Eat," he orders. "You didn't eat yesterday."

Oh, bossy Fifty!

"That's because you were being an arse."

Mrs. Jones drops something that clatters into the sink, making me jump. Christian seems oblivious to the noise. Ignoring her, he stares at me impassively.

"Arse or not—eat." His tone is serious. No arguing with him.

"Okay! Picking up spoon, eating granola," I mutter like a petulant teenager. I reach for the Greek yogurt and spoon some onto my cereal, followed by a handful of blueberries. I glance at Mrs. Jones and she catches my eye. I smile, and she responds with a warm smile of her own. She has provided me with my breakfast of choice, which was introduced to me on our honeymoon.

"I may have to go to New York later in the week." Christian's announcement interrupts my reverie.

"Oh."

"It'll mean an overnight. I want you to come with me."

"Christian, I won't get the time off."

He gives me his oh-really-but-I'm-the-boss stare.

I sigh. "I know you own the company, but I've been away for three weeks. Please. How can you expect me to run the business if I'm never there? I'll be fine here. I'm assuming you'll take Taylor with you, but Sawyer and Ryan will be here—" I stop, because Christian is grinning at me. "What?" I snap.

"Nothing. Just you," he says.

I frown. Is he laughing at me? Then a nasty thought pops into my mind. "How are you getting to New York?"

"The company jet, why?"

"I just wanted to check if you were taking *Charlie Tango*." My voice is quiet, and a shiver runs down my spine. I remember the last time he flew his helicopter. A wave of nausea hits me as I recall the anxious hours I spent waiting for news. That was possibly the lowest point in my life. I notice Mrs. Jones has stilled, too. I try to dismiss the idea.

"I wouldn't fly to New York in *Charlie Tango*. She doesn't have that kind of range. Besides, she won't be back from the engineers for another two weeks."

Thank heavens. My smile is partly from relief, but also the knowledge that the demise of *Charlie Tango* has occupied a great deal of Christian's thoughts and time over the last few weeks.

"Well, I'm glad she's nearly fixed, but—" I stop. Can I tell him how nervous I'll be when he flies next time?

"What?" he asks as he finishes his omelet.

I shrug.

"Ana?" he says, more sternly.

"I just . . . you know. Last time you flew in her . . . I thought, we thought, you'd—" I can't finish the sentence, and Christian's expression softens.

"Hey." He caresses my face with the backs of his knuckles. "That was sabotage." A dark expression crosses his face, and for a moment I wonder if he knows who was responsible.

"I couldn't bear to lose you," I murmur.

"Five people have been fired because of that, Ana. It won't happen again."

"Five?"

He nods, his face serious.

Holy crap!

"That reminds me. There's a gun in your desk."

He frowns at my non sequitur and probably at my accusatory tone, though I don't mean it that way. "It's Leila's," he says finally.

"It's fully loaded."

"How do you know?" His frown deepens.

"I checked it yesterday."

He scowls at me. "I don't want you messing with guns. I hope you put the safety back on."

I blink at him, momentarily stupefied. "Christian, there's no safety on that revolver. Don't you know anything about guns?"

His eyes widen. "Um . . . no."

Taylor coughs discreetly from the entrance. Christian nods at him.

"We have to go," Christian says. He stands, distracted, and slips on his gray jacket. I follow him into the hallway.

He has Leila's gun. I am stunned by this news and briefly wonder what's happened to her. Is she still in—where is it? East somewhere. New Hampshire? I can't remember.

"Good morning, Taylor," Christian says.

"Good morning, Mr. Grey, Mrs. Grey." He nods at us both, but he's careful not to look me in the eye. I'm grateful, recalling my state of undress when we bumped into each other last night.

"I am just going to brush my teeth," I mutter. Christian always brushes his teeth before breakfast. I don't understand why.

"YOU SHOULD ASK TAYLOR to teach you how to shoot," I say as we travel down in the elevator. Christian gazes down at me, amused.

"Should I now?" he says dryly.

"Yes."

"Anastasia, I despise guns. My mom has patched up too many victims of gun crime, and my dad is vehemently antigun. I grew up with their ethos. I support at least two gun control initiatives here in Washington."

"Oh. Does Taylor carry a gun?"

Christian's mouth thins.

"Sometimes."

"You don't approve?" I ask, as Christian ushers me out of the elevator on the ground floor.

"No," he says, tight-lipped. "Let's just say that Taylor and I hold very different views with regard to gun control." I'm with Taylor on this.

Christian holds the foyer door open for me and I head out to the car. He has not let me drive alone to SIP since he found out that *Charlie Tango* was sabotaged. Sawyer smiles pleasantly, holding the door open for me as Christian and I climb into the car.

"Please." I reach across and grasp Christian's hand.

"Please what?"

"Learn how to shoot."

He rolls his eyes at me. "No. End of discussion, Anastasia."

And again I am a child to be scolded. I open my mouth to say something cutting, but decide I don't want to start my workday in a bad mood. I fold my arms instead and glimpse Taylor regarding me in the rearview mirror. He looks away, concentrating on the road in front, but shakes his head a little, in obvious frustration.

Hmm . . . Christian drives him crazy, too, sometimes. The thought makes me smile, and my mood is saved.

"Where is Leila?" I ask as Christian gazes out of his window.

"I told you. She's in Connecticut with her folks." He glances at me.

"Did you check? After all, she does have long hair. It could have been her driving the Dodge."

"Yes, I checked. She's enrolled in an art school in Hamden. She started this week."

"You've spoken to her?" I whisper, all the blood draining from my face.

Christian whips his head around at the tone of my voice.

"No. Flynn has." He searches my face for a clue to my thoughts.

"I see," I murmur, relieved.

"What?"

"Nothing."

Christian sighs. "Ana. What is it?"

I shrug, not wanting to admit to my irrational jealousy.

Christian continues, "I'm keeping tabs on her, checking that she stays on her side of the continent. She's better, Ana. Flynn has referred her to a shrink in New Haven, and all the reports are very positive. She's always been interested in art, so . . ." He stops, his face still searching mine. And in that moment I suspect that he is paying for her art classes. Do I want to know? Should I ask him? I mean, it's not as if he can't afford it, but why does he feel the obligation? I sigh. Christian's baggage hardly compares to Bradley Kent from biology class and his half-assed attempts to kiss me. Christian reaches for my hand.

"Don't sweat this, Anastasia," he murmurs, and I return his reassuring squeeze. I know he's doing what he thinks is right.

MIDMORNING I HAVE A break in meetings. As I pick up the phone to call Kate, I notice an e-mail from Christian.

From: Christian Grey
Subject: Flattery
Date: August 23 2011 09:54
To: Anastasia Grey

Mrs. Grey

I have received three compliments on my new haircut. Compliments from my staff are new. It must be the ridiculous smile I'm wearing whenever I think about last night. You are indeed a wonderful, talented, beautiful woman.

And all mine.

Christian Grey
CEO, Grey Enterprises Holdings, Inc.

I melt reading it.

From: Anastasia Grey
Subject: Trying to Concentrate Here
Date: August 23 2011 10:48
To: Christian Grey

Mr. Grey

I am trying to work and don't want to be distracted by delicious memories.

Is now the time to confess that I used to cut Ray's hair regularly? I had no idea it would be such useful training.

And yes, I am yours and you, my dear, overbearing husband who refuses to exercise his constitutional right under the Second Amendment to bear arms, are mine. But don't worry because I shall protect you. Always.

Anastasia Grey
Editor, SIP

From: Christian Grey
Subject: Annie Oakley
Date: August 23 2011 10:53
To: Anastasia Grey

Mrs. Grey

I am delighted to see you have spoken to the IT dept and changed your name. :D

I shall sleep safe in my bed knowing that my gun-toting wife sleeps beside me.

Christian Grey
CEO & Hoplophobe, Grey Enterprises Holdings, Inc.

Hoplophobe? What the hell is that?

From: Anastasia Grey
Subject: Long Words
Date: August 23 2011 10:58
To: Christian Grey

Mr. Grey

Once more you dazzle me with your linguistic prowess.

In fact, your prowess in general, and I think you know what I'm referring to.

Anastasia Grey
Editor, SIP

From: Christian Grey
Subject: Gasp!
Date: August 23 2011 11:01
To: Anastasia Grey

Mrs. Grey

Are you flirting with me?

Christian Grey
Shocked CEO, Grey Enterprises Holdings, Inc.

From: Anastasia Grey
Subject: Would you rather . . .
Date: August 23 2011 11:04
To: Christian Grey

I flirted with someone else?

Anastasia Grey
Brave Editor, SIP

From: Christian Grey
Subject: Grrrrr
Date: August 23 2011 11:09
To: Anastasia Grey

NO!

Christian Grey
Possessive CEO, Grey Enterprises Holdings, Inc.

From: Anastasia Grey
Subject: Wow . . .
Date: August 23 2011 11:14
To: Christian Grey

Are you growling at me? 'Cause that's kinda hot.

Anastasia Grey
Squirming (in a good way) Editor, SIP

From: Christian Grey
Subject: Beware

Date: August 23 2011 11:16
To: Anastasia Grey

Flirting and toying with me, Mrs. Grey?

I may pay you a visit this afternoon.

Christian Grey
Priapic CEO, Grey Enterprises Holdings, Inc.

From: Anastasia Grey
Subject: Oh No!
Date: August 23 2011 11:20
To: Christian Grey

I'll behave. I wouldn't want my boss's boss's boss getting on top of me at work. ;)

Now let me get on with my job. My boss's boss's boss may fire my ass.

Anastasia Grey
Editor, SIP

From: Christian Grey
Subject: &*%$&*&*
Date: August 23 2011 11:23
To: Anastasia Grey

Believe me when I say there are a great many things he'd like to do to your ass right now. Firing you is not one of them.

Christian Grey
CEO & Ass man, Grey Enterprises Holdings, Inc.

His response makes me giggle.

From: Anastasia Grey
Subject: Go Away!
Date: August 23 2011 11:26
To: Christian Grey

Don't you have an empire to run?

Stop bothering me.

My next appointment is here.

I thought you were a breast man . . .

Think about my ass, and I'll think about yours . . .

ILY x

Anastasia Grey
Now Moist Editor, SIP

I cannot help my despondent mood as Sawyer drives me to the office on Thursday. Christian's threatened business trip to New York has happened, and though he's been gone only a few hours, I miss him already. I fire up my computer, and there's an e-mail waiting for me. My mood lifts immediately.

From: Christian Grey
Subject: Miss You Already

Date: August 25 2011 04:32
To: Anastasia Grey

Mrs. Grey

You were adorable this morning.

Behave while I'm away.

I love you.

Christian Grey
CEO, Grey Enterprises Holdings, Inc.

This will be the first night we've slept apart since our wedding. I intend to have a few cocktails with Kate—that should help me sleep. Impulsively, I e-mail him back, although I know that he's still flying.

From: Anastasia Grey
Subject: Behave Yourself!
Date: August 25 2011 09:03
To: Christian Grey

Let me know when you land—I'll worry until you do.

And I shall behave. I mean how much trouble can I get into with Kate?

Anastasia Grey
Editor, SIP

I hit "send" and sip my latte, courtesy of Hannah. Who knew I'd grow to love coffee? Despite the fact that I'm going out this evening with Kate, I feel like a chunk of me is missing. At the moment, it's thirty-five thousand feet somewhere above the Midwest en route to New York. I didn't know I would feel this unsettled and anxious just because Christian's away. Surely over time I won't feel this loss and uncertainty, will I? I let out a heavy sigh and continue with my work.

Around lunchtime, I start manically checking my e-mail and my BlackBerry for a text. Where is he? Has he landed safely? Hannah asks if I want lunch, but I'm too apprehensive and wave her away. I know it's irrational, but I need to be sure he's arrived safely.

My office phone rings, startling me. "Ana St—Grey."

"Hi." Christian's voice is warm with a trace of amusement. Relief floods through me.

"Hi." I'm grinning from ear to ear. "How was your flight?"

"Long. What are you doing with Kate?"

Oh no. "We're just going out for a quiet drink."

Christian says nothing.

"Sawyer and the new woman—Prescott—are coming to watch over us," I offer, trying to placate him.

"I thought Kate was coming to the apartment."

"She is after a quick drink." *Please let me go out!*

Christian sighs heavily. "Why didn't you tell me?" he says quietly. Too quietly.

I mentally kick myself. "Christian, we'll be fine. I have Ryan, Sawyer, and Prescott here. It's only a quick drink."

Christian remains resolutely silent, and I know he's not happy. "I've seen her only a few times since you and I met. Please. She's my best friend."

"Ana, I don't want to keep you from your friends. But I thought she was coming back to the apartment."

"Okay," I acquiesce. "We'll stay in."

"Only while this lunatic is out there. Please."

"I've said okay," I mutter in exasperation, rolling my eyes.

Christian snorts softly down the phone. "I always know when you're rolling your eyes at me."

I scowl at the receiver. "Look, I'm sorry. I didn't mean to worry you. I'll tell Kate."

"Good," he breathes, his relief evident. I feel guilty for worrying him.

"Where are you?"

"On the tarmac at JFK."

"Oh, so you just landed."

"Yes. You asked me to call the moment I landed."

I smile. My subconscious glares at me. *See? He does what he says he's going to do.*

"Well, Mr. Grey, I'm glad one of us is punctilious."

He laughs. "Mrs. Grey, your gift for hyperbole knows no bounds. What am I going to do with you?"

"I am sure you'll think of something imaginative. You usually do."

"Are you flirting with me?"

"Yes."

I sense his grin. "I'd better go. Ana, do as you're told, please. The security team knows what they're doing."

"Yes, Christian, I will." I sound exasperated again. *Jeez, I get the message.*

"I'll see you tomorrow evening. I'll call you later."

"To check up on me?"

"Yes."

"Oh, Christian!" I scold him.

"*Au revoir*, Mrs. Grey."

"*Au revoir*, Christian. I love you."

He inhales sharply. "And I you, Ana."

Neither of us hangs up.

"Hang up, Christian," I whisper.

"You're a bossy little thing, aren't you?"

"Your bossy little thing."

"Mine," he breathes. "Do as you're told. Hang up."

"Yes, Sir." I hang up and grin stupidly at the phone.

A few moments later, an e-mail appears in my in-box.

From: Christian Grey
Subject: Twitching Palms
Date: August 25 2011 13:42 EDT
To: Anastasia Grey

Mrs. Grey

You are as entertaining as ever on the phone.

I mean it. Do as you're told.

I need to know you're safe.

I love you.

Christian Grey
CEO, Grey Enterprises Holdings, Inc.

Honestly, he's the bossy one. But one phone call and all my anxiety has disappeared. He's arrived safely and he's fussing about me as usual. I hug myself momentarily. God, I love that man. Hannah knocks on my door, distracting me, and brings me back to the now.

KATE LOOKS GORGEOUS. In her tight white jeans and red camisole, she's ready to rock the town. She's chatting animatedly with Claire in Reception when I make my entrance.

"Ana!" she cries, scooping me up in a Kate hug. She holds me at arm's length.

"Don't you look the mogul's wife? Who would have thought, little Ana Steele? You look so . . . sophisticated!" She grins. I roll my eyes at her. I'm wearing a pale cream shift dress with a navy belt and navy pumps.

"It's good to see you, Kate." I hug her back.

"So, where are we going?"

"Christian wants us to go back to the apartment."

"Aw, really? Can't we sneak a quick cocktail at the Zig Zag Café? I've booked us a table."

I open my mouth to protest.

"Please?" she whines and pouts prettily. She must be picking this up from Mia. She never pouts normally. I'd really like a cocktail at the Zig Zag. We had such fun the last time we went there, and it's close to Kate's apartment.

I hold up my index finger. "One."

She grins. "One." She links her arm in mine, and we stroll out to the car, which is parked at the curb with Sawyer at the wheel. We're followed by Miss Belinda Prescott, who's new to the security team—a tall African American with a no-nonsense attitude. I've yet to warm to her, maybe because she's too cool and professional. The jury's definitely out, but like the rest of the team, she's been hand-picked by Taylor. She's dressed like Sawyer, in a dark somber pantsuit.

"Can you take us to the Zig Zag, please, Sawyer?"

Sawyer turns to look at me, and I know he wants to say something. He's obviously been given his orders. He hesitates.

"The Zig Zag Café. We'll have only one drink."

I give Kate a sideways glance, and she's glaring at Sawyer. Poor man.

"Yes, ma'am."

"Mr. Grey requested you go back to the apartment," Prescott pipes up.

"Mr. Grey isn't here," I snap. "The Zig Zag, please."

"Ma'am," Sawyer replies with a sideways glance at Prescott, who wisely holds her tongue.

Kate gapes at me as if she can't believe her eyes and ears. I purse my lips and shrug. Okay, so I'm a little more assertive than I used to be. Kate nods as Sawyer pulls out into the early evening traffic.

"You know the additional security is driving Grace and Mia crazy," Kate says casually.

I gawk at her, baffled.

"You didn't know?" She seems incredulous.

"Know what?"

"Security for all of the Greys has been tripled. Gazillioned, even."

"Really?"

"He hasn't told you?"

I flush. "No." *Damn it, Christian!* "Do you know why?"

"Jack Hyde."

"What about Jack? I thought he was just after Christian." I gasp. *Jeez. Why hasn't he told me?*

"Since Monday," Kate says.

Last Monday? *Hmm . . . we identified Jack on Sunday. But why all the Greys?*

"How do you know all this?"

"Elliot."

Of course.

"Christian hasn't told you any of this, has he?"

I flush once more. "No."

"Oh, Ana, how annoying."

I sigh. As ever, Kate has hit the nail squarely on the head in her usual sledgehammer style. "Do you know why?" If Christian's not going to tell me, then maybe Kate will.

"Elliot said it's something to do with information stored on Jack Hyde's computer when he was at SIP."

Holy crap. "You're kidding." A surge of anger pulses through me. How does Kate know about this when I don't?

I glance up to see Sawyer eyeing me in the rearview mirror. The red light turns to green and he surges forward, focusing on the road ahead. I hold my finger up to my lips and Kate nods. I bet Sawyer knows, too, and I don't.

"How's Elliot?" I ask to change the subject.

Kate grins stupidly, telling me all I need to know.

Sawyer pulls up at the end of the passageway that leads down to the Zig Zag Café, and Prescott opens my door. I scoot out and Kate slides out after me. We link arms and meander down the passage, followed by Prescott, who's wearing a thunderous expression

on her face. Oh, for heaven's sake, it's just a drink. Sawyer drives
off to park the car.

"SO HOW DOES ELLIOT know Gia?" I ask, taking a sip of my second strawberry mojito. The bar is intimate and cozy, and I don't
want to leave. Kate and I have not stopped talking. I had forgotten
how much I like hanging with her. It's liberating to be out, relaxing, enjoying Kate's company. I contemplate texting Christian,
then dismiss the idea. He'll just be mad and make me go home
like an errant child.

"Don't talk to me about that bitch!" Kate splutters.

Kate's reaction makes me laugh.

"What's so funny, Steele?" she snaps, but not seriously.

"I feel the same way."

"You do?"

"Yes. She was all over Christian."

"She had a fling with Elliot." Kate pouts.

"No!"

She nods, her lips pressed together in the patented Katherine
Kavanagh scowl.

"It was brief. Last year, I think. She's a social climber. No wonder she has her sights set on Christian."

"Christian is taken. I told her to leave him alone or I would
fire her."

Kate gapes at me once more, stunned. I nod proudly, and she
lifts her glass to salute me, impressed and beaming.

"Mrs. Anastasia Grey! Way to go!" We clink.

"DOES ELLIOT OWN A gun?"

"No. He's very antigun." Kate stirs her third drink.

"Christian, too. I think it was Grace and Carrick's influence,"
I mutter. I'm feeling a little tipsy.

"Carrick's a good man." Kate nods.

"He wanted a prenup," I mutter sadly.

"Oh, Ana." She reaches across the table and grasps my arm.
"He was only looking out for his boy. As we both know, you have

gold digger tattooed on your forehead." She smiles at me, and I poke my tongue out at her, then giggle.

"Mature, Mrs. Grey," she says, grinning. She sounds like Christian. "You'll do the same for your son one day."

"My son?" It hadn't even crossed my mind that my kids will be rich. Holy crap. They'll want for nothing. I mean . . . nothing. This needs further thought—but not right now. I glance at Prescott and Sawyer seated nearby, watching us and the evening crowd from a side table while they each nurse a glass of sparkling mineral water.

"Do you think we should eat?" I ask.

"No. We should drink," Kate says.

"Why are you in such a drinking mood?"

"Because I don't see enough of you anymore. I didn't know you'd up and marry the first guy who turned your head." She pouts again. "Honestly, you married so quickly that I thought you were pregnant."

I giggle. "Everyone thought I was pregnant. Let's not rehash that conversation again. Please! And I have to use the restroom."

Prescott accompanies me. She says nothing. She doesn't have to. Disapproval radiates off her like a lethal isotope.

"I haven't been out on my own since I got married," I mutter wordlessly at the closed stall door. I make a face, knowing that she's standing on the other side of the door, waiting while I pee. What precisely is Hyde going to do in a bar anyway? Christian is just overreacting as usual.

"KATE, IT'S LATE. WE should go."

It's ten fifteen, and I have downed my fourth strawberry mojito. I am definitely feeling the effects of the alcohol, warm and fuzzy. Christian will be fine. Eventually.

"Sure, Ana. It's been so good to see you. You just seem so much more, I don't know . . . confident. Marriage obviously agrees with you."

My face warms. Coming from Miss Katherine Kavanagh, this is indeed a compliment.

"It does," I whisper, and because I've probably had too much to drink, tears prick the backs of my eyes. Could I be any happier? In spite of all his baggage, his nature, his Fiftyness, I have met and married the man of my dreams. I quickly change the subject to stem my sentimental thoughts, because I know I will cry otherwise.

"I have really enjoyed this evening." I grasp Kate's hand. "Thank you for dragging me out!" We hug. As she releases me, I nod at Sawyer and he hands Prescott the keys to the car.

"I'm sure Miss Goody-Two-Shoes Prescott has told Christian I'm not at home. He'll be mad," I mutter to Kate. And maybe he'll think of some delicious way to punish me . . . hopefully.

"Why are you grinning like a loon, Ana? You like making Christian mad?"

"No. Not really. But it's easily done. He's very controlling sometimes." *Most of the time.*

"I've noticed," Kate says wryly.

WE PULL UP OUTSIDE Kate's apartment. She hugs me hard.

"Don't be a stranger," she whispers and kisses my cheek. Then she's out of the car. I wave, feeling strangely homesick. I have missed girl talk. It's fun and relaxing, and it reminds me that I'm still young. I must make more of an effort to see Kate, but the truth is, I love being in my bubble with Christian. Last night we attended a charity dinner together. There were so many men in suits and well-groomed elegant women talking about real estate prices and the failing economy and the plunging stock markets. I mean, it was dull, really dull. So it's refreshing to let my hair down with someone my own age.

My stomach rumbles. I still haven't eaten. *Shit—Christian!* I scramble through my purse and fish out my BlackBerry. *Holy crap—five missed calls!* One text . . .

WHERE THE HELL ARE YOU?

And one e-mail.

From: Christian Grey
Subject: Angry. You've Not Seen Angry
Date: August 26 2011 00:42 EST
To: Anastasia Grey

Anastasia

Sawyer tells me that you are drinking cocktails in a bar
when you said you wouldn't.

Do you have any idea how mad I am at the moment?

I'll see you tomorrow.

Christian Grey
CEO, Grey Enterprises Holdings, Inc.

My heart sinks. Oh shit! I really am in trouble. My subconscious glares at me, then shrugs, wearing her you-made-your-bed-
you-lie-in-it face. What did I expect? I contemplate calling him,
but it's late and he's probably asleep . . . or pacing. I decide a quick
text may be enough.

*I'M STILL IN ONE PIECE. I HAD A NICE TIME.
MISSING YOU—PLEASE DON'T BE MAD*

I gaze at my BlackBerry, willing him to respond, but it's ominously silent. I sigh.

Prescott pulls up outside Escala and Sawyer gets out to hold
the door open for me. As we stand waiting for the elevator, I take
the opportunity to quiz him.

"What time did Christian call you?"

Sawyer flushes. "About nine thirty, ma'am."

"Why didn't you interrupt my conversation with Kate so I could speak with him?"

"Mr. Grey told me not to."

I purse my lips. The elevator arrives, and we ride up in silence. I'm suddenly grateful that Christian has a whole night to recover from his conniption, and that he's on the other side of the country. It gives me some time. On the other hand . . . I miss him.

The doors to the elevator open, and for a split second I stare at the foyer table.

What is wrong with this picture?

The vase of flowers lies smashed into fragments all over the floor of the foyer, water and flowers and chunks of china are strewn everywhere, and the table is overturned. My scalp prickles and Sawyer grabs my arm and pulls me back into the elevator.

"Stay there," he hisses, drawing a gun. He steps into the foyer and disappears from my field of vision.

I cower in the back of the elevator.

"Luke!" I hear Ryan call from inside the great room. "Code blue!"

Code blue?

"You have the perp?" Sawyer calls back. "Jesus H. Christ!"

I flatten myself against the elevator wall. *What the hell is going on?* Adrenaline spikes through my body, and my heart leaps into my throat. I hear soft voices, and a moment later Sawyer reappears in the foyer, standing in the puddle of water. He holsters his gun.

"You can come in, Mrs. Grey," he says gently.

"What's happened, Luke?" My voice is barely a whisper.

"We've had a visitor." He takes my elbow, and I'm grateful for the support—my legs have turned to jelly. I walk with him through the open double doors.

Ryan is standing at the entrance of the great room. A cut above his eye is bleeding, and there's another on his mouth. He looks roughed up, his clothes disheveled. But what's more shocking is Jack Hyde slumped at his feet.

CHAPTER TEN

My heart is pounding and blood thrums loudly in my eardrums; the alcohol flowing through my system amplifies the sound.

"Is he—" I gasp, unable to finish the sentence and gazing wide-eyed and terrified at Ryan. I can't even look at the prone figure on the floor.

"No, ma'am. Just knocked out cold."

Relief floods through me. *Oh, thank God.*

"And you?" I ask, gazing at Ryan. I realize I don't know his first name. He's panting as if he's run a marathon. He wipes the corner of his mouth, removing the trace of blood, and a faint bruise is forming on his cheek.

"He put up one hell of a fight, but I'm okay, Mrs. Grey." He smiles reassuringly. If I knew him better, I'd say he looked a little smug.

"And Gail? Mrs. Jones?" *Oh no . . . is she okay? Has she been harmed?*

"I'm here, Ana." Glancing behind me, I see she's in a night-dress and robe, her hair loose, her face ashen and her eyes wide— like mine, I imagine.

"Ryan woke me. Insisted I come in here." She points behind her into Taylor's office. "I'm fine. Are you okay?"

I nod briskly and realize she's probably just come out of the panic room that adjoins Taylor's office. Who knew we'd need it so soon? Christian had insisted on its installation shortly after our engagement—and I had rolled my eyes. Now, seeing Gail standing in the doorway, I'm grateful for his foresight.

A creak from the door to the foyer distracts me. It's hanging off its hinges. What the hell happened to that?

"Was he alone?" I ask Ryan.

"Yes, ma'am. You wouldn't be standing here if he wasn't, I can assure you." Ryan sounds vaguely affronted.

"How did he get in?" I ask, ignoring his tone.

"Through the service elevator. He's got quite a pair, ma'am."

I stare down at Jack's slumped figure. He's wearing a uniform of sorts—coveralls, I think.

"When?"

"About ten minutes ago. I caught him on the security monitor. He was wearing gloves . . . kinda strange in August. I recognized him and decided to give him access. That way I knew we'd have him. You weren't here and Gail was safe, so I figured it was now or never." Ryan looks very pleased with himself once more, and Sawyer scowls at him in disapproval.

Gloves? The thought distracts me, and I glance once more at Jack. Yes, he's wearing brown leather gloves. Creepy.

"What now?" I try to dismiss the ramifications from my mind.

"We need to secure him," Ryan replies.

"Secure him?"

"In case he wakes." Ryan glances at Sawyer.

"What do you need?" asks Mrs. Jones, stepping forward. She's recovered her composure.

"Something to restrain him—cord or rope," Ryan replies.

Cable ties. I flush as memories of the night before invade my mind. Reflexively, I rub my wrists and glance quickly down at them. No, no bruising. Good.

"I have something. Cable ties. Will they do?"

All eyes turn to me.

"Yes, ma'am. Perfect," Sawyer says, serious and straight-faced. I want the floor to swallow me up, but I turn and head for our bedroom. Sometimes you just have to brazen things out. Perhaps it's the combination of fear and alcohol making me audacious.

When I return, Mrs. Jones is surveying the mess in the foyer and Miss Prescott has joined the security team. I hand the ties to Sawyer, who slowly, and with unnecessary care, ties Hyde's hands behind his back. Mrs. Jones disappears into the kitchen and returns with a first aid kit. She takes Ryan's arm, leads him into the doorway of the great room, and starts tending to the cut above his eye. He flinches as she dabs it with an antiseptic wipe. Then I notice the Glock on the floor with a silencer attached. *Holy shit! Jack was armed?* Bile rises in my throat and I fight it down.

"Don't touch, Mrs. Grey," says Prescott when I bend to pick it up. Sawyer emerges from Taylor's office wearing latex gloves.

"I'll take care of that, Mrs. Grey," he says.

"It's his?" I ask.

"Yes, ma'am," says Ryan, wincing once more from Mrs. Jones's ministrations. Holy crap. Ryan fought an armed man in my home. I shudder at the thought. Sawyer bends and gingerly picks up the Glock.

"Should you be doing that?" I ask.

"Mr. Grey would expect it, ma'am." Sawyer slides the gun into a Ziploc bag then squats to pat down Jack. He pauses and partially pulls a roll of duct tape from the man's pocket. Sawyer blanches and pushes the tape back into Hyde's pocket.

Duct tape? My mind idly registers as I watch the proceedings with fascination and an odd detachment. Then bile rises to my throat again as I realize the implications. Rapidly, I dismiss them from my head. *Don't go there, Ana!*

"Should we call the police?" I mutter, trying to hide my fear. I want Hyde out of my home, sooner rather than later.

Ryan and Sawyer glance at each other.

"I think we should call the police," I say, rather more forcefully, wondering what's going on between Ryan and Sawyer.

"I've just tried Taylor, and he's not answering his cell. Maybe he's asleep." Sawyer checks his watch. "It's one forty-five in the morning on the East Coast."

Oh no.

"Have you called Christian?" I whisper.

"No, ma'am."

"Were you calling Taylor for instructions?"

Sawyer looks momentarily embarrassed. "Yes, ma'am."

Part of me bristles. This man—I glance down at Hyde again—has invaded my home, and he needs to be removed by the police. But looking at the four of them, into their anxious eyes, I decide I must be missing something, so I decide to call Christian. My scalp prickles. I know he's mad at me—really, really mad at me—and I falter at the thought of what he'll say. And how he'll stress because he's not here and can't be here until tomorrow evening. I know I've worried him enough this evening. Perhaps I shouldn't call him. And then it occurs to me. Shit. *What if I'd been here?* I pale at the thought. Thank heavens I was out. Maybe I won't be in so much trouble after all.

"Is he okay?" I ask, pointing at Jack.

"He'll have an aching skull when he wakes," Ryan says, gazing down at Jack with contempt. "But we need paramedics here to make sure."

I reach into my purse and pull out my BlackBerry, and before I can give too much thought to the extent of Christian's anger, I dial his number. It goes straight to voice mail. He must have switched it off because he's so mad. I cannot think what to say. Turning away, I walk down the hallway a little, away from everyone.

"Hi. It's me. Please don't be mad. We've had an incident at the apartment. But it's under control, so don't worry. No one is hurt. Call me." I hang up.

"Call the police," I tell Sawyer. He nods, takes out his cell, and makes the call.

OFFICER SKINNER IS DEEP in conversation with Ryan at the dining room table. Officer Walker is with Sawyer in Taylor's office. I don't know where Prescott is, perhaps in Taylor's office. Detective Clark is barking questions at me as we sit on the couch in the great room. He's tall, dark, and would be good-looking if it weren't for his permanent scowl. I suspect he's been woken and dragged from his warm bed because the home of one of Seattle's most influential and wealthy businessmen has been breached.

"He used to be your boss?" Clark asks tersely.

"Yes."

I am tired—beyond tired—and I want to go to bed. I still haven't heard from Christian. On the plus side, the paramedics have removed Hyde. Mrs. Jones hands Detective Clark and me each a cup of tea.

"Thanks." Clark turns to me. "And where is Mr. Grey?"

"New York. On business. He'll be back tomorrow evening—I mean this evening." It's after midnight.

"Hyde is known to us," Detective Clark murmurs. "I'll need you to come down to the station to make a statement. But that can wait. It's late and there are a couple of reporters camped out on the sidewalk. Do you mind if I look around?"

"Of course not," I offer, relieved his questioning is finished. I shudder at the thought of the photographers outside. Well, they won't be a problem until tomorrow. I remind myself to call Mom and Ray just in case they hear anything and worry.

"Mrs. Grey, may I suggest you go to bed?" Mrs. Jones says, her voice warm and full of concern.

Looking into her warm, kind eyes, I suddenly feel an over-whelming need to cry. She reaches over and rubs my shoulder.

"We're safe now," she murmurs. "This will all look better in the morning, once you've had some sleep. And Mr. Grey will be back tomorrow evening."

I glance nervously up at her, keeping my tears at bay. Christian is going to be so mad.

"Can I get you anything before you go to bed?" she asks.

I realize how hungry I am. "I'd love something to eat."

She smiles broadly. "Sandwich and some milk?"

I nod with gratitude, and she heads into the kitchen. Ryan is still with Officer Skinner. In the foyer, Detective Clark is examining the mess outside the elevator. He looks thoughtful, despite his scowl. And suddenly I feel homesick—homesick for Christian. Holding my head in my hands, I wish fervently that he were here. He'd know what to do. *What an evening.* I want to crawl into his lap, have him hold me and tell me that he loves me, even though I don't do as I'm told—but that won't be possible until this evening. Inwardly I roll my eyes . . . Why didn't he tell me about the increased security for everyone? What exactly is on Jack's computer? He's so frustrating, but right now, I just don't care. I want my husband. I miss him.

"Here you are, Ana dear." Mrs. Jones interrupts my inner turmoil. When I glance up at her, she hands me a peanut butter and jelly sandwich, her eyes twinkling. I haven't had one of these for years. I smile shyly and dig in.

When I finally crawl into bed, I curl up on Christian's side, dressed in his T-shirt. Both his pillow and his T-shirt smell of him, and as I drift off I silently wish him safe passage home . . . and a good mood.

I WAKE WITH A start. It's light and my head is aching, throbbing at my temples. Oh no. I hope I don't have a hangover. Cautiously, I open my eyes and notice the bedroom chair has moved, and Christian is sitting in it. He's wearing his tux, and the end of his bow tie is peeping out of the breast pocket. I wonder if I'm dreaming. His left arm is draped over the chair, and in his hand he holds a cut-glass tumbler of amber liquid. Brandy? Whiskey? I have no idea. One long leg is crossed at the ankle over his knee. He's wearing black socks and dress shoes. His right elbow rests on the arm of the chair, his hand up to his chin, and he's slowly running his index finger rhythmically back and forth over his lower lip. In the early morning light, his eyes burn with grave intensity, but his general expression is completely unreadable.

My heart almost stops. He's here. How did he get here? He must have left New York last night. How long has he been here watching me sleep?

"Hi," I whisper.

He regards me coolly, and my heart stutters once more. *Oh no.* He moves his long fingers away from his mouth, tosses back the remainder of his drink, and places the glass on the bedside table. I half expect him to kiss me, but he doesn't. He sits back, continuing to regard me, his expression impassive.

"Hello," he says finally, his voice hushed. And I know he's still mad. Really mad.

"You're back."

"It would appear so."

Slowly I pull myself up into a sitting position, not taking my eyes off him. My mouth is dry. "How long have you been sitting there watching me sleep?"

"Long enough."

"You're still mad." I can hardly speak the words.

He gazes at me, as if considering his response. "Mad," he says, as if testing the word, weighing up its nuances, its meaning. "No, Ana. I am way, *way* beyond mad."

Holy crap. I try to swallow, but it's hard with a dry mouth.

"Way beyond mad . . . that doesn't sound good."

He gazes at me, completely impassive, and doesn't respond. A stark silence stretches between us. I reach over to my glass of water and take a welcome sip, trying to bring my erratic heart rate under control.

"Ryan caught Jack." I try a different tack, and I place my glass beside his on the bedside table.

"I know," he says icily.

Of course, he knows. "Are you going to be monosyllabic for long?"

His eyebrows move fractionally, registering his surprise as if he hadn't expected this question. "Yes," he says finally.

Oh . . . okay. What to do? Defense—the best form of attack. "I'm sorry I stayed out."

"Are you?"

"No," I mutter after a pause, because it's true.

"Why say it then?"

"Because I don't want you to be mad at me."

He sighs heavily, as if he's been holding this tension for a thousand hours, and runs his hand through his hair. He looks beautiful. Mad, but beautiful. I drink him in—Christian's back—angry, but in one piece.

"I think Detective Clark wants to talk to you."

"I'm sure he does."

"Christian, please . . ."

"Please what?"

"Don't be so cold."

His eyebrows rise in surprise once more. "Anastasia, cold is not what I'm feeling at the moment. I'm burning. Burning with rage. I don't know how to deal with these"—he waves his hand, searching for the word—"feelings." His tone is bitter.

Oh shit. His honesty disarms me. All I want to do is crawl into his lap. It's all I've wanted to do since I came home last night. *To hell with this.* I move, taking him by surprise and climbing awkwardly into his lap, where I curl up. He doesn't push me away, which is what I'd feared. After a beat, he folds his arms around me and buries his nose in my hair. He smells of whiskey. *How much did he drink?* He smells of body wash, too. He smells of Christian. I wrap my arms around his neck and nuzzle his throat, and he sighs once more, deeply this time.

"Oh, Mrs. Grey. What am I going to do with you?" He kisses the top of my head. I close my eyes, relishing the contact with him.

"How much have you had to drink?"

He stills. "Why?"

"You don't normally drink hard liquor."

"This is my second glass. I've had a trying night, Anastasia. Give a man a break."

I smile. "If you insist, Mr. Grey," I breathe into his neck. "You smell heavenly. I slept on your side of the bed because your pillow smells of you."

He nuzzles my hair. "Did you now? I wondered why you were on this side. I'm still mad at you."

"I know."

His hand rhythmically strokes my back.

"And I'm mad at you," I whisper.

He pauses. "And what, pray, have I done to deserve your ire?"

"I'll tell you later when you're no longer burning with rage." I kiss his throat. He closes his eyes and leans into my kiss but makes no move to kiss me back. His arms tighten around me, squeezing me.

"When I think of what might have happened . . ." His voice is barely a whisper. Broken, raw.

"I'm okay."

"Oh, Ana." It's almost a sob.

"I'm okay. We're all okay. A bit shaken. But Gail is fine. Ryan is fine. And Jack is gone."

He shakes his head. "No thanks to you," he mutters.

What? I lean back and glare at him. "What do you mean?"

"I don't want to argue about it right now, Ana."

I blink. Well, maybe *I* do, but I decide against it. At least he's talking to me. I nestle into him once more. His fingers move to my hair and start playing with it.

"I want to punish you," he whispers. "Really beat the shit out of you," he adds.

My heart leaps into my mouth. *Fuck.* "I know," I whisper as my scalp prickles.

"Maybe I will."

"I hope not."

He hugs me tighter. "Ana, Ana, Ana. You'd try the patience of a saint."

"I could accuse you of many things, Mr. Grey, but being a saint isn't one of them."

Finally I am blessed with his reluctant chuckle. "Fair point well made as ever, Mrs. Grey." He kisses my forehead and shifts.

"Back to bed. You had a late night, too." He moves quickly, picking me up and depositing me back on the bed.

"Lie down with me?"

"No. I have things to do." He reaches down and collects the glass. "Go back to sleep. I'll wake you in a couple of hours."

"Are you still mad at me?"

"Yes."

"I'll go back to sleep, then."

"Good." He pulls the duvet over me and kisses my forehead once more. "Sleep."

And because I'm so groggy from the night before, relieved that he's back, and emotionally fatigued by our early morning encounter, I do exactly as I'm told. As I drift off, I'm curious though grateful, given the nasty taste in my mouth, to know why he hasn't deployed his usual coping mechanism and leaped on me to have his wicked way.

"THERE'S SOME ORANGE JUICE for you here," Christian says, and my eyes flutter open again. I have had the most restful two hours of sleep I can remember, and I wake refreshed, my head no longer throbbing. The orange juice is a welcome sight—as is my husband. He's in his sweats. And I'm momentarily zapped back to the Heathman Hotel and the first time I ever woke up with him. His gray tank top is damp with his sweat. Either he's been working out in the basement gym or he's been for a run, but he shouldn't look this good after a workout.

"I'm going to take a shower," he murmurs and disappears into the bathroom. I frown. He's still distant. He's either distracted by all that's happened, or still mad, or . . . what? I sit up and reach for the orange juice, drinking it down too quickly. It's delicious, ice cold, and it makes my mouth a much better place. I clamber out of bed, anxious to close the distance—real and metaphysical—between my husband and me. I glance quickly at the alarm. It's eight o'clock. I strip off Christian's T-shirt and follow him into the bathroom. He's in the shower, washing his hair, and I don't hesitate. I slip in behind him, and he stiffens the moment I wrap my arms around him—my front to his wet, muscular back. I ignore his reaction, holding him tightly, and press my cheek flat against him, closing my eyes. After a moment, he shifts so we are both under the cascade of hot water and carries on washing his hair. I let the water wash over me as I cradle the man I love. I think of all the times he's fucked me and all the times he's made love to me in here. I frown. He's never been this quiet. Turning my head, I start to trail kisses across his back. His body stiffens again.

"Ana," he warns.

"Hmm."

My hands travel slowly down over his taut stomach to his belly. He places both his hands on mine and brings them to an abrupt halt. He shakes his head.

"Don't," he warns.

I release him, immediately. *He's saying no?* My mind goes into free fall—has this ever happened before? My subconscious shakes her head, her lips pursed. She glares at me over her half-moon glasses, wearing her you've-really-fucked-up-this-time look. I feel like I've been slapped, hard. Rejected. And a lifetime of insecurity spawns the ugly thought that *he doesn't want me anymore.* I gasp as the pain sears through me. Christian turns, and I'm relieved to see he's not completely oblivious to my charms. Grasping my chin, he tilts my head back, and I find myself gazing into his wary, gray eyes.

"I'm still fucking mad at you," he says, his voice quiet and serious. *Shit!* Leaning down, he rests his forehead against mine, closing his eyes. I reach up and caress his face.

"Don't be mad at me, please. I think you're overreacting," I whisper.

He straightens, blanching. My hand falls free to my side.

"Overreacting?" he snarls. "Some fucking lunatic gets into my apartment to kidnap my wife, and you think I'm overreacting!" The restrained menace in his voice is frightening, and his eyes blaze as he stares at me as if *I'm* the fucking lunatic.

"No . . . um, that's not what I was referring to. I thought this was about me staying out."

He closes his eyes once more as if in pain and shakes his head.

"Christian, I wasn't here." I try to appease and reassure him.

"I know," he whispers, opening his eyes. "And all because you can't follow a simple, fucking request." His tone is bitter and it's my turn to blanch. "I don't want to discuss this now, in the shower. I am still fucking mad at you, Anastasia. You're making me question my judgment." He turns and promptly leaves the shower, grabbing a towel on the way and stalking out of the bathroom, leaving me bereft and chilled under the hot water.

Crap. Crap. Crap.

Then the significance of what he's just said dawns on me. *Kidnap?* Fuck. Jack wanted to kidnap me? I recall the duct tape and not wanting to think too deeply about why Jack had it. Does Christian have more information? Hurriedly I wash myself, then shampoo and rinse my hair. I want to know. I need to know. I am not going to let him keep me in the dark about this.

Christian's not in the bedroom when I come out. Jeez, he dresses quickly. I do the same, throwing on my favorite plum dress and black sandals, and I'm conscious that I've chosen this outfit because Christian likes it. I vigorously towel-dry my hair, then braid it and wind it into a bun. Fitting diamond studs into my ears, I dash to the bathroom to apply a little mascara and glance at myself in the mirror. *I'm pale. I'm always pale.* I take a deep steadying breath. I need to face the consequences of my rash decision to actually enjoy myself with my friend. I sigh, knowing that Christian won't see it that way.

Christian is nowhere to be seen in the great room. Mrs. Jones is busying herself in the kitchen.

"Good morning, Ana," she says sweetly.

"Morning." I smile broadly at her. I am Ana again!

"Tea?"

"Please."

"Anything to eat?"

"Please. I'd like an omelet this morning."

"With mushrooms and spinach?"

"And cheese."

"Coming up."

"Where's Christian?"

"Mr. Grey's in his study."

"Has he had breakfast?" I glance at the two places set on the breakfast bar.

"No, ma'am."

"Thanks."

Christian is on the phone, dressed in a white shirt with no tie, looking every bit the relaxed CEO. How deceptive appearances can be. Perhaps he's not going into the office after all. He glances up when I appear in the doorway but shakes his head at me, indicating that I am not welcome. *Shit* . . . I turn and wander dejectedly back to the breakfast bar. Taylor appears, snappily dressed in a somber suit, looking like he's had eight hours of uninterrupted sleep.

"Morning, Taylor," I murmur, trying to gauge his mood and see if he'll offer me any visual cues about what has been going on.

"Good morning, Mrs. Grey," he replies, and I hear the sympathy in those four words. I smile compassionately back at him, knowing he had to endure an angry, frustrated Christian returning to Seattle way ahead of schedule.

"How was the flight?" I dare to ask.

"Long, Mrs. Grey." His brevity speaks volumes. "May I ask how you are?" he adds, his tone softening.

"I'm good."

He nods. "If you'll excuse me." He heads toward Christian's study. Hmm. Taylor's allowed in, but not me.

"Here you go." Mrs. Jones places my breakfast in front of me. My appetite has vanished, but I eat anyway, not wishing to offend her.

By the time I've finished what I can of my breakfast, Christian has still not emerged from his study. Is he avoiding me?

"Thanks, Mrs. Jones," I murmur, sliding off the barstool and making my way to the bathroom to clean my teeth. As I brush them, I'm reminded of Christian's sulk over the wedding vows. He holed up in his study then, too. Is that what this is? Him sulking? I shudder as I recall his subsequent nightmare. Will that happen again? We really need to talk. I need to know about Jack and about the increased security for the Greys—all the details that have been kept from me, but not from Kate. Obviously Elliot talks to her.

I glance at my watch. It's eight fifty—I'm late for work. I finish brushing my teeth, apply a little lip gloss, grab my lightweight black jacket, and head back to the great room. I am relieved to see Christian there, eating his breakfast.

"You're going?" he says when he sees me.

"To work? Yes, of course." Bravely, I walk toward him and rest my hands on the edge of the breakfast bar. He gazes at me blankly.

"Christian, we've hardly been back a week. I have to go to work."

"But—" He stops and rakes his hand through his hair. Mrs. Jones walks quietly out of the room. *Discreet, Gail, discreet.*

"I know we have a great deal to talk about. Perhaps if you've calmed down, we can do it this evening."

His mouth pops open with dismay. "Calmed down?" His voice is eerily soft.

I flush. "You know what I mean."

"No, Anastasia, I don't know what you mean."

"I don't want to fight. I was coming to ask you if I could take my car."

"No. You can't," he snaps.

"Okay." I acquiesce immediately.

He blinks. He was obviously expecting a fight. "Prescott will accompany you." His tone is slightly less belligerent.

Damn it, not Prescott. I want to pout and protest but decide against it. Surely now that Jack has been caught we can cut back on our security.

I remember my mom's "words of wisdom" talk the day before my wedding. *Ana, honey, you really have to choose your battles. It'll be the same with your kids when you have them.* Well, at least he's letting me go to work.

"Okay," I mutter. And because I don't want to leave him like this with so much unresolved and so much tension between us, I step tentatively toward him. He stiffens, his eyes widening, and for a moment he looks so vulnerable it pulls at some deep, dark place in my heart. *Oh, Christian, I'm so sorry.* I kiss him chastely on the side of his mouth. He closes his eyes as if relishing my touch.

"Don't hate me," I whisper.

He grabs my hand. "I don't hate you."

"You haven't kissed me," I whisper.

He eyes me suspiciously. "I know," he mutters.

I'm desperate to ask him why, but I'm not sure I want to know the answer. Abruptly he stands and grabs my face between his hands, and in a flash his lips are hard on mine. I gasp with surprise, inadvertently granting his tongue access. He takes full advantage, invading my mouth, claiming me, and just as I'm beginning to respond he releases me, his breathing quickening.

"Taylor will take you and Prescott to SIP," he says, his eyes flaring with need. "Taylor!" he calls. I flush, trying to recover some composure.

"Sir." Taylor is standing in the doorway.

"Tell Prescott Mrs. Grey is going to work. Can you drive them, please?"

"Certainly." Turning on his heel, Taylor disappears.

"If you could try to stay out of trouble today, I would appreciate it," Christian mutters.

"I'll see what I can do." I smile sweetly. A reluctant half smile tugs at Christian's lips, but he doesn't give in to it.

"I'll see you later, then," he says coolly.

"Laters," I whisper.

Prescott and I take the service elevator down to the basement garage in order to avoid the media outside. Jack's arrest and the fact that he was apprehended in our apartment are now public knowledge. As I settle into the Audi, I wonder if there will be more paparazzi waiting at SIP like the day our engagement was announced.

We drive a while in silence, until I remember to call first Ray and then my mom to reassure them that Christian and I are safe. Mercifully, both calls are short, and I hang up just as we arrive outside SIP. As I feared, there's a small crowd of reporters and photographers lying in wait. They turn as one, looking expectantly at the Audi.

"Are you sure you want to do this, Mrs. Grey?" Taylor asks. Part of me just wants to go home, but that means spending the day with Mr. Burning Rage. I hope that with a little time, he will gain some perspective. Jack is in police custody, so Fifty should be happy, but he's not. Part of me understands why; too much of this is out of his control, including me, but I don't have time to think about this now.

"Take me around to the delivery entrance, please, Taylor."

"Yes, ma'am."

IT'S ONE O'CLOCK AND I've managed to immerse myself in work all morning. There's a knock and Elizabeth pops her head around the door.

"Can I have a moment?" she asks brightly.

"Sure," I mutter, surprised at her unscheduled visit.

She enters and sits down, tossing her long black hair over her shoulder. "I just wanted to check you're okay. Roach asked me to pay you a visit," she adds hurriedly as her face reddens. "I mean with all that went on last night."

Jack Hyde's arrest is all over the newspapers, but no one seems to have made the connection yet with the fire at GEH.

"I'm fine," I answer, trying not to think too deeply about how I feel. Jack wanted to harm me. Well, that's not news. He's tried before. It's Christian I'm more concerned about.

I glance quickly at my e-mail. There's still nothing from him. I don't know if I were to send him an e-mail, whether I'd just be provoking Mr. Burning Rage further.

"Good," Elizabeth answers, and her smile actually touches her eyes for a change. "If there's anything I can do—anything you need—let me know."

"Will do."

Elizabeth stands. "I know how busy you are, Ana. I'll let you get back to it."

"Um . . . thanks."

That has to have been the briefest, most pointless meeting in the Western Hemisphere today. Why did Roach send her here? Perhaps he's worried, given I'm his boss's wife. I shake off the dark thoughts and reach for my BlackBerry in the hope that there might be a message from Christian. As I do, my work e-mail pings.

From: Christian Grey
Subject: Statement
Date: August 26 2011 13:04
To: Anastasia Grey

Anastasia

Detective Clark will be visiting your office today at 3 pm to take your statement.

I have insisted that he should come to you, as I don't want you going to the police station.

Christian Grey
CEO, Grey Enterprises Holdings, Inc.

I gaze at his e-mail for a full five minutes, trying to think of a light and witty response to lift his mood. I draw a complete blank, and opt for brevity instead.

From: Anastasia Grey
Subject: Statement
Date: August 26 2011 13:12
To: Christian Grey

Okay.

A x

Anastasia Grey
Editor, SIP

I stare at the screen for another five minutes, anxious for his response, but there's nothing. Christian is not in the mood to play today.

I sit back. Can I blame him? My poor Fifty was probably frantic, back in the early hours of this morning. Then a thought occurs to me. He was in his tux when I woke this morning. What time did he decide to come back from New York? He normally leaves functions between ten and eleven. Last night at that hour, I was still at large with Kate.

Did Christian come home because I was out or because of the Jack incident? If he left because I was out having a good time, he would have had no idea about Jack, about the police, nothing—until he landed in Seattle. It's suddenly very important to me to find out. If Christian came back merely because I was out, then he was overreacting. My subconscious sucks her teeth, wearing her harpy face. Okay, I'm glad he's back, so maybe it's irrelevant. But still—Christian must have had one hell of a shock when he landed. No wonder he's so confused today. His earlier words come back to me. *"I am still fucking mad at you, Anastasia. You're making me question my judgment."*

I have to know—did he come back because of Cocktailgate or because of the fucking lunatic?

From: Anastasia Grey
Subject: Your Flight
Date: August 26 2011 13:24
To: Christian Grey

What time did you decide to come back to Seattle yesterday?

Anastasia Grey
Editor, SIP

From: Christian Grey
Subject: Your Flight
Date: August 26 2011 13:26
To: Anastasia Grey

Why?

Christian Grey
CEO, Grey Enterprises Holdings, Inc.

From: Anastasia Grey
Subject: Your Flight
Date: August 26 2011 13:29
To: Christian Grey

Call it curiosity.

Anastasia Grey
Editor, SIP

From: Christian Grey
Subject: Your Flight
Date: August 26 2011 13:32
To: Anastasia Grey

Curiosity killed the cat.

Christian Grey
CEO, Grey Enterprises Holdings, Inc.

From: Anastasia Grey
Subject: Huh?
Date: August 26 2011 13:35
To: Christian Grey

What is that oblique reference to? Another threat?

You know where I am going with this, don't you?

Did you decide to return because I went out for a drink
with my friend after you asked me not to, or did you return
because a madman was in your apartment?

Anastasia Grey
Editor, SIP

I stare at my screen. There's no response. I glance at the clock
on my computer. One forty-five and still no response.

From: Anastasia Grey
Subject: Here's the Thing . . .
Date: August 26 2011 13:56
To: Christian Grey

I will take your silence as an admission that you did indeed
return to Seattle because I CHANGED MY MIND. I am an
adult female and went for a drink with my friend. I did not
understand the security ramifications of CHANGING MY
MIND because YOU NEVER TELL ME ANYTHING. I found
out from Kate that security has, in fact, been stepped up
for all the Greys, not just us. I think you generally overreact
where my safety is concerned, and I understand why, but
you're like the boy crying wolf.

I never have a clue about what is a real concern or merely something that is perceived as a concern by you. I had two of the security detail with me. I thought both Kate and I would be safe. Fact is, we were safer in that bar than at the apartment. Had I been FULLY INFORMED of the situation, I would have taken a different course of action.

I understand your concerns are something to do with material that was on Jack's computer here—or so Kate believes. Do you know how annoying it is to find out my best friend knows more about what's going on with you than I do? And I am your WIFE. So are you going to tell me? Or will you continue to treat me like a child, guaranteeing that I continue to behave like one?

You are not the only one who is fucking pissed. Okay?

Ana

Anastasia Grey
Editor, SIP

I hit "send." *There—stick that in your pipe and smoke it, Grey.* I take a deep breath. I have worked myself up into quite a rage. Here I was feeling sorry and guilty for behaving badly. Well, no longer.

From: Christian Grey
Subject: Here's the Thing . . .
Date: August 26 2011 13:59
To: Anastasia Grey

As ever, Mrs. Grey, you are forthright and challenging in e-mail.

Perhaps we can discuss this when you get home to **OUR** apartment.

You should watch your language. I am still fucking pissed,
too.

Christian Grey
CEO, Grey Enterprises Holdings, Inc.

Watch my language! I scowl at my computer, realizing this
is getting me nowhere. I don't respond, but pick up a manu-
script recently received from a promising new author and begin
to read.

MY MEETING WITH DETECTIVE Clark is uneventful. He is less
growly than the night before, maybe because he's managed some
sleep. Or maybe he just prefers working during the day.

"Thank you for your statement, Mrs. Grey."

"You're welcome, Detective. Is Hyde in police custody yet?"

"Yes, ma'am. He was released from the hospital earlier this
morning. With what he's charged with, he should be with us for a
while." He smiles, his dark eyes crinkling in the corners.

"Good. This has been an anxious time for my husband and
me."

"I spoke at length with Mr. Grey this morning. He's very
relieved. Interesting man, your husband."

You have no idea.

"Yes, I think so." I offer him a polite smile, and he knows he's
being dismissed.

"If you think of anything, you can call me. Here's my card."
He wrestles a card out of his wallet and hands it to me.

"Thank you, Detective. I'll do that."

"Good day to you, Mrs. Grey."

"Good day."

As he leaves, I wonder exactly what Hyde has been charged
with. No doubt Christian won't tell me. I purse my lips.

WE RIDE IN SILENCE to Escala. Sawyer is driving this time, Prescott at his side, and my heart grows heavier and heavier as we head back. I know Christian and I are going to have an almighty fight, and I don't know if I have the energy.

As I ride in the elevator from the garage with Prescott beside me, I try to marshal my thoughts. What do I want to say? I think I said it all in my e-mail. Perhaps he'll give me some answers. I hope so. I can't help my nerves. My heart is pounding, my mouth is dry, and my palms are sweaty. I don't want to fight. But sometimes he's so difficult, and I need to stand my ground.

The elevator doors slide open, revealing the foyer, and it's once more neat and tidy. The table is upright and a new vase is in place with a gorgeous array of pale pink and white peonies. I quickly check the paintings as we wander through—the Madonnas all look to be intact. The broken foyer door is fixed and operational once more, and Prescott kindly opens it for me. She's been so quiet today. I think I prefer her this way.

I drop my briefcase in the hall and head into the great room. I stop. *Holy fuck.*

"Good evening, Mrs. Grey," Christian says softly. He's standing by the piano, dressed in a tight black T-shirt and jeans . . . *those* jeans—the ones he wore in the playroom. *Oh my.* They are overwashed pale blue denim, snug, ripped at the knee, and hot. He saunters over to me, his feet bare, the top button of the jeans undone, his smoldering eyes never leaving mine.

"Good to have you home. I've been waiting for you."

CHAPTER ELEVEN

H ave you now?" I whisper. My mouth goes drier still, my
heart pounding in my chest. Why's he dressed like this?
What does it mean? Is he still sulking?

"I have." His voice is kitten soft, but he's smirking as he strolls
closer to me.

He looks hot—his jeans hanging that way from his hips. Oh
no, I'm not going to be distracted by Mr. Sex-on-Legs. I try to
gauge his mood as he stalks toward me. Angry? Playful? Lustful?
Gah! It's impossible to tell.

"I like your jeans," I murmur. He grins a disarming wolfish
grin that doesn't reach his eyes. *Shit—he's still mad.* He's wearing
these to distract me. He halts in front of me, and I'm seared by
his intensity. He gazes down, wide unreadable eyes burning into
mine. I swallow.

"I understand you have issues, Mrs. Grey," he says silkily, and
he pulls something from the back pocket of his jeans. I can't tear
my gaze from his, but hear him unfold a piece of paper. He holds
it up, and glancing briefly in its direction, I recognize my e-mail.
My gaze returns to his, as his eyes blaze bright with anger.

"Yes, I have issues," I whisper, feeling breathless. I need distance if we're going to discuss this. But before I can step back,
he leans down and runs his nose along mine. My eyes flutter to a
close as I welcome his unexpected, gentle touch.

"So do I," he whispers against my skin, and I open my eyes
at his words. He straightens and gazes intently at me once more.

"I think I'm familiar with your issues, Christian." My voice
is wry, and he narrows his eyes, suppressing the amusement that
sparks there momentarily. Are we going to fight? I take a precau-

tionary step back. I must physically distance myself from him—
from his smell, his look, his distracting body in those hot jeans.
He frowns as I move away.

"Why did you fly back from New York?" I whisper. Let's get
this over and done with.

"You know why." His tone carries a warning ring.

"Because I went out with Kate?"

"Because you went back on your word, and you defied me,
putting yourself at unnecessary risk."

"Went back on my word? Is that how you see it?" I gasp, ignoring the rest of his sentence.

"Yes."

Holy crap. Talk about overreaction! I start to roll my eyes but
stop when he scowls at me. "Christian, I changed my mind," I
explain slowly, patiently, as if he's a child. "I'm a woman. We're
renowned for it. That's what we do."

He blinks at me as if he doesn't comprehend this.

"If I had thought for one minute that you would cancel your
business trip . . ." Words fail me. I realize I don't know what to say.
I am momentarily catapulted back to the argument over our vows.
I never promised to obey you, Christian. But I hold my tongue,
because deep down I'm glad he came back. In spite of his fury, I'm
glad he's here in one piece, angry and smoldering in front of me.

"You changed your mind?" He can't hide his contemptuous
disbelief.

"Yes."

"And you didn't think to call me?" He glares at me, incredulous, before continuing. "What's more, you left the security detail
short here and put Ryan at risk."

Oh. I hadn't thought about that.

"I should have called, but I didn't want to worry you. If I had,
I'm sure you would have forbidden me to go, and I've missed Kate.
I wanted to see her. Besides, it kept me out of the way when Jack
was here. Ryan shouldn't have let him in." This is so confusing. If
Ryan hadn't, Jack would still be at large.

Christian's eyes gleam wildly, then shut, his face tightening as if in pain. *Oh no.* He shakes his head, and before I know it he has folded me in his arms, pulling me hard against him.

"Oh, Ana," he whispers as he tightens his hold on me so that I can barely breathe. "If something were to happen to you—" His voice is barely a whisper.

"It didn't," I manage to say.

"But it could have. I've died a thousand deaths today thinking about what might have happened. I was so mad, Ana. Mad at you. Mad at myself. Mad at everyone. I can't remember being this angry . . . except—" He stops again.

"Except?" I prompt.

"Once in your old apartment. When Leila was there."

Oh. I don't want to think about that.

"You were so cold this morning," I murmur. My voice cracks on the last word as I remember the hideous feeling of rejection in the shower. His hands move to the nape of my neck, loosening their grip on me, and I take a deep breath. He pulls my head back.

"I don't know how to deal with this anger. I don't think I want to hurt you," he says, his eyes wide and wary. "This morning, I wanted to punish you, badly, and—" He stops, lost for words I think, or too afraid to say them.

"You were worried you'd hurt me?" I finish his sentence for him, not believing that he'd hurt me for a minute, but relieved, too. A small vicious part of me feared it was because he didn't want me anymore.

"I didn't trust myself," he says quietly.

"Christian, I know you'd never hurt me. Not physically, anyway." I clasp his head between my hands.

"Do you?" he asks, and there's skepticism in his voice.

"Yes. I knew what you said was an empty, idle threat. I know you're not going to beat the shit out of me."

"I wanted to."

"No you didn't. You just thought you did."

"I don't know if that's true," he murmurs.

"Think about it," I urge, wrapping my arms around him once more and nuzzling his chest through the black T-shirt. "About how you felt when I left. You've told me often enough what that did to you. How it altered your view of the world, of me. I know what you've given up for me. Think about how you felt about the cuff marks on our honeymoon."

He stills, and I know he's processing this information. I tighten my arms around him, my hands on his back, feeling his taut, toned muscles beneath his T-shirt. Gradually he relaxes as the tension slowly ebbs away.

Is this what's been worrying him? That he'll hurt me? Why do I have more faith in him than he has in himself? I don't understand; surely we've moved on. He's normally so strong, so in control, but without that, he's lost. *Oh, Fifty, Fifty, Fifty—I'm sorry.* He kisses my hair, I turn my face up to his, and his lips find mine, searching, taking, giving, begging—for what, I don't know. I just want to feel his mouth on mine, and I return his kiss passionately.

"You have such faith in me," he whispers after he breaks away.

"I do." He strokes my face with the backs of his knuckles and the tip of his thumb, gazing intently into my eyes. His anger has gone. My Fifty is back from wherever he's been. It's good to see him. I glance up and smile shyly.

"Besides," I whisper, "you don't have the paperwork."

His mouth drops open in amused shock, and he clutches me to his chest again.

"You're right. I don't." He laughs.

We stand in the middle of the great room, locked in our embrace, just holding each other.

"Come to bed," he whispers, after heaven knows how long.

Oh my . . .

"Christian, we need to talk."

"Later," he urges softly.

"Christian, please. Talk to me."

He sighs. "About what?"

"You know. You keep me in the dark."

"I want to protect you."

"I'm not a child."

"I am fully aware of that, Mrs. Grey." He runs his hands down my body and cups my backside. Flexing his hips, he presses his growing erection into me.

"Christian!" I scold. "Talk to me."

He sighs once more with exasperation. "What do you want to know?" His voice is resigned as he releases me. I balk—*I didn't mean you had to let me go*. Taking my hand, he reaches down to pick up my e-mail from the floor.

"Lots of things," I mutter, as I let him lead me to the couch.

"Sit," he orders. Some things never change, I muse, doing as I'm told. Christian sits beside me, and leaning forward, puts his head in his hands.

Oh no. Is this too hard for him? Then he sits up, rakes both hands through his hair, and turns to me, at once expectant and reconciled to his fate.

"Ask me," he says simply.

Oh. Well, that was easier than I thought. "Why the additional security for your family?"

"Hyde was a threat to them."

"How do you know?"

"From his computer. It held personal details about me and the rest of my family. Especially Carrick."

"Carrick? Why him?"

"I don't know yet. Let's go to bed."

"Christian, tell me!"

"Tell you what?"

"You are so . . . exasperating."

"So are you." He glares.

"You didn't ramp up the security when you first found out there was information about your family on the computer. So what happened? Why now?"

Christian narrows his eyes at me.

"I didn't know he was going to attempt to burn down my building, or—" He stops. "We thought it was an unwelcome obses-
sion, but you know"—he shrugs—"when you're in the public eye,
people are interested. It was random stuff: news reports on me
from when I was at Harvard—my rowing, my career. Reports on
Carrick—following his career, following my mom's career—and to
some extent, Elliot and Mia."

How strange.

"You said *or*," I prompt.

"Or what?"

"You said, 'attempt to burn down my building, or . . .' Like you
were going to say something else."

"Are you hungry?"

What? I frown at him, and my stomach rumbles.

"Did you eat today?" His voice is sterner and his eyes frost.

I'm betrayed by my flush.

"As I thought." His voice is clipped. "You know how I feel
about you not eating. Come," he says. He stands and holds out
his hand. "Let me feed you." And he shifts again . . . this time his
voice full of sensual promise.

"Feed me?" I whisper, as everything south of my navel lique-
fies. *Hell.* This is such a typically mercurial diversion from what
we've been discussing. *Is that it? Is that all I'm getting out of him
for now?* Leading me over to the kitchen, Christian grabs a barstool and hefts it around to the other side of the island.

"Sit," he says.

"Where's Mrs. Jones?" I ask, noticing her absence for the first
time as I perch on the stool.

"I've given her and Taylor the night off."

Oh.

"Why?"

He gazes at me for a beat, and his arrogant amusement is back.
"Because I can."

"So you're going to cook?" My voice betrays my incredulity.

"Oh, ye of little faith, Mrs. Grey. Close your eyes."

Wow. I thought we were going to have a full-on fight, and here we are, playing in the kitchen.

"Close them," he orders.

I roll them first, then oblige.

"Hmm. Not good enough," he mutters. I open one eye and see him take a plum-colored silk scarf out of the back pocket of his jeans. It matches my dress. *Holy cow.* I look quizzically at him. *When did he get that?*

"Close," he orders again. "No peeking."

"You're going to blindfold me?" I mutter, shocked. All of a sudden I'm breathless.

"Yes."

"Christian—" He places a finger upon my lips, silencing me. *I want to talk.*

"We'll talk later. I want you to eat now. You said you were hungry." He lightly kisses my lips. The silk of the scarf is soft against my eyelids as he ties it securely at the back of my head.

"Can you see?" he asks.

"No," I mutter, figuratively rolling my eyes. He chuckles softly.

"I can tell when you're rolling your eyes . . . and you know how that makes me feel."

I purse my lips. "Can we just get this over and done with?" I snap.

"Such impatience, Mrs. Grey. So eager to talk." His tone is playful.

"Yes!"

"I must feed you first," he says and brushes his lips over my temple, calming me instantly.

Okay . . . have it your way. I resign myself to my fate and listen to his movements around the kitchen. The fridge door opens, and Christian places various dishes on the countertop behind me. He pads over to the microwave, pops something in, and turns it on. My curiosity is piqued. I hear the toaster lever drop, the turn of the control, and the quiet tick of the timer. Hmm—toast?

"Yes. I am eager to talk," I murmur, distracted. An assortment of exotic, spicy aromas fills the kitchen, and I shift in my chair.

"Be still, Anastasia." He's close to me again. "I want you to behave . . . ," he whispers.

Oh my.

"And don't bite your lip." Gently he tugs my bottom lip free of my teeth, and I can't help my smile.

Next, I hear the sharp pop of a cork being drawn from a bottle and the gentle glug of wine being poured into a glass. Then a moment of silence followed by a quiet click and the soft hiss of white noise from the surround-sound speakers as they come to life. A loud twang of a guitar begins a song I don't know. Christian turns the volume down to background level. A man starts to sing, his voice deep, low, and sexy.

"A drink first, I think," Christian whispers, diverting me from the song. "Head back." I tip my head back. "Farther," he prompts.

I oblige, and his lips are on mine. Cool crisp wine flows into my mouth. I swallow reflexively. *Oh my.* Memories flood back of not so long ago—me trussed up on my bed in Vancouver before I graduated with a hot, angry Christian not appreciating my e-mail. *Hmm . . . have times changed?* Not much. Except now I recognize the wine, Christian's favorite—a Sancerre.

"Hmm," I murmur in appreciation.

"You like the wine?" he whispers, his breath warm on my cheek. I'm bathed in his proximity, his vitality, the heat radiating from his body, even though he doesn't touch me.

"Yes," I breathe.

"More?"

"I always want more, with you."

I almost hear his grin. It makes me grin, too. "Mrs. Grey, are you flirting with me?"

"Yes."

His wedding ring clinks against the glass as he takes another sip of wine. Now that is a sexy sound. This time he pulls my head right back, cradling me. He kisses me once more, and greedily I swallow the wine he gives me. He smiles as he kisses me again.

"Hungry?"

"I think we've already established that, Mr. Grey."

The troubadour on the iPod is singing about wicked games. *Hmm . . . How apt.*

The microwave pings, and Christian releases me. I sit upright. The food smells spicy: garlic, mint, oregano, rosemary, and lamb, I think. The door to the microwave opens, and the appetizing smell grows stronger.

"Shit! Christ!" Christian curses, and a dish clatters onto the countertop.

Oh Fifty! "You okay?"

"Yes!" he snaps, his voice tight. A moment later, he's standing beside me once more.

"I just burned myself. Here." He cases his index finger into my mouth. "Maybe you could suck it better."

"Oh." Clasping his hand, I draw his finger slowly from my mouth. "There, there," I soothe, and leaning forward I blow, cooling his finger, then kiss it gently twice. He stops breathing. I reinsert it into my mouth and suck gently. He inhales sharply, and the sound travels straight to my groin. He tastes as delicious as ever, and I realize that this is his game—the slow seduction of his wife. I thought he was mad, and now . . . ? This man, my husband, is so confusing. But this is how I like him. Playful. Fun. Sexy as hell. He's given me some answers, but I'm greedy. I want more, but I want to play, too. After the anxiety and tension of today, and the nightmare of last night with Jack, this is a welcome diversion.

"What are you thinking?" Christian murmurs, stopping my thoughts in their tracks as he pulls his finger out of my mouth.

"How mercurial you are."

He stills beside me. "Fifty Shades, baby," he says eventually and plants a tender kiss at the corner of my mouth.

"My Fifty Shades," I whisper. Grabbing his T-shirt, I pull him back to me.

"Oh no you don't, Mrs. Grey. No touching . . . not yet." He takes my hand, pries it off his T-shirt, and kisses each finger in turn.

"Sit up," he commands.

I pout.

"I will spank you if you pout. Now open wide."

Oh shit. I open my mouth, and he pops in a forkful of spicy hot lamb covered in a cool, minty, yogurt sauce. Mmm. I chew.

"You like?"

"Yes."

He makes an appreciative noise, and I know he's eating and enjoying, too.

"More?"

I nod. He gives me another forkful, and I chew it enthusiastically. He puts the fork down and he tears . . . bread, I think.

"Open," he orders.

This time it's pita bread and hummus. I realize Mrs. Jones—or maybe even Christian—has been shopping at the delicatessen I discovered about five weeks ago only two blocks from Escala. I chew gratefully. Christian in a playful mood increases my appetite.

"More?" he asks.

I nod. "More of everything. Please. I'm starving."

I hear his delighted grin. Slowly and patiently he feeds me, occasionally kissing a morsel of food from the corner of my mouth or wiping it off with his fingers. Intermittently, he offers me a sip of wine in his unique way.

"Open wide, then bite," he murmurs. I follow his command. Hmm—one of my favorites, stuffed vine leaves. Even cold they are delicious, though I prefer them heated up, but I don't want to risk Christian burning himself again. He feeds it to me slowly, and when I've finished I lick his fingers clean.

"More?" he asks, his voice low and husky.

I shake my head. I'm full.

"Good," he whispers against my ear, "because it's time for my

favorite course. You." He scoops me up in his arms, surprising me
so much I squeal.

"Can I take the blindfold off?"

"No."

I almost pout, then remember his threat and think better of it.

"Playroom," he murmurs.

Oh—I don't know if that's a good idea.

"You up for the challenge?" he asks. And because he's used
the word *challenge*, I can't say no.

"Bring it on," I murmur, desire and something that I don't want
to name thrumming through my body. He carries me through the
door, then up the stairs to the second floor.

"I think you've lost weight," he mutters disapprovingly. I have?
Good. I remember his comment when we arrived back from our
honeymoon, and how much it smarted. Jeez—was that just a week
ago?

Outside the playroom, he slides me down his body and sets me
on my feet, but keeps his arm wrapped around my waist. Briskly
he unlocks the door.

It always smells the same: polished wood and citrus. It's actually become a comforting smell. Releasing me, Christian turns
me around until I'm facing away from him. He undoes the scarf,
and I blink in the soft light. Gently, he pulls the hairpins from my
updo, and my braid falls free. He grasps it and tugs gently so I have
to step back against him.

"I have a plan," he whispers in my ear, sending delicious shivers down my spine.

"I thought you might," I answer. He kisses me beneath my
ear.

"Oh, Mrs. Grey, I do." His tone is soft, mesmerizing. He tugs
my braid to the side and plants a trail of soft kisses down my throat.

"First we have to get you naked." His voice hums low in his
throat and resonates through my body. I want this—whatever he
has planned. I want to connect the way we know how. He turns
me around to face him. I glance down at his jeans, the top but-

ton still undone, and I can't help myself. I brush my index finger around the waistband, avoiding his T-shirt, feeling the hairs of his happy trail tickle my knuckle. He inhales sharply, and I look up to meet his eyes. I stop at the unfastened button. His eyes darken to a deeper gray . . . *oh my.*

"You should keep these on," I whisper.

"I fully intend to, Anastasia."

And he moves, grabbing me with one hand on the back of my neck and the other around my backside. He pulls me against him, then his mouth is on mine, and he's kissing me like his life depends on it.

Whoa!

He walks me backward, our tongues entwined, until I feel the wooden cross behind me. He leans into me, the contours of his body pressing into mine.

"Let's get rid of this dress," he says, peeling my dress up my thighs, my hips, my belly . . . deliciously slowly, the material skimming over my skin, skimming over my breasts.

"Lean forward," he says.

I comply, and he pulls my dress over my head and discards it on the floor, leaving me in my sandals, panties, and bra. His eyes blaze as he grasps both my hands and raises them over my head. He blinks once and tilts his head to one side, and I know he's asking for my permission. *What is he going to do to me?* I swallow, then nod, and a trace of an admiring, almost proud, smile touches his lips. He clips my wrists into the leather cuffs on the bar above and produces the scarf once more.

"Think you've seen enough." He wraps it around my head, blindfolding me again, and I feel a frisson run through me as all my other senses heighten; the sound of his soft breathing, my own excited response, the blood pulsing in my ears, Christian's scent mixed with the citrus and polish in the room—all are brought into sharper focus because I can't see. His nose touches mine.

"I'm going to drive you wild," he whispers. His hands grasp my hips, and he moves down, removing my panties as his hands glide down my legs. *Drive me wild . . . wow.*

"Lift your feet, one at a time." I oblige and he removes first my panties, then each sandal in turn. Gently grasping my ankle, he tugs my leg gently to the right.

"Step," he says. He cuffs my right ankle to the cross, then proceeds to do the same with my left. I am helpless, spread-eagled on the cross. Standing, Christian steps toward me, and my body is bathed in his warmth once more, though he doesn't touch me. After a moment he grasps my chin, tilts my head up, and kisses me chastely.

"Some music and toys, I think. You look beautiful like this, Mrs. Grey. I may take a moment to admire the view." His voice is soft. Everything clenches deep inside.

After a moment, maybe two, I hear him pad quietly to the museum chest and open one of the drawers. The butt drawer? I have no idea. He takes something out and places it on the top, followed by something else. The speakers spring to life, and after a moment the strains of a single piano playing a soft, lilting melody fill the room. It's familiar—Bach, I think—but I don't know what piece it is. Something about the music makes me apprehensive. Perhaps because the music is too cool, too detached. I frown, trying to grasp why it unsettles me, but Christian grasps my chin, startling me, and tugs gently so that I release my bottom lip. I smile, trying to reassure myself. Why do feel uneasy? Is it the music?

Christian runs his hand from my chin, along my throat, and down my chest to my breast. Using his thumb he pulls on the cup, freeing my breast from the restraint of my bra. He makes a low, appreciative humming noise in his throat and kisses my neck. His lips follow the path of his fingers to my breast, kissing and sucking all the way. His fingers move to my left breast, releasing it from my bra. I moan as he skates his thumb across my left nipple, and his lips close around my right, tugging and teasing gently until both nipples are long and hard.

"Ah."

He doesn't stop. With exquisite care, he slowly increases the intensity on each. I pull fruitlessly against my restraints as sharp pleasure spikes from my nipples to my groin. I try to squirm but I can hardly move, and it makes the torture all the more intense.

"Christian," I plead.

"I know," he murmurs, his voice hoarse. "This is what you make me feel."

What? I groan, and he begins again, subjecting my nipples to his sweet agonizing touch over and over—taking me closer.

"Please," I mewl.

He makes a low primal sound in his throat, then stands, leaving me bereft, breathless, and squirming against my restraints. He runs his hands down my sides, one pausing on my hip while the other travels down my belly.

"Let's see how you're doing," he croons softly. Gently, he cups my sex, brushing his thumb across my clitoris and making me cry out. Slowly, he inserts one, then two fingers inside me. I groan and thrust my hips forward, eager to meet his fingers and the palm of his hand.

"Oh, Anastasia, you're so ready," he says.

He circles his fingers inside me, around and around, while his thumb strokes my clitoris, back and forth, once more. It's the only point on my body where he's touching me, and all the tension, all the anxiety of the day, is concentrated on this one part of my anatomy.

Holy shit . . . it's intense . . . and strange . . . the music . . . I begin to build . . . Christian shifts, his hand still moving against and in me, and I hear a low buzzing noise.

"What?" I gasp.

"Hush," he soothes, and his lips are on mine, effectively silencing me. I welcome the warmer, more intimate contact, kissing him voraciously. He breaks the contact and the buzzing noise gets nearer.

"This is a wand, baby. It vibrates."

He holds it against my chest, and it feels like a large ball-like object vibrating against me. I shiver as it moves across my skin, down between my breasts, across to first one, then the other nipple, and I'm awash with sensation, tingling everywhere, synapses firing as dark, dark need pools at the base of my belly.

"Ah," I groan while Christian's fingers continue to move inside me. *I'm close . . . all this stimulation . . .* Tilting my head back, I moan loudly and Christian stills his fingers. All sensation stops.

"No! Christian," I plead, trying to thrust my hips forward for some friction.

"Still, baby," he says while my impending orgasm melts away. He leans forward once more and kisses me.

"Frustrating, isn't it?" he murmurs.

Oh no! Suddenly I understand his game.

"Christian, please."

"Hush," he says and kisses me. And he starts to move again—wand, fingers, thumb—a lethal combination of sensual torture. He shifts so his body brushes against mine. He's still dressed, and the soft denim of his jeans brushes against my leg, his erection at my hip. So tantalizingly close. He brings me to the brink again, my body singing with need, and stops.

"No," I mewl loudly.

He plants soft wet kisses on my shoulder as he withdraws his fingers from me, and moves the wand down. It oscillates over my stomach, my belly, onto my sex, against my clitoris. Fuck, it's intense.

"Ah!" I cry out, pulling hard on the restraints.

My body is so sensitized I feel I am going to explode, and just as I am, Christian stops again.

"Christian!" I cry out.

"Frustrating, yes?" he murmurs against my throat. "Just like you. Promising one thing and then . . ." His voice trails off.

"Christian, please!" I beg.

He pushes the wand against me again and again, stopping just at the vital moment each time. *Ah!*

"Each time I stop, it feels more intense when I start again. Right?"

"Please," I whimper. My nerve endings are screaming for release.

The buzzing stops and Christian kisses me. He runs his nose down mine. "You are the most frustrating woman I have ever met."

No, No, No.

"Christian, I never promised to obey you. Please, please—"

He moves in front of me, grabs my behind and pushes his hips against me, making me gasp—his groin rubbing into mine, the buttons of his jeans pressing into me, barely containing his erection. With one hand he pulls off the blindfold and grasps my chin, and I blink up into his scorching eyes.

"You drive me crazy," he whispers, flexing his hips against me once, twice, three times more, causing my body to spark—ready to burn. And again he denies me. I want him so badly. I need him so badly. I close my eyes and mutter a prayer. I can't help but feel I'm being punished. I'm helpless and he's ruthless. Tears spring to my eyes. I don't know how far he's going to take this.

"Please," I whisper once more.

But he gazes down at me, implacable. He's just going to continue. For how long? Can I play this game? No. No. No—I can't do this. I know he's not going to stop. He's going to continue to torture me. His hand travels down my body once more. No . . . And the dam bursts—all the apprehension, the anxiety, and the fear from the last couple of days overwhelming me anew as tears spring to my eyes. I turn away from him. This is not love. It's revenge.

"Red," I whimper. "Red. Red." The tears course down my face. He stills. "No!" He gasps, stunned. "Jesus Christ, no."

He moves quickly, unclipping my hands, clasping me around my waist and leaning down to unclip my ankles, while I put my head in my hands and weep.

"No, no, no. Ana, please. No."

Picking me up, he moves to the bed, sitting down and cradling me in his lap while I sob inconsolably. I'm overwhelmed . . . my body wound up to breaking point, my mind a blank, and my emotions scattered to the wind. He reaches behind him, drags the satin sheet off the four-poster bed, and drapes it around me. The cool sheets feel alien and unwelcome against my sensitized skin. He wraps his arms around me, hugging me close, rocking me gently backward and forward.

"I'm sorry. I'm sorry," Christian murmurs, his voice raw. He kisses my hair over and over again. "Ana, forgive me, please."

Turning my face into his neck, I continue to cry, and it's a cathartic release. So much has happened over the last few days— fires in computer rooms, car chases, careers planned out for me, slutty architects, armed lunatics in the apartment, arguments, his anger—and Christian has been away. I hate Christian going away . . . I use the corner of the sheet to wipe my nose and gradually become aware that the clinical tones of Bach are still echoing around the room.

"Please switch the music off." I sniff.

"Yes, of course." Christian shifts, not letting me go, and pulls the remote out of his back pocket. He presses a button and the piano music ceases, to be replaced by my shuddering breaths. "Better?" he asks.

I nod, my sobs easing. Christian wipes my tears away gently with his thumb.

"Not a fan of Bach's Goldberg Variations?" he asks.

"Not that piece."

He gazes down at me, trying and failing to hide the shame in his eyes.

"I'm sorry," he says again.

"Why did you do that?" My voice is barely audible as I try to process my scrambled thoughts and feelings.

He shakes his head sadly and closes his eyes. "I got lost in the moment," he says unconvincingly.

I frown at him, and he sighs. "Ana, orgasm denial is a standard tool in— You never—" He stops. I shift in his lap, and he winces.

Oh. I flush. "Sorry," I mutter.

He rolls his eyes, then leans back suddenly, taking me with him, so that we're both lying on the bed, me in his arms. My bra is uncomfortable, and I adjust it.

"Need a hand?" he asks quietly.

I shake my head. I don't want him to touch my breasts. He shifts so he's looking down at me, and tentatively raising his hand, he strokes his fingers gently down my face. Tears pool in my eyes again. How can he be so callous one minute and so tender the next?

"Please don't cry," he whispers.

I'm dazed and confused by this man. My anger has deserted me in my hour of need . . . I feel numb. I want to curl up in a ball and withdraw. I blink, trying to hold back my tears as I gaze into his harrowed eyes. I take a shuddering breath, my eyes not leaving his. What am I going to do with this controlling man? Learn to be controlled? I don't think so . . .

"I never what?" I ask.

"Do as you're told. You changed your mind; you didn't tell me where you were. Ana, I was in New York, powerless and livid. If I'd been in Seattle I'd have brought you home."

"So you are punishing me?"

He swallows, then closes his eyes. He doesn't have to answer, and I know that punishing me was his exact intention.

"You have to stop doing this," I murmur.

His brow furrows.

"For a start, you only end up feeling shittier about yourself."

He snorts. "That's true," he mutters. "I don't like to see you like this."

"And I don't like feeling like this. You said on the *Fair Lady* that you hadn't married a submissive."

"I know. I know." His voice is soft and raw.

"Well stop treating me like one. I'm sorry I didn't call you. I won't be so selfish again. I know you worry about me."

He gazes at me, scrutinizing me closely, his eyes bleak and

anxious. "Okay. Good," he says eventually. He leans down, but pauses before his lips touch mine, silently asking if it's allowed. I raise my face to his, and he kisses me tenderly.

"Your lips are always so soft when you've been crying," he murmurs.

"I never promised to obey you, Christian," I whisper.

"I know."

"Deal with it, please. For both our sakes. And I will try to be more considerate of your . . . controlling tendencies."

He looks lost and vulnerable, completely at sea.

"I'll try," he murmurs, his voice burning with sincerity.

I sigh, a long shuddering sigh. "Please do. Besides, if I *had* been here . . ."

"I know," he says and blanches. Lying back, he puts his free arm over his face. I curl around him and lay my head on his chest. We both lie silent for a few moments. His hand moves to the end of my braid. He pulls the tie from it, freeing my hair, and gently, rhythmically combs his fingers through it. This is what this is really about—his fear . . . his irrational fear for my safety. An image of Jack Hyde slumped on the floor in the apartment with a Glock comes to mind . . . well, maybe not so irrational, which reminds me . . .

"What did you mean earlier, when you said *or*?" I ask.

"Or?"

"Something about Jack."

He peers down at me. "You don't give up, do you?"

I rest my chin on his sternum, enjoying the soothing caress of his fingers in my hair.

"Give up? Never. Tell me. I don't like being kept in the dark. You seem to have some overblown idea that I need protecting. You don't even know how to shoot—I do. Do you think I can't handle whatever it is you won't tell me, Christian? I've had your stalker ex-sub pull a gun on me, your pedophile ex-lover harass me—and don't look at me like that," I snap when he scowls at me. "Your mother feels the same way about her."

"You talked to my mother about Elena?" Christian's voice raises a few octaves.

"Yes, Grace and I talked about her."

He gapes at me.

"She's very upset about it. Blames herself."

"I can't believe you spoke to my mother. Shit!" He lies down and puts his arm over his face again.

"I didn't go into any specifics."

"I should hope not. Grace doesn't need all the gory details. Christ, Ana. My dad, too?"

"No!" I shake my head vehemently. I don't have that kind of relationship with Carrick. His comments about the prenup still sting. "Anyway, you're trying to distract me—again. Jack. What about him?"

Christian lifts his arm briefly and gazes at me, his expression unreadable. Sighing, he puts his arm back over his face.

"Hyde is implicated in *Charlie Tango*'s sabotage. The investigators found a partial print—just partial, so they couldn't make a match. But then you recognized Hyde in the server room. He has convictions as a minor in Detroit, and the prints matched his."

My mind reels as I try to absorb this information. Jack brought down *Charlie Tango*? But Christian is on a roll. "This morning, a cargo van was found in the garage here. Hyde was the driver. Yesterday, he delivered some shit to that new guy who's moved in. The guy we met in the elevator."

"I don't remember his name."

"Me neither." Christian says. "But that's how Hyde managed to get into the building legitimately. He was working for a delivery company—"

"And? What's so important about the van?"

Christian says nothing.

"Christian, tell me."

"The cops found . . . things in the van." He stops again and tightens his hold around me.

"What things?"

He's quiet for several moments, and I open my mouth to prompt him, but he speaks. "A mattress, enough horse tranquilizer to take down a dozen horses, and a note." His voice has softened to barely a whisper while horror and revulsion roll off him.

Holy fuck.

"Note?" My voice mirrors his.

"Addressed to me."

"What did it say?"

Christian shakes his head, indicating he doesn't know or that he won't divulge its contents.

Oh.

"Hyde came here last night with the intention of kidnapping you." Christian freezes, his face taut with tension. As he says those words, I recall the duct tape, and a shudder runs through me, though deep down this is not news to me.

"Shit," I mutter.

"Quite," Christian says tightly.

I try to remember Jack in the office. Was he always insane? How did he think he could get away with this? I mean, he was pretty creepy, but this unhinged?

"I don't understand why," I murmur. "It doesn't make sense to me."

"I know. The police are digging further, and so is Welch. But we think Detroit is the connection."

"Detroit?" I gaze at him, confused.

"Yeah. There's something there."

"I still don't understand."

Christian lifts his face and gazes at me, his expression unreadable. "Ana, I was born in Detroit."

CHAPTER TWELVE

I thought you were born here in Seattle," I murmur. My mind races. What does this have to do with Jack? Christian raises the arm covering his face, reaches behind him, and grabs one of the pillows. Placing it under his head, he settles back and gazes at me with a wary expression. After a moment he shakes his head.

"No. Elliot and I were both adopted in Detroit. We moved here shortly after my adoption. Grace wanted to be on the West Coast, away from the urban sprawl, and she got a job at Northwest Hospital. I have very little memory of that time. Mia was adopted here."

"So Jack is from Detroit?"

"Yes."

Oh . . . "How do you know?"

"I ran a background check when you went to work for him."

Of course he did. "Do you have a manila file on him, too?" I smirk.

Christian's mouth twists as he hides his amusement. "I think it's pale blue." His fingers continue to run through my hair. It's soothing.

"What does it say in his file?"

Christian blinks. Reaching down he strokes my cheek. "You really want to know?"

"Is it that bad?"

He shrugs. "I've known worse," he whispers.

No! Is he referring to himself? And the image I have of Christian as a small, dirty, fearful, lost boy comes to mind. I curl around him, holding him tighter, pulling the sheet over him, and I lay my cheek against his chest.

"What?" he asks, puzzled by my reaction.

"Nothing," I murmur.

"No, no. This works both ways, Ana. What is it?"

I glance up, assessing his apprehensive expression. Resting my cheek upon his chest once more, I decide to tell him. "Sometimes I picture you as a child . . . before you came to live with the Greys."

Christian stiffens. "I wasn't talking about me. I don't want your pity, Anastasia. That part of my life is done. Gone."

"It's not pity," I whisper, appalled. "It's sympathy and sorrow— sorrow that anyone could do that to a child." I take a deep steadying breath as my stomach twists and tears prick my eyes anew. "That part of your life is not done, Christian—how can you say that? You live every day with your past. You told me yourself—fifty shades, remember?" My voice is barely audible.

Christian snorts and runs his free hand through his hair, though he remains silent and tense beneath me.

"I know it's why you feel the need to control me. Keep me safe."

"And yet you choose to defy me," he murmurs, baffled, his hand stilling in my hair.

I frown. *Holy cow! Do I do that deliberately?* My subconscious removes her half-moon glasses and chews the end, pursing her lips and nodding. I ignore her. This is confusing—I'm his wife, not his submissive, not some company he's acquired. I'm not the crack whore who was his mother . . . *Fuck.* The thought is sickening. Dr. Flynn's words come back to me:

"Just keep doing what you're doing. Christian is head over heels . . . It's a delight to see."

That's it. I'm just doing what I've always done. Isn't that what Christian found attractive in the first place?

Oh, this man is so confusing.

"Dr. Flynn said I should give you the benefit of the doubt. I think I do—I'm not sure. Perhaps it's my way of bringing you into the here and now—away from your past," I whisper. "I don't know. I just can't seem to get a handle on how far you'll overreact."

He's silent for a moment. "Fucking Flynn," he mutters to himself.

"He said I should continue to behave the way I've always behaved with you."

"Did he now?" Christian says dryly.

Okay. Here goes nothing. "Christian, I know you loved your mom, and you couldn't save her. It wasn't your job to do that. But I'm not her."

He freezes again. "Don't," he whispers.

"No, listen. Please." I raise my head to stare into wide eyes that are paralyzed with fear. He's holding his breath. *Oh, Christian . . .* My heart constricts. "I'm not her. I'm much stronger than she was. I have you, and you're so much stronger now, and I know you love me. I love you, too," I whisper.

His brow creases as if my words were not what he expected. "Do you still love me?" he asks.

"Of course I do. Christian, I will always love you. No matter what you do to me." Is this the reassurance he wants?

He exhales and closes his eyes, placing his arm over his face again, but hugging me closer, too.

"Don't hide from me." Reaching up, I grasp his hand and pull his arm away from his face. "You've spent your life hiding. Please don't, not from me."

He looks at me with incredulity and frowns. "Hiding?"

"Yes."

He shifts suddenly, rolling over onto his side and moving me so that I am lying beside him on the bed. He reaches up, smoothes my hair off my face, and tucks it behind my ear.

"You asked me earlier today if I hated you. I didn't understand why, and now—" He stops, staring down at me as if I'm a complete conundrum.

"You still think I hate you?" Now my voice is incredulous.

"No." He shakes his head. "Not now." He looks relieved. "But I need to know . . . why did you safe-word, Ana?"

I blanch. What can I tell him? That he frightened me. That I didn't know if he'd stop. That I begged him—and he didn't stop. That I didn't want things to escalate . . . like—like that one time in here. I shudder as I recall him whipping me with his belt.

I swallow. "Because . . . because you were so angry and distant and . . . cold. I didn't know how far you'd go."

His expression is unreadable.

"Were you going to let me come?" My voice is barely a whisper, and I feel a blush steal over my cheeks, but I hold his gaze.

"No," he says eventually.

Holy crap. "That's . . . harsh."

His knuckle gently grazes my cheek. "But effective," he murmurs. He gazes down at me as if he's trying to see into my soul, his eyes darkening. After an eternity, he murmurs, "I'm glad you did."

"Really?" I don't understand.

His lips twist in a sad smile. "Yes. I don't want to hurt you. I got carried away." He reaches down and kisses me. "Lost in the moment." He kisses me again. "Happens a lot with you."

Oh? And for some bizarre reason the thought pleases me . . . I grin. Why does that make me happy? He grins, too.

"I don't know why you're grinning, Mrs. Grey."

"Me neither."

He wraps himself around me and places his head on my chest. We are a tangle of naked and denim-clad limbs and satin red sheets. I stroke his back with one hand and run the fingers of my other hand through his hair. He sighs and relaxes in my arms.

"It means I can trust you . . . to stop me. I never want to hurt you," he murmurs. "I need—" He halts.

"You need what?"

"I need control, Ana. Like I need you. It's the only way I can function. I can't let go of it. I can't. I've tried . . . And yet, with you . . ." He shakes his head in exasperation.

I swallow. This is the heart of our dilemma—his need for control and his need for me. I refuse to believe these are mutually exclusive.

"I need you, too," I whisper, hugging him tighter. "I'll try, Christian. I'll try to be more considerate."

"I want you to need me," he murmurs.

Holy cow!

"I do!" My voice is impassioned. I need him so much. I love him so much.

"I want to look after you."

"You do. All the time. I missed you so much while you were away."

"You did?" He sounds so surprised.

"Yes, of course. I hate you going away."

I sense his smile. "You could have come with me."

"Christian, please. Let's not rehash that argument. I want to work."

He sighs as I run my fingers gently through his hair.

"I love you, Ana."

"I love you, too, Christian. I will always love you."

We both lie still in the quiet after our storm. Listening to the steady beat of his heart, I drift exhausted into sleep.

I WAKE WITH A start, disoriented. Where am I? The playroom. The lights are still on, softly illuminating the bloodred walls. Christian moans again, and I realize this is what woke me.

"No," he groans. He's sprawled out beside me, his head back, his eyes screwed shut, his face contorted in anguish.

Holy shit. He's having a nightmare.

"No!" he cries out again.

"Christian, wake up." I struggle to sit up, kicking off the sheet. Kneeling beside him, I grab his shoulders and shake him as tears spring to my eyes.

"Christian, please. Wake up!"

His eyes spring open, gray and wild, his pupils enlarged with fear. He stares vacantly up at me.

"Christian, you're having a nightmare. You're home. You're safe."

He blinks, looks around frantically, and frowns as he takes in our surroundings. Then his eyes are back on mine. "Ana," he breathes, and with no preamble whatsoever he grabs my face with both hands, pulls me down onto his chest, and kisses me. Hard. His tongue invades my mouth, and he tastes of desperation and need. Barely giving me a chance to breathe, he rolls over, his lips locked to mine so that he's pressing me into the hard mattress of the four-poster. One of his hands clasps my jaw, the other spreads out on top of my head, keeping me still as his knee parts my legs and he nestles, still clothed in his jeans, between my thighs.

"Ana," he gasps, as if he can't believe I'm there with him. He gazes down at me for a split second, allowing me a moment to breathe. Then his lips are on mine again, plundering my mouth, taking all I have to give. He groans loudly, flexing his hips into me. His erection sheathed in denim pushes into my soft flesh. *Oh . . .* I moan, and all the pent-up sexual tension of earlier erupts, resurfacing with a vengeance, flushing my system with desire and need. Driven by his demons, he urgently kisses my face, my eyes, my cheeks, along my jaw.

"I'm here," I whisper, trying to calm him, our heated, panting breath mingling. I wrap my arms around his shoulders as I grind my pelvis against his in welcome.

"Oh, Ana," he pants, his voice rough and low. "I need you."

"Me, too," I whisper urgently, my body desperate for his touch. I want him. I want him now. I want to heal him. I want to heal me . . . I need this. His hand reaches down and tugs on the button of his fly, fumbling momentarily, then freeing his erection.

Holy shit. I was asleep less than a minute ago.

He shifts, staring down at me for a split second, suspended above me.

"Yes. Please," I breathe, my voice hoarse and needy.

And in one swift move he buries himself inside me.

"Ah!" I cry out, not from any pain, but from surprise at his alacrity.

He groans, and his lips find mine again as he pushes into me,

over and over, his tongue possessing me, too. He moves frantically, compelled by his fear, his lust, his desire, his—love? I don't
know, but I meet him thrust for thrust, welcoming him.

"Ana," he growls almost inarticulately, and he comes power-
fully, pouring himself into me, his face strained, his body rigid,
before he collapses with his full weight onto me, panting, and he
leaves me hanging . . . again.

Holy shit. This is not my night. I hold him, drawing in a lung-
ful of air and practically writhing with need beneath him. He
eases out of me and holds me for minutes . . . many minutes.
Finally he shakes his head and leans up on his elbows, taking
some of his weight. He gazes down at me as if seeing me for the
first time.

"Oh, Ana. Sweet Jesus." He bends and kisses me tenderly.

"You okay?" I breathe, caressing his lovely face. He nods, but
he looks shaken and most definitely stirred. My own lost boy. He
frowns and stares intently into my eyes as if finally registering
where he is.

"You?" he asks, concern in his voice.

"Um . . ." I wriggle beneath him, and after a moment he
smiles, a slow carnal smile.

"Mrs. Grey, you have needs," he murmurs. He kisses me
swiftly, then scoots off the bed.

Kneeling on the floor at the end of the bed, he reaches up,
grabs me just above the knees, and pulls me toward him so my
behind is on the edge of the bed.

"Sit up," he murmurs. I struggle into a sitting position, my hair
falling like a veil around me, down to my breasts. His gray gaze
holds mine as he gently pushes my legs apart as far as they'll go. I
lean back on my hands—knowing full well what he's going to do.
But . . . he's just . . . um . . .

"You are so fucking beautiful, Ana," he breathes, and I watch
his copper-haired head dip and plant a trail of kisses up my right
thigh, heading north. My whole body clenches in anticipation.
He glances up at me, his eyes darkening through long lashes.

"Watch," he rasps, then his mouth is on me.

Oh my. I cry out as the world is concentrated at the apex of my thighs, and it's so erotic—*Fuck*—watching him. Watching his tongue against what feels like the most sensitive part of my body. And he shows no mercy, teasing and taunting, worshipping me. My body tenses and my arms start to tremble from the strain of staying upright.

"No . . . ah," I murmur. Gently, he eases one long finger inside me, and I can bear it no more, collapsing back onto the bed, relishing his mouth and fingers on and in me. Slowly and gently, he massages that sweet, sweet spot deep inside me. And that's it—I'm gone. I explode around him, crying out an incoherent rendition of his name as my intense orgasm arches my back off the bed. I think I see stars it's such a visceral primal feeling . . . Vaguely I'm aware that he's nuzzling my belly, giving me soft, sweet kisses. Reaching down, I caress his hair.

"I'm not finished with you yet," he murmurs. And before I've fully come back to Seattle, planet Earth, he's reaching for me, grasping my hips, and pulling me off the bed to where's he's kneeling, into his waiting lap and onto his waiting erection.

I gasp as he fills me. *Holy cow* . . .

"Oh, baby," he breathes as he wraps his arms around me and stills, cradling my head and kissing my face. He flexes his hips, and pleasure spikes hot and hard from deep within me. He reaches for my behind and lifts me, rocking his groin upward.

"Ah," I moan, and his lips are on mine again as he slowly, oh so slowly, lifts and rocks . . . lifts and rocks. I throw my arms around his neck, surrendering to his gentle rhythm and to wherever he'll take me. I flex my thighs, riding him . . . he feels so good. Leaning backward, I tilt my head back, my mouth open wide in a silent expression of my pleasure, reveling in his sweet lovemaking.

"Ana," he breathes, and he leans down, kissing my throat. Holding me tight, slowly easing in and out, pushing me . . . higher and higher . . . so exquisitely timed—a fluid carnal force. Blissful pleasure radiates outward from deep, deep inside me as he holds me so intimately.

"I love you, Ana," he whispers close to my ear, his voice low and harsh, and he lifts me again—up, down, up, down. I curl my hands back around his neck into his hair.

"I love you, too, Christian." Opening my eyes, I find he's gazing at me, and all I see is his love, shining bright and bold in the soft glow of the playroom light, his nightmare seemingly forgotten. And as I feel my body build toward my release, I realize this is what I wanted—this connection, this demonstration of our love.

"Come for me, baby," he whispers, his voice low. I screw my eyes shut as my body tightens at the low sound of his voice, and I come loudly, spiraling into an intense climax. He stills, his forehead against mine, as he softly whispers my name, wraps his arms around me, and finds his own release.

HE LIFTS ME GENTLY and lays me on the bed. I lie in his arms, wrung out and finally sated. He nuzzles my neck.

"Better now?" he whispers.

"Hmm."

"Shall we go to bed, or do you want to sleep here?"

"Hmm."

"Mrs. Grey, talk to me." He sounds amused.

"Hmm."

"Is that the best you can do?"

"Hmm."

"Come. Let me put you to bed. I don't like sleeping here."

Reluctantly, I shift and turn to face him. "Wait," I whisper. He blinks at me, looking all wide-eyed and innocent, and at the same time thoroughly fucked and pleased with himself.

"Are you okay?" I ask.

He nods, smiling smugly like an adolescent boy. "I am now."

"Oh, Christian," I scold and gently stroke his lovely face. "I was talking about your nightmare."

His expression freezes momentarily, then he closes his eyes and tightens his arms around me, burying his face in my neck.

"Don't," he whispers, his voice hoarse and raw. My heart

lurches and twists once more in my chest, and I clutch him tightly, running my hands down his back and through his hair.

"I'm sorry," I whisper, alarmed by his reaction. Holy fuck—how can I keep up with these mood swings? What the hell was his nightmare about? I don't want to cause him any more pain by making him relive the details. "It's okay," I murmur softly, desperate to bring him back to the playful boy of a moment ago. "It's okay," I repeat over and over soothingly.

"Let's go to bed," he says quietly after a while, and he pulls away from me, leaving me empty and aching as he rises from the bed. I scramble after him, keeping the satin sheet wrapped around me, and bend to pick up my clothes.

"Leave those," he says, and before I know it, he's scooped me up in his arms. "I don't want you to trip over this sheet and break your neck." I put my arms around him, marveling that he's recovered his composure, and nuzzle him as he carries me downstairs to our bedroom.

MY EYES SPRING OPEN. Something is wrong. Christian is not in bed, though it's still dark. Glancing at the radio alarm, I see it's three twenty in the morning. Where's Christian? Then I hear the piano.

Quickly slipping out of bed, I grab my robe and run down the hallway to the great room. The tune he's playing is so sad—a mournful lament that I've heard him play before. I pause in the doorway and watch him in a pool of light while the achingly sorrowful music fills the room. He finishes, then starts the piece again. Why such a plaintive tune? I wrap my arms around myself and listen spellbound as he plays. But my heart aches. *Christian, why so sad? Is it because of me? Did I do this?* When he finishes, only to start a third time, I can bear it no longer. He doesn't look up as I near the piano, but shifts to one side so I can sit beside him on the piano bench. He continues to play, and I put my head on his shoulder. He kisses my hair but doesn't stop playing until he's finished the piece. I peek up at him and he's staring down at me, warily.

"Did I wake you?" he asks.

"Only because you were gone. What's that piece called?"

"It's Chopin. It's one of his preludes in E minor." Christian pauses. "It's called 'Suffocation' . . ."

Reaching over, I take his hand. "You're really shaken by all this, aren't you?"

He snorts. "A deranged asshole gets into my apartment to kid-nap my wife. She won't do as she's told. She drives me crazy. She safe-words on me." He closes his eyes briefly, and when he opens them again, they are stark and raw. "Yeah, I'm pretty shaken up."

I squeeze his hand. "I'm sorry."

He presses his forehead against mine. "I dreamed you were dead," he whispers.

What?

"Lying on the floor—so cold—and you wouldn't wake up."

Oh, Fifty.

"Hey—it was just a bad dream." Reaching up, I clasp his head in my hands. His eyes burn into mine and the anguish in them is sobering. "I'm here and I'm cold without you in bed. Come back to bed, please." I take his hand and stand, waiting to see if he'll fol-low me. Finally he stands, too. He's wearing his pajama bottoms, and they hang in that way he has, and I want to run my fingers along the inside of his waistband, but I resist and lead him back to the bedroom.

WHEN I WAKE HE'S curled around me, sleeping peacefully. I relax and enjoy his enveloping heat, his skin on my skin. I lie very still, not wanting to disturb him.

Boy, what an evening. I feel like I've been run over by a train—the freight train that is my husband. Hard to believe that the man lying beside me, looking so serene and young in his sleep, was so tortured last night . . . and so tortured me last night. I gaze up at the ceiling, and it occurs to me that I always think of Christian as strong and dominating—yet the reality is he's so fragile, my lost boy. And the irony is that he looks upon me as fragile—and I don't think I am. Compared to him *I'm* strong.

But am I strong enough for both of us? Strong enough to do what I'm told and give him some peace of mind? I sigh. He's not asking that much of me. I flit through our conversation of last night. Did we decide anything other than to both try harder? The bottom line is that I love this man, and I need to chart a course for both of us. One that lets me keep my integrity and independence but still be more for him. I am his *more,* and he is mine. I resolve to make a special effort this weekend not to give him cause for concern.

Christian stirs and lifts his head off my chest, looking sleepily at me.

"Good morning, Mr. Grey." I smile.

"Good morning, Mrs. Grey. Did you sleep well?" He stretches out beside me.

"Once my husband stopped making that terrible racket on the piano, yes, I did."

He smiles his shy smile, and I melt. "Terrible racket? I'll be sure to e-mail Miss Kathie and let her know."

"Miss Kathie?"

"My piano teacher."

I giggle.

"That's a lovely sound," he says. "Shall we have a better day today?"

"Okay," I agree. "What do you want to do?"

"After I have made love to my wife, and she's cooked me breakfast, I'd like to take her to Aspen."

I gape at him. "Aspen?"

"Yes."

"Aspen, Colorado?"

"The very same. Unless they've moved it. After all, you did pay twenty-four thousand dollars for the experience."

I grin at him. "That was your money."

"Our money."

"It was your money when I made the bid." I roll my eyes.

"Oh, Mrs. Grey, you and your eye rolling," he whispers as he runs his hand up my thigh.

"Won't it take hours to get to Colorado?" I ask to distract him.

"Not by jet," he says silkily as his hand reaches my behind.

Of course, my husband has a jet. How could I forget? His hand continues to skim up my body, lifting my nightdress as it goes, and soon I've forgotten everything.

TAYLOR DRIVES US ONTO the tarmac at Sea-Tac and around to where the GEH jet is waiting. It's a gray day in Seattle, but I refuse to let the weather dampen my soaring spirits. Christian is in a much better mood. He's excited about something—lit up like Christmas and twitching like a small boy with a big secret. I wonder what scheme he's concocted. He looks dreamy, all tousled hair, white T-shirt, and black jeans. Not CEO-like at all today. He takes my hand as Taylor glides to a stop at the foot of the jet steps.

"I have a surprise for you," he murmurs and kisses my knuckles.

I grin at him. "Good surprise?"

"I hope so." He smiles warmly.

Hmm . . . what can it be?

Sawyer leaps out from the front and opens my door. Taylor opens Christian's, then retrieves our cases from the trunk. Stephan is waiting at the top of the stairs when we enter the aircraft. I glance into the cockpit and see First Officer Beighley flipping switches on the imposing instrument panel.

Christian and Stephan shake hands. "Good morning, sir." Stephan smiles.

"Thanks for doing this on such short notice." Christian grins back at him. "Our guests here?"

"Yes, sir."

Guests? I turn and gasp. Kate, Elliot, Mia, and Ethan are all smiling and sitting in the cream-colored leather seats. Wow! I spin around to Christian.

"Surprise!" he says.

"How? When? Who?" I mumble inarticulately, trying to contain my delight and elation.

"You said you didn't see enough of your friends." He shrugs and gives me a lopsided, apologetic smile.

"Oh, Christian, thank you." I throw my arms around his neck and kiss him hard in front of everyone. He puts his hands on my hips, hooking his thumbs through the belt loops of my jeans, and deepens the kiss.

Oh my.

"Keep this up and I'll drag you into the bedroom," he murmurs.

"You wouldn't dare," I whisper against his lips.

"Oh, Anastasia." He grins, shaking his head. He releases me and without further preamble, stoops down, grabs my thighs, and lifts me over his shoulder.

"Christian, put me down!" I smack his behind.

I briefly catch Stephan's smile as he turns and heads into the cockpit. Taylor is standing at the doorway, trying to stifle his grin. Ignoring my pleas and my futile struggles, Christian strides through the narrow cabin past Mia and Ethan, who are facing each other in the single seats, and past Kate and Elliot, who is whooping like a demented gibbon.

"If you'll excuse me," he says to our four guests. "I need to have a word with my wife in private."

"Christian!" I shout. "Put me down!"

"All in good time, baby."

I have a brief view of Mia, Kate, and Elliot laughing. *Damn it!* This is not funny, it's embarrassing. Ethan gawks at us, mouth open and utterly shocked, as we disappear into the cabin.

Christian closes the cabin door behind him and releases me, letting me slide down his body slowly, so that I feel every hard sinew and muscle. He gives me his boyish grin, thoroughly pleased with himself.

"That was quite a show, Mr. Grey." I cross my arms and regard him with faux indignation.

"That was fun, Mrs. Grey." And his grin widens. *Oh boy.* He looks so young.

"Are you going to follow through?" I arch a brow, unsure how I feel about this. I mean, the others will hear us, for heaven's sake. Suddenly, I feel shy. Glancing anxiously at the bed, I feel a blush steal across my cheeks as I recall our wedding night. We talked so much yesterday, did so much yesterday. I feel as if we leaped some unknown hurdle—but that's the problem. It's unknown. My eyes find Christian's intense but amused gaze, and I'm unable to keep a straight face. His grin is too infectious.

"I think it might be rude to keep our guests waiting," he says silkily as he steps toward me. *When did he start to care what people think?* I step back against the cabin wall and he imprisons me, the heat from his body holding me in place. He leans down and runs his nose along mine.

"Good surprise?" he whispers, and there's a hint of anxiety in his voice.

"Oh, Christian, fantastic surprise." I run my hands up his chest, curl them around his neck, and kiss him.

"When did you organize this?" I ask when I pull away from him, stroking his hair.

"Last night, when I couldn't sleep. I e-mailed Elliot and Mia, and here they are."

"It's very thoughtful. Thank you. I'm sure we'll have a great time."

"I hope so. I thought it would be easier to avoid the press in Aspen than at home."

The paparazzi! He's right. If we'd stayed in Escala, we'd have been imprisoned. A shiver runs down my spine as I recollect the snapping cameras and dazzling flashes of the few photographers Taylor sped through this morning.

"Come. We'd better take our seats—Stephan will be taking off shortly." He offers me his hand and together we walk back into the cabin.

Elliot cheers as we enter. "That sure was speedy in-flight service!" he calls mockingly.

Christian ignores him.

"Please be seated, ladies and gentlemen, as we'll shortly begin taxiing for takeoff." Stephan's voice echoes calmly and authoritatively around the cabin. The brunette woman—*um . . . Natalie?*—who was on the flight for our wedding night appears from the galley and gathers up the discarded coffee cups. *Natalia . . . Her name's Natalia.*

"Good morning Mr. Grey, Mrs. Grey," she says with a purr. Why does she make me uncomfortable? Maybe it's that she's a brunette. By his own admission, Christian doesn't usually employ brunettes because he finds them attractive. He gives Natalia a polite smile as he slides in behind the table and sits down facing Elliot and Kate. I swiftly hug Kate and Mia and give Ethan and Elliot a wave before sitting down and buckling up beside Christian. He puts his hand on my knee and gives it an affectionate squeeze. He seems relaxed and happy, even though we're with company. Idly, I wonder why he can't always be like this—not controlling at all.

"Hope you packed your hiking boots," he says, his voice warm.

"We're not going skiing?"

"That would be a challenge, in August," he says, amused.

Oh, of course.

"Do you ski, Ana?" Elliot interrupts us.

"No."

Christian moves his hand from my knee to clasp my hand.

"I'm sure my little brother can teach you." Elliot winks at me. "He's pretty fast on the slopes, too."

And I can't help my blush. When I glance up at Christian, he's gazing impassively at Elliot, but I think he's trying to suppress his mirth. The plane surges forward and starts taxiing toward the runway.

Natalia runs through the plane's safety procedures in a clear, ringing voice. She's dressed in a neat navy short-sleeved shirt and matching pencil skirt. Her makeup is immaculate—she really is quite pretty. My subconscious raises a plucked-to-within-an-inch-of-its-life eyebrow at me.

"You okay?" Kate asks me pointedly. "I mean, following the Hyde business?"

I nod. I don't want to think or talk about Hyde, but Kate seems to have other plans.

"So why did he go postal?" she asks, cutting to the heart of the matter in her inimitable style. She tosses her hair behind her as she prepares to investigate further.

Eyeing her coolly, Christian shrugs. "I fired his ass," he says bluntly.

"Oh? Why?" Kate tilts her head to one side, and I know she's in full Nancy Drew mode.

"He made a pass at me," I mutter. I try to kick Kate's ankle beneath the table and miss. Shit!

"When?" Kate glares at me.

"Ages ago."

"You never told me he made a pass at you!" she splutters.

I shrug apologetically.

"It can't just be a grudge about that, surely. I mean his reaction is way too extreme," Kate continues, but now she directs her questions at Christian. "Is he mentally unstable? What about all the information he has on you Greys?" Her grilling Christian this way makes my hackles rise, but she's already established that I know nothing, so she can't ask me. The thought is annoying.

"We think there's a connection with Detroit," Christian says mildly. Too mildly. *Oh no, Kate, please give it up for now.*

"Hyde is from Detroit, too?"

Christian nods.

The plane accelerates, and I tighten my grip on Christian's hand. He glances at me reassuringly. He knows I hate takeoffs and landings. He squeezes my hand and his thumb strokes my knuckles, calming me.

"What *do* you know about him?" Elliot asks, oblivious to the fact that we are hurtling down the runway in a small jet about to launch itself into the sky, and equally oblivious to Christian's growing exasperation with Kate. Kate leans forward, listening attentively.

"This is off the record," Christian says directly to her. Kate's mouth sets in a subtle but thin line. I swallow. *Oh shit.*

"We know a little about him," Christian continues. "His dad died in a brawl in a bar. His mother drank herself into oblivion. He was in and out of foster homes as a kid . . . in and out of trouble, too. Mainly boosting cars. Spent time in juvie. His mom got back on track through some outreach program, and Hyde turned himself around. Won a scholarship to Princeton."

"Princeton?" Kate's curiosity is piqued.

"Yep. He's a bright boy." Christian shrugs.

"Not that bright. He got caught," Elliot mutters.

"But surely he can't have pulled this stunt alone?" Kate asks.

Christian stiffens beside me. "We don't know yet." His voice is very quiet. *Holy crap.* There could be someone working with him? I turn and gape in horror at Christian. He squeezes my hand once more but doesn't look me in the eye. The plane lifts smoothly into the air, and I get that horrible sinking feeling in my stomach.

"How old is he?" I ask Christian, leaning close so only he can hear. Much as I'd like to know what's going on, I don't want to encourage Kate's questions. I know they're irritating Christian, and I'm sure she's on his shit list since Cocktailgate.

"Thirty-two. Why?"

"Curious, that's all."

Christian's jaw tightens. "Don't be curious about Hyde. I'm just glad the fucker's locked up." It's almost a reprimand, but I choose to ignore his tone.

"Do *you* think he's working with someone?" The thought that someone else might be involved makes me sick. It would mean this isn't over.

"I don't know," Christian answers, and his jaw tightens once more.

"Maybe someone who has a grudge against you?" I suggest. Holy shit. I hope it's not the bitch troll. "Like Elena?" I whisper. I realize I've muttered her name out loud, but only he can hear. I glance anxiously at Kate, but she's deep in conversation with Elliot, who looks pissed at her. Hmm.

"You do like to demonize her, don't you?" Christian rolls his eyes and shakes his head in disgust. "She may hold a grudge, but she wouldn't do this kind of thing." He pins me with a steady gray gaze. "Let's not discuss her. I know she's not your favorite topic of conversation."

"Have you confronted her?" I whisper, not sure if I really want to know.

"Ana, I haven't spoken to her since my birthday party. Please, drop it. I don't want to talk about her." He raises my hand and brushes my knuckles with his lips. His eyes burn into mine, and I know I shouldn't pursue this line of questioning right now.

"Get a room," Elliot teases. "Oh right—you already have, but you didn't need it for long."

Christian glances up and pins Elliot with a cool glare. "Fuck off, Elliot," he says without malice.

"Dude, just telling you how it is." Elliot's eyes light up with mirth.

"Like you'd know," Christian murmurs sardonically, raising an eyebrow.

Elliot grins, enjoying the banter. "You married your first girl-friend." Elliot gestures at me.

Oh shit. Where is this going? I flush.

"Can you blame me?" Christian kisses my hand again.

"No." Elliot laughs and shakes his head.

I flush, and Kate slaps Elliot's thigh.

"Stop being an ass," she scolds him.

"Listen to your girlfriend," Christian says to Elliot, grinning, and his earlier concern seems to have disappeared. My ears pop as we gain altitude, and the tension in the cabin dissipates as the plane levels out. Kate scowls at Elliot. Hmm . . . is something up between them? I'm not sure.

Elliot is right. I snort at the irony. I am—was—Christian's first girlfriend, and now I'm his wife. The fifteen and the evil Mrs. Robinson—they don't count. But then Elliot doesn't know about them, and clearly Kate hasn't told him. I smile at her, and she gives me a conspiratorial wink. My secrets are safe with Kate.

"Okay, ladies and gentlemen, we'll be cruising at an altitude of approximately thirty-two thousand feet, and our estimated flight time is one hour and fifty-six minutes," Stephan announces. "You are now free to move around the cabin."

Natalia appears abruptly from the galley.

"May I offer anyone coffee?" she asks.

CHAPTER THIRTEEN

We land smoothly at Sardy Field at 12:25 p.m. (MST). Stephan brings the plane to a halt a little way from the main terminal, and through the windows I spot a large VW minivan waiting for us.

"Good landing." Christian grins and shakes Stephan's hand as we get ready to file out of the jet.

"It's all about the density altitude, sir." Stephan smiles back. "Beighley here is good at math."

Christian nods at Stephan's first officer. "You nailed it, Beighley. Smooth landing."

"Thank you, sir." She grins smugly.

"Enjoy your weekend, Mr. Grey, Mrs. Grey. We'll see you tomorrow." Stephan steps aside to let us disembark and, taking my hand, Christian leads me down the aircraft steps to where Taylor is waiting by the vehicle.

"Minivan?" says Christian in surprise as Taylor slides open the door.

Taylor gives him a tight, contrite smile and a slight shrug.

"Last minute, I know," Christian says, immediately placated. Taylor returns to the plane to retrieve our luggage.

"Want to make out in the back of the van?" Christian murmurs to me, a mischievous gleam in his eye.

I giggle. Who is this man, and what has he done with Mr. Unbelievably Angry of the last couple of days?

"Come on, you two. Get in," Mia says from behind us, oozing impatience beside Ethan. We climb in, stagger to the double seat at the back, and sit down. I snuggle against Christian, and he puts his arm around the back of my seat. "Comfortable?" he murmurs as Mia and Ethan take the seat in front of us.

"Yes." I smile and he kisses my forehead. And for some unfathomable reason I feel shy with him today. *Why?* Last night? Being with company? I can't put my finger on it.

Elliot and Kate join us last as Taylor opens the liftgate to load the luggage. Five minutes later, we are on our way.

I gaze out the window as we head toward Aspen. The trees are green, but a whisper of the coming fall is evident here and there in the yellowing tips of the leaves. The sky is a clear crystal blue, though there are darkening clouds to the west. All around us in the distance loom the Rockies, the highest peak directly ahead. They're lush and green, and the highest are capped with snow and look like a child's drawing of mountains.

We're in the winter playground of the rich and famous. *And I own a house here.* I can barely believe it. And from deep within my psyche, the familiar unease that's always present when I try to wrap my head around Christian's wealth looms and taunts me, making me feel guilty. What have I done to deserve this lifestyle? I've done nothing, nothing except fall in love.

"Have you been to Aspen before, Ana?" Ethan turns and asks, dragging me out of my reverie.

"No, first time. You?"

"Kate and I used to come here a lot when we were teens. Dad's a keen skier. Mom less so."

"I'm hoping my husband will teach me how to ski." I glance up at my man.

"Don't bet on it," Christian mutters.

"I won't be that bad!"

"You might break your neck." His grin gone.

Oh. I don't want to argue and sour his good mood, so I change the subject. "How long have you had this place?"

"Nearly two years. It's yours now, too, Mrs. Grey," he says softly.

"I know," I whisper. But somehow I don't feel the courage of my convictions. Leaning in, I kiss his jaw and nestle once more at his side, listening to him laugh and joke with Ethan and Elliot. Mia chimes in occasionally, but Kate is quiet, and I wonder if she's brooding about Jack Hyde or something else. Then I remember. Aspen . . . Christian's house here was redesigned by Gia Matteo and rebuilt by Elliot. I wonder if that's what's preoccupying Kate. I can't ask her in front of Elliot, given his history with Gia. Does Kate even know about Gia's connection to the house? I frown, wondering what could be bothering her, and resolve to ask her when we're on our own.

We drive through the center of Aspen and my mood brightens as I take in the town. There are squat buildings of mostly red-brick, Swiss-style chalets, and numerous little turn-of-the-century houses painted in fun colors. Plenty of banks and designer shops, too, betraying the affluence of the local populace. Of course Christian fits in here.

"Why did you choose Aspen?" I ask him.

"What?" He regards me quizzically.

"To buy a place."

"Mom and Dad used to bring us here when we were kids. I learned to ski here, and I like the place. I hope you do, too—otherwise we'll sell the house and choose somewhere else."

Simple as that!

He tucks a loose strand of hair behind my ear. "You look lovely today," he murmurs.

My cheeks heat. I'm just wearing my traveling gear: jeans and a T-shirt with a lightweight navy blue jacket. *Damn it.* Why does he make me feel shy?

He kisses me, a tender, sweet, loving kiss.

Taylor drives us on out of town, and we start to climb the other side of the valley, twisting along a mountain road. The higher we go, the more excited I get, and Christian tenses beside me.

"What's wrong?" I ask as we round a bend.

"I hope you like it," he says quietly. "We're here."

Taylor slows and turns through a gateway made of gray, beige, and red stones. He heads down the driveway and finally pulls up outside the impressive house. Double fronted with high-pitched roofs and built of dark wood and the same mixed stone as the gateway. It's stunning—modern and stark, very much Christian's style.

"Home," he mouths at me as our guests start piling out of the van.

"Looks good."

"Come. See," he says, an excited, though anxious, gleam in his eyes as if he's about to show me his science project or something.

Mia runs up the steps to where a woman stands in the doorway. She's tiny and her raven-colored hair is dusted with gray. Mia flings her arms around her neck and hugs her tightly.

"Who's that?" I ask as Christian helps me out of the van.

"Mrs. Bentley. She lives here with her husband. They look after the place."

Holy cow . . . more staff?

Mia is making introductions—Ethan, then Kate. Elliot hugs Mrs. Bentley, too. As Taylor unloads the van, Christian takes my hand and leads me to the front door.

"Welcome back, Mr Grey." Mrs. Bentley smiles.

"Carmella, this is my wife, Anastasia," Christian says proudly. His tongue caresses my name, making my heart stutter.

"Mrs. Grey." Mrs. Bentley nods a respectful greeting. I hold out my hand and we shake. It's no surprise to me that she's much more formal with Christian than the rest of the family.

"I hope you've had a pleasant flight. The weather is supposed to be fine all weekend, though I'm not sure." She eyes the darkening gray clouds behind us. "Lunch is ready whenever you want." She smiles again, her dark eyes twinkling, and I warm to her immediately.

"Here." Christian grabs me and lifts me off my feet.

"What are you doing?" I squeal.

"Carrying you over yet another threshold, Mrs. Grey."

I grin as he carries me into the wide hallway, and after a brief kiss, he sets me gently down onto the hardwood floor. The interior decor is stark and reminds me of the great room at Escala—all white walls, dark wood, and contemporary abstract art. The hallway opens up into a large sitting area where three off-white leather couches surround a stone fireplace that dominates the room. The only color is from the soft cushions scattered on the couches. Mia grabs Ethan's hand and drags him farther into the house. Christian narrows his eyes at their departing figures, his mouth thinning. He shakes his head, then turns to me.

Kate whistles loudly. "Nice place."

I glance around to see Elliot helping Taylor with our luggage. I wonder again if she knows that Gia had a hand in this place.

"Tour?" Christian asks me, and whatever was going through his mind about Mia and Ethan is gone. He's radiating excitement—or is it anxiety? It's difficult to tell.

"Sure." Once again I'm overwhelmed by the wealth. How much did this place cost? And I have contributed nothing to it. Briefly I'm transported back to the first time Christian took me to Escala. I was overwhelmed then. *You got used to it,* my subconscious hisses at me.

Christian frowns but takes my hand, leading me through the various rooms. The state-of-the-art kitchen is all pale marble countertops and black cupboards. There's an impressive wine cellar, and an expansive den downstairs, complete with a large plasma screen TV, soft couches . . . and a billiards table. I gape at it and blush when Christian catches me.

"Fancy a game?" he asks, a wicked gleam in his eye. I shake my head, and his brow furrows once more. Taking my hand again, he leads me up to the first floor. There are four bedrooms upstairs, each with an en suite bathroom.

The master suite is something else. The bed is huge, bigger than the bed at home, and faces an enormous picture window looking out over Aspen and toward the verdant mountains.

"That's Ajax Mountain . . . or Aspen Mountain, if you like," Christian says, eyeing me warily. He's standing in the doorway, his thumbs hooked through the belt loops on his black jeans.

I nod.

"You're very quiet," he murmurs.

"It's lovely, Christian." And suddenly I'm aching to be back at Escala.

In five long strides he's standing in front of me, tugging at my chin, and releasing my lower lip from the grip of my teeth.

"What is it?" he asks, his eyes searching mine.

"You're very rich."

"Yes."

"Sometimes, it just takes me by surprise how wealthy you are."

"We are."

"We are," I mutter automatically.

"Don't stress about this, Ana, please. It's just a house."

"And what did Gia do here, exactly?"

"Gia?" He raises his eyebrows in surprise.

"Yes. She remodeled this place?"

"She did. She designed the den downstairs. Elliot did the build." He rakes his hand through his hair and frowns at me. "Why are we talking about Gia?"

"Did you know she had a fling with Elliot?"

Christian gazes at me for a moment, his expression unreadable. "Elliot's fucked most of Seattle, Ana."

I gasp.

"Mainly women, I understand," Christian jokes. I think he's amused by my expression.

"No!"

Christian nods. "It's none of my business." He holds his palms up.

"I don't think Kate knows."

"I'm not sure he broadcasts that information. Kate seems to be holding her own."

I'm shocked. Sweet, unassuming, blond, blue-eyed Elliot? I stare in disbelief.

Christian tilts his head to one side, scrutinizing me. "This can't just be about Gia's or Elliot's promiscuity."

"I know. I'm sorry. After all that's happened this week, it's just . . ." I shrug, feeling tearful all of a sudden. Christian seems to sag with relief. Pulling me into his arms, he holds me tightly, his nose in my hair.

"I know. I'm sorry, too. Let's relax and enjoy ourselves, okay? You can stay here and read, watch god-awful TV, shop, go hiking—fishing even. Whatever you want to do. And forget what I said about Elliot. That was indiscreet of me."

"Goes some way to explain why he's always teasing you," I murmur, nuzzling his chest.

"He really has no idea about my past. I told you, my family assumed I was gay. Celibate, but gay."

I giggle and begin to relax in his arms. "I thought you were celibate. How wrong I was." I wrap my arms around him, marveling at the ridiculousness of Christian's being gay.

"Mrs. Grey, are you smirking at me?"

"Maybe a little." I acquiesce. "You know, what I don't understand is why you have this place."

"What do you mean?" He kisses my hair.

"You have the boat, which I get, you have the place in New York for business—but why here? It's not like you shared it with anyone."

Christian stills and is silent for several beats. "I was waiting for you," he says softly, his eyes dark gray and luminous.

"That's . . . that's such a lovely thing to say."

"It's true. I didn't know it at the time." He smiles his shy smile.

"I'm glad you waited."

"You are worth waiting for, Mrs. Grey." He tips my chin up with his finger, leans down, and kisses me tenderly.

"So are you." I smile. "Though I feel like I cheated. I didn't have to wait long for you at all."

He grins. "Am I that much of a prize?"

"Christian, you are the state lottery, the cure for cancer, and the three wishes from Aladdin's lamp all rolled into one."

He raises a brow.

"When will you realize this?" I scold him. "You were a very eligible bachelor. And I don't mean all this." I wave dismissively at our plush surroundings. "I mean in here." I place my hand over his heart, and his eyes widen. My confident, sexy husband has gone, and I'm facing my lost boy. "Believe me, Christian, please," I whisper and clasp his face, pulling his lips to mine. He groans, and I don't know if it's hearing what I've said or his usual primal response. I claim him, my lips moving against his, my tongue invading his mouth.

When we're both breathless, he pulls away, eyeing me doubtfully.

"When are you going to get it through your exceptionally thick skull that I love you?" I ask, exasperated.

He swallows. "One day," he says.

This is progress. I smile and am rewarded with his answering shy smile.

"Come. Let's have some lunch—the others will be wondering where we are. We can discuss what we all want to do."

"OH NO!" KATE SAYS suddenly.

All eyes turn to her.

"Look," she says, pointing to the picture window. Outside, rain has started pouring down. We are sitting around the dark wood table in the kitchen, having consumed an Italian feast of a mixed antipasto, prepared by Mrs. Bentley, and a bottle or two of Frascati. I'm replete and a little buzzed from the alcohol.

"There goes our hike," Elliot mutters, sounding vaguely relieved. Kate scowls at him. Something is definitely up with them. They have been relaxed with all of us but not with each other.

"We could go into town," Mia pipes up. Ethan smirks at her.

"Perfect weather for fishing," Christian suggests.

"I'll go fish," Ethan says.

"Let's split up." Mia claps her hands. "Girls, shopping—boys, outdoor boring stuff."

I glance at Kate, who regards Mia indulgently. Fishing or shopping? Jeez, what a choice.

"Ana, what do you want to do?" Christian asks.

"I don't mind," I lie.

Kate catches my eye and mouths "shopping." Perhaps she wants to talk.

"But I'm more than happy to go shopping." I smile wryly at Kate and Mia. Christian smirks. He knows I hate shopping.

"I can stay here with you, if you'd like," he murmurs, and something dark unfurls in my belly at his tone.

"No, you go fish," I answer. Christian needs boy time.

"Sounds like a plan," Kate says, rising from the table.

"Taylor will accompany you," Christian says, and it's a given—not up for discussion.

"We don't need babysitting," Kate retorts bluntly, direct as ever.

I put my hand on Kate's arm. "Kate, Taylor should come."

She frowns, then shrugs, and for once in her life holds her tongue.

I smile timidly at Christian. His expression remains impassive. Oh, I hope he's not mad at Kate.

Elliot frowns. "I need to pick up a battery for my watch in town." He glances quickly at Kate, and I spot his slight blush. She doesn't notice because she is pointedly ignoring him.

"Take the Audi, Elliot. When you come back we can go fishing," Christian says.

"Yeah," Elliot mutters, but he seems distracted. "Good plan."

"IN HERE." GRABBING MY hand, Mia hauls me into a designer boutique that's all pink silk and faux-French distressed rustic furniture. Kate follows us while Taylor waits outside, sheltering under the awning from the rain. Aretha is belting out "Say a Little Prayer" over the store's hi-fi system. I love this song. I should put it on Christian's iPod.

"This will look wonderful on you, Ana." Mia holds up a scrap of silver material. "Here, try it on."

"Um . . . it's a bit short."

"You'll look fantastic in it. Christian will love it."

"You think?"

Mia beams at me. "Ana, you have legs to die for, and if we go clubbing tonight"—she smiles, sensing an easy kill—"you'll look hot for your husband."

I blink at her, slightly shocked. We're going *clubbing*? I don't do clubbing.

Kate laughs at my expression. She seems more relaxed now that she's away from Elliot. "We should throw some shapes this evening," she says.

"Go try it on," Mia orders, and reluctantly I head for the changing room.

WHILE I WAIT FOR Kate and Mia to emerge from the dressing room, I stroll to the shop window and look out, unseeing, across the main street. The soul compilation continues: Dionne Warwick is singing "Walk on By." Another great song—one of my mother's favorites. I glance down at The Dress in my hand. *Dress* is perhaps an overstatement. It's backless and very short, but Mia has declared it a winner, perfect for dancing the night away. Apparently, I need shoes, too, and a large chunky necklace, which we'll source next. Rolling my eyes, I reflect once more on how lucky I am to have Caroline Acton, my own personal shopper.

Through the boutique window I'm distracted by the sight of Elliot. He has appeared on the other side of the leafy main street, climbing out of a large Audi. He dives into a store as if to duck out of the rain. Looks like a jewelry store . . . maybe he's looking for that watch battery. He emerges a few minutes later and not alone—with a woman.

Fuck! He's talking to Gia! *What the hell is she doing here?*

As I watch, they hug briefly and she holds her head back, laughing animatedly at something he says. He kisses her cheek and then runs to the waiting car. She turns and heads down the street, and I gape after her. *What was that about?* I turn anxiously toward the dressing rooms, but there's still no sign of Kate or Mia.

I glance at Taylor, where he's waiting outside the store. He catches my eye, then shrugs. He's witnessed Elliot's little encounter, too. I blush, embarrassed to have been caught snooping. Turning back, Mia and Kate emerge, both of them laughing. Kate looks at me quizzically.

"What's wrong, Ana?" she asks. "You gone cold on the dress? You look sensational in it."

"Um, no."

"Are you okay?" Kate's eyes widen.

"I'm fine. Shall we pay?" I head to the cashier, joining Mia, who has chosen two skirts.

"Good afternoon, ma'am." The young sales assistant—who has more gloss coating her lips than I have ever seen in one place— smiles at me. "That'll be eight hundred and fifty dollars."

What? For this scrap of material! I blink at her and meekly hand over my black Amex.

"Mrs. Grey," Ms. Lip Gloss purrs.

I follow Kate and Mia in a daze for the next two hours, warring with myself. Should I tell Kate? My subconscious firmly shakes her head. Yes, I should tell her. No, I shouldn't. It could just have been an innocent meeting. *Shit.* What should I do?

"WELL, DO YOU LIKE the shoes, Ana?" Mia has her fists on her hips.

"Um . . . yeah, sure."

I end up with a pair of unfeasibly high Manolo Blahniks with straps that look like they are made from mirrors. They match the dress perfectly and set Christian back just over a thousand dollars. I'm luckier with the long silver chain that Kate insists I buy; it's a bargain at eighty-four dollars.

"Getting used to having money?" Kate asks, not unkindly, as we walk back to the car. Mia has skipped ahead.

"You know this isn't me, Kate. I'm kind of uncomfortable about all this. But I'm reliably informed it's part of the package." I purse my lips at her, and she puts her arm around me.

"You'll get used to it, Ana," she says sympathetically. "You'll look great."

"Kate, how are you and Elliot getting along?" I ask.

Her wide blue eyes dart to mine.

Oh no.

She shakes her head. "I don't want to talk about it now." She nods toward Mia. "But things are—" She doesn't finish her sentence.

This is unlike my tenacious Kate. *Shit.* I knew something was up. Do I tell her what I saw? What did I see? Elliot and Miss Well-Groomed-Sexual-Predator talking, hugging, and that kiss on the cheek. Surely they are just old friends? No, I won't tell her. Not right now. I give her my I-completely-understand-and-will-respect-your-privacy nod. She reaches for my hand and gives it a grateful squeeze, and there it is—a swift glimpse of pain and hurt in her eyes that she quickly stifles with a blink. I feel a sudden surge of protectiveness for my dear friend. What the hell is Elliot Manwhore Grey playing at?

ONCE BACK AT THE house, Kate decides we deserve cocktails after our shopping extravaganza and whips up some strawberry daiquiris for us. We curl up on the sitting room couches in front of the blazing log fire.

"Elliot has just been a little distant lately," Kate murmurs, gazing into the flames. Kate and I finally have a moment to ourselves as Mia puts away her purchases.

"Oh?"

"And I think I'm in trouble for getting you into trouble."

"You heard about that?"

"Yes. Christian called Elliot; Elliot called me."

I roll my eyes. *Oh, Fifty, Fifty, Fifty.*

"I'm sorry. Christian is . . . protective. You haven't seen Elliot since Cocktailgate?"

"No."

"Oh."

"I really like him, Ana," she whispers. And for one dreadful minute I think she's going to cry. This is not like Kate. Does this mean the return of the pink pajamas? She turns to me.

"I've fallen in love with him. At first I thought it was just the great sex. But he's charming and kind and warm and funny. I could see us growing old together—you know . . . kids, grandkids—the works."

"Your happily ever after," I whisper.

She nods sadly.

"Maybe you should talk to him. Try to find some alone time here. Find out what's eating him."

Who's eating him, my subconscious snarls. I slap her down, shocked at the waywardness of my own thoughts.

"Perhaps you guys could go for a walk tomorrow morning?"

"We'll see."

"Kate, I hate seeing you like this."

She smiles weakly, and I lean over to hug her. I resolve not to mention Gia, though I might mention it to the manwhore himself. How can he mess with my friend's affections like this?

Mia returns, and we move on to safer territory.

THE FIRE HISSES AND spits sparks onto the hearth as I feed it the last log. We're almost out of wood. Even though it's summer, the fire is very welcome on this wet day.

"Mia, do you know where the wood for the fire is kept?" I ask as she sips her daiquiri.

"I think it's in the garage."

"I'll go find some. It'll give me an opportunity to explore."

The rain has eased off when I venture outside and head to the three-car garage adjoining the house. The side door is unlocked and I enter, switching on the light to fight the gloom. The fluorescent strips ping noisily to life.

There's a car in the garage, and I realize it's the Audi I saw Elliot in this afternoon. There are also two snowmobiles. But what really grabs my attention are the two trail bikes, both 125cc.

Memories of Ethan bravely endeavoring to teach me how to ride last summer flash through my mind. Unconsciously, I rub my arm where I badly bruised it in a fall.

"You ride?" Elliot asks from behind me.

I whirl around. "You're back."

"It would appear so." He grins, and I realize that Christian might say the same thing to me—but without the huge, heart-melting grin. "Well?" he asks.

Manwhore! "Sort of."

"Do you want a go?"

I snort. "Um, no . . . I don't think Christian would be very happy if I did."

"Christian's not here." Elliot smirks—*oh, it's a family trait*—and waves his arm to indicate we're alone. He strolls toward the nearest bike and swings a long denim-clad leg over the saddle, sitting astride and grabbing the handlebars.

"Christian has, um . . . issues about my safety. I shouldn't."

"You always do what he says?" Elliot has a wicked sparkle in his baby-blue eyes, and I see a glimmer of the bad boy . . . the bad boy Kate has fallen in love with. The bad boy from Detroit.

"No." I arch an admonishing brow at him. "But I'm trying to put that right. He has enough to worry about without adding me to the mix. Is he back?"

"I don't know."

"You didn't go fishing?"

Elliot shakes his head. "I had some business to deal with in town."

Business! Holy shit—groomed blonde business! I inhale sharply and gape at him.

"If you don't want to ride, what are you doing in the garage?" Elliot is intrigued.

"I'm looking for wood for the fire."

"There you are. Oh, Elliot—you're back." Kate interrupts us.

"Hey, baby." He smiles broadly.

"Catch anything?"

I scrutinize Elliot's reaction. "No. I had a few things to take care of in town." And for one brief moment, I see a flash of uncertainty cross his face.

Oh shit.

"I came out to see what was keeping Ana." Kate looks at us, confused.

"We were just shooting the breeze," Elliot says, and the tension crackles between them.

We all pause as we hear a car pull up outside. *Oh! Christian's back. Thank heavens.* The garage door opener whirs loudly into action, startling us all, and the door slowly lifts to reveal Christian and Ethan unloading a black flatbed truck. Christian stops when he sees us standing in the garage.

"Garage band?" he asks sardonically as he wanders in, heading straight for me.

I grin. I am relieved to see him. Beneath his wading jacket, he's wearing the coveralls I sold him at Clayton's.

"Hi," he says, looking quizzically at me and ignoring both Kate and Elliot.

"Hi. Nice coveralls."

"Lots of pockets. Very handy for fishing." His voice is soft and seductive, for my ears only, and when he gazes down at me, his expression is hot.

I flush, and he smiles a huge, no-holds-barred, all-for-me smile.

"You're wet," I murmur.

"It was raining. What are you guys doing in the garage?" Finally he acknowledges that we are not alone.

"Ana came to fetch some wood." Elliot arches an eyebrow. Somehow he manages to make that sentence sound smutty. "I tried to tempt her to take a ride." He is master of the double entendre.

Christian's face falls, and my heart stills.

"She said no. That you wouldn't like it," Elliot says kindly—and innuendo-free.

Christian's gray gaze swings back to me. "Did she, now?" he murmurs.

"Listen, I'm all for standing around discussing what Ana did next, but shall we go back inside?" Kate snaps. She stoops down, snatches up two logs, and turns on her heel, stomping toward the door. Oh shit. Kate is mad—but I know it's not at me. Elliot sighs and, without a word, follows her out. I gaze after them, but Christian distracts me.

"You can ride a motorcycle?" he asks, his voice laced with disbelief.

"Not very well. Ethan taught me."

His eyes frost immediately. "You made the right decision," he says, his voice much cooler. "The ground's very hard at the moment, and the rain's made it treacherous and slippery."

"Where do you want the fishing gear?" Ethan calls from outside.

"Leave it, Ethan—Taylor will take care of it."

"What about the fish?" Ethan continues, his voice vaguely taunting.

"You caught a fish?" I ask, surprised.

"Not me. Kavanagh did." And Christian pouts . . . prettily.

I burst out laughing.

"Mrs. Bentley will deal with that," he calls back. Ethan grins and heads into the house.

"Am I amusing you, Mrs. Grey?"

"Very much so. You're wet . . . Let me run you a bath."

"As long as you join me." He leans down and kisses me.

I FILL THE LARGE egg-shaped tub in the en suite bathroom and pour in some expensive bath oil, which starts to foam immediately. The aroma is heavenly . . . jasmine, I think. Back in the bedroom, I start to hang The Dress while the bath fills.

"Did you have a good time?" Christian asks as he enters the room. He's just in a T-shirt and sweatpants, his feet bare. He closes the door behind him.

"Yes," I murmur, drinking him in. I have missed him. Ridiculous—it's only been what, a few hours?

He cocks his head to one side and gazes at me. "What is it?"

"I was thinking how much I've missed you."

"You sound like you have it bad, Mrs. Grey."

"I have, Mr. Grey."

He strolls toward me until he's standing in front of me. "What did you buy?" he whispers, and I know it's to change the topic of conversation.

"A dress, some shoes, a necklace. I spent a great deal of your money." I glance up at him guiltily.

He's amused. "Good," he murmurs and tucks a stray lock of hair behind my ear. "And for the billionth time, our money." He tugs my chin, releasing my lip from my teeth, and runs his index finger down the front of my T-shirt, down my sternum, between my breasts, down my stomach, and over my belly to the hem.

"You won't be needing this in the bath," he whispers, and gripping the hem of my T-shirt in both hands slowly pulls it up. "Lift your arms."

I comply, not taking my eyes off his, and he drops my T-shirt on the floor.

"I thought we were just having a bath." My pulse quickens.

"I want to make you good and dirty first. I've missed you, too." He leans down and kisses me.

"SHIT, THE WATER!" I struggle to sit up, all postorgasmic and dazed.

Christian doesn't release me.

"Christian, the bath!" I gaze down at him from my prone position across his chest.

He laughs. "Relax—it's a wet room." He rolls over and kisses me quickly. "I'll switch off the faucet."

He climbs gracefully off the bed and strolls into the bathroom. My eyes greedily follow him all the way. Hmm . . . my husband, naked and soon to be wet. I bound out of bed.

———   ———

WE SIT AT OPPOSITE ends of the bath, which is very full—so full that whenever we move, water laps over the side and splashes to the floor. It's very decadent. Even more decadent is Christian washing my feet, massaging the soles, pulling gently on my toes. He kisses each one and gently bites my little toe.

"Aaah!" I feel it—*there*, in my groin.

"Like that?" he breathes.

"Hmm," I mumble incoherently.

He starts massaging again. Oh, this feels good. I close my eyes.

"I saw Gia in town," I murmur.

"Really? I think she has a place here," he says dismissively. He's not interested in the slightest.

"She was with Elliot."

Christian stops massaging. That got his attention. When I open my eyes his head is inclined to one side, like he doesn't understand.

"What do you mean with Elliot?" he asks, perplexed rather than concerned.

I explain what I saw.

"Ana, they're just friends. I think Elliot is pretty stuck on Kate." He pauses, then adds more quietly, "In fact, I *know* he's pretty stuck on her." And he gives me his I-have-no-idea-why look.

"Kate is gorgeous." I bristle, championing my friend.

He snorts. "Still glad it was you who fell into my office." He kisses my big toe, releases my left foot, and picks up my right before beginning the massage process again. His fingers are so strong and supple, I relax again. I do not want to fight about Kate. I close my eyes and let his fingers work their magic on my feet.

I GAPE AT MYSELF in the full-length mirror, not recognizing the vixen that stares back at me. Kate has gone all out and played Barbie with me this evening, styling my hair and makeup. My hair is full and straight, my eyes ringed with kohl, my lips scarlet red. I look . . . hot. I'm all legs, especially in the high-heeled Manolos and my indecently short dress. I need Christian to approve, though I have a horrible feeling he won't like so much of my flesh exposed. In view of our *entente cordiale,* I decide I should ask him. I pick up my BlackBerry.

From: Anastasia Grey
Subject: Does My Butt Look Big in This?
Date: August 27 2011 18:53 MST
To: Christian Grey

Mr. Grey

I need your sartorial advice.

Yours

Mrs. G x

From: Christian Grey
Subject: Peachy
Date: August 27 2011 18:55 MST
To: Anastasia Grey

Mrs. Grey

I seriously doubt it.

But I will come and give your butt a thorough examination just to make sure.

Yours in anticipation

Mr. G x

Christian Grey,
CEO Grey Enterprises Holdings and Butt Inspectorate, Inc.

As I read his e-mail, the bedroom door opens, and Christian freezes on the threshold. His mouth pops open and his eyes widen.

Holy crap . . . this could go either way.

"Well?" I whisper.

"Ana, you look . . . Wow."

"You like it?"

"Yes, I guess so." He's a little hoarse. Slowly he steps into the room and closes the door. He's wearing black jeans and a white shirt, but with a black jacket. He looks divine. He stalks slowly toward me, but as soon as he reaches me, he puts his hands on my shoulders and turns me around to face the full-length mirror, while he stands behind me. My gaze finds his in the glass, then he glances down, fascinated by my naked back. His finger glides down my spine and reaches the edge of my dress at the small of my back, where pale flesh meets silver cloth.

"This is very revealing," he murmurs.

His hand skims lower, over my backside and down to my naked thigh. He pauses, gray eyes burning intently into blue. Then slowly he trails his fingers back up to the hem of my skirt.

Watching his long fingers move lightly, teasingly across my skin, feeling the tingles they leave in their wake, my mouth forms a perfect O.

"It's not far from here." He touches the hem, then moves his fingers higher. "To here," he whispers. I gasp as his fingers stroke my sex, moving tantalizingly over my panties, feeling me, teasing me.

"And your point is?" I whisper.

"My point is . . . it's not far from here"—his fingers glide over my panties, then one is inside, against my soft dampened flesh—"to here. And then . . . to here." He slips a finger inside me.

I gasp and make a soft mewling sound.

"This is mine," he murmurs in my ear. Closing his eyes, he moves his finger slowly in and out of me. "I don't want anyone else to see this."

My breath stutters, my panting matching the rhythm of his finger. Watching him in the mirror, doing this . . . it's beyond erotic.

"So be a good girl and don't bend down, and you should be fine."

"You approve?" I whisper.

"No, but I'm not going to stop you from wearing it. You look stunning, Anastasia." Abruptly he withdraws his finger, leaving me wanting more, and he moves around to face me. He places the tip of his invading finger on my lower lip. Instinctively, I pucker my lips and kiss it, and I'm rewarded with a wicked grin. He puts his finger in his mouth and his expression informs me that I taste good . . . real good. I flush. Will it always shock me when he does that?

He grasps my hand.

"Come," he orders softly. I want to retort that I was about to, but in light of what happened in the playroom yesterday, I decide against it.

WE ARE WAITING FOR dessert in a plush, exclusive restaurant in town. It's been a lively evening so far, and Mia is determined it should continue and that we must go clubbing. Right now she's sitting silently for once, hanging on Ethan's every word as he and Christian talk. Mia is obviously infatuated with Ethan, and Ethan is . . . well, it's difficult to tell. I don't know if they are just friends or if there's something more.

Christian seems at ease. He's been talking animatedly with Ethan. They obviously bonded over the fly-fishing. They're talking about psychology, mainly. Ironically, Christian sounds the more knowledgeable. I snort softly as I half listen to their conversation, sadly acknowledging that his expertise is the result of his experience with so many shrinks.

You're the best therapy. His words, whispered while we were making love once, echo in my head. Am I? *Oh, Christian, I hope so.*

I glance over at Kate. She looks beautiful, but then she always does. She and Elliot are less lively. He seems nervous, his jokes a little too loud and his laugh a little off. Have they had a fight? What's eating him? Is it that woman? My heart sinks at the thought that he might hurt my best friend. I glance at the entrance, half expecting to see Gia calmly saunter her well-groomed ass across the restaurant to us. My mind is playing tricks, I suspect it's the amount of alcohol I've had. My head is beginning to ache.

Abruptly, Elliot startles us all by standing and pulling his chair back so it scrapes across the tile floor. All eyes turn to him. He gazes down at Kate for one moment and then drops to one knee beside her.

Oh. My. God.

He reaches for her hand, and silence settles like a blanket over the entire restaurant as everyone stops eating, stops talking, stops walking, and stares.

"My beautiful Kate, I love you. Your grace, your beauty, and your fiery spirit have no equal, and you have captured my heart. Spend your life with me. Marry me."

Holy shit!

CHAPTER FOURTEEN

The attention of the entire restaurant is trained on Kate and Elliot, waiting with bated breath as one. The anticipation is unbearable. Silence stretches like a taut rubber band. The atmosphere is oppressive, apprehensive, and yet hopeful.

Kate stares blankly at Elliot as he gazes up at her, his eyes wide with longing—fear even. *Holy crap, Kate! Put him out of his misery. Please.* Jeez—he could have asked her privately.

A single tear trickles down her cheek, though she remains expressionless. Shit! Kate crying? Then she smiles, a slow disbelieving I've-found-Nirvana smile.

"Yes," she whispers, a breathy, sweet acceptance—not Kate-like at all. For one nanosecond there's a pause as the entire restaurant exhales a collective sigh of relief, and then the noise is deafening. Spontaneous applause, cheering, catcalls, whooping, and suddenly I have tears rolling down my face, smudging my Barbie-meets-Joan-Jett makeup.

Oblivious to the commotion around them, the two are locked in their own little world. From his pocket Elliot produces a small box, opens it, and presents it to Kate. A ring. And from what I can see, an exquisite ring, but I need a closer look. Is that what he was doing with Gia? Choosing a ring? *Shit!* Oh, I'm so glad I didn't tell Kate.

Kate looks from the ring to Elliot, then throws her arms around his neck. They kiss, remarkably chaste for them, and the crowd goes wild. Elliot stands and acknowledges the approbation with a surprisingly graceful bow and then, wearing a huge self-satisfied grin, sits back down. I can't take my eyes off them. Taking the ring out of its box, Elliot gently slides it onto Kate's finger, and they kiss once more.

Christian squeezes my hand. I didn't realize I'd been gripping his so tightly. I release him, a little embarrassed, and he shakes his hand, mouthing, "Ow."

"Sorry. Did you know about this?" I whisper.

Christian smiles, and I know that he did. He summons the waiter. "Two bottles of the Cristal please. The 2002 if you have it."

I smirk at him.

"What?" he asks.

"Because the 2002 is so much better than the 2003," I tease.

He laughs. "To the discerning palate, Anastasia."

"You have a very discerning palate, Mr. Grey, and singular tastes." I smile.

"That I do, Mrs. Grey." He leans in close. "You taste best," he whispers, and he kisses a certain spot behind my ear, sending little shivers down my spine. I blush scarlet and fondly remember his earlier demonstration of the quite literal shortcomings of my dress.

Mia is the first up to hug Kate and Elliot, and we all take turns congratulating the happy couple. I clutch Kate in a fierce hug.

"See? He was just worried about his proposal," I whisper.

"Oh, Ana." She giggle-sobs.

"Kate, I am so happy for you. Congratulations."

Christian is behind me. He shakes Elliot's hand, then— surprising both Elliot and me—pulls him into a hug. I can only just catch what he says.

"Way to go, Lelliot," he murmurs. Elliot says nothing, for once stunned into silence, then warmly returns his brother's hug.

Lelliot?

"Thanks, Christian," Elliot chokes out.

Christian gives Kate a brief, if awkward, almost arm's-length hug. I know that Christian's attitude toward Kate is tolerant, at best, and ambivalent most of the time, so this is progress. Releasing her, he says, so quietly only she and I can hear, "I hope you are as happy in your marriage as I am in mine."

"Thank you, Christian. I hope so, too," she says graciously.

The waiter has returned with the champagne, which he proceeds to open with an understated flourish.

Christian holds his champagne flute aloft.

"To Kate and my dear brother, Elliot—congratulations."

We all sip, well, I glug. Hmm, Cristal tastes so good, and I'm reminded of the first time I drank it at Christian's club and later, our eventful elevator journey to the first floor.

Christian frowns at me. "What are you thinking about?" he whispers.

"The first time I drank this champagne."

His frown becomes more quizzical.

"We were at your club," I prompt.

He grins. "Oh yes. I remember." He winks at me.

"Elliot, have you set a date?" Mia pipes up.

Elliot gives his sister an exasperated stare. "I've only just asked Kate, so we'll get back to you on that, 'kay?"

"Oh, make it a Christmas wedding. That would be so romantic, and you'd have no trouble remembering your anniversary." Mia claps her hands.

"I'll take that under advisement." Elliot smirks at her.

"After the champagne, can we please go clubbing?" Mia turns and gives Christian her biggest, brown-eyed look.

"I think we should ask Elliot and Kate what they'd like to do."

As one, we turn expectantly to them. Elliot shrugs and Kate turns puce. Her carnal intent toward her fiancé is so clear I nearly spit four-hundred-dollar champagne all over the table.

ZAX IS THE MOST exclusive nightclub in Aspen—or so says Mia. Christian strolls to the front of the short line with his arm wrapped around my waist and is immediately granted access. I wonder briefly if he owns the place. I glance at my watch—eleven thirty in the evening, and I'm feeling fuzzy. The two glasses of champagne and several glasses of Pouilly-Fumé during our meal are starting to have an effect, and I'm grateful Christian has his arm around me.

"Mr. Grey, welcome back," says a very attractive, leggy blonde in black satin hot pants, matching sleeveless shirt, and a little red bow tie. She smiles broadly, revealing perfect all-American teeth between scarlet lips that match her bow tie. "Max will take your coat."

A young man dressed entirely in black, fortunately not satin, smiles as he offers to take my coat. His dark eyes are warm and inviting. I am the only one wearing a coat—Christian insisted I take Mia's trench coat to cover my behind—so Max has to deal only with me.

"Nice coat," he says, gazing at me intently.

Beside me Christian bristles and fixes Max with a back-off-now glare. He reddens and quickly hands Christian my coat check ticket.

"Let me show you to your table." Miss Satin Hot Pants flutters her eyelashes at my husband, flicks her long blonde hair, and sashays through the entryway. I tighten my grip around Christian, and he gazes down at me questioningly for a moment, then smirks as we follow Miss Satin Hot Pants into the bar.

The lighting is muted, the walls are black, and the furnishings deep red. There are booths flanking two sides of the walls and a large U-shaped bar in the middle. It's busy, given that we're here off-season, but not too crowded with the well-heeled of Aspen out for a good time on a Saturday night. The dress code is relaxed, and for the first time I feel a little over . . . um, underdressed. I'm not sure which. The floor and walls vibrate with the music pulsing from the dance floor behind the bar, and lights are whirling and flashing on and off. In my heady state, I idly think it's an epileptic's nightmare.

Satin Hot Pants leads us to a corner booth that's been roped off. It's near the bar with access to the dance floor. Clearly the best seats in the house.

"There'll be someone along to take your order shortly." She gives us her full megawatt smile and, with a final flutter of eyelashes at my husband, sashays back from where she came. Mia is already jigging from foot to foot, itching to get onto the dance floor, and Ethan takes pity on her.

"Champagne?" Christian asks as they head off, holding hands, toward the dance floor. Ethan gives him a thumbs-up and Mia nods enthusiastically.

Kate and Elliot sit back on the soft velvet seating, hand in hand. They look so happy, their features soft and radiant in the glow from the tea lights flickering in crystal holders on the low table. Christian gestures for me to sit, and I scoot in beside Kate. He takes a seat beside me and anxiously scans the room.

"Show me your ring." I raise my voice over the music. I will be hoarse by the time we leave. Kate beams at me and holds up her hand. The ring is exquisite, a single solitaire in a fine elaborate claw with tiny diamonds on either side. It has a retro Victorian look to it.

"It's beautiful."

She nods in delight and, reaching over, squeezes Elliot's thigh. He leans down and kisses her.

"Get a room," I call out.

Elliot grins.

A young woman with short dark hair and a mischievous smile, wearing the regulation black satin hot pants, comes to take our order.

"What do you want to drink?" Christian asks.

"You're not picking up the tab for this, too," Elliot grumbles.

"Don't start that shit, Elliot," Christian says mildly.

Despite the objections of Kate, Elliot, and Ethan, Christian has paid for the meal we just consumed. He simply waved them aside and would not hear of anyone else paying. I gaze at him lovingly. My Fifty Shades . . . always in control.

Elliot opens his mouth to say something but, wisely perhaps, closes it again.

"I'll have a beer," he says.

"Kate?" Christian asks.

"More champagne, please. The Cristal is delicious. But I'm sure Ethan would prefer a beer." She smiles sweetly—*yes, sweetly*—at Christian. She is incandescent with happiness. I feel it radiating off her, and it's a pleasure to bask in her joy.

"Ana?"

"Champagne, please."

"Bottle of Cristal, three Peronis, and a bottle of iced mineral water, six glasses," he says in his usual authoritative, no-nonsense manner.

It's kinda hot.

"Thank you, sir. Coming right up." Miss Hot Pants Number Two gives him a gracious smile, but he's spared the fluttering of eyelashes, though her cheeks redden a little.

I shake my head in resignation. *He's mine, girlfriend.*

"What?" he asks me.

"She didn't flutter her eyelashes at you." I smirk.

"Oh. Was she supposed to?" he asks, failing to hide his mirth.

"Women usually do." My tone is ironic.

He grins. "Mrs. Grey, are you jealous?"

"Not in the slightest." I pout at him. And I realize in that moment that I am beginning to tolerate women ogling my husband. Almost. Christian clasps my hand and kisses my knuckles.

"You have nothing to be jealous of, Mrs. Grey," he murmurs close to my ear, his breath tickling me.

"I know."

"Good."

The waitress returns, and moments later I'm sipping another glass of champagne.

"Here." Christian hands me a glass of water. "Drink this."

I frown at him and see, rather than hear, his sigh.

"Three glasses of white wine at dinner and two of champagne, after a strawberry daiquiri and two glasses of Frascati at lunchtime. Drink. Now, Ana."

How does he know about the cocktails this afternoon? I scowl at him. But actually he does have a point. Taking the glass of water, I down it in a most unladylike manner to register my protest at being told what to do . . . again. I wipe my hand across the back of my mouth.

"Good girl," he says, smirking. "You've vomited on me once already. I don't wish to experience that again in a hurry."

"I don't know what you're complaining about. You got to sleep with me."

He smiles and his eyes soften. "Yeah, I did."

Ethan and Mia are back.

"Ethan's had enough, for now. Come on, girls. Let's hit the floor. Strike a pose, throw some shapes, work off the calories from the chocolate mousse."

Kate stands immediately. "Coming?" she asks Elliot.

"Let me watch you," he says. And I have to look away quickly, blushing at the look he gives her. She grins as I stand.

"I'm going to burn some calories," I say, and leaning down I whisper in Christian's ear, "You can watch me."

"Don't bend over," he growls.

"Okay." I stand abruptly. Whoa! Head rush, and I clutch Christian's shoulder as the room shifts and tilts a little.

"Perhaps you should have some more water," Christian murmurs, a warning clear in his voice.

"I'm fine. These seats are low and my heels are high."

Kate takes my hand, and taking a deep breath I follow her and Mia, perfectly poised, onto the dance floor.

The music is pulsing, a techno beat with a thumping bass line. The dance floor isn't crowded, which means we have some space. The mix is eclectic—young and old alike dancing the night away. I have never been a good dancer. In fact, it's only since I've been with Christian that I dance at all. Kate hugs me.

"I'm so happy," she shouts over the music, and she starts to dance. Mia is doing what Mia does, grinning at the pair of us, throwing herself around. Jeez, she's taking up a lot of room on the dance floor. I glance back toward the table. Our men are watching us. I start to move. It's a pulsing rhythm. I close my eyes and surrender to it.

I open my eyes to find the dance floor filling up. Kate, Mia, and I are forced closer together. And to my surprise I find I'm actually enjoying myself. I begin to move a little more . . . bravely. Kate gives me two thumbs up, and I beam back at her.

I close my eyes. Why did I spend the first twenty years of my life not doing this? I chose reading over dancing. *Jane Austen didn't have great music to move to and Thomas Hardy . . . jeez, he'd have felt guilty as sin that he wasn't dancing with his first wife.* I giggle at the thought.

It's Christian. He has given me this confidence in my body and how I can move it.

Suddenly, there are two hands on my hips. I grin. Christian has joined me. I wiggle, and his hands move to my behind and squeeze, then back to my hips.

I open my eyes. And Mia is gaping at me in horror. *Shit . . . Am I that bad?* I reach down to hold Christian's hands. They're hairy. *Fuck!* They're not his. I whirl around, and towering over me is a blond giant with more teeth than is natural and a leering smile to showcase them.

"Get your hands off me!" I scream over the pounding music, apoplectic with rage.

"Come on, sugar, it's just some fun." He smiles, holding his apelike hands up, his blue eyes gleaming under the pulsing ultra-violet lights.

Before I know what I'm doing, I slap him hard across the face. *Ow! Shit . . . my hand.* It stings. "Get away from me!" I shout. He gazes down at me, cupping his red cheek. I thrust my unin-jured hand in front of his face, spreading my fingers to show him my rings.

"I'm married, you asshole!"

He shrugs rather arrogantly and gives me a halfhearted, apolo-getic smile.

I glance around frantically. Mia is at my right, glaring at Blond Giant. Kate is lost in the moment doing her thing. Christian is not at the table. *Oh, I hope he's gone to the restroom.* I step back into a front I know well. *Oh shit.* Christian puts his arm around my waist and moves me to his side.

"Keep your fucking hands off my wife," he says. He's not shout-ing, but somehow he can be heard over the music.

Holy shit!

"She can take care of herself," Blond Giant shouts. His hand moves from his cheek where I've slapped him, and Christian hits him. It's like I'm watching it in slow motion. A perfectly timed punch to the chin that moves at such speed, but with so little wasted energy, Blond Giant doesn't see it coming. He crumples to the floor like the scumbag he is.

Fuck.

"Christian, no!" I gasp in panic, standing in front of him to hold him back. Shit, he'll kill him. "I already hit him," I shout over the music. Christian doesn't look at me. He's glaring at my assailant with a malevolence I've not seen before flaring in his eyes. Well, maybe once before after Jack Hyde made a pass at me.

The other dancers move outward like a ripple in a pond, clearing space around us, keeping a safe distance. Blond Giant scrambles to his feet as Elliot joins us.

Oh no! Kate is with me, gaping at all of us. Elliot grasps Christian's arm as Ethan appears, too.

"Take it easy, okay? Didn't mean any harm." Blond Giant holds his hands up in defeat, beating a hasty retreat. Christian's eyes follow him off the dance floor. He does not look at me.

The song changes from the explicit lyrics of "Sexy Bitch" to a pulsing techno dance number with a woman singing with an impassioned voice. Elliot looks down at me, then across at Christian, and, releasing Christian, pulls Kate into a dance. I put my arms around Christian's neck until he finally makes eye contact, his eyes still blazing—primal and feral. A glimpse of a brawling adolescent. *Holy shit.*

He scrutinizes my face. "Are you okay?" he asks finally.

"Yes." I rub my palm, trying to dispel the sting, and bring my hands down to his chest. My hand is throbbing. I have never slapped anyone before. What possessed me? Touching me wasn't the worst crime against humanity. Was it?

Yet deep down I know why I hit him. It's because I instinctively knew how Christian would react to seeing some stranger pawing me. I knew he'd lose his precious self-control. And the thought that some stupid nobody could derail my husband, my love, well, it makes me mad. Really mad.

"Do you want to sit down?" Christian asks over the pulsing beat.

Oh, come back to me, please.

"No. Dance with me."

He looks at me impassively, saying nothing.

Touch me . . . the woman sings.

"Dance with me." He's still mad. "Dance. Christian, please." I take his hands. Christian glares after the guy, but I start to move against him, weaving myself around him.

The throng of dancers has circled us once more, although there's now a two-foot exclusion zone around us.

"You hit him?" Christian asks, standing stock-still. I take his fisted hands.

"Of course I did. I thought it was you, but his hands were hairier. Please dance with me."

As Christian gazes at me, the fire in his eyes slowly changes, evolves into something else, something darker, something hotter. Suddenly, he grabs my wrists and pulls me flush against him, pinning my hands behind my back.

"You wanna dance? Let's dance," he growls close to my ear, and as he rolls his hips around into me, I can do nothing but follow, his hands holding mine against my backside.

Oh . . . Christian can move, really move. He keeps me close, not letting me go, but his hands gradually relax on mine, freeing me. My hands creep around, up his arms, feeling his bunched muscles through his jacket, up to his shoulders. He presses me against him, and I follow his moves as he slowly, sensually dances with me in time to the pulsing beat of the club music.

The moment he grabs my hand and spins me first one way, then the other, I know he's back with me. I grin. He grins.

We dance together and it's liberating—fun. His anger forgotten, or suppressed, he whirls me around with consummate skill

in our small space on the dance floor, never letting go. He makes
me graceful, that's his skill. He makes me sexy, because that's
what he is. He makes me feel loved, because in spite of his fifty
shades, he has a wealth of love to give. Watching him now, enjoying himself . . . one could be forgiven for thinking he doesn't
have a care in the world. I know his love is clouded with issues of
overprotectiveness and control, but it doesn't make me love him
any less.

I am breathless when the song morphs to another.

"Can we sit?" I gasp.

"Sure." He leads me off the dance floor.

"You've made me rather hot and sweaty," I whisper as we
return to the table.

He pulls me into his arms. "I like you hot and sweaty. Though
I prefer to make you hot and sweaty in private," he purrs, and a
lascivious smile tugs at his lips.

As I sit, it's as if the incident on the dance floor never happened. I'm vaguely surprised we haven't been thrown out. I
glance around the bar. No one is looking at us, and I can't see
Blond Giant. Maybe he left, or maybe he's been thrown out. Kate
and Elliot are being indecent on the dance floor, Ethan and Mia
less so. I take another sip of champagne.

"Here." Christian puts another glass of water before me and
regards me intently. His expression is expectant—*drink it. Drink
it now.*

I do as I'm told. Besides, I'm thirsty.

He lifts a bottle of Peroni from the ice bucket on the table and
takes a long drink.

"What if there had been press here?" I ask.

Christian knows immediately that I'm referring to his knocking Blond Giant on his ass.

"I have expensive lawyers," he says coolly, all at once arrogance personified.

I frown at him. "But you're not above the law, Christian. I did
have the situation under control."

His eyes frost. "No one touches what's mine," he says with chilling finality, as if I'm missing the obvious.

Oh . . . I take another sip of my champagne. All of a sudden I feel overwhelmed. The music is loud, pounding, my head and feet are aching, and I feel woozy.

He grasps my hand. "Come, let's go. I want to get you home," he says. Kate and Elliot join us.

"You going?" Kate asks, and her voice is hopeful.

"Yes," Christian says.

"Good, we'll come with you."

AS WE WAIT AT the coat check for Christian to retrieve my trench coat, Kate quizzes me.

"What happened with that guy on the dance floor?"

"He was feeling me up."

"I opened my eyes and you'd hit him."

I shrug. "Well, I knew Christian would go thermonuclear, and that could potentially ruin your evening." I'm still processing how I feel about Christian's behavior. At the time, I was worried that it could have been worse.

"Our evening," she clarifies. "He is rather hot-headed, isn't he?" Kate adds dryly, staring at Christian as he collects my coat.

I snort and smile. "You could say that."

"I think you handle him well."

"Handle?" I frown. Do I *handle* Christian?

"Here." Christian holds my coat open for me so that I can put it on.

"WAKE UP, ANA." CHRISTIAN is shaking me gently. We've arrived back at the house. Reluctantly I open my eyes and stagger from the minivan. Kate and Elliot have disappeared, and Taylor is standing patiently beside the vehicle.

"Do I need to carry you?" Christian asks.

I shake my head.

"I'll fetch Miss Grey and Mr. Kavanagh," Taylor says.

Christian nods, then leads me to the front door. My feet are throbbing, and I stumble after him. At the front door he bends down, grasps my ankle, and gently pries off first one shoe, then the other. *Oh, the relief.* He straightens and gazes down at me, holding my Manolos.

"Better?" he asks, amused.

I nod.

"I had delightful visions of these around my ears," he murmurs, staring down wistfully at my shoes. He shakes his head and, taking my hand once more, leads me through the darkened house and up the stairs to our bedroom.

"You're wrecked, aren't you?" he says softly, staring down at me.

I nod. He starts to unbuckle the belt on my trench coat.

"I'll do it," I mutter, making a halfhearted attempt to brush him off.

"Let me."

I sigh. I had no idea I was this tired.

"It's the altitude. You're not used to it. And the drinking, of course." He smirks, divests me of my coat, and throws it on one of the bedroom chairs. Taking my hand, he leads me into the bathroom. *Why are we going in here?*

"Sit," he says.

I sit on the chair and close my eyes. I hear him as he messes around with bottles on the vanity unit. I am too tired to open my eyes to find out what he's doing. A moment later he tips my head back, and I open my eyes in surprise.

"Eyes closed," Christian says. *Holy crap*, he's holding a cotton ball! Gently, he wipes it over my right eye. I sit stunned as he methodically removes my makeup.

"Ah. There's the woman I married," he says after a few wipes.

"You don't like makeup?"

"I like it well enough, but I prefer what's beneath it." He kisses my forehead. "Here. Take these." He puts some Advil into my palm and hands me a glass of water.

I look and pout.

"Take them," he orders.

I roll my eyes, but do as I'm told.

"Good. Do you need a private moment?" he asks sardonically.

I snort. "So coy, Mr. Grey. Yes, I need to pee."

He laughs. "You expect me to leave?"

I giggle. "You want to stay?"

He cocks his head to one side, his expression amused.

"You are one kinky son of a bitch. Out. I don't want you to watch me pee. That's a step too far." I stand and wave him out of the bathroom.

WHEN I EMERGE FROM the bathroom, he's changed into his pajama bottoms. Hmm . . . Christian in PJs. Mesmerized, I gaze at his abdomen, his muscles, his happy trail. It's distracting. He strides over to me.

"Enjoying the view?" he asks wryly.

"Always."

"I think you're slightly drunk, Mrs. Grey."

"I think, for once, I have to agree with you, Mr. Grey."

"Let me help you out of what little there is of this dress. It really should come with a health warning." He turns me around and undoes the single button at the neck.

"You were so mad," I murmur.

"Yes. I was."

"At me?"

"No. Not at you." He kisses my shoulder. "For once."

I smile. *Not mad at me.* This is progress. "Makes a nice change."

"Yes. It does." He kisses my other shoulder, then tugs my dress down over my backside and onto the floor. He removes my panties at the same time, leaving me naked. Reaching up, he takes my hand.

"Step," he commands, and I step out of the dress, holding his hand for balance.

He stands and tosses my dress and panties onto the chair with Mia's trench coat.

"Arms up," he says softly. He slips his T-shirt over my head and pulls it down, covering me up. I am ready for bed.

He pulls me into his arms and kisses me, my minty breath mingling with his.

"As much as I'd love to bury myself in you, Mrs. Grey—you've had too much to drink, you're at nearly eight thousand feet, and you didn't sleep well last night. Come. Get into bed." He pulls back the duvet and I climb in. He covers me up and kisses my forehead once more.

"Close your eyes. When I come back to bed, I'll expect you to be asleep." It's a threat, a command . . . it's Christian.

"Don't go," I plead.

"I have some calls to make, Ana."

"It's Saturday. It's late. Please."

He runs his hands through his hair. "Ana, if I come to bed with you now, you won't get any rest. Sleep." He's adamant. I close my eyes and his lips brush my forehead once more.

"Good night, baby," he breathes.

Images of the day flash through my mind . . . Christian hauling me over his shoulder in the plane. His anxiety as to whether or not I'd like the house. Making love this afternoon. The bath. His reaction to my dress. Decking Blond Giant—my palm tingles at the memory. And then Christian putting me to bed.

Who would have thought? I grin widely, the word *progress* running around my brain as I drift.

CHAPTER FIFTEEN

I am too warm. Christian warm. His head is on my shoulder, and he's breathing softly on my neck while he sleeps, his legs threaded through mine, his arm around my waist. I linger on the edge of consciousness, aware that if I wake fully I'll wake him, too, and he doesn't sleep enough. Hazily my mind wanders through the events of yesterday evening. I drank too much—boy, did I drink too much. I'm amazed Christian let me. I smile as I remember him putting me to bed. That was sweet, real sweet, and unexpected. I conduct a quick mental inventory of how I'm feeling. Stomach? Fine. Head? Surprisingly, fine, but fuzzy. My palm is still red from last night. Sheesh. Idly I think about Christian's palms when he's spanked me. I squirm and he wakes.

"What's wrong?" Sleepy gray eyes search mine.

"Nothing. Good morning." I run the fingers of my uninjured hand through his hair.

"Mrs. Grey, you look lovely this morning," he says, kissing my cheek, and I light up from within.

"Thank you for taking care of me last night."

"I like taking care of you. It's what I want to do," he says quietly, but his eyes betray him as triumph flares in their gray depths. It's like he's won the World Series or the Super Bowl.

Oh, my Fifty.

"You make me feel cherished."

"That's because you are," he murmurs, and my heart clenches.

He clasps my hand and I wince. He releases me immediately, alarmed. "The punch?" he asks. His eyes frost as he scrutinizes mine, and his voice is laced with sudden anger.

"I slapped him. I didn't punch him."

"That fucker!"

I thought we'd dealt with this last night.

"I can't bear that he touched you."

"He didn't hurt me, he was just inappropriate. Christian, I'm okay. My hand's a little red, that's all. Surely you know what that's like?" I smirk, and his expression changes to one of amused surprise.

"Why, Mrs. Grey, I am very familiar with that." His lips twist in amusement. "I could reacquaint myself with that feeling this minute, should you so wish."

"Oh, stow your twitching palm, Mr. Grey." I stroke his face with my injured hand, my fingers caressing his sideburn. Gently I tug the little hairs. It distracts him, and he takes my hand and plants a tender kiss on my palm. Miraculously, the pain disappears.

"Why didn't you tell me this hurt last night?"

"Um . . . I didn't really feel it last night. It's okay now."

His eyes soften and his mouth twists. "How are you feeling?"

"Better than I deserve."

"That's quite a right arm you have there, Mrs. Grey."

"You'd do well to remember that, Mr. Grey."

"Oh, really?" He rolls suddenly so that he's fully on top of me, pressing me into the mattress, holding my wrists above my head. He gazes down at me.

"I'd fight you any day, Mrs. Grey. In fact, subduing you in bed is a fantasy of mine." He kisses my throat.

What?

"I thought you subdued me all the time." I gasp as he nibbles my earlobe.

"Hmm . . . but I'd like some resistance," he murmurs, his nose skirting my jaw.

Resistance? I still. He stops, releasing my hands, and leans up on his elbows.

"You want me to fight you? Here?" I whisper, trying to contain my surprise. Okay—my shock. He nods, his eyes hooded but wary as he gauges my reaction.

"Now?"

He shrugs, and I see the idea flit through his mind. He gives me his shy smile and nods again, slowly.

Oh my . . . He's tense, lying on top of me, and his growing erection is digging tantalizingly into my soft, willing flesh, distracting me. What's this about? Brawling? Fantasy? Will he hurt me? My inner goddess shakes her head—*Never.*

"Is this what you meant about coming to bed angry?"

He nods once more, his eyes still wary.

Hmm . . . my Fifty wants to rumble.

"Don't bite your lip," he warns.

Compliantly, I release my lip. "I think you have me at a disadvantage, Mr. Grey." I bat my lashes and squirm provocatively beneath him. This could be fun.

"Disadvantage?"

"Surely you've already got me where you want me?"

He smirks and presses his groin into mine once more.

"Good point well made, Mrs. Grey," he whispers and quickly kisses my lips. Abruptly he shifts and takes me with him, rolling over so I'm straddling him. I grab his hands, pinning them to the side of his head, and ignore the protesting ache from my hand. My hair falls in a chestnut veil around us, and I move my head so that the strands tickle his face. He jerks his face away but doesn't try to stop me.

"So, you want to play rough?" I ask, skimming my crotch over his.

His mouth opens and he inhales sharply.

"Yes." He hisses, and I release him.

"Wait." I reach over for the glass of water beside the bed. Christian must have left it here. It's cool and sparkling—too cool to have been sitting here for long—and I wonder when he came to bed.

As I take a long draft, Christian trails his fingers in small circles up my thighs, leaving tingling skin in their wake before he cups and squeezes my naked behind. Hmm.

Taking a leaf from his impressive repertoire, I lean forward and kiss him, pouring clear cool water into his mouth.

He drinks. "Very tasty, Mrs. Grey," he murmurs, sporting a boyish and playful grin.

After placing the glass back on the bedside table, I remove his hands from my backside and pin them by his head once more.

"So I'm supposed to be unwilling?" I smirk.

"Yes."

"I'm not much of an actress."

He grins. "Try."

I lean down and kiss him chastely. "Okay, I'll play," I whisper, trailing my teeth along his jaw, feeling his prickly stubble beneath my teeth and my tongue.

Christian makes a low, sexy sound in his throat and moves, tossing me onto the bed beside him. I cry out in surprise, then he's on top of me, and I start to struggle as he makes a grab for my hands. Roughly, I place my hands on his chest, pushing with all my might, trying to move him, while he endeavors to pry my legs apart with his knee.

I continue pushing at his chest—*Jeez, he's heavy*—but he doesn't flinch, doesn't freeze as he once might have. *He's enjoying this!* He attempts to grab my wrists, and finally captures one, despite my valiant attempts to twist it free. It's my sore hand, so I surrender it to him, but I grab his hair with my other hand and pull hard.

"Ah!" He yanks his head free and gazes down at me, his eyes wild and carnal.

"Savage," he whispers, his voice laced with salacious delight.

In response to this one whispered word, my libido explodes, and I stop acting. Again I struggle in vain to wrest my hand out of his hold. At the same time I try to hook my ankles together and attempt to buck him off me. He's too heavy. *Gah!* It's frustrating and hot.

With a groan, Christian captures my other hand. He holds both my wrists in his left hand, and his right travels leisurely—

insolently, almost—down my body, fondling and feeling as it goes, tweaking my nipple on the way.

I yelp in response, pleasure spiking short, sharp, and hot from my nipple to my groin. I make another fruitless attempt to buck him off, but he's just too *on me*.

When he tries to kiss me I jerk my head to the side so he can't. Promptly his insolent hand moves from the hem of my T-shirt up to my chin, holding me in place as he runs his teeth along my jaw, mirroring what I did to him earlier.

"Oh, baby, fight me," he murmurs.

I twist and writhe, trying to free myself from his merciless hold, but it's hopeless. He's much stronger than me. He's gently biting at my lower lip as his tongue tries to invade my mouth. And I realize I don't want to resist him. I want him—now, like I always do. I stop fighting and fervently return his kiss. I don't care that I haven't brushed my teeth. I don't care that we're supposed to be playing some game. Desire, hot and hard, surges through my bloodstream, and I'm lost. Unhooking my ankles, I wrap my legs around his hips and use my heels to push his pajamas down over his behind.

"Ana," he breathes, and he kisses me everywhere. And we're no longer wrestling, but all hands and tongues and touch and taste, quick and urgent.

"Skin," he murmurs hoarsely, his breathing labored. He drags me up and tugs off my T-shirt in one swift move.

"You," I whisper while I'm upright, because it's all I can think of to say. I seize the front of his pajamas and yank them down, freeing his erection. I grab and squeeze him. He's hard. The air whistles through his teeth as he inhales sharply, and I revel in his response.

"Fuck," he murmurs. He leans back, lifting my thighs, tipping me down onto the bed as I pull and squeeze him tightly, running my hand up and down him. Feeling a bead of moisture on his tip, I swirl it around with my thumb. As he lowers me to the mattress, I slip my thumb in my mouth to taste him while his hands travel up my body, caressing my hips, my stomach, my breasts.

"Taste good?" he asks as he hovers over me, eyes blazing.

"Yes. Here." I push my thumb into his mouth, and he sucks and bites the pad. I groan, grasp his head, and pull him down to me so I can kiss him. Wrapping my legs around him, I push his pajamas off his legs with my feet, then cradle him with my legs around his waist. His lips trail from across my jaw to my chin, nipping softly.

"You're so beautiful." He dips his head lower to the base of my throat. "Such beautiful skin." His breath is soft as his lips glide down to my breasts.

What? I am panting, confused—wanting, now waiting. I thought this was going to be quick.

"Christian." I hear the quiet plea in my voice and reach down, fisting my hands in his hair.

"Hush," he whispers and circles my nipple with his tongue before pulling it into his mouth and tugging hard.

"Ah!" I moan and squirm, tilting my pelvis up to tempt him. He grins against my skin and turns his attention to my other breast.

"Impatient, Mrs. Grey?" He then sucks hard on my nipple. I tug his hair. He groans and peers up. "I'll restrain you," he warns.

"Take me," I beg.

"All in good time," he murmurs against my skin. His hand travels down at an infuriatingly slow speed to my hip as he worships my nipple with his mouth. I moan loudly, my breath short and shallow, and I try once more to entice him into me, rocking against him. He's thick and heavy and close, but he's taking his own sweet leisurely time with me.

Fuck this. I struggle and twist, determined to buck him off me again.

"What the—"

Grabbing my hands, Christian pins them down on the bed, my arms spread wide, and rests his full body weight on me, completely subduing me. I am breathless, wild.

"You wanted resistance," I say, panting. He rears up over me and gazes down, his hands still locked around my wrists. I place my heels under his behind and push. He doesn't move. *Gah!*

"You don't want to play nice?" he asks, astonished, his eyes alight with excitement.

"I just want you to make love to me, Christian." Could he be any more obtuse? First we're fighting and wrestling, then he's all tender and sweet. It's confusing. I'm in bed with Mr. Mercurial.

"Please." I press my heels against his backside once more. Burning gray eyes search mine. *Oh, what is he thinking?* He looks momentarily bewildered and confused. He releases my hands and sits back on his heels, pulling me into his lap.

"Okay, Mrs. Grey, we'll do this your way." He lifts me up and slowly lowers me onto him so I'm straddling him.

"Ah!" This is it. This is what I want. This is what I need. Curling my arms around his neck, I twist my fingers in his hair, glorying in the feeling of him inside me. I start to move. Taking control, taking him at my pace, at my speed. He moans, and his lips find mine, and we're lost.

I TRAIL MY FINGERS through the hair on Christian's chest. He lies on his back, still and quiet beside me as we both catch our breath. His hand thrums rhythmically down my back.

"You're quiet," I whisper and kiss his shoulder. He turns and looks at me, his expression giving nothing away. "That was fun." *Shit, is something wrong?*

"You confound me, Ana."

"Confound you?"

He shifts so that we're face to face. "Yes. You. Calling the shots. It's . . . different."

"Good different or bad different?" I trail a finger over his lips. His brow furrows, as if he doesn't quite understand the question. Absentmindedly, he kisses my finger.

"Good different," he says, but he doesn't sound convinced.

"You've never indulged this little fantasy before?" I blush as I say it. Do I really want to know any more about my husband's colorful . . . um, kaleidoscopic sex life before me? My subconscious eyes me warily over her tortoiseshell half-moon specs. *Do you really want to go there?*

"No, Anastasia. You can touch me." It's a simple explanation that speaks volumes. Of course, the fifteen couldn't.

"Mrs. Robinson could touch you." I murmur the words before my brain registers what I've said. *Shit. Why did I mention her?*

He stills. His eyes widen with his oh-no-where's-she-going-with-this expression. "That was different," he whispers.

Suddenly I want to know. "Good different or bad different?"

He gazes at me. Doubt and possibly pain flit across his face, and fleetingly he looks like a man drowning.

"Bad, I think." His words are barely audible.

Holy shit!

"I thought you liked it."

"I did. At the time."

"Not now?"

He gazes at me, eyes wide, then slowly shakes his head.

Oh my . . . "Oh, Christian." I'm overwhelmed by the feelings that swamp me. My lost boy. I launch myself at him and kiss his face, his throat, his chest, his little round scars. He groans, pulls me to him, and kisses me passionately. And very slowly, and tenderly, at his pace, he makes love to me once more.

"ANA TYSON. PUNCHING ABOVE your weight!" Ethan applauds as I head into the kitchen for breakfast. He's sitting with Mia and Kate at the breakfast bar while Mrs. Bentley cooks waffles. Christian is nowhere to be seen.

"Good morning, Mrs. Grey." Mrs. Bentley smiles. "What would you like for breakfast?"

"Good morning. Whatever's going, thank you. Where's Christian?"

"Outside." Kate gestures with her head toward the backyard. I wander over to the window that looks out over the yard and the mountains beyond. It's a clear, powder-blue summer day, and my beautiful husband is about twenty feet away in deep discussion with some guy.

"That's Mr. Bentley he's talking to," calls Mia from the break-fast bar. I turn to look at her, distracted by her sulky tone. She looks venomously at Ethan. *Oh dear.* I wonder once more what's going on between them. Frowning, I turn my attention back to my husband and Mr. Bentley.

Mrs. Bentley's husband is fair-haired, dark eyed, and wiry, dressed in work pants and an Aspen Fire Department T-shirt. Christian is dressed in his black jeans and T-shirt. As the two men amble across the lawn toward the house, lost in their conversa-tion, Christian casually bends to pick up what looks like a bamboo cane that must have been blown over or discarded in the flower bed. Pausing, Christian absentmindedly holds out the cane at arm's length as if weighing it carefully and swipes it through the air, just once.

Oh . . .

Mr. Bentley appears to see nothing odd in his behavior. They continue their discussion, nearer to the house this time, then pause once more, and Christian repeats the gesture. The tip of the cane hits the ground. Glancing up, Christian sees me stand-ing at the window. Suddenly I feel as if I'm spying on him. He stops. I give him an embarrassed wave, then turn and walk back to the breakfast bar.

"What were you doing?" asks Kate.

"Just watching Christian."

"You have got it bad." She snorts.

"And you don't, oh soon-to-be sister-in-law?" I reply, grinning and trying to bury the disquieting visual of Christian wielding a cane. I am startled when Kate leaps up and hugs me.

"Sister!" she exclaims, and it's hard not to be swept up in her joy.

"Hey, sleepyhead." Christian wakes me. "We're about to land. Buckle up."

I fumble sleepily for my seat belt, but Christian fastens it for me. He kisses my forehead before settling back into his seat. I lean my head on his shoulder again and close my eyes.

An impossibly long hike and a picnic lunch on top of a spectacular mountain have exhausted me. The rest of our party is quiet, too—even Mia. She looks despondent, as she has all day. I wonder how her campaign with Ethan is going. I don't even know where they slept last night. My eyes catch hers, and I give a small are-you-okay smile. She gives me a brief sad smile in return and goes back to her book. I peek up at Christian through my lashes. He's working on a contract or something, reading it through and annotating the margins. But he seems relaxed. Elliot is snoring softly beside Kate.

I have yet to corner Elliot and quiz him about Gia, but it's been impossible to pry him away from Kate. Christian isn't interested enough to ask, which is irritating, but I haven't pressed him. We've been enjoying ourselves too much. Elliot rests his hand possessively on Kate's knee. She looks radiant, and to think that only yesterday afternoon she was so unsure of him. What did Christian call him? Lelliot. Perhaps that's a family nickname? It was sweet, better than manwhore. Abruptly, Elliot opens his eyes and gazes straight at me. I blush, caught staring.

He grins. "I sure love your blush, Ana," he teases, stretching. Kate gives me her self-satisfied, cat-ate-the-canary smile.

First Officer Beighley announces our approach to Sea-Tac, and Christian clasps my hand.

———

"How was your weekend, Mrs. Grey?" Christian asks once we're in the Audi heading back to Escala. Taylor and Ryan are up front.

"Good, thank you." I smile, feeling shy all of a sudden.

"We can go anytime. Take anyone you wish to take."

"We should take Ray. He'd like the fishing."

"That's a good idea."

"How was it for you?" I ask.

"Good," he says after a moment, surprised by my question, I think. "Real good."

"You seemed to relax."

He shrugs. "I knew you were safe."

I frown. "Christian, I'm safe most of the time. I've told you before, you'll keel over at forty if you keep up this level of anxiety. And I want to grow old and gray with you." I grasp his hand. He looks at me as if he can't comprehend what I'm saying. He gently kisses my knuckles and changes the subject.

"How's your hand?"

"It's better, thank you."

He smiles. "Very good, Mrs. Grey. You ready to face Gia again?"

Oh crap. I'd forgotten we were seeing her this evening to go over the final plans. I roll my eyes. "I might want to keep you out of the way, keep you safe." I smirk.

"Protecting me?" Christian is laughing at me.

"As ever, Mr. Grey. From all sexual predators," I whisper.

Christian is brushing his teeth when I crawl into bed. Tomorrow we go back to reality—back to work, the paparazzi, and to Jack in custody but with the possibility that he has an accomplice. *Hmm* . . . Christian was vague about that. Does he know? And if he did know, would he tell me? I sigh. Getting information out of Christian is like pulling teeth, and we've had such a lovely weekend. Do I want to ruin the feel-good moment by trying to drag the information out of him?

It's been a revelation to see him out of his normal environment, outside this apartment, relaxed and happy with his family. I wonder vaguely if it's because we're here in this apartment with all its memories and associations that he gets wound up. Maybe we should move.

I snort. *We are moving*—we're having a huge house refurbished on the coast. Gia's plans are complete and approved, and Elliot's team starts building next week. I chuckle as I recall Gia's shocked expression when I told her that I'd seen her in Aspen. Turns out it was nothing but coincidence. She'd camped out at her holiday place to work solely on our plans. For one awful moment I'd thought she'd had a hand in choosing the ring, but apparently not. But I still don't trust Gia. I want to hear the same story from Elliot. At least she kept her distance from Christian this time.

I look out at the night sky. I will miss this view. This panoramic vista . . . Seattle at our feet, so full of possibilities, yet so far removed. Maybe that's Christian's problem—he's been too isolated from real life for too long, thanks to his self-imposed exile. Yet with his family around him, he is less controlling, less anxious—freer, happier. I wonder what Flynn would make of all that. Holy crap! Maybe that's the answer. Maybe he needs his own family. I shake my head in denial—we're too young, too new to all this. Christian strides into the room, looking his usual gorgeous but pensive self.

"Everything okay?" I ask.

He nods distractedly as he climbs into bed.

"I'm not looking forward to going back to reality," I murmur.

"No?"

I shake my head and caress his lovely face. "I had a wonderful weekend. Thank you."

He smiles softly. "You're my reality, Ana," he murmurs and kisses me.

"Do you miss it?"

"Miss what?" he asks, perplexed.

"You know. The caning . . . and stuff," I whisper, embarrassed.

He stares at me, his gaze impassive. Then doubt crosses his face, his where-is-she-going-with-this look.

"No Anastasia, I don't." His voice is steady and quiet. He caresses my cheek. "Dr. Flynn said something to me when you left, something that's stayed with me. He said I couldn't be that way if you weren't so inclined. It was a revelation." He stops and frowns. "I didn't know any other way, Ana. Now I do. It's been educational."

"Me, educate you?" I scoff.

His eyes soften. "Do you miss it?" he asks.

Oh! "I don't want you to hurt me, but I like to play, Christian. You know that. If you wanted to do something . . ." I shrug, gazing at him.

"Something?"

"You know, with a flogger or your crop—" I stop, blushing.

He raises his brow, surprised. "Well . . . we'll see. Right now, I'd like some good old-fashioned vanilla." His thumb skirts my bottom lip, and he kisses me once more.

From: Anastasia Grey
Subject: Good Morning
Date: August 29 2011 09:14
To: Christian Grey

Mr. Grey

I just wanted to tell you that I love you.

That is all.

Yours Always

A x

Anastasia Grey
Editor, SIP

From: Christian Grey
Subject: Banishing Monday Blues

Date: August 29 2011 09:18
To: Anastasia Grey

Mrs. Grey

What gratifying words to hear from one's wife (errant or not)
on a Monday morning.

Let me assure you that I feel exactly the same way.

Sorry about the dinner this evening. I hope it won't be too
tedious for you.

x

Christian Grey,
CEO, Grey Enterprises Holdings, Inc.

Oh yes. The American Shipbuilding Association dinner. I roll
my eyes . . . More stuffed shirts. Christian really does take me to
the most fascinating functions.

From: Anastasia Grey
Subject: Ships That Pass in the Night
Date: August 29 2011 09:26
To: Christian Grey

Dear Mr. Grey

I am sure you can think of a way to spice up the dinner . . .

Yours in anticipation

Mrs. G. x

Anastasia (nonerrant) Grey
Editor, SIP

From: Christian Grey
Subject: Variety Is the Spice of Life
Date: August 29 2011 09:35
To: Anastasia Grey

Mrs. Grey

I have a few ideas . . .

x

Christian Grey
CEO, Grey Enterprises Holdings, Inc. Now Impatient for
the ASA Dinner, Inc.

All the muscles in my belly clench. Hmm . . . I wonder what he'll
dream up. Hannah knocks on the door, interrupting my reverie.

"Ready to go through your schedule for this week, Ana?"

"Sure. Sit." I smile, recovering my equilibrium, and minimize
my e-mail program. "I've had to move a couple of appointments.
Mr. Fox next week and Dr.—"

My phone rings, interrupting her. It's Roach. He asks me up
to his office.

"Can we pick this up in twenty minutes?"

"Of course."

From: Christian Grey
Subject: Last Night

Date: August 30 2011 09:24
To: Anastasia Grey

Was . . . fun.

Who would have thought the ASA annual dinner could be so stimulating?

As ever, you never disappoint, Mrs. Grey.

I love you.

x

Christian Grey
In awe, CEO, Grey Enterprises Holdings, Inc.

From: Anastasia Grey
Subject: I Love a Good Ball Game . . .
Date: August 30 2011 09:33
To: Christian Grey

Dear Mr. Grey

I have missed the silver balls.

You never disappoint.

That is all.

Mrs. G. x

Anastasia Grey
Editor, SIP

Hannah taps on my door, interrupting my erotic thoughts of the previous evening. *Christian's hands . . . his mouth.*

"Come in."

"Ana, Mr. Roach's PA just called. He'd like you to attend a meeting this morning. It means I have to move some of your appointments again. Is that okay?"

His tongue.

"Sure. Yes," I mutter, trying to halt my wayward thoughts. She grins and ducks out of my office . . . leaving me with my delicious memory of last night.

From: Christian Grey
Subject: Hyde
Date: September 1 2011 15:24
To: Anastasia Grey

Anastasia

For your information, Hyde has been refused bail and remanded in custody. He's charged with attempted kidnapping and arson. As yet no date has been set for the trial.

Christian Grey
CEO, Grey Enterprises Holdings, Inc.

From: Anastasia Grey
Subject: Hyde
Date: September 1 2011 15:53
To: Christian Grey

That's good news.

Does this mean you'll lighten up on security?

I really don't see eye to eye with Prescott.

Ana x

Anastasia Grey
Editor, SIP

From: Christian Grey
Subject: Hyde
Date: September 1 2011 15:59
To: Anastasia Grey

No. Security will remain in place. No arguments.

What's wrong with Prescott? If you don't like her, we'll replace her.

Christian Grey
CEO, Grey Enterprises Holdings, Inc.

I scowl at his high-handed e-mail. Prescott isn't that bad.

From: Anastasia Grey
Subject: Keep Your Hair On!
Date: September 1 2011 16:03
To: Christian Grey

I was just asking (rolls eyes). And I'll think about Prescott.

Stow that twitchy palm!

Ana x

Anastasia Grey
Editor, SIP

From: Christian Grey
Subject: Don't Tempt Me
Date: September 1 2011 16:11
To: Anastasia Grey

I can assure you, Mrs. Grey, that my hair is very firmly attached—has this not been demonstrated often enough by your good self?

My palm, however, is twitching.

I might do something about that tonight.

x

Christian Grey
Not bald yet CEO, Grey Enterprises Holdings, Inc.

From: Anastasia Grey
Subject: Squirm
Date: September 1 2011 16:20
To: Christian Grey

Promises, promises . . .

Now stop pestering me. I am trying to work; I have an impromptu meeting with an author. Will try not to be distracted by thoughts of you during the meeting.

A x

Anastasia Grey
Editor, SIP

From: Anastasia Grey
Subject: Sailing & Soaring & Spanking
Date: September 5 2011 09:18
To: Christian Grey

Husband

You sure know how to show a girl a good time.

I shall of course be expecting this kind of treatment every weekend.

You are spoiling me. I love it.

Your wife

xox

Anastasia Grey
Editor, SIP

From: Christian Grey
Subject: My Life's Mission . . .
Date: September 5 2011 09:25
To: Anastasia Grey

Is to spoil you, Mrs. Grey.

And keep you safe because I love you.

Christian Grey
Smitten CEO, Grey Enterprises Holdings, Inc.

Oh my. Could he be any more romantic?

From: Anastasia Grey
Subject: My Life's Mission . . .
Date: September 5 2011 09:33
To: Christian Grey

Is to let you—because I love you, too.

Now stop being so sappy.

You are making me cry.

Anastasia Grey
Equally Smitten Editor, SIP

The following day, I gaze at the calendar on my desk. Only five days until September 10—my birthday. I know we are driving out to the house to see how Elliot and his crew are progressing. Hmm . . . I wonder if Christian has any other plans? I smile at the thought. Hannah taps on my door.

"Come in."

Prescott is hovering outside. *Odd . . .*

"Hi, Ana," says Hannah. "There's a Leila Williams here to see you? She says it's personal."

"Leila Williams? I don't know a . . ." My mouth goes dry, and Hannah's eyes widen at my expression.

Leila? Fuck. What does she want?

CHAPTER SIXTEEN

D o you want me to send her away?" Hannah asks, alarmed at my expression.

"Um, no. Where is she?"

"In Reception. She's not alone. She's accompanied by another young woman."

Oh!

"And Miss Prescott wants to talk to you," Hannah adds.

I'm sure she does. "Send her in."

Hannah stands aside, and Prescott enters my office. She's on a mission, bristling with professional efficiency.

"Give me a moment, Hannah. Prescott, take a seat."

Hannah closes the door, leaving Prescott and me alone.

"Mrs. Grey, Leila Williams is on your proscribed list of visitors."

"What?" *I have a proscribed list?*

"On our watch list, ma'am. Taylor and Welch have been quite specific about not letting her come into contact with you."

I frown, not understanding. "Is she dangerous?"

"I can't say, ma'am."

"Why do I even know that she's here?"

Prescott swallows and for a moment looks awkward. "I was on a restroom break. She came in, spoke directly to Claire, and Claire called Hannah."

"Oh. I see." I realize that even Prescott has to pee, and I laugh. "Oh dear."

"Yes, ma'am." Prescott gives me an embarrassed grin, and it's the first time I've seen a chink in her armor. She has a lovely smile.

"I need to talk to Claire about protocol again," she says, her tone weary.

"Sure. Does Taylor know she's here?" I cross my fingers unconsciously, hoping she hasn't told Christian.

"I left a brief voice message for him."

Oh. "Then I have only a short time. I'd like to know what she wants."

Prescott gazes at me for a moment. "I must advise against it, ma'am."

"She's here to see me for a reason."

"I'm supposed to prevent that, ma'am." Her voice is soft but resigned.

"I really want to hear what she has to say." My tone is more forceful than I intend.

Prescott stifles her sigh. "I'd like to search them both before you do."

"Okay. Can you do that?"

"I'm here to protect you, Mrs. Grey, so yes, I can. I'd also like to stay with you while you talk."

"Okay." I'll grant her this concession. Besides, last time I met Leila, she was armed. "Go ahead."

Prescott rises.

"Hannah," I call.

Hannah opens the door too quickly. She must have been hovering outside.

"Can you check to see if the meeting room is free, please?"

"I already have, and it's good to go."

"Prescott, can you search them in there? Is it private enough?"

"Yes, ma'am."

"I'll be there in five minutes, then. Hannah, show Leila Williams and whomever she's with into the meeting room."

"Will do." Hannah looks anxiously from Prescott to me. "Shall I cancel your next meeting? It's at four, but it's across town."

"Yes," I murmur, distracted. Hannah nods and then leaves.

What the hell does Leila want? I don't think she's here to do me any harm. She didn't in the past when she had the opportunity. *Christian is going to go nuts.* My subconscious purses her lips, primly crosses her legs, and nods. I need to tell him that I am doing this. I type a quick e-mail, then pause, checking the time. I feel a momentary pang of regret. We've been getting along so well since Aspen. I press "send."

From: Anastasia Grey
Subject: Visitors
Date: September 6 2011 15:27
To: Christian Grey

Christian

Leila is here to see me. I will see her with Prescott.

I'll use my newly acquired slapping skills with my now-healed hand, should I need to.

Try, and I mean try, not to worry.

I am a big girl.

Will call once we've spoken.

A x

Anastasia Grey
Editor, SIP

Hurriedly, I hide my BlackBerry in my desk drawer. I stand, smoothing my gray pencil skirt over my hips, pinch my cheeks to give them some color, and undo the next button on my gray silk blouse. Okay, I'm ready. After taking a deep breath, I head out of my office to meet the infamous Leila, ignoring "Your Love Is King" humming gently from inside my desk.

Leila looks much better. More than better—she's very attractive. There's a rosy bloom to her cheeks, and her brown eyes are bright, her hair clean and shiny. She's dressed in a pale pink blouse and white pants. She stands as soon as I enter the meeting room, as does her friend—another dark-haired young woman with soft brown eyes, the color of brandy. Prescott hovers in the corner, not taking her eyes off Leila.

"Mrs. Grey, thank you so much for seeing me." Leila's voice is soft but clear.

"Um . . . Sorry about the security," I mutter, because I cannot think what else to say. I wave a hand distractedly at Prescott.

"This is my friend, Susi."

"Hi." I nod at Susi. She looks like Leila. She looks like me. *Oh no. Another one.*

"Yes," Leila says, as if reading my thoughts. "Susi knows Mr. Grey, too."

What the hell am I supposed to say to that? I give her a polite smile.

"Please, sit," I murmur.

There's a knock on the door. It's Hannah. I motion her in, knowing full well why she's disturbing us.

"Sorry to interrupt, Ana. I have Mr. Grey on the line?"

"Tell him I'm busy."

"He was quite insistent," she says fearfully.

"I am sure he was. Would you apologize to him, and say I'll call him back very shortly?"

Hannah hesitates.

"Hannah, please."

She nods and scurries out of the room. I turn back to the two women sitting in front of me. They are both staring at me in awe. It's uncomfortable.

"What can I do for you?" I ask.

Susi speaks. "I know this is all kinds of weird, but I wanted to meet you, too. The woman who captured Chris—"

I hold up my hand, stopping her in mid-sentence. I do not want to hear this. "Um . . . I get the picture," I mutter.

"We call ourselves the sub club." She grins at me, her eyes shining with mirth.

Oh my God.

Leila gasps and gapes at Susi, at once amused and appalled. Susi winces. I suspect Leila's kicked her under the table.

What the hell am I supposed to say to that? I glance nervously at Prescott, who remains impassive, her eyes never leaving Leila.

Susi seems to remember herself. She blushes, then nods and stands. "I'll wait in Reception. This is Lulu's show." I can tell she's embarrassed.

Lulu?

"You'll be okay?" she asks Leila, who smiles up at her. Susi gives me a large, open, genuine smile and exits the room.

Susi and Christian . . . it's not a thought I wish to dwell on. Prescott takes her phone out of her pocket and answers it. I didn't hear it ring.

"Mr. Grey," she says. Leila and I turn to look at her. Prescott closes her eyes as if in pain.

"Yes, sir," she says, stepping forward, and hands me the phone.

I roll my eyes. "Christian," I murmur, trying to contain my exasperation. I stand and stride briskly out of the room.

"What the fuck are you playing at?" he shouts. He's seething.

"Don't shout at me."

"What do you mean don't shout at you?" he shouts, louder this time. "I gave specific instructions which you have completely disregarded—again. Hell, Ana, I am fucking furious."

"When you are calmer, we will talk about this."

"Don't you hang up on me," he hisses.

"Good-bye, Christian." I hang up and switch off Prescott's phone.

Holy shit. I don't have long with Leila. Taking a deep breath, I reenter the meeting room. Both Leila and Prescott look up at me expectantly, and I hand Prescott her phone.

"Where were we?" I ask Leila as I sit back down opposite her. Her eyes widen slightly.

Yes. Apparently, I *handle* him, I want to say to her. But I don't think she wants to hear that.

Leila fiddles nervously with the ends of her hair. "First, I wanted to apologize," she says softly.

Oh . . .

She glances up and registers my surprise. "Yes," she says quickly. "And to thank you for not pressing charges. You know— for your car and in your apartment."

"I know you weren't . . . um, well," I murmur, reeling. I hadn't expected an apology.

"No, I wasn't."

"You're feeling better now?" I ask gently.

"Much. Thank you."

"Does your doctor know you're here?"

She shakes her head.

Oh.

She looks suitably guilty. "I know I'll have to deal with the fallout for this later. But I had to get some things, and I wanted to see Susi, and you, and . . . Mr. Grey."

"You want to see Christian?" My stomach free-falls to the floor. *That's why she's here.*

"Yes. I wanted to ask you if that would be okay."

Holy fuck. I gape at her, and I want to tell her that it's not okay. I don't want her anywhere near my husband. Why is she here? To assess the opposition? To unsettle me? Or perhaps she needs this as some sort of closure?

"Leila." I flounder, exasperated. "It's not up to me, it's up to Christian. You'll need to ask him. He doesn't need my permission. He's a grown man . . . most of the time."

She gazes at me for a fraction of a beat as if surprised by my reaction and then laughs softly, nervously twiddling the ends of her hair.

"He's repeatedly refused all my requests to see him," she says quietly.

Oh shit. I'm in more trouble than I thought.

"Why is it so important for you to see him?" I ask gently.

"To thank him. I'd be rotting in a stinking prison psychiatric facility if it wasn't for him. I know that." She glances down and runs her finger along the edge of the table. "I suffered a serious psychotic episode, and without Mr. Grey and John—Dr. Flynn . . ." She shrugs and gazes at me once more, her face full of gratitude.

Once again I'm speechless. What does she expect me to say? Surely she should be saying these things to Christian, not me.

"And for art school. I can't thank him enough for that."

I knew it! Christian *is* funding her classes. I remain expressionless, tentatively exploring my feelings for this woman now that she's confirmed my suspicions about Christian's generosity. To my surprise, I feel no ill will toward her. It's a revelation, and I'm glad she's better. Now, hopefully, she can move on with her life and out of ours.

"Are you missing classes right now?" I ask, because I'm interested.

"Only two. I head home tomorrow."

Oh good. "What are your plans, while you're here?"

"Pick up my belongings from Susi, return to Hamden. Continue painting and learning. Mr. Grey already has a couple of my paintings."

What the hell! My stomach plunges into the basement once more. *Are they hanging in my living room?* I bridle at the thought.

"What sort of painting do you do?"

"Abstracts, mainly."

"I see." My mind flits through the now-familiar paintings in the great room. Two by his ex-sub . . . possibly.

"Mrs. Grey, can I speak frankly?" she asks, completely oblivious to my warring emotions.

"By all means," I mutter, glancing at Prescott, who looks like she's relaxed a little. Leila leans forward as if to impart a long-held secret.

"I loved Geoff, my boyfriend who died earlier this year." Her voice drops to a sad whisper.

Holy shit, she's getting personal.

"I'm so sorry," I mutter automatically, but she continues as if she hasn't heard me.

"I loved my husband . . . and one other," she murmurs.

"My husband." The words are out of my mouth before I can stop them.

"Yes." She mouths the word.

This is not news to me. When she lifts her brown eyes to mine, they are wide with conflicting emotions, and the overriding one seems to be apprehension . . . of my reaction, perhaps? But my overwhelming response to this poor young woman is compassion. Mentally I run through all the classical literature I can think of that deals with unrequited love. Swallowing hard, I clutch the moral high ground.

"I know. He's very easy to love," I whisper.

Her wide eyes widen further in surprise, and she smiles. "Yes. He is—was." She corrects herself quickly and blushes. Then she giggles so sweetly that I can't help myself. I giggle, too. Yes, Christian Grey makes us giggly. My subconscious rolls her eyes at me in despair and goes back to reading her dog-eared copy of *Jane Eyre*. I glance at my watch. Deep down I know Christian will be here soon.

"You'll get your chance to see Christian."

"I thought I would. I know how protective he can be." She smiles.

So this is her scheme. She's very shrewd. *Or manipulative*, whispers my subconscious. "This is why you're here to see me?"

"Yes."

"I see." And Christian is playing right into her hands. Reluctantly, I have to acknowledge that she knows him well.

"He seemed very happy. With you," she says.

What? "How would you know?"

"From when I was in the apartment," she adds cautiously.

Oh hell . . . how could I forget that?

"Were you there often?"

"No. But he was very different with you."

Do I want to hear this? A shudder runs through me. My scalp prickles as I recall my fear when she was the unseen shadow in our apartment.

"You know it's against the law. Trespassing."

She nods, gazing down at the table. She runs a fingernail along the edge. "It was only a few times, and I was lucky not to get caught. Again, I need to thank Mr. Grey for that. He could have had me thrown in jail."

"I don't think he'd do that," I murmur.

Suddenly there is a flurry of activity outside the meeting room, and instinctively I know that Christian is in the building. A moment later he bursts through the door, and before he closes it, I catch Taylor's eye as he stands patiently outside. Taylor's mouth is set in a grim line, and he doesn't return my tight smile. Oh hell, even he's mad at me.

Christian's burning gray gaze pins first me then Leila to our chairs. His demeanor is quietly determined, but I know better, and I suspect Leila does, too. The menacing cool glint in his eyes reveals the truth—he's emanating rage, though he hides it well. In his gray suit, with his dark tie loosened and the top button of his white shirt undone, he looks at once businesslike and casual . . . and hot. His hair is in disarray—no doubt because he's been running his hands through it in exasperation.

Leila looks nervously down at the edge of the table, running her index finger along the edge again as Christian looks from me to her and then to Prescott.

"You," he says to Prescott in a soft tone. "You're fired. Get out now."

I blanch. Oh no—this isn't fair.

"Christian—" I make to stand up.

He holds his index finger up at me in warning. "Don't," he says, his voice so ominously quiet that I'm immediately silenced and rooted to my seat. Bowing her head, Prescott walks briskly out of the room to join Taylor. Christian shuts the door behind her and walks to the edge of the table. *Crap! Crap! Crap!* That was my fault. Christian stands opposite Leila, and, placing both hands on the wooden surface, he leans forward.

"What the fuck are you doing here?" he growls at her.

"Christian!" I gasp. He ignores me.

"Well?" he demands.

Leila peeks up at him through long lashes, her eyes wide, her face ashen, her rosy glow gone.

"I wanted to see you, and you wouldn't let me," she whispers.

"So you came here to harass my wife?" His voice is quiet. Too quiet.

Leila looks down at the table again.

He stands, glowering at her. "Leila, if you come anywhere near my wife again, I will cut off all support. Doctors, art school, medical insurance—all of it—gone. Do you understand?"

"Christian—" I try again. But he silences me with a chilling look. Why is he being so unreasonable? My compassion for this sad woman blooms.

"Yes," she says, her voice just audible.

"What's Susannah doing in Reception?"

"She came with me."

He runs a hand through his hair, glaring at her.

"Christian, please," I beg him. "Leila just wants to say thank you. That's all."

He ignores me, concentrating his wrath on Leila. "Did you stay with Susannah while you were sick?"

"Yes."

"Did she know what you were doing while you were staying with her?"

"No. She was away on vacation."

He strokes his index finger over his lower lip. "Why do you need to see me? You know you should send any requests through Flynn. Do you need something?" His tone has softened, maybe by a fraction.

Leila runs her finger along the edge of the table again.

Stop bullying her, Christian!

"I had to know." And for the first time she looks up directly at him.

"Had to know what?" he snaps.

"That you're okay."

He gapes at her. "That I'm okay?" he scoffs, disbelieving.

"Yes."

"I'm fine. There, question answered. Now Taylor will run you to Sea-Tac so you can go back to the East Coast. And if you take one step west of the Mississippi, it's all gone. Understand?"

Holy fuck . . . Christian! I gape at him. What the fuck is eating him? He cannot confine her to one side of the country.

"Yes. I understand," Leila says quietly.

"Good." Christian's tone is more conciliatory.

"It might not be convenient for Leila to go back now. She has plans," I object, outraged on her behalf.

Christian glares at me. "Anastasia," he warns, his voice icy, "this does not concern you."

I scowl at him. Of course it concerns me. She's in my office. There must be more to this than I know. He's not being rational.

Fifty Shades, my subconscious hisses at me.

"Leila came to see me, not you," I murmur petulantly.

Leila turns to me, her eyes impossibly wide.

"I had my instructions, Mrs. Grey. I disobeyed them." She glances nervously at my husband, then back at me.

"This is the Christian Grey I know," she says, her tone sad and wistful. Christian frowns at her, while all the breath evaporates from my lungs. I can't breathe. Was Christian like this with her all the time? Was he like this with me, at first? I find it hard to remember. Giving me a forlorn smile, Leila rises from the table.

"I'd like to stay until tomorrow. My flight is at noon," she says quietly to Christian.

"I'll have someone collect you at ten to take you to the airport."

"Thank you."

"You're at Susannah's?"

"Yes."

"Okay."

I glare at Christian. He can't dictate to her like this . . . and how does he know where Susannah lives?

"Good-bye, Mrs. Grey. Thank you for seeing me."

I stand and hold out my hand. She takes it gratefully and we shake.

"Um . . . good-bye. Good luck," I mutter, because I'm not sure what the protocol is for saying farewell to my husband's ex-submissive.

She nods and turns to him. "Good-bye, Christian."

Christian's eyes soften a little. "Good-bye, Leila." His voice is low. "Dr. Flynn, remember."

"Yes, Sir."

He opens the door to usher her out, but she halts in front of him and looks up. He stills, watching her warily.

"I'm glad you're happy. You deserve to be," she says and leaves before he can reply. He frowns after her, then nods to Taylor, who follows Leila toward the reception area. Closing the door, Christian gazes uncertainly at me.

"Don't even think about being angry with me," I hiss. "Call Claude Bastille and kick the shit out of him or go see Flynn."

His mouth drops open; he's surprised by my outburst and his brow creases once more.

"You promised you wouldn't do this." Now his tone is accusatory.

"Do what?"

"Defy me."

"No I didn't. I said I'd be more considerate. I told you she was here. I had Prescott search her, and your other little friend, too. Prescott was with me the entire time. Now you've fired the poor woman, when she was only doing what I asked. I told you not to worry, yet here you are. I don't remember receiving your papal bull decreeing that I couldn't see Leila. I didn't know that my visitors were subject to a proscribed list." My voice rises with indignation as I warm to my cause. Christian regards me, his expression unreadable. After a moment his mouth twists.

"Papal bull?" he says, amused, and he visibly relaxes. I wasn't aiming to lighten our conversation, yet here he is smirking at me, and that makes me madder. The exchange between him and his ex was painful to witness. How could he be so cold with her?

"What?" he asks, exasperated, as my face remains resolutely straight.

"You. Why were you so callous toward her?"

He sighs and shifts, stepping toward me and perching on the table.

"Anastasia," he says, as if to a child, "you don't understand. Leila, Susannah—all of them—they were a pleasant, diverting pastime. But that's all. You are the center of my universe. And the last time you two were in a room together, she had you at gunpoint. I don't want her anywhere near you."

"But, Christian, she was ill."

"I know that, and I know she's better now, but I'm not giving her the benefit of the doubt anymore. What she did was unforgivable."

"But you've just played right into her hands. She wanted to see you again, and she knew you'd come running if she came to see me."

Christian shrugs as if he doesn't care. "I don't want you tainted with my old life."

What?

"Christian . . . you are who you are because of your old life, your new life, whatever. What touches you, touches me. I accepted that when I agreed to marry you, because I love you."

He stills. I know he finds it hard to hear this.

"She didn't hurt me. She loves you, too."

"I don't give a fuck."

I gape at him, shocked. And I'm shocked that he still has the capacity to shock me. *This is the Christian Grey I know.* Leila's words rattle around my head. His reaction to her was so cold, so much at odds with the man I've come to know and love. I frown, recalling the remorse he felt when she had her breakdown, when he thought he might in some way be responsible for her pain. I swallow, remembering, too, that he bathed her. My stomach twists painfully at the thought, and bile rises in my throat. How can he say he doesn't care about her? He did back then. What's changed? Sometimes, like now, I just don't understand him. He operates on a level far, far removed from mine.

"Why are you championing her cause all of a sudden?" he asks, mystified and irritable.

"Look, Christian, I don't think Leila and I will be swapping recipes and knitting patterns anytime soon. But I didn't think you'd be so heartless to her."

His eyes frost. "I told you once, I don't have a heart," he mutters.

I roll my eyes—oh, now he *is* being adolescent.

"That's just not true, Christian. You're being ridiculous. You do care about her. You wouldn't be paying for art classes and the rest of that stuff if you didn't."

Suddenly, it's my lifetime ambition to make him realize this. It's painstakingly obvious that he cares. Why does he deny it? It's like his feelings for his birth mother. *Oh shit—of course.* His feelings for Leila and his other submissives are tangled up with his feelings for his mother. *I like to whip little brown-haired girls like you because you all look like the crack whore.* No wonder he's so mad. I sigh and shake my head. Paging Dr. Flynn, please. How can he not see this?

My heart swells for him momentarily. My lost boy . . . Why is it so hard for him to get back in touch with the humanity, the compassion, he showed Leila when she had her breakdown?

He glares at me, his eyes glittering with anger. "This discussion is over. Let's go home."

I glance at my watch. It's four twenty-three. I have work to do. "It's too early," I mutter.

"Home," he insists.

"Christian." My voice is weary. "I'm tired of having the same argument with you."

He frowns as if he doesn't understand.

"You know," I elucidate, "I do something you don't like, and you think of some way to get back at me. Usually involving some of your kinky fuckery, which is either mind-blowing or cruel." I shrug, resigned. This is exhausting and confusing.

"Mind-blowing?" he asks.

What?

"Usually, yes."

"What was mind-blowing?" he asks, his eyes now shimmering with amused sensual curiosity. And I know he's trying to distract me.

Crap! I do not want to discuss this in SIP's meeting room. My subconscious examines her finely manicured nails with disdain. *Shouldn't have brought the subject up, then.*

"You know." I blush, irritated with both him and myself.

"I can guess," he whispers.

Holy crap. I'm trying to castigate him and he's confounding me. "Christian, I—"

"I like to please you." He delicately traces his thumb over my bottom lip.

"You do," I acknowledge, my voice a whisper.

"I know," he says softly. He leans forward and whispers in my ear, "It's the one thing I do know." Oh, he smells good. He leans back and gazes down at me, his lips curled in an arrogant, I-so-own-you smile.

Pursing my lips, I strive to appear unaffected by his touch. He is so artful at diverting me from anything painful, or anything he doesn't want to address. *And you let him,* my subconscious pipes up unhelpfully, gazing over her copy of *Jane Eyre.*

"What was mind-blowing, Anastasia?" he prompts, a wicked gleam in his eye.

"You want the list?" I ask.

"There's a list?" He's pleased.

Oh, this man is exhausting. "Well, the handcuffs," I mumble, my mind catapulting back to our honeymoon.

He furrows his brow and grasps my hand, tracing the pulse point on my wrist with his thumb.

"I don't want to mark you."

Oh . . .

His lips curl in a slow carnal smile. "Come home." His tone is seductive.

"I have work to do."

"Home," he says, more insistent.

We gaze at each other, molten gray into bewildered blue, testing each other, testing our boundaries and our wills. I search his eyes for some understanding, trying to fathom how this man can go from raging control freak to seductive lover in one breath. His eyes grow larger and darker, his intention clear. Softly, he caresses my cheek.

"We could stay here." His voice is low and husky.

Oh no. No. No. No. Not in the office. "Christian, I don't want to have sex here. Your mistress has just been in this room."

"She was never my mistress," he growls, his mouth flattening into a grim line.

"That's just semantics, Christian."

He frowns, his expression puzzled. The seductive lover has gone. "Don't overthink this, Ana. She's history," he says dismissively.

I sigh . . . maybe he's right. I just want him to admit to himself that he cares for her. A chill grips my heart. *Oh no.* This is why it's important to me. Suppose *I* do something unforgivable. Suppose I don't conform. Will I be history, too? If he can turn like this, when he was so concerned and upset when Leila was ill . . . could he turn against me? I gasp, recalling the fragments of a dream: gilt mirrors and the sound of his heels clicking on the marbled floor as he leaves me standing alone in opulent splendor.

"No . . ." The word is out of my mouth in whispered horror before I can stop it.

"Yes," he says, and grasping my chin, he leans down and plants a tender kiss on my lips.

"Oh, Christian, you scare me sometimes." I grasp his head in my hands, twist my fingers into my hair, and pull his lips to mine. He stills for a moment as his arms fold around me.

"Why?"

"You could turn away from her so easily . . ."

He frowns. "And you think I might turn away from you, Ana? Why the hell would you think that? What's brought this on?"

"Nothing. Kiss me. Take me home," I plead. And as his lips touch mine, I am lost.

———

"Oh please," I beg, as Christian blows gently on my sex.

"All in good time," he murmurs.

I pull on my restraints and groan loudly in protest from his carnal assault. I'm trussed up in soft leather cuffs, each elbow bound to each knee, and Christian's head bobs and weaves between my legs, his masterful tongue teasing me, relentless. I open my eyes and gaze unseeing at our bedroom ceiling, which is bathed in the soft late afternoon light. His tongue moves round and round, swirling and curling over and around the center of my universe. I want to straighten my legs and struggle in a vain attempt to control the pleasure. But I can't. My fingers fist in his hair and I tug hard to fight his sublime torture.

"Don't come," he murmurs in warning against me, his soft breath on my warm, wet flesh as he resists my fingers. "I will spank you if you come."

I moan.

"Control, Ana. It's all about control." His tongue renews its erotic incursion.

Oh, he knows what he's doing. I am helpless to resist or stop my slavish reaction, and I try—really try—but my body detonates under his merciless ministrations, and his tongue doesn't stop as he wrings every last ounce of debilitating pleasure from me.

"Oh, Ana," he scolds. "You came." His voice is soft with his triumphant reprimand. He flips me onto my front, and I shakily support myself on my forearms. He smacks me hard on my behind.

"Ah!" I cry out.

"Control," he admonishes, and, grabbing my hips, he thrusts himself into me. I cry out again, my flesh still quivering from the aftershocks of my orgasm. He stills while deep inside me and, leaning over, unclips first one, then the second cuff. He wraps his arm around me and pulls me into his lap, his front to my back, and his hand curls beneath my chin around my throat. I revel in the feeling of fullness.

"Move," he orders.

I moan and rise up and down on his lap.

"Faster," he whispers.

And I move faster and faster. He groans and his hand tips my head back as he nibbles my neck. His other hand travels leisurely across my body, from my hip, down to my sex, down to my clitoris . . . still sensitive from his earlier lavish attention. I whimper as his fingers close around me, teasing me once more.

"Yes, Ana," he rasps softly in my ear. "You are mine. Only you."

"Yes," I breathe as my body tightens again, closing around him, cradling him in the most intimate way.

"Come for me," he demands.

And I let go, my body obediently following his command. He holds me still as my climax rips through me and I call out his name.

"Oh, Ana, I love you," he groans and follows my lead as he bucks into me, finding his own release.

HE KISSES MY SHOULDER and smoothes my hair from my face. "Does that make the list, Mrs. Grey?" he murmurs. I am lying, barely conscious, flat on my belly on our bed. Christian gently kneads my backside. He's propped up beside me on one elbow.

"Hmm."

"Is that a yes?"

"Hmm." I smile.

He grins and kisses me again, and reluctantly I roll on my side to face him.

"Well?" he asks.

"Yes. It makes the list. But it's a long list."

His face nearly splits in two, and he leans forward to kiss me gently. "Good. Shall we have dinner?" His eyes glow with love and humor.

I nod. I am famished. I reach over to gently pull the little hairs on his chest. "I want you to tell me something," I whisper.

"What?"

"Don't get mad."

"What is it, Ana?"

"You do care."

His eyes widen, and all trace of his good humor vanishes.

"I want you to admit that you care. Because the Christian I know and love would care."

He stills, his eyes not leaving mine, and I'm witness to his internal struggle as if he's about to make the judgment of Solomon. He opens his mouth to say something, then closes it again as some fleeting emotion crosses his face . . . pain, maybe.

Say it, I will him.

"Yes. Yes, I care. Happy?" His voice is barely a whisper.

Oh, thank fuck for that. It's a relief. "Yes. Very."

He frowns. "I can't believe I'm talking to you now, here in our bed, about—"

I put my finger to his lips. "We're not. Let's eat. I'm hungry."

He sighs and shakes his head. "You beguile and bewilder me, Mrs. Grey."

"Good." I lean up and kiss him.

From: Anastasia Grey
Subject: The List
Date: September 9 2011 09:33
To: Christian Grey

That's definitely at the top.

:D

A x

Anastasia Grey
Editor, SIP

From: Christian Grey
Subject: Tell Me Something New
Date: September 9 2011 09:42
To: Anastasia Grey

You've said that for the last three days.

Make your mind up.

Or . . . we could try something else.

;)

Christian Grey
CEO, Enjoying This Game, Grey Enterprises Holdings, Inc.

I grin at my screen. The last few evenings have been . . . entertaining. We have relaxed again, Leila's brief interruption forgotten. I haven't quite worked up the courage to ask if any of her
paintings hang on the walls—and frankly, I don't really care. My
BlackBerry buzzes and I answer, expecting Christian.

"Ana?"

"Yes?"

"Ana, honey. It's José Senior."

"Mr. Rodriguez! Hi!" My scalp prickles. What does José's dad
want with me?

"Honey, I'm sorry to call you at work. It's Ray." His voice falters.

"What is it? What's happened?" My heart leaps into my throat.

"Ray's been in an accident."

Oh no. Daddy. I stop breathing.

"He's in the hospital. You'd better get here quick."

CHAPTER SEVENTEEN

M r. Rodriguez, what's happened?" My voice is hoarse and thick with unshed tears. *Ray. Sweet Ray. My dad.* "He's been in a car accident."

"Okay, I'll come . . . I'll come now." Adrenaline has flooded my bloodstream, leaving panic in its wake. I'm finding it difficult to breathe.

"They've transferred him to Portland."

Portland? What the hell is he doing in Portland?

"They airlifted him, Ana. I'm heading there now. OHSU. Oh, Ana, I didn't see the car. I just didn't see it . . ." His voice cracks.

Mr. Rodriguez—no!

"I'll see you there." Mr. Rodriguez chokes and the line goes dead.

A dark dread seizes me by the throat, overwhelming me. Ray. No. No. I take a deep steadying breath, pick up the phone, and call Roach. He answers on the second ring.

"Ana?"

"Jerry. It's my father."

"Ana, what happened?"

I explain, barely pausing to breathe.

"Go. Of course, you must go. I hope your father's okay."

"Thank you. I'll keep you informed." Inadvertently I slam the phone down, but right now I couldn't care less.

"Hannah!" I call, aware of the anxiety in my voice. Moments later she pokes her head around the door to find me packing my purse and grabbing papers to stuff into my briefcase.

"Yes, Ana?" She frowns.

"My father has been in an accident. I have to go."

"Oh dear—"

"Cancel all my appointments today. And Monday. You'll have to finish prepping the e-book presentation—notes are in the shared file. Get Courtney to help if you have to."

"Yes," Hannah whispers. "I hope he's okay. Don't worry about anything here. We'll muddle through."

"I have my BlackBerry."

The concern etched on her pinched, pale face is almost my undoing.

Daddy.

I grab my jacket, purse, and briefcase. "I'll call you if I need anything."

"Do, please. Good luck, Ana. Hope he's okay."

I give her a small tight smile, fighting to maintain my composure, and exit my office. I try hard not to run all the way to Reception. Sawyer leaps to his feet when I arrive.

"Mrs. Grey?" he asks, confused by my sudden appearance.

"We're going to Portland—now."

"Okay, ma'am," he says, frowning, but opens the door.

Moving is good.

"Mrs. Grey," Sawyer asks as we race toward the parking lot. "Can I ask why we're making this unscheduled trip?"

"It's my dad. He's been in an accident."

"I see. Does Mr. Grey know?"

"I'll call him from the car."

Sawyer nods and opens the rear door to the Audi SUV, and I climb in. With shaking fingers, I reach for my BlackBerry and dial Christian's cell.

"Mrs. Grey." Andrea's voice is crisp and businesslike.

"Is Christian there?" I breathe.

"Um . . . he's somewhere in the building, ma'am. He's left his BlackBerry charging with me."

I groan silently with frustration.

"Can you tell him I called, and that I need to speak with him? It's urgent."

"I could try to track him down. He does have a habit of wandering off sometimes."

"Just get him to call me, please," I beg, fighting back tears.

"Certainly, Mrs. Grey." She hesitates. "Is everything all right?"

"No," I whisper, not trusting my voice. "Please, just get him to call me."

"Yes, ma'am."

I hang up. I cannot contain my anguish any longer. Pulling my knees up to my chest, I curl up on the rear seat, and tears ooze, unwelcome, down my cheeks.

"Where in Portland, Mrs. Grey?" Sawyer asks gently.

"OHSU," I choke out. "The big hospital."

Sawyer pulls out into the street and heads for the I-5, while I keen softly in the back of the car, muttering wordless prayers. *Please let him be okay. Please let him be okay.*

My phone rings, "Your Love Is King" startling me from my mantra.

"Christian," I gasp.

"Christ, Ana. What's wrong?"

"It's Ray—he's been in an accident."

"Shit!"

"Yes. I am on my way to Portland."

"Portland? Please tell me Sawyer is with you."

"Yes, he's driving."

"Where is Ray?"

"At OHSU."

I hear a muffled voice in the background. "Yes, Ros," Christian snaps angrily. "I know! Sorry, baby—I can be there in about three hours. I have business I need to finish here. I'll fly down."

Oh shit. Charlie Tango is back in commission and last time Christian flew her . . .

"I have a meeting with some guys over from Taiwan. I can't blow them off. It's a deal we've been hammering out for months."

Why do I know nothing about this?

"I'll leave as soon as I can."

"Okay," I whisper. And I want to say that it's okay, stay in Seattle and sort out your business, but the truth is I want him with me.

"Oh, baby," he whispers.

"I'll be okay, Christian. Take your time. Don't rush. I don't want to worry about you, too. Fly safely."

"I will."

"Love you."

"I love you, too, baby. I'll be with you as soon as I can. Keep Luke close."

"Yes, I will."

"I'll see you later."

"Bye." After hanging up, I hug my knees once more. I know nothing about Christian's business. What the hell is he doing with the Taiwanese? I gaze out the window as we pass King County International Airport/Boeing Field. He must fly safely. My stomach knots anew and nausea threatens. Ray *and* Christian. I don't think my heart could take that. Leaning back, I start my mantra again: *Please let him be okay. Please let him be okay.*

"MRS. GREY." SAWYER'S VOICE rouses me. "We're on the hospital grounds. I just have to find the ER."

"I know where it is." My mind flits back to my last visit to OHSU, when, on my second day, I fell off a stepladder at Clayton's, twisting my ankle. I recall Paul Clayton hovering over me and shudder at the memory.

Sawyer pulls up to the drop-off point and leaps out to open my door.

"I'll go park, ma'am, and come find you. Leave your briefcase, I'll bring it."

"Thank you, Luke."

He nods, and I walk briskly into the buzzing ER reception area. The receptionist at the desk gives me a polite smile, and within a few moments, she's located Ray and is sending me to the OR on the third floor.

OR? Fuck! "Thank you," I mutter, trying to focus on her directions to the elevators. My stomach lurches as I almost run toward them.

Let him be okay. Please let him be okay.

The elevator is agonizingly slow, stopping on each floor. *Come on . . . Come on!* I will it to move faster, scowling at the people strolling in and out and preventing me from getting to my dad.

Finally, the doors open on the third floor, and I rush to another reception desk, this one staffed by nurses in navy uniforms.

"Can I help you?" asks one officious nurse with a myopic stare.

"My father, Raymond Steele. He's just been admitted. He's in OR 4, I think." Even as I say the words, I am willing them not to be true.

"Let me check, Miss Steele."

I nod, not bothering to correct her as she gazes intently at her computer screen.

"Yes. He's been in for a couple of hours. If you'd like to wait, I'll let them know that you're here. The waiting room's there." She points toward a large white door helpfully labeled WAITING ROOM in bold blue lettering.

"Is he okay?" I ask, trying to keep my voice steady.

"You'll have to wait for one of the attending doctors to brief you, ma'am."

"Thank you," I mutter—but inside I am screaming, *I want to know now!*

I open the door to reveal a functional, austere waiting room, where Mr. Rodriguez and José are seated.

"Ana!" Mr. Rodriguez gasps. His arm is in a cast, and his cheek is bruised on one side. He's in a wheelchair with one of his legs in a cast, too. I gingerly wrap my arms around him.

"Oh, Mr. Rodriguez," I sob.

"Ana, honey." He pats my back with his uninjured arm. "I'm so sorry," he mumbles, his hoarse voice cracking.

Oh no.

"No, Papa," José says softly in admonishment as he hovers behind me. When I turn, he pulls me into his arms and holds me.

"José," I mutter. And I'm lost—tears falling as all the tension, fear, and heartache of the last three hours surface.

"Hey, Ana, don't cry." José gently strokes my hair. I wrap my arms around his neck and softly weep. We stand like this for ages, and I'm so grateful that my friend is here. We pull apart when Sawyer joins us in the waiting room. Mr. Rodriguez hands me a tissue from a conveniently placed box, and I dry my tears.

"This is Mr. Sawyer. Security," I murmur. Sawyer nods politely to José and Mr. Rodriguez, then moves to take a seat in the corner.

"Sit down, Ana." José ushers me to one of the vinyl-covered armchairs.

"What happened? Do we know how he is? What are they doing?"

José holds up his hands to halt my barrage of questions and sits down beside me. "We don't have any news. Ray, Dad, and I were on a fishing trip to Astoria. We were hit by some stupid fucking drunk—"

Mr. Rodriguez tries to interrupt, stammering an apology.

"*Cálmate*, Papa!" José snaps. "I don't have a mark on me, just a couple of bruised ribs and a knock on the head. Dad . . . well, Dad broke his wrist and ankle. But the car hit the passenger side and Ray."

Oh no, *no* . . . Panic swamps my limbic system again. No, no, no. My body shudders and chills as I imagine what's happening to Ray in the OR.

"He's in surgery. We were taken to the community hospital in Astoria, but they airlifted Ray here. We don't know what they're doing. We're waiting for news."

I start to shake.

"Hey, Ana, you cold?"

I nod. I'm in my white sleeveless shirt and black summer jacket, and neither provides warmth. Gingerly, José pulls off his leather jacket and wraps it around my shoulders.

"Shall I get you some tea, ma'am?" Sawyer is by my side. I nod gratefully, and he disappears from the room.

"Why were you fishing in Astoria?" I ask.

José shrugs. "The fishing's supposed to be good there. We were having a boys' get-together. Some bonding time with my old man before academia heats up for my final year." José's dark eyes are large and luminous with fear and regret.

"You could have been hurt, too. And Mr. Rodriguez . . . worse." I gulp at the thought. My body temperature drops further, and I shiver once more. José takes my hand.

"Hell, Ana, you're freezing."

Mr. Rodriguez inches forward and takes my other hand in his good one.

"Ana, I am so sorry."

"Mr. Rodriguez, please. It was an accident . . ." My voice fades to a whisper.

"Call me José," he corrects me. I give him a weak smile, because that's all I can manage. I shiver once more.

"The police took the asshole into custody. Seven in the morning and the guy was out of his skull," José hisses in disgust.

Sawyer reenters, bearing a paper cup of hot water and a separate tea bag. *He knows how I take my tea!* I'm surprised, and glad for the distraction. Mr. Rodriguez and José release my hands as I gratefully take the cup from Sawyer.

"Do either of you want anything?" Sawyer asks Mr. Rodriguez and José. They both shake their heads, and Sawyer resumes his seat in the corner. I dunk my tea bag in the water and, rising shakily, dispose of the used bag in a small trashcan.

"What's taking them so long?" I mutter to no one in particular as I take a sip.

Daddy . . . Please let him be okay. Please let him be okay.

"We'll know soon enough, Ana," José says gently. I nod and take another sip. I take my seat again beside him. We wait . . . and wait. Mr. Rodriguez with his eyes closed, praying I think, and José holding my hand and squeezing it every now and then. I slowly sip my tea. It's not Twinings, but some cheap nasty brand, and it tastes disgusting.

I remember the last time I waited for news. The last time I thought all was lost, when *Charlie Tango* went missing. Closing my eyes, I offer up a silent prayer for the safe passage of my husband. I glance at my watch: 2:15 p.m. He should be here soon. My tea is cold . . . Ugh!

I stand up and pace, then sit down again. Why haven't the doctors been to see me? I take José's hand, and he gives mine another reassuring squeeze. *Please let him be okay. Please let him be okay.*

Time crawls so slowly.

Suddenly the door opens, and we all glance up expectantly, my stomach knotting. *Is this it?*

Christian strides in. His face darkens momentarily when he notices my hand in José's.

"Christian!" I gasp and leap up, thanking God he's arrived safely. Then I'm wrapped in his arms, his nose in my hair, and I'm inhaling his scent, his warmth, his love. A small part of me feels calmer, stronger, and more resilient because he's here. Oh, the difference his presence makes to my peace of mind.

"Any news?"

I shake my head, unable to speak.

"José." He nods a greeting.

"Christian, this is my father, José Senior."

"Mr. Rodriguez—we met at the wedding. I take it you were in the accident, too?"

José briefly retells the story.

"Are you both well enough to be here?" Christian asks.

"We don't want to be anywhere else," Mr. Rodriguez says, his voice quiet and laced with pain. Christian nods. Taking my hand, he sits me down, then takes a seat beside me.

"Have you eaten?" he asks.

I shake my head.

"Are you hungry?"

I shake my head.

"But you're cold?" he asks, eyeing José's jacket.

I nod. He shifts in his chair, but wisely says nothing.

The door opens again, and a young doctor in bright blue scrubs enters. He looks exhausted and harrowed.

All the blood disappears from my head as I stumble to my feet.

"Ray Steele," I whisper as Christian stands beside me, putting his arm around my waist.

"You're his next of kin?" the doctor asks. His bright blue eyes almost match his scrubs, and under any other circumstances I would have found him attractive.

"I'm his daughter, Ana."

"Miss Steele—"

"Mrs. Grey," Christian interrupts him.

"My apologies," the doctor stammers, and for a moment I want to kick Christian. "I'm Dr. Crowe. Your father is stable, but in critical condition."

What does that mean? My knees buckle beneath me, and only Christian's supporting arm prevents me from falling to the floor.

"He suffered severe internal injuries," Dr. Crowe says, "principally to his diaphragm, but we've managed to repair them, and we were able to save his spleen. Unfortunately, he suffered a cardiac arrest during the operation because of blood loss. We managed to get his heart going again, but this remains a concern. However, our gravest concern is that he suffered severe contusions to the head, and the MRI shows that he has swelling in his brain. We've induced a coma to keep him quiet and still while we monitor the brain swelling."

Brain damage? No.

"It's standard procedure in these cases. For now, we just have to wait and see."

"And what's the prognosis?" Christian asks coolly.

"Mr. Grey, it's difficult to say at the moment. It's possible he could make a complete recovery, but that's in God's hands now."

"How long will you keep him in a coma?"

"That depends on how his brain responds. Usually seventy-two to ninety-six hours."

Oh, so long! "Can I see him?" I whisper.

"Yes, you should be able to see him in about half an hour. He's been taken to the ICU on the sixth floor."

"Thank you, Doctor."

Dr. Crowe nods, turns, and leaves us.

"Well, he's alive," I whisper to Christian. And the tears start to roll down my face once more.

"Sit down," Christian orders gently.

"Papa, I think we should go. You need to rest. We won't know anything for a while," José murmurs to Mr. Rodriguez, who gazes blankly at his son. "We can come back this evening, after you've rested. That's okay, isn't it, Ana?" José turns, imploring me.

"Of course."

"Are you staying in Portland?" Christian asks. José nods.

"Do you need a ride home?"

José frowns. "I was going to order a cab."

"Luke can take you."

Sawyer stands, and José looks confused.

"Luke Sawyer," I murmur in clarification.

"Oh . . . Sure. Yeah, we'd appreciate it. Thanks, Christian."

Standing, I hug Mr. Rodriguez and José in quick succession.

"Stay strong, Ana," José whispers in my ear. "He's a fit and healthy man. The odds are in his favor."

"I hope so." I hug him hard. Then, releasing him, I shrug off his jacket and hand it back to him.

"Keep it, if you're still cold."

"No, I'm okay. Thanks." Glancing nervously up at Christian, I see that he's regarding us impassively. Christian takes my hand.

"If there's any change, I'll let you know right away," I say as José pushes his father's wheelchair toward the door Sawyer is holding open.

Mr. Rodriguez raises his hand, and they pause in the doorway. "He'll be in my prayers, Ana." His voice wavers. "It's been so good to reconnect with him after all these years. He's become a good friend."

"I know."

And with that they leave. Christian and I are alone. He caresses my cheek. "You're pale. Come here." He sits down on the chair and pulls me onto his lap, folding me into his arms again, and I go willingly. I snuggle up against him, feeling oppressed by my stepfather's misfortune, but grateful that my husband is here to comfort me. He gently strokes my hair and holds my hand.

"How was *Charlie Tango*?" I ask.

He grins. "Oh, she was yar," he says, quiet pride in his voice. It makes me smile properly for the first time in several hours, and I glance at him, puzzled.

"Yar?"

"It's a line from *The Philadelphia Story*. Grace's favorite film."

"I don't know it."

"I think I have it on Blu-Ray at home. We can watch it and make out." He kisses my hair and I smile once more.

"Can I persuade you to eat something?" he asks.

My smile disappears. "Not now. I want to see Ray first."

His shoulders slump, but he doesn't push me.

"How were the Taiwanese?"

"Amenable," he says.

"Amenable how?"

"They let my buy their shipyard for less than the price I was willing to pay."

He's bought a shipyard? "That's good?"

"Yes. That's good."

"But I thought you had a shipyard, over here."

"I do. We're going to use that to do the fitting-out. Build the hulls in the Far East. It's cheaper."

Oh. "What about the workforce at the shipyard here?"

"We'll redeploy. We should be able to keep redundancies to a minimum." He kisses my hair. "Shall we check on Ray?" he asks, his voice soft.

THE ICU ON THE sixth floor is a stark, sterile, functional ward with whispered voices and bleeping machinery. Four patients are each housed in their own separate hi-tech area. Ray is at the far end.

Daddy.

He looks so small in his large bed, surrounded by all this tech-
nology. It's a shock. My dad has never been so diminished. There's
a tube in his mouth, and various lines pass through drips into a
needle in each arm. A small clamp is attached to his finger. I wonder vaguely what that's for. His leg is on top of the sheets, encased
in a blue cast. A monitor displays his heart rate: *beep, beep, beep.*
It's beating strong and steady. This I know. I move slowly toward
him. His chest is covered in a large, pristine bandage that disappears beneath the thin sheet that protects his modesty.

I realize that the tube pulling at the right corner of his mouth
leads to a ventilator. Its noise is weaving with the *beep, beep, beep* of
his heart monitor into a percussive rhythmic beat. Sucking, expelling, sucking, expelling, sucking, expelling in time with the beeps.
There are four lines on the screen of his heart monitor, each moving steadily across, demonstrating clearly that Ray is still with us.

Oh, Daddy.

Even though his mouth is distorted by the ventilator tube, he
looks peaceful, lying there fast asleep.

A petite young nurse stands to one side, checking his monitors.

"Can I touch him?" I ask her, tentatively reaching for his hand.

"Yes." She smiles kindly. Her badge says KELLIE RN, and she
must be in her twenties. She's blonde with dark, dark eyes.

Christian stands at the end of the bed, watching me carefully
as I clasp Ray's hand. It's surprisingly warm, and that's my undoing. I sink onto the chair by the bed, place my head gently against
Ray's arm, and start to sob.

"Oh, Daddy. Please get better," I whisper. "Please."

Christian puts his hand on my shoulder and gives it a reassuring squeeze.

"All Mr. Steele's vitals are good," Nurse Kellie says quietly.

"Thank you," Christian murmurs. I glance up in time to see
her gape. She's finally gotten a good look at my husband. I don't
care. She can gape at Christian all she likes as long as she makes
my father well again.

"Can he hear me?" I ask.

"He's in a deep sleep. But who knows?"

"Can I sit for a while?"

"Sure thing." She smiles at me, her cheeks pink from a telltale blush. Incongruously, I find myself thinking blonde is not her true color.

Christian gazes down at me, ignoring her. "I need to make a call. I'll be outside. I'll give you some alone time with your dad."

I nod. He kisses my hair and walks out of the room. I hold Ray's hand, marveling at the irony that it's only now when he's unconscious and can't hear me that I really want to tell him how much I love him. This man has been my constant. My rock. And I've never thought about it until now. I'm not flesh of his flesh, but he's my dad, and I love him so very much. My tears trail down my cheeks. *Please, please get better.*

Very quietly, so as not to disturb anyone, I tell him about our weekend in Aspen and about last weekend when we were soaring and sailing aboard *The Grace.* I tell him about our new house, our plans, about how we hope to make it ecologically sustainable. I promise to take him with us to Aspen so he can go fishing with Christian and assure him that Mr. Rodriguez and José will both be welcome, too. *Please be here to do that, Daddy. Please.*

Ray remains immobile, the ventilator sucking and expelling and the monotonous but reassuring *beep, beep, beep* of his heart monitor his only response.

When I look up, Christian is sitting quietly at the end of the bed. I don't know how long he's been there.

"Hi," he says, his eyes glowing with compassion and concern.

"Hi."

"So, I'm going fishing with your dad, Mr. Rodriguez, and José?" he asks.

I nod.

"Okay. Let's go eat. Let him sleep."

I frown. I don't want to leave him.

"Ana, he's in a coma. I've given our cell numbers to the nurses here. If there's any change, they'll call us. We'll eat, check into a hotel, rest up, then come back this evening."

THE SUITE AT THE Heathman looks just as I remember it. How often have I thought about that first night and morning I spent with Christian Grey? I stand in the entrance to the suite, paralyzed. Jeez, it all started here.

"Home away from home," says Christian, his voice soft, putting my briefcase down beside one of the overstuffed couches.

"Do you want a shower? A bath? What do you need, Ana?" Christian gazes at me, and I know he's rudderless—my lost boy dealing with events beyond his control. He's been withdrawn and contemplative all afternoon. This is a situation he cannot manipulate and predict. This is real life in the raw, and he's kept himself from that for so long, he's exposed and helpless now. My sweet, sheltered Fifty Shades.

"A bath. I'd like a bath," I murmur, aware that keeping him busy will make him feel better, useful even. *Oh, Christian—I'm numb and I'm cold and I'm scared, but I'm so glad you're here with me.*

"Bath. Good. Yes." He strides into the bedroom and out of sight into the palatial bathroom. A few moments later, the roar of water gushing to fill the tub echoes from the room.

Finally, I galvanize myself to follow him into the bedroom. I'm dismayed to see several bags from Nordstrom on the bed. Christian reenters, sleeves rolled up, tie and jacket discarded.

"I sent Taylor to get some things. Nightwear. You know," he says, eyeing me warily.

Of course he did. I nod my approval to make him feel better. *Where is Taylor?*

"Oh, Ana," Christian murmurs. "I've not seen you like this. You're normally so brave and strong."

I don't know what to say. I merely gaze wide-eyed at him. I have nothing to give right now. I think I'm in shock. I wrap my arms around myself, trying to keep the pervading cold at bay, even though I know it's a fruitless task as this cold comes from within. Christian pulls me into his arms.

"Baby, he's alive. His vital signs are good. We just have to be patient," he murmurs. "Come." He takes my hand and leads me into the bathroom. Gently, he slips my jacket off my shoulders and places it on the bathroom chair, then, turning back, he undoes the buttons on my shirt.

THE WATER IS DELICIOUSLY warm and fragrant, the smell of lotus blossom heavy in the warm, sultry air of the bathroom. I lie between Christian's legs, my back to his front, my feet resting on top of his. We're both quiet and introspective, and I'm finally feeling warm. Intermittently Christian kisses my hair as I absentmindedly pop the bubbles in the foam. His arm is wrapped around my shoulders.

"You didn't get into the bath with Leila, did you? That time you bathed her?" I ask.

He stiffens and snorts, his hand tightening on my shoulder where it rests. "Um . . . no." He sounds astounded.

"I thought so. Good."

He tugs gently at my hair knotted in a crude bun, tilting my head around so he can see my face. "Why do you ask?"

I shrug. "Morbid curiosity. I don't know . . . seeing her this week."

His face hardens. "I see. Less of the morbid." His tone is reproachful.

"How long are you going to support her?"

"Until she's on her feet. I don't know." He shrugs. "Why?"

"Are there others?"

"Others?"

"Exes who you support."

"There was one, yes. No longer though."

"Oh?"

"She was studying to be a doctor. She's qualified now and has someone else."

"Another Dominant?"

"Yes."

"Leila says you have two of her paintings," I whisper.

"I used to. I didn't really care for them. They had technical merit, but they were too colorful for me. I think Elliot has them. As we know, he has no taste."

I giggle, and he wraps his other arm around me, sloshing water over the side of the bath.

"That's better," he whispers and kisses my temple.

"He's marrying my best friend."

"Then I'd better shut my mouth," he says.

I FEEL MORE RELAXED after our bath. Wrapped in my soft Heathman robe, I gaze at the various bags on the bed. Jeez, this must be more than nightwear. Tentatively, I peek into one. A pair of jeans and a pale blue hooded sweatshirt, my size. Holy cow . . . Taylor's bought a whole weekend's worth of clothes, and he knows what I like. I smile, remembering this is not the first time he's shopped for clothes for me when I was at the Heathman.

"Apart from harassing me at Clayton's, have you ever actually gone into a store and just bought stuff?"

"Harassing you?"

"Yes. Harassing me."

"You were flustered, if I recall. And that young boy was all over you. What was his name?"

"Paul."

"One of your many admirers."

I roll my eyes, and he smiles a relieved, genuine smile and kisses me.

"There's my girl," he whispers. "Get dressed. I don't want you getting cold again."

"READY," I MURMUR. CHRISTIAN is working on the Mac in the study area of the suite. He's dressed in black jeans and a gray cable-knit sweater, and I'm wearing the jeans, the hoodie, and a white T-shirt.

"You look so young," Christian says softly, glancing up, his eyes glowing. "And to think you'll be a whole year older tomorrow." His voice is wistful. I give him a sad smile.

"I don't feel much like celebrating. Can we go see Ray now?"

"Sure. I wish you'd eat something. You barely touched your food."

"Christian, please. I'm just not hungry. Maybe after we've seen Ray. I want to wish him good night."

AS WE ARRIVE AT the ICU, we meet José leaving. He's alone.

"Ana, Christian, hi."

"Where's your dad?"

"He was too tired to come back. He was in a car accident this morning," José grins ruefully. "And his painkillers have kicked in. He was out for the count. I had to fight to get in to see Ray since I'm not next of kin."

"And?" I ask anxiously.

"He's good, Ana. Same . . . but all good."

Relief floods my system. No news is good news.

"See you tomorrow, birthday girl?"

"Sure. We'll be here."

José eyes Christian quickly, then pulls me into a brief hug. "*Mañana.*"

"Good night, José."

"Good-bye, José," Christian says. José nods and walks down the corridor. "He's still nuts about you," Christian says quietly.

"No he's not. And even if he is . . ." I shrug because right now I just don't care.

Christian gives me a tight smile, and my heart melts.

"Well done," I murmur.

He frowns.

"For not frothing at the mouth."

He gapes at me, wounded—but amused, too. "I've never frothed. Let's see your dad. I have a surprise for you."

"Surprise?" My eyes widen in alarm.

"Come." Christian takes my hand, and we push open the double doors of the ICU.

Standing at the end of Ray's bed is Grace, deep in discussion with Crowe and a second doctor, a woman I've not seen before. Seeing us, Grace grins.

Oh, thank heavens.

"Christian." She kisses his cheek, then turns to me and folds me in her warm embrace.

"Ana. How are you holding up?"

"I'm fine. It's my father I'm worried about."

"He's in good hands. Dr. Sluder is an expert in her field. We trained together at Yale."

Oh . . .

"Mrs. Grey," Dr. Sluder greets me very formally. She's short-haired and elfin with a shy smile and a soft southern accent. "As the lead physician for your father, I'm pleased to tell you that all is on track. His vital signs are stable and strong. We have every faith that he'll make a complete recovery. The brain swelling has stopped, and shows signs of decreasing. This is very encouraging after such a short time."

"That's good news," I murmur.

She smiles warmly at me. "It is, Mrs. Grey. We're taking real good care of him.

"Great to see you again, Grace."

Grace smiles. "Likewise, Lorraina."

"Dr. Crowe, let's leave these good people to visit with Mr. Steele." Crowe follows in Dr. Sluder's wake to the exit.

I glance over at Ray, and for the first time since his accident, I feel more hopeful. Dr. Sluder and Grace's kind words have rekindled my hope.

Grace takes my hand and squeezes gently. "Ana, sweetheart, sit with him. Talk to him. It's all good. I'll visit with Christian in the waiting room."

I nod. Christian smiles his reassurance, and he and his mother leave me with my beloved father sleeping peacefully to the gentle lullaby of his ventilator and heart monitor.

I SLIP CHRISTIAN'S WHITE T-shirt on and get into bed.

"You seem brighter," Christian says cautiously as he pulls on his pajamas.

"Yes. I think talking to Dr. Sluder and your mom made a big difference. Did you ask Grace to come here?"

Christian slides into bed and pulls me into his arms, turning me to face away from him.

"No. She wanted to come and check on your dad herself."

"How did she know?"

"I called her this morning."

Oh.

"Baby, you're exhausted. You should sleep."

"Hmm," I murmur in agreement. He's right. I'm so tired. It's been an emotional day. I crane my head around and gaze at him a beat. *We're not going to make love?* And I'm relieved. In fact, he's had a totally hands-off approach with me all day. I wonder if I should be alarmed by this turn of events, but since my inner goddess has left the building and taken my libido with her, I'll think about it in the morning. I turn over and snuggle against Christian, wrapping my leg over his.

"Promise me something," he says softly.

"Hmm?" It's a question that I am too tired to articulate.

"Promise me you'll eat something tomorrow. I can just about tolerate you wearing another man's jacket without frothing at the mouth, but, Ana . . . you must eat. Please."

"Hmm," I acquiesce. He kisses my hair. "Thank you for being here," I mumble and sleepily kiss his chest.

"Where else would I be? I want to be wherever you are, Ana. Being here makes me think of how far we've come. And the night I first slept with you. What a night that was. I watched you for hours. You were just . . . yar," he breathes. I smile against his chest.

"Sleep," he murmurs, and it's a command. I close my eyes and drift.

CHAPTER EIGHTEEN

I stir, opening my eyes to a bright September morning. Warm and comfortable between clean, crisp sheets, I take a moment to orient myself and am overwhelmed by a sense of déjà vu. Of course, I'm at the Heathman.

"Shit! Daddy!" I gasp out loud, recalling with a gut-wrenching surge of apprehension that twists my heart and starts it pounding why I'm in Portland.

"Hey." Christian is sitting on the edge of the bed. He strokes my cheek with his knuckles, instantly calming me. "I called the ICU this morning. Ray had a good night. It's all good," he says reassuringly.

"Oh, good. Thank you," I mutter, sitting up.

He leans in and presses his lips to my forehead. "Good morning, Ana," he whispers and kisses my temple.

"Hi," I mutter. He's up and dressed in a black T-shirt and blue jeans.

"Hi," he replies, his eyes soft and warm. "I want to wish you happy birthday. Is that okay?"

I offer him a tentative smile and caress his cheek. "Yes, of course. Thank you. For everything."

His brow furrows. "Everything?"

"Everything."

He looks momentarily confused, but it's fleeting and his eyes widen with anticipation. "Here." He hands me a small, exquisitely wrapped box with a tiny gift card.

In spite of the worry I feel about my father, I sense Christian's anxiety and excitement, and it's infectious. I read the card.

For all our firsts on your first birthday as my beloved wife.
I love you.
C x

Oh my, how sweet is that? "I love you, too," I murmur, smiling at him.

He grins. "Open it."

Unwrapping the paper carefully so it doesn't tear, I find a beautiful red leather box. *Cartier.* It's familiar, thanks to my second-chance earrings and my watch. Cautiously, I open the box to discover a delicate charm bracelet of silver or platinum or white gold—I don't know, but it's absolutely enchanting. Attached to it are several charms: the Eiffel Tower; a London black cab; a helicopter—*Charlie Tango*; a glider—the soaring, a catamaran—*The Grace*; a bed; and an ice cream cone? I look up at him, bemused.

"Vanilla?" He shrugs apologetically, and I can't help but laugh. Of course.

"Christian, this is beautiful. Thank you. It's yar."

He grins.

My favorite is the heart. It's a locket.

"You can put a picture or whatever in that."

"A picture of you." I glance at him through my lashes. "Always in my heart."

He smiles his lovely, heartbreakingly shy smile.

I fondle the last two charms: a letter C—oh yes, I was his first girlfriend to use his first name. I smile at the thought. And finally, there's a key.

"To my heart and soul," he whispers.

Tears prick my eyes. I launch myself at him, curling my arms around his neck and settling into his lap. "It's such a thoughtful present. I love it. Thank you," I murmur against his ear. Oh, he smells so good—clean, of fresh linen, body wash, and Christian. Like home, my home. My threatened tears begin to fall.

He groans softly and enfolds me in his embrace.

"I don't know what I'd do without you." My voice cracks as I try to hold back the overwhelming swell of emotion.

He swallows hard and tightens his hold on me. "Please don't cry."

I sniff in a rather unladylike way. "I'm sorry. I'm just so happy and sad and anxious at the same time. It's bittersweet."

"Hey." His voice is feather soft. Tipping my head back, he plants a gentle kiss on my lips. "I understand."

"I know," I whisper, and I'm rewarded with his shy smile again.

"I wish we were in happier circumstances and at home. But we're here." He shrugs apologetically once more. "Come, up you go. After breakfast, we'll check on Ray."

ONCE DRESSED IN MY new jeans and T-shirt, my appetite makes a brief but welcome return during breakfast in our suite. I know Christian is pleased to see me eating my granola and Greek yogurt.

"Thank you for ordering my favorite breakfast."

"It's your birthday," Christian says softly. "And you have to stop thanking me." He rolls his eyes in exasperation, but fondly, I think.

"I just want you to know that I appreciate it."

"Anastasia, it's what I do." His expression is serious—of course, Christian in command and control. How could I forget . . . Would I want him any other way?

I smile. "Yes, it is."

He gives me a puzzled look, then shakes his head. "Shall we go?"

"I'll just brush my teeth."

He smirks. "Okay."

Why is he smirking? The thought nags me as I head into the bathroom. A memory springs unbidden to my mind. I used his toothbrush after I first spent the night with him. I smirk and grab his toothbrush in homage to that first time. Gazing at myself as I brush my teeth, I'm pale, too pale. But then I'm always pale. The last time I was here I was single, and now I'm married at twenty-two! I'm getting old. I rinse out my mouth.

Holding up my wrist, I shake it, and the charms on my bracelet give a satisfying rattle. How does my sweet Fifty always know
exactly the right thing to give me? I take a deep breath, attempt-
ing to stem the emotion still lurking in my system, and gaze down
at the bracelet once more. I bet it cost a fortune. *Ah . . . well*. He
can afford it.

As we walk to the elevators, Christian takes my hand and
kisses my knuckles, his thumb brushing over *Charlie Tango* on
my bracelet. "You like?"

"More than like. I love it. Very much. Like you."

He smiles and kisses my knuckles once more. I feel lighter
than I did yesterday. Perhaps because it's morning and the world
always seems a more hopeful place than it does in the dead of
night. Or maybe it's my husband's sweet wake-up. Or maybe it's
knowing that Ray is no worse.

As we step into the empty elevator, I glance up at Christian.
His eyes flicker quickly down to mine, and he smirks again.

"Don't," he whispers as the doors shut.

"Don't what?"

"Look at me like that."

"Fuck the paperwork," I mutter, grinning.

He laughs, and it's such a carefree, boyish sound. He tugs me
into his arms and tilts my head up. "Someday, I'll rent this elevator
for a whole afternoon."

"Just the afternoon?" I arch my brow.

"Mrs. Grey, you are greedy."

"When it comes to you, I am."

"I'm very glad to hear it." He kisses me gently.

And I don't know if it's because we are in *this* elevator or
because he's not touched me in more than twenty-four hours
or if he's just my intoxicating husband, but desire unwinds and
stretches lazily deep in my belly. I run my fingers into his hair and
deepen the kiss, pushing him against the wall and bringing my
body flush against his.

He groans into my mouth and cups my head, cradling me as
we kiss—really kiss, our tongues exploring the oh-so-familiar but

still oh-so-new, oh-so-exciting territory that is the other's mouth. My inner goddess swoons, bringing my libido back from purdah. I caress his dear, dear face in my hands.

"Ana," he breathes.

"I love you, Christian Grey. Don't forget that," I whisper as I gaze into darkening gray eyes.

The elevator comes smoothly to a halt and the doors open.

"Let's go and see your father before I decide to rent this today." He kisses me quickly, takes my hand, and leads me into the lobby.

As we walk past the concierge, Christian gives a discreet signal to the kindly middle-aged man standing behind the desk. He nods and picks up his phone. I glance questioningly at Christian, and he gives me his secret smile. I frown at him, and for a moment he looks nervous.

"Where's Taylor?" I ask.

"We'll see him shortly."

Of course, he's probably fetching the car. "Sawyer?"

"Running errands."

What errands?

Christian avoids the revolving door, and I know it's so he doesn't have to release my hand. The thought warms me. Outside it's a mild late-summer morning, but the scent of the coming fall is in the breeze. I glance around, looking for the Audi SUV and Taylor. No sign. Christian's hand tightens around mine, and I look up at him. He seems anxious.

"What is it?"

He shrugs. The hum of an approaching car engine distracts me. It's throaty . . . familiar. As I turn to find the source of the noise, it stops suddenly. Taylor is climbing out of a sleek white sports car parked in front of us.

Oh shit! It's an R8. I whip my head back to Christian, who's watching me warily. *"You can buy me one for my birthday . . . a white one, I think."*

"Happy birthday," he says, and I know he's gauging my reaction. I gape at him because that's all I can do. He holds out a key.

"You are completely over the top," I whisper. *He's bought me a fucking Audi R8! Holy shit. Just like I asked!* My face splits in a huge grin, and I jump up and down on the spot in a moment of unguarded and unbridled overexcitement. Christian's expression mirrors mine, and I dance forward into his waiting arms. He swings me around.

"You have more money than sense!" I whoop. "I love it! Thank you." He stops and dips me low suddenly, startling me, so that I have to grasp his upper arms.

"Anything for you, Mrs. Grey." He grins down at me. *Oh my.* What a very public display of affection. He bends and kisses me. "Come. Let's go see your dad."

"Yes. And I get to drive?"

He grins down at me. "Of course. It's yours." He stands me up and releases me, and I hurry around to the driver's door.

Taylor opens it for me, smiling broadly. "Happy birthday, Mrs. Grey."

"Thank you, Taylor." I startle him by giving him a swift hug, which he returns awkwardly. He's still blushing when I climb into the car, and he closes the door promptly once I'm inside.

"Drive safe, Mrs. Grey," he says gruffly. I beam up at him, barely able to contain my excitement.

"Will do," I promise, putting the key in the ignition as Christian stretches out beside me.

"Take it easy. Nobody chasing us now," he warns. When I turn the key, the engine thunders to life. I check the rearview and side mirrors, and spotting a rare moment of clear traffic, execute a huge perfect U-turn and roar off in the direction of OSHU.

"Whoa!" Christian exclaims, alarmed.

"What?"

"I don't want you in the ICU beside your father. Slow down," he growls, not to be argued with. I ease off the accelerator and grin at him.

"Better?"

"Much," he mutters, trying hard to look stern—and failing miserably.

RAY'S CONDITION IS THE same. Seeing him grounds me after the heady road trip here. *I really should drive more carefully.* You can't legislate for every drunk driver in this world. I must ask Christian what's become of the asshole who hit Ray—I'm sure he knows. In spite of the tubes, my father looks comfortable, and I think he has a little more color in his cheeks. While I tell him about my morning, Christian wanders off to the waiting room to make phone calls.

Nurse Kellie hovers, checking Ray's lines and making notes on his chart. "All his signs are good, Mrs. Grey." She smiles kindly at me.

"That's very encouraging."

A little later Dr. Crowe appears with two nursing assistants and says warmly, "Mrs. Grey, time to take your father up to radiology. We're giving him a CT scan. To see how his brain is doing."

"Will you be long?"

"Up to an hour."

"I'll wait. I'd like to know."

"Sure thing, Mrs. Grey."

I wander into the thankfully empty waiting room where Christian is talking on the phone, pacing. As he speaks, he gazes out the window at the panoramic view of Portland. He turns to me when I shut the door, and he looks angry.

"How far above the limit? . . . I see . . . All charges, everything. Ana's father is in the ICU—I want you to throw the fucking book at him, Dad . . . Good. Keep me informed." He hangs up.

"The other driver?"

He nods. "Some drunken trailer trash from southeast Portland." He sneers, and I'm shocked by his terminology and his derisory tone. He walks over to me, and his tone softens.

"Finished with Ray? Do you want to go?"

"Um . . . no." I peer up at him, still reeling at his display of contempt.

"What's wrong?"

"Nothing. Ray's being taken to radiology for a CT scan to check the swelling in his brain. I'd like to wait for the results."

"Okay. We'll wait." He sits down and holds out his arms. As we're alone, I go willingly and curl up in his lap.

"This is not how I envisaged spending today," Christian murmurs into my hair.

"Me neither, but I'm feeling more positive now. Your mom was very reassuring. It was kind of her to come last night."

Christian strokes my back and rests his chin on my head. "My mom is an amazing woman."

"She is. You're very lucky to have her."

Christian nods.

"I should call my mom. Tell her about Ray," I murmur and Christian stiffens. "I'm surprised she hasn't called me." I frown in a moment of realization. In fact, I feel hurt. It's my birthday after all, and she was there when I was born. Why hasn't she called?

"Maybe she did," Christian says. I fish my BlackBerry out of my pocket. It shows no missed calls, but quite a few texts: happy birthdays from Kate, José, Mia, and Ethan. Nothing from my mother. I shake my head despondently.

"Call her now," he says softly. I do, but there's no reply, just the answering machine. I don't leave a message. How can my own mother forget my birthday?

"She's not there. I'll call later when I know the results of the brain scan."

Christian tightens his arms around me, nuzzling my hair once more, and wisely makes no comment on my mother's lack of maternal concern. I feel rather than hear the buzz of his BlackBerry. He doesn't let me stand up but fishes it awkwardly out of his pocket.

"Andrea," he snaps, businesslike again. I make another move to stand and he stops me, frowning and holding me tightly around my waist. I nestle back against his chest and listen to the one-sided conversation.

"Good . . . ETA is what time? . . . And the other, um . . . packages?" Christian glances at his watch. "Does the Heathman have all the details? . . . Good . . . Yes. It can hold until Monday morning, but e-mail it just in case—I'll print, sign, and scan it back to you . . . They can wait. Go home, Andrea . . . No, we're good, thank you." He hangs up.

"Everything okay?"

"Yes."

"Is this your Taiwan thing?"

"Yes." He shifts beneath me.

"Am I too heavy?"

He snorts. "No, baby."

"Are you worried about the Taiwan thing?"

"No."

"I thought it was important."

"It is. The shipyard here depends on it. There are lots of jobs at stake."

Oh!

"We just have to sell it to the unions. That's Sam and Ros's job. But the way the economy's heading, none of us have a lot of choice."

I yawn.

"Am I boring you, Mrs. Grey?" He nuzzles my hair again, amused.

"No! Never . . . I'm just very comfortable on your lap. I like hearing about your business."

"You do?" He sounds surprised.

"Of course." I lean back to gaze directly at him. "I like hearing any bit of information you deign to share with me." I smirk, and he regards me with amusement and shakes his head.

"Always hungry for more information, Mrs. Grey."

"Tell me," I urge him as I snuggle up against his chest again.

"Tell you what?"

"Why you do it."

"Do what?"

"Work the way you do."

"A guy's got to earn a living." He's amused.

"Christian, you earn more than a living." My voice is full of irony. He frowns and is quiet for a moment. I think he's not going to divulge any secrets, but he surprises me.

"I don't want to be poor," he says, his voice low. "I've done that. I'm not going back there again. Besides . . . it's a game," he murmurs. "It's about winning. A game I've always found very easy."

"Unlike life," I murmur to myself. Then I realize I said the words out loud.

"Yes, I suppose." He frowns. "Though it's easier with you."

Easier with me? I hug him tightly. "It can't all be a game. You're very philanthropic."

He shrugs, and I know he's growing uncomfortable. "About some things, maybe," he says quietly.

"I love philanthropic Christian," I murmur.

"Just him?"

"Oh, I love megalomaniac Christian, too, and control freak Christian, sexpertise Christian, kinky Christian, romantic Christian, shy Christian . . . the list is endless."

"That's a whole lot of Christians."

"I'd say at least fifty."

He laughs. "Fifty Shades," he murmurs into my hair.

"My Fifty Shades."

He shifts, tipping my head back, and kisses me. "Well, Mrs. Shades, let's see how your dad is doing."

"Okay."

"CAN WE GO FOR a drive?"

Christian and I are back in the R8, and I'm feeling giddily buoyant. Ray's brain is back to normal—all swelling gone. Dr. Sluder has decided to wake him from his coma tomorrow. She says she's pleased with his progress.

"Sure." Christian grins at me. "It's your birthday—we can do anything you want."

Oh! His tone makes me turn and gaze at him. His eyes are dark.

"Anything?"

"Anything."

How much promise can he load into one word? "Well, I want to drive."

"Then drive, baby." He grins, and I grin back.

My car handles like a dream, and as we hit the I-5, I subtly put my foot down, forcing us both back in our seats.

"Steady, baby," Christian warns.

AS WE DRIVE BACK into Portland, an idea occurs to me.

"Have you planned lunch?" I ask Christian tentatively.

"No. You're hungry?" He sounds hopeful.

"Yes."

"Where do you want to go? It's your day, Ana."

"I know just the place."

I pull up near the gallery where José exhibited his work and park right outside Le Picotin restaurant, where we went after José's show.

Christian grins. "For one minute I thought you were going to take me to that dreadful bar you drunk dialed me from."

"Why would I do that?"

"To check the azaleas are still alive." He arches a sardonic brow.

I blush. "Don't remind me! Besides . . . you still took me to your hotel room." I smirk.

"Best decision I ever made," he says, his eyes soft and warm.

"Yes. It was." I lean over and kiss him.

"Do you think that supercilious fucker is still waiting tables?" Christian asks.

"Supercilious? I thought he was fine."

"He was trying to impress you."

"Well, he succeeded."

Christian's mouth twists in amused disgust.

"Shall we go see?" I offer.

"Lead on, Mrs. Grey."

AFTER LUNCH AND A quick detour to the Heathman to pick up Christian's laptop, we return to the hospital. I spend the afternoon with Ray, reading aloud from one of the manuscripts I've been sent. My only accompaniment is the sound of the machinery keeping him alive, keeping him with me. Now that I know he's making progress, I can breathe a little easier and relax. I'm hopeful. He just needs time to get well. I've got time—I can give him that. I wonder idly if I should try calling Mom again, but decide to do it later. I hold Ray's hand loosely as I read to him, squeezing it occasionally, willing him to be well. His fingers feel soft and warm beneath my touch. He still has the indentation on his finger where he wore his wedding ring—even after all this time.

An hour or two later, I don't know how long, I glance up to see Christian, laptop in hand, standing at the end of Ray's bed with Nurse Kellie.

"It's time to go, Ana."

Oh. I clasp Ray's hand tightly. I don't want to leave him.

"I want to feed you. Come. It's late." Christian sounds insistent.

"I'm about to give Mr. Steele a sponge bath," Nurse Kellie says.

"Okay." I concede. "We'll be back tomorrow morning."

I kiss Ray on his cheek, feeling his unfamiliar stubble beneath my lips. I don't like it. *Keep getting better, Daddy. I love you.*

"I THOUGHT WE'D DINE downstairs. In a private room," Christian says, a gleam in his eye as he opens the door to our suite.

"Really? Finish what you started a few months ago?"

He smirks. "If you're very lucky, Mrs. Grey."

I laugh. "Christian, I don't have anything dressy to wear."

He smiles, holds out his hand, and leads me into the bedroom. He opens the wardrobe to reveal a large white dress bag hanging inside.

"Taylor?" I ask.

"Christian," he replies, forceful and wounded at once. His tone makes me laugh. Unzipping the bag, I find a navy satin dress and ease it out. It's gorgeous—fitted, with thin straps. It looks small.

"It's lovely. Thank you. I hope it fits."

"It will," he says confidently. "And here"—he picks up a shoebox—"shoes to match." He gives me a wolfish smile.

"You think of everything. Thank you." I stretch up and kiss him.

"I do." He hands me yet another bag.

I gaze at him quizzically. Inside is a black strapless bodysuit with a central panel of lace. He caresses my face, tilts my chin, and kisses me.

"I look forward to taking this off you later."

FRESH OUT OF MY bath, washed, shaved, and feeling pampered, I sit on the edge of the bed and start up the hair dryer. Christian wanders into the bedroom. I think he's been working.

"Here, let me," he says, pointing to the chair in front of the dressing table.

"Dry my hair?"

He nods. I blink at him.

"Come," he says, regarding me intently. I know that expression, and I know better than to disobey. Slowly and methodically he dries my hair, one lock at a time with his usual skill.

"You're no stranger to this," I murmur. His smile is reflected in the mirror, but he says nothing and continues to brush through my hair. Hmm . . . it's very relaxing.

WHEN WE STEP INTO the elevator on our way to dinner, we are not alone. Christian looks delicious in his signature white linen shirt, black jeans and jacket. No tie. The two women inside shoot admiring glances at him and less generous ones at me. I hide my smile. *Yes, ladies, he's mine.* Christian takes my hand and pulls me close as we travel in silence down to the mezzanine level.

It's busy, full of people dressed up for the evening, sitting around chatting and drinking, starting their Saturday night. I am grateful that I fit in. The dress hugs me, skimming over my curves and holding everything in place. I have to say, I feel . . . attractive wearing it. I know Christian approves.

At first, I think we're heading for the private dining room where we first discussed the contract, but he leads me past that doorway and on to the far end, where he opens the door to another wood-paneled room.

"*Surprise!*"

Oh my. Kate and Elliot, Mia and Ethan, Carrick and Grace, Mr. Rodriguez and José, and my mother and Bob are all there raising their glasses. I stand gaping at them, speechless. *How? When?* I turn in consternation to Christian, and he squeezes my hand. My mom steps forward and wraps her arms around me. *Oh, Mom!*

"Darling, you look beautiful. Happy birthday."

"Mom!" I sob, embracing her. *Oh, Mommy.* Tears stream down my face despite the audience, and I bury my face in her neck.

"Honey, darling. Don't cry. Ray will be okay. He's such a strong man. Don't cry. Not on your birthday." Her voice cracks, but she maintains her composure. She grasps my face in her hands and with her thumbs wipes away my tears.

"I thought you'd forgotten."

"Oh, Ana! How could I? Seventeen hours of labor is not something you easily forget."

I giggle through my tears, and she smiles.

"Dry your eyes, honey. Lots of people are here to share your special day."

I sniffle, not wanting to look at anyone else in the room, embarrassed and thrilled that everyone has made such an effort to come and see me.

"How did you get here? When did you arrive?"

"Your husband sent his plane, darling." She grins, impressed. And I laugh. "Thank you for coming, Mom." She wipes my

nose with a tissue as only a mother would. "Mom!" I scold, com-
posing myself.

"That's better. Happy birthday, darling." She steps aside while
everyone lines up to hug me and wish me happy birthday.

"He's doing well, Ana. Dr. Sluder is one of the best in the
country. Happy birthday, angel." Grace hugs me.

"You cry all you want to, Ana—it's your party." José embraces
me.

"Happy birthday, darling girl." Carrick smiles, cupping my
face.

"S'up babe? Your old man will be fine." Elliot enfolds me in
his arms. "Happy birthday."

"Okay." Taking my hand, Christian pulls me from Elliot's
embrace. "Enough fondling my wife. Go fondle your fiancée."

Elliot grins wickedly at him and winks at Kate.

A waiter I hadn't noticed before presents Christian and me
with glasses of pink champagne.

Christian clears his throat. "This would be a perfect day if Ray
were here with us, but he's not far away. He's doing well, and I
know he'd like you to enjoy yourself, Ana. To all of you, thank you
for coming to share my beautiful wife's birthday, the first of many
to come. Happy birthday, my love." Christian raises his glass to me
amid a chorus of "happy birthday's", and I have to fight again to
keep my tears at bay.

I WATCH THE ANIMATED conversations around the dinner table.
It's strange to be cocooned in the bosom of my family, knowing the
man I consider my father is on a life support machine in the cold
clinical environs of the ICU. I'm detached from the proceedings
but grateful that they're all here. Watching the sparring between
Elliot and Christian, José's ready warm wit, Mia's excitement and
her enthusiasm for the food, Ethan slyly watching her. I think he
likes her . . . though it's hard to tell. Mr. Rodriguez is sitting back,
like me, enjoying the conversations. He looks better. Rested. José
is very attentive to him, cutting his food, keeping his glass filled.

Having his surviving parent come so close to death has made José appreciate Mr. Rodriguez more . . . I know.

I gaze at Mom. She's in her element, charming, witty, and warm. I love her so much. I must remember to tell her. Life is so precious, I realize that now.

"You okay?" Kate asks in an uncharacteristically gentle voice.

I nod and clasp her hand. "Yes. Thanks for coming."

"You think Mr. Megabucks could keep me away from you on your birthday? We got to fly in the helicopter!" She grins.

"Really?"

"Yes. All of us. And to think Christian can fly it."

I nod.

"That's kinda hot."

"Yeah, I think so."

We grin.

"Are you staying here tonight?" I ask.

"Yes. We all are, I think. You knew nothing about this?"

I shake my head.

"Smooth, isn't he?"

I nod.

"What did he get you for your birthday?"

"This." I hold up my bracelet.

"Oh, cute!"

"Yes."

"London, Paris . . . ice cream?"

"You don't want to know."

"I can guess."

We laugh, and I blush, recalling Ben & Jerry's & Ana.

"Oh . . . and an R8."

Kate spits her wine rather unattractively down her chin, making us both laugh some more.

"Over the top bastard, isn't he?" She giggles.

FOR DESSERT I AM presented with a sumptuous chocolate cake blazing with twenty-two silver candles and a rousing chorus of

"Happy Birthday." Grace watches Christian singing with the rest of my friends and family, and her eyes shine with love. Catching my eye, she blows me a kiss.

"Make a wish," Christian whispers to me. In one breath I blow out all the candles, fervently willing my father better. *Daddy, get well. Please get well. I love you so.*

AT MIDNIGHT, MR. RODRIGUEZ and José take their leave.

"Thank you so much for coming." I hug José tightly.

"Wouldn't miss it for the world. Glad Ray's heading in the right direction."

"Yes. You, Mr. Rodriguez, and Ray have to come fishing with Christian in Aspen."

"Yeah? Sounds cool." José grins before he leaves to fetch his father's coat, and I crouch down to say good-bye to Mr. Rodriguez.

"You know, Ana, there was a time . . . well, I thought you and José . . ." His voice fades, and he looks at me, his dark gaze intense but loving.

Oh no.

"I'm very fond of your son, Mr. Rodriguez, but he's like a brother to me."

"You would have made one fine daughter-in-law. And you do. To the Greys." He smiles wistfully and I blush.

"I hope you'll settle for friend."

"Of course. Your husband is a fine man. You chose well, Ana."

"I think so," I whisper. "I love him so." I hug Mr. Rodriguez.

"Treat him good, Ana."

"I will," I promise.

CHRISTIAN CLOSES THE DOOR to our suite.

"Alone at last," he murmurs, leaning back against the door, watching me.

I step toward him and run my fingers over the lapels of his jacket. "Thank you for a wonderful birthday. You really are the most thoughtful, considerate, generous husband."

"My pleasure."

"Yes . . . your pleasure. Let's do something about that," I whisper. Tightening my hands around his lapels, I pull his lips to mine.

———

After a communal breakfast, I open all my presents, then give a series of cheery good-byes to all the Greys and Kavanaghs who will be returning to Seattle via *Charlie Tango*. My mom, Christian, and I head up to the hospital with Taylor driving, since the three of us would not fit into my R8. Bob has declined to visit, and I'm secretly glad. It'd be just too weird, and I'm sure Ray wouldn't appreciate Bob seeing him at anything less than his best.

Ray looks much the same. Hairier. Mom is shocked when she sees him, and together we cry a little more.

"Oh, Ray." She squeezes his hand and gently strokes his face, and I'm moved to see her love for her ex-husband. I'm glad I have tissues in my purse. We sit beside him, me holding her hand while she holds his.

"Ana, there was a time when this man was the center of my world. The sun rose and set with him. I'll always love him. He's taken such good care of you."

"Mom—" I choke, and she strokes my face and tucks a lock of hair behind my ear.

"You know I'll always love Ray. We just drifted apart." She sighs. "And I just couldn't live with him." She gazes down at her fingers, and I wonder if she's thinking about Steve, Husband Number Three, who we don't talk about.

"I know you love Ray," I whisper, drying my eyes. "They're going to bring him out of his coma today."

"Good. I'm sure he'll be fine. He's so stubborn. I think you learned it from him."

I smile. "Have you been talking to Christian?"

"Does he think you're stubborn?"

"I believe so."

"I'll tell him it's a family trait. You look so good together, Ana. So happy."

"We are, I think. Getting there, anyway. I love him. He's the center of my world. The sun rises and sets with him for me, too."

"He obviously adores you, darling."

"And I adore him."

"Make sure you tell him. Men need to hear that stuff just like we do."

I INSIST ON GOING to the airport with Mom and Bob to say good-bye. Taylor follows in the R8, and Christian drives the SUV. I'm sorry they can't stay longer, but they have to get back to Savannah. It's a tearful good-bye.

"Take good care of her, Bob," I whisper as he hugs me.

"Sure will, Ana. And you look after yourself."

"Will do." I turn to my mother. "Good-bye, Mom. Thank you for coming," I whisper, my voice hoarse. "I love you so much."

"Oh, my darling girl, I love you, too. And Ray will be fine. He's not ready to shuffle off this mortal coil just yet. There's probably a Mariners game he can't miss."

I giggle. She's right. I resolve to read the sports pages of the Sunday newspaper to Ray that evening. I watch her and Bob climb the steps into the GEH jet. She gives me a tearful wave, then she's gone. Christian wraps his arm around my shoulder.

"Let's head back, baby," he murmurs.

"Will you drive?"

"Sure."

WHEN WE RETURN TO the hospital that evening, Ray looks different. It takes me a moment to realize that the suck and push of the ventilator has vanished. Ray is breathing on his own. Relief floods through me. I stroke his stubbly face and take out a tissue to gently wipe the spittle from his mouth.

Christian stalks off to find Dr. Sluder or Dr. Crowe for an update, while I take my familiar seat beside his bed to keep a watchful vigil.

I unfold the sports section of the Sunday *Oregonian* and conscientiously begin reading out the report about the Sounders soccer game against Real Salt Lake. By all accounts, it was a wild game, but the Sounders were defeated by an own goal from Kasey Keller. I grip Ray's hand firmly in mine as I read it through.

"And the final score, Sounders one, Real Salt Lake two."

"Hey, Annie, we lost? No!" Ray rasps, and he squeezes my hand.

Daddy!

CHAPTER NINETEEN

Tears stream down my face. He's back. My daddy is back.

"Don't cry, Annie." Ray's voice is hoarse. "What's happening?"

I take up his hand in both of mine and cradle it against my face. "You've been in an accident. You're in the hospital in Portland."

Ray frowns, and I don't know if it's because he's uncomfortable with my uncharacteristic display of affection or because he can't remember the accident.

"Do you want some water?" I ask, though I'm not sure if I'm allowed to give him any. He nods, bewildered. My heart swells. I stand up and lean over him, kissing his forehead. "I love you, Daddy. Welcome back."

He waves his hand, embarrassed. "Me, too, Annie. Water." I run the short distance to the nurses' station.

"My dad—he's awake!" I beam at Nurse Kellie, who smiles back.

"Page Dr. Sluder," she says to her colleague and hurriedly makes her way around the desk.

"He wants water."

"I'll bring him some."

I skip back to my father's bed, I feel so lighthearted. His eyes are closed when I reach him, and I immediately worry that he's slipped back into a coma.

"Daddy?"

"I'm here," he mutters, and his eyes flutter open as Nurse Kellie appears with a jug of ice chips and a glass.

"Hello, Mr. Steele. I'm Kellie, your nurse. Your daughter tells me you're thirsty."

IN THE WAITING ROOM, Christian is staring fixedly at his laptop, deep in concentration. He glances up when I close the door.

"He's awake," I announce. He smiles, and the tension around his eyes vanishes. Oh . . . I hadn't noticed before. Has he been tense all this time? He sets his laptop aside, stands, and embraces me.

"How is he?" he asks as I wrap my arms around him.

"Talking, thirsty, bewildered. He doesn't remember the accident at all."

"That's understandable. Now that he's awake, I want to get him moved to Seattle. Then we can go home, and my mom can keep an eye on him."

Already?

"I'm not sure he's well enough to be moved."

"I'll talk to Dr. Sluder. Get her opinion."

"You miss home?"

"Yes."

"Okay."

"YOU HAVEN'T STOPPED SMILING," Christian says as I pull up outside the Heathman.

"I'm very relieved. And happy."

Christian grins. "Good."

The light is fading, and I shiver as I step out into the cool, crisp evening and hand my key to the parking valet. He's eyeing my car with lust, and I don't blame him. Christian puts his arm around me.

"Shall we celebrate?" he asks as we enter the foyer.

"Celebrate?"

"Your dad."

I giggle. "Oh, him."

"I've missed that sound." Christian kisses my hair.

"Can we just eat in our room? You know, have a quiet night in?"

"Sure. Come." Taking my hand, he leads me to the elevators.

"THAT WAS DELICIOUS," I murmur with satisfaction as I push my plate away, replete for the first time in ages. "They sure know how to make a fine tarte tatin here."

I am freshly bathed and wearing only Christian's T-shirt and my panties. In the background, Christian's iPod is on shuffle and Dido is warbling on about white flags.

Christian eyes me speculatively. His hair is still damp from our bath, and he's wearing just his black T-shirt and jeans. "That's the most I've seen you eat the entire time we've been here," he says.

"I was hungry."

He leans back in his chair with a self-satisfied smirk and takes a sip of his white wine. "What would you like to do now?" His voice is soft.

"What do you want to do?"

He raises an eyebrow, amused. "What I always want to do."

"And that is?"

"Mrs. Grey, don't be coy."

Reaching across the dining table, I grasp his hand, turn it over, and skim my index finger over his palm. "I'd like you to touch me with this." I run my finger up his index finger.

He shifts in his chair. "Just that?" His eyes darken and heat at once.

"Maybe this?" I run my finger up his middle finger and back to his palm. "And this." My nail traces his ring finger. "Definitely this." My finger stops at his wedding ring. "This is very sexy."

"Is it, now?"

"It sure is. It says *this man is mine*." And I skim the small callus that has already formed on his palm beneath the ring. He leans forward and cups my chin with his other hand.

"Mrs. Grey, are you seducing me?"

"I hope so."

"Anastasia, I'm a given." His voice is low. "Come here." He

tugs my hand, pulling me onto his lap. "I like having unfettered access to you." He runs a hand up my thigh to my behind. He grasps the nape of my neck with his other hand and kisses me, holding me firmly in place.

He tastes of white wine and apple pie and Christian. I run my fingers through his hair, holding him to me while our tongues explore and curl and twist around each other, my blood heating in my veins. We're breathless when Christian pulls away.

"Let's go to bed," he murmurs against my lips.

"Bed?"

He pulls back farther and tugs my hair so I am looking up at him. "Where would you prefer, Mrs. Grey?"

I shrug, feigning indifference. "Surprise me."

"You're feisty this evening." He runs his nose along mine.

"Maybe I need to be restrained."

"Maybe you do. You're getting mighty bossy in your old age." He narrows his eyes, but can't disguise the latent humor there.

"What are you going to do about it?" I challenge.

His eyes glitter. "I know what I'd like to do about it. Depends if you're up to it."

"Oh, Mr. Grey, you've been very gentle with me these last couple of days. I'm not made of glass, you know."

"You don't like gentle?"

"With you, of course. But you know . . . variety is the spice of life." I bat my lashes at him.

"You're after something less gentle?"

"Something life-affirming."

He raises his brows in surprise. "Life-affirming," he repeats, astonished humor in his voice.

I nod. He gazes at me for a moment. "Don't bite your lip," he whispers, then rises suddenly with me in his arms. I gasp and grab his biceps, fearful that he'll drop me. He walks over to the smallest of the three couches and deposits me on it.

"Wait here. Don't move." He gives me a brief, hot, intense look and turns on his heel, stalking toward the bedroom. Oh . . . Christian barefoot. Why are his feet so hot? He's back a few moments later, taking me by surprise as he leans over me from behind.

"I think we'll dispense with this." He grabs my T-shirt and drags it over my head, leaving me naked except for my panties. He pulls my ponytail back and kisses me.

"Stand up," he orders against my lips and releases me. I comply immediately. He lays a towel out on the sofa.

Towel?

"Take your panties off."

I swallow but do as I'm told, discarding them by the sofa.

"Sit." He grabs my ponytail again and pulls my head back. "You'll tell me to stop if this gets too much, yes?"

I nod.

"Say it." His voice is stern.

"Yes," I squeak.

He smirks. "Good. So, Mrs. Grey . . . by popular demand, I'm going to restrain you." His voice drops to a breathless whisper. Desire streaks through my body like lightning simply at those words. Oh, my sweet Fifty—on the sofa?

"Bring your knees up," he commands softly. "And sit right back."

I rest my feet on the edge of the sofa, my knees up in front of me. He reaches for my left leg, and taking the belt from one of the bathroom robes, he ties one end above my knee.

"Bathrobes?"

"I'm improvising." He smirks again and fastens the slipknot above my knee and ties the other end of the soft belt around the finial at the back corner of the sofa, effectively parting my legs.

"Don't move," he warns and repeats the process with my right leg, tying the second cord to the other finial.

Oh my . . . I am sitting up, splayed out on the sofa, legs spread wide.

"Okay?" Christian asks softly, gazing down at me from behind the sofa.

I nod, expecting him to tie my hands, too. But he refrains. He bends and kisses me.

"You have no idea how hot you look right now," he murmurs and rubs his nose against mine. "Change of music, I think." He stands and strolls casually over to the iPod dock.

How does he do this? Here I am, trussed up and horny as hell, while he's so cool and calm. He's just in my field of vision, and I watch the flex and pull of the muscles of his back under his T-shirt as he changes the song. Immediately, a sweet, almost childlike female voice starts to sing about watching me.

Oh, I like this song.

Christian turns and his eyes lock on mine as he moves around to the front of the sofa and sinks gracefully to his knees in front of me.

Suddenly, I feel very exposed.

"Exposed? Vulnerable?" he asks with his uncanny ability to voice my unspoken words. His hands are on his knees. I nod.

Why doesn't he touch me?

"Good," he murmurs "Hold out your hands." I can't look away from his mesmerizing eyes as I do what he asks. Christian pours a little oily liquid onto each palm from a small clear bottle. It's scented—a rich, musky, sensuous scent that I can't place.

"Rub your hands." I squirm beneath his hot, heavy gaze. "Keep still," he warns.

Oh my.

"Now, Anastasia, I want you to touch yourself."

Holy cow.

"Start at your throat and work down."

I hesitate.

"Don't be shy, Ana. Come. Do it." The humor and challenge in his expression is plain to see, along with his desire.

The sweet voice sings that there's nothing sweet about her. I place my hands against my throat and let them slide down to the top of my breasts. The oil makes them glide effortlessly over my skin. My hands are warm.

"Lower," Christian murmurs, his eyes darkening. He doesn't touch me.

My hands cup my breasts.

"Tease yourself."

Oh my. I tug gently on my nipples.

"Harder," Christian urges. He sits immobile between my thighs, just watching me. "Like I would," he adds, his eyes shining darkly. My muscles clench deep in my belly. I groan in response and pull harder on my nipples, feeling them stiffen and lengthen beneath my touch.

"Yes. Like that. Again."

Closing my eyes I pull hard, rolling and twisting them between my fingers. I moan.

"Open your eyes."

I blink up at him.

"Again. I want to see you. See you enjoy your touch."

Oh fuck. I repeat the process. This is so . . . erotic.

"Hands. Lower."

I squirm.

"Keep still, Ana. Absorb the pleasure. Lower." His voice is low and husky, tempting and beguiling at once.

"You do it," I whisper.

"Oh, I will—soon. You. Lower. Now." Christian, exuding sensuality, runs his tongue along his teeth. *Holy fuck . . .* I writhe, pulling on the restraints.

He shakes his head, slowly. "Still." He rests his hands on my knees, holding me in place. "Come on, Ana—lower."

My hands glide down over my belly.

"Lower," he mouths, and he is carnality personified.

"Christian, please."

His hands glide down from my knees, skimming my thighs, moving toward my sex. "Come on, Ana. Touch yourself."

My left hand skims over my sex, and I rub in a slow circle, my mouth an O as I pant.

"Again," he whispers.

I groan louder and repeat the move and tip my head back, gasping.

"Again."

I moan loudly, and Christian inhales sharply. Grabbing my hands, he bends down, running his nose and then his tongue back and forth at the apex of my thighs.

"Ah!"

I want to touch him, but when I try to move my hands, his fingers tighten around my wrists.

"I'll restrain these, too. Keep still."

I groan. He releases me, then eases his middle two fingers inside me, the heel of his hand resting against my clitoris.

"I'm going to make you come quickly, Ana. Ready?"

"Yes," I pant.

He starts to move his fingers, his hand, up and down, rapidly, assaulting both that sweet spot inside me and my clitoris at the same time. Ah! The feeling is intense—really intense. Pleasure builds and spikes throughout the lower half of my body. I want to stretch my legs, but I can't. My hands claw at the towel beneath me.

"Surrender," Christian whispers.

I explode around his fingers, crying out incoherently. He presses the heel of his hand against my clitoris as the aftershocks run through my body, prolonging the delicious agony. Vaguely, I'm aware that he's untying my legs.

"My turn," he murmurs, and flips me over so I am facedown on the sofa with my knees on the floor. He spreads my legs and slaps me hard across my behind.

"Ah!" I yelp, and he slams into me.

"Oh, Ana," he hisses through clenched teeth as he starts to move. His fingers grip me hard around my hips as he grinds into me over and over. And I'm building again. *No . . . Ah . . .*

"Come on, Ana!" Christian shouts, and I shatter once more, pulsing around him and crying out as I come.

"LIFE-AFFIRMING ENOUGH FOR YOU?" Christian kisses my hair.

"Oh yes," I murmur, gazing up at the ceiling. I am lying on my husband, my back to his front, both of us on the floor beside the sofa. He's still dressed.

"I think we should go again. No clothes for you this time."

"Christ, Ana. Give a man a chance."

I giggle and he chuckles. "I'm glad Ray's conscious. Seems all your appetites are back," he says, not disguising the smile in his voice.

I turn over and scowl at him. "Are you forgetting about last night and this morning?" I pout.

"Nothing forgettable about either of those." He grins, and when he does, he looks so young and carefree and happy. He cups my behind. "You have a fantastic ass, Mrs. Grey."

"So do you." I arch a brow at him. "Though yours is still under cover."

"And what are you going to do about that, Mrs. Grey?"

"Why, I'm going to undress you, Mr. Grey. All of you."

He grins.

"And I think there's a lot that's sweet about you," I murmur, referring to the song still playing on repeat. His smile fades.

Oh no.

"You are," I whisper. I lean down and kiss the corner of his mouth. He closes his eyes and tightens his arms around me.

"Christian, you are. You made this weekend so special—in spite of what happened to Ray. Thank you."

He opens his large, serious gray eyes, and his expression tugs at my heart.

"Because I love you," he murmurs.

"I know. I love you, too." I caress his face. "And you're precious to me, too. You do know that, don't you?"

His stills, looking lost.

Oh, Christian . . . my sweet Fifty.

"Believe me," I whisper.

"It's not easy." His voice is almost inaudible.

"Try. Try hard, because it's true." I stroke his face once more, my fingers brushing against his sideburns. His eyes are gray oceans of loss and hurt and pain. I want to climb into his body and hold him. Anything to stop that look. When will he realize that he means the world to me? That he's more than worthy of my love, the love of his parents—his siblings? I have told him over and over, and yet here we are as Christian gives me his lost, abandoned look. Time. It will just take time.

"You'll get cold. Come." He rises gracefully to his feet and pulls me up to stand beside him. I slip my arm around his waist as we wander back into the bedroom. I won't push him, but since Ray's accident, it's become more important to me that he knows how much I love him.

As we enter the bedroom, I frown, desperate to recover the very welcome lighthearted mood of only a few moments ago.

"Shall we watch TV?" I ask.

Christian snorts. "I was hoping for round two." And my mercurial Fifty is back. I arch my brow and stop by the bed.

"Well, in that case, I think I'll be in charge."

He gapes at me, and I push him onto the bed and quickly straddle him, pinning his hands down beside his head.

He grins up at me. "Well, Mrs. Grey, now that you've got me, what are you going to do with me?"

I lean down and whisper in his ear, "I am going to fuck you with my mouth."

He closes his eyes, inhaling sharply, and I run my teeth gently along his jaw.

Christian is working at the computer. It's a bright early morning, and he's tapping out an e-mail, I think.

"Good morning," I murmur shyly from the doorway. He turns and smiles at me.

"Mrs. Grey. You're up early." He holds open his arms.

I bolt across the suite and curl into his lap. "As are you."

"I was just working." He shifts as he kisses my hair.

"What?" I ask, sensing something wrong.

He sighs. "I got an e-mail from Detective Clark. He wants to talk to you about that fucker Hyde."

"Really?" I sit back to gaze at Christian.

"Yes. I told him you're in Portland for the time being, so he'll have to wait. But he says he'd like to interview you here."

"He's coming here?"

"Apparently so." Christian looks bemused.

I frown. "What's so important that it can't wait?"

"Exactly."

"When's he coming?"

"Today. I'll e-mail him back."

"I have nothing to hide. I wonder what he wants to know?"

"We'll find out when he gets here. I'm intrigued, too." Christian shifts again. "Breakfast will be here shortly. Let's eat, then we can go and see your dad."

I nod. "You can stay here if you want. I can see you're busy."

He scowls. "No, I want to come with you."

"Okay." I grin, wrap my arms around his neck, and kiss him.

RAY IS BAD-TEMPERED. It's a joy. He's itchy, scratchy, impatient, and uncomfortable.

"Dad, you've been in a major car accident. It will take time to heal. Christian and I want to move you to Seattle."

"I don't know why you're bothering with me. I'll be fine here on my own."

"Don't be ridiculous." I squeeze his hand fondly, and he has the grace to smile at me.

"Do you need anything?"

"I could murder a doughnut, Annie."

I grin indulgently at him. "I'll get you a doughnut or two. We'll go to Voodoo."

"Great!"

"You want some decent coffee, too?"

"Hell yeah!"

"Okay, I'll go get some."

_____

CHRISTIAN IS ONCE MORE in the waiting room, talking on the phone. He really should set up office in here. Weirdly, he's by himself, although the other ICU beds are occupied. I wonder if Christian's frightened off the other visitors. He hangs up.

"Clark will be here at four this afternoon."

I frown. What could be so urgent? "Okay. Ray wants coffee and doughnuts."

Christian laughs. "I think I would too if I'd been in an accident. Ask Taylor to go."

"No, I'll go."

"Take Taylor with you." His voice is stern.

"Okay." I roll my eyes and he glares. Then he smirks and cocks his head to one side.

"There's no one here." His voice is deliciously low, and I know he's threatening to spank me. I am about to dare him, when a young couple enters the room. She is weeping softly.

I shrug apologetically at Christian, and he nods. He picks up his laptop, takes my hand, and leads me out of the room. "They need the privacy more than we do," Christian murmurs. "We'll have our fun later."

Outside Taylor is waiting patiently. "Let's all go get coffee and doughnuts."

_____

At four o'clock precisely there's a knock on the suite door. Taylor ushers in Detective Clark, who looks more bad-tempered than usual. He always seems to look bad-tempered. Perhaps it's the way his face is set.

"Mr. Grey, Mrs. Grey, thank you for seeing me."

"Detective Clark." Christian shakes his hand and directs him to a seat. I sit down on the sofa where I enjoyed myself so much last night. The thought makes me blush.

"It's Mrs. Grey I wish to see," Clark says pointedly to Christian and to Taylor, who is stationed beside the door. Christian glances and then nods almost imperceptibly at Taylor, who turns and leaves, shutting the door behind him.

"Anything you wish to say to my wife you can say in front of me." Christian's voice is cool and businesslike. Detective Clark turns to me.

"Are you sure you'd like your husband to be present?"

I frown at him. "Of course. I have nothing to hide. You are just interviewing me?"

"Yes, ma'am."

"I'd like my husband to stay."

Christian sits beside me, radiating tension.

"All right," murmurs Clark, resigned. He clears his throat. "Mrs. Grey, Mr. Hyde maintains that you sexually harassed him and made several lewd advances toward him."

Oh! I almost burst out laughing, but put my hand on Christian's thigh to restrain him as he shifts forward in his seat.

"That's preposterous," Christian splutters. I squeeze Christian's leg to silence him.

"That's not true," I state calmly. "In fact, it was the other way around. He propositioned me in a very aggressive manner, and he was fired."

Detective Clark's mouth flattens briefly into a thin line before he continues.

"Hyde alleges that you fabricated a tale about sexual harassment in order to get him fired. He says that you did this because he refused your advances and because you wanted his job."

I frown. *Holy crap.* Jack is even more delusional than I thought.

"That's not true." I shake my head.

"Detective, please don't tell me you have driven all this way to harass my wife with these ridiculous accusations."

Detective Clark turns his steely blue glare on Christian. "I need to hear this from Mrs. Grey, sir," he says with quiet restraint. I squeeze Christian's leg once more, silently imploring him to keep his cool.

"You don't have to listen to this shit, Ana."

"I think I should let Detective Clark know what happened."

Christian gazes at me impassively for a beat, then waves his hand in a gesture of resignation.

"What Hyde says is simply not true." My voice sounds calm, although I feel anything but. I'm bewildered by these accusations and nervous that Christian might explode. *What's Jack's game?* "Mr. Hyde accosted me in the office kitchen one evening. He told me that it was thanks to him that I had been hired and that he expected sexual favors in return. He tried to blackmail me, using e-mails that I'd sent to Christian, who wasn't my husband then. I didn't know Hyde had been monitoring my e-mails. He's delusional—he even accused me of being a spy sent by Christian, presumably to help him take over the company. He didn't know that Christian had already bought SIP." I shake my head as I recall my distressing, tense encounter with Hyde. "In the end, I-I took him down."

Clark's eyebrows rise in surprise. "Took him down?"

"My father is ex-army. Hyde . . . um, touched me, and I know how to defend myself."

Christian glances at me with a brief look of pride.

"I see." Clark leans back on the sofa, sighing heavily.

"Have you spoken to any of Hyde's former personal assistants?" Christian asks almost genially.

"Yes, we have. But the truth is we can't get any of his assistants to talk to us. They all say he was an exemplary boss, even though none of them lasted more than three months."

"We've had that problem, too," Christian murmurs.

Oh? I gape at Christian, as does Detective Clark.

"My security chief. He's interviewed Hyde's past five PAs."

"And why's that?"

Christian gives him a steely glare. "Because my wife worked for him, and I run security checks on anyone my wife works with."

Detective Clark flushes. I shrug apologetically at him with a welcome-to-my-world smile.

"I see," Clark murmurs. "I think there's more to this than

meets the eye, Mr. Grey. We are conducting a more thorough search of his apartment tomorrow, so maybe something will present itself then. Though by all accounts he hasn't lived there for some time."

"You've searched already?"

"Yes. We're doing it again. A fingertip search this time."

"You've still not charged him with the attempted murder of Ros Bailey and myself?" Christian says softly.

What?

"We're hoping to find more evidence in regard to the sabotage of your aircraft, Mr. Grey. We need more than a partial print, and while he's in custody, we can build a case."

"Is this all you came down here for?"

Clark bristles. "Yes, Mr. Grey, it is, unless you've had any further thoughts about the note?"

Note? What note?

"No. I told you. It means nothing to me." Christian cannot hide his irritation. "And I don't see why we couldn't have done this over the phone."

"I think I told you I prefer a hands-on approach. And I'm visiting my great-aunt, who lives in Portland—two birds . . . one stone." Clark remains stony faced and unfazed by my husband's bad temper.

"Well, if we're all done, I have work to attend to." Christian stands and Detective Clark follows his cue.

"Thank you for your time, Mrs. Grey," he says politely.

I nod.

"Mr. Grey." Christian opens the door, and Clark leaves.

I sag into the sofa.

"Can you believe that asshole?" Christian explodes.

"Clark?"

"No. That fucker, Hyde."

"No, I can't."

"What's his fucking game?" Christian whispers through gritted teeth.

"I don't know. Do you think Clark believed me?"

"Of course he did. He knows Hyde is a fucked-up asshole."

"You're very sweary."

"Sweary?" Christian smirks. "Is that even a word?"

"It is now."

Unexpectedly he grins and sits down beside me, pulling me into his arms.

"Don't think about that fucker. Let's go see your dad and try to talk about the move tomorrow."

"He was adamant that he wanted to stay in Portland and not be a bother."

"I'll talk to him."

"I want to travel with him."

Christian gazes at me, and for a moment, I think he's going to say no. "Okay. I'll come, too. Sawyer and Taylor can take the cars. I'll let Sawyer drive your R8 tonight."

———

The following day Ray is examining his new surroundings—an airy, light room in the rehabilitation center of Northwest Hospital in Seattle. It's noon, and he looks sleepy. The journey, via helicopter no less, has exhausted him.

"Tell Christian I appreciate this," he says quietly.

"You can tell him yourself. He'll be along this evening."

"Aren't you going to work?"

"Probably. I just want to make sure you're settled in here."

"You get along. You don't need to worry about me."

"I like worrying about you."

My BlackBerry buzzes. I check the number—it's not one I recognize.

"You going to answer that?" Ray asks.

"No. I don't know who it is. The voice mail can take it for me. I brought you something to read." I indicate the pile of sports magazines on his bedside table.

"Thanks, Annie."

"You're tired, aren't you?"

He nods.

"I'll let you get some sleep." I kiss his forehead. "Laters, Daddy," I murmur.

"I'll see you later, honey. And thank you." Ray catches my hand and squeezes it gently. "I like that you call me Daddy. Takes me back."

Oh, Daddy. I return his squeeze.

AS I HEAD OUT the main doors toward the SUV where Sawyer is waiting, I hear my name being called.

"Mrs. Grey! Mrs. Grey!"

Turning, I see Dr. Greene hurrying toward me, looking her usual immaculate self, if a little flustered.

"Mrs. Grey, how are you? Did you get my message? I called earlier."

"No." My scalp prickles.

"Well, I was wondering why you'd canceled four appointments."

Four appointments? I gape at her. *I've missed four appointments! How?*

"Perhaps we should talk about this in my office. I was going out for lunch—do you have time right now?"

I nod meekly. "Sure. I . . ." Words fail me. I've missed four appointments? *I'm late for my shot. Shit.*

In a daze, I follow her back into the hospital and up to her office. How did I miss four appointments? I vaguely remember one being moved—Hannah mentioned it—but *four?* How could I miss four?

Dr. Greene's office is spacious, minimalistic, and well appointed.

"I'm so grateful you caught me before I left," I mumble, still shell-shocked. "My father's been in a car accident, and we've just moved him here from Portland."

"Oh, I'm so sorry. How's he doing?"

"He's doing okay, thank you. On the mend."

"That's good. And it explains why you canceled on Friday."

Dr. Greene wiggles the mouse on her desk, and her computer comes to life.

"Yes . . . it's been over thirteen weeks. You're cutting it a bit close. We'd better do a test before we give you another shot."

"A test?" I whisper, all the blood rushing from my head.

"A pregnancy test."

Oh no.

She reaches into the drawer of her desk. "You know what to do with this." She hands me a small container. "The restroom is just outside my office."

I get up as if in a trance, my whole body operating as if on automatic pilot, and stumble to the restroom.

Shit, shit, shit, shit, *shit*. How could I have let this happen . . . again? I suddenly feel sick and offer a silent prayer. *Please no. Please no. It's too soon. It's too soon. It's too soon.*

When I reenter Dr. Greene's office, she gives me a tight smile and waves me to the seat in front of her desk. I sit down and word-lessly hand her my sample. She dips a small white stick into it and watches. She raises her eyebrows as it turns pale blue.

"What does blue mean?" The tension is almost choking me.

She looks up at me, her eyes serious. "Well, Mrs. Grey, it means you're pregnant."

What? No. No. No. Fuck.

CHAPTER TWENTY

I gape at Dr. Greene, my world collapsing around me. A baby. A baby. I don't want a baby . . . not yet. *Fuck*. And I know deep down that Christian is going to freak.

"Mrs. Grey, you're very pale. Would you like a glass of water?"

"Please." My voice is barely audible. My mind is racing. Pregnant? When?

"I take it you're surprised."

I nod mutely at the good doctor as she hands me a glass of water from her conveniently placed water cooler. I take a welcome sip. "Shocked," I whisper.

"We could do an ultrasound to see how advanced the pregnancy is. Judging by your reaction, I suspect you're just a couple of weeks or so from conception—four or five weeks pregnant. I take it you haven't been suffering any symptoms?"

I shake my head mutely. *Symptoms?* I don't think so. "I thought . . . I thought this was a reliable form of contraceptive."

Dr. Greene arches a brow. "It normally is, *when* you remember to have the shot," she says coolly.

"I must have lost track of time." *Christian is going to freak*. I know it.

"Have you been bleeding at all?"

I frown. "No."

"That's normal for the Depo. Let's do an ultrasound shall we? I have time."

I nod, bewildered, and Dr. Greene directs me toward a black leather exam table behind a screen.

"If you'll just slip off your skirt, underwear, and cover yourself with the blanket on the table, we'll go from there," she says briskly.

Underwear? I was expecting an ultrasound scan over my belly. Why do I need to remove my panties? I shrug in consternation, then quickly do as she says and lie down beneath the soft white blanket.

"That's good." Dr. Greene appears at the end of the table, pulling the ultrasound machine closer. It's a hi-tech stack of computers. Sitting down, she positions the screen so that we can both see it and jogs the trackball on the keyboard. The screen pings into life.

"If you could lift and bend your knees, then part them wide," she says matter-of-factly.

I frown warily.

"This is a transvaginal ultrasound. If you're only just pregnant, we should be able to find the baby with this." She holds up a long white probe.

Oh, you have got *to be kidding!*

"Okay," I mutter, mortified, and do as she says. Greene pulls a condom over the wand and lubricates it with clear gel.

"Mrs. Grey, if you could relax."

Relax? I'm pregnant, damn it! How do you expect me to relax? I blush and endeavor to find my happy place . . . which has relocated somewhere near the lost island of Atlantis.

Slowly and gently she inserts the probe.

Holy fuck!

All I can see on the screen is the visual equivalent of white noise—although it's more sepia in color. Slowly, Dr. Greene moves the probe about, and it's very disconcerting.

"There," she murmurs. She presses a button, freezing the picture on the screen, and points to a tiny blip in the sepia storm.

It's a little blip. There's a tiny little blip in my belly. Tiny. Wow. I forget my discomfort as I stare dumbfounded at the blip.

"It's too early to see the heartbeat, but yes, you're definitely pregnant. Four or five weeks, I would say." She frowns. "Looks like the shot ran out early. Oh well, that happens sometimes."

I am too stunned to say anything. The little blip is a baby. A real honest to goodness baby. Christian's baby. My baby. Holy cow. A *baby!*

"Would you like me to print out a picture for you?"

I nod, still unable to speak, and Dr. Greene presses a button. Then she gently removes the wand and hands me a paper towel to clean myself.

"Congratulations, Mrs. Grey," she says as I sit up. "We'll need to make another appointment. I suggest in four weeks' time. Then we can ascertain the exact age of your baby and set a likely due date. You can get dressed now."

"Okay." I'm reeling and I dress hurriedly. I have a blip, a little blip. When I emerge from behind the screen, Dr. Greene is back at her desk.

"In the meantime, I'd like you to start this course of folic acid and prenatal vitamins. Here's a leaflet of dos and don'ts."

As she hands me a package of pills and a leaflet, she continues to talk at me, but I'm not listening. I'm in shock. Overwhelmed. Surely I should be happy. Surely I should be thirty . . . at least. This is too soon—far too soon. I try to quell my rising sense of panic.

I wish Dr. Greene a polite good-bye and head back down to the exit and out into the cool fall afternoon. I'm gripped suddenly by a creeping cold and deep sense of foreboding. Christian is going to freak, I know, but how much and how far, I have no idea. His words haunt me. *"I'm not ready to share you yet."* I pull my jacket tighter around me, trying to shake off the cold.

Sawyer leaps out of the SUV and holds open the door. He frowns when he sees my face, but I ignore his concerned expression.

"Where to, Mrs. Grey?" he asks gently.

"SIP." I nestle into the backseat of the car, closing my eyes and leaning my head on the headrest. I should be happy. I know I should be happy. But I'm not. This is too early. Far too early. What about my job? What about SIP? What about Christian and me? No. No. *No.* We'll be fine. He'll be fine. He loved baby

Mia—I remember Carrick telling me—he dotes on her now. Perhaps I should warn Flynn . . . Perhaps I shouldn't tell Christian. Perhaps I . . . perhaps I should end this. I halt my thoughts on that dark path, alarmed at the direction they're taking. Instinctively my hand sweeps down to rest protectively over my belly. *No. My little Blip.* Tears spring to my eyes. What am I going to do?

A vision of a little boy with copper-colored hair and bright gray eyes running through the meadow at the new house invades my thoughts, teasing and tantalizing me with possibilities. He's giggling and squealing with delight as Christian and I chase him. Christian swings him high in his arms and carries him on his hip as we walk hand in hand back to the house.

My vision morphs into Christian turning away from me in disgust. I'm fat and awkward, heavy with child. He paces the long hall of mirrors, away from me, the sound of his footsteps echoing off the silvered glass, walls, and floor. *Christian* . . .

I jerk awake. *No.* He's going to freak out.

When Sawyer pulls up outside SIP, I leap out and head into the building.

"Ana, great to see you. How's your dad?" Hannah asks as soon as I reach my office. I regard her coolly.

"He's better, thank you. Can I see you in my office?"

"Sure." She looks surprised as she follows me in. "Is everything okay?"

"I need to know if you've moved or canceled any appointments with Dr. Greene."

"Dr. Greene? Yes, I have. About two or three of them. Mostly because you were in other meetings or running late. Why?"

Because now I'm fucking pregnant! I scream at her in my head. I take a deep, steadying breath. "If you move any appointments, will you make sure I know? I don't always check my calendar."

"Sure," Hannah says quietly. "I'm sorry. Have I done something wrong?"

I shake my head and sigh loudly. "Can you make me some tea? Then let's discuss what's been happening while I've been away."

"Sure. I'll jump to it." Brightening, she heads out of the office.

I gaze after her departing figure. "You see that woman?" I talk quietly to the blip. "She might be the reason you're here." I pat my belly, then feel like a complete idiot, because I am talking to the blip. *My* tiny little Blip. I shake my head, exasperated at myself and at Hannah . . . though deep down I know I can't really blame Hannah. Despondently I switch on my computer. There's an e-mail from Christian.

From: Christian Grey
Subject: Missing You
Date: September 13 2011 13:58
To: Anastasia Grey

Mrs. Grey

I've been back in the office for only three hours, and I'm missing you already.

Hope Ray has settled into his new room okay. Mom is going to see him this afternoon and check up on him.

I'll collect you around six this evening, and we can go and see him before heading home.

Sound good?

Your loving husband

Christian Grey
CEO, Grey Enterprises Holdings, Inc.

I type a quick response.

From: Anastasia Grey
Subject: Missing You
Date: September 13 2011 14:10
To: Christian Grey

Sure.

x

Anastasia Grey
Editor, SIP

From: Christian Grey
Subject: Missing You
Date: September 13 2011 14:14
To: Anastasia Grey

Are you okay?

Christian Grey
CEO, Grey Enterprises Holdings, Inc.

No, Christian, I'm not. I'm freaking out about you freaking out.
I don't know what to do. But I am not going to tell you via e-mail.

From: Anastasia Grey
Subject: Missing You
Date: September 13 2011 14:17
To: Christian Grey

Fine. Just busy.

See you at six.

x

Anastasia Grey
Editor, SIP

When will I tell him? Tonight? Maybe after sex? Maybe during sex. No, that might be dangerous for both of us. When he's asleep? I put my head in my hands. What the hell am I going to do?

———

"Hi," Christian says warily as I climb into the SUV.

"Hi," I murmur.

"What's wrong?" He frowns. I shake my head as Taylor sets off toward the hospital.

"Nothing." *Maybe now?* I could tell him now when we're in a contained space and Taylor is with us.

"Is work all right?" Christian continues to probe.

"Yes. Fine. Thanks."

"Ana, what's wrong?" His tone is a little more forceful, and I chicken out.

"I've just missed you, that's all. And I've been worried about Ray."

Christian visibly relaxes. "Ray's good. I spoke to Mom this afternoon and she's impressed with his progress." Christian grasps my hand. "Boy, your hand is cold. Have you eaten today?"

I blush.

"Ana," Christian scolds me, annoyed.

Well, I haven't eaten because I know you're going to go bat-shit crazy when I tell you I'm pregnant.

"I'll eat this evening. I haven't really had time."

He shakes his head in frustration. "Do you want me to add 'feed my wife' to the security detail's list of duties?"

"I'm sorry. I'll eat. It's just been a weird day. You know, moving Dad and all."

His lips press into a hard line, but he says nothing. I gaze out the window. *Tell him!* My subconscious hisses. No. I'm a coward.

Christian interrupts my reverie. "I may have to go to Taiwan."

"Oh. When?"

"Later this week. Maybe next week."

"Okay."

"I want you to come with me."

I swallow. "Christian, please. I have my job. Let's not rehash this argument again."

He sighs and pouts like a sulky teenager. "Thought I'd ask," he mutters petulantly.

"How long will you go for?"

"Not more than a couple of days. I wish you'd tell me what's bothering you."

How can he tell? "Well, now that my beloved husband is going away . . ."

Christian kisses my knuckles. "I won't be away for long."

"Good." I smile weakly at him.

RAY IS MUCH BRIGHTER and a lot less grumpy when we see him. I'm touched by his quiet gratitude to Christian, and for a moment I forget about my impending news as I sit and listen to them talk fishing and the Mariners. But he tires easily.

"Daddy, we'll leave you to sleep."

"Thanks, Ana honey. I like that you drop by. Saw your mom today, too, Christian. She was very reassuring. And she's a Mariners fan."

"She's not crazy about fishing, though," Christian says wryly as he rises.

"Don't know many women who are, eh?" Ray grins.

"I'll see you tomorrow, okay?" I kiss him. My subconscious

purses her lips. *That's provided Christian hasn't locked you away . . . or worse.* My spirits take a nosedive.

"Come." Christian holds out his hand, frowning at me. I take it and we leave the hospital.

I PICK AT MY food. It's Mrs. Jones's chicken chasseur, but I'm just not hungry. My stomach is knotted in a tight ball of anxiety.

"Damn it! Ana, will you tell me what's wrong?" Christian pushes his empty plate away, irritated. I gaze at him. "Please. You're driving me crazy."

I swallow and try to subdue the panic rising in my throat. I take a deep, steadying breath. It's now or never. "I'm pregnant."

He stills, and very slowly all the color drains from his face. "What?" he whispers, ashen.

"I'm pregnant."

His brow furrows with incomprehension. "How?"

How . . . *how?* What sort of ridiculous question is that? I blush and give him a quizzical how-do-you-think look.

His stance changes immediately, his eyes hardening to flint. "Your shot?" he snarls.

Oh, shit.

"Did you forget your shot?"

I just gaze at him, unable to speak. Fuck, he's mad—really mad.

"Christ, Ana!" He bangs his fist on the table, making me jump, and stands so abruptly he almost knocks the dining chair over. "You have one thing, one thing to remember. Shit! I don't fucking believe it. How could you be so stupid?"

Stupid! I gasp. Shit. I want to tell him that the shot was ineffective, but words fail me. I gaze down at my fingers. "I'm sorry," I whisper.

"Sorry? Fuck!" he says again.

"I know the timing's not very good."

"Not very good!" he shouts. "We've known each other five fucking minutes. I wanted to show you the fucking world and now . . . Fuck. Diapers and vomit and shit!" He closes his eyes. I think he's trying to contain his temper and losing the battle.

"Did you forget? Tell me. Or did you do this on purpose?" His eyes blaze and anger emanates off him like a force field.

"No," I whisper. I can't tell him about Hannah—he'd fire her.

"I thought we'd agreed on this!" he shouts.

"I know. We had. I'm sorry."

He ignores me. "This is why. This is why I like control. So shit like this doesn't come along and fuck everything up."

No . . . Little Blip. "Christian, please don't shout at me." Tears start to slip down my face.

"Don't start with waterworks now," he snaps. "Fuck." He runs a hand through his hair, pulling at it as he does. "You think I'm ready to be a father?" His voice catches, and it's a mixture of rage and panic.

And it all becomes clear, the fear and loathing writ large in his eyes—his rage is that of a powerless adolescent. *Oh, Fifty, I am so sorry. It's a shock for me, too.*

"I know neither one of us is ready for this, but I think you'll make a wonderful father," I choke. "We'll figure it out."

"How the fuck do you know!" he shouts, louder this time. "Tell me how!" His eyes burn as so many emotions cross his face. It's fear that's most prominent.

"Oh, fuck this!" Christian bellows dismissively and holds his hands up in a gesture of defeat. He turns on his heel and stalks toward the foyer, grabbing his jacket as he leaves the great room. His footsteps echo off the wooden floor, and he disappears through the double doors into the foyer, slamming the door behind him and making me jump once more.

I am alone with the silence—the still, silent emptiness of the great room. I shudder involuntarily as I gaze numbly at the closed doors. *He's walked out on me. Shit!* His reaction is far worse than I could ever have imagined. I push my plate away and fold my arms on the table, letting my head sink into them while I weep.

"ANA, DEAR." MRS. JONES is hovering beside me.

I sit up quickly, dashing the tears from my face.

"I heard. I'm sorry," she says gently. "Would you like an herbal tea or something?"

"I'd like a glass of white wine."

Mrs. Jones pauses for a fraction of a second, and I remember Blip. Now I can't drink alcohol. Can I? I must study the dos and don'ts Dr. Greene gave me.

"I'll get you a glass."

"Actually, I'll have a cup of tea, please." I wipe my nose. She smiles kindly.

"Cup of tea coming up." She clears our plates and heads over to the kitchen area. I follow her and perch on a stool, watching her prepare my tea.

She places a steaming mug in front of me. "Is there anything else I can get for you, Ana?"

"No, this is fine, thank you."

"Are you sure? You didn't eat much."

I gaze up at her. "I'm just not hungry."

"Ana, you should eat. It's not just you anymore. Please let me fix you something. What would you like?" She looks so hopefully at me. But really, I can't face anything.

My husband has just walked out on me because I'm pregnant, my father has been in a major car accident, and there's Jack Hyde the nutcase trying to make out that I sexually harassed him. I suddenly have an uncontrollable urge to giggle. *See what you've done to me, Little Blip!* I caress my belly.

Mrs. Jones smiles indulgently at me. "Do you know how far along you are?" she asks softly.

"Very newly pregnant. Four or five weeks, the doctor isn't sure."

"If you won't eat, then at least you should rest."

I nod, and taking my tea, I head into the library. It's my refuge. I dig my BlackBerry out of my purse and contemplate calling Christian. I know it's a shock for him—but he really did overreact. *When does he not overreact?* My subconscious arches a finely plucked brow at me. I sigh. Fifty Shades of fucked up.

"Yes, that's your daddy, Little Blip. Hopefully he'll cool off and come back . . . soon."

I pull out the leaflet of dos and don'ts and sit down to read. I can't concentrate. Christian's never walked out on me before. He's been so thoughtful and kind over the last few days, so loving and now . . . Suppose he never comes back? *Shit!* Perhaps I should call Flynn. I don't know what to do. I'm at a loss. He's so fragile in so many ways, and I knew he'd react badly to the news. He was so sweet this weekend. All those circumstances way beyond his control, yet he managed fine. But this news was too much.

Ever since I met him, my life has been complicated. Is it him? Is it the two of us together? Suppose he doesn't get past this? Suppose he wants a divorce? Bile rises in my throat. No. I mustn't think this way. He'll be back. He will. I know he will. I know, regardless of the shouting and his harsh words, that he loves me . . . yes. And he'll love you, too, Little Blip.

Leaning back in my chair, I start to doze.

I WAKE COLD AND disoriented. Shivering, I check my watch: eleven in the evening. *Oh yes . . . You.* I pat my belly. Where's Christian? Is he back? Stiffly I ease out of the armchair and go in search of my husband.

Five minutes later, I realize he's not home. I hope nothing's happened to him. Memories of the long wait when *Charlie Tango* went missing flood back.

No, no, no. Stop thinking like this. He's probably gone to . . . where? Who would he go and see? Elliot? Or maybe he's with Flynn. I hope so. I find my BlackBerry back in the library, and I text him.

Where are you?

I head into the bathroom and run myself a bath. I am so cold.

HE STILL HASN'T RETURNED when I climb out of the bath. I change into one of my 1930s-style satin nightdresses and my robe and head to the great room. On the way, I pop into the spare bedroom. Perhaps this could be Little Blip's room. I am startled by the thought and stand in the doorway, contemplating this reality.

Will we paint it blue or pink? The sweet thought is soured by the fact that my errant husband is so pissed at the idea. Grabbing the duvet from the spare bed, I head into the great room to keep vigil.

SOMETHING WAKES ME. A sound.

"Shit!"

It's Christian in the foyer. I hear the table scrape across the floor again.

"Shit!" he repeats, more muffled this time.

I scramble up in time to see him stagger through the double doors. *He's drunk.* My scalp prickles. *Shit, Christian drunk?* I know how much he hates drunks. I leap up and run toward him.

"Christian, are you okay?"

He leans against the jamb of the foyer doors. "Mrs. Grey," he slurs.

Crap. He's *very* drunk. I don't know what to do.

"Oh . . . you look mighty fine, Anastasia."

"Where have you been?"

He puts his finger to his lips and smiles crookedly at me. "Shh!"

"I think you'd better come to bed."

"With you . . ." He snickers.

Snickering! Frowning, I gently put my arm around his waist because he can hardly stand, let alone walk. Where has he been? How did he get home?

"Let me help you to bed. Lean on me."

"You are very beautiful, Ana." He leans on me and sniffs my hair, almost knocking both of us over.

"Christian, walk. I am going to put you to bed."

"Okay," he says, as if he's trying to concentrate.

We stumble down the corridor and finally make it into the bedroom.

"Bed," he says, grinning.

"Yes, bed." I maneuver him to the edge, but he holds me.

"Join me," he says.

"Christian, I think you need some sleep."

"And so it begins. I've heard about this."

I frown. "Heard about what?"

"Babies mean no sex."

"I'm sure that's not true. Otherwise we'd all come from one-child families."

He gazes down at me. "You're funny."

"You're drunk."

"Yes." He smiles, but his smile changes as he thinks about it, and a haunted expression crosses his face, a look that chills me to the bone.

"Come on, Christian," I say gently. I hate his expression. It speaks of horrid, ugly memories that no child should see. "Let's get you into bed." I push him gently, and he flops down onto the mattress, sprawling in all directions and grinning up at me, his haunted expression gone.

"Join me," he slurs.

"Let's get you undressed first."

He grins widely, drunkenly. "Now you're talking."

Holy cow. Drunk Christian is cute and playful. I'll take him over mad-as-hell Christian anytime.

"Sit up. Let me take your jacket off."

"The room is spinning."

Shit . . . is he going to throw up? "Christian, sit up!"

He smirks up at me. "Mrs. Grey, you are a bossy little thing . . ."

"Yes. Do as you're told and sit up." I put my hands on my hips. He grins again, struggles up onto his elbows, then sits up in a most un-Christian-like, gawky fashion. Before he can flop down again, I grab his tie and wrestle him out of his gray jacket, one arm at a time.

"You smell good."

"You smell of hard liquor."

"Yes . . . bour-bon." He pronounces the syllables with such exaggeration that I have to stifle a giggle. Discarding his jacket on the floor beside me, I make a start on his tie. He rests his hands on my hips.

"I like the feel of this fabric on you, Anastay-shia," he says, slurring his words. "You should always be in satin or silk." He runs his hands up and down my hips, then jerks me forward, pressing his mouth against my belly.

"And we have an invader in here."

I stop breathing. Holy cow. He's talking to Little Blip.

"You're going to keep me awake, aren't you?" he says to my belly.

Oh my. Christian looks up at me through his long dark lashes, gray eyes blurred and cloudy. My heart constricts.

"You'll choose him over me," he says sadly.

"Christian, you don't know what you're talking about. Don't be ridiculous—I am not choosing anyone over anyone. And he might be a she."

He frowns. "A she . . . Oh, God." He flops back down on the bed and covers his eyes with his arm. I have managed to loosen his tie. I undo one shoelace and yank off his shoe and sock, then the other. When I stand, I see why I've met no resistance—Christian has passed out completely. He's sound asleep and snoring softly.

I stare at him. He's so goddamned beautiful, even drunk and snoring. His sculptured lips parted, one arm above his head, ruffling his messy hair, his face relaxed. He looks young—but then he is young; my young, stressed-out, drunk, unhappy husband. The thought rests heavily in my heart.

Well, at least he's home. I wonder where he went. I'm not sure I have the energy or the strength to move him or undress him any further. He's on top of the duvet, too. Heading back into the great room, I pick up the duvet I was using and bring it back to our bedroom.

He's still fast asleep, still wearing his tie and his belt. I climb onto the bed beside him, remove his tie, and gently undo the top button of his shirt. He mumbles something incoherently in his sleep, but he doesn't wake. Carefully, I unbuckle his belt and pull it through the belt loops, and after some difficulty it's off. His shirt has come dislodged from his pants, revealing a hint of his happy trail. I can't resist. I bend and kiss it. He shifts, flexing his hips forward, but stays asleep.

I sit up and gaze at him again. *Oh, Fifty, Fifty, Fifty . . . what am I going to do with you?* I brush my fingers through his hair—it's so soft—and kiss his temple.

"I love you, Christian. Even when you're drunk and you've been out God knows where, I love you. I'll always love you."

"Hmm," he murmurs. I kiss his temple once more, then get off the bed and cover him up with the spare duvet. I can sleep beside him, sideways across the bed . . . *Yes, I'll do that.*

First I'll sort out his clothes, though. I shake my head and pick up his socks and tie and fold his jacket over my arm. As I do, his BlackBerry falls to the floor. I pick it up and inadvertently unlock it. It opens on the texts screen. I can see my text, and above it, another.

Fuck. My scalp prickles.

> *It was good to see you. I understand now.
> Don't fret. You'll make a wonderful father.*

It's from *her*. Mrs. Elena Bitch Troll Robinson.
Shit. That's where he went. He's been to see *her*.

CHAPTER TWENTY-ONE

I gape at the text, then look up at the sleeping form of my husband. He's been out until one thirty in the morning drinking— with *her*! He snores softly, sleeping the sleep of a seemingly innocent, oblivious drunk. He looks so serene.

Oh no, no, no. My legs turn to jelly, and I sink slowly to the chair beside the bed in disbelief. Raw, bitter, humiliating betrayal lances through me. How could he? How could he go to her? Scalding, angry tears ooze down my cheeks. His wrath and fear, his need to lash out at me I can understand, and forgive—just. But this . . . this treachery is too much. I pull my knees up against my chest and wrap my arms around them, protecting me and protecting my Little Blip. I rock to and fro, weeping softly.

What did I expect? I married this man too quickly. I knew it—I knew it would come to this. Why. Why. *Why?* How could he do this to me? He knows how I feel about that woman. How could he turn to her? How? The knife twists slowly and painfully deep in my heart, lacerating me. Will it always be this way?

Through my tears, his prostrate figure blurs and shimmers. *Oh, Christian.* I married him because I love him, and deep down I know that he loves me. I know he does. His achingly sweet birthday present comes to mind.

For all our firsts on your first birthday as my beloved wife. I love you. C x

No, no, no—I can't believe that it will always be this way, two steps forward and three steps back. But that's how it's always been with him. After each setback, we move forward, inch by inch. He will come around . . . he will. But will I? Will I recover from this . . . from this treachery? I think about how he's been this last, horrible, wonderful weekend. His quiet strength while my step-dad lay broken and comatose in the ICU . . . my surprise party, bringing my family and friends together . . . dipping me down low outside the Heathman and kissing me in full public view. *Oh, Christian, you strain all my trust, all my faith . . . and I love you.*

But it's not just me now. I place my hand on my belly. No, I will not let him do this to me and our Blip. Dr. Flynn said I should give him the benefit of the doubt—well, not this time. I dash the tears from my eyes and wipe my nose with the back of my hand.

Christian stirs and rolls over, pulling his legs up from the side of the bed, and curls up beneath the duvet. He stretches out a hand as if searching for something, then grumbles and frowns but settles back to sleep, his arm outstretched.

Oh, Fifty. What am I going to do with you? And what the hell were you doing with the Bitch Troll? I need to know.

I glance once more at the offending text and quickly hatch a plan. Taking a deep breath, I forward the text to my BlackBerry. Step one complete. I quickly check the other recent texts, but see only messages from Elliot, Andrea, Taylor, Ros, and me. None from Elena. Good, I think. I exit the text screen, relieved that he hasn't been texting her, and my heart lurches into my throat. *Oh my.* The wallpaper on his phone is photograph upon photograph of me, a patchwork of tiny Anastasias in various poses—our honeymoon, our recent weekend sailing and soaring, and a few of José's photos, too. When did he do this? It must have been recently.

I notice his e-mail icon, and an idea slithers enticingly into my mind . . . *I could read Christian's e-mails.* See if he's been talking to *her.* Should I? Sheathed in jade-green silk, my inner goddess nods emphatically, her mouth set in a scowl. Before I can stop myself, I invade his privacy.

There are hundreds and hundreds of e-mails. I spin down through them, and they look dull as ditchwater . . . mostly from Ros, Andrea, and me, and various executives in his company. None from Bitch Troll. While I'm at it, I'm relieved to see there are none from Leila either.

One e-mail catches my eye. It's from Barney Sullivan, Christian's IT guy, and the subject line is: Jack Hyde. I glance guiltily at Christian, but he's still snoring gently. I've never heard him snore. I open the e-mail.

From: Barney Sullivan
Subject: Jack Hyde
Date: September 13 2011 14:09
To: Christian Grey

CCTV around Seattle tracks the white van from South Irving Street. Before that I can find no trace, so Hyde must have been based in that area.

As Welch has told you the unsub car was rented with a false license by an unknown female, though nothing that ties it to the South Irving Street area.

Details of known GEH and SIP employees who live in the area are in the attached file, which I have forwarded to Welch, too.

There was nothing on Hyde's SIP computer about his former PAs.

As a reminder, here is a list of what was retrieved from Hyde's SIP computer.

Greys' Home Addresses:
Five properties in Seattle
Two properties in Detroit

Detailed Resumés for:
Carrick Grey
Elliot Grey

Christian Grey
Dr. Grace Trevelyan
Anastasia Steele
Mia Grey

Newspaper and online articles relating to:
Dr. Grace Trevelyan
Carrick Grey
Christian Grey
Elliot Grey

Photographs:
Carrick Grey
Dr. Grace Trevelyan
Christian Grey
Elliot Grey
Mia Grey

I'll continue my investigation, see what else I can find.

B Sullivan
Head of IT, GEH

This odd e-mail momentarily sidetracks me from my night of woe. I click on the attachment to check through the names on the list, but it's obviously huge, too big to open on the BlackBerry.

What am I doing? It's late. I've had a tiring day. There are no e-mails from the Bitch Troll or Leila Williams, and I take some cold comfort from that. I glance quickly at the alarm clock: it's just after two in the morning. Today has been a day of revelations. I am to be a mother, and my husband has been fraternizing with the enemy. Well, let him stew. I am not sleeping here with him. He can wake up alone tomorrow. After placing his BlackBerry on the bedside table, I retrieve my purse from beside the bed and, after one last look at my angelic, sleeping Judas, I leave the bedroom.

The spare playroom key is in its usual place in the cabinet in the utility room. I grab it and scoot upstairs. From the linen closet, I retrieve a pillow, duvet, and sheet, then unlock the play-room door and enter, switching the lights to dim. Odd that I find the smell and ambience of this room so comforting, considering I safe-worded the last time we were in here. I lock the door behind me, leaving the key in the lock. I know that tomorrow morning Christian will be frantic to find me, and I don't think he'll look in here if the door's locked. Well, it will serve him right.

I curl up on the Chesterfield couch, wrap myself in the duvet, and drag my BlackBerry from my purse. Checking my texts, I find the one from the evil Bitch Troll that I forwarded from Christian's phone. I press "forward" and type:

*WOULD YOU LIKE MRS. LINCOLN TO JOIN US
WHEN WE EVENTUALLY DISCUSS THIS TEXT SHE
SENT TO YOU? IT WILL SAVE YOU RUNNING TO
HER AFTERWARD. YOUR WIFE*

I press "send" and switch the volume to mute. I huddle under my duvet. For all my bravado, I'm overwhelmed by the enormity of Christian's deceit. This should be a happy time. Jeez, we're going to be parents. Briefly, I relive telling Christian that I'm preg-nant and fantasize that he falls to his knees with joy in front of me, pulling me into his arms and telling me how much he loves me and our Little Blip.

Yet here I am, alone and cold in a BDSM fantasy playroom. Suddenly I feel old, older than my years. Taking on Christian was always going to be a challenge, but he really has surpassed himself this time. What was he thinking? Well, if he wants a fight, I'll give him a fight. No way am I going to let him get away with running off to see that monstrous woman whenever we have a problem. He's going to have to choose—her or me and our Little Blip. I sniffle softly, but because I'm so exhausted, I soon fall asleep.

I WAKE WITH A start, momentarily disoriented . . . *Oh yes—I'm in the playroom.* Because there are no windows, I have no idea what time it is. The door handle rattles.

"Ana!" Christian shouts from outside the door. I freeze, but he doesn't come in. I hear muffled voices, but they move away. I exhale and check the time on my BlackBerry. It's seven fifty, and I have four missed calls and two voice messages. The missed calls are mostly from Christian, but there's also one from Kate. *Oh no.* He must have called her. I don't have time to listen to them. I don't want to be late for work.

I wrap the duvet around me and pick up my purse before making my way to the door. Unlocking it slowly, I peek outside. No sign of anyone. *Oh shit . . .* Perhaps this is a bit melodramatic. I roll my eyes at myself, take a deep breath, and head downstairs.

Taylor, Sawyer, Ryan, Mrs. Jones, and Christian are all standing in the entrance to the great room, and Christian is issuing rapid-fire instructions. As one they all turn and gape at me. Christian is still wearing the clothes he slept in last night. He looks disheveled, pale, and heart-stoppingly beautiful. His large gray eyes are wide, and I don't know if he's fearful or angry. It's difficult to tell.

"Sawyer, I'll be ready to leave in about twenty minutes," I mutter, wrapping the duvet tighter around me for protection.

He nods, and all eyes turn to Christian, who is still staring intensely at me.

"Would you like some breakfast, Mrs. Grey?" Mrs. Jones asks. I shake my head.

"I'm not hungry, thank you." She purses her lips but says nothing.

"Where were you?" Christian asks, his voice low and husky. Suddenly Sawyer, Taylor, Ryan, and Mrs. Jones scatter, scurrying into Taylor's office, into the foyer, and into the kitchen like terrified rats from a sinking ship.

I ignore Christian and march toward our bedroom.

"Ana," he calls after me, "answer me." I hear his footsteps behind me as I walk into the bedroom and continue into our bathroom. Quickly, I lock the door.

"Ana!" Christian pounds on the door. I turn on the shower. The door rattles. "Ana, open the damned door."

"Go away!"

"I'm not going anywhere."

"Suit yourself."

"Ana, please."

I climb into the shower, effectively blocking him out. Oh, it's warm. The healing water cascades over me, cleansing the exhaustion of the night off my skin. *Oh my.* This feels so good. For a moment, for one short moment, I can pretend all is well. I wash my hair and by the time I've finished, I feel better, stronger, ready to face the freight train that is Christian Grey. I wrap my hair in a towel, briskly dry myself with another towel, and wrap it around me.

I unlock the door and open it to find Christian leaning against the wall opposite, his hands behind his back. His expression is wary, that of a hunted predator. I stride past him and into our walk-in closet.

"Are you ignoring me?" Christian asks in disbelief as he stands on the threshold of the closet.

"Perceptive, aren't you?" I murmur absentmindedly as I search for something to wear. Ah, yes—my plum dress. I slide it off the hanger, choose my high black stiletto boots, and head for the bedroom. I pause for Christian to step out of my way, which he does, eventually—his intrinsic good manners taking over. I sense his eyes boring into me as I walk over to my chest of drawers, and I peek at him in the mirror, standing motionless in the doorway, watching me. In an act worthy of an Oscar winner, I let my towel fall to the floor and pretend that I am oblivious to my naked body. I hear his restrained gasp and ignore it.

"Why are you doing this?" he asks. His voice is low.

"Why do you think?" My voice is velvet soft as I pull out a pretty pair of black lace La Perla panties.

"Ana—" He stops as I shimmy into them.

"Go ask your Mrs. Robinson. I'm sure she'll have an explanation for you," I mutter as I search for the matching bra.

"Ana, I've told you before, she's not my—"

"I don't want to hear it, Christian." I wave my hand dismissively. "The time for talking was yesterday, but instead you decided to rant and get drunk with the woman who abused you for years. Give her a call. I am sure she'll be more than willing to listen to you now." I find the matching bra and slowly pull it on and fasten it. Christian walks farther into the bedroom and places his hands on his hips.

"Why were you snooping on me?" he says.

In spite of my resolve I flush. "That's not the point, Christian," I snap at him. "Fact is, the going gets tough and you run to her."

His mouth settles into a grim line. "It wasn't like that."

"I'm not interested." Picking a pair of black thigh-highs with lacey tops, I retreat to the bed. I sit, point my toe, and gently ease the gossamer material up to my thigh.

"Where were you?" he asks, his eyes following my hands up my legs, but I continue to ignore him as I slowly roll on the other stocking. Standing, I bend to towel-dry my hair. Through my parted thighs, I can see his bare feet, and I sense his intense gaze. When I've finished, I stand and step back to the chest of drawers, where I grab my hairdryer.

"Answer me." Christian's voice is low and husky.

I switch on the hairdryer so I can no longer hear him and watch him through my lashes in the mirror as I finger dry my hair. He glares at me, eyes narrow and cool, chilling even. I look away, focusing on the task at hand and trying to suppress the shiver that runs through me. I swallow hard and concentrate on drying my hair. He's still mad. He goes out with that damned woman, and he's mad at *me*? *How dare he!* When my hair looks wild and untamed, I stop. Yes . . . I like it. I switch off the hairdryer.

"Where were you?" he whispers, his tone arctic.

"What do you care?"

"Ana, stop this. Now."

I shrug, and Christian moves quickly across the room toward me. I whirl around, stepping back as he reaches out.

"Don't touch me," I snap and he freezes.

"Where were you?" he demands. His hands fist at his side.

"I wasn't out getting drunk with my ex," I seethe. "Did you sleep with her?"

He gasps. "*What*? No!" He gapes at me and has the gall to look wounded and angry at the same time. My subconscious breathes a small, welcome sigh of relief.

"You think I'd cheat on you?" His tone is one of moral outrage.

"You did," I snarl. "By taking our very private life and spilling your spineless guts to that woman."

His mouth drops open. "Spineless. That's what you think?" His eyes blaze.

"Christian, I saw the text. That's what I know."

"That text was not meant for you," he growls.

"Well, fact is I saw it when your BlackBerry fell out of your jacket while I was undressing you because you were too drunk to undress yourself. Do you have any idea how much you've hurt me by going to see that woman?"

He pales momentarily, but I'm on a roll, my inner bitch unleashed.

"Do you remember last night when you came home? Remember what you said?"

He stares at me blankly, his face frozen.

"Well, you were right. I do choose this defenseless baby over you. That's what any loving parent does. That's what your mother should have done for you. And I am sorry that she didn't—because we wouldn't be having this conversation right now if she had. But you're an adult now—you need to grow up and smell the fucking coffee and stop behaving like a petulant adolescent.

"You may not be happy about this baby. I'm not ecstatic, given the timing and your less-than-lukewarm reception to this new life, this flesh of your flesh. But you can either do this with me, or I'll do it on my own. The decision is yours.

"While you wallow in your pit of self-pity and self-loathing, I'm going to work. And when I return I'll be moving my belongings to the room upstairs."

He blinks at me, shocked.

"Now, if you'll excuse me, I'd like to finish getting dressed." I am breathing hard.

Very slowly, Christian retreats one step, his demeanor hardening. "Is that what you want?" he whispers.

"I don't know what I want anymore." My tone mirrors his, and it takes a monumental effort to feign disinterest while I casually dip the tips of my fingers into my moisturizer and smooth it gently over my face. I peer at myself in the mirror. Blue eyes wide, face pale, but cheeks flushed. *You're doing great. Don't back down now. Don't back down now.*

"You don't want me?" he whispers.

Oh no . . . oh no you don't, Grey.

"I'm still here aren't I?" I snap. Taking my mascara, I apply some first to my right eye.

"You've thought about leaving?" His words are barely audible.

"When one's husband prefers the company of his ex-mistress, it's usually not a good sign." I pitch the disdain at just the right level, evading his question. Lip gloss now. I pout my shiny lips at the image in the mirror. *Stay strong, Steele . . . um—Grey.* Holy fuck, I can't even remember my name. I pick up my boots, stride over to the bed once more, and quickly put them on, tugging them up over my knees. Yep. I look hot just in underwear and boots. I know. Standing, I gaze dispassionately at him. He blinks at me, and his eyes travel swiftly and greedily down my body.

"I know what you're doing here," he murmurs, and his voice has acquired a warm, seductive edge.

"Do you?" And my voice cracks. *No, Ana . . . hold on.*

He swallows and takes a step forward. I step back and hold my hands up.

"Don't even think about it, Grey," I whisper menacingly.

"You're my wife," he says softly, threateningly.

"I'm the pregnant woman you abandoned yesterday, and if you touch me I will scream the place down."

His eyebrows rise in disbelief. "You'd scream?"

"Bloody murder." I narrow my eyes.

"No one would hear you," he murmurs, his gaze intense, and briefly I'm reminded of our morning in Aspen. No. No. No.

"Are you trying to frighten me?" I mutter, breathless, deliberately trying to derail him.

It works. He stills and swallows. "That wasn't my intention." He frowns.

I can barely breathe. If he touches me, I will succumb. I know the power he wields over me and over my traitorous body. I know. I hang on to my anger.

"I had a drink with someone I used to be close to. We cleared the air. I am not going to see her again."

"You sought her out?"

"Not at first. I tried to see Flynn. But I found myself at the salon."

"And you expect me to believe you're not going to see her again?" I cannot contain my fury as I hiss at him. "What about the next time I step across some imaginary line? This is the same argument we have over and over again. Like we're on some Ixion's wheel. If I fuck up again, are you going to run back to her?"

"I am not going to see her again," he says with a chilling finality. "She finally understands how I feel."

I blink at him. "What does that mean?"

He straightens and runs a hand through his hair, exasperated and angry and mute. I try a different tack.

"Why can you talk to her and not to me?"

"I was mad at you. Like I am now."

"You don't say!" I snap. "Well I am mad at you right now. Mad at you for being so cold and callous yesterday when I needed you. Mad at you for saying I got knocked up deliberately, when I didn't. Mad at you for betraying me." I manage to suppress a sob. His mouth drops open in shock, and he closes his eyes briefly as if I'd slapped him. I swallow. *Calm down, Anastasia.*

"I should have kept better track of my shots. But I didn't do it on purpose. This pregnancy is a shock to me, too." I mutter, trying for a modicum of civility. "It could be that the shot failed."

He glares at me, silent.

"You really fucked up yesterday," I whisper, my anger boiling over. "I've had a lot to deal with over the last few weeks."

"You really fucked up three or four weeks ago. Or whenever you forgot your shot."

"Well, God forbid I should be perfect like you!"

Oh stop, stop, stop. We stand glowering at each other.

"This is quite a performance, Mrs. Grey," he whispers.

"Well, I'm glad that even knocked up I'm entertaining."

He stares at me blankly. "I need a shower," he murmurs.

"And I've provided enough of a floor show."

"It's a mighty fine floor show," he whispers. He steps forward, and I step back again.

"Don't."

"I hate that you won't let me touch you."

"Ironic, huh?"

His eyes narrow once more. "We haven't resolved much, have we?"

"I'd say not. Except that I'm moving out of this bedroom."

His eyes flare and widen briefly. "She doesn't mean anything to me."

"Except when you need her."

"I don't need her. I need you."

"You didn't yesterday. That woman is a hard limit for me, Christian."

"She's out of my life."

"I wish I could believe you."

"For fuck's sake, Ana."

"Please let me get dressed."

He sighs and runs a hand through his hair once more. "I'll see you this evening," he says, his voice bleak and devoid of feeling.

And for a brief moment I want to take him in my arms and soothe him . . . but I resist because I'm just too mad. He turns and heads for the bathroom. I stand frozen until I hear the door close.

I stagger to the bed and flop down on it. I did not resort to tears, shouting, or murder, nor did I succumb to his sexpertise. I deserve a Congressional Medal of Honor, but I feel so low. Shit. We resolved nothing. We're on the edge of a precipice. Is our marriage at stake here? Why can't he see what a complete and utter ass he's been by running to that woman? And what does he mean when he says he'll never see her again? How on Earth am I supposed to believe that? I glance at the radio alarm—eight thirty. *Shit!* I'll don't want to be late. I take a deep breath.

"Round Two was a stalemate, Little Blip," I whisper, patting my belly. "Daddy may be a lost cause, but I hope not. Why, oh why, did you come so early, Little Blip? Things were just getting good." My lip trembles, but I take a deep cleansing breath and bring my rolling emotions under control.

"Come on. Let's go kick ass at work."

I DON'T SAY GOOD-BYE to Christian. He's still in the shower when Sawyer and I leave. As I gaze out the darkened windows of the SUV, my composure slips and my eyes water. My mood is reflected in the gray, dreary sky, and I feel a strange sense of foreboding. We didn't actually discuss the baby. I have had less than twenty-four hours to assimilate the news of Little Blip. Christian has had even less time. "He doesn't even know your name." I caress my belly and wipe tears from my face.

"Mrs. Grey." Sawyer interrupts my reverie. "We're here."

"Oh. Thanks, Sawyer."

"I'm going to make a run to the deli, ma'am. Can I get you anything?"

"No. Thank you, no. I'm not hungry."

HANNAH HAS MY LATTE waiting for me. I take one sniff of it and my stomach roils.

"Um . . . can I have tea, please?" I mutter, embarrassed. I knew there was a reason I never really liked coffee. Jeez, it smells foul.

"You okay, Ana?"

I nod and scurry into the safety of my office. My BlackBerry buzzes. It's Kate.

"Why was Christian looking for you?" she asks with no pre-amble at all.

"Good morning, Kate. How are you?"

"Cut the crap, Steele. What gives?" The Katherine Kavanagh Inquisition begins.

"Christian and I had a fight, that's all."

"Did he hurt you?"

I roll my eyes. "Yes, but not the way you're thinking." I cannot deal with Kate at the moment. I know I will cry, and right now I am so proud of myself for not breaking down this morning. "Kate, I have a meeting. I'll call you back."

"Good. You're all right?"

"Yes." No. "I'll call you later, okay?"

"Okay, Ana, have it your own way. I'm here for you."

"I know," I whisper and fight the backlash of emotion at her kind words. *I am not going to cry. I am not going to cry.*

"Ray okay?"

"Yes," I whisper the word.

"Oh, Ana," she whispers.

"Don't."

"Okay. Talk later."

"Yes."

DURING THE COURSE OF the morning, I sporadically check my e-mails, hoping for word from Christian. But there's nothing. As the day wears on, I realize that he's not going to contact me at all and that he's still mad. Well, I'm still mad, too. I throw myself into my work, pausing only at lunchtime for a cream cheese and salmon bagel. It's extraordinary how much better I feel once I've eaten something.

At five o'clock Sawyer and I set off for the hospital to see Ray. Sawyer is extra vigilant, and even oversolicitous. It's irritating. As we approach Ray's room, he hovers over me.

"Shall I get you some tea while you visit with your father?" he asks.

"No thanks, Sawyer. I'll be fine."

"I'll wait outside." He opens the door for me, and I'm grateful to get away from him for a moment. Ray is sitting up in bed reading a magazine. He's shaved, wearing a pajama top—he looks like his old self.

"Hey, Annie." He grins. And his face falls.

"Oh, Daddy . . ." I rush to his side, and in a very uncharacteristic move, he opens his arms wide and hugs me.

"Annie?" he whispers. "What is it?" He holds me tight and kisses my hair. As I'm in his arms, I realize how rare these moments between us have been. *Why is that?* Is that why I like to crawl into Christian's lap? After a moment, I pull away from him and sit down in the chair beside the bed. Ray's brow is furrowed with concern.

"Tell your old man."

I shake my head. He doesn't need my problems right now.

"It's nothing, Dad. You look well." I clasp his hand.

"Feeling more like myself, though this leg in a cast is bitchin'."

"Bitchin'?" His word prompts my smile.

He smiles back. "Bitchin' sounds better than itchin'."

"Oh, Dad, I am so glad you're okay."

"Me, too, Annie. I'd like to bounce some grandchildren on this bitchin' knee one day. Wouldn't want to miss that for the world."

I blink at him. *Shit.* Does he know? And I fight the tears that prick the corners of my eyes.

"You and Christian getting along?"

"We had a fight," I whisper, trying to speak past the knot in my throat. "We'll work it out."

He nods. "He's a fine man, your husband," Ray says reassuringly.

"He has his moments. What did the doctors say?" I don't want to talk about my husband right now; he's a painful topic of conversation.

BACK AT ESCALA, CHRISTIAN is not home.

"Christian called and said that he'd be working late," Mrs. Jones informs me apologetically.

"Oh. Thanks for letting me know." Why couldn't he tell me? Jeez, he really is taking his sulk to a whole new level. I am briefly reminded of the fight over our wedding vows and the major tantrum he had then. But I'm the aggrieved one here.

"What would you like to eat?" Mrs. Jones has a determined, steely glint in her eye.

"Pasta."

She smiles. "Spaghetti, penne, fusilli?"

"Spaghetti, your Bolognese."

"Coming up. And Ana . . . you should know Mr. Grey was frantic this morning when he thought you'd left. He was beside himself." She smiles fondly.

Oh . . .

HE'S STILL NOT HOME by nine. I am sitting at my desk in the library, wondering where he is. I call him.

"Ana," he says, his voice cool.

"Hi."

He inhales softly. "Hi," he says, his voice lower.

"Are you coming home?"

"Later."

"Are you in the office?"

"Yes. Where did you expect me to be?"

With her. "I'll let you go."

We both hang on the line, the silence stretching and tightening between us.

"Good night, Ana," he says eventually.

"Good night, Christian."

He hangs up.

Oh shit. I gaze at my BlackBerry. I don't know what he expects me to do. I'm not going to let him walk all over me. Yes, he's mad, fair enough. I'm mad. But we are where we are. I haven't run off loose-lipped to my ex-pedo lover. I want him to acknowledge that that is not an acceptable way to behave.

I sit back in my chair, gazing at the billiards table in the library, and recall fun times playing snooker. I place my hand on my belly. Maybe it's just too early. Maybe this is not meant to be . . . And even as I think that, my subconscious is screaming *no!* If I terminate this pregnancy, I will never forgive myself—or Christian. "Oh, Blip, what have you done to us?" I can't face talking to Kate. I can't face talking to anyone. I text her, promising to call soon.

By eleven, I can no longer keep my eyelids open. Resigned, I head up to my old room. Curling up beneath the duvet, I finally let myself go, sobbing into my pillow, great heaving unladylike sobs of grief . . .

MY HEAD IS HEAVY when I wake. Crisp fall light shines through the great windows of my room. Glancing at my alarm I see it's seven thirty. My immediate thought is *Where's Christian?* I sit up and swing my legs out of bed. On the floor beside the bed is Christian's silver-gray tie, my favorite. It wasn't there when I went to bed last night. I pick it up and stare at it, caressing the silky material between my thumbs and forefingers, then hug it against my cheek. He was here, watching me sleep. And a glimmer of hope sparks deep inside me.

MRS. JONES IS BUSY in the kitchen when I arrive downstairs.

"Good morning," she says brightly.

"Morning. Christian?" I ask.

Her face falls. "He's already left."

"So he did come home?" I need to check, even though I have his tie as evidence.

"He did," she pauses. "Ana, please forgive me for speaking out of turn, but don't give up on him. He's a stubborn man."

I nod and she stops. I'm sure my expression tells her I do not want to discuss my errant husband right now.

WHEN I ARRIVE AT work, I check my e-mails. My heart leaps into overdrive when I see there's one from Christian.

From: Christian Grey
Subject: Portland
Date: September 15 2011 06:45
To: Anastasia Grey

Ana,

I am flying down to Portland today.

I have some business to conclude with WSU.

I thought you would want to know.

Christian Grey
CEO, Grey Enterprises Holdings, Inc.

Oh. Tears prick my eyes. That's it? My stomach flips. Shit! I am going to be sick. I race to the powder room and make it just in time, depositing my breakfast into the toilet. I sink to the floor of the cubicle and put my head in my hands. Could I be any more miserable? After a while, there's a gentle knock on the door.

"Ana?" It's Hannah.

Fuck. "Yes?"

"Are you okay?"

"I'll be out in a moment."

"Boyce Fox is here to see you."

Shit. "Show him into the meeting room. I'll be there in a minute."

"Do you want some tea?"

"Please."

AFTER MY LUNCH—ANOTHER CREAM cheese and salmon bagel, which I manage to keep down—I sit staring listlessly at my computer, looking for inspiration and wondering how Christian and I are going to resolve this huge problem.

My BlackBerry buzzes, making me jump. I glance at the screen—it's Mia. Jeez, that's all I need, her gushing and enthusiasm. I hesitate, wondering if I could just ignore it, but courtesy wins out.

"Mia," I answer brightly.

"Well, hello there, Ana—long time no speak." The male voice is familiar. *Fuck!*

My scalp prickles and all the hair on my body stands to attention as adrenaline floods through my system and my world stops spinning.

It's Jack Hyde.

CHAPTER TWENTY-TWO

J ack." My voice has disappeared, choked by fear. How is he
out of jail? Why does he have Mia's phone? The blood drains
from my face, and I feel dizzy.

"You do remember me," he says, his tone soft. I sense his bitter
smile.

"Yes. Of course." My answer is automatic as my mind races.

"You're probably wondering why I called you."

"Yes."

Hang up.

"Don't hang up. I've been having a chat with your little sister-
in-law."

What? Mia! No! "What have you done?" I whisper, trying to
quell my fear.

"Listen here, you prick-teasing, gold-digging whore. You
fucked up my life. Grey fucked up my life. You *owe* me. I have the
little bitch with me now. And you, that cocksucker you married,
and his whole fucking family are going to pay."

Hyde's contempt and bile shock me. *His family?* What the
hell?

"What do you want?"

"I want his money. I really want his fucking money. If things
had been different, it could have been me. So *you're* going to get
it for me. I want five million dollars, today."

"Jack, I don't have access to that kind of money."

He snorts his derision. "You have two hours to get it. That's
it—two hours. Tell no one or this little bitch gets it. Not the cops.
Not your prick of a husband. Not his security team. I will know if
you do. Understand?" He pauses and I try to respond, but panic
and fear seal my throat.

"You understand!" he shouts.

"Yes," I whisper.

"Or I will kill her."

I gasp.

"Keep your phone with you. Tell no one or I'll fuck her up before I kill her. You have two hours."

"Jack, I need longer. Three hours. How do I know that you have her?"

The line goes dead. I gape in horror at the phone, my mouth parched with fear, leaving the nasty metallic taste of terror. *Mia, he has Mia. Or does he?* My mind whirs at the obscene possibility, and my stomach roils again. I think I'm going to be sick, but I inhale deeply, trying to steady my panic, and the nausea passes. My mind rockets through the possibilities. *Tell Christian? Tell Taylor? Call the police? How will Jack know? Does he actually have Mia?* I need time, time to think—but I can accomplish that only by following his instructions. I grab my purse and head for the door.

"Hannah, I have to go out. I am not sure how long I'll be. Cancel my appointments this afternoon. Let Elizabeth know I have to deal with an emergency."

"Sure, Ana. Everything okay?" Hannah frowns, concern etched on her face as she watches me flee.

"Yes," I call back distractedly, hurrying toward Reception, where Sawyer is waiting.

"Sawyer." He leaps up from the armchair at the sound of my voice and frowns when he sees my face.

"I'm not feeling well. Please take me home."

"Sure, ma'am. Do you want to wait here while I get the car?"

"No, I'll come with you. I'm in a hurry to get home."

I GAZE OUT THE window in stark terror as I go over my plan. Get home. Change. Find checkbook. Escape from Ryan and Sawyer somehow. Go to bank. Hell, how much room does five million dollars take up? What will it weigh? Will I need a suitcase?

Should I telephone the bank in advance? Mia. *Mia.* What if he, doesn't have Mia? How can I check? If I call Grace it will raise her suspicions, and possibly endanger Mia. He said he would know. I glance out the back window of the SUV. Am I being followed? My heart races as I examine the cars following us. They look innocuous enough. *Oh, Sawyer, drive faster. Please.* My eyes flicker to meet his in the rearview mirror and his brow creases.

Sawyer presses a button on his Bluetooth headset to answer a call. "T . . . I wanted to let you know Mrs. Grey is with me." Sawyer's eyes meet mine once more before he looks back at the road and continues. "She's unwell. I'm taking her back to Escala . . . I see . . . sir." Sawyer's eyes flick from the road to mine in the rearview mirror again. "Yes," he agrees and hangs up.

"Taylor?" I whisper.

He nods.

"He's with Mr. Grey?"

"Yes, ma'am." Sawyer's look softens in sympathy.

"Are they still in Portland?"

"Yes, ma'am."

Good. I have to keep Christian safe. My hand strays down to my belly, and I rub it consciously. And you, Little Blip. Keep you both safe.

"Can we hurry please? I'm not feeling well."

"Yes, ma'am." Sawyer presses the accelerator and our car glides through the traffic.

MRS. JONES IS NOWHERE to be seen when Sawyer and I arrive at the apartment. Since her car is missing from the garage, I assume she's running errands with Ryan. Sawyer heads for Taylor's office while I bolt to Christian's study. Stumbling in panic around his desk, I wrench open the drawer to find the checkbooks. Leila's gun slides forward into view. I feel an incongruous twinge of annoyance that Christian has not secured this weapon. He knows nothing about guns. *Jeez, he could get hurt.*

After a moment's hesitation, I grab the pistol, check to ensure it's loaded, and tuck it into the waistband of my black slacks. I may need it. I swallow hard. I've only ever practiced on targets. I've never fired a gun at anyone; I hope Ray will forgive me. I turn my attention to tracking down the right checkbook. There are five, and only one is in the names of C. Grey and Mrs. A. Grey. I have about fifty-four thousand dollars in my own account. I have no idea how much money is in this one. But Christian must be good for five million dollars, surely. Perhaps there's money in the safe? Crap. I have no idea of the number. Didn't he mention the combination was in his filing cabinet? I try the cabinet, but it's locked. *Shit.* I'll have to stick to plan A.

I take a deep breath and, in a more composed but determined manner, stride to our bedroom. The bed has been made, and for a moment, I feel a pang. Perhaps I should have slept here last night. What is the point of arguing with someone who, by his own admission, is Fifty Shades? He's not even talking to me now. No—I do not have time to think about this.

Quickly, I change out of my slacks, pulling on jeans, a hooded sweatshirt, and a pair of sneakers, and put the gun in the waistband of my jeans, at my back. From the closet I fish out a large soft duffel bag. Will five million dollars fit into this? Christian's gym bag is lying there on the floor. I open it, expecting to find it full of dirty laundry, but no—his gym kit is clean and fresh. Mrs. Jones does indeed get everywhere. I dump the contents onto the floor and stuff his gym bag into my duffel. There, that should do it. I check that I have my driver's license as identification for the bank and check the time. It's been thirty-one minutes since Jack called. Now I just have to get out of Escala without Sawyer seeing me.

I make my way slowly and quietly to the foyer, aware of the CCTV camera, which is trained on the elevator. I think Sawyer's still in Taylor's office. Cautiously, I open the foyer door, making as little noise as possible. Shutting it quietly behind me, I stand on the very threshold, up against the door, out of the view of the CCTV lens. I fish my cell phone out of my purse and call Sawyer.

"Mrs. Grey."

"Sawyer, I'm in the room upstairs, will you give me a hand with something?" I keep my voice low, knowing he's just down the hallway on the other side of this door.

"I'll be right with you, ma'am," he says, and I hear his confusion. I've never telephoned him for help before. My heart is in my throat, pounding in a jarring, frenetic rhythm. Will this work? I hang up and listen as his footsteps cross the hallway and go up the stairs. I take another deep, steadying breath and briefly contemplate the irony of escaping from my own home like a felon.

Once Sawyer's reached the upstairs landing, I race to the elevator and punch the call button. The doors slide open with the too-loud ping that announces the elevator is ready. I dash inside and frantically stab the button for the basement garage. After an agonizing pause, the doors slowly start to slide shut, and as they do I hear Sawyer's cries.

"Mrs. Grey!" Just as the elevator doors close, I see him skid into the foyer. "Ana!" he shouts in disbelief. But he's too late, and he disappears from view.

The elevator sinks smoothly down to the garage level. I have a couple of minutes' start on Sawyer, and I know he'll try to stop me. I glance longingly at my R8 as I rush to the Saab, open the door, toss the duffel bag onto the passenger seat, and slide into the driver's seat.

I start the car, and the tires squeal as I race to the entrance and wait eleven agonizing seconds for the barrier to lift. The instant it's clear I drive out, catching sight of Sawyer in my rearview mirror as he dashes out of the service elevator into the garage. His bewildered, injured expression haunts me as I turn off the ramp onto Fourth Avenue.

I let out my long-held breath. I know Sawyer will call Christian or Taylor, but I'll deal with that when I have to—I don't have time to dwell on it now. I squirm uncomfortably in my seat, knowing in my heart of hearts that Sawyer's probably lost his job. *Don't dwell*. I have to save Mia. I have to get to the bank and collect five million dollars. I glance in the rearview mirror, nervously anticipating the sight of the SUV bursting forth from the garage, but as I drive away, there's no sign of Sawyer.

THE BANK IS SLEEK, modern, and understated. There are hushed tones, echoing floors, and pale green etched glass everywhere. I stride to the information desk.

"May I help you, ma'am?" The young woman gives me a bright, insincere smile, and for a moment I regret changing into jeans.

"I'd like to withdraw a large sum of money."

Ms. Insincere Smile arches an even more insincere eyebrow.

"You have an account with us?" She fails to hide her sarcasm.

"Yes," I snap. "My husband and I have several accounts here. His name is Christian Grey."

Her eyes widen fractionally and insincerity gives way to shock. Her eyes sweep up and down me once more, this time with a combination of disbelief and awe.

"This way, ma'am," she whispers, and leads me to a small, sparsely furnished office walled with more green-etched glass.

"Please take a seat." She gestures to a black leather chair by a glass desk bearing a state-of-the-art computer and phone. "How much will you be withdrawing today, Mrs. Grey?" she asks pleasantly.

"Five million dollars." I look her straight in the eye as if I ask for this amount of cash every day.

She blanches. "I see. I'll fetch the manager. Oh, forgive me for asking, but do you have ID?"

"I do. But I'd like to speak to the manager."

"Of course, Mrs. Grey." She scurries out. I sink into the seat, and a wave of nausea washes over me as the gun presses uncomfortably into the small of my back. *Not now. I can't be sick now.* I take a deep cleansing breath, and the wave passes. Nervously, I check my watch. Twenty-five past two.

A middle-aged man enters the room. He has a receding hairline, but wears a sharp, expensive charcoal suit and matching tie. He holds out his hand.

"Mrs. Grey. I'm Troy Whelan." He smiles, we shake, and he sits down at the desk opposite me.

"My colleague tells me you'd like to withdraw a large amount of money."

"That's correct. Five million dollars."

He turns to his sleek computer and taps in a few numbers.

"We normally ask for some notice for large amounts of money." He pauses and flashes me a reassuring but supercilious smile. "Fortunately, however, we hold the cash reserve for the entire Pacific Northwest," he boasts. *Jeez, is he trying to impress me?*

"Mr. Whelan, I'm in a hurry. What do I need to do? I have my driver's license, and our joint account checkbook. Do I just write a check?"

"First things first, Mrs. Grey. May I see the ID?" He switches from jovial show-off to serious banker.

"Here." I hand over my license.

"Mrs. Grey . . . this says Anastasia Steele."

Oh shit.

"Oh . . . yes. Um."

"I'll call Mr. Grey."

"Oh no, that won't be necessary." *Shit!* "I must have something with my married name." I rifle through my purse. What do I have with my name on it? I pull out my wallet, open it, and find a photograph of Christian and me, on the bed in *Fair Lady*'s cabin. *I can't show him that!* I dig out my black Amex.

"Here."

"Mrs. Anastasia Grey," Whelan reads. "Yes, that should do." He frowns. "This is highly irregular, Mrs. Grey."

"Do you want me to let my husband know that your bank has been less than cooperative?" I square my shoulders and give him my most forbidding stare.

He pauses, momentarily reassessing me, I think. "You'll need to write a check, Mrs. Grey."

"Sure. This account?" I show him my checkbook, trying to quell my pounding heart.

"That'll be fine. I'll also need you to complete some additional paperwork. If you'll excuse me for a moment?"

I nod, and he rises and stalks out of the office. Again, I release my held breath. I had no idea this would be so difficult. Clumsily, I open my checkbook and pull a pen out of my purse. Do I just make it out to cash? I have no idea. With shaking fingers I write: *Five million dollars. $5,000,000.*

Oh God, I hope I'm doing the right thing. Mia, think of Mia. I can't tell anyone.

Jack's chilling, repugnant words haunt me. *"Tell no one or I'll fuck her up before I kill her."*

Mr. Whelan returns, pale-faced and sheepish.

"Mrs. Grey? Your husband wants to speak with you," he murmurs and points to the phone on the glass table between us.

What? No.

"He's on line one. Just press the button. I'll be outside." He has the grace to look embarrassed. Benedict Arnold has nothing on Whelan. I scowl at him, feeling the blood drain from my face again as he shuffles out of the office.

Shit! Shit! *Shit!* What am I going to say to Christian? He'll know. He'll intervene. He's a danger to his sister. My hand trembles as I reach for the phone. I hold it against my ear, trying to calm my erratic breathing, and press the button for line one.

"Hi," I murmur, trying in vain to steady my nerves.

"You're leaving me?" Christian's words are an agonized, breathless whisper.

What?

"No!" My voice mirrors his. *Oh no. Oh no. Oh no—how can he think that?* The money? He thinks I'm going because of *the money?* And in a moment of horrific clarity, I realize the only way I'm going to keep Christian at arm's length, out of harm's way, and to save his sister . . . is to lie.

"Yes," I whisper. And searing pain lances through me, tears springing to my eyes.

He gasps, almost a sob. "Ana, I—" He chokes.

No! My hand clutches my mouth as I stifle my warring emotions. "Christian, please. Don't." I fight back tears.

"You're going?" he says.

"Yes."

"But why the cash? Was it always the money?" His tortured voice is barely audible.

No! Tears roll down my face. "No," I whisper.

"Is five million enough?"

Oh please, stop!

"Yes."

"And the baby?" His voice is a breathless echo.

What? My hand moves from my mouth to my belly. "I'll take care of the baby," I murmur. *My Little Blip . . . our Little Blip.*

"This is what you want?"

No!

"Yes."

He inhales sharply. "Take it all," he hisses.

"Christian," I sob. "It's for you. For your family. Please. Don't."

"Take it all, Anastasia."

"Christian—" And I nearly cave. Nearly tell him—about Jack, about Mia, about the ransom. *Just trust me, please!* I silently beg him.

"I'll always love you." His voice is hoarse. He hangs up.

"Christian! No . . . I love you, too." And all the stupid shit that we put each other through over the last few days fades into insignificance. I promised I'd never leave him. I am not leaving you. I am saving your sister. I slump into the chair, weeping copiously into my hands.

I am interrupted by a timid knock on the door. Whelan enters, though I haven't acknowledged him. He looks everywhere but at me. He's mortified.

You called him, you bastard! I glare at him.

"Your husband has agreed to liquidate five million dollars worth of his assets, Mrs. Grey. This is highly irregular but as our main client . . . he was insistent . . . very insistent." He pauses and flushes. Then frowns at me and I don't know if it's because Christian is being highly irregular or that Whelan doesn't know how to deal with a weeping woman in his office.

"Are you all right?" He asks.

"Do I look all right?" I snap.

"I'm sorry, ma'am. Some water?"

I nod, sullenly. I have just left my husband. Well, Christian thinks I have. My subconscious purses her lips. *Because you told him so.*

"I'll have my colleague bring you some while I prepare the money. If you could just sign here, ma'am . . . and make the check out to cash and sign that, too."

He places a form on the table. I scrawl my signature along the dotted line of the check, then the form. *Anastasia Grey.* Teardrops fall on the desk, narrowly missing the paperwork.

"I'll take those, ma'am. It will take us about half an hour to prepare the money."

I quickly check my watch. Jack said two hours—that should take us to two hours. I nod to Whelan, and he tiptoes out of the office, leaving me to my misery.

A few moments, minutes, hours later—I don't know—Miss Insincere Smile reenters with a carafe of water and a glass.

"Mrs. Grey," she says softly as she places the glass on the desk and fills it.

"Thank you." I take the glass and drink gratefully. She exits, leaving me with my jumbled, frightened thoughts. I will fix things with Christian somehow . . . if it's not too late. At least he's out of the picture. Right now I have to concentrate on Mia. Suppose Jack is lying? Suppose he doesn't have her? Surely I should call the police.

"Tell no one or I'll fuck her up before I kill her." I can't. I sit back in the chair, feeling the reassuring presence of Leila's pistol at my waist, digging into my back. Who would have thought I'd ever feel grateful that Leila once pulled a gun on me? Oh, Ray, I'm so glad you taught me how to shoot.

Ray! I gasp. He'll be expecting me to visit this evening. Perhaps I can simply dump the money with Jack. He can run while I take Mia home. *Oh, this sounds absurd!*

My BlackBerry jumps to life, "Your Love Is King" filling the room. *Oh no!* What does Christian want? To twist the knife in my wounds?

"Was it always the money?"

Oh, Christian—how could you think that? Anger flares in my gut. Yes, anger. It helps. I send the call to voice mail. I'll deal with my husband later.

There's a knock on the door.

"Mrs. Grey." It's Whelan. "The money is ready."

"Thank you." I stand up and the room spins momentarily. I clutch the chair.

"Mrs. Grey, are you feeling okay?"

I nod and give him a back-off-now-mister stare. I take another deep, calming breath. *I have to do this. I have to do this. I must save Mia.* I pull the hem of my hooded sweatshirt down, concealing the butt of the pistol in the back of my jeans.

Mr. Whelan frowns but holds open the door, and I propel myself forward on my shaking limbs.

Sawyer is waiting at the entrance, scanning the public area. *Shit!* Our eyes meet, and he frowns at me, gauging my reaction. Oh, he's mad. I hold up my index finger in a with-you-in-a-minute gesture. He nods and answers a call on his cell phone. *Shit! I bet that's Christian.* I turn abruptly, almost colliding with Whelan right behind me, and bolt back into the little office.

"Mrs. Grey?" Whelan sounds confused as he follows me back in.

Sawyer could blow this whole plan. I gaze up at Whelan.

"There's someone out there I don't want to see. Someone following me."

Whelan's eyes widen.

"Do you want me to call the police?"

"No!" Holy fuck, no. What am I going to do? I glance at my

watch. It's nearly three fifteen. Jack will call at any moment. *Think, Ana, think!* Whelan gazes at me in growing desperation and bewilderment. He must think I'm crazy. *You are crazy,* my subconscious snaps.

"I need to make a call. Could you give me some privacy, please?"

"Certainly," Whelan answers—grateful, I think, to leave the room. When he's closed the door, I call Mia's cell phone with trembling fingers.

"Well, if it isn't my paycheck," Jack answers scornfully.

I don't have time for his bullshit. "I have a problem."

"I know. Your security followed you to the bank."

What? How the hell does he know?

"You'll have to lose him. I have a car waiting at the back of the bank. Black SUV, a Dodge. You have three minutes to get there." *The Dodge!*

"It may take longer than three minutes." My heart leaps into my throat once more.

"You're bright for a gold-digging whore, Grey. You figure it out. And dump your cell phone once you reach the vehicle. Got it, bitch?"

"Yes."

"Say it!" he snaps.

"I've got it."

He hangs up.

Shit! I open the door to find Whelan waiting patiently outside.

"Mr. Whelan, I'll need some help taking the bags to my car. It's parked outside, at the back of the bank. Do you have an exit at the rear?"

He frowns.

"We do, yes. For staff."

"Can we leave that way? I can avoid the unwelcome attention at the door."

"As you wish, Mrs. Grey. I'll have two clerks help with the bags and two security guards to supervise. If you could follow me?"

"I have one more favor to ask you."

"By all means, Mrs. Grey."

TWO MINUTES LATER MY entourage and I are out on the street, heading over to the Dodge. Its windows are blacked out, and I can't tell who's at the wheel. But as we approach, the driver's door swings open, and a woman clad in black with a black cap pulled low over her face climbs gracefully out of the car. *Elizabeth from the office! What the hell.* She moves to the rear of the SUV and opens the trunk. The two young bank clerks carrying the money sling the heavy bags into the back.

"Mrs. Grey." She has the nerve to smile as if we are off on a friendly jaunt.

"Elizabeth." My greeting is arctic. "Nice to see you outside work."

Mr. Whelan clears this throat.

"Well, it's been an interesting afternoon, Mrs. Grey," he says. And I am forced to observe the social niceties of shaking his hand and thanking him while my mind reels. *Elizabeth?* Why is she mixed up with Jack? Whelan and his team disappear back into the bank, leaving me alone with the head of personnel at SIP, who's involved in kidnapping, extortion, and very possibly other felonies. Why?

Elizabeth opens the rear passenger door and ushers me in.

"Your phone, Mrs. Grey?" she asks, watching me warily. I hand it to her, and she tosses it into a nearby trash can.

"That will throw the dogs off the scent," she says smugly.

Who *is* this woman? Elizabeth slams my door shut and climbs into the driver's seat. I glance anxiously behind me as she pulls out into traffic, going east. Sawyer is nowhere to be seen.

"Elizabeth, you have the money. Call Jack. Tell him to let Mia go."

"I think he wants to thank you in person."

Shit! I glare at her stonily in the rearview mirror.

She pales and an anxious scowl mars her otherwise lovely face.

"Why are you doing this, Elizabeth? I thought you didn't like Jack."

She glances at me again briefly in the mirror, and I see a fleeting look of pain in her eyes.

"Ana, we'll get along just fine if you keep your mouth shut."

"But you can't do this. This is so wrong."

"Quiet," she says, but I sense her unease.

"Does he have some kind of hold on you?" I ask. Her eyes shoot to mine and she slams on the brakes, throwing me forward so hard that I hit my face against the headrest of the front seat.

"I said be quiet," she snarls. "And I suggest you put on your seat belt."

And in that moment I know that he does. Something so awful that she's prepared to do this for him. I wonder briefly what that could be. Theft from the company? Something from her private life? Something sexual? I shudder at the thought. Christian said that none of Jack's PAs would talk. Perhaps it's the same story with all of them. *That's why he wanted to fuck me, too.* Bile rises in my throat with revulsion at the thought.

Elizabeth heads away from downtown Seattle and up into the hills to the east. Before long we're driving through residential streets. I catch sight of one of the street signs: SOUTH IRVING STREET. She takes a sharp left onto a deserted street with a dilapidated children's playground on one side and a large concrete parking lot flanked by a row of squat, empty brick buildings on the other. Elizabeth pulls into the parking lot and stops outside the last of the brick units.

She turns to me. "Showtime," she murmurs.

My scalp prickles as fear and adrenaline course through my body.

"You don't have to do this," I whisper back. Her mouth flattens into a grim line, and she climbs out of the car.

This is for Mia. This is for Mia. I quickly pray, *Please let her be okay, please let her be okay.*

"Get out," Elizabeth snaps, yanking the rear passenger door open.

Shit. As I clamber out, my legs are shaking so hard I wonder if I can stand. The cool late afternoon breeze carries the scent of the coming fall and the chalky, dusty smell of derelict buildings.

"Well, lookee here." Jack emerges from a small, boarded-up doorway on the left of the building. His hair is short. He's removed his earrings and he's wearing a suit. A *suit?* He ambles toward me, oozing arrogance and hate. My heart rate spikes.

"Where's Mia?" I stammer, my mouth so dry I can hardly form the words.

"First things first, bitch," Jack sneers, coming to a halt in front of me. I can practically taste his contempt. "The money?"

Elizabeth is checking the bags in the trunk. "There's a hell of a lot of cash here," she says in awe, zipping and unzipping each bag.

"And her cell?"

"In the trash."

"Good," Jack snarls, and from nowhere he lashes out, back-handing me hard across the face. The ferocious, unprovoked blow knocks me to the ground, and my head bounces with a sickening thud off the concrete. Pain explodes in my head, my eyes fill with tears, and my vision blurs as the shock of the impact resonates, unleashing agony that pulses through my skull.

I scream a silent cry of suffering and shocked terror. Oh no— *Little Blip.* Jack follows through with a swift, vicious kick to my ribs, and my breath is blasted from my lungs by the force of the blow. Scrunching my eyes tightly, I try to fight the nausea and pain, to fight for a precious breath. *Little Blip, Little Blip, oh my Little Blip—*

"That's for SIP, you fucking bitch!" Jack screams.

I pull my legs up, huddling into a ball and anticipating the next blow. *No. No. No.*

"Jack!" Elizabeth screeches. "Not here. Not in broad daylight for fuck's sake!"

He pauses.

"The bitch deserves it!" he gloats to Elizabeth. And it gives me one precious second to reach around and pull the gun from the waistband of my jeans. Shakily, I aim at him, squeeze the trigger, and fire. The bullet hits him just above the knee, and he collapses in front of me, crying out in agony, clutching his thigh as his fingers redden with his blood.

"Fuck!" Jack bellows. I turn to face Elizabeth, and she's gaping at me in horror and raising her hands above her head. She blurs . . . darkness closes in. *Shit* . . . She's at the end of a tunnel. Darkness consuming her. Consuming me. From far away, all hell breaks loose. Cars screeching . . . brakes . . . doors . . . shouting . . . running . . . footsteps. The gun drops from my hand.

"Ana!" Christian's voice . . . Christian's voice . . . Christian's agonized voice. Mia . . . *save Mia.*

"ANA!"

Darkness . . . peace.

CHAPTER TWENTY-THREE

There is only pain. My head, my chest . . . burning pain. My side, my arm. Pain. Pain and hushed words in the gloom. *Where am I?* Though I try, I cannot open my eyes. The whispered words become clearer . . . a beacon in the darkness.

"Her ribs are bruised, Mr. Grey, and she has a hairline fracture to her skull, but her vital signs are stable and strong."

"Why is she still unconscious?"

"Mrs. Grey has had a major contusion to her head. But her brain activity is normal, and she has no cerebral swelling. She'll wake when she's ready. Just give her some time."

"And the baby?" The words are anguished, breathless.

"The baby's fine, Mr. Grey."

"Oh, thank God." The words are a litany . . . a prayer. "Oh, thank God."

Oh my. He's worried about the baby . . . the baby? . . . *Little Blip.* Of course. My Little Blip. I try in vain to move my hand to my belly. Nothing moves, nothing responds.

"And the baby? . . . Oh, thank God."

Little Blip is safe.

"And the baby? . . . Oh, thank God."

He cares about the baby.

"And the baby? . . . Oh, thank God."

He wants the baby. Oh, thank God. I relax, and unconsciousness claims me once more, stealing me away from the pain.

EVERYTHING IS HEAVY AND aching: limbs, head, eyelids, nothing will move. My eyes and mouth are resolutely shut, unwilling to open, leaving me blind and mute and aching. As I surface from the fog, consciousness hovers, a seductive siren just out of reach. Sounds become voices.

"I'm not leaving her."

Christian! He's here . . . I will myself to wake—his voice is strained, an agonized whisper.

"Christian, you should sleep."

"No, Dad. I want to be here when she wakes up."

"I'll sit with her. It's the least I can do after she saved my daughter."

Mia!

"How's Mia?"

"She's groggy . . . scared and angry. It'll be a few hours before the Rohypnol is completely out of her system."

"Christ."

"I know. I'm feeling seven kinds of foolish for relenting on her security. You warned me, but Mia is so stubborn. If it wasn't for Ana here . . ."

"We all thought Hyde was out of the picture. And my crazy, stupid wife—Why didn't she tell me?" Christian's voice is full of anguish.

"Christian, calm down. Ana's a remarkable young woman. She was incredibly brave."

"Brave and headstrong and stubborn and stupid." His voice cracks.

"Hey," Carrick murmurs, "don't be so hard on her, or yourself, son . . . I'd better get back to your mom. It's after three in the morning, Christian. You really should try to sleep."

The fog closes in.

THE FOG LIFTS BUT I have no sense of time.

"If you don't take her across your knee, I sure as hell will. What the hell was she thinking?"

"Trust me, Ray, I just might do that."

Dad! He's here. I fight the fog . . . fight . . . But I spiral down once more into oblivion. *No . . .*

"DETECTIVE, AS YOU CAN see, my wife is in no state to answer any of your questions." Christian is angry.

"She's a headstrong young woman, Mr. Grey."

"I wish she'd killed the fucker."

"That would have meant more paperwork for me, Mr. Grey . . ."

"Miss Morgan is singing like the proverbial canary. Hyde's a real twisted son of a bitch. He has a serious grudge against your father and you . . ."

The fog surrounds me once more, and I'm dragged down . . . down. *No!*

"WHAT DO YOU MEAN you weren't talking?" It's Grace. She sounds angry. I try to move my head, but I'm met with a resounding, listless silence from my body.

"What did you do?"

"Mom—"

"Christian! What did you do?"

"I was so angry." It's almost a sob . . . No.

"Hey . . ."

The world dips and blurs and I'm gone.

I HEAR SOFT GARBLED voices.

"You told me you'd cut all ties." Grace is talking. Her voice is quiet, admonishing.

"I know." Christian sounds resigned. "But seeing her finally put it all in perspective for me. You know . . . with the child. For the first time I felt . . . What we did . . . it was wrong."

"What *she* did, darling . . . Children will do that to you. Make you look at the world in a different light."

"She finally got the message . . . and so did I . . . I hurt Ana," he whispers.

"We always hurt the ones we love, darling. You'll have to tell her you're sorry. And mean it and give her time."

"She said she was leaving me."

No. No. No!

"Did you believe her?"

"At first, yes."

"Darling, you always believe the worst of everyone, including yourself. You always have. Ana loves you very much, and it's obvious you love her."

"She was mad at me."

"I'm sure she was. I'm pretty mad at you right now. I think you can only be truly mad at someone you really love."

"I thought about it, and she's shown me over and over how much she loves me . . . to the point of putting her own life in danger."

"Yes, she has, darling."

"Oh, Mom, why won't she wake up?" His voice cracks. "I nearly lost her."

Christian! There are muffled sobs. No . . .

Oh . . . the darkness closes in. *No—*

"IT'S TAKEN TWENTY-FOUR YEARS for you to let me hold you like this . . ."

"I know, Mom . . . I'm glad we talked."

"Me too, darling. I'm always here. I can't believe I'm going to be a grandmother."

Grandma!

Sweet oblivion beckons.

HMM. HIS STUBBLE SOFTLY scrapes the back of my hand as he squeezes my fingers.

"Oh, baby, please come back to me. I'm sorry. Sorry for everything. Just wake up. I miss you. I love you . . ."

I try. I try. I want to see him. But my body disobeys me, and I fall asleep once more.

I HAVE A PRESSING need to pee. I open my eyes. I'm in the clean, sterile environment of a hospital room. It's dark except for a sidelight, and all is quiet. My head and my chest ache, but more than that, my bladder is bursting. I need to pee. I test my limbs. My right arm smarts, and I notice the IV attached to it on the inside of my elbow. I shut my eyes quickly. Turning my head—I'm pleased that it responds to my will—I open my eyes again. Christian is asleep, sitting beside me and leaning on my bed with his head on his folded arms. I reach out, grateful once more that my body responds, and run my fingers through his soft hair.

He startles awake, raising his head so suddenly that my hand falls weakly back onto the bed.

"Hi," I croak.

"Oh, Ana." His voice is choked and relieved. He grasps my hand, squeezing it tightly and holding it up against his rough, stubbled cheek.

"I need to use the bathroom," I whisper.

He gapes, then frowns at me for a moment. "Okay."

I struggle to sit up.

"Ana, stay still. I'll call a nurse." He quickly stands, alarmed, and reaches for a buzzer on the bedside.

"Please," I whisper. *Why do I ache everywhere?* "I need to get up." *Jeez, I feel so weak.*

"Will you do as you're told for once?" he snaps, exasperated.

"I really need to pee," I rasp. My throat and mouth are so dry.

A nurse bustles into the room. She must be in her fifties, though her hair is jet black. She wears overlarge pearl earrings.

"Mrs. Grey, welcome back. I'll let Dr. Bartley know you're awake." She makes her way to my bedside. "My name is Nora. Do you know where you are?"

"Yes. Hospital. I need to pee."

"You have a catheter."

What? Oh, this is gross. I glance anxiously at Christian, then back to the nurse.

"Please. I want to get up."

"Mrs. Grey."

"Please."

"Ana," Christian warns. I struggle to sit up once more.

"Let me remove your catheter. Mr. Grey, I am sure Mrs. Grey would like some privacy." She looks pointedly at Christian, dismissing him.

"I'm not going anywhere." He glares back at her.

"Christian, please," I whisper, reaching out and grasping his hand. Briefly he squeezes my hand, then gives me an exasperated look. "Please," I beg.

"Fine!" he snaps and runs his hand through his hair. "You have two minutes," he hisses at the nurse, and he leans down and kisses my forehead before turning on his heel and leaving the room.

CHRISTIAN BURSTS BACK INTO the room two minutes later as Nurse Nora is helping me out of bed. I'm dressed in a thin hospital gown. I don't remember being stripped.

"Let me take her," he says and strides toward us.

"Mr. Grey, I can manage," Nurse Nora scolds him.

He gives her a hostile glare. "Damn it, she's my wife. I'll take her," he says through gritted teeth as he moves the IV stand out of his way.

"Mr. Grey!" she protests.

He ignores her, leans down, and gently lifts me off the bed. I wrap my arms around his neck, my body complaining. *Jeez, I ache everywhere.* He carries me to the en suite bathroom while Nurse Nora follows us, pushing the IV stand.

"Mrs. Grey, you're too light," he mutters disapprovingly as he sets me gently on my feet. I sway. My legs feel like Jell-O. Christian flips the light switch, and I'm momentarily blinded by the fluorescent lamp that pings and flickers to life.

"Sit before you fall," he snaps, still holding me.

Tentatively, I sit down on the toilet.

"Go." I try to wave him out.

"No. Just pee, Ana."

Could this be any more embarrassing? "I can't, not with you here."

"You might fall."

"Mr. Grey!"

We both ignore the nurse.

"Please," I beg.

He raises his hands in defeat. "I'll stand outside, door open." He takes a couple of paces back until he's standing just outside the door with the angry nurse.

"Turn around, please," I ask. Why do I feel so ridiculously shy with this man? He rolls his eyes but complies. And when his back is turned . . . I let go, and savor the relief.

I take stock of my injuries. My head hurts, my chest aches where Jack kicked me, and my side throbs where he pushed me to the ground. Plus I'm thirsty and hungry. *Jeez, really hungry.* I finish up, thankful that I don't have to get up to wash my hands, as the sink is close. I just don't have the strength to stand.

"I'm done," I call, drying my hands on the towel.

Christian turns and comes back in and before I know it, I'm in his arms again. I have missed these arms. He pauses and buries his nose in my hair.

"Oh, I've missed you, Mrs. Grey," he whispers, and with Nurse Nora fussing behind him, he lays me back on the bed and releases me—reluctantly, I think.

"If you've quite finished, Mr. Grey, I'd like to check over Mrs. Grey now." Nurse Nora is mad.

He stands back. "She's all yours," he says in a more measured tone.

She huffs at him and then turns her attention back to me.

Exasperating isn't he?

"How do you feel?" she asks me, her voice laced with sympathy and a trace of irritation, which I suspect is for Christian's benefit.

"Sore and thirsty. Very thirsty," I whisper.

"I'll fetch you some water once I've checked your vitals and Dr. Bartley has examined you."

She reaches for a blood pressure cuff and wraps it around my

upper arm. I glance anxiously up at Christian. He looks dreadful—
haunted, even—as if he hasn't slept for days. His hair is a mess,
he hasn't shaved for a long time, and his shirt is badly wrinkled.
I frown.

"How are you feeling?" Ignoring the nurse, he sits down on
the bed out of arm's reach.

"Confused. Achy. Hungry."

"Hungry?" He blinks in surprise.

I nod.

"What do you want to eat?"

"Anything. Soup."

"Mr. Grey, you'll need the doctor's approval before Mrs. Grey
can eat."

He gazes at her impassively for a moment, then takes his
BlackBerry out of his pants pocket and presses a number.

"Ana wants chicken soup . . . Good . . . Thank you." He hangs up.

I glance at Nora, whose eyes narrow at Christian.

"Taylor?" I ask quickly.

Christian nods.

"Your blood pressure is normal, Mrs. Grey. I'll fetch the doctor." She removes the cuff and, without so much as another word,
stalks out of the room, radiating disapproval.

"I think you made Nurse Nora mad."

"I have that effect on women." He smirks.

I laugh, then stop suddenly as pain radiates through my chest.
"Yes, you do."

"Oh, Ana, I love to hear you laugh."

Nora returns with a pitcher of water. We both fall silent, gazing at each other as she pours out a glass and hands it to me.

"Small sips now," she warns.

"Yes, ma'am," I mutter and take a welcome sip of cool water.
Oh my. It tastes perfect. I take another, and Christian watches me
intently.

"Mia?" I ask.

"She's safe. Thanks to you."

"They did have her?"

"Yes."

All the madness was for a reason. Relief spirals through my body. *Thank God, thank God, thank God she's okay.* I frown.

"How did they get her?"

"Elizabeth Morgan," he says simply.

"No!"

He nods. "She picked her up at Mia's gym."

I frown, still not understanding.

"Ana, I'll fill you in on the details later. Mia is fine, all things considered. She was drugged. She's groggy now and shaken up, but by some miracle she wasn't harmed." Christian's jaw clenches. "What you did"—he runs his hand through his hair—"was incredibly brave and incredibly stupid. You could have been killed." His eyes blaze a bleak, chilling gray, and I know he's restraining his anger.

"I didn't know what else to do," I whisper.

"You could have told me!" he says vehemently, fisting his hands in his lap.

"He said he'd kill her if I told anyone. I couldn't take that risk."

Christian closes his eyes, dread etched in his face.

"I have died a thousand deaths since Thursday."

Thursday?

"What day is it?"

"It's almost Saturday," he says, checking his watch. "You've been unconscious for more than twenty-four hours."

Oh.

"And Jack and Elizabeth?"

"In police custody. Although Hyde is here under guard. They had to remove the bullet you left in him," Christian says bitterly. "I don't know where in this hospital he is, fortunately, or I'd probably kill him myself." His face darkens.

Oh shit. Jack is here?

"That's for SIP you fucking bitch!" I pale. My empty stomach convulses, tears prick my eyes, and a deep shudder runs through me.

"Hey." Christian scoots forward, his voice filled with concern. Taking the glass from my hand, he tenderly folds me into his arms. "You're safe now," he murmurs against my hair, his voice hoarse.

"Christian, I'm so sorry." My tears start to fall.

"Hush." He strokes my hair, and I weep into his neck.

"What I said. I was never going to leave you."

"Hush, baby, I know."

"You do?" His admission halts my tears.

"I worked it out. Eventually. Honestly, Ana, what were you *thinking*?" His tone is strained.

"You took me by surprise," I mutter into his shirt collar. "When we spoke at the bank. Thinking I was leaving you. I thought you knew me better. I've said to you over and over I would never leave."

"But after the appalling way I've behaved—" His voice is barely audible, and his arms tighten around me. "I thought for a short time that I'd lost you."

"No, Christian. Never. I didn't want you to interfere and put Mia's life in danger."

He sighs, and I don't know if it's from anger, exasperation, or hurt.

"How did you work it out?" I ask quickly to distract him from his line of thought.

He tucks my hair behind my ear. "I'd just touched down in Seattle when the bank called. Last I'd heard, you were ill and going home."

"So you were in Portland when Sawyer called you from the car?"

"We were just about to take off. I was worried about you," he says softly.

"You were?"

He frowns. "Of course I was." He skirts his thumb over my bottom lip. "I spend my life worrying about you. You know that."

Oh, Christian!

"Jack called me at the office," I murmur. "He gave me two

hours to get the money." I shrug. "I had to leave, and it just seemed the best excuse."

Christian's mouth presses into a hard line. "And you gave Sawyer the slip. He's mad at you, as well."

"As well?"

"As well as me."

I tentatively touch his face, running my fingers over his stubble. He closes his eyes, leaning into my fingers.

"Don't be mad at me. Please," I whisper.

"I am so mad at you. What you did was monumentally stupid. Bordering on insane."

"I told you, I didn't know what else to do."

"You don't seem to have any regard for your personal safety. And it's not just you now," he adds angrily.

My lip trembles. He's thinking about our Little Blip.

The door opens, startling us both, and a young African American woman in a white coat over gray scrubs strides in.

"Good evening, Mrs. Grey. I'm Dr. Bartley."

She starts to examine me thoroughly, shining a light in my eyes, making me touch her fingers, then my nose while closing first one eye and then the other, and checking all my reflexes. But her voice is soft and her touch gentle; she has a warm bedside manner. Nurse Nora joins her, and Christian wanders to the corner of the room and makes some calls while the two of them tend to me. It's hard to concentrate on Dr. Bartley, Nurse Nora, and Christian at the same time, but I hear him call his father, my mother, and Kate to say I'm awake. Finally, he leaves a message for Ray.

Ray. Oh shit . . . A vague memory of his voice comes back to me. He was here—yes, while I was still unconscious.

Dr. Bartley checks my ribs, her fingers probing gently but firmly.

I wince.

"These are bruised, not cracked or broken. You were very lucky, Mrs. Grey."

I scowl. *Lucky?* Not the word I would have chosen. Christian glowers at her, too. He mouths something at me. I think it's *foolhardy,* but I'm not sure.

"I'll prescribe some painkillers. You'll need them for this and for the headache you must have. But all's looking as it should, Mrs. Grey. I suggest you get some sleep. Depending on how you feel in the morning, we may let you go home. My colleague Dr. Singh will be attending you then."

"Thank you."

There's a knock on the door, and Taylor enters bearing a black cardboard box with *Fairmont Olympic* emblazoned in cream on the side.

Holy cow!

"Food?" Dr. Bartley says, surprised.

"Mrs. Grey is hungry," Christian says. "This is chicken soup."

Dr. Bartley smiles. "Soup will be fine, just the broth. Nothing heavy." She looks pointedly at both of us, then exits the room with Nurse Nora.

Christian pulls the wheeled tray over to me, and Taylor places the box on it.

"Welcome back, Mrs. Grey."

"Hello, Taylor. Thank you."

"You're most welcome, ma'am." I think he wants to say more, but he holds off.

Christian is unpacking the box, producing a thermos, soup bowl, side plate, linen napkin, soupspoon, a small basket of bread rolls, silver salt and pepper shakers . . . The Olympic has gone all-out.

"This is great, Taylor." My stomach is rumbling. I am famished.

"Will that be all?" he asks.

"Yes, thanks," Christian says, dismissing him.

Taylor nods.

"Taylor, thank you."

"Anything else I can get you, Mrs. Grey?"

I glance at Christian. "Just some clean clothes for Christian." Taylor smiles. "Yes, ma'am."

Christian glances down at his shirt, bemused.

"How long have you been wearing that shirt?" I ask.

"Since Thursday morning." He gives me a crooked smile. Taylor exits.

"Taylor's real pissed at you, too," Christian adds grumpily, unscrewing the lid of the thermos and pouring creamy chicken soup into the bowl.

Taylor, too! But I don't dwell on that as my chicken soup distracts me. It smells delicious, and steam curls invitingly from its surface. I take a taste and it's everything it promised to be.

"Good?" Christian asks, perching on the bed again.

I nod enthusiastically and don't stop. My hunger is primal. I pause only to wipe my mouth with the linen napkin.

"Tell me what happened—after you realized what was going on."

Christian runs his hand through his hair and shakes his head. "Oh, Ana, it's good to see you eat."

"I'm hungry. Tell me."

He frowns. "Well, after the bank called and I thought my world had completely fallen apart—" He can't hide the pain in his voice.

I stop eating. *Oh shit.*

"Don't stop eating, or I'll stop talking," he whispers, his tone adamant as he glares at me. I continue with my soup. *Okay, okay . . . Damn, it tastes good.* Christian's gaze softens and after a beat, he resumes.

"Anyway, shortly after you and I had finished our conversation, Taylor informed me that Hyde had been granted bail. How, I don't know, I thought we'd managed to thwart any attempts at bail. But that gave me a moment to think about what you'd said . . . and I knew something was seriously wrong."

"It was never about the money," I snap suddenly, an unexpected surge of anger flaring in my belly. My voice rises. "How could you even think that? It's never been about your fucking money!" My head starts to pound and I wince. Christian gapes at me for a split second, surprised by my vehemence. He narrows his eyes.

"Mind your language," he growls. "Calm down and eat."

I glare mutinously at him.

"Ana," he warns.

"That hurt me more than anything, Christian," I whisper. "Almost as much as you seeing that woman."

He inhales sharply, as if I've slapped him, and all of a sudden, he looks exhausted. Closing his eyes briefly, he shakes his head, resigned.

"I know." He sighs. "And I'm sorry. More than you know." His eyes are luminous with contrition. "Please, eat. While your soup is still hot." His voice is soft and compelling, and I do as he asks. He breathes a sigh of relief.

"Go on," I whisper, between bites of the illicit fresh white bread roll.

"We didn't know Mia was missing. I thought maybe he was blackmailing you or something. I called you back, but you didn't answer." He scowls. "I left you a message and then called Sawyer. Taylor started tracking your cell. I knew you were at the bank, so we headed straight there."

"I don't know how Sawyer found me. Was he tracking my cell, too?"

"The Saab is fitted with a tracking device. All our cars are. By the time we got near the bank, you were already on the move, and we followed. Why are you smiling?"

"On some level I knew you'd be stalking me."

"And that is amusing because?" he asks.

"Jack had instructed me to get rid of my cell. So I borrowed Whelan's cell, and that's the one I threw away. I put mine into one of the duffel bags so you could track your money."

Christian sighs. "Our money, Ana," he says quietly. "Eat."

I wipe my soup bowl with the last of my bread and pop it into my mouth. For the first time in a long while, I feel replete in spite of our conversation.

"Finished."

"Good girl."

There's a knock on the door and Nurse Nora enters once more, carrying a small paper cup. Christian clears away my plate and starts putting all the items back into the box.

"Pain relief." Nora smiles, showing me the white pill in the paper cup.

"Is this okay to take? You know—with the baby?"

"Yes, Mrs. Grey. It's Lortab—it's fine; it won't affect the baby."

I nod gratefully. My head is pounding. I swallow it down with a sip of water.

"You ought to rest, Mrs. Grey." Nurse Nora looks pointedly at Christian.

He nods.

No! "You're going?" I exclaim, panic setting in. *Don't go— we've just started talking!*

Christian snorts. "If you think for one moment I'm going to let you out of my sight, Mrs. Grey, you are very much mistaken."

Nora huffs but hovers over me and readjusts my pillows so that I have to lie down.

"Good night, Mrs. Grey," she says, and with one last censorious glance at Christian, she leaves.

He raises an eyebrow as she closes the door.

"I don't think Nurse Nora approves of me."

He stands by the bed, looking tired, and despite the fact that I want him to stay, I know I should try to persuade him to go home.

"You need rest, too, Christian. Go home. You look exhausted."

"I'm not leaving you. I'll doze in this armchair."

I scowl at him, then shift onto my side.

"Sleep with me."

He frowns. "No. I can't."

"Why not?"

"I don't want to hurt you."

"You won't hurt me. Please, Christian."

"You have an IV."

"Christian. Please."

He gazes at me, and I can tell he's tempted.

"Please." I lift up the blankets, inviting him into the bed.

"Fuck it." He slips off his shoes and socks, and gingerly climbs in beside me. Gently, he wraps his arm around me, and I lay my head on his chest. He kisses my hair.

"I don't think Nurse Nora will be very happy with this arrangement," he whispers conspiratorially.

I giggle, then stop as pain lances through my chest. "Don't make me laugh. It hurts."

"Oh, but I love that sound," he says a little sadly, his voice low. "I'm sorry, baby, so, so sorry." He kisses my hair again and inhales deeply, and I don't know what he's apologizing for . . . making me laugh? Or the mess we're in? I rest my hand over his heart, and he gently places his hand on mine. We are both silent for a moment.

"Why did you go see that woman?"

"Oh, Ana." He groans. "You want to discuss that now? Can't we drop this? I regret it, okay?"

"I need to know."

"I'll tell you tomorrow," he mutters, irritated. "Oh, and Detective Clark wants to talk to you. Just routine. Now go to sleep."

He kisses my hair. I sigh heavily. I need to know why. At least he says he regrets it. That's something, my subconscious agrees. She's in an agreeable mood today, it seems. Ugh, Detective Clark. I shudder at the thought of reliving Thursday's events for him.

"Do we know why Jack was doing all this?"

"Hmm," Christian murmurs. I'm soothed by the slow rise and fall of his chest, gently rocking my head, lulling me to sleep as his breathing slows. And while I drift I try to make sense of the fragments of conversations I heard while I was on the edge of consciousness, but they slither through my mind, remaining steadfastly elusive, taunting me from the edges of my memory. Oh, it's frustrating and exhausting . . . and . . .

NURSE NORA'S MOUTH IS pursed and her arms folded in hostility. I hold my finger up to my lips.

"Please let him sleep," I whisper, squinting in the early morning light.

"This is your bed. Not his," she hisses sternly.

"I slept better because he was here," I insist, rushing to my husband's defense. Besides, it's true. Christian stirs, and Nurse Nora and I freeze.

He mumbles in his sleep, "Don't touch me. No more. Only Ana."

I frown. I have rarely heard Christian talk in his sleep. Admittedly, that might be because he sleeps less than I do. I've only ever heard his nightmares. His arms tighten around me, squeezing me, and I wince.

"Mrs. Grey—" Nurse Nora glowers.

"Please," I beg.

She shakes her head, turns on her heel, and leaves, and I snuggle up against Christian again.

WHEN I WAKE, CHRISTIAN is nowhere to be seen. The sun is blazing through the windows, and I can now really appreciate the room. *I have flowers!* I didn't notice them the night before. Several bouquets. I wonder idly who they're from.

A soft knock distracts me, and Carrick peeks around the door. He beams when he sees that I'm awake.

"May I come in?" he asks.

"Of course."

He strides into the room and over to me, his soft, gentle blue eyes assessing me shrewdly. He's wearing a dark suit—he must be working. He surprises me by leaning down and kissing my forehead.

"May I sit?"

I nod, and he perches on the edge of the bed and takes my hand.

"I don't know how to thank you for my daughter, you crazy, brave, darling girl. What you did probably saved her life. I will be forever in your debt." His voice wavers, filled with gratitude and compassion.

Oh . . . I don't know what to say. I squeeze his hand but remain mute.

"How are you feeling?"

"Better. Sore." I say, for honesty's sake.

"Have they given you meds for the pain?"

"Lor . . . something."

"Good. Where's Christian?"

"I don't know. When I woke up, he was gone."

"He won't be far away, I'm sure. He wouldn't leave you while you were unconscious."

"I know."

"He's a little mad at you, as he should be." Carrick smirks. Ah, this is where Christian gets it from.

"Christian is always mad at me."

"Is he?" Carrick smiles, pleased—as if this is a good thing. His smile is infectious.

"How's Mia?"

His eyes cloud and his smile vanishes. "She's better. Mad as hell. I think anger is a healthy reaction to what happened to her."

"Is she here?"

"No, she's back at home. I don't think Grace will let her out of her sight."

"I know how that feels."

"You need watching, too," he admonishes. "I don't want you taking any more silly risks with your life or the life of my grand-child."

I flush. *He knows!*

"Grace read your chart. She told me. Congratulations."

"Um . . . thank you."

He gazes down at me, and his eyes soften, though he frowns at my expression.

"Christian will come around," he says gently. "This will be the best thing for him. Just . . . give him some time."

I nod. *Oh . . . They've spoken.*

"I'd better go. I'm due in court." He smiles and rises. "I'll check in on you later. Grace speaks highly of Dr. Singh and Dr. Bartley. They know what they're doing."

He leans down and kisses me once more. "I mean it, Ana. I can never repay what you've done for us. Thank you."

I look up at him, blinking back tears, suddenly overwhelmed, and he strokes my cheek affectionately. Then he turns on his heel and leaves.

Oh my. I'm reeling from his gratitude. Perhaps now I can let the prenup debacle go. My subconscious nods sagely in agreement with me yet again. I shake my head and gingerly get out of bed. I'm relieved to find that I am much steadier on my feet than I was yesterday. In spite of Christian sharing the bed, I have slept well and feel refreshed. My head still aches, but it's a dull nagging pain, nothing like the pounding yesterday. I'm stiff and sore, but I just need a bath. I feel grimy. I head into the en suite.

"ANA!" CHRISTIAN SHOUTS.

"I'm in the bathroom," I call as I finish brushing my teeth. That feels better. I ignore my reflection in the mirror. *Crap, I look a mess.* When I open the door, Christian is by the bed, holding a tray of food. He's transformed. Dressed entirely in black, he's shaved, showered, and looks well rested.

"Good morning, Mrs. Grey," he says brightly. "I have your breakfast." He looks so boyish and much happier.

Wow. I smile broadly as I climb back into bed. He pulls over the tray on wheels and lifts the cover to reveal my breakfast: oatmeal with dried fruits, pancakes with maple syrup, bacon, orange juice, and Twinings English breakfast tea. My mouth waters; I'm so hungry. I down the orange juice in a few gulps and dig into the oatmeal. Christian sits down on the edge of the bed to watch. He smirks.

"What?" I ask with my mouth full.

"I like to watch you eat," he says. But I don't think that's what he's smirking about. "How are you feeling?"

"Better," I mutter between mouthfuls.

"I've never seen you eat like this."

I glance up at him, and my heart sinks. We have to address

the very tiny elephant in the room. "It's because I'm pregnant, Christian."

He snorts, and his mouth twists into an ironic smile. "If I knew getting you knocked up was going to make you eat, I might have done it earlier."

"Christian Grey!" I gasp and set the oatmeal down.

"Don't stop eating," he warns.

"Christian, we need to talk about this."

He stills. "What's there to say? We're going to be parents." He shrugs, desperately trying to look nonchalant, but all I can see is his fear. Pushing the tray aside, I crawl down the bed to him and take his hands in mine.

"You're scared," I whisper. "I get it."

He gazes at me, impassive, his eyes wide and all his earlier boyishness stripped away.

"I am, too. That's normal," I whisper.

"What kind of father could I possibly be?" His voice is hoarse, barely audible.

"Oh, Christian." I stifle a sob. "One that tries his best. That's all any of us can do."

"Ana—I don't know if I can . . ."

"Of course you can. You're loving, you're fun, you're strong, you'll set boundaries. Our child will want for nothing."

He's frozen, staring at me, doubt etched on his beautiful face.

"Yes, it would have been ideal to have waited. To have longer, just the two of us. But we'll be three of us, and we'll all grow up together. We'll be a family. Our own family. And your child will love you unconditionally, like I do." Tears spring to my eyes.

"Oh, Ana," Christian whispers, his voice anguished and pained. "I thought I'd lost you. Then I thought I'd lost you again. Seeing you lying on the ground, pale and cold and unconscious—it was all my worst fears realized. And now here you are—brave and strong . . . giving me hope. Loving me after all that I've done."

"Yes, I do love you, Christian, desperately. I always will."

Gently taking my head between his hands, he wipes my tears

away with his thumbs. He gazes into my eyes, gray to blue, and all I see is his fear and wonder and love.

"I love you, too," he breathes. And he kisses me sweetly, tenderly, like a man who adores his wife. "I'll try to be a good father," he whispers against my lips.

"You'll try, and you'll succeed. And let's face it; you don't have much choice in the matter, because Blip and I are not going anywhere."

"Blip?"

"Blip."

He raises his eyebrows. "I had the name Junior in my head."

"Junior it is, then."

"But I like Blip." He smiles his shy smile and kisses me once more.

CHAPTER TWENTY-FOUR

M uch as I'd like to kiss you all day, your breakfast is getting cold," Christian murmurs against my lips. He
gazes down at me, now amused, except his eyes are
darker, sensual. Holy cow, he's switched again. My Mr. Mercurial.

"Eat," he orders, his voice soft. I swallow, a reaction to his
smoldering look, and crawl back into bed, avoiding snagging my
IV line. He pushes the tray in front of me. The oatmeal is cold,
but the pancakes under the cover are fine—in fact, they're mouth-
watering.

"You know," I mutter between mouthfuls, "Blip might be a
girl."

Christian runs his hand through his hair. "Two women, eh?"
Alarm flashes across his face, and his dark look vanishes.

Oh crap. "Do you have a preference?"

"Preference?"

"Boy or girl."

He frowns. "Healthy will do," he says quietly, clearly discon-
certed by the question. "Eat," he snaps, and I know he's trying to
avoid the subject.

"I'm eating, I'm eating . . . Jeez, keep your hair on, Grey." I
watch him carefully. The corners of his eyes are crinkled with
worry. He's said he'll try, but I know he's still freaked out by the
baby. *Oh, Christian, so am I.* He sits down in the armchair beside
me, picking up the *Seattle Times.*

"You made the papers again, Mrs. Grey." His tone is bitter.

"Again?"

"The hacks are just rehashing yesterday's story, but it seems
factually accurate. You want to read it?"

I shake my head. "Read it to me. I'm eating."

He smirks and proceeds to read the article aloud. It's a report on Jack and Elizabeth, depicting them as a modern-day Bonnie and Clyde. It briefly covers Mia's kidnapping, my involvement in Mia's rescue, and the fact that both Jack and I are in the same hospital. How does the press get all this information? I must ask Kate.

When Christian finishes, I say, "Please read something else. I like listening to you."

He obliges and reads me a report about a booming bagel business and the fact that Boeing has had to cancel the launch of some plane. Christian frowns as he reads. But listening to his soothing voice as I eat, secure in the knowledge that I am fine, Mia is safe, and my Little Blip is safe, I feel a precious moment of peace despite all that has happened over the last few days.

I understand that Christian is scared about the baby, but I don't understand the depth of his fear. I resolve to talk to him some more about this. See if I can put his mind at ease. What puzzles me is that he hasn't lacked for positive role models as parents. Both Grace and Carrick are exemplary parents, or so they seem. Maybe it was the Bitch Troll's interference that damaged him so badly. I'd like to think so. But in truth I think it goes back to his birth mom, though I'm sure Mrs. Robinson didn't help. I halt my thoughts as I nearly recall a whispered conversation. *Damn!* It hovers on the edge of my memory from when I was unconscious. Christian talking with Grace. It melts away into the shadows of my mind. *Oh, it's so frustrating.*

I wonder if Christian will ever volunteer the reason he went to see her or if I'll have to push him. I'm about to ask when there's a knock on the door.

Detective Clark makes an apologetic entry into the room. He's right to be apologetic—my heart sinks when I see him.

"Mr. Grey, Mrs. Grey. Am I interrupting?"

"Yes," snaps Christian.

Clark ignores him. "Glad to see you're awake, Mrs. Grey. I

need to ask you a few questions about Thursday afternoon. Just routine. Is now a convenient time?"

"Sure," I mumble, but I do not want to relive Thursday's events.

"My wife should be resting." Christian bristles.

"I'll be brief, Mr. Grey. And it means I'll be out of your hair sooner rather than later."

Christian stands and offers Clark his chair, then sits down beside me on the bed, takes my hand, and squeezes it reassuringly.

HALF AN HOUR LATER, Clark is done. I've learned nothing new, but I have recounted the events of Thursday to him in a halting, quiet voice, watching Christian go pale and grimace at some parts.

"I wish you'd aimed higher," Christian mutters.

"Might have done womankind a service if Mrs. Grey had," Clark agrees.

What?

"Thank you, Mrs. Grey. That's all for now."

"You won't let him out again, will you?"

"I don't think he'll make bail this time, ma'am."

"Do we know who posted his bail?" Christian asks.

"No sir. It was confidential."

Christian frowns, but I think he has his suspicions. Clark rises to leave just as Dr. Singh and two interns enter the room.

AFTER A THOROUGH EXAMINATION, Dr. Singh declares me fit to go home. Christian sags with relief.

"Mrs. Grey, you'll have to watch for worsening headaches and blurry vision. If that occurs you must return to the hospital immediately."

I nod, trying to contain my delight at going home.

As Dr. Singh leaves, Christian asks her for a quick word in the corridor. He keeps the door ajar as he asks her a question. She smiles.

"Yes, Mr. Grey, that's fine."

He grins and returns to the room a happier man.

"What was all that about?"

"Sex," he says, flashing a wicked grin.

Oh. I blush. "And?"

"You're good to go." He smirks.

Oh, Christian!

"I have a headache." I smirk right back.

"I know. You'll be off limits for a while. I was just checking."

Off limits? I frown at the momentary stab of disappointment I feel. I'm not sure I want to be off limits.

Nurse Nora joins us to remove my IV. She glares at Christian. I think she's one of the few women I've met who is oblivious to his charms. I thank her when she leaves with my IV stand.

"Shall I take you home?" Christian asks.

"I'd like to see Ray first."

"Sure."

"Does he know about the baby?"

"I thought you'd want to be the one to tell him. I haven't told your mom either."

"Thank you." I smile, grateful that he hasn't stolen my thunder.

"My mom knows," Christian adds. "She saw your chart. I told my dad but no one else. Mom said couples normally wait for twelve weeks or so . . . to be sure." He shrugs.

"I'm not sure I'm ready to tell Ray."

"I should warn you, he's mad as hell. Said I should spank you."

What? Christian laughs at my appalled expression. "I told him I'd be only too willing to oblige."

"You didn't!" I gasp, though an echo of a whispered conversation tantalizes my memory. Yes, Ray was here while I was unconscious . . .

He winks at me. "Here, Taylor brought you some clean clothes. I'll help you dress."

AS CHRISTIAN PREDICTED, RAY is furious. I don't ever remember him being this mad. Christian has wisely decided to leave us alone. For such a taciturn man, Ray fills his hospital room with his invective, berating me for my irresponsible behavior. I am twelve years old again.

Oh, Dad, please calm down. Your blood pressure is not up to this.

"And I've had to deal with your mother," he grumbles, waving both of his hands in exasperation.

"Dad, I'm sorry."

"And poor Christian! I've never seen him like that. He's aged. We've both aged years over the last couple of days."

"Ray, I'm sorry."

"Your mother is waiting for your call," he says in a more measured tone.

I kiss his cheek, and finally he relents from his tirade.

"I'll call her. I really am sorry. But thank you for teaching me to shoot."

For a moment, he regards me with ill-concealed paternal pride. "I'm glad you can shoot straight," he says, his voice gruff. "Now go on home and get some rest."

"You look well, Dad." I try to change the subject.

"You look pale." His fear is suddenly evident. His look mirrors Christian's from last night, and I grasp his hand.

"I'm okay. I promise I won't do anything like that again."

He squeezes my hand and pulls me into a hug. "If anything happened to you," he whispers, his voice hoarse and low. Tears prick my eyes. I am not used to displays of emotion from my stepfather.

"Dad, I'm good. Nothing that a hot shower won't cure."

WE LEAVE THROUGH THE rear exit of the hospital to avoid the paparazzi gathered at the entrance. Taylor leads us to the waiting SUV.

Christian is quiet as Sawyer drives us home. I avoid Sawyer's gaze in the rearview mirror, embarrassed that the last time I saw him was at the bank when I gave him the slip. I call my mom, who sobs and sobs. It takes most of the journey home to calm her down, but I succeed by promising that we'll visit soon. Throughout my conversation with her, Christian holds my hand, brushing his thumb across my knuckles. He's nervous . . . something's happened.

"What's wrong?" I ask when I'm finally free from my mother.

"Welch wants to see me."

"Welch? Why?"

"He's found something out about that fucker Hyde." Christian's lip curls into a snarl, and a frisson of fear passes through me. "He didn't want to tell me on the phone."

"Oh."

"He's coming here this afternoon from Detroit."

"You think he's found a connection?"

Christian nods.

"What do you think it is?"

"I have no idea." Christian's brow furrows, perplexed.

Taylor pulls into the garage at Escala and stops by the elevator to let us out before he parks. In the garage, we can avoid the attention of the waiting photographers. Christian ushers me out of the car. Keeping his arm around my waist, he leads me to the waiting elevator.

"Glad to be home?" he asks.

"Yes," I whisper. But as I stand in the familiar surroundings of the elevator, the enormity of what I've been through crashes over me, and I start to shake.

"Hey—" Christian wraps his arms around me and pulls me close. "You're home. You're safe," he says, kissing my hair.

"Oh, Christian." A dam I didn't even know was in place bursts, and I start to sob.

"Hush now," Christian whispers, cradling my head against his chest.

But it's too late. I weep, overwhelmed, into his T-shirt, recalling Jack's vicious attack—*"That's for SIP, you fucking bitch!"*— telling Christian I was leaving—*"You're leaving me?"*—and my fear, my gut-wrenching fear for Mia, for myself, and for Little Blip.

When the doors of the elevator slide open, Christian picks me up like a child and carries me into the foyer. I wrap my arms around his neck and cling to him, keening quietly.

He carries me through to our bathroom and gently settles me on the chair. "Bath?" he asks.

I shake my head. No . . . no . . . not like Leila.

"Shower?" His voice is choked with concern.

Through my tears, I nod. I want to wash away the grime of the last few days, wash away the memory of Jack's attack. *"You gold-digging whore."* I sob into my hands as the sound of the water cascading from the shower echoes off the walls.

"Hey," Christian croons. Kneeling in front of me, he pulls my hands away from my tearstained cheeks and cups my face in his hands. I gaze at him, blinking away my tears.

"You're safe. You both are," he whispers.

Blip and me. My eyes brim with tears again.

"Stop, now. I can't bear it when you cry." His voice is hoarse. His thumbs wipe my cheeks, but my tears still flow.

"I'm sorry, Christian. Just sorry for everything. For making you worry, for risking everything—for the things I said."

"Hush, baby, please." He kisses my forehead. "I'm sorry. It takes two to tango, Ana." He gives me a crooked smile. "Well, that's what my mom always says. I said things and did things I'm not proud of." His gray eyes are bleak but penitent. "Let's get you undressed." His voice is soft. I wipe my nose with the back of my hand, and he kisses my forehead once more.

Briskly he strips me, taking particular care as he pulls my T-shirt over my head. But my head is not too sore. Leading me to the shower, he peels off his own clothing in record time before stepping into the welcome hot water with me. He pulls me into his arms and holds me, holds me for the longest time, as the water gushes over us, soothing us both.

He lets me cry into his chest. Occasionally he kisses my hair, but he doesn't let go, he just rocks me gently beneath the warm water. To feel his skin against mine, his chest hair against my cheek . . . this man I love, this self-doubting, beautiful man, the man I could have lost through my own recklessness. I feel empty and aching at the thought but grateful that he's here, still here— despite everything that's happened.

He has some explaining to do, but right now I want to revel in the feel of his comforting, protective arms around me. And in that moment it occurs to me; any explanations on his part have to come from him. I can't force him—he's got to want to tell me. I won't be cast as the nagging wife, constantly trying to wheedle information out of her husband. It's just exhausting. I know he loves me. I know he loves me more than he's ever loved anyone, and for now, that's enough. The realization is liberating. I stop crying and step back.

"Better?" he asks.

I nod.

"Good. Let me look at you," he says, and for a moment I don't know what he means. But he takes my hand and examines the arm I fell on when Jack hit me. There are bruises on my shoulder and scrapes at my elbow and wrist. He kisses each of them. He grabs a washcloth and shower gel from the rack, and the sweet familiar scent of jasmine fills my nostrils.

"Turn around." Gently, he proceeds to wash my injured arm, then my neck, my shoulders, my back, and my other arm. He turns me sideways, and traces his long fingers down my side. I wince as they skate over the large bruise at my hip. Christian's eyes harden and his lips thin. His anger is palpable as he whistles through his teeth.

"It doesn't hurt," I murmur to reassure him.

Blazing gray eyes meet mine. "I want to kill him. I nearly did," he whispers cryptically. I frown, then shiver at his bleak expression. He squirts more shower gel on the washcloth and with tender, aching gentleness, he washes my side and my behind, then, kneeling, moves down my legs. He pauses to examine my knee. His lips brush over the bruise before he returns to washing my legs and my feet. Reaching down, I caress his head, running my fingers through his wet hair. He stands, and his fingers trace the outline of the bruise on my ribs where Jack kicked me.

"Oh, baby," he groans, his voice filled with anguish, his eyes dark with fury.

"I'm okay." I pull his head down to mine and kiss his lips. He's hesitant to reciprocate, but as my tongue meets his, his body stirs against me.

"No," he whispers against my lips, and he pulls back. "Let's get you clean."

His face is serious. *Damn* . . . He means it. I pout, and the atmosphere between us lightens in an instant. He grins and kisses me briefly.

"Clean," he emphasizes. "Not dirty."

"I like dirty."

"Me, too, Mrs. Grey. But not now, not here." He grabs the shampoo, and before I can persuade him otherwise, he's washing my hair.

I LOVE CLEAN, TOO. I feel refreshed and reinvigorated, and I don't know if it's from the shower, the crying, or my decision to stop hassling Christian about everything. He wraps me in a large towel and drapes one around his hips while I gingerly dry my hair. My head aches, but it's a dull persistent pain that is more than manageable. I have some painkillers from Dr. Singh, but she's asked me not to use them unless I have to.

As I dry my hair, I think about Elizabeth.

"I still don't understand why Elizabeth was involved with Jack."

"I do," Christian mutters darkly.

This is news. I frown up at him, but I'm distracted. He's drying his hair with a towel, his chest and shoulders still wet with beads of water that glint beneath the halogens. He pauses and smirks.

"Enjoying the view?"

"How do you know?" I ask, trying to ignore that I've been caught staring at my own husband.

"That you're enjoying the view?" he teases.

"No," I scold. "About Elizabeth."

"Detective Clark hinted at it."

I give him my tell-me-more expression, and another nagging memory from when I was unconscious surfaces. Clark was in my room. I wish I could remember what he said.

"Hyde had videos. Videos of all of them. On several USB flash drives."

What? I frown, my skin tightening across my forehead.

"Videos of him fucking her and fucking all his PAs."

Oh!

"Exactly. Blackmail material. He likes it rough." Christian frowns, and I watch confusion followed by disgust cross his face. He pales as his disgust turns to self-loathing. Of course—Christian likes it rough, too.

"Don't." The word is out of my mouth before I can stop it.

His frown deepens. "Don't what?" He stills and regards me with apprehension.

"You aren't *anything* like him."

Christian's eyes harden, but he says nothing, confirming that's exactly what he's thinking.

"You're not." My voice is adamant.

"We're cut from the same cloth."

"No, you're not," I snap, though I understand why he might think so. *"His dad died in a brawl in a bar. His mother drank herself into oblivion. He was in and out of foster homes as a kid, in and out of trouble, too—mainly boosting cars. Spent time in juvie."* I recall the information Christian revealed on the plane to Aspen.

"You both have troubled pasts, and you were both born in Detroit. That's it, Christian." I fist my hands on my hips.

"Ana, your faith in me is touching, especially in light of the last few days. We'll know more when Welch is here." He's dismissing the subject.

"Christian—"

He stops me with a kiss. "Enough," he breathes, and I remember the promise I made to myself not to hound him for information.

"And don't pout," he adds. "Come. Let me dry your hair."

And I know the subject is closed.

AFTER DRESSING IN SWEATPANTS and a T-shirt, I sit between Christian's legs as he dries my hair.

"So did Clark tell you anything else while I was unconscious?"

"Not that I recall."

"I heard a few of your conversations."

The hairbrush stills in my hair.

"Did you?" he asks, his tone nonchalant.

"Yes. My dad, your dad, Detective Clark . . . your mom."

"And Kate?"

"Kate was there?"

"Briefly, yes. She's mad at you, too."

I turn in his lap. "Stop with the *everyone is mad at Ana* crap, okay?"

"Just telling you the truth," Christian says, bemused by my outburst.

"Yes, it was reckless, but you know, your sister was in danger."

His face falls. "Yes. She was." Switching off the hairdryer, he puts it down on the bed beside him. He grasps my chin.

"Thank you," he says, surprising me. "But no more recklessness. Because next time, I will spank the living shit out of you."

I gasp.

"You wouldn't!"

"I would." He's serious. Holy cow. Deadly serious. "I have your stepfather's permission." He smirks. He's teasing me! Or is he? I launch myself at him, and he twists so that I fall onto the bed and into his arms. As I land, pain from my ribs shoots through me and I wince.

Christian pales. "Behave!" he admonishes, and for a moment he's angry.

"Sorry," I mumble, caressing his cheek.

He nuzzles my hand and kisses it gently. "Honestly, Ana, you really have no regard for your own safety." He tugs up the hem of my T-shirt, then rests his fingers on my belly. I stop breathing. "It's not just you anymore," he whispers, trailing his fingertips along the waistband of my sweats, caressing my skin. Desire explodes unexpected, hot, and heavy in my blood. I gasp and Christian tenses, halting his fingers and gazing down at me. He moves his hand up and tucks a stray lock of hair behind my ear.

"No," he whispers.

What?

"Don't look at me like that. I've seen the bruises. And the answer's no." His voice is firm, and he kisses my forehead.

I squirm. "Christian," I whine.

"No. Get into bed." He sits up.

"Bed?"

"You need rest."

"I need you."

He closes his eyes and shakes his head as if it's a great effort of will. When he opens them again, his eyes are bright with his resolve. "Just do as you're told, Ana."

I'm tempted to take off all my clothes, but then I remember the bruises and know I won't win that way.

Reluctantly, I nod. "Okay." I deliberately give him an exaggerated pout.

He grins, amused. "I'll bring you some lunch."

"You're going to cook?" I nearly expire.

He has the grace to laugh. "I'm going to heat something up. Mrs. Jones has been busy."

"Christian, I'll do it. I'm fine. Jeez, I want sex—I can certainly cook." I sit up awkwardly, trying to hide the flinch caused by my smarting ribs.

"Bed!" Christian's eyes flash, and he points to the pillow.

"Join me," I murmur, wishing I were wearing something a little more alluring than sweatpants and a T-shirt.

"Ana, get into bed. Now."

I scowl, stand up, and let my pants drop unceremoniously to the floor, glaring at him the whole time. His mouth twitches with humor as he pulls the duvet back.

"You heard Dr. Singh. She said rest." His voice is gentler. I slip into bed and fold my arms in frustration. "Stay," he says, clearly enjoying himself.

My scowl deepens.

MRS. JONES'S CHICKEN STEW is, without doubt, one of my favorite dishes. Christian eats with me, sitting cross-legged in the middle of the bed.

"That was very well heated." I smirk and he grins. I'm replete and sleepy. Was this his plan?

"You look tired." He picks up my tray.

"I am."

"Good. Sleep." He kisses me. "I have some work I need to do. I'll do it in here if that's okay with you."

I nod . . . fighting a losing battle with my eyelids. I had no idea chicken stew could be so exhausting.

IT'S DUSK WHEN I wake. Pale pink light floods the room. Christian is sitting in the armchair, watching me, gray eyes luminous in the ambient light. He's clutching some papers. His face is ashen.

Holy cow! "What's wrong?" I ask immediately, sitting up and ignoring my protesting ribs.

"Welch has just left."

Oh shit. "And?"

"I lived with the fucker," he whispers.

"Lived? With Jack?"

He nods, his eyes wide.

"You're related?"

"No. Good God, no."

I shuffle over and pull the duvet back, inviting him into bed beside me, and to my surprise he doesn't hesitate. He kicks off his shoes and slides in alongside me. Wrapping one arm around me, he curls up, resting his head in my lap. I'm stunned. *What's this?*

"I don't understand," I murmur, running my fingers through his hair and gazing down at him. Christian closes his eyes and furrows his brow as if he's straining to remember.

"After I was found with the crack whore, before I went to live with Carrick and Grace, I was in the care of Michigan State. I lived in a foster home. But I can't remember anything about that time."

My mind reels. A foster home? This is news to both of us.

"For how long?" I whisper.

"Two months or so. I have no recollection."

"Have you spoken to your mom and dad about it?"

"No."

"Perhaps you should. Maybe they could fill in the blanks."

He hugs me tightly. "Here." He hands me the papers, which turn out to be two photographs. I reach over and switch on the bedside light so I can examine them in detail. The first photo is of a shabby house with a yellow front door and a large gabled window in the roof. It has a porch and a small front yard. It's an unremarkable house.

The second photo is of a family—at first glance, an ordinary blue-collar family—a man and his wife, I think, and their children. The adults are both dressed in dowdy, overwashed blue T-shirts. They must be in their forties. The woman has scraped-back blonde hair, and the man a severe buzz-cut, but they are both smiling warmly at the camera. The man has his hand draped over the shoulders of a sullen teenage girl. I gaze at each of the children: two boys—identical twins, about twelve—both with sandy blond hair, grinning broadly at the camera; there's another boy, who's smaller, with reddish blond hair, scowling; and hiding behind him, a copper-haired gray-eyed little boy. Wide-eyed and scared, dressed in mismatched clothes, and clutching a child's dirty blanket.

Fuck. "This is you," I whisper, my heart lurching into my throat. I know Christian was four when his mother died. But this child looks much younger. He must have been severely malnourished. I stifle a sob as tears spring to my eyes. *Oh, my sweet Fifty.*

Christian nods. "That's me."

"Welch brought these photos?"

"Yes. I don't remember any of this." His voice is flat and lifeless.

"Remember being with foster parents? Why should you? Christian, it was a long time ago. Is this what's worrying you?"

"I remember other things, from before and after. When I met my mom and dad. But this . . . It's like there's a huge chasm."

My heart twists and understanding dawns. My darling control freak likes everything in its place, and now he's learned he's missing part of the jigsaw.

"Is Jack in this picture?"

"Yes, he's the older kid." Christian's eyes are still screwed shut, and he's clinging to me as if I'm a life raft. I run my fingers through his hair while I gaze at the older boy, who is glaring, defiant and arrogant, at the camera. I can see it's Jack. But he's just a kid, a sad eight- or nine-year-old, hiding his fear behind his hostility. A thought occurs to me.

"When Jack called to tell me he had Mia, he said if things had been different, it could have been him."

Christian closes his eyes and shudders. "That fucker!"

"You think he did all this because the Greys adopted you instead of him?"

"Who knows?" Christian's tone is bitter. "I don't give a fuck about him."

"Perhaps he knew we were seeing each other when I went for that job interview. Perhaps he planned to seduce me all along." Bile rises in my throat.

"I don't think so," Christian mutters, his eyes now open. "The searches he did on my family didn't start until a week or so after you began your job at SIP. Barney knows the exact dates. And, Ana, he fucked all his assistants and taped them." Christian closes his eyes and tightens his grip on me once more.

Suppressing the tremor that runs through me, I try to recall my various conversations with Jack when I first started at SIP. I knew deep down he was bad news, yet I ignored all my instincts. Christian's right—I have no regard for my own safety. I remember the fight we had about me going to New York with Jack. Jeez—I could have ended up on some sordid sex tape. The thought is nauseating. And in that moment I recall the photographs Christian kept of his submissives.

Oh shit. *"We're cut from the same cloth."* No, Christian, you're not, you're nothing like him. He's still curled around me like a small boy.

"Christian, I think you should talk to your mom and dad." I am reluctant to move him, so I shift and slide back into the bed until we are eye to eye.

A bewildered gray gaze meets mine, reminding me of the child in the photograph.

"Let me call them," I whisper. He shakes his head. "Please," I beg. Christian stares at me, pain and self-doubt reflected in his eyes as he considers my request. *Oh, Christian, please!*

"I'll call them," he whispers.

"Good. We can go to see them together, or you can go. Whichever you prefer."

"No. They can come here."

"Why?"

"I don't want you going anywhere."

"Christian, I'm up for a car journey."

"No." His voice is firm, but he gives me an ironic smile. "Anyway, it's Saturday night, they're probably at some function."

"Call them. This news has obviously upset you. They might be able to shed some light." I glance at the radio alarm. It's almost seven in the evening. He regards me impassively for a moment.

"Okay," he says, as if I've issued him a challenge. Sitting up, he picks up the bedside phone.

I wrap my arm around him and rest my head on his chest as he makes the call.

"Dad?" I register his surprise that Carrick has answered the phone. "Ana's good. We're home. Welch has just left. He found out the connection . . . the foster home in Detroit . . . I don't remember any of that." Christian's voice is almost inaudible as he mutters the last sentence. My heart constricts once more. I hug him, and he squeezes my shoulder.

"Yeah . . . You will? . . . Great." He hangs up. "They're on their way." He sounds surprised, and I realize that he's probably never asked them for help.

"Good. I should get dressed."

Christian's arm tightens around me. "Don't go."

"Okay." I snuggle into his side again, stunned by the fact that he's just told me a great deal about himself—entirely voluntarily.

AS WE STAND AT the threshold of the great room, Grace wraps me gently in her arms.

"Ana, Ana, darling Ana," she whispers. "Saving two of my children. How can I ever thank you?"

I blush, touched and embarrassed in equal measure by her words. Carrick hugs me, too, kissing my forehead.

Then Mia grabs me, squashing my ribs. I wince and gasp, but she doesn't notice. "Thank you for saving me from those assholes."

Christian scowls at her. "Mia! Careful! She's in pain."

"Oh! Sorry."

"I'm good," I mutter, relieved when she releases me.

She looks fine. Impeccably dressed in tight black jeans and a pale pink frilly blouse. I'm glad I'm wearing my comfortable wrap dress and flats. At least I look reasonably presentable.

Racing over to Christian, Mia curls her arm around his waist.

Wordlessly, he hands Grace the photo. She gasps, her hand flying to her mouth to contain her emotion as she instantly recognizes Christian. Carrick wraps his arm around her shoulders as he, too, examines it.

"Oh, darling." Grace caresses Christian's cheek.

Taylor appears. "Mr. Grey? Miss Kavanagh, her brother, and your brother are coming up, sir."

Christian frowns. "Thank you, Taylor," he mutters, bemused.

"I called Elliot and told him we were coming over." Mia grins. "It's a welcome-home party."

I sneak a sympathetic glance at my poor husband as both Grace and Carrick glare at Mia in exasperation.

"We'd better get some food together," I declare. "Mia, will you give me a hand?"

"Oh, I'd love to."

I usher her toward the kitchen area as Christian leads his parents into his study.

KATE IS APOPLECTIC WITH righteous indignation that's aimed at me and Christian, but most of all Jack and Elizabeth.

"What were you *thinking*, Ana?" she shouts as she confronts me in the kitchen, causing all eyes in the room to turn and stare.

"Kate, please. I've had the same lecture from everyone!" I snap back. She glares at me, and for one minute I think I'm going to be subjected to a Katherine Kavanagh how-not-to-succumb-to-kidnappers lecture, but instead she folds me in her arms.

"Jeez—sometimes you don't have the brains you were born with, Steele," she whispers. As she kisses my cheek, there are tears in her eyes. *Kate!* "I've been so worried about you."

"Don't cry. You'll set me off."

She stands back and wipes her eyes, embarrassed, then takes a deep breath and composes herself. "On a more positive note, we've set a date for our wedding. We thought next May? And of course I want you to be my matron of honor."

"Oh . . . Kate . . . Wow. Congratulations!" *Crap—Little Blip . . . Junior!*

"What is it?" she asks, misinterpreting my alarm.

"Um . . . I'm just so happy for you. Some good news for a change." I wrap my arms around her and pull her into a hug. Shit, shit, *shit*. When is Blip due? Mentally I calculate my due date. Dr. Greene said I was four or five weeks. So—sometime in May? *Shit.*

Elliot hands me a glass of champagne.

Oh. Shit.

Christian emerges from his study, looking ashen, and follows his parents into the great room. His eyes widen when he sees the glass in my hand.

"Kate," he greets her coolly.

"Christian." She is equally cool. I sigh.

"Your meds, Mrs. Grey." He eyes the glass in my hand.

I narrow my eyes. *Dammit. I want a drink.* Grace smiles as she joins me in the kitchen, collecting a glass from Elliot on the way.

"A sip will be fine," she whispers with a conspiratorial wink at me, and lifts her glass to clink mine. Christian scowls at both of us, until Elliot distracts him with news of the latest match between the Mariners and the Rangers.

Carrick joins us, putting his arms around us both, and Grace kisses his cheek before joining Mia on the sofa.

"How is he?" I whisper to Carrick as he and I stand in the kitchen watching the family lounge on the sofa. I note with surprise that Mia and Ethan are holding hands.

"Shaken," Carrick murmurs to me, his brow furrowing, his face serious. "He remembers so much of his life with his birth mother; many things I wish he didn't. But this—" He stops. "I hope we've helped. I'm glad he called us. He said you told him to." Carrick's gaze softens. I shrug and take a hasty sip of champagne.

"You're very good for him. He doesn't listen to anyone else."

I frown. I don't think that's true. The unwelcome specter of the Bitch Troll looms large in my mind. I know Christian talks to Grace, too. I heard him. Again I feel a moment's frustration as I try to fathom their conversation in the hospital, but it still eludes me.

"Come and sit down, Ana. You look tired. I'm sure you weren't expecting all of us here this evening."

"It's great to see everyone." I smile. Because it's true, it *is* great. I'm an only child who has married into a large and gregarious family, and I love it. I snuggle up next to Christian.

"One sip," he hisses at me and takes my glass from my hand.

"Yes, Sir." I bat my lashes, disarming him completely. He puts his arm around my shoulders and returns to his baseball conversation with Elliot and Ethan.

"MY PARENTS THINK YOU walk on water," Christian mutters as he drags off his T-shirt.

I'm curled up in bed watching the floorshow. "Good thing you know differently." I snort.

"Oh, I don't know." He slips out of his jeans.

"Did they fill in the gaps for you?"

"Some. I lived with the Colliers for two months while Mom and Dad waited for the paperwork. They were already approved for adoption because of Elliot, but the wait's required by law to see if I had any living relatives who wanted to claim me."

"How do you feel about that?" I whisper.

He frowns. "About having no living relatives? Fuck that. If they were anything like the crack whore . . ." He shakes his head in disgust.

Oh, Christian! You were a child, and you loved your mom.

He slides on his pajamas, climbs into bed, and gently pulls me into his arms.

"It's coming back to me. I remember the food. Mrs. Collier could cook. And at least we know now why that fucker is so hung up on my family." He runs his free hand through his hair. "Fuck!" he says, suddenly turning to gape at me.

"What?"

"It makes sense now!" His eyes are full of recognition.

"What?"

"Baby Bird. Mrs. Collier used to call me Baby Bird."

I frown. "That makes sense?"

"The note," he says, gazing at me. "The ransom note that fucker left. It went something like 'Do you know who I am? Because I know who you are, Baby Bird.'"

This makes no sense to me at all.

"It's from a kid's book. Christ. The Colliers had it. It was called . . . *Are You My Mother?* Shit." His eyes widen. "I loved that book."

Oh. I know that book. My heart lurches—*Fifty!*

"Mrs. Collier used to read it to me."

I am at a loss as to what to say.

"Christ. He knew . . . that fucker knew."

"Will you tell the police?"

"Yes. I will. Christ knows what Clark will do with that information." Christian shakes his head as if trying to clear his thoughts. "Anyway, thank you for this evening."

Whoa. Gear change. "For what?"

"Catering for my family at a moment's notice."

"Don't thank me, thank Mia. And Mrs. Jones, she keeps the pantry well stocked."

He shakes his head as if in exasperation. At me? Why?

"How are you feeling, Mrs. Grey?"

"Good. How are you feeling?"

"I'm fine." He frowns . . . not understanding my concern.

Oh . . . in that case. I trail my fingers down his stomach to his oh-so-happy trail.

He laughs and grabs my hand. "Oh no. Don't get any ideas."

I pout, and he sighs. "Ana, Ana, Ana, what am I going to do with you?" He kisses my hair.

"I have some ideas." I squirm beside him and wince as pain radiates through my upper body from my bruised ribs.

"Baby, you've been through enough. Besides, I have a bedtime story for you."

Oh?

"You wanted to know . . ." He trails off, closes his eyes, and swallows.

All the hair on my body stands on end. *Shit.*

He begins in a soft voice. "Picture this, an adolescent boy looking to earn some extra money so he can continue his secret drinking habit." He shifts onto his side so that we're lying facing each other, and he's gazing into my eyes.

"So I was in the backyard at the Lincolns', clearing some rubble and trash from the extension Mr. Lincoln had just added to their place . . ."

Holy fuck . . . he's talking.

CHAPTER TWENTY-FIVE

I can barely breathe. Do I want to hear this? Christian closes his eyes and swallows. When he opens them again, they are bright but diffident, full of disquieting memories.

"It was a hot summer day. I was working hard." He snorts and shakes his head, suddenly amused. "It was backbreaking work shifting that rubble. I was on my own, and Ele—Mrs. Lincoln appeared out of nowhere and brought me some lemonade. We exchanged small talk, and I made some smart-ass remark . . . and she slapped me. She slapped me so hard." Unconsciously, his hand moves to his face and he caresses his cheek, his eyes clouding at the memory. *Holy shit!*

"But then she kissed me. And when she finished, she slapped me again." He blinks, seemingly still confounded even after all this time.

"I'd never been kissed before or hit like that."

Oh. She pounced. On a kid.

"Do you want to hear this?" Christians asks.

Yes . . . No . . .

"Only if you want to tell me." My voice is small as I lie facing him, my mind reeling.

"I'm trying to give you some context."

I nod in what I hope is an encouraging manner. But I suspect I may look like a statue, frozen and wide-eyed with shock.

He frowns, his eyes searching mine, trying to gauge my reaction. Then he turns onto his back and stares up at the ceiling.

"Well, naturally, I was confused and angry and horny as hell. I mean, a hot older woman comes on to you like that—" He shakes his head as if he still can't believe it.

Hot? I feel queasy.

"She went back into the house, leaving me in the backyard. She acted as if nothing had happened. I was at a total loss. So I went back to work, loading the rubble into the Dumpster. When I left that evening, she asked me to come back the next day. She didn't mention what had happened. So the next day I went back. I couldn't wait to see her again," he whispers, as if it's a dark confession . . . because frankly it is.

"She didn't touch me when she kissed me," he murmurs and turns his head to gaze at me. "You have to understand . . . my life was hell on earth. I was a walking hard-on, fifteen years old, tall for my age, hormones raging. The girls at school—" He stops, but I've got the picture: a scared, lonely, but attractive adolescent. My heart twists.

"I was angry, so fucking angry at everyone, at myself, my folks. I had no friends. My therapist at the time was a total asshole. My folks, they kept me on a tight leash; they didn't understand." He stares back up at the ceiling and runs a hand through his hair. I itch to run my fingers through his hair, too, but I stay still.

"I just couldn't bear anyone to touch me. I couldn't. Couldn't bear anyone near me. I used to fight . . . fuck, did I fight. I got into some god-awful brawls. I was expelled from a couple of schools. But it was a way to let off steam. To tolerate some kind of physical contact." He stops again. "Well, you get the idea. And when she kissed me, she only grabbed my face. She didn't touch me." His voice is barely audible.

She must have known. Perhaps Grace had told her. *Oh, my poor Fifty.* I have to fold my hands beneath my pillow and rest my head on it in order to resist the urge to hold him.

"Well, the next day I went back to the house, not knowing what to expect. And I'll spare you the gory details, but there was more of the same. And that's how our relationship started."

Oh, fuck, this is painful to hear.

He shifts again onto his side so he's facing me.

"And you know something, Ana? My world came into focus. Sharp and clear. Everything. It was exactly what I needed. She was a breath of fresh air. Making the decisions, taking all that shit away from me, letting me breathe."

Holy shit.

"And even when it was over, my world stayed in focus because of her. And it stayed that way until I met you."

What the hell am I supposed to say to that? Tentatively, he smoothes a stray lock of hair behind my ear.

"You turned my world on its head." He closes his eyes, and when he opens them again, they are raw. "My world was ordered, calm, and controlled, then you came into my life with your smart mouth, your innocence, your beauty, and your quiet temerity . . . and everything before you was just dull, empty, mediocre . . . it was nothing."

Oh my.

"I fell in love," he whispers.

I stop breathing. He caresses my cheek.

"So did I," I murmur with the little breath I have left.

His eyes soften. "I know," he mouths.

"You do?"

"Yes."

Hallelujah! I smile shyly at him. "Finally," I whisper.

He nods. "And it's put everything into perspective for me. When I was younger, Elena was the center of my world. There was nothing I wouldn't do for her. And she did a lot for me. She stopped my drinking. Made me work hard at school . . . You know, she gave me a coping mechanism I hadn't had before, allowed me to experience things that I never thought I could."

"Touch," I whisper.

He nods. "After a fashion."

I frown, wondering what he means.

He hesitates at my reaction.

Tell me! I will him.

"If you grow up with a wholly negative self-image, thinking you're some kind of reject, an unlovable savage, you think you deserve to be beaten."

Christian . . . you are none of those things.

He pauses and runs his hand through his hair. "Ana, it's much easier to wear your pain on the outside . . ." Again, it's a confession.

Oh.

"She channeled my anger." His mouth presses together in a bleak line. "Mostly inward—I realize that now. Dr. Flynn's been on and on about this for some time. It was only recently that I saw our relationship for what it was. You know . . . on my birthday."

I shudder as the unwelcome memory of Elena and Christian verbally eviscerating each other at Christian's birthday party surfaces unwelcome in my mind.

"For her that side of our relationship was about sex and control and a lonely woman finding some kind of comfort with her boy toy."

"But you like control," I whisper.

"Yes. I do. I always will, Ana. It's who I am. I surrendered it for a brief while. Let someone make all my decisions for me. I couldn't do it myself—I wasn't in a fit state. But through my submission to her, I found myself and found the strength to take charge of my life . . . take control and make my own decisions."

"Become a Dom?"

"Yes."

"Your decision?"

"Yes."

"Dropping out of Harvard?"

"My decision, and it was the best decision I ever made. Until I met you."

"Me?"

"Yes." His lips quirk up in a soft smile. "The best decision I ever made was marrying you."

Oh my. "Not starting your company?"

He shakes his head.

"Not learning to fly?"

He shakes his head. "You," he mouths. He caresses my cheek with his knuckles. "She knew," he whispers.

I frown. "She knew what?"

"That I was head over heels in love with you. She encouraged me to go down to Georgia to see you, and I'm glad she did. She thought you'd freak out and leave. Which you did."

I pale. I'd rather not think about that.

"She thought I needed all the trappings of the lifestyle I enjoyed."

"The Dom?" I whisper.

He nods. "It enabled me to keep everyone at arm's length, gave me control, and kept me detached, or so I thought. I'm sure you've worked out why," he adds softly.

"Your birth mom?"

"I didn't want to be hurt again. And then you left me." His words are barely audible. "And I was a mess."

Oh no.

"I've avoided intimacy for so long—I don't know how to do this."

"You're doing fine," I murmur. I trace his lips with my index finger. He purses them into a kiss. *You're talking to me.*

"Do you miss it?" I whisper.

"Miss it?"

"That lifestyle."

"Yes, I do."

Oh!

"But only insofar as I miss the control it brings. And frankly, your stupid stunt"—he stops—"that saved my sister," he whispers, his words full of relief, awe, and disbelief. "That's how I know."

"Know?"

"Really know that you love me."

I frown. "You do?"

"Yes. Because you risked so much . . . for me, for my family."

My frown deepens. He reaches over and traces his finger over the middle of my brow above my nose.

"You have a V here when you frown," he murmurs. "It's very soft to kiss. I can behave so badly . . . and yet you're still here."

"Why are you surprised I'm still here? I told you I wasn't going to leave you."

"Because of the way I behaved when you told me you were pregnant." He runs his finger down my cheek. "You were right. I am an adolescent."

Oh shit . . . I did say that. My subconscious glares at me. *His doctor said that!*

"Christian, I said some awful things." He puts his index finger over my lips.

"Hush. I deserved to hear them. Besides, this is my bedtime story." He rolls onto his back again.

"When you told me you were pregnant—" He stops. "I'd thought it would be just you and me for a while. I'd considered children, but only in the abstract. I had this vague idea we'd have a child sometime in the future."

Just one? No . . . Not an only child. Not like me. Perhaps now's not the best time to bring that up.

"You are still so young, and I know you're quietly ambitious."
Ambitious? Me?

"Well, you pulled the rug out from under me. Christ, was that unexpected. Never in a million years, when I asked you what was wrong, did I expect you to be pregnant." He sighs. "I was so mad. Mad at you. Mad at myself. Mad at everyone. And it took me back, that feeling of nothing being in my control. I had to get out. I went to see Flynn, but he was at some school parents' evening." Christian pauses and arches an eyebrow.

"Ironic," I whisper. Christian smirks in agreement.

"So I walked and walked and walked, and I just . . . found myself at the salon. Elena was leaving. She was surprised to see me. And, truth be told, I was surprised to find myself there. She could tell I was mad and asked me if I wanted a drink."

Oh shit. We've cut to the chase. My heart doubles in speed. *Do I really want to know this?* My subconscious glares at me, a plucked eyebrow raised in warning.

"We went to a quiet bar I know and had a bottle of wine. She apologized for the way she behaved the last time she saw us. She's hurt that my mom will have nothing to do with her anymore—it's narrowed her social circle—but she understands. We talked about the business, which is doing fine, in spite of the recession . . . I mentioned that you wanted kids."

I frown. "I thought you let her know I was pregnant."

He regards me, his face guileless. "No, I didn't."

"Why didn't you tell me that?"

He shrugs. "I never got the chance."

"Yes, you did."

"I couldn't find you the next morning, Ana. And when I did, you were so mad at me . . ."

Oh yes. "I was."

"Anyway, at some point in the evening—about halfway through the second bottle—she leaned over to touch me. And I froze," he whispers, throwing his arm over his eyes.

My scalp tingles. *What's this?*

"She saw that I recoiled from her. It shocked both of us." His voice is low, too low.

Christian, look at me! I tug at his arm and he lowers it, turning to gaze into my eyes. Shit. His face is pale, his eyes wide.

"What?" I breathe.

He frowns and swallows.

Oh . . . what isn't he telling me? Do I want to know?

"She made a pass at me." He's shocked, I can tell.

All the breath is sucked from my body. I feel winded, and I think my heart has stopped. *That fucking Bitch Troll!*

"It was a moment, suspended in time. She saw my expression, and she realized how far she'd crossed the line. I said . . . no. I haven't thought of her like that for years, and besides"—he swallows—"I love you. I told her, I love my wife."

I gaze at him. I don't know what to say.

"She backed right off. Apologized again, made it seem like a joke. I mean, she said she's happy with Isaac and with the business and she doesn't bear either of us any ill will. She said she missed my friendship, but she could see that my life was with you now. And how awkward that was, given what happened the last time we were all in the same room. I couldn't have agreed with her more. We said our good-byes—our final good-byes. I said I wouldn't see her again, and she went on her way."

I swallow, fear gripping my heart. "Did you kiss?"

"No!" he snorts. "I couldn't bear to be that close to her."

Oh. Good.

"I was miserable. I wanted to come home to you. But . . . I knew I'd behaved badly. I stayed and finished the bottle, then started on the bourbon. While I was drinking, I remembered your saying to me some time ago, 'If that was my son . . .' And I got to thinking about Junior and about how Elena and I started. And it made me feel . . . uncomfortable. I'd never thought of it like that before."

A memory blossoms in my mind—a whispered conversation from when I was half-conscious—Christian's voice: *"But seeing her finally put it all in perspective for me. You know . . . with the child. For the first time I felt . . . What we did . . . it was wrong."* He'd been speaking to Grace.

"That's it?"

"Pretty much."

"Oh."

"Oh?"

"It's over?"

"Yes. It's been over since I laid eyes on you. I finally realized it that night and so did she."

"I'm sorry," I mutter.

He frowns. "What for?"

"Being so angry the next day."

He snorts. "Baby, I understand angry." He pauses, then sighs. "You see, Ana, I want you to myself. I don't want to share you. What we have, I've never had before. I want to be the center of your universe, for a while at least."

Oh, Christian. "You are. That's not going to change."

He gives me an indulgent, sad, resigned smile. "Ana," he whispers. "That's just not true."

Tears prick my eyes.

"How can it be?" he murmurs.

Oh no.

"Shit—don't cry, Ana. Please, don't cry." He caresses my face.

"I'm sorry." My lower lip trembles, and he brushes his thumb over it, soothing me.

"No, Ana, no. Don't be sorry. You'll have someone else to love as well. And you're right. That's how it should be."

"Blip will love you, too. You'll be the center of Blip's—Junior's world," I whisper. "Children love their parents unconditionally, Christian. That's how they come into the world. Programmed to love. All babies . . . even you. Think about that children's book you liked when you were small. You still wanted your mom. You loved her."

He furrows his brow and withdraws his hand, fisting it against his chin.

"No," he whispers.

"Yes. You did." My tears flow freely now. "Of course you did. It wasn't an option. That's why you're so hurt."

He stares at me, his expression raw.

"That's why you're able to love me," I murmur. "Forgive her. She had her own world of pain to deal with. She was a shitty mother, and you loved her."

He gazes at me, saying nothing, eyes haunted—by memories I can't begin to fathom.

Oh, please don't stop talking.

Eventually he says, "I used to brush her hair. She was pretty."

"One look at you and no one would doubt that."

"She was a shitty mother." His voice is barely audible.

I nod and he closes his eyes. "I'm scared I'll be a shitty father."

I stroke his dear face. *Oh, my Fifty, Fifty, Fifty.* "Christian, do you think for one minute I'd let you be a shitty father?"

He opens his eyes and gazes at me for what feels like an eternity. He smiles as relief slowly illuminates his face. "No, I don't think you would." He caresses my face with the backs of his knuckles, gazing at me in wonder. "God, you're strong, Mrs. Grey. I love you so much." He kisses my forehead. "I didn't know I could."

"Oh, Christian," I whisper, trying to contain my emotion.

"Now, that's the end of your bedtime story."

"That's some bedside story . . . "

He smiles wistfully, but I think he's relieved. "How's your head?"

"My head?" *Actually, it's about to explode with all you've told me!*

"Does it hurt?"

"No."

"Good. I think you should sleep now."

Sleep! How can I sleep after all that?

"Sleep," he says sternly. "You need it."

I pout. "I have one question."

"Oh? What?" He eyes me warily.

"Why have you suddenly become all . . . forthcoming, for want of a better word?"

He frowns.

"You're telling me all this, when getting information out of you is normally a pretty harrowing and trying experience."

"It is?"

"You know it is."

"Why am I being forthcoming? I can't say. Seeing you practically dead on the cold concrete, maybe. The fact I'm going to be a father. I don't know. You said you wanted to know, and I don't want Elena to come between us. She can't. She's the past, and I've said that to you so many times."

"If she hadn't made a pass at you . . . would you still be friends?"

"That's more than one question."

"Sorry. You don't have to tell me." I flush. "You've already volunteered more than I ever thought you would."

His gaze softens. "No, I don't think so, but she's felt like unfinished business since my birthday. She stepped over the line, and I'm done. Please, believe me. I'm not going to see her again. You said she's a hard limit for you. That's a term I understand," he says with quiet sincerity.

Okay. I'm going to let this go now. My subconscious sags into her armchair. *Finally!*

"Good night, Christian. Thank you for the enlightening bedtime story." I lean over to kiss him, and our lips touch briefly, but he pulls back when I try to deepen the kiss.

"Don't," he whispers. "I am desperate to make love to you."

"Then do."

"No, you need to rest, and it's late. Go to sleep." He switches off the bedside light, plunging us into darkness.

"I love you unconditionally, Christian," I murmur as I cuddle into his side.

"I know," he whispers, and I sense his shy smile.

I wake with a start. Light is flooding the room, and Christian is not in bed. I glance at the clock and see it's seven fifty-three. I take a deep breath and wince as my ribs smart, though not as badly as yesterday. I think I could go to work. *Work—yes.* I want to go to work.

It's Monday, and I spent all of yesterday lounging about in bed. Christian let me go out only briefly to see Ray. Honestly, he's still such a control freak. I smile fondly. *My control freak.* He's been attentive and loving and chatty . . . and hands-off since I arrived home. I scowl. I am going to have to do something about this. My head doesn't hurt, the pain around my ribs has eased—though, admittedly, laughing has to be undertaken with caution—but I'm frustrated. I think this is the longest I've gone without sex since . . . well, since the first time.

I think we've both recovered our equilibrium. Christian is much more relaxed; his long bedtime story seems to have laid some ghosts to rest, for him *and* for me. We'll see.

I shower quickly, and once I'm dry, I browse carefully through my clothes. I want something sexy. Something that might galvanize Christian into action. Who would have thought such an insatiable man could actually exercise so much self-control? I don't really want to dwell on how Christian learned such discipline over his body. We haven't spoken of the Bitch Troll once since his confession. I hope we never do. To me she's dead and buried.

I choose an almost indecently short black skirt and a white silk blouse with a frill. I slide on thigh-highs with lacy tops and my black Louboutin pumps. A little mascara and lip gloss for a natural look, and after a ferocious brushing, I leave my hair loose. Yes. This should do it.

Christian is eating at the breakfast bar. His forkful of omelet stops in midair when he sees me. He frowns.

"Good morning, Mrs. Grey. Going somewhere?"

"Work." I smile sweetly.

"I don't think so." Christian snorts with amused derision. "Dr. Singh said a week off."

"Christian, I am not spending the day lounging in bed on my own. So I may as well go to work. Good morning, Gail."

"Mrs. Grey." Mrs. Jones tries to hide a smile. "Would you like some breakfast?"

"Please."

"Granola?"

"I'd prefer scrambled eggs with whole wheat toast."

Mrs. Jones grins and Christian registers his surprise.

"Very good, Mrs. Grey," Mrs. Jones says.

"Ana, you are not going to work."

"But—"

"No. It's simple. Don't argue." Christian is adamant. I glare at him, and only then do I notice that he's in the same pajama bottoms and T-shirt he was wearing last night.

"Are you going to work?" I ask.

"No."

Am I going crazy? "It is Monday, right?"

He smiles. "Last time I looked."

I narrow my eyes. "Are you playing hooky?"

"I'm not leaving you here on your own to get into trouble. And Dr. Singh said it would be a week before you could go back to work. Remember?"

I slide onto a barstool beside him and hoist my skirt up a little. Mrs. Jones places a cup of tea in front of me.

"You look good," Christian says. I cross my legs. "Very good. Especially here." He traces a finger over the bare flesh that shows above my thigh-highs. My pulse quickens as his finger runs across my skin. "This skirt is very short," he murmurs, vague disapproval in his voice as his eyes follow his finger.

"Is it? I hadn't noticed."

Christian gazes at me, his mouth twisted in an amused yet exasperated smirk.

"Really, Mrs. Grey?"

I blush.

"I'm not sure this look is suitable for the workplace," he murmurs.

"Well, since I'm not going to work, that's a moot point."

"Moot?"

"Moot," I mouth.

Christian smirks again and resumes eating his omelet. "I have a better idea."

"You do?"

He glances at me through long lashes, gray eyes darkening. I inhale sharply. *Oh my. About time.*

"We can go see how Elliot's getting on with the house."

What? Oh! Tease! I vaguely remember we were supposed to do that before Ray was injured.

"I'd love to."

"Good." He grins.

"Don't you have to work?"

"No. Ros is back from Taiwan. That all went well. Today, everything's fine."

"I thought *you* were going to Taiwan."

He snorts again. "Ana, you were in the hospital."

"Oh."

"Yeah—oh. So today I'm spending some quality time with my wife." He smacks his lips together as he takes a sip of coffee.

"Quality time?" I can't disguise the hope in my voice.

Mrs. Jones places my scrambled eggs in front of me, again failing to hide her smile.

Christian smirks. "Quality time." He nods.

I am too hungry to flirt anymore with my husband.

"It's good to see you eat," he murmurs. Rising, he leans over and kisses my hair. "I'm going to shower."

"Um . . . can I come and scrub your back?" I mumble through a mouth full of toast and scrambled egg.

"No. Eat."

Leaving the breakfast bar, he tugs his T-shirt over his head, treating me to the sight of his finely sculptured shoulders and naked back as he saunters out of the great room. I stop mid-chew. He's doing this on purpose. *Why?*

CHRISTIAN IS RELAXED ON the drive north. We've just left Ray and Mr. Rodriguez watching soccer on the new flat-screen television that I suspect Christian has bought for Ray's hospital room.

Christian has been laid back ever since "the talk." It's as if a weight has been lifted; Mrs. Robinson's shadow no longer looms so large over us, maybe because I've decided to let it go—or because he has, I don't know. But I feel closer to him now than I ever have before. Perhaps because he's finally confided in me. I hope he continues to do so. And he's more accepting of the baby, too. He hasn't gone out and bought a crib yet, but I have high hopes.

I gaze at him, drinking him in as he drives. He looks casual, cool . . . sexy with his tousled hair, Ray-Bans, pinstripe jacket, white linen shirt, and jeans.

He glances at me and clasps my leg above the knee, his fingers stroking gently. "I'm glad you didn't change."

I did slip on a denim jacket and change to flats, but I'm still wearing the short skirt. His hand lingers above my knee. I put my hand on his.

"Are you going to continue to tease me?"

"Maybe." Christian smiles.

"Why?"

"Because I can." He grins, boyish as ever.

"Two can play that game," I whisper.

His fingers move tantalizingly up my thigh. "Bring it on, Mrs. Grey." His grin broadens.

I pick up his hand and put it back on his knee. "Well, you can keep your hands to yourself."

He smirks. "As you wish, Mrs. Grey."

Damn it. This game is going to backfire on me.

CHRISTIAN TURNS INTO THE driveway of our new house. He stops at the keypad and punches in a number, and the ornate white metal gates swing open. We roar up the tree-lined lane under leaves that are a blend of green, yellow, and burnished copper. The tall grass in the meadow is turning gold, but there are still a few yellow wildflowers dotted among the grass. It's a beautiful day. The sun is shining, and the salty tang of the Sound is mixed with the scent of the coming fall in the air. This is such a tranquil and beautiful place. And to think we're going to make our home here.

The lane curves around, and our house comes into view. Several large trucks, sides emblazoned with GREY CONSTRUCTION, are parked out front. The house is decked in scaffolding, and several workmen in hard hats are busy on the roof.

Christian pulls up outside the portico and switches off the engine. I can sense his excitement.

"Let's go find Elliot."

"Is he here?"

"I hope so. I'm paying him enough."

I snort, and Christian grins as we get out of the car.

"Yo, bro!" Elliot shouts from somewhere. We both glance around.

"Up here!" He's up on the roof, waving down at us and beaming from ear to ear. "About time we saw you here. Stay where you are. I'll be right down."

I glance at Christian, who shrugs. A few minutes later, Elliot appears at the front door.

"Hey, bro." He shakes Christian's hand. "And how are you, little lady?" He picks me up and swings me around.

"Better, thanks," I giggle breathlessly, my ribs protesting. Christian frowns at him, but Elliot ignores him.

"Let's head over to the site office. You'll need one of these." He taps his hard hat.

THE HOUSE IS A shell. The floors are covered in a hard fibrous material that looks like burlap; some of the original walls have disappeared and new ones have taken their place. Elliot leads us through, explaining what's happening, while men—and a few women—work everywhere around us. I'm relieved to see the stone staircase with its intricate iron balustrade is still in place and draped completely in white dust sheets.

In the main living area, the back wall has been removed to make way for Gia's glass wall, and work is beginning on the terrace. In spite of the mess, the view is still stunning. The new work is sympathetic and in keeping with the old-world charm of the house . . . Gia's done well. Elliot patiently explains the processes and gives us a rough time frame for each. He's hoping we can be in by Christmas, although Christian thinks this is optimistic.

Holy cow—Christmas overlooking the Sound. I can't wait. A bubble of excitement blooms inside me. I have visions of us trimming an enormous tree while a copper-haired little boy looks on in wonder.

Elliot finishes our tour in the kitchen. "I'll leave you two to roam. Be careful. This is a building site."

"Sure. Thanks, Elliot," Christian murmurs, taking my hand. "Happy?" he asks once Elliot has left us alone. I am gazing at this empty shell of a room and wondering where I will hang the pepper pictures that we bought in France.

"Very. I love it. You?"

"Ditto." He grins.

"Good. I was thinking of the pepper pictures in here."

Christian nods. "I want to put up José's portraits of you in this house. You need to decide where they should go."

I blush. "Somewhere I won't see them often."

"Don't be like that." He scolds me, brushing his thumb across my bottom lip. "They're my favorite pictures. I love the one in my office."

"I have no idea why," I murmur and kiss the pad of his thumb.

"Worse things to do than look at your beautiful smiling face all day. Hungry?" he asks.

"Hungry for what?" I whisper.

He smirks, his eyes darkening. Hope and desire unfurl in my veins.

"Food, Mrs. Grey." And he plants a swift kiss on my lips.

I give him my faux pout and sigh. "Yes. These days I'm always hungry."

"The three of us can have a picnic."

"Three of us? Is someone joining us?"

Christian cocks his head to one side. "In about seven or eight months."

Oh . . . Blip. I grin goofily at him.

"I thought you might like to eat alfresco."

"In the meadow?" I ask.

He nods.

"Sure." I grin.

"This will be a great place to raise a family," he murmurs, gazing down at me.

Family! More than one? Dare I mention this now?

He spreads his fingers over my belly. *Holy shit.* I hold my breath and place my hand over his.

"It's hard to believe," he whispers, and for the first time I hear wonder in his voice.

"I know. Oh—here, I have evidence. A picture."

"You do? Baby's first smile?"

I pull out the ultrasound of Blip from my wallet.

"See?"

Christian examines it closely, staring for several seconds. "Oh . . . Blip. Yeah, I see." He sounds distracted, awed.

"Your child," I whisper.

"Our child." He counters.

"First of many."

"Many?" Christian's eyes widen with alarm.

"At least two."

"Two?" He tests the word. "Can we just take this one child at a time?"

I grin. "Sure."

We head back outside into the warm fall afternoon.

"When are you going to tell your folks?" Christian asks.

"Soon," I murmur. "I thought about telling Ray this morning, but Mr. Rodriguez was there." I shrug.

Christian nods and opens the hood of the R8. Inside are a wicker picnic basket and the tartan blanket we bought in London.

"Come," he says, taking the basket and blanket in one hand and holding the other out to me. Together we walk into the meadow.

"SURE, ROS, GO FOR it." Christian hangs up. That's the third call he's taken during our picnic. He's kicked off his shoes and socks and is watching me, arms on his raised knees. His jacket lies discarded on top of mine, as we're warm in the sun. I lie beside him, stretched out on the picnic blanket, both of us surrounded by tall golden and green grass far from the noise at the house and hidden from the prying eyes of the construction workers. We are in our own bucolic haven. He feeds me another strawberry, and I chew and suck it gratefully, gazing at his darkening eyes.

"Tasty?" he whispers.

"Very."

"Had enough?"

"Of strawberries, yes."

His eyes glitter dangerously, and he grins. "Mrs. Jones packs a mighty fine picnic," he says.

"That she does," I whisper.

Shifting suddenly, he lies down so his head is resting on my belly. He closes his eyes and seems content. I tangle my fingers in his hair.

He sighs heavily, then scowls and checks the number on the screen of his buzzing BlackBerry. He rolls his eyes and takes the call.

"Welch," he snaps. He tenses, listens for a second or two, then suddenly bolts upright.

"Twenty-four/seven . . . Thanks," he says through gritted teeth and hangs up. The change in his mood is instant. Gone is my teasing, flirtatious husband, replaced by a cold, calculating master of the universe. He narrows his eyes for a moment, then gives me a cool, chilling smile. A shiver runs down my back. He picks up his BlackBerry and presses a speed dial.

"Ros, how much stock do we own in Lincoln Timber?" He kneels up.

My scalp prickles. *Oh no, what's this?*

"So, consolidate the shares into GEH, then fire the board . . . except the CEO . . . I don't give a fuck . . . I hear you, just do it . . . thank you . . . keep me informed." He hangs up and gazes at me impassively for a moment.

Holy shit! Christian is mad.

"What's happened?"

"Linc," he murmurs.

"Linc? Elena's ex?"

"The same. He's the one who posted Hyde's bail."

I gape at Christian in shock. His mouth is pressed in a hard line.

"Well—he'll look like an idiot," I murmur, dismayed. "I mean, Hyde committed another crime while out on bail."

Christian's eyes narrow and he smirks. "Fair point well made, Mrs. Grey."

"What did you just do?" I kneel, facing him.

"I fucked him over."

Oh! "Um . . . that seems a little impulsive," I murmur.

"I'm an in-the-moment kind of guy."

"I'm aware of that."

His eyes narrow and his lips thin. "I've had this plan in my back pocket for a while," he says dryly.

I frown. "Oh?"

He pauses, seeming to weigh something in his mind, then takes a deep breath.

"Several years back, when I was twenty-one, Linc beat his wife to a pulp. He broke her jaw, her left arm, and four of her ribs because she was fucking me." His eyes harden. "And now I learn he posted bail for a man who tried to kill me, kidnapped my sister, and fractured my wife's skull. I've had enough. I think it's payback time."

I blanch. *Holy shit.* "Fair point well made, Mr. Grey," I whisper.

"Ana, this is what I do. I'm not usually motivated by revenge, but I cannot let him get away with this. What he did to Elena . . . well, she should have pressed charges, but she didn't. That was her prerogative.

"But he's seriously crossed the line with Hyde. Linc's made this personal by going after my family. I'm going to crush him, break up his company right under his nose, and sell the pieces to the highest bidder. I am going to bankrupt him."

Oh . . .

"Besides." Christian smirks. "We'll make good money out of the deal."

I stare into blazing gray eyes that soften suddenly.

"I didn't mean to frighten you," he whispers.

"You didn't," I lie.

He arches a brow, amused.

"You just took me by surprise," I whisper, then swallow. Christian is really quite scary sometimes.

He brushes his lips against mine. "I will do anything to keep you safe. Keep my family safe. Keep this little one safe," he murmurs and splays his hand out over my belly in a gentle caress.

Oh . . . I stop breathing. Christian gazes down at me, his eyes darkening. His lips part as he inhales and, in a deliberate move, the tips of his fingers brush against my sex.

Holy shit. Desire detonates like an incendiary device igniting my bloodstream. I grasp his head, my fingers weaving into his hair, and tug hard so my lips find his. He gasps, surprised by my assault, giving my tongue free passage into his mouth. He groans and kisses me back, his lips and tongue hungry for mine, and for a moment we consume each other, lost in tongues and lips and breaths and sweet, sweet sensation as we rediscover each other.

Oh, I want this man. It's been too long. I want him here, now, in the open air, in our meadow.

"Ana," he breathes, entranced, and his hand skims over my backside to the hem of my skirt. I scramble to unbutton his shirt, all fingers and thumbs.

"Whoa, Ana—stop." He pulls back, his jaw clenched, and grabs my hands.

"No." My teeth clamp gently around his lower lip and I tug. "No," I murmur again, gazing at him. I release him. "I want you."

He inhales sharply. He's torn, his indecision writ large in his luminous gray eyes.

"Please, I need you." Every pore of my being is begging. *This is what we do.*

He groans in defeat as his mouth finds mine, molding my lips to his. One hand cradles my head while the other skims down my body to my waist, and he eases me onto my back and stretches out beside me, never breaking contact with my mouth.

He pulls back, hovering over me and gazing down. "You are so beautiful, Mrs. Grey."

I caress his lovely face. "So are you, Mr. Grey. Inside and out."

He frowns, and my fingers trace the furrow in his brow.

"Don't frown. You are to me, even when you're angry," I whisper.

He groans once more, and his mouth captures mine, pushing me into the soft grass beneath the blanket.

"I've missed you," he whispers, and his teeth graze my jaw. My heart soars.

"I've missed you, too. Oh, Christian." I fist one hand in his hair and clutch his shoulder with the other.

His lips move to my throat, leaving tender kisses in their wake, and his fingers follow, deftly undoing each button of my blouse. Tugging my blouse apart, he kisses the soft swell of my breasts. He murmurs appreciatively, low in his throat, and the sound echoes through my body to my deep dark places.

"Your body's changing," he whispers. His thumb teases my nipple until it's erect and straining against my bra. "I like," he adds. I watch his tongue taste and trace the line between my bra and my breast, tantalizing and teasing me. Taking my bra cup delicately between his teeth, he pulls it down, freeing my breast and nuzzling my nipple with his nose in the process. It puckers at his touch and from the chill of the gentle fall breeze. His lips close around me, and he sucks long and hard.

"Ah!" I groan, inhaling sharply, then wincing as pain radiates outward from my bruised ribs.

"Ana!" Christian exclaims and glares down at me, concern etched on his face. "This is what I'm talking about," he admonishes. "Your lack of self-preservation. I don't want to hurt you."

"No . . . don't stop," I whimper. He stares at me, warring with himself. "Please."

"Here." Abruptly he moves, and I'm sitting astride him, my short skirt now bunched up around my hips. His hands glide over the tops of my thigh-highs.

"There. That's better, and I can enjoy the view." He reaches up and hooks his long index finger into my other bra cup, freeing that breast, too. He grasps both of my breasts, and I throw my head back, pushing them into his welcome, expert hands. He teases me, tugging and rolling my nipples until I cry out, then sits up so we're nose to nose, his greedy gray eyes on mine. He kisses me, his fingers still teasing me. I scramble for his shirt, undoing the first two buttons, and it's like sensory overload—I want to be kissing him everywhere, undressing him, making love with him all at once.

"Hey—" He gently grasps my head and pulls back, eyes dark and full of sensual promise. "There's no rush. Take it slow. I want to savor you."

"Christian, it's been so long." I'm panting.

"Slow," he whispers, and it's a command. He kisses the right corner of my mouth. "Slow." He kisses the left corner. "Slow, baby." He tugs my bottom lip with his teeth. "Let's take this slow." He unfurls his fingers in my hair, keeping me in place as his tongue invades my mouth, seeking, tasting, calming . . . inflaming. Oh, my man can kiss.

I caress his face, my fingers moving tentatively down to his chin and then to his throat, and I start again on the buttons of his shirt, taking my time, as he continues to kiss me. Slowly I pull his shirt apart, my fingers trailing over his clavicles, feeling their way across his warm, silky skin. I push him gently back until he's lying beneath me. Sitting up, I gaze down at him, aware that I'm squirming against his growing erection. *Hmm.* I trace my fingers across his lips to his jaw, then down his neck and over his Adam's apple to that little dip at the base of his throat. *My beautiful man.* I lean down, and my kisses follow the tips of my fingers. My teeth graze his jaw and kiss his throat. He closes his eyes.

"Ah." He groans and tilts his head back, giving me easier access to the base of his throat, his mouth slack and open in silent veneration. Christian lost and aroused is just so exhilarating . . . and so arousing to me.

My tongue trails down his sternum, twirling through his chest hair. *Hmm.* He tastes so good. He smells so good. Intoxicating. I kiss first one, then two of his small round scars, and he grasps my hips, so my fingers halt on his chest as I gaze down at him. His breathing is harsh.

"You want this? Here?" he breathes, his eyes hooded with a heady combination of love and lust.

"Yes," I murmur, and my lips and tongue graze across his chest to his nipple. I pull and roll it gently with my teeth.

"Oh, Ana," he whispers and, circling my waist, he lifts me, tugging at his button and fly so he springs free. He sits me down again, and I push against him, delighting in the feel of him hot and hard beneath me. He runs his hands up my thighs, pausing where my thigh-highs stop and my flesh begins, his hands running small, teasing circles at the tops of my thighs so that the tips of his thumbs touch me . . . touch me where I want to be touched. I gasp.

"I hope you're not attached to your underwear," he murmurs, his eyes wild and bright. His fingers trace the elastic along my belly and then slide inside, teasing me, before grabbing my panties tightly and pushing his thumbs through the delicate material. My panties disintegrate. His hands splay out on my thighs, and his thumbs brush against my sex once more. He flexes his hips so his erection rubs against me.

"I can feel how wet you are." His voice is tinged with carnal appreciation, and he suddenly sits up, his arm around my waist again, so we're nose to nose. He rubs his nose against mine.

"We're going to take this slow, Mrs. Grey. I want to feel all of you." He lifts me, and with exquisite, frustrating, slow ease, lowers me onto him. I feel each blessed inch of him fill me.

"Ah—" I moan incoherently as I reach out to clasp his arms. I try to lift myself off him for some welcome friction, but he holds me in place.

"All of me," he whispers and tilts his pelvis, pushing himself into me all the way. I throw my head back and let out a strangled cry of pure pleasure.

"Let me hear you," he murmurs. "No—don't move, just feel."

I open my eyes, my mouth frozen in a silent *Ah!* And he's gazing at me, hooded, licentious gray eyes into dazed blue. He shifts, rolling his hips, but holds me in place.

I groan. His lips are at my throat, kissing me.

"This is my favorite place. Buried in you," he murmurs against my skin.

"Please, move," I plead.

"Slow, Mrs. Grey." He flexes his hips again and pleasure radiates through me. I cup his face and kiss him, consuming him.

"Love me. Please, Christian."

His teeth skim my jaw up to my ear. "Go," he whispers, and he lifts me up and down. My inner goddess is unleashed, and I push him down on the ground and start to move, savoring the feeling of him inside me . . . riding him . . . riding him hard. With his hands around my waist he matches my rhythm. I have missed this . . . the heady feeling of him beneath me, inside me . . . the sun on my back, the sweet smell of fall in the air, the gentle autumnal breeze. It's a heady fusion of senses: touch, taste, smell, and the sight of my beloved husband beneath me.

"Oh, Ana." He groans, eyes closed, head back, mouth open.

Ah . . . I love this. And inside, I'm building . . . building . . . climbing . . . higher. Christian's hands move to my thighs, and delicately his thumbs press at their apex, and I explode around him over and over and over and over, and I collapse, sprawled on his chest as he cries out in turn, letting go and calling out my name with love and joy.

HE CUDDLES ME AGAINST his chest, cradling my head. *Hmm.* Closing my eyes, I savor the feel of his arms around me. My hand is on his chest, feeling the steady beat of his heart as it slows and calms. I kiss and nuzzle him, and marvel briefly that not long ago he would not have let me do this.

"Better?" he whispers. I raise my head. He's grinning broadly.

"Much. You?" My answering grin reflects his.

"I've missed you, Mrs. Grey." He's serious for a moment.

"Me, too."

"No more heroics, eh?"

"No," I promise.

"You should always talk to me," he whispers.

"Back at you, Grey."

He smirks. "Fair point well made. I'll try." He kisses my hair.

"I think we're going to be happy here," I whisper, closing my eyes again.

"Yep. You, me and . . . Blip. How do you feel, incidentally?"

"Fine. Relaxed. Happy."

"Good."

"You?"

"Yeah, all those things," he murmurs.

I look up at him, trying to gauge his expression.

"What?" he asks.

"You know, you're very bossy when we have sex."

"Are you complaining?"

"No. I'm just wondering . . . you said you missed it."

He stills, gazing at me. "Sometimes," he whispers.

Oh. "Well, we'll have to see what we can do about that," I murmur and kiss him lightly on his lips, curling around him like a vine. Images of us together, in the playroom; the Tallis, the table, on the cross, shackled to the bed . . . I love his kinky fuckery—our kinky fuckery. Yes. I can do that stuff. I can do that for him, with him. *I can do that for me.* My skin tingles as I remember the riding crop.

"I like to play, too," I murmur, and glancing up, I'm treated to his shy smile.

"You know, I'd really like to test your limits," he whispers.

"My limits for what?"

"Pleasure."

"Oh, I think I'd like that."

"Well, maybe when we get home," he whispers, leaving that promise hanging between us.

I nuzzle him once more. I love him so.

———————

It's been two days since our picnic. Two days since the promise of *well, maybe when we get home* was made. Christian is still treating me like I'm made of glass. He still won't let me go to work, so I have been working from home. I put the stack of query letters I've been reading aside on my desk and sigh. Christian and I haven't been back in the playroom since I safe-worded. And he's said he misses it. Well, so do I . . . especially now that he wants to explore my limits. I flush, thinking what that could possibly entail. I glance at the billiards table . . . Yes, I can't wait to explore those.

My thoughts are interrupted by soft, lyrical music that fills the apartment. Christian is playing the piano; not one of his usual laments but a sweet melody, a hopeful melody—one that I recognize, but have never heard him play.

I tiptoe to the archway of the great room and watch Christian at the piano. It's dusk. The sky is an opulent pink, and the light is reflected off his burnished copper hair. He looks his beautiful breathtaking self, concentrating as he plays, unaware of my presence. He's been so forthcoming over the last few days, so attentive—offering small insights into his day, his thoughts, his plans. It's as if he's breached a dam and started talking.

I know he'll come to check on me in a few minutes, and it gives me an idea. Excited, I steal away, hoping that he still hasn't noticed me, and race to our room, stripping off my clothes as I go, until I'm wearing nothing but pale blue lace panties. I find a pale blue camisole and slip into it quickly. It will hide my bruise. Diving into the closet, I pull out Christian's faded jeans—his playroom jeans, my favorite jeans—from the drawer. From my bedside table I pick up my BlackBerry, fold the jeans neatly, and kneel by the bedroom door. The door is ajar, and I can hear the strains of another piece, one I don't know. But it's another hopeful tune; it's lovely. Quickly I type an e-mail.

From: Anastasia Grey
Subject: My Husband's Pleasure
Date: September 21 2011 20:45
To: Christian Grey

Sir

I await your instructions.

Yours always

Mrs. G x

I press "send."

A few moments later the music stops abruptly. My heart lurches and starts pounding. I wait and wait and eventually my BlackBerry buzzes.

From: Christian Grey
Subject: My Husband's Pleasure <—— love this title, baby
Date: September 21 2011 20:48
To: Anastasia Grey

Mrs. G

I'm intrigued. I'll come find you.

Be ready.

Christian Grey
Anticipative CEO, Grey Enterprises Holdings, Inc.

Be ready! My heart starts to pound and I begin to count. Thirty-seven seconds later the door opens. I'm looking down at his bare feet as they pause on the threshold. *Hmm.* He says nothing. For ages he says nothing. *Oh shit.* I resist the urge to look up at him and keep my eyes downcast.

Finally, he reaches down and picks up his jeans. He stays silent but heads into the walk-in closet while I remain stock-still. *Oh my . . . this is it.* My heart is thundering, and I relish the rush of adrenaline that spikes through my body. I squirm as my excitement builds. What will he do to me? A few moments later he's back, wearing the jeans.

"So you want to play?" he murmurs.

"Yes."

He says nothing, and I risk a quick glance . . . up his jeans, his denim clad thighs, the soft bulge at his fly, the open button at the waist, his happy trail, his navel, his chiseled abdomen, his chest hair, his gray eyes blazing, and his head cocked to one side. He's arching an eyebrow. *Oh shit.*

"Yes what?" he whispers.

Oh.

"Yes, Sir."

His eyes soften. "Good girl," he murmurs, and he caresses my head. "I think we'd better get you upstairs now," he adds. My insides liquefy, and my belly clenches in that delicious way.

He takes my hand and I follow him through the apartment and up the stairs. Outside the playroom door, he halts and bends and kisses me gently before grasping my hair hard.

"You know, you're topping from the bottom," he murmurs against my lips.

"What?" I don't understand what he's talking about.

"Don't worry. I'll live with it," he whispers, amused, and he runs his nose along my jaw and gently bites my ear. "Once inside, kneel, like I've shown you."

"Yes . . . Sir."

He gazes down at me, eyes shining with love, wonder, and wicked thoughts.

Jeez . . . Life is never going to be boring with Christian, and I'm in this for the long haul. I love this man: my husband, my lover, father of my child, my sometimes Dominant . . . my Fifty Shades.

EPILOGUE

The Big House, May 2014

I lie on our tartan picnic blanket and gaze up at the clear, blue, summer sky, my view framed by meadow flowers and tall green grasses. The heat of the afternoon summer sun warms my skin, my bones, and my belly, and I relax, my body turning to Jell-O. This is comfortable. Hell no . . . this is wonderful. I savor the moment, a moment of peace, a moment of pure and utter contentment. I should feel guilty for feeling this joy, this completeness, but I don't. Life right here, right now, is good, and I've learned to appreciate it and live in the moment like my husband. I smile and squirm as my mind drifts to the delicious memory of last night at our home in Escala . . .

The strands of the flogger skim across my swollen belly at an aching, languorous pace.

"Have you had enough yet, Ana?" Christian whispers in my ear.

"Oh, please." I beg, pulling on the restraints above my head as I stand blindfolded and tethered to the grid in the playroom.

The flogger's sweet sting bites into my behind.

"Please what?"

I gasp. "Please, Sir."

Christian places his hand over my ringing skin and rubs gently.

"There. There. There." His words are soft. His hand moves south and around, and his fingers slide inside me.

I groan.

"Mrs. Grey," he breathes, and his teeth pull on my earlobe. "You're so ready."

His fingers slide in and out of me, hitting that spot, that sweet, sweet spot again. The flogger clatters onto the floor and his hand moves over my belly and up to my breasts. I tense. They are sensitive.

"Hush," Christian says, cupping one, and he gently brushes his thumb over my nipple.

"Ah."

His fingers are gentle and enticing, and pleasure spirals out from my breast, down, down . . . deep down. I tilt my head back, pushing my nipple into his palm, and moan once more.

"I like to hear you," Christian whispers. His erection is at my hip, the buttons of his fly pressing into my flesh as his fingers continue their relentless assault: in, out, in, out—keeping a rhythm. "Shall I make you come like this?" he asks.

"No."

His fingers stop moving inside me.

"Really, Mrs. Grey? Is it up to you?" His fingers tighten around my nipple.

"No . . . No, Sir."

"That's better."

"Ah. Please," I beg.

"What do you want, Anastasia?"

"You. Always."

He inhales sharply.

"All of you," I add, breathless.

He eases his fingers out of me, pulls me around to face him, and removes the blindfold. I blink up into darkening gray eyes that burn into mine. His index fingers trace my bottom lip, and he pushes his index and middle fingers into my mouth, letting me taste the salty tang of my arousal.

"Suck," he whispers. I swirl my tongue around and between his fingers.

Hmm . . . even I taste good on his fingers.

His hands skim up my arms to the cuffs above my head, and he unclips them, freeing me. Turning me around so I'm facing the wall, he tugs on my braid, pulling me into his arms. He angles my head to one side and skims his lips up my throat to my ear while holding me flush against him.

"I want in your mouth." His voice is soft and seductive. My body, ripe and ready, clenches deep inside. The pleasure is sweet and sharp.

I moan. Turning to face him, I pull his head down to mine and kiss him hard, my tongue invading his mouth, tasting and savoring him. He groans, places his hands on my behind and tugs me against him, but only my pregnant belly touches him. I bite his jaw and trail kisses down his throat and run my fingers down to his jeans. He tilts his head back, exposing more of his throat to me, and I run my tongue down to his chest and through his chest hair.

"Ah."

I tug the waistband of his jeans, the buttons popping, and he grasps my shoulders as I sink to my knees in front of him.

As I gaze up at him through my lashes, he stares down at me. His eyes are dark, his lips parted, and he inhales deeply when I free him and ensnare him with my mouth. I love doing this to Christian. Watching him come apart, hearing his breath hitch, and the soft moans he makes deep in his throat. I close my eyes and suck hard, pressing down on him, relishing his taste and his breathless gasp.

He grasps my head, stilling me, and I sheath my teeth with my lips and push him deeper into my mouth.

"Open your eyes and look at me," he orders, his voice low.

Blazing eyes meet mine and he flexes his hips, filling my mouth to the back of my throat then withdrawing quickly. He pushes into me again and I reach up to grab him. He stops and holds me in place.

"Don't touch or I'll cuff you again. I just want your mouth," he growls.

Oh my. *Like that is it?* I put my hands behind my back and gaze up at him innocently with my mouth full.

"Good girl," he says, smirking down at me, his voice hoarse. He eases back, and holding me gently but firmly, he pushes into me again. "You have such a fuckable mouth, Mrs. Grey." He closes his eyes and eases into my mouth as I squeeze him between my lips, running my tongue over and around him. I take him deeper and withdraw, again and again and again, the air hissing between his teeth.

"Ah! Stop," he says, and he pulls out of me, leaving me wanting more. He grasps my shoulders and pulls me to my feet. Grabbing my braid, he kisses me hard, his persistent tongue greedy and giving at once. Suddenly he releases me, and before I know it, he's lifted me into his arms and moved over to the four-poster. Gently, he lays me down so that my behind is just on the edge of the bed.

"Wrap your legs around my waist," he orders. I do and pull him toward me. He leans down, hands either side of my head, and still standing, very slowly eases himself into me.

Oh, that feels so good. I close my eyes and revel in his slow possession.

"Okay?" he asks, his concern evident in his tone.

"Oh, God, Christian. Yes. Yes. Please." I tighten my legs around him and push against him. He groans. I clasp his arms, and he flexes his hips slowly at first, in, out.

"Christian, please. Harder—I won't break."

He groans and starts to move, really move, pounding into me again and again. Oh, it's heavenly.

"Yes," I gasp, tightening my hold on him as I start to build . . . He moans, grinding into me with renewed determination . . . and I'm close. *Oh, please. Don't stop.*

"Come on, Ana," he groans through gritted teeth, and I explode around him, my orgasm going on and on and on. I call out his name and Christian stills, groaning loudly, as he climaxes inside me.

"Ana," he cries.

CHRISTIAN LIES BESIDE ME, his hand caressing my belly, his long fingers splayed out wide.

"How's my daughter?"

"She's dancing." I laugh.

"Dancing? Oh yes! Wow. I can feel her." He grins as Blip Two somersaults inside me.

"I think she likes sex already."

Christian frowns. "Really?" he says dryly. He moves so his lips are against my bump. "There'll be none of that until you're thirty, young lady."

I giggle. "Oh, Christian, you are such a hypocrite."

"No, I'm an anxious father." He gazes up at me, his brow furrowed, betraying his anxiety.

"You're a wonderful father, as I knew you would be." I caress his lovely face, and he gives me his shy smile.

"I like this," he murmurs, stroking then kissing my belly. "There's more of you."

I pout. "I don't like more of me."

"It's great when you come."

"Christian!"

"And I'm looking forward to the taste of breast milk again."

"Christian! You are such a kinky—"

He swoops on me suddenly, kissing me hard, throwing his leg over mine, and grabbing my hands so they are above my head. "You love the kinky fuckery," he whispers, and he runs his nose down mine.

I grin, caught in his infectious, wicked smile. "Yes, I love the kinky fuckery. And I love you. Very much."

I jerk awake, woken by a high-pitched squeal of delight from my son, and even though I can't see him or Christian, I grin like an idiot with my glee. Ted has woken from his nap, and he and Christian are romping nearby. I lie quietly, still marveling at Christian's capacity for play. His patience with Teddy is extraordinary—much more so than with me. I snort. But then, that's how it should be. And my beautiful little boy, the apple of his mother's and father's eyes, knows no fear. Christian, on the other hand, is still too overprotective—of both of us. My sweet, mercurial, controlling Fifty.

"Let's find Mommy. She's here in the meadow somewhere."

Ted says something I don't hear, and Christian laughs freely, happily. It's a magical sound, filled with his paternal joy. I can't resist. I struggle up onto my elbows to spy on them from my hiding place in the long grass.

Christian is swinging Ted around and around, making him squeal once more in delight. He stops, launches him high into the air—I stop breathing—then he catches him. Ted shrieks with childish abandon and I breathe a sigh of relief. Oh, my little man, my darling little man, always on the go.

" 'Gain, Daddy!" he squeals. Christian obliges, and my heart leaps into my mouth once more as he tosses Teddy into the air and then catches him again, clutching him close. Christian kisses Ted's copper-colored hair and blows a kiss on his cheek, then tickles him mercilessly for a moment. Teddy howls with laughter, squirming and pushing against Christian's chest, wanting out of his arms. Grinning, Christian sets him on the ground.

"Let's find Mommy. She's hiding in the grass."

Ted beams, enjoying the game, and looks around the meadow. Grasping Christian's hand, he points to somewhere I'm not, and it makes me giggle. I lie back down quickly, delighting in this game.

"Ted, I heard Mommy. Did you hear her?"

"Mommy!"

I giggle-snort at Ted's imperious tone. Jeez—so like his dad, and he's only two.

"Teddy!" I call back, gazing up at the sky with a ridiculous grin on my face.

"Mommy!"

All too soon I hear their footsteps trampling through the meadow, and first Ted then Christian bursts through the long grass.

"Mommy!" Ted screeches as if he's found the lost treasure of the Sierra Madre, and he leaps on me.

"Hey, baby boy!" I cradle him against me and kiss his chubby cheek. He giggles and kisses me in return, then struggles out of my arms.

"Hello, Mommy." Christian smiles down at me.

"Hello, Daddy." I grin, and he picks Ted up and sits down beside me with our son in his lap.

"Gently with Mommy," he admonishes Ted. I smirk—the irony is not lost on me. From his pocket, Christian produces his Black-Berry and gives it to Ted. This will probably win us five minutes of peace, maximum. Teddy studies it, his little brow furrowed. He looks so serious, blue eyes concentrating hard, just like his daddy does when he reads his e-mails. Christian nuzzles Ted's hair, and my heart swells to look at them both. Two peas in a pod: my son sitting quietly—for a few moments at least—in my husband's lap. My two favorite men in the whole world.

Of course, Ted is the most beautiful and talented child on the planet, but then I am his mother so I would think that. And Christian is . . . well, Christian is just himself. In white T-shirt and jeans, he looks as hot as usual. What did I do to win such a prize?

"You look well, Mrs. Grey."

"As do you, Mr. Grey."

"Isn't Mommy pretty?" Christian whispers in Ted's ear. Ted swats him away, more interested in Daddy's BlackBerry.

I giggle. "You can't get around him."

"I know." Christian grins and kisses Ted's hair. "I can't believe he'll be two tomorrow." His tone is wistful. Reaching across, he spreads his hand over my bump. "Let's have lots of children," he says.

"One more at least." I grin, and he caresses my belly.

"How is my daughter?"

"She's good. Asleep, I think."

"Hello, Mr. Grey. Hi, Ana."

We both turn to see Sophie, Taylor's ten-year-old daughter, appear out of the long grass.

"Soeee," Ted squeals with delighted recognition. He struggles out of Christian's lap, discarding the BlackBerry.

"I have some popsicles from Gail," Sophie says. "Can I give one to Ted?"

"Sure," I say. Oh dear, this is going to be messy.

"Pop!" Ted holds out his hands and Sophie passes one to him. It's dripping already.

"Here—let Mommy see." I sit up, take the popsicle from Ted, and quickly slip it into my mouth, licking off the excess juice. Hmm . . . cranberry, cool and delicious.

"Mine!" Ted protests, his voice ringing with indignation.

"Here you go." I hand him back a slightly less runny popsicle, and it goes straight into his mouth. He grins.

"Can Ted and I go for a walk?" Sophie asks.

"Sure."

"Don't go too far."

"No, Mr. Grey." Sophie's hazel eyes are wide and serious. I think she's a little frightened of Christian. She holds her hand out, and Teddy takes it willingly. They trudge away together through the long grass.

Christian watches them.

"They'll be fine, Christian. What harm could come to them here?" He frowns at me momentarily, and I crawl over into his lap.

"Besides, Ted is completely smitten with Sophie."

Christian snorts and nuzzles my hair. "She's a delightful child."

"She is. So pretty, too. A blonde angel."

Christian stills and places his hands on my belly. "Girls, eh?" There's a hint of trepidation in his voice. I curl my hand behind his head.

"You don't have to worry about your daughter for at least another three months. I have her covered here. Okay?"

He kisses me behind my ear and scrapes his teeth around the edge to the lobe.

"Whatever you say, Mrs. Grey." Then he bites me. I yelp.

"I enjoyed last night," he says. "We should do that more often."

"Me, too."

"And we could, if you stopped working . . ."

I roll my eyes and he tightens his arms around me and grins into my neck.

"Are you rolling your eyes at me, Mrs. Grey?" His threat is implicit but sensual, making me squirm, but as we're in the middle of the meadow with the kids nearby, I ignore his invitation.

"Grey Publishing has an author on the *New York Times* bestsellers list—Boyce Fox's sales are phenomenal, the e-book side of our business has exploded, and I finally have the team I want around me."

"And you're making money in these difficult times," Christian adds, his voice reflecting his pride. "But . . . I like you barefoot and pregnant and in my kitchen."

I lean back so I can see his face. He gazes down at me, eyes bright.

"I like that, too," I murmur, and he kisses me, his hands still spread across my bump.

Seeing he's in a good mood, I decide to broach a delicate subject. "Have you thought any more about my suggestion?"

He stills. "Ana, the answer is no."

"But Ella is such a lovely name."

"I am not naming my daughter after my mother. No. End of discussion."

"Are you sure?"

"Yes." Grasping my chin, he gazes earnestly down at me, radiating exasperation. "Ana, give it up. I don't want my daughter tainted by my past."

"Okay. I'm sorry." Shit . . . I don't want to anger him.

"That's better. Stop trying to fix it," he mutters. "You got me to admit I loved her, you dragged me to her grave. Enough."

Oh no. I twist in his lap to straddle him and grasp his head in my hands.

"I'm sorry. Really. Don't be angry with me, please." I kiss him, then kiss the corner of his mouth. After a beat, he points to the other corner, and I smile and kiss it. He points to his nose. I kiss that. He grins and places his hands on my backside.

"Oh, Mrs. Grey—what am I going to do with you?"

"I'm sure you'll think of something," I murmur. He grins and, twisting suddenly, he pushes me down onto the blanket.

"How about I do it now?" he whispers with a salacious smile.

"Christian!" I gasp.

Suddenly there's a high-pitched cry from Ted. Christian leaps to his feet with a panther's easy grace and races toward the source of the sound. I follow at a more leisurely pace. Secretly, I'm not as concerned as Christian—it was not a cry that would make me take the stairs two at a time to find out what's wrong.

Christian swings Teddy up into his arms. Our little boy is crying inconsolably and pointing to the ground, where the remains of his popsicle lie in a soggy mess, melting into the grass.

"He dropped it," Sophie says, sadly. "He could have had mine, but I've finished it."

"Oh, Sophie darling, don't worry." I stroke her hair.

"Mommy!" Ted wails, holding his hands out to me. Christian reluctantly lets him go as I reach for him.

"There, there."

"Pop," he sobs.

"I know, baby boy. We'll go see Mrs. Taylor and get another one." I kiss his head . . . oh, he smells so good. He smells of my baby boy.

"Pop," he sniffs. I take his hand and kiss his sticky fingers.

"I can taste your popsicle here on your fingers."

Ted stops crying and examines his hand.

"Put your fingers in your mouth."

He does. "Pop!"

"Yes. Popsicle."

He grins. My mercurial little boy, just like his dad. Well, at least he has an excuse—he's only two.

"Shall we go see Mrs. Taylor?" He nods, smiling his beautiful baby smile. "Will you let Daddy carry you?" He shakes his head and wraps his arms around my neck, hugging me tightly, his face pressed against my throat.

"I think Daddy wants to taste popsicle, too," I whisper in Ted's little ear. Ted frowns at me, then looks at his hand and holds it out to Christian. Christian smiles and puts Ted's fingers in his mouth.

"Hmm . . . tasty."

Ted giggles and reaches up, wanting Christian to hold him. Christian grins at me and takes Ted in his arms, settling him on his hip.

"Sophie, where's Gail?"

"She was in the big house."

I glance at Christian. His smile has turned bittersweet, and I wonder what he's thinking.

"You're so good with him," he murmurs.

"This little one?" I ruffle Ted's hair. "It's only because I have the measure of you Grey men." I smirk at my husband.

He laughs. "Yes, you do, Mrs. Grey."

Teddy squirms out of Christian's hold. Now he wants to walk, my stubborn little man. I take one of his hands, and his dad takes the other, and together we swing Teddy between us all the way back to the house, Sophie skipping along in front of us.

I wave to Taylor who, on a rare day off, is outside the garage, dressed in jeans and a wife-beater, as he tinkers with an old motorbike.

———————

I pause outside the door to Ted's room and listen as Christian reads to Ted. "I am the Lorax! I speak for the trees . . ."

WHEN I PEEK IN, Teddy is fast asleep while Christian continues to read. He glances up when I open the door and closes the book. He puts his finger to his lips and switches on the baby monitor beside Ted's crib. He adjusts Ted's bedclothes, strokes his cheek, then straightens up and tiptoes over to me without making a sound. It's hard not to giggle at him.

Out in the hallway, Christian pulls me into his embrace. "God, I love him, but it's great when he's asleep," he murmurs against my lips.

"I couldn't agree with you more."

He gazes down at me, eyes soft. "I can hardly believe he's been with us for two years."

"I know." I kiss him, and for a moment, I'm transported back to Teddy's birth: the emergency caesarian, Christian's crippling anxiety, Dr. Greene's no-nonsense calm when my Little Blip was in distress. I shudder inwardly at the memory.

———

"Mrs. Grey, you've been in labor for fifteen hours now. Your contractions have slowed in spite of the Pitocin. We need to do a C-section—the baby is in distress." Dr. Greene is adamant.

"About fucking time!" Christian growls at her. Dr. Greene ignores him.

"Christian, quiet." I squeeze his hand. My voice is low and weak and everything is fuzzy—the walls, the machines, the green-gowned people . . . I just want to go to sleep. But I have something important to do first . . . Oh yes. "I wanted to push him out myself."

"Mrs. Grey, please. C-section."

"Please, Ana," Christian pleads.

"Can I sleep then?"

"Yes, baby, yes." It's almost a sob, and Christian kisses my forehead.

"I want to see the Lil' Blip."

"You will."

"Okay," I whisper.

"Finally," Dr. Greene mutters. "Nurse, page the anesthesiologist. Dr. Miller, prep for a C-section. Mrs. Grey, we are going to move you to the OR."

"Move?" Christian and I speak at once.

"Yes. Now."

And suddenly we're moving—quickly, the lights on the ceiling blurring into one long bright strip as I'm whisked across the corridor.

"Mr. Grey, you'll need to change into scrubs."

"What?"

"Now, Mr. Grey."

He squeezes my hand and releases me.

"Christian," I call, panic setting in.

We are through another set of doors, and in no time a nurse is setting up a screen across my chest. The door opens and closes, and there's so many people in the room. It's so loud . . . I want to go home.

"Christian?" I search the faces in the room for my husband.

"He'll be with you in a moment, Mrs. Grey."

A moment later, he's beside me, in blue scrubs, and I reach for his hand.

"I'm frightened," I whisper.

"No, baby, no. I'm here. Don't be frightened. Not my strong Ana." He kisses my forehead, and I can tell by the tone of his voice that something's wrong.

"What is it?"

"What?"

"What's wrong?"

"Nothing's wrong. Everything's fine. Baby, you're just exhausted." His eyes burn with fear.

"Mrs. Grey, the anesthesiologist is here. He's going to adjust your epidural, and then we can proceed."

"She's having another contraction."

Everything tightens like a steel band around my belly. Shit! I crush Christian's hand as I ride it out. This is what's tiring—enduring this pain. I am so tired. I can feel the numbing liquid spread . . . spread down. I concentrate on Christian's face. On the furrow between his brows. He's tense. He's worried. *Why is he worried?*

"Can you feel this, Mrs. Grey?" Dr. Greene's disembodied voice is coming from behind the curtain.

"Feel what?"

"You can't feel it."

"No."

"Good. Dr. Miller, let's go."

"You're doing well, Ana."

Christian is pale. There is sweat on his brow. He's scared. *Don't be scared, Christian. Don't be scared.*

"I love you," I whisper.

"Oh, Ana," he sobs. "I love you, too, so much."

I feel a strange pulling deep inside. Like nothing I've felt before. Christian looks over the screen and blanches, but stares, fascinated.

"What's happening?"

"Suction! Good . . ."

Suddenly, there's a piercing angry cry.

"You have a boy, Mrs. Grey. Check his Apgar."

"Apgar is nine."

"Can I see him?" I gasp.

Christian disappears from view for a second and reappears a moment later, holding my son, swathed in blue. His face is pink and covered in white mush and blood. My baby. My Blip . . . Theodore Raymond Grey.

When I glance at Christian, he has tears in his eyes.

"Here's your son, Mrs. Grey," he whispers, his voice strained and hoarse.

"Our son," I breathe. "He's beautiful."

"He is," Christian says and plants a kiss on our beautiful boy's forehead beneath a shock of dark hair. Theodore Raymond Grey is oblivious. Eyes closed, his earlier crying forgotten, he's asleep. He is the most beautiful sight I have ever seen. So beautiful, I begin to weep.

"Thank you, Ana," Christian whispers, and there are tears in his eyes, too.

———

"What is it?" Christian tilts my chin back.

"I was just remembering Ted's birth."

Christian blanches and cups my belly.

"I am not going through that again. Elective caesarian this time."

"Christian, I—"

"No, Ana. You nearly fucking died last time. No."

"I did not nearly die."

"No." He's emphatic and not to be argued with, but as he gazes down at me, his eyes soften. "I like the name Phoebe," he whispers, and runs his nose down mine.

"Phoebe Grey? Phoebe . . . Yes. I like that, too." I grin up at him.

"Good. I want to set up Ted's present." He takes my hand, and we head downstairs. His excitement radiates off him; Christian has been waiting for this moment all day.

"DO YOU THINK HE'LL like it?" His apprehensive gaze meets mine.

"He'll love it. For about two minutes. Christian, he's only two."

Christian has finished setting up the wooden train set he bought Teddy for his birthday. He's had Barney at the office convert two of the little engines to run on solar power like the helicopter I gave Christian a few years ago. Christian seems anxious for the sun to rise. I suspect that's because he wants to play with the train set himself. The layout covers most of the stone floor of our outdoor room.

Tomorrow we will have a family party for Ted. Ray and José will be coming and all the Greys, including Ted's new cousin Ava, Kate and Elliot's two-month-old daughter. I look forward to catching up with Kate and seeing how motherhood is agreeing with her.

I gaze up at the view as the sun sinks behind the Olympic Peninsula. It's everything Christian promised it would be, and I get the same joyful thrill seeing it now as I did the first time. It's simply stunning: twilight over the Sound. Christian pulls me into his arms.

"It's quite a view."

"It is," Christian answers, and when I turn to look at him, he's gazing at me. He plants a soft kiss on my lips. "It's a beautiful view," he murmurs. "My favorite."

"It's home."

He grins and kisses me again. "I love you, Mrs. Grey."

"I love you, too, Christian. Always."

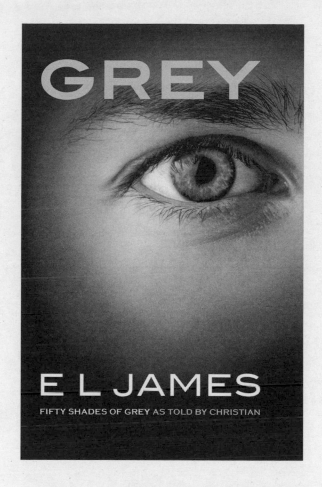

Read on to see the world of Fifty Shades
through the eyes of Christian Grey...

I have three cars. They go fast across the floor. So fast. One is red. One is green. One is yellow. I like the green one. It's the best. Mommy likes them, too. I like when Mommy plays with the cars and me. The red is her best. Today she sits on the couch staring at the wall. The green car flies into the rug. The red car follows. Then the yellow. Crash! But Mommy doesn't see. I do it again. Crash! But Mommy doesn't see. I aim the green car at her feet. But the green car goes under the couch. I can't reach it. My hand is too big for the gap. Mommy doesn't see. I want my green car. But Mommy stays on the couch staring at the wall. *Mommy. My car.* She doesn't hear me. *Mommy.* I pull her hand and she lies back and closes her eyes. *Not now, Maggot. Not now,* she says. My green car stays under the couch. It's always under the couch. I can see it. But I can't reach it. My green car is fuzzy. Covered in gray fur and dirt. I want it back. But I can't reach it. I can never reach it. My green car is lost. Lost. And I can never play with it again.

I open my eyes and my dream fades in the early-morning light. *What the hell was that about?* I grasp at the fragments as they recede, but fail to catch any of them.

Dismissing it, like I do most mornings, I climb out of bed and find some newly laundered sweats in my walk-in closet. Outside, a leaden sky promises rain, and I'm not in the mood to be rained on during my run today. I head upstairs to my gym, switch on the TV for the morning business news, and step onto the treadmill.

My thoughts stray to the day. I've nothing but meetings, though I'm seeing my personal trainer later for a workout at my office— Bastille is always a welcome challenge.

Maybe I should call Elena?

Yeah. Maybe. We can do dinner later this week.

I stop the treadmill, breathless, and head down to the shower to start another monotonous day.

"TOMORROW," I MUTTER, DISMISSING Claude Bastille as he stands at the threshold of my office.

"Golf, this week, Grey." Bastille grins with easy arrogance, knowing that his victory on the golf course is assured.

I scowl at him as he turns and leaves. His parting words rub salt into my wounds because, despite my heroic attempts during our workout today, my personal trainer has kicked my ass. Bastille is the only one who can beat me, and now he wants another pound of flesh on the golf course. I detest golf, but so much business is done on the fairways, I have to endure his lessons there, too . . . and though I hate to admit it, playing against Bastille does improve my game.

As I stare out the window at the Seattle skyline, the familiar ennui seeps unwelcome into my consciousness. My mood is as flat and gray as the weather. My days are blending together with no distinction, and I need some kind of diversion. I've worked all weekend, and now, in the continued confines of my office, I'm restless. I shouldn't feel this way, not after several bouts with Bastille. But I do.

I frown. The sobering truth is that the only thing to capture my interest recently has been my decision to send two freighters of cargo to Sudan. This reminds me—Ros is supposed to come back to me with numbers and logistics. *What the hell is keeping her?* I check my schedule and reach for the phone.

Damn. I have to endure an interview with the persistent Miss Kavanagh for the WSU student newspaper. *Why the hell did I agree to this?* I loathe interviews—inane questions from ill-informed, envious people intent on probing my private life. *And she's a student.* The phone buzzes.

"Yes," I snap at Andrea, as if she's to blame. At least I can keep this interview short.

"Miss Anastasia Steele is here to see you, Mr. Grey."

"Steele? I was expecting Katherine Kavanagh."

"It's Miss Anastasia Steele who's here, sir."

I hate the unexpected. "Show her in."

Well, well . . . Miss Kavanagh is unavailable. I know her father, Eamon, the owner of Kavanagh Media. We've done business together, and he seems like a shrewd operator and a rational human being. This interview is a favor to him—one that I mean to cash in on later when it suits me. And I have to admit I was vaguely curious about his daughter, interested to see if the apple has fallen far from the tree.

A commotion at the door brings me to my feet as a whirl of long chestnut hair, pale limbs, and brown boots dives headfirst into my office. Repressing my natural annoyance at such clumsiness, I hurry over to the girl who has landed on her hands and knees on the floor. Clasping slim shoulders, I help her to her feet.

Clear, embarrassed eyes meet mine and halt me in my tracks. They are the most extraordinary color, powder blue, and guileless, and for one awful moment, I think she can see right through me and I'm left . . . exposed. The thought is unnerving, so I dismiss it immediately.

She has a small, sweet face that is blushing now, an innocent pale rose. I wonder briefly if all her skin is like that—flawless— and what it would look like pink and warmed from the bite of a cane.

Damn.

I stop my wayward thoughts, alarmed at their direction. *What the hell are you thinking, Grey?* This girl is much too young. She gapes at me, and I resist rolling my eyes. *Yeah, yeah, baby, it's just a face, and it's only skin deep.* I need to dispel that admiring look from those eyes but let's have some fun in the process!

"Miss Kavanagh. I'm Christian Grey. Are you all right? Would you like to sit?"

There's that blush again. In command once more, I study her. She's quite attractive—slight, pale, with a mane of dark hair barely contained by a hair tie.

A brunette.

Yeah, she's attractive. I extend my hand as she stutters the beginning of a mortified apology and places her hand in mine. Her skin is cool and soft, but her handshake surprisingly firm.

"Miss Kavanagh is indisposed, so she sent me. I hope you don't mind, Mr. Grey." Her voice is quiet with a hesitant musicality, and she blinks erratically, long lashes fluttering.

Unable to keep the amusement from my voice as I recall her less-than-elegant entrance into my office, I ask who she is.

"Anastasia Steele. I'm studying English literature with Kate, um . . . Katherine . . . um . . . Miss Kavanagh, at WSU Vancouver."

A bashful, bookish type, eh? She looks it: poorly dressed, her slight frame hidden beneath a shapeless sweater, an A-line brown skirt, and utilitarian boots. *Does she have any sense of style at all?* She looks nervously around my office—everywhere but at me, I note, with amused irony.

How can this young woman be a journalist? She doesn't have an assertive bone in her body. She's flustered, meek . . . submissive. Bemused at my inappropriate thoughts, I shake my head and wonder if first impressions are reliable. Muttering some platitude, I ask her to sit, then notice her discerning gaze appraising my office paintings. Before I can stop myself, I find I'm explaining them. "A local artist. Trouton."

"They're lovely. Raising the ordinary to extraordinary," she says dreamily, lost in the exquisite, fine artistry of Trouton's work. Her profile is delicate—an upturned nose, soft, full lips—and in her words she has captured my sentiments exactly. *Raising the ordinary to extraordinary.* It's a keen observation. Miss Steele is bright.

I agree and watch, fascinated, as that flush creeps slowly over her skin once more. As I sit down opposite her, I try to bridle my thoughts. She fishes some crumpled sheets of paper and a digital recorder out of her large bag. She's all thumbs, dropping the damned thing twice on my Bauhaus coffee table. It's obvious she's never done this before, but for some reason I can't fathom, I find it amusing. Under normal circumstances her maladroitness would irritate the hell out of me, but now I hide my smile beneath my index finger and resist the urge to set it up for her myself.

As she fumbles and grows more and more flustered, it occurs to me that I could refine her motor skills with the aid of a riding crop. Adeptly used, it can bring even the most skittish to heel. The errant thought makes me shift in my chair. She peeks up at me and bites down on her full bottom lip.

Fuck! How did I not notice how inviting that mouth is?

"S-Sorry, I'm not used to this."

I can tell, baby, but right now I don't give a damn because I can't take my eyes off your mouth.

"Take all the time you need, Miss Steele." I need another moment to marshal my wayward thoughts.

Grey . . . stop this, now.

"Do you mind if I record your answers?" she asks, her face candid and expectant.

I want to laugh. "After you've taken so much trouble to set up the recorder, you ask me now?"

She blinks, her eyes large and lost for a moment, and I'm overcome by an unfamiliar twinge of guilt.

Stop being such a shit, Grey. "No, I don't mind." I don't want to be responsible for that look.

"Did Kate, I mean, Miss Kavanagh, explain what the interview was for?"

"Yes, to appear in the graduation issue of the student newspaper, as I shall be giving the commencement address at this year's graduation ceremony." Why the hell I've agreed to do *that*, I don't know. Sam in PR tells me that WSU's environmental sciences department needs the publicity in order to attract additional fund-

556   E L James

ing to match the grant I've given them, and Sam will go to any
lengths for media exposure.

Miss Steele blinks once more, as if this is news to her—and she
looks disapproving. Hasn't she done any background work for this
interview? She should know this. The thought cools my blood.
It's . . . displeasing, not what I expect from someone who's imposing on my time.

"Good. I have some questions, Mr. Grey." She tucks a lock of
hair behind her ear, distracting me from my annoyance.

"I thought you might," I say dryly. Let's make her squirm.
Obligingly, she does, then pulls herself upright and squares her
small shoulders. She means business. Leaning forward, she presses
the start button on the recorder and frowns as she glances down at
her crumpled notes.

"You're very young to have amassed such an empire. To what
do you owe your success?"

Surely she can do better than this. What a dull question.
Not one iota of originality. It's disappointing. I trot out my usual
response about having exceptional people working for me. People
I trust, insofar as I trust anyone, and pay well—blah, blah, blah . . .
But Miss Steele, the simple fact is, I'm brilliant at what I do. For
me it's like falling off a log. Buying ailing, mismanaged companies
and fixing them, keeping some or, if they're really broken, stripping their assets and selling them off to the highest bidder. It's
simply a question of knowing the difference between the two, and
invariably it comes down to the people in charge. To succeed in
business you need good people, and I can judge a person, better
than most.

"Maybe you're just lucky," she says quietly.

Lucky? A frisson of annoyance runs through me. *Lucky?* How
dare she? She looks unassuming and quiet, but this question? No
one has ever suggested that I was lucky. Hard work, bringing people with me, keeping a close watch on them, and second-guessing
them if I need to, and if they aren't up to the task, ditching them.
*That's what I do, and I do it well. It's nothing to do with luck!
Well, to hell with that.* Flaunting my erudition, I quote the words

of Harvey Firestone, my favorite industrialist. "The growth and development of people is the highest calling of leadership."

"You sound like a control freak," she says, and she's perfectly serious.

What the hell? Maybe she *can* see through me.

"Control" is my middle name, sweetheart.

I glare at her, hoping to intimidate her. "Oh, I exercise control in all things, Miss Steele." And I'd like to exercise it over you, right here, right now.

That attractive blush steals across her face, and she bites that lip again. I ramble on, trying to distract myself from her mouth.

"Besides, immense power is acquired by assuring yourself, in your secret reveries, that you were born to control things."

"Do you feel that you have immense power?" she asks in a soft, soothing voice, but she arches a delicate brow with a look that conveys her censure. Is she deliberately trying to goad me? Is it her questions, her attitude, or the fact that I find her attractive that's pissing me off? My annoyance grows.

"I employ over forty thousand people. That gives me a certain sense of responsibility—power, if you will. If I were to decide I was no longer interested in the telecommunications business and sell, twenty thousand people would struggle to make their mortgage payments after a month or so."

Her mouth pops open at my response. That's more like it. *Suck it up, baby.* I feel my equilibrium returning.

"Don't you have a board to answer to?"

"I own my company. I don't have to answer to a board." She should know this.

"And do you have any interests outside your work?" she continues hastily, correctly gauging my reaction. She knows I'm pissed, and for some inexplicable reason this pleases me.

"I have varied interests, Miss Steele. Very varied." Images of her in assorted positions in my playroom flash through my mind: shackled on the cross, spread-eagled on the four-poster, splayed over the whipping bench. And behold—there's that blush again. It's like a defense mechanism.

"But if you work so hard, what do you do to chill out?"

"Chill out?" Those words out of her smart mouth sound odd but amusing. Besides, when do I get time to chill out? She has no idea what I do. But she looks at me again with those ingenuous big eyes, and to my surprise I find myself considering her question. *What do I do to chill out?* Sailing, flying, fucking . . . testing the limits of attractive brunettes like her, and bringing them to heel . . . The thought makes me shift in my seat, but I answer her smoothly, omitting a few favorite hobbies.

"You invest in manufacturing. Why, specifically?"

"I like to build things. I like to know how things work: what makes things tick, how to construct and deconstruct. And I have a love of ships. What can I say?" They transport food around the planet.

"That sounds like your heart talking, rather than logic and facts."

Heart? Me? Oh no, baby.

My heart was savaged beyond recognition a long time ago. "Possibly. Though there are people who'd say I don't have a heart."

"Why would they say that?"

"Because they know me well." I give her a wry smile. In fact, no one knows me that well, except maybe Elena. I wonder what she would make of little Miss Steele here. The girl is a mass of contradictions: shy, awkward, obviously bright, and arousing as hell.

Yes, okay, I admit it. I find her alluring.

She recites the next question by rote. "Would your friends say you're easy to get to know?"

"I'm a very private person. I go a long way to protect my privacy. I don't often give interviews." Doing what I do, living the life I've chosen, I need my privacy.

"Why did you agree to do this one?"

"Because I'm a benefactor of the university, and for all intents and purposes, I couldn't get Miss Kavanagh off my back. She badgered and badgered my PR people, and I admire that kind of tenacity." But I'm glad it's you who turned up and not her.

"You also invest in farming technologies. Why are you interested in this area?"

"We can't eat money, Miss Steele, and there are too many people on this planet who don't have enough food." I stare at her, poker-faced.

"That sounds very philanthropic. Is that something you feel passionately about? Feeding the world's poor?" She regards me with a puzzled look, as if I'm a conundrum, but there's no way I want her seeing into my dark soul. This is not an area open to discussion. *Move it along, Grey.*

"It's shrewd business," I mutter, feigning boredom, and I imagine fucking that mouth to distract myself from all thoughts of hunger. Yes, her mouth needs training, and I imagine her on her knees before me. Now, that thought is appealing.

She recites her next question, dragging me away from my fantasy. "Do you have a philosophy? If so, what is it?"

"I don't have a philosophy as such. Maybe a guiding principle— Carnegie's: 'A man who acquires the ability to take full possession of his own mind may take possession of anything else to which he is justly entitled.' I'm very singular, driven. I like control—of myself and those around me."

"So you want to possess things?"

Yes, baby. You, for one. I frown, startled by the thought.

"I want to deserve to possess them, but yes, bottom line, I do."

"You sound like the ultimate consumer." Her voice is tinged with disapproval, pissing me off again.

"I am."

She sounds like a rich kid who's had all she ever wanted, but as I take a closer look at her clothes—she's dressed in clothes from some cheap store like Old Navy or H&M—I know that isn't it. She hasn't grown up in an affluent household.

I could really take care of you.

Where the hell did that thought come from?

Although, now that I consider it, I do need a new sub. It's been, what—two months since Susannah? And here I am, salivating over this woman. I try an agreeable smile. Nothing wrong with consumption—after all, it drives what's left of the American economy.

"You were adopted. How much do you think that's shaped the way you are?"

What does this have to do with the price of oil? What a ridiculous question. If I'd stayed with the crack whore, I'd probably be dead. I blow her off with a non-answer, trying to keep my voice level, but she pushes me, demanding to know how old I was when I was adopted.

Shut her down, Grey!

My tone goes cold. "That's a matter of public record, Miss Steele."

She should know this, too. Now she looks contrite as she tucks an escaped strand of hair behind her ear. *Good.*

"You've had to sacrifice family life for your work."

"That's not a question," I snap.

She startles, clearly embarrassed, but she has the grace to apologize and she rephrases the question: "Have you had to sacrifice family life for your work?"

What do I want with a family? "I have a family. I have a brother, a sister, and two loving parents. I'm not interested in extending my family beyond that."

"Are you gay, Mr. Grey?"

What the hell!

I cannot believe she's said that out loud! Ironically, the question even my own family will not ask. How dare she! I have a sudden urge to drag her out of her seat, bend her over my knee, spank her, and then fuck her over my desk with her hands tied behind her back. That would answer her ridiculous question. I take a deep calming breath. To my vindictive delight, she appears to be mortified by her own question.

"No, Anastasia, I'm not." I raise my eyebrows, but keep my expression impassive. *Anastasia.* It's a lovely name. I like the way my tongue rolls around it.

"I apologize. It's, um . . . written here." She's at it again with the hair behind the ear. Obviously it's a nervous habit.

Are these not her questions? I ask her, and she pales. Damn, she really is attractive, in an understated sort of way.

"Er . . . no. Kate—Miss Kavanagh—she compiled the questions."

"Are you colleagues on the student paper?"

"No. She's my roommate."

No wonder she's all over the place. I scratch my chin, debating whether or not to give her a really hard time.

"Did you volunteer to do this interview?" I ask, and I'm rewarded with her submissive look: she's nervous about my reaction. I like the effect I have on her.

"I was drafted. She's not well." Her voice is soft.

"That explains a great deal."

There's a knock at the door, and Andrea appears.

"Mr. Grey, forgive me for interrupting, but your next meeting is in two minutes."

"We're not finished here, Andrea. Please cancel my next meeting."

Andrea gapes at me, looking confused. I stare at her. *Out! Now!* I'm busy with little Miss Steele here.

"Very well, Mr. Grey," she says, recovering quickly, and turning on her heel, she leaves us.

I turn my attention back to the intriguing, frustrating creature on my couch. "Where were we, Miss Steele?"

"Please, don't let me keep you from anything."

Oh no, baby. It's my turn now. I want to know if there are any secrets to uncover behind that lovely face.

"I want to know about you. I think that's only fair." As I lean back and press my fingers to my lips, her eyes flick to my mouth and she swallows. *Oh yes—the usual effect.* And it is gratifying to know she isn't completely oblivious of my charms.

"There's not much to know," she says, her blush returning.

I'm intimidating her. "What are your plans after you graduate?"

"I haven't made any plans, Mr. Grey. I just need to get through my final exams."

"We run an excellent internship program here."

What possessed me ever to say that? It's against the rules, Grey. Never fuck the staff . . . But you're not fucking this girl.

She looks surprised, and her teeth sink into that lip again. Why is that so arousing?

"Oh. I'll bear that in mind," she replies. "Though I'm not sure I'd fit in here."

"Why do you say that?" I ask. *What's wrong with my company?*

"It's obvious, isn't it?"

"Not to me." I'm confounded by her response. She's flustered again as she reaches for the recorder.

Shit, she's going. Mentally I run through my schedule for that afternoon—there is nothing that won't keep. "Would you like me to show you around?"

"I'm sure you're far too busy, Mr. Grey, and I do have a long drive."

"You're driving back to Vancouver?" I glance out the window. It's one hell of a drive, and it's raining. She shouldn't be driving in this weather, but I can't forbid her. The thought irritates me. "Well, you'd better drive carefully." My voice is sterner than I intend. She fumbles with the recorder. She wants out of my office, and to my surprise, I don't want her to go.

"Did you get everything you need?" I ask in a transparent effort to prolong her stay.

"Yes, sir," she says quietly. Her response floors me—the way those words sound, coming out of that smart mouth—and briefly I imagine that mouth at my beck and call.

"Thank you for the interview, Mr. Grey."

"The pleasure's been all mine," I respond—truthfully, because I haven't been this fascinated by anyone for a while. The thought is unsettling. She stands and I extend my hand, eager to touch her.

"Until we meet again, Miss Steele." My voice is low as she places her hand in mine. Yes, I want to flog and fuck this girl in my playroom. Have her bound and wanting . . . needing me, trusting me. I swallow.

It ain't going to happen, Grey.

"Mr. Grey." She nods and withdraws her hand quickly, too quickly.

I can't let her go like this. It's obvious she's desperate to leave. It's irritating, but inspiration hits me as I open my office door.

"Just ensuring you make it through the door," I quip.

Her lips form a hard line. "That's very considerate, Mr. Grey," she snaps.

Miss Steele bites back! I grin behind her as she exits, and follow her out. Both Andrea and Olivia look up in shock. *Yeah, yeah. I'm just seeing the girl out.*

"Did you have a coat?" I ask.

"A jacket."

I give Olivia a pointed look and she immediately leaps up to retrieve a navy jacket, passing it to me with her usual simpering expression. Christ, Olivia is annoying—mooning over me all the time.

Hmm. The jacket is worn and cheap. Miss Anastasia Steele should be better dressed. I hold it up for her, and as I pull it over her slim shoulders, I touch the skin at the base of her neck. She stills at the contact and pales.

Yes! She is affected by me. The knowledge is immensely pleasing. Strolling over to the elevator, I press the call button while she stands fidgeting beside me.

Oh, I could stop your fidgeting, baby.

The doors open and she scurries in, then turns to face me. She's more than attractive. I would go as far as to say she's beautiful.

"Anastasia," I say, in good-bye.

"Christian," she answers, her voice soft. And the elevator doors close, leaving my name hanging in the air between us, sounding odd and unfamiliar, but sexy as hell.

I need to know more about this girl.

"Andrea," I bark as I return to my office. "Get me Welch on the line, now."

As I sit at my desk and wait for the call, I look at the paintings on the wall of my office, and Miss Steele's words drift back to me.

"Raising the ordinary to extraordinary." She could so easily have been describing herself.

My phone buzzes. "I have Mr. Welch on the line for you."

"Put him through."

"Yes, sir."

"Welch, I need a background check."

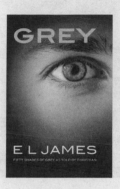

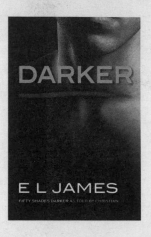